PRAISE FOR
PAUL BLACK'S THE TELS TRILOGY.

WINNER for genre fiction in the Writer's Digest's International Book Awards.

Gold and Silver medalist for science fiction, ForeWord Magazine's Book of the Year.

"Dallas writer Paul Black makes his first foray into the world of science fiction with The Tels. It's a HIGHLY ORIGINAL novel set in the near future and IT MOVES AT LIGHTNING SPEED. Mr. Black has quite an imagination and puts it to good use. The MIND-BENDING PLOT centers on Jonathan Kortel, who is approached by a shadowy group called the Tels, who covet his telekinetic gifts. The ENSUING ACTION IS BIZARRE enough to read like something straight out of The X-Files."

~ *Steve Powers, Dallas Morning News*

"(The Tels) is WRITTEN SO SPLENDIDLY, at times I forgot I was reading science fiction – with the emphasis on fiction. The characters are realistic, and the hero is someone you relate to, worry about and wonder if he's going to be able to cope with the reality that is set before him. This is definitely ONE OF THE BEST SCIENCE FICTION NOVELS I've ever read...the BOOK IS REMARKABLE."

~ *Marilyn Meredith, Writer's Digest's 11th Annual Book Awards*

"...Soulware was a BRILLIANTLY EMBROIDERED STORY, mixing science and fiction in a plausible and entertaining way...I absolutely LOVED THIS BOOK!"

~ *Ismael Manzano, G-POP.net*

"A riveting science fiction novel...an imaginatively skilled storyteller."

**"*The Tels* is an addictive read...
manages to capture the reader in the first
ten pages...*The Tels* has it all."**

"Black rises above the Trekkie laser tag spastics found in your typical sci-fi novels resting on the grocery store racks. His sensibilities broaden from machine gun testosterone to discreet fatherhood, from errant sexuality to wry humor. HE DELIVERS A CHARGE OF VENTURE RARELY FOUND IN FIRST-TIME WRITERS. And THE TELS HITS THE MARK as a solid adventure serial, leaving you hanging for the next publication."

~ Brian Adams, Collegian

"The Tels is an ADDICTIVE READ from first-time novelist Paul Black, a promising new storyteller on the sci-fi scene. He manages to capture the reader in the first ten pages. He introduces us to a set of intriguing characters in a totally believable possible future. There is a grittiness and sensuality to his writing that pours out of every word in the book. Whether it's his description of the preparation of a good meal, the seduction of a beautiful woman, or a fight to the death, THE TELS HAS IT ALL. Even people who don't read sci-fi will want to read this book. The action is great and would make one hell of a movie. Is Hollywood listening? Paul Black has a winner on his hands. I can hardly wait for the next installment."

~ Cynthia A., About Towne, ITCN

"Soulware doesn't miss a beat as it continues Jonathan's story, the story of his quest to find out exactly who he really is and why the Tels are so interested in him. The ending makes it clear that there's more to come, and readers who crave their science-fiction with a hint of weirdness can look forward to the next book in the series."

~ Steve Powers, Dallas Morning News

THE TELS

WINNER OF THE *WRITER'S DIGEST* BOOK AWARD

SOULWARE

PAUL BLACK

NEXUS POINT

NOVEL INSTINCTS
Publishers of Fine Genre Fiction

This book is a work of fiction. Names, characters, places, and incidents either are products of the author's imagination or are used fictitiously. Any resemblance to actual events or locations or persons, living or dead, is entirely coincidental.

NOVEL INSTINCTS PUBLISHING
6008 Ross Avenue
Dallas, Texas 75206
www.novelinstincts.com and www.paulblackbooks.com

This book can be ordered on the web at all major retail sites including www.barnesandnoble.com and www.amazon.com.

ISBN: 978-0-9726007-9-8
1. Fiction / Science Fiction / High Tech 2. Fiction / Near-Future

Library of Congress Control Numbers:
The Tels (2003): 2003092612
Soulware (2005): 2004097635
Nexus Point (2007): 2007921887

Printed in the United States of America.
10 9 8 7 6 5 4 3 2 1

This book's body text was typeset in Garamond Three, 11pt/12pt, and its page numbers and titles in Futura Light, Medium and Heavy.

AUTHOR'S NOTE

~

The Tels, Soulware and *Nexus Point* will always have a special place in my heart, especially *The Tels*. It was my first book and in many ways it taught me how to write. Written before 9-11 and published in 2002, it's ironic how its themes of mass destruction and terrorists attacks were ahead of their time. My vision of the future has become somewhat dated, but there are still many intriguing ideas to enjoy. You'll also find that the books are written in different styles...book one is written in third-person omniscient, while books two and three are written in alternating POVs. I was playing with different techniques at the time and to be honest, I like the alternating POV the best. In the end, this series is about one person's struggle with love and destiny. And isn't that what all good books are about? I like to think so. I hope you enjoy the series as much as I did writing it. Now sit back, relax and get ready to enter the fascinating world of The Tels!

WINNER of Writer's Digest's 2003 Book of the Year for Genre Fiction
FINALIST for Science Fiction Independent Publishers Book Awards.

"...this is definitely **ONE OF THE BEST SCIENCE FICTION NOVELS** I've ever
read...the book is remarkable."

~ *Marilyn Meredith, Writer's Digest's 11th Annual Book Awards*

Book 1

THE TELS

Originally published in 2003

Thank you, God... 1

JONATHAN felt his heart beginning to beat harder with each sudden jerk of the toggle, and the booming bass emanating from the car's MuzSat link only intensified the pounding in his chest. The Interway was clear, and Tarris piloted the car like he was raging on some biovid game, high into the bonus levels. He calmly hummed as they slipped through the hot Midwestern night.

"Well?!" Jonathan yelled over the deafening sounds of Nymphia Scooter Pie, this week's flavor for Tarris.

"Well what?" Tarris shot back and brought the music down a click.

Tarris had been Jonathan's friend ever since the "event," three years ago. He was older, cooler and could drive. And if you could drive, then in this little town you were free.

"How does it feel?"

"Oh, the car?" Tarris asked dryly.

Even Tarris's name was cool. He was of the generation whose parents had abandoned the typical names that had permeated the culture for the last hundred and fifty years or so in favor of techno-names. Sharp-edged names. Names that melded the cultures, even the world, into a standard, much like the Internet did a century earlier. And he was Jonathan's friend and brother figure, even, he dared think, a father figure. At least as much a father figure as a 17-year-old can be.

"The car handles as it should," he said.

"Yeah?..." Jonathan pressed.

"Damn right it does!" And with that, Tarris asked the car to accelerate beyond the legal Interway limit.

"How did you do that? I thought these models were unalterable."

"Don't worry, Jonny, just a little retroengineering trick my dad taught me." (Jonathan hated that version of his name.) "My dad says that even after alterations, the biochip's constructs can't be permanent. They just regenerate and reconfigure to the factory specs and before you know it, original car. Just like it was right out of the tank."

The car Tarris piloted was as much a car of the last century as milk that was actually milked. Or a building that was actually built. The Biolution of the mid-21st century had changed much of life. The way the world was headed in the first half of the century, who would have guessed it? The Biolution was predicted, but nobody expected it would happen this fast. And with consequences such as the event.

It was hard for Jonathan to hold back, to swallow the pain every time the event was mentioned. Every time he thought about it. He swallowed. Hard. Thinking he could gulp down the fear. But he knew what would come next.

The tears.

He used to run. Anywhere where he could be alone. Then came the rush of memories, of faces, of a life he knew he would never have. The stolen life he would never reflect upon. The life he should have had with his mother and father. And their Hawaiian home where he used to play, three years ago.

Where he had played was now what the world called "ground zero," still dominating the news. Even if Jonathan could, he would never be able to outrun the event. In many respects, it forever changed the world. Much as, the history pads said, the atom bomb did in the mid-20th century. But what the pads left unsaid is what his grandfather called the "collateral damage." The shattered lives of thousands of relatives and friends left behind, alive.

No one saw it coming. The world's collective fear of terrorism had waned by the mid-21st century. Individualism and information had been interwoven, due in part to the Internet revolution. But the Biolution made the bandwidth issues of the late-20th and early 21st centuries a thing of the past. The world had been lulled into a false sense of security, thinking there wasn't any problem the collective intelligence networks of the G-12 couldn't find and solve. The Biochip ushered in a flood of technology that changed almost every aspect of life. Information didn't flow; it ran like a torrent. And the world, it seemed, rode along helplessly like tourists shooting rapids in a giant, guideless river raft.

The Biolution affected everything in its path. Like a monstrous Midwestern thunderstorm, it swept across the human landscape. Even the most sacred of resources could not escape its effect. The corpulent oil industry that dominated the world since the late-19th century was irrevocably changed. Gas now could be synthetically made with biotechnology, cheaply and without end. The power of the Arab nations disappeared almost overnight and, with it, the collective grip they held on the throat of the world. This demotion in world ranking was more than their Arab pride could take. Their radical fringe elements joined forces and set out to teach the world a lesson in Arab anger. No one knew how important this lesson would be.

~

"Hey, are you crying, Jonny boy?" Tarris asked, glancing at his younger friend while piloting the vehicle through a series of sharp "S" curves.

"No! I just got crap in my eye. I need to raise this window; your driving is freaking me."

"Aw, don't worry, Jonny boy," Tarris said with that look.

Jonathan knew that look.

"Tarris is captain tonight, we're free to sail!"

"Are you riding?" Jonathan asked, though he already knew the answer. For all his strengths, Tarris had one weakness. He loved to ride. But the drugs of the latter century had evolved into a new form. A bioform. And it scared Jonathan when Tarris was riding. The phrase was true. You didn't take a drug, the drug took you. For a ride. Good or bad, you rode. And because of their biomatrix structures, each biodrug reacted differently with each individual. The effects were only somewhat predictable. That was their allure. The unknowing. The surprise inside each box. That's also why some called it Cracker Jack. Jack, for short.

"Just a little tonight...come on, it's our first time sailing this piece. I gotta have an edge, little buddy," Tarris begged. "You understand, don't you?"

Jonathan understood all too well. It wasn't the first time he had been along for a ride. Usually it went smoothly. The Tarris Jonathan knew just became more of himself. Funnier, sillier – and the girls loved this Tarris. But if it went badly, the friend he knew disappeared. The bioconstructs of the drug altered his persona, and it wasn't pretty. But tonight looked clear. Clear of the Tarris Jonathan had come to call The Mean Man.

"Hottttt damn," Tarris screamed as he, the drug, and the car all synced into perfect harmony, "let's sail toooonight!" And as his hand passed over the car's interface pad, he lightly touched the BR button, changed the ratio, caused the car to punch forward and threw Jonathan back against the seat. Tarris pushed the car to its design limits, weaving in and out of the Interway traffic, throwing the boys from side to side. The scene outside the window blurred, and the car seemed to float above the ground through the "S" curves. Tarris was piloting like it was his last ride. Jonathan couldn't tell if the cause was the altered state of the car's system or of Tarris, but whatever it was, the car reacted with pinpoint accuracy to all of his commands. After 12 miles of riding Tarris's high, Jonathan couldn't take any more.

"Tarris!" Jonathan screamed. "Tarris, please slow down!" He gripped the leather, leaving indents no biochips could reconstruct, and as he watched his friend reach the height of his ride, he began to pray. He hadn't prayed since the death of his parents. He had given up on a God he thought had abandoned him. Had abandoned man. What kind of God would allow something like the event to happen? Right now, though, he was reconsidering. If there was a God, Jonathan could have used just a little of his grace tonight.

"Now that's what I call a bitchin' killer ride!" the 17-year-old blared. And with that, Tarris grazed the ratio button again, and the car eased into legal speed without so much as a change in G.

"Open those eyes, little buddy," Tarris said. He piloted the car off the Interway and into the urban flow.

Jonathan looked up from his conversation with the Almighty and saw that his friend wasn't riding anymore. He couldn't tell specifically how he knew; he just knew when Tarris was coming off. Or "jerking off" as Tarris liked to put it.

"This is your captain speaking. That was one bitchin' killer ride, folks." Tarris burst out laughing.

"Yeah, you were the captain tonight, Tarris," Jonathan nervously agreed.

"And you...you're sitting there praying...." Tarris roared as he slapped the car's toggle to a beat only he was hearing. Neither of them saw the lights of the two-ton recycle hauler entering their road's interface space.

"Shit, Tarris!"

Jonathan's heart almost exploded from his chest as he turned and realized the fate that awaited them both. In the 20-foot space between their car and the poly-bio grillwork of the hauler, Jonathan saw what was surely the end of his life. No force on earth was going to stop it.

"Shit!" Tarris screamed, and his hands danced on the protocol pad of the vehicle. But it was too late. In the chaos of the moment, Tarris had tried everything he knew, which, at 17, wasn't much. Looking past Jonathan's head to the hauler's enormous grill, all he knew now was that it was over.

While Jonathan stared at the last thing he would see in his life, he felt his fear transform. The blood rushed from his head and an intense heat took over his body. In the nanosecond before the hauler's grill impacted the window, Jonathan's vision changed to white, then to colors that twinkled, then swirled. Then it all collapsed to black.

Dead black.

~

To Jonathan, the black space seemed like purgatory. He woke to Tarris shaking his arm and an immense pain gripping not only his head, but his mind.

"Jonathan! Jonathan, wake up!" Tarris said.

Jonathan could hardly make out his friend's voice. As Tarris came into focus his face was white, but his demeanor was calm.

"Hey little guy," Tarris asked softly. "Are you all right?"

Jonathan surfaced to the moment to find himself, Tarris and the car unharmed. He pulled himself up to look out what he thought would be a shattered window of high-impact plastic only to see that the hauler was facing them about 50 feet away. Its grillwork undamaged, it just sat there, chugging like a bull ready to charge.

"What happened?" Jonathan asked through a cough, his throat dry and raw.

"Your captain saved the day! Now let's get the hell out of here!" Tarris jerked the toggle, and the car obeyed.

It was quiet inside the cabin as the car hummed along the surface of the road. Its systems were struggling with the recent input of event data that seemed to defy known physics. Both boys reflected on what could have been.

"What happened Tarris...really?"

"Well..." Tarris confessed, "I thought we were gone for sure, but the car just jerked itself about and that recycler bounced off us, sort of."

"What?..."

"Hey, who cares what happened, just that it did. Or we would be a tangle of biomatter right now, you got that, buddy? Hey, are you okay?" Tarris reached over to wipe away the little river of blood coming from Jonathan's right nostril. He was doing his big brother routine.

Jonathan jerked away. "I'm okay. I must have hit something."

"Really? I saw you when we were spinning, and you didn't hit a damn thing. In fact, you didn't even move."

It was quiet again in the cabin. Both boys just stared straight ahead. Tarris was watching the system readouts imbedded in the windshield as he piloted the car home. Jonathan's head pounded, and his clothes were drenched in sweat. He knew the captain hadn't done a damn thing to save this ship. But if Tarris hadn't saved it, who had? Or what had? Jonathan leaned back into the coolness of the leather, and only one thought managed to come into his pain-addled brain.

Thank you, God.

Working the crowd...2

"**WHAT** the hell is she doing?" Jimbo asked.

"It is hard to say," his partner answered.

James McCarris, or Jimbo as his friends called him, was a Level 5 – a pretty low level for a Recruiter, but Jimbo had shown promise and the patience required of the job. His partner, on the other hand, was a Level 8. Very rare and very powerful. He was considered the best of the best. There were no other levels that a human could achieve. Of course, Levels 9 and 10 existed, but only as the last levels of the 1 through 10 Tel chart. And Level 10 was considered unattainable. Beyond the human genome. Beyond evolution. Beyond comprehension. But there were a few in the government who believed the day would come. Far off for sure. Possibly in a century or two, though, a human would go beyond the mere movement of an object, beyond the multi-grav aspects to change physical properties, most likely at the molecular level.

These were the Tels, a group of humans who had split from the pack, who had begun an evolutionary divergence from their brothers and sisters. They were headed down a new genetic path, one that would take them into another realm.

A telekinetic realm.

They were discovered in the 20th century after World War Two. Reports came out of the war of men and women who had performed extraordinary acts of strength disguised as courage. Some seemingly had moved objects without lifting a finger. After the war, the rumors continued to circulate: a child lifts a car off a dying parent, a woman stops a combine from shredding her son. These reports had always been part of the culture, but a skeptical world had dismissed them as tabloid fodder. But there were those in the governments of the superpowers who took these rumors seriously. They discovered the potential of these people. They organized branches of their governments that even their military didn't know about – so secretive, they existed in shadow. The belief was that these new humans had the potential to be the saving factor for mankind. They were the next leap. The race that would take humans to the stars.

In America, this branch was known simply as the Agency.

~

"Is she trying to move that truck? Shit, partner, she's only six." Jimbo whistled and made a clicking sound with his mouth.

His partner hated that sound. It always reconfirmed that Jimbo was from the South. *It must be,* he often thought, *genetically encoded in Southerners to make this sound after what they think is a profound statement.* To him it sounded more like Jimbo was trying to get a horse to move.

"I do not think that this little girl has the potential," Jimbo's partner said, tapping the netpad off and slipping it back into his overcoat pocket. "Her time would be better spent playing with her dolls." He turned to walk back to their car.

"Why aren't they qualifying these Potentials," Jimbo complained, "before we spend six months with them?"

"Because currently there is no other way to effectively monitor Potentials without disclosing who we are or exposing either ourselves or them to harm. We cannot just abduct them, run the biodiogs and dump them back into their lives. You know the Agency's directive as well as I do!"

Jimbo knew it. Every Tel knew it. It was the key to their existence and survival. Directive 1: Never expose the Agency, yourself or a fellow member to a Potential, until such time as a Recruiter affirms the readiness of the Potential.

"Our work here is done," Jimbo's partner said, opening the car door.

"Back to the hotel?"

"No, I am hungry. Let us stop and get some dinner, shall we?" He quietly lit a cigarette, leaned back against the seat and piloted the car into the Interway, never touching a single system's button or the toggle stick.

Jimbo had gotten used to his partner's idiosyncrasies. As a Level 8, his partner could do things most Tels couldn't. Driving a car without the physical interface all humans required, for instance. Now starting a car, even driving it, was simple and achievable for most Level 5's. But to navigate the complex Interway, to dialog with the Interway's control systems, to smoke a cigarette, and to hold an intense conversation – that was reserved for a Level 8.

"How do you do that?" Jimbo asked enviously.

"Do what?" his partner answered. He stared out the window and let the smoke linger in the air before he mentally condensed the particles into a speck the size of a pinhead that floated gently to the car floor. "Smoke?"

"No. You know what I'm talking about..."

"You mean do what I am doing right now?"

"Yes!" Jimbo said impatiently. "It's nerve-racking. What if you miss a data input? What if your mind wanders for just a millisecond? What if something comes up in the road you aren't aware of?"

"Aware?" his partner demanded.

Jimbo knew he had crossed the line.

"What do you know of being aware?"

"Look...I..."

"That is your problem," his partner said coolly, settling back into the seat. "You are too busy looking instead of sensing."

Here comes the lesson, Jimbo thought.

"If you spent less time using your vision sense and developed your seventh sense, you would not be asking such questions....You would already have the answer."

And he was right. It took more than the gift. It took a deep, genetic, almost instinctual sensing of your abilities. Only a few Tels had this capacity.

Oh, lucky me, I get the Dean of Telekinesis as my partner. But Jimbo knew deep down, his partner could teach him well.

~

It was late in the evening, and the streets were void of the current of traffic that made Chicago one of the busiest cities in the world. Jimbo's partner deftly piloted the car to the curb's edge. Another Recruiter had recommended the restaurant to the senior Tel. He had said that it was...special.

"You sure this is good?" Jimbo asked. His partner fired off a look that Jimbo could swear he felt in the base of his neck. "You know, you don't have to keep demonstrating your supreme powers, oh Great One," he said, reaching to rub where he thought he felt the sensation.

"I am sorry, James," his partner answered. With that, he took his cigarette from his mouth, snuffed it out and let it fall into the recycling container at the corner. He never used his hands.

"Gotta watch that," Jimbo warned. "We're in public now."

"Yes we are, a public of which we are not a part."

"Yeah...well, let's go eat." Jimbo turned his collar up to the brisk Lake Michigan wind, and they stepped into the restaurant.

The exposed brick walls of the old renovated warehouse had captured every smell from every dish, and the cool of the street gave way to the inviting warmth from the kitchen. A young man was busy busing a table. He turned to greet the new customers with that "I'll be right with you" look.

"Smells great, I'm starved," Jimbo said. His partner said nothing and kept watching the young man.

"Welcome to Kortel's, gentlemen," the young man said, wiping his hands on his well-stained apron. "Two for dinner?"

"Yes, please," Jimbo's partner said, removing his coat, and they were led to a small two-top by a window.

"Man, I could use a drink," Jimbo said.

"Hmmm..." his partner mused, sitting down.

Jimbo knew that tone. "What are you sensing?"

"I am not sure...someone in here..."

Jimbo leaned closer to read his partner's actions. He was in hunt mode, and his Level 8 senses were on point. Level 8's not only had the gift, but in some cases they had the sense. His partner read the menu, but he was more focused on who was triggering the "effect," as members called it. The effect was the displacement of the gravitational field created by all Tels, Potentials or Members. Some in the Agency thought Level 8's sensed an electromagnetic change much the way dogs and cats sensed the coming of an earthquake. Others believed it was genetic. An innate sensitivity to their own species. Their own kind. Whatever it was, his partner was truly intrigued by this one.

"Is the Force strong, Obi Wan?" Jimbo asked.

"What?"

"Never mind. Ancient trivia. Come on, let's order and then you can get back to hunting."

The menu was simple, but the dishes were complex. As Jimbo looked around the restaurant, he saw that everything was edge food.

"You see what I see?" he declared.

"Yes, I do." his partner said. "Want to leave?"

"No, no. I'm too damn hungry now to go looking for another place. I'll get over it."

"I thought you were against biofoods."

"Yes and no. I know it customizes the flavors to your body's chemical profile, and I do like the unique combinations, but..."

"But what?"

"It's just..."

"It is just that you are a Southern boy who likes the way foods used to taste. Like mom used to make. Am I right?"

"Very funny..."

"If you must know, I tend to concur with you."

"Well, I'll be damned," Jimbo exclaimed. "I never thought I'd see the day you would come down to my level."

"Oh, I believe we share more than you think."

"Oh really? Like what?..."

"Gentlemen," the young man interrupted, "can I start you off with a drink this evening?" He was looking distracted as he watched the workings of the restaurant.

"You bet. I'll take a beer – draft if you've got it," Jimbo said.

"Nothing for me, thank you," his partner said, carefully looking the young man up and down like a med scanner.

"Very good, I'll be back with your drink and tell you our specials then. Take a look at the appetizers tonight, gentlemen. I think you'll find we have a little something for everyone."

Jimbo waited for him to leave. "Will you loosen up, please!" he scolded. "Oh, I'm sorry, we're in hunt mode, aren't we..."

"We are not, but yes...I am." His partner continued to track the young man to the kitchen. He watched him place the order into his netpad, all the while working the crowd like he owned the place.

"It's him, isn't it?" Jimbo asked, following his partner's stare.

"I am not sure...the heat from the kitchen and the fact that I am famished makes isolating the effect difficult. I do believe, though, he might be just a 'Displacer.'"

A Displacer was Agency slang for someone who displaced the gravitational field around themselves but could no more move an object than a dog could. Level 8's usually could tell the difference between a Displacer and a true Potential.

"Maybe I could use a drink after all." Jimbo's partner trained his attention at the young man, who instantly stopped what he was doing, looked over to their table and began walking back. This time he paid no attention at all to the crowd.

"Is...there something you gentlemen need?" He had a puzzled look on his face.

"Why yes," Jimbo's partner said, "you are so perceptive. I would like a Scotch, a house blend would do, thank you. Oh, and with ice only, please."

"Very good, sir." The young man slowly turned to go, his gaze momentarily lingering on the Recruiter.

"That was totally out of protocol! Are you crazy? Jerking him like that," declared Jimbo.

"Yes, yes I know..." his partner said, casually looking over the menu. "I think I will have the steak tonight. And you?"

"I'm waiting to hear the specials, or can you sense them for me?"

His partner slowly looked up over the top of his menu.

"Okay, okay...lighten up, for God's sake," Jimbo said. "You're too serious sometimes. You have to relax once in a while. You said it yourself, you can't pick up on him because you're tired and hungry. Give your Level 8 self a break now and then."

Jimbo's partner only partially listened. This Level 5 Tel, assigned to him just under a year ago, served his needs, but what he really needed was someone on his own level. Someone like his old partner. Now that Indian could hunt.

"Here you go, gentlemen," the young man interrupted, "a draft of our best beer, locally brewed, I might add. And a Scotch for you, sir." He set both drinks down and pulled out his netpad. "Tonight, we have a roasted duck, altered to your special tastes, and the fish is developed from the finest biofarms in Canada. Both come with an asparagus salad and roasted corn from an actual soil farm not too far from here. All of our foods, gentlemen, come with their genetic seals, assurance of their purity and flavor."

"I will have your filet, young man, and please prepare it the old-fashioned way. You do have an actual flame grill?" Jimbo's partner asked.

"Oh, yes sir, we do. Probably the only one in the area!"

"That is what I was told. And my friend will have?..."

"I'll have the fish," Jimbo said. "What does it simulate?"

"It will be swordfish tonight. It's especially good, if I do say so. I programmed it myself."

"Great, I'll have that!"

"Very good, I'll have your salads out in a moment." He turned and headed toward the kitchen while entering the order into his netpad.

"I don't know," Jimbo said. "He doesn't seem that special to me."

"You might be right on this one, James. Then again, he could be The Infinite Tel. We never really know at first sense, do we?"

"The Infinite Tel? Have you been drinking?" Jimbo asked. "Oh, I guess you are."

They both laughed as they leaned back and took sips from their drinks.

~

Jimbo's partner had been trained to believe there were no Tels greater than him. All Level 8's were. And this training was effective. As a young Tel entering the Agency, he had been separated from the general group. They had said he was special. Unique. And they had a reason to cull him from his peers. His level was well-suited for "certain" assignments. Only later would he find their true use for his uniqueness. But by then, it would be too late.

"Hey," Jimbo said, "when we get back to the Agency, I'm going to take a little time off. How ,bout you?"

"I do not believe I will."

"All work and no play makes for a dull Tel..."

"Yes, well, I have a certain commitment with the Agency."

"Yeah, what's up with that anyway? You're always referencing 'your commitment.'" Jimbo mockingly gestured quotations with his hands.

"Get to my level and you will understand."

"Here you go," the young man said, returning suddenly. "Only the finest in natural soil-grown salads. The dirt in this area is some of the cleanest we've ever scanned."

"Say," Jimbo inquired, "who has the bioknowledge to create these dishes? I thought this kind of food was reserved for New York or Tokyo?"

"We're asked that all the time. Actually I'm the one. This is my restaurant. I'm so sorry, I'm Jonathan Kortel. I'm principle partner and head chef. Many of the dishes here are my own personal coding." He shook Jimbo's hand, but stopped at his partner's. "Have we met before?"

"No, young man, I do not believe we have," he answered.

Jonathan hesitated. He reached to take the senior Tel's hand, and an arc of static electricity jumped between them just before their hands met. They held for a moment, each man curiously studying the other.

"Well, enjoy your salads," Jonathan said nervously. "Monis will bring you your entrees." He summoned a young, bald, street urchin of a girl to their table. He spoke quietly into her ear and rushed off to the kitchen. This time, he didn't work the crowd.

The kitchen...3

"**JONATHAN**, you look like you just saw a ghost!" declared Toto, the sous chef.

"Or he just saw my ex-wife!" answered Hector, the big Mexican who held reign over Kitchen Kortel.

Jonathan smiled and reverted to being an owner. "Yeah, that's real damn funny, Hector. How many tables are left? Let's hustle it up people, we've got five eight-tops and twelve four-tops, solid."

Jonathan wasn't worried, though. He and Hector went back. Their days of trial in the trendy cafe scene had given them their chops. Those early years had been rough, and to prove it, Hector boasted the burn scars no bioderm could regenerate. They developed a symbiotic relationship. One couldn't perform without the other. Jonathan knew the code and could crack it to make a dish special. But Hector had the magic to bring hydro-grown biopaste to a level that was beyond food. It was art. Tired of working the in-today, gone-tomorrow pace of big city restaurants, they decided to strike out on their own.

Jonathan had inherited talent for writing code and the delicate encryptions necessary to develop complex food algorithms from his parents. They had been independent research scientists working on the island of Hawaii's alarming loss of plant life. Yet, Jonathan didn't really need to work. The settlement from their death and the money left to him by his grandparents meant he could have slid through life. But that wasn't his way.

For his part, Hector had grown up in the streets outside the largest urban center on the planet, Mexico City. His father was a chef, as his grandfather was before him. And little Hector had been groomed to be a chef, but a chef of the new era in food. The bio era. Hector had the talent, but it was evident early on that his promise lay on the organic side, not the biotech side. He amazed even the old chefs of the city, mastering dishes that would have taken others years to learn. Eschewing the traditional route through the famous culinary school El Mercardo, Hector began at the bottom, saying if it had been good for his grandfather, it was good for him. He worked his way up through the ranks, struggled in the toughest of kitchens, and learned what it was like to create the traditional foods of his country. The old way. The original way. How can you develop foods, he would ask, in the bio form if you don't know what it's supposed to look like, smell like and, above all, taste like? To create them with your hands. To smell the chorizo under your fingernails and feel the sting of the jalapeño in your eyes. He had learned the foundation of his country's foods, and it made him proud.

Jonathan and Hector had built Kortel's into a Chicago landmark: the place to go for a food experience you could only get this side of a flight to Hong Kong or London. Their clients were loyal, and they spread the word of the two young men who had created a fusion between bio and food. But tonight, Hector sensed something wrong.

"You okay there, Jonathan?" Hector asked. "You don't look so good."

"Yeah. I just feel weird. Kinda tingly all over."

"You just need to be laid...and by my sister!" said Enrique, Hector's line chef, right hand and cousin.

The kitchen burst into laughter like a group of sailors who were riding. It was at these times Jonathan felt the techno chasm between himself and the men who turned his coding into a dining experience. Even Hector, who had shared so much with him, gave him that "you-couldn't-be-here-without-us" look. But that was rare. And as quickly as Jonathan had sensed it, Hector's deep voice returned the kitchen to business.

"Come on, *vatos*, we have art to make!" And the kitchen snapped back into its synchronized rhythm.

~

"This was a good day, eh, Jonathan?" Hector asked.

"What...yeah, it was Hector, it was..." Jonathan said distractedly while he tapped his netpad to enter the customer codes for the night's tally.

"You should get back into the kitchen. You were very good at one time," the big Mexican said softly.

Jonathan looked up pensively. He did need to get back to the essence of his craft. "Maybe I do, Hector, but who would run this place? It can't run itself, unless you got a spare hundred million lying around. Then it could, and we could just sit back at the bar and relax."

Hector laughed. The restaurant was quiet. The crew was beginning to clean up, and some of the regulars were still at the bar, waiting to be shooed out like cattle from a holding pen.

Just then a scream came from the kitchen that would drain the blood from any soul. It was Enrique. Both Hector and Jonathan knew the sound. A kitchen is a dangerous place. Hector heard his blood cousin's pain and swung around, navigating his large frame through the maze of stacked chairs and tables. Jonathan was at his heels.

"*Chinga tu madre!* I'm on fire, man!" Enrique screamed. The grease he was cleaning had caught fire, and the flames had jumped to the sleeve of his shirt.

Hector burst into the kitchen and reached for one of the extinguishers. Callis, the night washer, grabbed for the other one across the kitchen. By now, flames had engulfed the shirt and, with it, Enrique's upper body.

"Aurgh, my face! My face!" Enrique yelled in that guttural tone instinctually recognized at the primal level. He desperately tried to escape, violently twisting in place, trapped between the antique grill and the prep island. His hands banged out an eerie sound as they flailed against the pots suspended from the ceiling.

"My cousin, I'm here!" Hector yelled. Both he and Callis raised their extinguishers in sync, their fingers dancing across the system pads to program the grease setting. They lunged toward Enrique, but instantly recoiled. The flames leaped from his body and tore away what was left of his shirt. Enrique crouched down, thinking he was now fully engulfed, while the ball of fire hung suspended in the air, roaring as it consumed the shirt. Then, like some cheap magic trick, the flames vanished in a small puff of smoke. Hector and Callis stared dumbstruck, their extinguishers at the ready. Enrique was still crouching and flailing at the phantom flames.

"Help me, goddamn it, don't just stand there!"

"Stand up, my cousin," Hector said slowly. "You're not on fire anymore." The night washer crossed himself, said a Hail Mary and slowly backed out of the kitchen.

Enrique picked himself up and looked himself over for burned skin. "Qué paso?"

"I don't know," Hector said, embracing his cousin in one of his Hector hugs. "Are you all right?"

"I think my arm is burned a little." He quickly rolled his arm over to view the blisters the flames had left behind.

"Jonathan!" Hector barked. "Get the bioderm from the med kit...Jonathan?"

They all turned to see Jonathan standing like a statue at the wash station, staring blankly into the middle of the kitchen. His eyes were bright and wildly open, and his right hand was clenched as if in severe pain. A little trail of blood flowed from his right nostril.

"Jonathan?..." Hector said uncertainly, taking a step toward him.

Jonathan snapped back to the moment. He grabbed his head, his mind numb with pain, and stumbled forward, almost falling into Hector's arms.

"Oh, shit..." he groaned.

"Jonathan? Callis, get the bioderm, now!"

"Don't!" Jonathan yelled. "I'm okay. I'm okay...I'll go get it!"

Jonathan pushed away from Hector, averting his face and wiping the blood from his lip. Hector looked at Jonathan, then back to his cousin, then back to Jonathan, who was now coming around the prep station with the biomed kit.

"What the hell is going on here?" Hector demanded.

Jonathan looked up from attending to Enrique's burns. "You need to go to the hospital," he said quietly to Enrique. Hector was still standing by the wash station with his hands on his hips.

"Callis, can you take Enrique to the hospital?" Jonathan asked.

Callis just stood in the doorway in shock.

"Hector, will you tell him!" Jonathan demanded, and Hector said something only the other Mexican could understand.

Callis grabbed Enrique by the arm and led him out of the kitchen. Hector spoke to the washer, who nodded his head and disappeared out the back door.

After years of working with these men, Jonathan had learned a little Spanish. But what Hector had said escaped him. "What was that all about?"

"Nothing, Jonathan, nothing..."

"Nothing my ass. What did you say to him?"

"I said 'quit acting like you've seen the devil, you Catholic shit, and take him to the hospital.'"

"The devil?"

"Yes, the devil!"

"I...I..."

"I'm not the devil?" Hector offered.

"Yes, I'm definitely not the devil!" Jonathan slumped on the stool by the prep station. "But I don't know what I am," he said under his breath.

"Jonathan, what are you saying?"

"I don't know, Hector....What was that?"

"How should I know! An act of God? A miracle? Why, what do you think?"

It was hard for Jonathan to speak about it. All his life he had experienced these little "episodes." These magic tricks. The pencil in third grade. The book thrown at his mom. The recycle truck with Tarris. The elevator ride with the girl in New York.

"It can't be me," Jonathan said in anguish. Anger filled his eyes as he held back the deep realization of what was happening. "This is not me, goddamn it!"

A glass jar filled with their finest soil-grown herbs exploded on the prep shelf. Hector jumped as the glass shards ricocheted about the kitchen. Jonathan never looked up. His mind was too focused.

Hector put his hand on his friend's shoulder. "Jonathan, it's impossible. You're not some freak, man. Enrique just threw the shirt off in his struggle, and it burned up before our eyes. I've seen this kind of shit on the TVids."

Jonathan continued to stare.

"I told that asshole Gonzalez not to pressure those jars too tight," Hector said. He glared back toward the shelf. "Shit, I'll get him to clean this up in the morning. Let's go get a drink, partner."

~

It was past two in the morning when Hector and Jonathan pulled up to the bar, having said nothing to each other the whole way over. The argon sign flashed "Blind Monkey." They walked to the front door, which was padded with riveted red vinyl and, as Jonathan reached, swung out to meet him. Hector didn't notice. Jonathan just smiled. They pushed though the crowd of street smack, tech workers, market jockeys and young riders. They squeezed to the bar and secured a space amongst the night dead.

"Oban," Hector said. "And I'll take a Tequila Screw, Caesar."

Caesar grinned. He knew their drinks, because they were his regulars, kind of celebs in their business.

"Tough day, boys?" he asked, wiping a clean glass for the Scotch.

Jonathan said nothing and continued to stare into the mirror behind the bar.

"I'll say," Hector answered. "How's business been?"

"Crazy," Caesar said. "It's this weather. Brings them in every time."

"I love it!" Hector yelled, and he threw back his tequila. "Jonathan, come on. You haven't said two words. Have your drink and let's forget about it."

"Guess you're right. Sorry, Hector. What am I thinking?" Jonathan laughed and sipped his Scotch. He studied his reflection in the mirror. He knew what he was thinking.

He was a freak.

One week later...4

"**GOOD** morning, gentlemen."

The Unit Director's in a good mood, thought Jimbo.

"So our little girl wasn't who we thought?" he asked them.

"No, I do not think she had the potential," Jimbo's partner said, casually looking out the window.

"Well," replied the director, opening a new file pad, "it's better to be cautious and right than expeditious and wrong."

"Yes, sir," Jimbo chimed. Both Level 8's just looked at him.

"Let's forget about her for the moment, shall we? We have something else to discuss." He spun the file pad around to face the two Recruiters.

Jimbo was pissed. He needed a break and was tired of being hostage to his partner's "commitment" to the Agency.

"We have a special case for you boys. This is Jonathan Kortel." The file pad's screen displayed a vid of Jonathan going about his business: working with a customer, buying supplies at the markets, entering his home. A gravitational flux level was displayed that tracked to the vid like a time code.

Jimbo whistled. "Man, this boy's grav flux is off the chart. Say!" he said. He leaned closer to the vid screen. "This is the guy from the restaurant we were at." He slapped his partner's shoulder.

"Yes he is," the Unit Director said. His eyes narrowed at the senior Tel. "You had a sensing there, didn't you?"

"Yes, Stewart, I did."

"And your report says this was a different sensing than for the usual Potential. "Yes..."

"What does your gut say?"

The Unit Director preferred this phrase, even though the gut was hardly the organ that did the sensing. Jimbo's partner hated it.

"My gut says we need to try one of Mr. Kortel's specials again. He is quite a chef. My meal was excellent. And yours, James?"

"Yeah, fine...but sir, I didn't get a feel for this guy being all that special."

His partner cracked a grin.

"And why was that, Jim?" the Unit Director asked.

Jimbo froze for a second. "Just a feeling...sir."

"Excellent, Jim. Keep working on your Sense. We're going to get you to a Level 6, I know it," he said mockingly. "Now take this and study it. I want you two in the field by the end of the week. That will be all."

Both Recruiters rose from their chairs.

"Please stay..." he directed Jimbo's partner.

"I'll see you at the terminal, James," his partner said. Jimbo nodded and closed the door on the way out.

The Unit Director gestured for him to sit back down.

"What do you think...what do you really think?" he asked the senior Tel.

"I think, Stewart, we have a Potential here." His disinfor-mation was calculated, because he had left out just a little bit of data in his report. He had sensed Jonathan right from the start. Usually his seventh sense would pick up the "effect." But as soon as he had entered the restaurant, it wasn't just his seventh sense that felt the pulse; it was more like his entire being reacted to a sudden shift – a shift that was deep, rich and different. Almost on a genetic level. Not like anything he had ever felt or sensed before. This wasn't the usual electromagnetic field displacements of the typical Potential. This was...harmonic.

Like music.

"So you don't think we have something special here? Look at his readings, like his Field Flux. My God, look at his APT Waves!" The Unit Director spun the file pad around mentally.

The senior Tel snapped the lid of the file pad shut. He raised it until it was level with the Unit Director's face and moved it against his nose, pressing him back against his chair.

"No, I do not think we do," he said, hands still folded. "But if you insist, Stewart, I will take this child you have assigned me, and we will discover what is really going on in Chicago."

"Good," the Unit Director said in a nasal voice. "Now get going!"

The senior Tel slowly rose from his seat, lit a cigarette and calmly strolled out of the room. When the door clicked shut, the file pad dropped into the Unit Director's lap.

Liquid Courage...5

MORE than two weeks had passed since the incident in the kitchen. Callis had resigned, but this was *no problema*, since there were plenty of other desperate men and women who needed Hector's pity. Even though the U.S. and Mexico had merged years ago, the Rio Grande might just as well be an ocean for those without status. The social and economic imbalances that had widened the gulf between the two countries was predicted to disappear with the creation of the super nation. Instead, things remained the same as they had for centuries. The Biolution did not reach the third world, much less the second, as fast as it had engulfed the first. By the time biotechnology had reached the interior of Mexico, the former United States was decades ahead. Hector wanted to close the gap, one person at a time.

The kitchen had begun to treat Jonathan differently, and Hector had noticed. It wasn't that they feared him. It wasn't even that they believed the rumor that he had floated while eating the flames with his mind. No, it was that there had always been a bond between the bioprogrammer and his army. Now, the troops were worried that their general was changing, and they didn't understand how or why.

The night had begun as a typical night. The four-top by the fireplace complained about the service. The sous chef almost cut off his finger. The biofridges were at 60 percent limit. The new hostess had overbooked the eight o'clock hour, and the city food inspector was entertaining his girlfriend without noticing his wife in booth number five.

"Jonathan, you know it's Enrique's birthday today?" Hector quizzed while he put the finish on the last Saffron Salmon for the night.

"Oh shit," Jonathan said, embarrassed. "That's right. What's going on after close?"

Hector's broad smile said it all. "What else? Liquid, my friend...Liquid!"

~

Liquid Courage was the place for out-of-town conventioneers to play, the hot-wired salesman to close the deal, or anyone who had the available cash to entertain the sexiest women the city could offer. Part Vegas show club, part sex bar and part oasis to the rich; to play the Liquid life took money, lots of money, because its girls were pros. Every military boy riding or bachelor saying farewell to his freedom paid homage at its doors. And that was just to get in. Once inside, true players went straight for The Den. The Den was the gate to empyrean. If you had the cash, you lived your dreams.

Usually Enrique and the boys stayed on the main floor, where the circus of sin was choreographed and monitored. But tonight, the crew of Kitchen Kortel wanted a deeper drink of the Liquid life.

"To The Den, *cabrones*!" Enrique raised his fist and the troops followed.

Jonathan hung back, soaking in the energy of the main floor. Dancers were spinning or hanging, and the whole place undulated to the intense bass rhythms of the latest chart risers from Africa, Cuba and the Pacific Rim. Liquid Courage was like a circus gone horribly wrong. It occupied the space between reality and fantasy. Beautiful women hung in the air, their bodies floating, and nothing more than crystal sequins covered what the imagination already had seen. The floor dancers intertwined themselves around men and women who where either riding or drunk. Everyone's chip cards had already been swiped at the door, so freedom ruled.

"Gentlemen, do we have reservations?" the Den's doorman yelled over TransDust, a recent German import from the Euroclub scene.

"Yes, we do. It's under Kortel!" Enrique screamed back, as VIPs with dancers slid past them through the door.

The doorman studied his netpad and snapped it shut. "First timers," he cooed at the Den's bouncer, whose sex was up for debate. They kissed and coolly looked at Enrique, whose attention was captured by their ever-changing, living tattoos.

"Welcome to the Den, gentlemen. Anari is waiting. She will show you to your table." His pale hand passed over the door's small antique lion head knocker. A hot beam of light streamed from the knocker to the knob, and the door slowly swung open.

Inside the Den, the music changed. The hard-driving sounds of TransDust fell away as Anari closed the door. The Den was carved out of what appeared to be solid rock, which even felt cool and damp to the touch. But it couldn't have been. They were 40 stories above the ground.

"Gentlemen, pleasssse," Anari said. She hung on the "S" to reveal a wicked smile. Her small Asian frame was wrapped in what appeared to be traditional Japanese silks, but as she moved the silks reconstituted to leave open areas of mesh shaped as animals. A tiger gave away a glimpse of her neck, an elephant her inner thigh, and a snake, her dark nipples. Biofabric. Living, programmable cloth that could reform its shape at the whim of the wearer. "Custom" was the word for retail. If you couldn't change for the customer, let the product do it for you.

"Here you are, gentlemen." She directed them to a large booth just off the Den's main stage. Jonathan slipped her his chipcard.

"Thank you, but no. Everything in the Den was taken care of when you entered Liquid Courage." She raised a plastic eyebrow and gently placed the chipcard back into Jonathan's hand.

"Tara will be right over to get your orders...enjoyyy." And again she hung on the "Y" as a crane transformed into a water buffalo and exposed a perfect set of breasts. Jonathan put his card away while she and her "porno kimono" disappeared into the recesses of the Den.

"Now that's service. Could she come work for us?" Toto asked.

Jonathan smiled. The Den had a deep rhythmic hum. The music laid like a thick blanket over the muffled conversations, and it was hard to make out where one ended and the other began. Oriental businessmen drank their sake while skinny topless Asian girls massaged their necks or whatever else their yen could buy. Jonathan could see that the Den was for the elite. The booths were a virtual library of the city's who's who. Carlos Souza, known for his aggressive soccer style, was holding court with four bioenhanced blondes who acted delighted to see him yet scanned the Den for their next victims. Mega-businessman Custus Carter was deep in conversation with a redhead with electric blue skin, who occasionally came up for air. Carrie Straw, a TVid news reader and underground bisexual, was still in her on-air makeup (not that she would stand out here). And Mayhem, former rock netstar turned sleazy netporn producer, was sporting his signature vintage kilt, crushed straw cowboy hat and sim-eel boots. He was busy riding the curve with his main girl chained to what was once his best asset.

How did I miss all this? Jonathan asked himself.

"Gentlemen, you're dry," Tara, a pretty little he/she announced, flipping open his/her netpad as he/she approached their booth. "Wait, I know what men like you need....You are men?"

They looked at each other and nodded.

"A Bucket of Sin!" he/she sang.

"Well, all right!" yelled Enrique." It is my birthday, god-damn it!"

"I see..." purred Tara. He/she reached over and grabbed his crotch. "You are a man." The men from Kitchen Kortel burst into howls and took turns reaching for Enrique's crotch, only to be batted desperately away.

On the stage, a lone dancer slowly swayed to the rough beat of Desperate Sense, a group that had been ahead of their time but never received much netplay. *What an odd choice for dance music,* Jonathan thought. The girl wrapped herself around the pole, pulled her legs up and locked her ankles together. She leaned back as casually as if she were sinking into her favorite chair and hung there upside down, alone, while Desperate Sense moaned its electric lament. She shifted her gaze to stare at Jonathan with that "I caught you" look and smiled softly, which caused her cheeks to push her eyes almost shut. She righted herself and swung down, ending perfectly in time with the song. Collecting her things from the stage, she stood up to unveil a tall, lean frame with proportional breasts and muscular legs. She rotated her shoulders back, looked about the room and slowly walked to the bar. Something about her gait intrigued Jonathan. It was predacious, almost sexual – like a cat stalking its prey.

When she reached the bar, a tall man in a sharply cut suit wrapped his arm around her waist and spoke into her ear. She pulled herself around him to face Jonathan's booth, but kept her face buried in the man's neck. The presentation of the Bucket of Sin distracted him for a moment. He grabbed his glass and turned back to find the dancer still listening to her mark, but looking right at him. Her curly blonde hair fell over her eyes like a wispy veil. She kissed the man's neck, her eyes never leaving Jonathan's. Suddenly self-aware, he quickly jerked his attention back to the table, which was deep into its third birthday toast. Girls were circling like ravenous vultures. He raised his glass to toast when he felt someone nestle beside him in the booth. It was the dancer. She didn't say a word, but motioned for him to finish.

"To Enrique," he declared. "One lucky *chinga el madre!*"

He felt her lean to his ear. "It's *chinga tu madre,*" she whispered, and then squeezed his arm almost affectionately.

He turned while sipping his drink, brushing up against her curls and coming face to face with her. She didn't pull back. She held her gaze. Jonathan was transfixed by her blue eyes. Blue eyes that she was born with, as far as he could tell. In fact, there didn't appear to be anything bioenhanced about her at all.

"Hello..." she started.

"Sorry...Hello. I'm Jonathan. And you are?..."

"I'm Nicki." She smiled, and her upper lip curled to expose a little gum above her teeth. She quickly corrected it and introduced a new smile. A model's fake smile, but pretty nonetheless. "This is my club smile..." she said, posing.

"I think I prefer the real smile," Jonathan said.

Taken aback, her smile disappeared and slowly returned as it first appeared. "Really? I don't look too gummy?" She laughed and cleared her throat with a small cough. She took a drag from her cigarette.

Pity, Jonathan thought, *so young, so pretty, and she's already going to need bioregeneration for her lungs.*

She blew her smoke up out of the booth. "First time?" she asked.

"To the Den, yes, but not to Liquid."

"Oh, great..."

"Your music, what an unusual selection."

"Desperate Sense? I love them. They were so far out front." She lit another cigarette. "You don't mind, do you?"

"No," Jonathan lied.

"I know it's a nasty habit, but I figure I can always get regen'd."

The glow of the lighter filled her face, and Jonathan saw for the first time how pretty she really was. A natural beauty. Not created at the hands of a biosurgeon.

"Let's down another Bucket!" she declared to the table, and the men cheered in approval.

"So how long have you been dancing?" Jonathan asked.

"You mean here, or total?"

"Total..."

"About five years..."

"How old are you...if I may ask?"

"How old are you?" she snapped back.

"Twenty-nine."

"Twenty-one," she whispered.

"You've been dancing since you were sixteen?"

"Shhh...I don't usually tell people that just because of that reaction."

"No, it's okay. I don't have any agenda. Just surprised."

"Are you from here?"

"No, I was born..." (*here it comes,* Jonathan thought) "...in Hawaii."

"Really..." she said, her mind already skipping past this small talk she had heard a million times before. Then it hit her, and she slowly turned to meet his look. She put out her cigarette and slid closer to him. She tilted her head as seriousness filled her face. Her eyes asked if he was all right, and he read them. She never said a word.

"I'm okay, really." But he wasn't. It was a general fact that Jonathan and the millions of survivors of the "event" would receive the world's grief till the generations were gone.

~

The event happened on a beautiful spring day in the islands of Hawaii. The islands woke up and went through their workday morning routine. Then at precisely noon, one million Hawaiians, tourists and military personnel (not to mention all animal, plant and aquatic life within a 300-mile radius) were vaporized. Or, more accurately, debiolized. This was the new term that became the word of the moment, probably of the century. Most people still clung to the old term, vaporized. They just couldn't wrap their minds around the idea that a bomb didn't blast. That there was no mushroom cloud, no rain of fire, no vaporizing of anything. Like an ice cream sundae on a hot afternoon, the congealing of matter that was once the Hawaiian Islands horrified the world and stumped scientists. They didn't really know what the people experienced. All matter simply began reforming. Or, as the TVids news analysts termed it, merging. Jonathan often wondered if the terrorists really knew what they were doing, or, worse yet, what they were creating. Even today, after years of analysis by the world's best scientific minds, everything on the islands (including his parents) was part of a giant biological sundae in the middle of the Pacific Ocean. A sundae that was still melting.

~

"I...I'm sorry..." she said and gently touched his knee.

He looked down at her hand and felt something he hadn't felt in a long time.

Compassion.

"Hey," she said, changing the moment, "wanna dance?"

From so close, Jonathan could see that her makeup was soft, not harsh like the other dancers. "Yes, I'd like that," he answered.

She took his hand and slowly pulled him from the booth. The men of Kitchen Kortel all "ooohed" as they left. She led him past other dark booths, filled with desperate patrons and hungry girls, to the last bar, which was dormant. It was used only for those parties where status was your invitation. On the way, he watched her stride with her shoulders pulled tight. The small of her lower back and the tops of her legs met in the most perfect ass Jonathan had ever seen. She looked back. Her face was serious, and her eyes were slits. But she wasn't smiling this time. She was a pro, and she meant business. She placed him in a large over-stuffed wingback and pushed him against the wall. Gently spreading his legs with her feet, she picked up right with the music. She first pulled her top over her head, letting her breasts bounce lightly with the beat. Then she turned and slid off her skirt, her soft skin an inch from Jonathan's chin. Spinning around she leaned over him, letting her hair fall over his head and face. She licked his ear and pressed her whole body against him. Jonathan didn't look at her breasts or any other part of her, as most marks do. He didn't grab or grope like the frat boys riding high on Jack. He delicately traced the curves of her body, with his focus on one thing.

Her crystal blue eyes.

A handful of times in her thousands of dances, a mark had played it cool. But even they were nothing compared to this one. Something in this one unnerved her, but intrigued her, too. He seemed into her, not her body. As she danced, she pressed and rubbed in sync to his touches. It was like they were dancing together, if that were possible for a stripper and her mark. The music stopped with their faces almost touching. They held for a moment, and then she leaned in and kissed him on the mouth, breaking her first rule (not to mention five of the city's).

Jonathan kissed back, and when he did, he felt a strange energy course through his body. She squeezed his hand.

"Hey you..." he whispered.

She slowly opened her eyes. He could sense that she had felt it, too. She smiled, but not the model smile. Just a small smile. The woman, not the dancer, was looking back.

"That was..." she replied, parting her lips just slightly as if to say something, yet holding back.

"Wonderful," Jonathan finished.

"Yes," she said. "Yes it was....What's your last name?"

"Kortel. And yours?" he asked softly.

"Tamara...Tamara Connor," she said, breaking the second of her rules.

They both waited, wondering.

"Well!" she said, going professional on him. "Welcome..." she leaned close to his face and whispered, "...to the Den, Mr. Kortel." She lightly kissed him again.

The music started up again.

~

When they returned to the booth, the men of Kitchen Kortel were in full swing. The music was pumping out harsh techno trash direct from the streets of Tel Aviv, and there were empty silver buckets strewn over the table. Half-naked girls were sprawled, standing or dancing, and the men were feeling no pain.

"I need to go freshen up," Tamara said. She let her hand fall from his.

"See you in a sec?" Jonathan asked.

"Yeahhh..." She held onto the "H" like she had just created that response custom for him.

Jonathan fell into the booth almost on top of Hector, who was halfway to the floor with a German/Latino fusion girl who couldn't stop giggling.

"God help me, don't tell my wife!" he pleaded to Jonathan.

"Don't worry," Jonathan assured. "What goes on here..." and the men answered in chorus, "...stays here!" Their roar of laughter shook the Den.

A sec turned into minutes. Jonathan looked around, but Tamara was gone. He slammed the last of his drink, got up to leave and continued to glance about the Den.

"Give her up, Jonathan," Hector said, barely conscious. "Take it from me, I know these type." And he did.

Jonathan shrugged at Hector, high-fived his men, at least those who could still raise their arms, and walked toward the Den's exit. The door opened without his request, and on the other side the doorman now worked a long line of young, drunk quarry. Jonathan scanned the club one last time for Tamara. The main floor was wall-to-wall press-the-flesh. As he neared the exit, he felt a hand slip a card into his front pants pocket.

"Call me," Tamara whispered, breaking her last and most important rule.

Tamara Connor...6

"**TODAY?!**" Jimbo yelled as he washed the three-hour flight off his face. His partner emerged from the stall.

"What is your hurry, James? We are going to take our time with this one."

"At least he has a profession we can enjoy. Remember that hydro-service guy? God, that place stank. Three months to find he's nothing but a damn fraud."

The two Recruiters left the airport and headed toward Jonathan's apartment.

"Did you pack the new gravscanner?" his partner asked as they entered the Interway.

"Yeah, and the Agency said to be careful with it. It's still a beta model."

"Excellent. We should be able to define his field ratio quite accurately now."

They slipped through the city, again reviewing Jonathan's preliminary data, searching for the footprint of the gift. All good Recruiters knew the drill. A Potential must be investigated thoroughly. Set-up begins by establishing a base. Jimbo had chosen a small hotel a block from Jonathan's loft. From there, they could monitor him almost without leaving the base. Biotechnology had created a cluster of equipment so sensitive it made surveillance virtually indetectable. But his partner preferred a different method. The old-fashioned way.

He called it hunting.

~

"It is the hunt, James, that makes recruiting interesting."

"I have to agree with you, partner." Jimbo said. He emptied the equipment case. "Don't get me wrong. I love this proprietary high-tech gear we get to play with. But the hunt is the best part. Especially when a Potential has the gift."

"That is an extraordinary moment, is it not?" his partner said. He methodically began transferring his clothes from suitcase to closet.

"The look on their faces when they discover what they really are...it's..."

"Rewarding, James?" his partner finished.

"Yeah, rewarding. I remember when they first told me. It was like a weight was lifted off my shoulders. And you know what else? For the first time, you feel like you've found your family. I know it's weird, but growing up, you have a sense that you're not really a part of the rest of the population. Know what I mean?"

"Exactly," his partner said, stopping the routine of setting up base. "They never understand, do they?"

They were the friends and family all Tels left behind. Tels would be "disconnected" from their families, according to the situation. The Agency had fingers throughout the information net, so that just about any disconnection could be backed up with the appropriate cover. Or, if the subject was a child, the arrogance of the Agency dictated that he or she just disappeared, only to find their holofaces on the side of milk containers. And in appropriate situations, the Agency could even fake a person's death. All in the name of the greater good. Once the gravity of their situation had sunk in, most new Potentials never looked back. Why should they? They weren't human; they were a new species. Humanlike, but not like them.

The Agency became your family.

"How about you? How did they disconnect you?" Jimbo asked.

"I was different," his partner reflected.

Forty years ago, Jimbo's partner had been singled out, like all Level 8 Potentials were. The Agency conducted tests that could calculate the current and potential level of any Tel. His partner was the highest ever recorded. Of course this information was restricted, even within the Agency. A Tel who displayed such a high-level potential was culled from the group to begin a different path than others in their class. And one as high as his partner was special, indeed.

Back then the world was a dangerous place. The Biolution was beginning, the third world felt cheated, and the key to the Arab cartel's power was threatened. The Agency saw a need for a special corps of men and women who could exercise their power for the security of the world. It was their duty to protect their human cousins from themselves. And if that meant that certain situations demanded difficult solutions, then the Agency had the answer. The perfect weapon for an imperfect world. It was kept secret from most in the Agency and hidden from other branches of government, but in an emergency these squads would be dispatched, always in twos. A foreign dignitary's brain hemorrhages at a state function. He collapses and dies before he hits the floor. A diplomat has a seizure at the signing of a weapons treaty. Simple. Clean. Perfect. Jimbo's partner had been one of the best.

"I was disconnected at a young age, James. My mother and father were poor. To them...I was killed in an accident."

"Oh...I'm sorry," Jimbo said, turning his attention back to the equipment.

"No need, James. They were better off because of it. I would have been too much for them to understand. My father was just a farmer." At that, his partner slowly closed his suitcase. "Well," he said, straightening his tie. "Let us go pay a visit to

Kortel's fine dining. Shall we?"

~

Jonathan reviewed the room from the kitchen. The two guys in black coats at the front door looked very familiar. He flipped Tamara's card through his fingers, reflecting on what Hector had said. It was slow, and they were going to lose some money tonight.

"Hector, can you close by yourself tonight?" Jonathan asked over his shoulder.

"Yes, yes...go and get it out of your system, my friend," Hector answered.

Jonathan turned around to see the big Mexican shaking his knife at him. Enrique sang a made-up Liquid Courage song under his breath.

Hector walked over. "Jonathan, she's just a stripper...probably got a kid..."

"...or two!" Enrique chimed in.

"Shut the hell up!" Hector snapped.

"It's Mr. Shut the Hell Up to you!" Enrique laughed.

"Yeah, yeah, whatever. Jonathan, seriously, do you really want to get involved with a girl like this? Take it from me, my friend, there're two types of dancers – ones that are screwed up and ones that are more screwed up. You with me?"

"I know, don't worry. I just want to have a little fun, that's all. I'll see ya in the morning." He slapped Hector in the chest with the back of his hand and headed out.

~

When Jonathan entered Liquid Courage it was oddly slow, but he had never been there before two in the morning. The main floor was sparsely filled with an odd juxtaposition of military and business types. He made his way to the Den, only to find the vampiresque doorman was nowhere around. He parked himself at the back bar and ordered a drink.

"Slow tonight?" he questioned the bar back. The kid turned to display a novel assortment of rings that interlocked through piercings in his head. He sounded like a wind chime when he spoke.

"Yeah, for a Tuesday, I guess. It'll pick up in an hour." He tossed the glass he had been cleaning over his head and caught it behind his back.

Jonathan was just getting settled when a finger dragged lightly across the back of his shoulders. He twisted around to find Tamara next to him. Her hair was straight and her makeup harsh. She wore a sexy evening dress cut to her navel, and the spiked dog collar added an odd 20th-century touch. Her hand came to rest on his.

"Hey, you..." she said.

"Hey," he replied. "Nice hair."

"You like?"

"Yes," he lied.

"So, what brings you to Club Liquid?" She smiled, and the harshness of her makeup softened.

He leaned closer and smiled back. "What do you think?"

"To see little ol' me?" she asked in her best Southern twang, putting her finger to her chin.

"Yes," he said seriously, slowly losing his smile.

Her smile shrank as well, and she adopted his demeanor like a mirror. Matching his seriousness, she tilted her head and slowly parted her lips. She pulled his hands up with hers and held them tight to her chest. "I was hoping you'd come back, Jonathan." She tugged him off the chair, towards the Den. With a wave of her hand over the knocker, she sent the beam of light dancing, and the door swung open. There was no one in the Den tonight.

"Anari sweetie, number 12?" she inquired.

Anari spread her arms and bowed, her ninja outfit hugging her small frame. "The Den is yours," she said, her mask muffling her voice.

Tamara led Jonathan by the hand deep into the Den to number 12. As they slid into the booth, Anari ninjaed through the room, landing by the table as they settled in. "A Crasher for Nicki and a Oban for Jonathan?" Her eyes darted between the two of them.

"Yes," Tamara answered, and Anari left the table.

"How did she know?" Jonathan asked.

"Your profile data is in the system. I'm sure she checked it on her netpad. She's the best. I should know." She raised one eyebrow and giggled.

"I don't want to know," Jonathan said, gesturing.

"Oh, I bet you'd watch." She poked him in the ribs with her finger.

"Hey, cool it, you." He groaned, and she poked him again. He grabbed her finger on the third strike, stopping it dead, and began to twist it.

"Owww..." she squealed.

He pulled her closer. They froze for a moment to take each other in.

"A Crasher for madame," Anari said, suddenly appearing. "And a Scotch with ice for the gentleman. Hiieee!" She ninja kicked her way back to the bar, battling an enemy only she could see.

"Jonathan...what an old name..." Tamara said softly.

"My parents were traditionalists, I think." Jonathan said, still holding onto her finger.

"I like it. It's Biblical. That's rare these days."

He let go of her finger and spread his hand. She answered his request and interlaced her fingers with his, never dropping her attention from him. She could tell that the mention of his parents triggered a stream of unwelcome memories. In his face, she saw the pain of the loss come forward, and she could tell that the wounds were deep. She squeezed his hand tighter.

"Does it hurt...still?" she quietly asked.

"I'd be a liar if I said it doesn't. Hell, it's still on the news almost every damn night."

"Oh, baby..."

She dropped her dancer's wall and touched his face. He turned away, but she brought his face around. Her tender feelings pushed through even the harsh makeup. They sat there quietly as she stroked his face and head. He closed his eyes and leaned into her touch. He felt a lump rising in his throat. A tear began to form at the edge of his eye. His instinct was to tighten up and man-out on her, but the moment felt so right. She felt so right. It had been a long time.

He let the tear fall.

She pretended not to notice.

Just then, the door of the Den burst open, and four fat fake cowboys strode inside, dusting themselves off like they had just brought a herd into Chicago. With a girl on each arm, they piled into the first booth they saw. Jonathan turned away and wiped the tear as if he were simply straightening his hair. The two of them sat up and sipped their drinks.

"So," he said, changing the mood. "What do you do for..." He stopped. Tamara was standing up, and he hadn't noticed that the music had started.

She put her finger to his lips and whispered in his ear. "Shhh, Mr. Kortel. I want you, right now." Her arms crossed her chest, pushing her breasts up and together. Her hands grabbed the sides of her dress and slowly slid it up and over her head. All she wore was a triangle of crystal sequins between her legs. They refracted a small spotlight that was aimed into the booth and sent red, blue and green bits of light to dance across the walls.

Now her makeup makes sense, Jonathan thought.

Her look was serious. Her hips swayed to the rhythm of the song, gradually coming closer and closer until they were grinding him into the back of the booth. She grabbed his hands and led them to her breasts. He pulled back — partly out of club protocol and partly out of fear. She held her grip. Tamara wanted him, and he felt it.

"It's okay, lover," she whispered.

Jonathan looked up at her. His hands followed her thighs to her waist. He pulled her close and gently kissed her breasts to the pace of the slow Latin beat. Then he bit down on one of her nipples, which hardened in his mouth. Her head dropped back and a soft moan escaped.

"Oh, God..." she sighed as she fell forward and kissed the top of his head. Jonathan bit harder. His fingers dug into her skin. She pulled away and kneeled between his legs. Tamara ran her chin down the front of his chest and across his stomach and stopped with her mouth pressing on the firmness in his pants.

It was her turn to bite down.

~

As the eighth song faded, Tamara lifted her head off his chest. She wasn't bothering to dance anymore. They sat in the booth just holding each other, having done about as much as they could without risking major jail time, not to mention a heavy fine.

"What...was..." She stopped herself.

"What, baby?..."

"What was that?" she asked seriously. She really wanted to know, because in all her years as a dancer she had never felt a connection like she had felt tonight.

Jonathan pulled her away and held her there. He knew from her eyes that they weren't "dancer" and "mark" anymore. They were more. Much more. In their passion, he had felt the same strange energy run through his body that he had felt before. She began to speak, but he motioned her to stop. He raised his hand, placed it on her heart, closed his eyes and imagined a ball of white light moving from his own heart, down his arm, through his hand and into her chest.

She jerked a little at the moment he imagined it entering.

He opened his eyes to find her trembling, his hand still at her heart. Her eyes were closed tight. A tear was crawling down her cheek.

"Shhh, it's all right," he whispered.

She fell onto his chest, and he held her tight. He didn't care what Hector said. He didn't care what his men would think. All he knew was that they had a connection he couldn't explain, and he wanted to be with her. Even if it was just for the night, he needed her like a drug addict needs his ride. She was his drug. And he was becoming addicted.

~

"Our specials tonight are roasted squid, bioenhanced for a true deep sea flavor. And..." the waitress flipped open her netpad, "...turkey? Guaranteed...to bring back...the memories of Thanksgiving." She looked up from her pad and shrugged.

"Are you new here, young lady?" Jimbo's partner quizzed.

"Yes sir, I'm sorry. I don't know the system yet. And to tell you the truth," she bent down to confide, "I'm a little nervous, this place being so famous and all."

"It is all right dear, you are doing fine. I will have the turkey."

"And I'll take the squid!" Jimbo announced. His partner looked up, surprised.

"I'm branching out, you said so yourself."

"Good, James, good," the senior Tel said, glancing about. He hailed a passing waiter. "Is Jonathan Kortel in tonight?"

"He was, sir, but he left early," the young waiter said. "May I tell him who was inquiring?"

"No, no, I am just a big fan of his programming."

"We all are, sir. He and Hector are the best."

"Yes, Hector...is he in?"

"Yes, he is. Would you like me to go ask if he has a moment?"

"That would be splendid, thank you." The waiter nodded in approval and hurried off to the kitchen.

"Taking a big risk here, boss," Jimbo warned.

"Sometimes, James, we have to take risks. The reward with this one will be substantial."

Hector, his large frame wrapped in his blood and biopaste-stained apron, sauntered through the restaurant like an Incan emperor. Usually Jonathan met with fans, but tonight, it was Hector's turn to tap his fifteen minutes.

"Gentlemen, welcome to Kortel's!" he bellowed. "I hope you find everything perfect?"

"We do indeed, sir," the senior Tel said, taking control. "This is our second time here."

"Are you in town for business or pleasure?"

"Business."

"Well, we love our loyal customers. What are we having?"

"The specials."

"Ah, good, the turkey is my programming tonight."

The senior Tel shifted in his seat. "And Mr. Kortel, is he off tonight?"

"Yes, he left early. He had a date." Hector chuckled.

"Really, the TVids say he is quite the bachelor catch. But he seems a workaholic..."

"Yes, we rib him for that. All work and no play, you know. But it's paid off." Hector spanned the room with his arms.

"Yes, your restaurant has quite the reputation. Tell me..." (Jimbo watched as his partner lifted one eyebrow, signaling he was about to demonstrate what a Level 8 could really do) "...where would one go if they were on a date?"

"Well...that's really not for me to sa..." Hector stammered. A small drop of sweat traversed his sideburn.

"I am sorry, what was that?" his partner asked, leaning closer.

Jimbo cringed as he watched the senior Tel exercise his level by surgically displacing the air pressure around Hector's head, pinpointing the exact area in the brain where the minimal amount of grav touch would deliver the maximum amount of effect.

"He's seeing someone at Liquid Courage..." Hector's voice trailed off, and he stared blankly into space.

"Oh, that is so wonderful to hear. It is good to see him getting out." The senior Tel released the grav pressure slowly so that Hector wouldn't jerk when the connection was severed.

Hector reached for his forehead, rubbing at the newly implanted pain.

"Are you all right?" the senior Tel inquired.

"Oh yes, this is a tough business. It's just been a long day. If you'll excuse me, I need to get back to the kitchen. Good night, gentlemen." He turned and slowly walked back to the kitchen.

Jimbo glared in contempt as his partner turned his attention to the menu.

"James, I just might have a dessert tonight," the senior Tel announced.

Jimbo just kept glaring.

~

"I have to go," Tamara whispered.

"What time is it?" Jonathan asked, checking his watch. "Shit, it's four in the morning!"

The Den had emptied, though neither of them noticed the wax and wane of patrons between eleven o'clock to three. They had withdrawn to the cocoon they had created for themselves. If they had crossed the line, they didn't care. The Den had become their sanctuary, and Anari was their gatekeeper. She slowly approached the booth.

"Last call, you two," Anari cautiously said.

"We're done, Anari," Jonathan said smiling.

"You both look well done, if you ask me."

"And no one did, sweetie," Tamara replied, stretching.

Jonathan began to reach for his chipcard.

"Don't worry, Jonathan," Anari said. "This has been compliments of Liquid Courage." She motioned to the Den's front door, where a man in a tailored, polybio European suit stood. His back was unusually straight, almost military in stature, and his drink reflected the lights from the club.

"Hey, isn't that the guy you were with the first night we met?" Jonathan asked Tamara. "You two were at the bar."

"Yeah, that's Joshua. He owns Club Courage." The man raised his glass to them, turned and left the Den.

"Well...I..." Jonathan began.

"Need to do nothing," she finished. "He has more money than God. If he wants to treat, let him. It's rare. Take it as a compliment, baby. I know him. He doesn't give them out very often." She kissed him on the cheek. "Let me walk you out."

"Why don't we..." he began, but she silenced him with a finger.

"I need you too, lover," she whispered. "But I can't tonight. I have to get up early. I have an important meeting."

"Cancel it," he urged.

"Believe me, I would...oh, I would so much." She pulled him close and kissed him. "But I can't, I just can't."

Jonathan held her away, searching her face for the real reason. For the first time that night, Tamara didn't meet his eyes. She knew what was coming. She had been here so often she had become dead to its consequence.

Jonathan lifted her chin, forcing her to acknowledge his look. He slowly smiled. "What's his name...or is it her name?"

Tamara looked up. "Nicole."

"And she's?..."

"Four."

He immediately read her anguish. "Tamara," he said, fumbling for the right words. "I'm not like that. I love children...really."

"Oh yeah," she said, toughening. "If you only knew how often I've heard that!" She turned away.

"Tamara!" He pulled her around, bringing her tight to his face. "Look at me. Listen very carefully...I don't lie. And I'm not going to run judgment on you, Tamara," he whispered. "I'm not like other guys you've met before."

Tamara studied his face. His sincerity cut through her cynicism deep into her heart. Why would a guy like this care about her? She reached up and touched his face.

No, she thought, *you're not like anyone I've met before.*

Hunting...7

"I take back everything I said earlier, hunting is boring. Give me the biotech shit any day!"

"They told me you were patient," his partner said through the haze of another of his custom Vietnamese cigarettes.

"I am. But it's four thirty in the morning! Hey, here's our boy."

They watched Jonathan and Tamara step to the street. The car jockeys were doing wind sprints to meet the demand pouring out of the building.

"She's hot!" Jimbo exclaimed. "Looks like our boy likes the strippers. Man, I can see why." He dialed up the vision reception of the field optics, standard issue for the Agency.

Jonathan kissed Tamara good night and shut the door of her car. She pulled away from the curb, then jerked to a stop. Jonathan went to her window.

"What are they saying?" asked Jimbo's partner.

Jimbo clicked the lens to Language Enhance drive.

"I can't get them. There's way too much interference...she's saying something about lunch...tomorrow...Blind Monkey...and...oh." Jimbo removed his eyes from the field optics.

"Well?" his partner pressed.

"None of our business, partner."

"It is our business, James."

Jimbo turned and faced him sternly. "It's none of our business."

The senior Tel studied his young associate for a moment. "Perhaps you are right. Follow her home."

"Her?"

"Yes, I believe we might be seeing a lot of Jonathan there."

~

Mornings in a restaurant such as Kortel's are dysfunctionally chaotic, at best.

Given the day, Hector could have five delivery men arguing about their orders, a waiter needing to be bailed out of jail, a serviceman checking the biopacks on the hydroponics, which had held the week's shrimp specials now spoiling in static water tanks that died at 2:30 that morning because the new bar back had never run a biosterilizer, or twelve cases of Chilean Merlot missing, even though they were counted at close last night. On this particular day the grill, which is the hallmark of the kitchen, refused to light no matter what Enrique tried. *Where the hell is Jonathan?*

"Has anyone seen our lover boy?" Hector asked.

Everyone looked up, their expressions more blank than the salmon biopaste from Canada.

"Has he even called?" Hector was desperate.

"No!" Enrique yelled over the laser drill's deafening sound.

"Is that fixed, yet?" Hector yelled.

"Almost!" Enrique crawled farther into the grill's small opening.

"I'm gonna kill..." Hector's netphone rang.

"Hector."

"Jonathan, where the hell are you?" Hector asked savagely.

"Hey, look, I'm sorry. I need a favor. I'm going to take a few days off, and before I get the lecture, just let me have it my way this time, okay?"

Hector hesitated. "Is she that special, my friend?"

"I...I don't know Hector. But I do know I need to play this out. Call it stupid, call it whatever you want, but there's something going on...it's hard to put into words. I'm not even sure what I'm doing. This might be a total disaster, but if I don't see where it goes, I'll never forgive myself. This one isn't open for debate, partner. You understand?"

"Jonathan, you know what I think? I think you need this. Go to her. Be with her. Fall in love with her if you want. You worked hard to build this restaurant, we worked hard, and you deserve the time. Take it, my friend. She is pretty. I can't blame you in the least. Hell, I'm envious. Shit, Jonathan, go screw her or love her or give yourself to her. But when you come back, I want one hundred percent of you. Now go, before I change my mind."

"Thanks, Hector, I'll see you soon."

Hector disconnected and stared at his netphone for a moment. "Hell, I am losing my mind....Okay you *vatos*, get this kitchen cooking. We have three hours before we open!" The big Mexican watched as the men of Kitchen Kortel slammed into gear. He loved his partner like a brother, which made the nagging feeling of trouble even more intense. Hector turned his attention to his crew. They were prepping the kitchen like army ants. Not once did they question when their general would return.

A test...8

JONATHAN leaned back against the headboard of his bed. The morning sun cascaded into the room with a clean light that made the metal surfaces glow yellow and gold.

The high loft ceilings contained cobwebs that predated the Biolution. On his side of town, artists and musicians filled the bodegas, not the pseudorich transworlders who flocked to the North Side like cranes to an oasis. He sat there wondering what was to come, what his next move should be. His dating history had been the typical list of social queens seeking "Mrs." degrees and bar chicks thinking sex was their ticket to happiness. Occasionally the errant nice girl came along, but there was never that special something, that strange energy.

Sipping his own specially programmed blend, Jonathan slipped to the window and looked down. The day had begun for the rest of Chicago, but not for him. He was still back in the booth, with her. As he watched the alluvion of the streets, he felt as if he were observing his own situation from above. He had nothing in common with her. He tried to imagine their future, if there was one. What would they talk about? What would they do? Did he really want to become an instant daddy? The loft's AI brought him back to the present.

"Jonathan, it's eleven o'clock. You should prepare for your lunch appointment."

"Thank you, Max. Do I have any netmail?"

"Yes, seven messages. Two from your lawyer. One from Tobby. One from the city inspection department. One from Dining magazine. Two from Terikia."

"God, what does she want?" he said under his breath. Terikia had been the last, and probably weirdest, one of all, and that had been almost ten months ago. "Max," he asked, stepping into the hydroshower, "what's the weather this week?"

"Today will be partly cloudy with a 10 percent chance of rain. The high will be 82 and the low will be 69. For tomorrow and the rest of the five-day extended forecast, expect continued sunny skies, highs in the lower 80s, lows in the high 60s. A cool front is approaching from the east..."

"Thank you, Max. How's the juice and milk?" he said over the rush of air and recycled water.

"They are within acceptable ranges. Would you like them chilled?"

"No, I was just wondering if we needed to get some new ones."

"The bread is at limit. The bioeggpaste is at half-life. The lettuce brick is acceptable. The hydrofruit is at..."

"Got it! Got it! Thank you, Max. Just do a rundown and order what we need. You know the drill."

"Yes, Jonathan. Will there be anything else?"

"Yeah, can you fast-forward me to tonight with Tamara?"

"Excuse me, sir?"

"Nothing. Thank you, Max."

Emerging from the hydroshower, Jonathan grabbed a towel. He still loved towels, even though no one used them anymore. He loved the way they felt against his body. The Biolution had changed so much of the contemporary home, and towels, along with toasters, ovens, refrigerators and about a thousand other labor-saving devices invented in the 20th century, gave way to the new generation of technology. Bioliving enhanced every facet of the home and had Martha Stewart's descendants rolling in their graves.

Jonathan examined himself in the mirror. He was in good shape; he should be for as much as he worked out. As with all males, his self-doubt and insecurities could be temporarily masked with a little attention to muscle tone and contemporary dermal care. He dressed casually in a pair of comfortable jeans, ergosandals and a light simwool sweater. He left the loft in the care of itself.

~

The Blind Monkey was jumping as usual for a midweek business crowd. Jonathan knew the staff, having frequented their bar after closing his kitchen. Deaka was working the front door, and he knew she wouldn't give him any grief. She smiled at him as he approached.

"Hey, Deaka."

"Hi, Jonathan. What brings you here in the middle of the day?"

"I'm meeting someone. She's kinda tall, curly blonde hair..."

"Has a kid with her?" She snapped her gum.

Jonathan hesitated. "Maybe..."

"Booth five, by the window." She pointed her netpad in the direction of the booth.

"Thanks." Jonathan began to walk past her, but Deaka slammed the netpad into his chest and stopped him in midstride.

"She's a knockout, Jonathan, but are you ready to become a daddy?" A broad, thin smile spread across Deaka's face.

"Screw you, Deaka."

"You tried." Her gum snapped like an antique .38 going off.

Jonathan saw Tamara sitting on the sunlit side of the booth, but he couldn't see little Nicole.

"Morning," he said, bending to kiss her.

"Hi, baby." She returned the kiss. Her hair was curly again, and her makeup was barely noticeable. She wore a man's collared shirt, old baggy pleated pants and work boots any construction guy would kill for. Jonathan couldn't decide whether it was a statement against being half-naked and having to perform as the perfect female or whether she just didn't care.

She reached across the table and took his hands. For a second they just sat there, letting the reality of what they were doing soak in. They were together – outside the club.

"Well?" he asked.

"Well what?" she replied.

"Where's Nicole?"

She smiled and poked her head under the booth. "Hey, silly, come up and meet someone."

A little head covered by curls appeared over the top of the table. Tamara brushed them back to reveal the face of a cherub who smiled at Jonathan, her eyes squinting shut. She was a perfect reproduction of her mother. Jonathan felt his heart go to the little girl, and, in an instant, he saw Tamara as a child. His eyes went back and forth between the two of them. Tamara's expression had changed. She knew exactly what he was thinking. His look gave it all away. She affectionately squeezed his hands.

"Hello, Mr. Kortel," the little voice said.

"Hello there," he said, clearing his throat. "I've heard a lot about you."

She giggled and disappeared back under the table.

"Shy one, isn't she?" Jonathan said.

"Not really," Tamara answered, slowly looking up at him, "when you get to know her."

"I hope I will," he replied.

~

They ordered sandwiches, and Nicole played with her horses under the booth. They talked about everything. Tamara had a tough life, being raised right in the city. Her father and mother had been small-time dealers in ride. Those were the early years, when the biodrugs were in their infancy. They had done time for it but had cleaned up their act some years back. Tamara had lived with her grandparents for awhile but later had become fairly close to her parents, especially her mom. Nicole was the product of a teen pregnancy that Tamara stubbornly wanted to see through. She had married the father, but that had lasted all of a month. She was wild, but she wasn't stupid. At 16 she had tested out of school with almost straight A's. She ran away from home, leaving Nicole in the care of her grandparents, and headed for Nevada.

"Why Nevada?" Jonathan asked.

Tamara leaned back and folded her arms tightly across her chest.

"Hey, that's okay. Your life is your life," he said.

"The Ranch..." she blurted.

The booth went silent.

Jonathan knew what that name meant. For more than 160 years, 12 owners, 3,821 girls and 73 million condoms had kept the Chicken Ranch the oldest working brothel in New America. Jonathan just looked at her. Half pity, half curiosity. He reached over and gathered her hands into his.

"For how long?" he asked.

"Not long. About a year." She stared blankly out the window.

"Was it..." he began.

"You know," she interrupted, staring out to the street. "You make great money for basically sitting around reading vidbooks. And it's very clean. Man, you wouldn't believe the tests...every other day." Her voice trailed off. She checked to see that Nicole wasn't listening.

"You know, I've done them all," she said quietly. "Young ones, dumb ones....You know who treats you the best? The old guys. They're real nice. Heck, you don't even have sex with them. They just want to talk. Three thousand dollars for 30 minutes of conversation about their dead wives." Her eyes remained blank.

They finished their meals. Jonathan didn't know what to say. He could see Tamara was distracted, mentally out in a past that still clearly impacted her life.

"Mommy, can we go?" Nicole said from below, tugging on Tamara's pant leg.

"Sure, baby. It's time." She gathered up her child and began to climb out of the booth. "I'm sorry," she said to Jonathan. Her mood changed as she hiked Nicole onto her hip. "I'm taking Nicole over to her grandmother's for the weekend. Meet me back at my place in about 40 minutes. Let's just go do something this afternoon....I don't care, maybe to the museum."

"It was good meeting you, Nicole," Jonathan said. "I hope I'll see you soon." He reached over and wiped away a little run that was coming out of Nicole's nose. She giggled and quickly buried her face into Tamara's neck. Tamara smiled, because no guy she knew would ever have done that.

She leaned over and kissed him on the cheek.

~

"Man, she's had it rough," Jimbo said, pulling the biomicro-transceiver out of his ear. The two Recruiters watched as Jonathan, Tamara and Nicole walked past their booth and out of the Blind Monkey. "Kortel doesn't have to worry about the competition. This sandwich is rank."

"I think we need a little test, James," his partner mused.

"Really?" Jimbo asked. He turned his attention to the window, where he could see Jonathan, Tamara and Nicole as they waited at the corner for the signal to change.

"James," his partner instructed, "I want you to watch those people." He pointed to a group of tourists crowded behind Tamara at the corner. "If they begin to pass her, hold them back." He looked at him seriously. "You *can* do this? It is in your level parameters?"

Jimbo nodded "yes" knowing that this was going to be a serious test, and it was neither the time nor the place for mistakes. Jonathan was about to undergo a severe test of GDRD – Gravitational Distortion Reflex Displacement. It was a standard test all Recruiters put their Potentials through, although this time Jimbo felt it was going to be "an extreme condition setup," which typically was reserved for tough cases and never used on the first test.

Jimbo sensed his partner was about to change the rules.

Tamara, holding Nicole in her arms, was talking with Jonathan, while down the street, a quarter-ton kit cab sped toward them, weaving in and out of traffic like a drunken linebacker heading toward their intersection.

"Be tight with your imaging, James, I may need you," his partner warned. The senior Tel began to focus a grav field for the kit cab.

Tamara struggled with Nicole's fussiness, and the tourists behind her grew impatient. The signal shifted. Tamara was first to step off the curb – possibly into oblivion.

"Steady, James, steady...watch them. They are about to move!" his partner said.

Twenty feet from the corner, the kit cab entered the imaging threshold for both Tels. The senior Tel converged the fields and pushed and displaced the kit cab into Tamara and Nicole's path. One of the tourists had already shoved his way around to Tamara's left side.

"James, that one," he said, pointing. "Watch that one for God's sake!"

The cab's pilot, trying desperately to overcome the unseen force that had taken over his cab, engaged the brake units. Their high-pitched squeal sent a pedestrian diving to the sidewalk. A woman screamed. A man anticipated the horror of the scene about to unfold and yelled out to God. Jimbo jerked the tourist circumnavigating Tamara back like a dog being yanked by its leash. He held the six others frozen in their steps. His partner, pushing against the tremendous force of the kit cab's technology, strained his level to its limits. Tamara looked to her right and saw the cab violently swerve in their direction. A scream so loud that the vessels in her vocal cords began to microhemorrhage erupted from her throat.

Jonathan jumped to the right of Tamara and Nicole, futilely trying to shield them with his body, as if he, alone, could absorb the impact from the quarter-ton vehicle. He was partially right. The thought of losing someone he so desperately wanted was the exact formula to trigger the "effect." To Jonathan, the scene went to white, then to colors that twinkled, then swirled. Then something different appeared.

Music.

Harmonic tones filled his mind, and he didn't black out as before. The whole scene slowly entered his consciousness frame by frame. Through the windshield of the kit cab, he could count every beat of the driver's heart in the vein that throbbed on his forehead. The man tore at the wheel, trying to turn away. Jonathan heard himself scream, "NO!" but never felt the sound in his throat. In that moment, the kit cab jerked away from them and back into traffic, throwing the pilot against the door window. His hands left the wheel and slapped him in the face. The cab swerved once, twice, then crashed into the side of a recycle hauler. The force of the impact lifted the cab's back end into the air.

In the time it took for a nerve to fire, the GDRD test was over.

People rushed to the kit cab pilot's aid. The tourists ran across the street. Jonathan stood motionless, halfway turned toward where the cab had been, yet still hugging Tamara and Nicole. Tamara clutched her child and trembled uncontrollably. Nicole was screaming, her face awash in tears and mucus.

Unlike any previous experience he had with the effect, this time Jonathan's eyes were open and his mind was focused. He knew what he had done, and he began to realize that his life was forever changed. A large trail of blood flowed from his nose to the edge of his mouth.

~

"Hmmm," the senior Tel said, casually observing the chaos of the accident engulf the corner. "This Potential is very strong, James."

James McCarris was sweating profusely. He slammed his palm down on the table and slapped at his coffee cup, sending it flying into the booth next to them. He stormed out of the Blind Monkey and charged down the sidewalk to get as far away as possible from the "accident" that had just happened at the corner. His partner scrambled after him. As Jimbo turned down an alley, his partner seized his shoulder. Jimbo, a big Southern man, quickly turned and brushed off the grip like dandruff. He grabbed a handful of coat and shirt and slammed his partner against the wet brick wall.

"You are one twisted asshole," he growled. He pressed his face within inches of his partner's. "If you ever put me in a situation like..."

Suddenly, Jimbo grabbed at his throat. Coughing for the air that should have been in his lungs, he dropped to one knee. His partner straightened up, adjusted his shirt and tie, and lit a cigarette.

"If I ever what, James?" he said contemptibly, holding Jimbo in a breathing limbo, letting in just enough air to keep him conscious. "Put you in a situation to where you get to test your level? Or where you get to truly see where we stand on the evolutionary scale?" He circled his struggling partner, seemingly uninterested in his agony. He blew three perfect little smoke rings. "James, the problem with you is you have not accepted your lot in life. You are a Tel. We are not like them! They are, as a species, over. Done! Finished!"

He bent down to meet Jimbo's contorted face. "James, please...look at me. I know it hurts, but it is for your own education. I cannot teach you if you are blinded by self-righteousness." He released his telekinetic grip at Jimbo's throat. "Now, let us go and work together on this case." He began walking away, leaving Jimbo struggling to his feet.

~

"Jonathan!" Tamara screamed. "Nicki!" She pulled the child close to her chest. Jonathan looked about, hoping no one had picked up what had just happened.

"It's okay, it's okay. We're fine. Come on. Let's get out of here!" He rushed them across the street toward the garage where they had parked. His thoughts were a torrent of images from his past. All the little clues: the pencil, the book, the tree, the hauler, the countless little "oddities"...the fire in the kitchen. It all came together. But to what? His mind raced as he gathered them into Tamara's car.

Tamara had calmed to the point where she began to get mad. "What the hell was that cabby doing?" she demanded.

"Just thank God he swerved in time," Jonathan lied. "Here, take Nicole to her grandmother's and meet me at my place."

Tamara stopped locking Nicole into her safety seat and looked back at Jonathan, framed in the car window.

"It's okay, baby," he gently said to her. "I want you to stay...with me tonight. Is that all right?"

Tamara tilted her head and intently studied Jonathan's face. She saw the seriousness in his eyes. Taking his hand, she smiled and silently nodded yes.

Who am I...9

JONATHAN watched Tamara inch her way past the accident, which had now become a circus of EMS's and city police. He walked toward the No. 6 L-Tram Station in a daze, not really sure what to do next. What was he supposed to do with this ability? Run the restaurant? Become a superhero and fight crime? *What the hell is going on,* he wondered. He began to question his whole understanding of the world and his place in it. Were there others like him? How would he know? Overwhelmed, he looked beyond the tall, century-old glass-skinned building that had made Chicago so famous and into the afternoon sky. "Where are you now?" he asked God.

Back down the sidewalk, a recycle can was strapped to a street sign. Jonathan spotted it. He focused his attention on the can, closed his eyes and imagined a ball of white energy leaping from the middle of his forehead and striking the can.

Nothing.

He tried again.

Again, nothing.

Frustrated, he remembered the music that had entered his mind just before he had moved the cab. He closed his eyes, focused his body energy, created the ball and listened for the music.

Nothing. Again.

"How the hell does this work?" he questioned under his breath.

Then it occurred to him that each episode happened under some sort of duress. *There must be a trigger,* he thought, *a common thread through all these events.*

Suddenly, a high-pitched screech caught Jonathan's attention. He looked across the street and saw an older woman vault out of the path of a WorldEx van. The woman had moved with all the speed and grace of a girl half her age. She also told the WorldEx driver where he could make his next delivery.

Then it hit him. Adrenaline.

Evolution's genetic leftover. Instinctual instructions blueprinted onto our genetic mapping that helped us survive the dawn of our existence. The cool, thick feeling all humans get when confronted with a stressful situation. Fight or flight.

Jonathan closed his eyes, focused his body energy, created the ball, listened for the music and tried to create an image that would trigger an adrenaline flow. He thought of Tamara being killed by the kit cab.

Like an instinctual trigger, his mind clicked, and he felt the blood drain from his face as adrenaline began to fill his system. Random musical tones rushed into his mind. His vision shifted from swirling colors to white. Then, as if he had kicked it with his foot, the can tore from the sign pole, its contents ejected into the street. A Channel 6 TVid truck swerved out of the way, its driver swearing at the can like it could actually hear.

A metallic taste filled Jonathan's mouth. He slowly opened his eyes and stared at the can as it came to a rest in the middle of the street. The warm afternoon sun highlighted the people rushing about. He was now resolved to the cold, hard reality that he was not like these people. He was something else – something off the evolutionary chart.

Way off.

He felt, at the same time, both empowered and scared. And he also felt something that had been with him since the death of his parents. An empty feeling of separation. But this time it was different. In the faces of the people walking past, he searched for some signs of himself, of his own humanity. But for the first time in his life, Jonathan Kortel felt disconnected from the world. Set apart in a sea of humanity.

He was, he felt, truly and totally alone.

Touched me...10

"**JAMES**, it looks like our Mr. Kortel has discovered his true nature," his partner said, removing the biomicrotransceiver from his ear and folding the field optics back into its case. The senior Tel lit another cigarette and watched from across the street as his Potential slowly walked away from the recycle can and headed toward the L-Tram Station.

Jimbo was silent.

"Please, James, get over what happened back there," his partner ordered. "This kind of behavior is not going to help us in this case."

"How do you want me to react? You nearly goddamn choked me to death!"

"James I am sorry for that, but sometimes a little pressure can make a bigger impression than words."

"Impression alright," Jimbo said, "on my damn windpipe!"

"James, you may not realize this, but I believe you have potential to be a great Recruiter. You did well earlier. Now lifting that tourist off the street may have been a bit extreme, but nonetheless, we did accomplish the test, and with no interventions."

An "intervention" was Agency slang for inadvertently exposing their real nature to outsiders. Jimbo's partner had never had an intervention in any of his cases, and he was going to keep it that way.

"In fact," his partner continued, "I think people believe that was a real accident back there. Your focus was good, your threshold field was contained, and your GFV was," he flipped open his netpad, "solid and stable. That is what being a professional is all about. You did very well, James."

Jimbo just smiled at his verbal pat on the head.

~

Jonathan unlocked the door to his loft and slowly stepped in. He glanced about the room, confronted by the evidence of a life he had come to enjoy. It all seemed so foreign to him now. He looked down at a pencil on the counter, and it instantly flew to his outstretched hand.

"Shit..." he sighed. He didn't even need to prep. He just asked it to come, and it did. He tried the sofa. It didn't budge. A vase. It slowly rose, hovered, and then crashed to the floor, shattering into hundreds of fragments.

"Damn..." he said sadly. It had been a gift from Hector. "...Guess I'd better get the hang of this." He tried various objects, probing the limits of his new ability, and began to find that certain sizes and weights he could move with no preparation, while others he couldn't. If he prepared, though, he could move big, heavy items with very little effort.

"Jonathan?"

"Yes, Max?"

"What are you doing?"

"Playing around..."

"Oh, very good. I will add this to my database. While you were out, you had three net messages from..."

"Max?"

"Yes, Jonathan?"

"Go off line for a while, please."

"Very good, sir."

Silence filled the loft.

He stood in the middle of the floor as the late afternoon light crept toward the wall. His eyes were closed. His mind was empty. He was listening to the universe. If he were truly the only one, he decided, then he was the first of a new breed of human. He breathed in and exhaled, raised his arms and held them out from his sides. He let his head fall back.

"Oh, God," he started, "show me what I need. This is going to be too big for me. I'm just a..."

The door tone hummed. Max was off line.

It hummed again.

"Max!"

"Sir, a Miss Tamara Connor is here to see you."

"Please," he smiled, "send her up. Thank you," he said under his breath, looking up.

~

When Jonathan opened the door to his loft, Tamara just stood there. She brushed her hair from her face. He looked at her oddly.

"What?" she asked.

He continued to look.

"I'm not in my heels, silly."

Jonathan blushed, having just realized her actual height.

"Nice place," she said. Her voice carried no hint of the near-death experience they had just been through. Jonathan watched her walk into the room. Nothing could change that walk. Even through her baggy clothes, it was as obvious as her beauty.

"Tamara," he said, "stand still for a moment."

She stopped and pulled her shoulders around. The late golden light from the large west windows washed over her. Her eyes focused on him almost like an animal's.

"God, you're beautiful," he said.

Tamara smiled, lowered her head and walked slowly toward him. He gathered her into his arms. She tilted her head and, as her curls fell away, Jonathan saw again the woman, not the dancer. Her eyes told him she wanted nothing else but to be with him that night. He kissed her gently and felt that same strange energy run from the base of his neck through his body. Then he kissed her a second time and, as he did, placed his hand to her heart. This time, though, he had control over his telekinetic delivery.

He felt her gasp against his lips.

"Oh God, baby...I need you," she said into his ear, holding his hand at her chest.

"I need you, too," he said. "I don't know why, but I do."

"Be careful," she whispered. "My world is a lot different than yours."

He pulled back to read her face. Brushing her hair aside, he didn't look at her, he looked into her.

"Tamara," he said, "I know."

~

The moonlight poured into the loft like milk as they made love. Tamara let go, and, for the first time in her life, she felt close to someone without the fear. She hardly knew this man, yet she felt closer to him than she ever had to anyone else. They both knew their connection seemed deeper. Truer. Like old souls. Jonathan made love to her as though these were his last days on earth. And as he held her in his arms, he had a sense that, after today, they might be.

~

"Tamara Connor. Tamara Connor. You have a netcall."

The loft was quiet.

"Excuse me, Tamara, you have a netcall."

"What?..." Tamara asked, blearily looking about the dark room and coughing lightly.

"It's Max, baby," Jonathan groaned. "Yeah, Max, what's up?"

"I'm sorry to wake the both of you, but Miss Connor has a netcall."

"Put it through. And no visual," Jonathan ordered.

"Mommy?..." the small voice asked.

"Nicki honey," Tamara replied. "It's four in the morning...what's the matter?"

"I can't sleep."

"It's okay, little one, now go see grandma and crawl into bed with her. Take Teddy Boo with you."

"Okay, mommy. Night-night."

"Good night, sweetie." Max disconnected the line as Tamara fell back against the pillows.

"You don't mind me giving her your code, do you? Jonathan?"

She turned to find her lover breathing quietly, hugging his pillow. The moonlight rippled over him as she ran her finger down the curves of his back. She lay there in the calm of the loft and looked at him, wondering if they would last.

"You've touched me like no one else has," she said softly. And she pulled the covers over herself and let the tears silently fall to the pillow.

Infant...11

JIMBO reclined against the headboard of the hotel bed and studied the netpad's data stream. Jonathan Kortel's telekinetic profile was scary. The GDRD test with the kit cab collected an immense amount of raw data, which revealed that Jonathan was at least a Level 8. His Gravity Field Flux ratios, ATP waves, Electromagnetic Displacement Grid readings, Wave Convergence Threshold and 20 other parameters were all at or near peak levels. The test also set a new tone in the approach the Recruiters would take with this particular Potential.

His partner was visibly disturbed by something he found in the data.

"What is it?" Jimbo asked.

His partner didn't look up. He sat there at the cramped hotel table, exhaustively picking apart Jonathan's data like a vulture on a dead carcass. Cigarette butts were piled in the ashtray, a reminder that his studies had not yielded the information he was desperate to find.

"Damn!" his partner exclaimed.

Jimbo, having never heard his partner swear before, looked up to see his partner's netpad floating about a foot off the hotel table. It held steady, then began to vibrate, building speed until it looked like a small flat blur, which is when it exploded. Parts radiated out in an almost perfect sphere, but they flew no farther than the circumference of a basketball. The pieces hung suspended where they were like some sort of horrendously difficult three-dimensional game. Finally they fell, bouncing and splintering about the tabletop.

His partner was seriously pissed.

"You alright there?" Jimbo asked.

"Yes," he said, still staring at the space the netpad had formerly occupied.

In the 22 years the senior Tel had been a Recruiter, he had reviewed more data on more Potentials than anyone in the Agency. He was known to have a keen sense of seeing clues to a Potential's promise in the data. And something within the terraquads of data on Jonathan Kortel clearly had him worried.

He snuffed out the last of his cigarette. "James, there is something here..."

"Or was here," Jimbo corrected.

"...that disturbs me. Mr. Kortel appears to be a Level 8. But look at his Field Threshold and his Imaging Threshold."

Jimbo flipped his netpad open and scanned down to the two charts.

"And?..." Jimbo questioned.

"Look at the peak levels in the FT and IT."

"Yeah?..."

"Now, see the tiny spike, right before the main MOT spike?"

"MOT?" Jimbo repeated, confused.

"Moment of Truth? James, really, you have heard that before?"

Jimbo remained silent, searching the spikes for what his partner had already found.

"I don't see it," he said with frustration.

"That little spike, James. I've never seen that before in all my years as a Recruiter."

"You used a contraction!" Jimbo was stunned.

"Excuse me?"

"You used a contraction. Shit, you are worried."

The room fell silent.

His partner kept staring.

~

The rest of the afternoon was quiet. Jimbo had fallen asleep while his partner continued to assay the results of the GDRD test. Jonathan Kortel appeared to be a Level 8, but the two spikes in his FT and IT charts said differently. He had shown an intense ability to tighten his Imaging Threshold almost to the width of a needle. And his Field Threshold was immense – at least twice the normal range. These two key bits of data pointed to only one thing: Jonathan Kortel was in the embryonic stages of developing to a Level 9. This was not good. There were only ten Level 8's in the world, and the appearance of a Level 9 changed the playing field altogether. As the highest testing Tel ever, Jimbo's partner felt something else from the data. Something he had never felt in his life.

Fear.

The introduction of a Level 9 would change the telekinetic world forever. Eights had set the standard for more than 70 years. Since the first discovery of a Level 8 early in the century, the Tel world had a standard that created balance and stability. If Jonathan Kortel was truly an infant Level 9, then the Tel Chart might require adjustment. Testing would be refined. Level assignments would shift. And the senior Tel's status would diminish. Jonathan Kortel could be the Gabriel, trumpeting a new era for mankind. At the moment, though, the senior Tel felt Jonathan was more like an infant wielding a charged Light-Force bioweapon. If his calculations were accurate, the curve for Jonathan's growth was beginning to increase...and at an alarming rate.

In a matter of days, he could achieve NTB.

"No Turning Back" was Agency-speak for the instant a Tel crossed the divide between awareness and acceptance. Most often, once a Tel accepted his or her condition, the LR, or Learn Rate, skyrocketed. There were no more emotional walls, no mental confusion – just a clear and present resolve to grow, develop and master their ability. Once Jonathan "crossed," the senior Tel feared he might not be able to control him. Having a live-wire Level 9 loose in the world would be a dangerous situation, and one the senior Tel was determined to avoid.

He watched the moon rise.

He smoked another cigarette.

~

Jonathan woke to the sound of rain hitting the metal roof. He rolled over looking for his lover.

"Hey, Tam?..." he quietly said, grabbing at the empty pillow.

He listened to the rain.

"Tamara?...Max!"

"Yes, sir?"

"Is Tamara in the loft?"

"No, sir. She left this morning at 8:37. She did leave you a message, however."

"Play it...please," Jonathan said cautiously.

Max engaged the message.

"Morning, baby..." her voice was somber and cool. "...Don't take this wrong. I...I really...last night was wonderful. It was so intense. We're so intense. You're the first guy that I've felt..." she hesitated, "...close to in a long time, maybe ever. When you touch me, it's almost too much. My feelings are...weird. I'm so drawn to you, it's like innate. I feel like we've known each other a long time....You know what I mean? Hey, look, I guess I'm freaking here just a little. It's not you....It's me. It's a little scary, sort of, I mean the intensity and all." She paused for a moment; the dead space killed Jonathan. "Baby, my life is so different from yours. Look at what I do. And there's Nicki. I can't hope that you'll learn to like her, even...love her. I can't ask that of you. Oh, Jonathan, I'm sorry....Bear with me for just a bit. I need some space. This is all too fast....I can't believe that I could..." her voice trailed off to a whisper. "...Umm, hey, I'm working tonight. Please come by. We'll talk. Take care, lover."

Max ended the message.

Jonathan was numb. His heart was collapsing from its own weight. He was beyond crying. The message cut right through him. He looked at a bowl filled with fruit, and it exploded, spraying yellow and green shards about the room. He slumped to the edge of the bed and cupped his head in his hands. The glass decanter given as the award for the Best New Chef in Chicago imploded, releasing its 30-year-old Scotch over the side table. The frame holding the only image he had of his parents shattered, slicing the photo into pieces. Oblivious to the destruction happening around him, he could think only of her.

Empty and alone, he stepped into the bathroom and glared at himself in the mirror. He drew back his fist, but the mirror shattered before he could throw the punch. Max asked repeatedly what was wrong. Jonathan's only reply was to switch him off at the system panel on the way to the hydroshower. He stood there frozen, with the air and water pulsing against his body. He brought his hands to his face to wipe away the previous night, but all he could do was smell their passion. Like a metaphor, she was right there at his fingertips.

MOT...12

ANARI sat at the bar resting her chin in her hand. Her bioshifting hair extension moved about her head to form intricate geometric shapes: first a multidimensional knot, then a ponytail in the shape of a real pony. She was bored out of her mind. The Den was empty, and the rent on her apartment was past due. Liquid Courage was suffering for a Saturday night. Gone were the BioUrologist Conventioneers who, for the last week, had swarmed over the city like drunken polyestered locusts. Gone, too, was their small contingent of lesbian doctors who had taken a liking to the club's "relaxed" policies on what could and couldn't be touched.

Anari wanted some action tonight. "Tebby, this isn't going to be good for me," she said with a yawn, her hair now in the shape of the Eiffel Tower. The young bar back laughed, and his rings clinked together in a sick tonal rhythm. On the main floor, a handful of military boys were betting who could slam the most Napalm Drops. At a four-top were the Too Blacks, slick, inner-city biodrug street repers suited up in their badest all-rain biogear just laughin' and slappin'. Except for the one or two horny husbands at the one-tops, club Liquid was dead.

Tamara was prepping in the locker room. She stared blankly into the mirror as the makeup artist sprayed the finishing highlights onto an intense palette of eye shadow. Tamara was there, but not there. Her mind was torn between the life she had and the life that Jonathan Kortel represented. He was 10 years older – not that that's bad, but she was still young and pretty wild for a single mother. She could not stop feeling the wonderful energy that had passed between them. Like a sexual hangover, it lingered in her system. She had never felt anything like it before, but its presence had both happy and scary overtones. Other dancers had always told her to find an older guy. They would be less put off by a single mom, they had said, than a guy her own age. But Tamara wanted someone real. Age was not as much an issue as the person. Her next move had never been far from her mind. Getting out of the professional sex trade had always been part of the plan, but how was another story. She had gone to a city college for a time and excelled in art. Art history and drawing were her favorite subjects, but what she could do with a degree in art history was up for debate in the 22nd century. As Blade put the final line on her eyelids, Tamara gazed at the eyes in the mirror. They look tired. After five years as a professional dancer, prostitute, student and single mother, Tamara's soul was beginning to show wear.

"Now, there we go!" Blade said smugly. "That's hot, if I do say so."

Being sexy for another screwed-up, drunk businessman was the last thing Tamara wanted to be doing. She leaned forward and intently studied the person looking back at her from the mirror.

"Honey, is it not what you wanted?" Blade asked, surprised.

Tamara didn't answer. "You're lying to yourself again," she said to her reflection. She closed her eyes and raised her hand to her heart. All she could feel was him.

~

Tamara had asked the VJ to track from her slow stuff. She wasn't in the spirit for any electro-funk from the African coast. It was 9:15, and Liquid was only at two stages. She came out as she had a million times before. There could have been two or two hundred marks; with the lights hitting her eyes for the first time, it all looked black to her. She slid over the stage floor and out to the edge that jutted into the crowd (if there had been one). A businessman on his VIDphone looked up in mid-conversation and gave her a thumbs-up. Tamara wanted to wretch. She bent over, her ass facing the Too Blacks, reached between her spread legs and slid her fingers from the center of her ass to the top of her thong. She straightened and glanced over her shoulder at the biodrug lords with the look she had been giving since she was 16.

"Okay, you freaks," Tamara said under her breath, and she started to dance as seductively as she could. The four-top repers came alive, banging their Buckets of Sin with their fists. Their gold jewelry reflected the stage lights, which had swung over to highlight their table. One got up and approached the main stage. Tamara danced over. She side-stepped right in front of him, then at the perfect moment in the song bent over backwards. Her legs spread wide apart, her back arched off the floor, she lay there humping the air. She slid her fingers up her crotch, past her breasts to the tip of her tongue.

The mark smiled at her and revealed his name in a perfect natural gold upper setting. "MR. COOL SHIT" was definitely a player.

He slipped out a Liquid five-C note as she crawled catlike towards him. She rubbed herself against him and purred in his ear.

"Say, baby," Mr. Cool Shit said, sliding her the note, "I'll see you at the next stage." He pinched her clitoris through her simmesh thong. Tamara didn't jump. She was a pro, but on the main floor, especially main stage, certain touching was way out of the zone. She smiled sex right back at him.

Tamara finished her set with her best pole work. Not one Liquid dollar. She picked up her things like an automaton, jumped off stage and sauntered to stage two.

As she passed the drug lords, Mr. Cool Shit smiled his name. She never took off her "come take me look" all the way to stage two. His gaze tracked her like a poacher.

The next girl on the main stage requested EuroTech dance crap. Tamara jammed to its beat like she was riding on Z Dust. Mr. Cool Shit rose from his table, high-fiving his brothers. He straightened his French biothread tie, pulled his cuffs out of his suit sleeves and approached stage two as if he owned Tamara. She read his look. She changed her dance to ensure he would tip and tip big. Mr. Cool Shit pulled out a wad of Liquid five hundreds as big as his fist.

Tamara pulled her thong down to the top of what little pubic hair she hadn't removed. Liquid was dead, and she needed the cash. Mr. Cool Shit laughed and licked his lips.

"Baby, I know that's right," he laughed as she bent down to greet him.

"Having a good time?" she purred.

"Damn straight." He slid two five-C notes into the front of her thong. They were so crisp they almost cut her skin.

"Yeah, baby..." she whispered into his ear, then licked it. With the taste of his poly-layered hair gel on her tongue, she stood and bent backwards, reaching for the floor. Mr. Cool Shit thought he'd test the standards of Liquid Courage. Her legs were spread, and her crotch was in his face. As soon as her hands touched the floor, Mr. Cool Shit pulled her thong aside and pressed his tongue into the gap. Startled, Tamara dropped to her back, leaving Mr. Cool Shit smiling his name and licking the air.

She kicked him across the face.

The force of the blow surprised even Tamara. Mr. Cool Shit's head snapped back so fast that his Czech-made Micro-Night Shades flew halfway to the main stage. He quickly pulled his head around and grabbed her ankle, his nails digging into her skin. He wasn't smiling his name any longer.

She kicked him again.

He slowly brought his head back and grinned. His name now was MR. COOL HIT. He spat blood and his "S" tooth onto the stage. "You fucking bitch whore!" he yelled. He jerked her forward by her ankle. His lieutenants jumped to their feet.

She kicked him for the last time.

"Oh, you gonna pay, bitch!" He threw open his suit coat and reached into it.

The VJ stopped the music. The club went silent. The dancer on the main stage crouched down on her 12-inch heels in the middle of the stage. She buried her face in her knees knowing too well what would come next.

Mr. Cool Hit pulled out a hand-held Light-Force bioweapon – not the standard issue for young drug lords climbing the corporate ladder out of the inner city. It was very light and very hard to get.

Its polycarbon and titanium housing reflected in Tamara's eyes. She didn't need to see the weapon to know that this reper was about to cap this little white girl's ass. In fear, she recoiled, slamming her forehead into the stage pole. Whether from pain or from her anticipated death, she shut her eyes tight and tears streamed down her cheeks. The light from the weapon's discharge filled her vision with white.

A girl screamed behind her.
She waited for the pain.

~

After a second, Tamara's mind recovered from her own death. The club remained silent. Nothing had happened. Still clutching the pole, she could taste blood running down her forehead into the corner of her mouth. She slowly opened her eyes and turned in the direction of the light blast.

There, two inches from her face, the end of the bioweapon beam floated motionless in the air. It was silent and glowed a brilliant white. It was as thin as a needle and protruded from the muzzle about three feet, which likewise was still in the hand of Mr. Cool Hit. His coat was flung open, suspended in midflap. His bloodied spittle was frozen in the air just in front of his open mouth, which appeared ready to finish a sentence. Even his stance was halted in midstep, his left foot four inches off the floor. The whole scene resembled a bad holoposter from some black Euro-action vid.

Tamara was shaking. Her legs buckled, and she crumpled to the base of the pole. The few people in the club were also standing motionless, but it was by their own choice. Mr Cool Hit's brothers, though, had fallen back into their chairs, stunned.

There was a scream at the rear of the club, near the back bar.

"Tamara!"

Fear had gripped Tamara so tightly, she could hardly make out the voice.

"Tamara!" Anari screamed again. "Look!"

Tamara followed the direction of the scream. There, next to Anari, was Jonathan. His head was tilted back, and his eyes were closed. Arms outstretched, his fists were clenched as tightly as his teeth. Blood poured from his ears, his nose and his eyes. His chest arched like he had been shot in the back, and he was floating.

Anari's hands were at her mouth as if she were about to gag. She looked back and forth between Jonathan and Tamara.

"Tamara, look! Look at him!" she screamed, pointing.

Tamara, and the whole of Liquid Courage, couldn't take their eyes from Jonathan. An admixture of blood and sweat dripped from him onto the floor three inches beneath his feet. No one moved. There was a gasp from one of the dancers.

Tamara carefully avoided the suspended Light-Force beam, climbed down from the stage and ran to her lover. Stopping short of him, the reality of the moment hit her hard.

Anari reached out to touch him. She jerked back.

"Oh my God, he's burning up!" she whispered.

Tamara cautiously approached. "Baby," she pleaded, her shock giving way to the need of the moment, "talk to me, please. Can you hear me?" She was beginning to cry.

"Are you all right?" Jonathan said hoarsely.

"Oh God, yes, yes baby, I am," she whispered to him, now only inches from his face.

His eyes opened, and his head fell forward. He caved to the floor, supporting himself on hands and knees, spitting blood onto Tamara's shoes. Simultaneously, the Light-Force bioweapon completed its discharge, and the wall mirror behind stage two debiolized into a gooey puddle. Mr. Cool Hit, released from Jonathan's telekinetic grip, finished his lunge toward the edge of the stage: "...ucking whore!"

Four standard Light-Force street handguns appeared from behind each bar, their high-pitched whines indicating that they would be fully charged in less than a second.

"Drop the weapon or you'll end up like the mirror!"

Mr. Cool Hit smarted out. His bioweapon hit the carpet without a sound.

Tamara knelt beside Jonathan. "Jonathan. Oh baby, what did you..."

"I couldn't see you die!" Jonathan cried. He tried to stand but was too exhausted. His spit out blood again.

Tamara touched his back. It was burning hot. He looked at her for the first time. Tears and blood created a web of small rivers over his face.

"Oh, Tamara," he reached up for her. "I had to stop it...I need you..." his voice faded.

Tamara gathered him into her arms and held him close. He was shaking. "I need you too, lover," she whispered into his ear. She squeezed him tightly, and he coughed blood down her back.

~

James McCarris was leaning forward on his elbows at a table just off the second stage. He was shocked at what he had just seen. His hands shook so badly that there was more of his drink on the table than in his glass. "Did you see that!? Did you see that!?" he said in disbelief.

His partner didn't respond. He was also visibly shaken by what he had just witnessed. Never in all his years had he seen someone like this. *Jonathan's Learn Rate curve*, he conjectured, *was off the planet.*

"Is that possible!? Can he really do that!?" There was fear in Jimbo's voice. "What the hell is going on here!?"

His partner couldn't talk. His mind was too busy calculating the parameters of what he was seeing. His netpad readings were running wild. Faster than he could scan, his mind had come to the realization of who, or what, he was confronting. Jonathan Kortel was something new, and his netpad couldn't define him.

"Sir..." Jimbo whispered in the dead silence of the club, "...he's faster than light! He's faster than goddamn light....He created a grav field that froze a Light-Force beam dead in its tracks....That can't be..." His voice trailed off. As Jimbo stared at the Light-Force beam suspended in air, the intensity of the situation tore at his mind. "Oh God..." he quietly uttered.

"That," his partner finally answered, "is what I believe we are dealing with here." He snapped his netpad shut.

With no interventions...13

JONATHAN surveyed the club, wiping the sweat and blood from his face. He felt about a dozen people staring at him. Tamara was holding him up. "I've got to get out of here," he coughed.

"Jonathan, you're hurt..." Tamara pleaded.

"Jonathan, listen to her," Anari said. "You are seriously screwed up. You're bleeding all over the place."

She was right. The blood wouldn't stop flowing from his nose, and he could taste it in his throat.

"I can't stay, don't you get it?!" he said, voice rising. "Look at what I just did! What the hell am I?!" He was now seriously freaking. He pushed Tamara off of him and stumbled backwards into the buffet table. Jerking about, he searched for the exit.

"Baby, don't. Please, let me help you!" Tamara cried.

Without a hand laid on them, small tables and chairs flew out of Jonathan's way as he stumbled toward the front of the club, coughing and spitting blood.

"Jonathan," Tamara screamed, "please don't go...please..."

Jonathan stopped, crumbling against a pillar, sending its hydro-grown plant crashing to the floor. He turned to see his love standing there, her shoulders slumped and arms to her sides. She was sobbing. Jonathan had never seen anyone look so helpless. She raised her eyes to him. Her makeup had melted into a nightmarish look.

"...I...I...think I love you," she said softly, not believing what she heard herself say.

Jonathan looked to her, then to the exit, and back to her. He knew he couldn't stay. Soon Liquid Courage would be a full-out media show of city police, VID trucks and young-gun reporters. And that was the last thing he could face. "I can't," he groaned. "I'm sorry, baby." Jonathan picked himself up and ran out into the lobby.

Tamara dropped to her knees.

~

The two Recruiters sat at their table and struggled with the input streaming into their senses. The laws of physics were supposed to define the property and nature of all matter. Tonight, though, the laws of physics at Club Courage were from another universe. Jonathan was definitely a Level 9, possibly heading toward Level 10, and he had just stumbled out of Liquid Courage into a very dangerous world.

That, Jimbo thought, *was some serious shit.*

"James, we have a containment issue here," the senior Tel declared.

"No shit, Hawkins!" Jimbo mocked.

"Shut this place down, James. Kill the power at the main grid for this floor and give me a grav field burst, from there to there." His sweeping gesture covered the whole of the main room. He looked at his colleague for the first time. "And James, I do not need to tell you the seriousness of this containment, do I?"

"No sir," Jimbo said soberly.

The two Tels, shifting gears into professional mode, slowly rose unnoticed from their chairs. This was the moment when all their training would be brought to bear. Jimbo did as he was told. All the doors slammed shut and locked. The lights in the club went out. A slow murmur began to build until it gave way to yells and panic.

"I am sorry, James," his partner said coldly through the blackness and confusion, "but some people are going to be hurt."

The senior Tel quietly went into telekinetic phase, whereupon silence fell over Liquid Courage for a second time that evening.

~

Not long before this, Anari had been consoling her best friend, who was kneeling on the floor. "Come on, sweetie, he'll be okay. He's not going to leave you," she lied.

Anari gathered Tamara and led her back to the Den. There wasn't a soul around. The two of them drew comfort from the thick granite and Teflon walls as they fell into a booth near the back. Tamara was visibly stunned. Appearing like she had just heard the news of a child's death, Tamara stared blankly forward. The events of the night played again and again in her head. She dug deep for the street toughness that had always served her well, but she couldn't seem to find it. To realize love and lose it all at the same time had taken its toll on the 21-year-old.

Then the lights went out in the Den.

"What the hell?..." Anari said under her breath. Anari was a "streetie." Her sixth sense kicked in, and she read the moment. "Come on!" she ordered and yanked Tamara out of the booth. Anari used her netpad light to guide them haltingly to the back of the Den. She waved her keycard at the exit door's system pad. No response. She tried again. Nothing.

"Shit!" Anari exclaimed. "In here!" They ran toward the biopaste locker near the kitchen. Anari grabbed the handle and yanked the door open. It hissed as it swung, blasting them with the sweet smell of the world's finest hydroponic-biopaste. They tumbled in, and Anari kicked the door shut. They leaned against the cool, 12-inch-thick lead wall. The usual hum of the biotanks was gone, and the pitch blackness concealed the size of the room.

Tamara reached through the darkness and took Anari's hand.

"Thanks, Anari," Tamara finally said.

"*No problema*, chicky."

They sat there quietly, waiting for the next chapter in an already strange night.

~

"James, the lights, please."

The low industrial hum of electricity returned to the club as the bar lights and stage spots grew back to full illumination. The two Tels stood like generals after a battle. The drug lord and his lieutenants, the businessman on the VIDphone, the four-top of military boys, the Liquid workers and freelance dancers: all were strewn about the club, unconscious. Some had fallen right where they stood. Others had landed in not-so-comfortable ways.

The senior Tel was clearly exhausted.

"You all right?" Jimbo asked, surveying the telekinetic carnage.

"Yes, James, just a little tired. Could you please see if anyone is seriously hurt." He collapsed into his chair.

Jimbo went from person to person, checking pulses and taking readings from his netpad. A petite Latina dancer had landed with her leg underneath her hip. It was fractured in three places.

"This looks bad, boss."

"Will she live?"

"Oh yeah, but she may not dance again." Jimbo moved on to the next victim, keeping a running tally. One broken wrist. Two cracked ribs. One guy was bleeding severely from the ears and nose. "Sir..."

"Yes, James," his partner answered, already knowing what Jimbo was going to say.

"I think we lost one here."

"What do the med readings say, goddamn it!"

"He's dead, sir."

His partner went silent and rubbed his forehead. "Okay, James, let's finish up," he finally said.

The senior Tel brushed back his salt-and-pepper hair. Assignments like this didn't help the aging process. He looked around at his handiwork. "James, they look so...fragile."

Jimbo finished his scans. If Jonathan Kortel was truly heading for Level 9 status, the Recruiters needed to act fast. The exponential rise in his LR was unnerving at best. No data had ever been recorded on a Level 9, much less a Level 10, and Level 10's were thought to be impossible to achieve. It appeared to the Recruiters that the impossible was possible.

"We're missing Tamara and the Asian," Jimbo said. "You want me to go find them?"

"No, James, we will deal with that containment issue later." He wiped the sweat from his brow. "For now, our concentration should be on finishing here and moving on to Jonathan."

To Jimbo, for the first time his partner looked his age. His hair was wet with sweat, his skin was pale, and he actually looked frail sitting in the club's oversized chair.

The senior Tel lifted his eyes to Jimbo with all the seriousness of his years. "This should appear, James, as an electrobiomicroburst. The building has enough net linkhubs. If we destroy the one on this floor, it could inflict this type of damage quite easily."

"What will they remember?" Jimbo asked.

"Well, I can tell you what they will definitely not remember. They will not remember the last 24 hours. And some may have severe motor-function challenges for the next week or two." His voice grew tired, and he looked in the direction of the bar back lying in a pool of his own blood.

"I am very sorry for that young man. This was not his affair."

"Let's go find the linkhub, sir," Jimbo suggested. "We haven't much time. Kortel's loose, and we're not getting any closer to him."

His partner nodded in agreement.

~

The blackness of the biopaste locker was calming, and, for Anari, a little calm was needed to regroup. Without warning, the low lights of the room came on. The soft drone of the biotank motors revved up, and their tiny bubbling sound resumed. Anari checked out Tamara.

"You look like shit, girlie!"

Tamara smiled, cracking the now dried makeup mask she was sporting. "Don't worry. I feel like shit, too."

Tamara's head pounded from the emotion of the night. She let it fall back against the wall and closed her eyes. At that moment, all she could think of was life without Jonathan. She had to get it together if she was going to salvage what was left of her life with him. "Let's go!" Tamara barked, her own street sense finally appearing.

They left the locker and headed back into the club. What they found was more surreal than what they had left. They cautiously checked the unconscious people.

"What happened here?" Anari asked, picking up and dropping the limp wrist of the night manager.

"Oh no!" screamed Tamara. "It's Tebby...I think he's...dead."

Anari ran to her side.

They stared down at the young bar back. One side of his face rested in a pool of deep red blood that was slowly fanning out. His eyes were open, his rings were silent, and he looked strangely peaceful.

"He was a cool dude," Anari said.

A groan came from the main stage.

They ran up to stage number one, where the lights were still trained on the dancer awakening from her telekinetic sleep. She sat up and crossed her legs, rubbing her face.

"Oh, man...god, what the hell am I doing here?" she asked gruffly.

Puzzled, Tamara glanced at Anari, then back to the dancer. "Where do you think you should be?" Tamara asked.

"I was at home, making some breakfast, which I never do..." she grabbed her head in pain. "Oh shit...what the hell is going on?" She looked around the club confused. Someone groaned at a two-top, and a cough came from the bar. Tamara and Anari watched as one by one, Liquid Courage began to wake up.

"She doesn't remember a thing," Tamara whispered to Anari.

"Yeah, like not a thing since yesterday. This is getting just a little weird."

Suddenly an explosion shook the building near the elevators. The force threw Tamara and Anari to their hands and knees. The piercing tone of the fire alarm system stung their ears. Emergency lights flooded the club, and the bitter taste of fire retardant began to fill the room.

"Let's get the hell out of here! This place is gonna be crawling with fire and police in about five minutes!" Tamara yelled over the hiss of retardant mist. They scrambled back toward the Den, and Anari noticed the young bar back on her way past. She realized that things would never be quite the same in the land of Liquid Courage.

To see a friend...14

"LIGHTS, Max."

The loft's lights grew in intensity. Jonathan's earlier telekinetic rampage was still in evidence. He had no time to waste. His ability was outpacing his control over it. He quickly began to pack.

"Will you be leaving for a time, sir?"

"Yes, Max, but I don't know for how long."

"Very good. I will notify the..."

"No! Max, that's all right. Don't change any of the loft's protocols."

"Yes, sir. Where are you going, sir?"

Jonathan stopped packing and looked out the large windows. The sun was beginning to rise over the city. "I'm going to see a dear friend."

"Why, sir?"

Taken aback by the intuitive question of his loft's AI, Jonathan hesitated for a second. "I can't tell you."

"Very good, sir. Will there be anything else?"

"You still have Tamara Connor's voice print in memory?"

"Yes, sir."

"Then the message I'm about to leave is for her ears only. Use her voice print as the only access to the message. Understood?"

"Perfectly, sir. Shall I encrypt it so no one can access it?"

"Yes, Max, that will be fine. Oh, and Max?"

"Yes, sir?"

"I want to amend my will. Please adjust it so that upon my death, my personal wealth – not the business holdings – is put in a trust for a Nicole Connor, at such time as she comes of age...blah, blah, blah. You know what to do. Access your legal database. It should all be in there. You still have her voice print and net address information?"

"Yes, sir. I will need your retina scan for authorization."

"I know. And make it accessible by her mother, Tamara Connor. Her net address is the same as Nicole's."

"Yes, sir."

"And Max, if any report of my death comes across the net in the next few days or weeks..." his voice trailed off.

"Sir?"

"Hell, just let Tamara know, will you please?"

"Very good, sir."

"Are you ready for my message?"

"Yes, sir."

~

While Jonathan dictated, he paced the room, solemnly reviewing the items that had been destroyed. So many years of memories, and it was all about to change. He picked up his gear bag and turned to go.

"Sir?"

"Yeah, Max?"

"Good luck."

Jonathan stopped. He thought he heard a trace of sadness in the AI's voice output.

"You can go off line now, Max, until you recognize the voice print of Hector, Tamara or Nicole."

Jonathan walked out the front door, headed for the one man who might know what was happening to him. Someone he could trust.

The message...15

ɪт was 3 a.m. when the Recruiters entered Jonathan's loft.

"Lights, please."

There was no response.

"Lights, please, Max," Jimbo repeated.

They waited.

"He's off line," Jimbo said.

"He is using a voice print ID matrix," his partner said, working his netpad. "No matter." The loft's basic functions came to life. He lit another cigarette and took a long drag. "What do you sense, James?"

Jimbo was studying the loft. As he walked about the living room, his hands grazed over certain items: a photo of Jonathan and Hector deep-sea fishing, a small Mexican mask, an old book by an 18th century author with the inscription: To Jonathan, love Dad. "Moby Dick..." Jimbo said under his breath.

"What, James?"

"Melville, Herman Melville. Moby Dick. I haven't seen this since I was a kid."

"One of the greatest works of human literature, James."

"Yeah, I loved this book." Jimbo studied the inscription.

"What are you sensing?" his partner questioned. "What is your seventh sense saying about Jonathan Kortel?"

Jimbo continued to touch and sense the essence of the man they were hunting. Like an old Southern bloodhound, he let his seventh sense take over his actions. When Potentials deny their abilities, they often run, and usually to someone close, such as a brother or sister. But Jonathan Kortel had no family. The Recruiters would have to rely on simple detective work to find their Potential, and Jonathan Kortel would be a difficult hunt.

His partner casually smoked as he watched his young associate track Jonathan's telekinetic "scent."

"It looks like he's in emotional pain," Jimbo announced.

"Oh, how is that?"

"Look at all this broken stuff. This is a clean, neat, put-together kind of guy. These trashed items are typical of a Potential struggling with his new ability."

"But..." his partner probed.

"But something's off. Most of these are very personal items. Potentials typically don't 'test out' on their personal stuff. They test out on things they can do without, junk, typically. He was distraught, probably over the dancer. Look here, this photo and this piece of art. And here, the Melville book. Why would he tear it apart?"

"Because?..." his partner quizzed.

"Because he's probably in love with her, and he's denying that. And he's in conflict with his new ability."

"And he is out there, somewhere, mentally unstable." His partner pointed to the large windows. "James, if our Jonathan Kortel is really developing into a Level 9, then the key to finding him will be Miss Connor."

"Max, play back..." Jimbo ordered.

"Oh, do not bother, James. Max is off line, and that is simple enough to correct, but I am sure Jonathan, being the excellent programmer that he is, has encrypted Max." He flipped open his netpad and began the hacking sequence to bring Max back on line. "Max?" he asked.

"Gentlemen, your presence is unauthorized. I will have to notify building security."

"Don't bother, Max." Jimbo said, still mulling through the loft. "They're off line to you."

"Max," the senior Tel asked, "where did Jonathan go?"

"I am unable to answer your request, sir."

"Yeah, yeah, we already knew you'd say that, too," Jimbo yelled from the back bedroom.

His partner was busy hacking into Max's matrix, downloading any of Jonathan's data that he could access into his netpad. "He has left her a message that is voice ID'd for her ears only, James, and these encryption codes are difficult." Frustrated, he snapped the netpad shut. "He is a damn good programmer."

"What about the other chef, Hector?" Jimbo asked.

"Possible. Go ahead and set up a VIDTrans there...and there," the senior Tel ordered, indicating a spot across the room. "I am sure Miss Connor will show up and retrieve his message. And when she does, Max's matrix will be exposed for our entry. We might get something, we might not. It is hard to say. But I do know this, she will lead us to him. I have a good feeling about her."

Jimbo's partner returned Max to his default settings while Jimbo set up the VIDTrans. Despite all their sophisticated equipment, they had failed to beat Jonathan's code. He had programmed Max's bioconstruct to be almost impossible for any hacker to breach without damage to the entire core matrix.

In the middle of the living room, Jimbo's partner stood gazing at the city through the loft's large windows. He was compressing his smoke into tiny little particle balls and letting them drop to the carpet, which he often did when his mind was working overtime.

"How you gonna play this one, boss?" Jimbo asked.

"James, if Jonathan is a Level 9, then we must be very careful not to...what is the word?"

"Spook him?"

"Yes...spook him. He will soon become very strong, stronger than I can control. So we have to befriend him, get him to trust us and trust the Agency. Pressure will not work on this one, James. Believe me. He is independent. And do you know what the most volatile factor is in this whole equation?" Morning light was beginning to stream into the loft. He blew a perfect smoke ring, letting it hang in front of him before compressing it into a little cube that floated into his outstretched hand. He slowly curled his fingers over the cube. "He might be in love, James. And that scares me the most."

Jimbo examined the system's panel to shut off the lights. "Say Max," he said impulsively, "why are you named Max?"

"I am named after Jonathan's brother."

"We have no record of him having a brother," the senior Tel quipped.

"He died in childbirth in Honolulu, Oahu, in the Hawaiian Islands."

The Tels exchanged a glance.

The senior Tel finished his cigarette, and they began to leave, but Jimbo stopped and stepped back into the loft. He walked toward the table and stretched out his hand. The book from Jonathan's father quietly flew into it. Jimbo turned it lovingly, caressing its soft leather cover.

"Call me Ishmael..." he said under his breath, pocketing the book in his coat.

~

Tamara woke to Anari standing on her head in the middle of the apartment. She was breathing softly in and out.

"Good morning, sunshine," Anari said, too cheery for the time of day.

"Morning," Tamara said, rubbing the sleep out of her eyes. "What are you doing?"

"My yoga," she answered. Anari fell over, spun around and ended up in full lotus position, with one finger to a nostril.

Tamara lit a cigarette and fell back against the bed.

Anari's apartment was a tiny 1-1 on the city's south side. Tamara had crashed there because, after dropping Nicole off at her grandmother's, she had been in no shape to deal with the late-night pilot crazies of the Interway. Anari was part Korean, part black and part anyone's guess. Having been found in a newspaper recycle bin at the end of Korea's last war with itself, she had been kicked from foster home to foster home. Her last and longest-lasting family was from the city. When she turned 18, she split and began a career in the late-night club scene. Doing everything from waitressing to dancing, she landed at Liquid Courage through a friend who knew

Joshua. Her apartment was sparsely furnished with a professional's attention to design.

Tamara closed her eyes and emptied her mind.

Anari screamed at the top of her lungs.

"What the hell are you doing?" Tamara said, covering her ears.

"Primal screaming."

"Primal whating?"

"Screaming. You should try it. It helps you get in touch with your real self. It's an old technique from 20th century pop psychology. I think it came out of that weird California thing...PEST, yeah, I think that's what it was called. I found it in an old book." She took a sip from her hydro-root celery tea.

Tamara gathered the blankets around her, clutching them for their innate security. She looked out the window and tried not to think of the events of last night. It was hard, though. The realization of what her lover was, of what he did (if she really knew), was almost too much to comprehend. She and Anari had said nothing on the ride back to her apartment. There had been no need. Anari had known Tamara for a long time and could read her like a netpad.

Anari handed her a cup of tea. "Hey, chicky, don't worry," she consoled.

"Don't worry?" Tamara took a long drag off her cigarette. "You did see what I saw last night, didn't you?" She sipped the tea and winced at its bitterness.

"I did!" Anari said. "But what did he do? If he did stop that Light-Force the reper was using, how? Some brain thing? I mean, come on, is Jonathan some gov experiment? How well do you know this guy, Tam?"

Tamara pulled in her knees tightly and began to rock. The end of her cigarette touched the blanket, which began to hiss from the burn.

"Oh shit!" Tamara batted wildly at the little burning threads that floated up from the blanket. "Anari, I'm so sorry, I'll get you a new one, really."

"Tam, don't worry...come on, it's just a blanket." Anari walked over and sat next to her. "Everything's going to be all right."

"Anari, that was telekinesis. Jonathan must be telekinetic, and if he can stop a weapon that powerful, he must be equally powerful..." She kept staring and rocking, unable to bring herself to finish the thought.

"What if he's, you know...not human?" Anari asked.

"You mean an alien? No, no way."

"No, I mean, a *different* human. Something from evolution, you know."

"He might be." Tamara closed her eyes. If her lover was more than human, then what did that make him? She put her hand to her heart and remembered the energy that flowed between them, the intense heat and tingling that filled her chest when he touched her. She had fallen in love with a man who could stop a weapon as powerful as a Light-Force, and she had no idea where he was.

One person might know, though.

"Max..." she said under her breath.

"What, Tam?"

"Come on, get dressed." Tamara said, toughing up. "We're heading out."

"Where?" Anari asked.

"To see a friend."

~

Tamara and Anari cautiously approached the door to Jonathan's loft.

"Are you sure he's not here?" Anari asked.

"I've called at least twenty times," Tamara said.

"Okay then. I'm following you, chicky,"

Tamara put out her cigarette.

"Max, it's me, Tamara Connor."

There was a long pause.

"Max, it's..."

"Good afternoon, Tamara." And the door unlatched.

The lights slowly came on as they entered.

"How are you today, Miss Connor? Who is your friend?"

"Max, this is Anari, and I'm fine, thanks."

They looked around the loft. Stepping through broken art and glass, Tamara was clearly disturbed.

"This place is trashed," Anari said.

"Yeah, and this isn't how he would have left it."

"Jonathan destroyed the items you see," Max interrupted.

"Why, Max?" Tamara asked.

"These are the physical, telekinetic results of the emotional duress he experienced after hearing your message."

"What did you say, girl?" Anari asked.

Tamara just stared.

"Girl?"

"I told him how I felt...then, I mean. Okay, I was freaked a little..." She lit up another cigarette.

"Well, by the looks of this place, you hurt him pretty bad."

Tamara scanned the room. Some, if not all, of Jonathan's favorite things were destroyed. He had told her about the mask that Hector had brought back to him. And the book his dad had given him as a child.

"Hey, where's the book?" Tamara said. She went to the table where Jonathan had kept it. "The book's gone. That's really strange."

"What book's that?" Anari asked.

"Moby Dick. It was real special to him. It was one of the only things he had from his father."

"Moby who? What is it, porn?"

Tamara shot Anari a look. "No. It's a classic."

"Tamara, there is a message for you," Max said.

"Really..." Tamara said slowly. "Please play it."

"Hey, you," Jonathan's holoimage appeared in the middle of the loft. He looked tired and his voice was rough. "I hope you're alone. But if not, well, it doesn't matter. Hi, Anari, if that's you." Anari smiled and looked over to Tamara. "Hey, baby, listen. What happened tonight was kind of an epiphany for me. All my life I've known that I was different in some way...I just couldn't put my finger on it. But some things have happened recently, and they've all culminated at the club with that reper pulling Light out on you." Jonathan's voice began to shake a little. "When he drew, I was talking to Anari. You need to thank her, baby, she really saved your life. She punched my arm so hard....It's still sore, girl, if you're in the room. Anyway, look, ah...I couldn't see you die in front of my eyes. I think I would have lost it right there. I've come to need you. You're like a drug to me, baby." Jonathan laughed and then coughed hard for a few seconds. "Sorry, I'm still feeling pretty bad. That last...hell, I don't even know what to call it. Episode...ah...telekinetic display? Whatever, it took it out of me. But you know, lover," his voice went soft, "I would have died to save you." He coughed again. "You looked so...helpless standing there. And when you told me you loved me, well...Hey, cover your ears, Anari, okay?...Tamara, listen carefully. I know we don't know each other, really, but what I do know has hit me deep. I'm not leaving you...like your message, I need a little space, too. This is a weird thing that's happening to me, and I have to get it together in order to deal with it. Do you understand? Please do. I'll be back, believe me. I need you too much. I would tell you where I'm going, but I have a feeling the less people know the better. Don't take offense to that, baby. I think it's for your own safety." He paused for a moment and folded his arms tightly across his chest. "Look, you should know that if news of my death comes down the net, Max has been instructed to contact you..."

Tamara closed her eyes.

"Oh hell, look, if I die, I'm giving Nicole most of my money. It's for both of you. Take care of her. Get her a great education. I don't have anyone, baby, you know that. The government would take most of it. I want you to have it." His voice cracked. "And baby, I wasn't asleep the other night...you've touched me too...I have to go now. Take care and be safe." Jonathan's holoimage disappeared.

Tamara stood motionless in the loft.

A little tear hung in the corner of Anari's eye. She saw that her friend had picked up a photo of Jonathan as a little boy. Anari could feel her pain without even asking. Tamara was about the only true friend Anari had, and it tore her up to see her this way.

"Hey, Tam...I..."

Tamara motioned for her to stop. She couldn't turn away from the photo of the young boy who had grown up to move mountains with his mind.

Tarris...16

AS the Airbus began its initial vert-descent into Albuquerque, Jonathan finished his drink. It was early evening, and the world always looked perfect from 58,000 feet. He had declined the use of the AB 800's workout room. Still fatigued from his telekinetic world premiere at the club the previous night, he chose the comfort of the plane's second-level sleeper stations. The blood had stopped flowing, and the pain in his mind had been fairly nominal considering he had just defied the speed of light. The plane's Rolls-Royce bioturbines emitted a low droning sound as the pilot corrected for turbulence over the Sangre de Cristo front range.

The last time Jonathan had seen Tarris was not long after the accident. Tarris had always been a wild child, and his drug habit had become a problem. He had been Jonathan's best friend until he left for college. He was always the one who could help him get straight on anything from complex quantum math to girls. He was the brother Jonathan had never had.

"Good evening, ladies and gentlemen. This is your first officer speaking. It looks like a beautiful evening in Albuquerque; the winds are calm, and there's a temperature of 82 degrees. We should be touching down in about 17 minutes. Flight attendants, please prepare the cabins for our initial vert-descent into New Mexico."

Tarris was a programming genius. He had taught Jonathan much of what made him the programmer he was today, and he was always flattered that Jonathan would reference him in interviews and articles. But Tarris's passion was gaming. He had developed the first holovid interface that didn't require the usual protocols that slowed uplink time off the net. He had worked for BioGame Industries, a huge Pacific Rim conglomerate that had its hands into everything from vertslots to holoporn. The gaming division was its brain trust, and Tarris was its golden child – at least until the time Tarris went for a midnight "century run" with the L.A. Ducati club. Jonathan had warned Tarris about riding and biking a long time ago. Tarris loved his drugs, and he loved his Ducati. But late one night about 10 years ago, he had mixed the two – and mixed them bad.

"Sir, please stow your VIDscreen, we'll be descending shortly. Thank you."

It had been a tough night for Tarris and his team. Marketing was putting on the pressure for a Christmas release date, but the complex programming for Stealth War, the new game for kids 13 and up, was too stubborn to comply. After months of testing, the game's download time was still too long. Marketing had made it clear that download time was the key to success in the Game category. And nobody knew the critical nature of download better than Tarris. Frustrated, he dismissed his team for the night and returned the netcall he had received from the Ducati Club of Los Angles. It was one call, he later would tell Jonathan, he wished he had never returned.

"Ah, ladies and gentlemen, this is your first officer again. We've been told by Albuquerque tower that we're going to experience some chop on our final vert-descent into the airport, so we're gonna ask that you return to your seats."

Tarris had met up with the club just outside L.A. *A run in the hills,* he had thought, *was just the thing to get the old brain clear again.* And a little recreational drug ride wouldn't hurt, either. He started the Ducati SS2300 and clicked it into its night-ride setting. Rolling into the Interway, he would tell Jonathan later, he felt his drug ride was going to be weird, but he didn't turn back.

As the pack wound its way through the California night, Tarris grew more and more uneasy with the drug he had taken. The usual effects of mild euphoria and enhanced senses had been replaced by paranoiac tension and a slight loss of motor skill. The Ducati SS was a smooth and solid bike, but it was still an aggressive machine, and you didn't jerk around with 600 pounds of biotechnology. Tarris began to lean into a typical Interway curve, and the new guy next to him looked over and pointed to his bike. Nothing unusual, except it was night, and they were redlining at 255 mph. For a fellow rider to divert his attention on a curve at that speed, something must definitely be wrong. Tarris braked. First mistake. In his fog of confusion, he used the front braking system. The biosport bike's onboard computer would have read the situation and applied the rear braking system at that speed and angle of attack, but Tarris, being the wild child, had disengaged the safety protocols. Second mistake. He said it made for a more authentic ride. Even with his self-inflating foam impact suit, the last thing Tarris remembered after that was coming out of post-op at L.A. County General.

~

The plane's vertical descent was flawless, and its touchdown hardly noticeable. Jonathan unbuckled, grabbed his gear and made his way to the exit. In the terminal, he pushed through throngs of teenage bioboarders, ski bums and Texas families struggling with vacation gear. Since the Biolution, a season with no snow was an impossibility, which made New Mexico the new Mecca for those who loved the slopes. It was June, and the season was still at full tilt.

The drive to Taos was always relaxing, and it was just what Jonathan needed. The sun was setting as the car slipped in and out of the dark shadows of the mountains. New Mexico was still relatively unspoiled, and he could see why Tarris had made his home here.

It was late when Jonathan came into Taos. What had been a small artist colony and vacation spot in the late 20th century had turned into a tourist's nightmare of Indian casinos, bioshirt shops and half-price ski outlets after the Biolution. Jonathan couldn't believe Tarris would have settled in a place like this. But his directions took him out of town toward Tres Piedras, population: 75.

It took another hour through the stark land before Jonathan saw renewed signs of human activity. He went around what little town there was and down a narrow gravel road. He drove through two sharp curves, past the shell of a burned-out antique propeller passenger plane, its tail section buried halfway into the side of a hill, and over a steep embankment. Jonathan stepped out of his car and looked over a compound of various metal-roofed buildings draped with black solar panels that reflected the dark night sky of New Mexico. Old tires and glass bottles filled some of the walls, and a dog barked off in the distance.

The dry night air had cooled quickly, and it felt good on Jonathan's face. Fresh. Crisp. Real.

He began the walk down the small hill to the compound. An antique rifle shot rang out, kicking up dirt at Jonathan's feet. Its sound echoed through the hills.

"Who the hell are you?" a voice called out from nowhere discernable.

"Tarris?"

"Jonathan? Jonathan Kortel?"

The door to the middle building burst open, flooding a small area of the ground with light. Tarris rolled out into it.

"What the hell are you doing here?" Tarris asked as Jonathan came down the hill into the compound.

"I needed a drink!" He bent down and hugged his boy-hood friend.

"You could have called!"

"Yeah, well, I'm off-line for a time. I'll tell you all about it."

"I want to hear! Must be pretty important to bring you all the way out here. Or is it *she's* pretty important?" Tarris laughed.

"Is that a new chair?" Jonathan said, changing the subject.

"Yeah, it's the best. It's almost like walking," Tarris said, rolling his eyes. "No, really, this thing is state-of-the-art. Check this out man, I designed it myself." Tarris rolled back a few feet and engaged the chair's system. Its biomedtronic technology made a soft hissing sound while lifting his body to a standing position. The chair's biopoly carbon tubing reformed into a support frame that molded against the back of his legs. The two small multiwheelbase platforms attached to his feet separated and became bootlike pads. The chair's back also shifted and wrapped partly around Tarris's midsection to provide support for his lower back. Throughout Tarris's legs and hips, implants controlled by an on-board computer matrix provided the interface connection for his brain to dialogue with his legs.

Tarris "walked" over to Jonathan. "Now," he said, his arms outstretched, "give your big brother a real hug."

~

Tarris poured Jonathan another Scotch. Light from a small lamp reflected off of Tarris's face. Jonathan could see that, for 33, his friend was looking older than his years. He had been beaten down. Whether by the accident or his harsh New Mexican environment was hard to say, but Jonathan could tell that the wild child of his boyhood had tamed a bit.

"Sounds like she's pretty special to you," Tarris said, sipping foam from the surface of his fresh margarita. He knew his friend, and he sensed Jonathan had revealed just the tip of the iceberg that really was bothering him.

"Yeah, she is..." Jonathan's voice wandered.

"Buddy, what is it?" Tarris said passionately. "It's me. Tarris. I know everything about you."

"No, you don't. There's more, Tarris...a lot more."

Jonathan talked for more than two hours. He told Tarris everything: the history of inexplicable experiences throughout his life, the kitchen fire and, finally, the Light-Force episode at Liquid Courage. Tarris sat motionless in his chair, quietly absorbing the anguish of his friend and sipping his margarita.

Jonathan ended his monologue by downing the last of his Scotch and watching the dying fire. The piñon smell was comforting, reminding him of the restaurant and the men of Kitchen Kortel. He finally looked over to Tarris, who had not taken his gaze from him.

"Am I a freak, Tarris?" Jonathan asked in a low voice.

His friend paused and focused on his margarita. Finally, he said, "Let me show you something, Jonathan." He scooted over to a bookshelf to the left of the fireplace, and rolling back, flipped through a large textbook. Finding the place, he handed it to Jonathan. "Here, buddy, read this."

Tarris rolled to another part of the house and started rummaging through a closet. Jonathan could hear him pulling boxes apart and swearing under his breath.

"Ohhh, it's gravity displacement. I wondered how it worked." Jonathan yelled over the commotion Tarris was making, "Where did you get this book?"

"It's from grad school. An old psych teacher had it, and he gave it to me. It goes into all sorts of paranormal shit. Here we go!" Tarris exclaimed, and he came rolling back down the hallway. He came up to the table brushing the dust off the book he had retrieved, but suddenly he stopped and stared at Jonathan reading.

"This is so interesting, do you really think I have..." Jonathan said, interrupting himself when he saw the smile on his friend's face.

"What?...What is it Tarris?"

"Do something."

"Well, I..."

"Come on, shit. We're out in the middle of nowhere. It's me, Tarris."

Jonathan smiled, put the book down and leaned forward on the table.

"So, you want to see something?" The buzz from the Scotch had kicked in.

Tarris nodded, still smiling.

Jonathan didn't move a muscle or close his eyes. He just kept looking at his friend. A moment passed.

Tarris lost his smile. "Hey, you're not bullshitting me..." Just then he rose off the brick floor in his chair. Tarris began to laugh. "Holy shit, Jonny! This is out of control!" He continued to rise until he hit his head on one of the room's *vigas*. "Okay, okay, bring me down!" Jonathan slowly lowered him to the floor, and Tarris motored back to the table as fast as his chair would take him. "What's it like?" Tarris asked.

"Well, that sort of stuff's not too tough anymore. I think I'm growing in ability. I've noticed that it gains strength each day. It's like it becomes more familiar, more comfortable to me. Like it's instinctual."

"Yeah, but man, you stopped a Light-Force weapon! That's damn fast, buddy. That's faster than light."

"Yeah, I know. That's one I can't explain. Yet." Jonathan reflectively jingled the ice cubes in his glass.

"I know how you did it. It was the extreme adrenaline rush you got from the fear of seeing your girl get killed by that reper." Tarris leaned within inches of Jonathan's face; his breath stank of tequila. "Love is a powerful thing. I should know." And he winked.

"Really?" Jonathan asked.

Tarris leaned back and smiled.

"Tarris, are you holding out on me? Who is she? What's her name?"

"Georgia. She'll be here later. She works the blackjack tables at The Diamond Horseshoe in Taos." He raised an eyebrow. "And you should see her in her uniform, mmm, shit, she is one fine woman, Jonathan." Tarris slammed his margarita and belched.

"Oh...here." Tarris threw Jonathan the other book. It landed in a dust cloud on his lap. "This might give you some more insight. Good night, buddy." He started to leave, but stopped and looked back. "Hey, Jonathan," he said with care in his eyes. "I'm glad you're here."

"Me too."

Tarris continued down the hall to the back of the house. Jonathan spun the book around to read its cover: Ten Things the Government Doesn't Want You to Know.

He flipped through chapters on aliens, the Challenger Explosion and the Kennedy assassinations, but one titled "The Tels" coldly grabbed his attention. It described a theory of a shadowy government agency staffed by men and women at various levels of telekinetic power. The Tel chart was explained, and the Agency's long history, starting in the early 1950s all the way to the present, was detailed as if it really existed. Jonathan finished and checked his watch. Two in the morning. He was tired. It had been a long trip, and the Scotch was tugging him toward the bed. As he looked around Tarris's home, he thought of Tamara and his message. "I miss you..." he said in the quiet of the living room. The fire crackled down to a pile of glowing, orange embers. He glanced down at the book. "Wouldn't that be the shits if you guys were real." He fell asleep as the fire died out.

~

Jonathan woke up to the scent of coffee brewing on a real flame stove. He looked around to find he was still in the chair, but he had been wrapped in a warm, natural wool Navaho blanket. Someone in the kitchen was humming a tune he couldn't quite make out.

"Good morning," she said.

"Good morning...Georgia?" Jonathan asked.

"Yes, I'm sure Tarris has told you all about me," she said over the whine of the blender.

"No, not really. We didn't get to it last night," Jonathan said, unwrapping himself from his Navaho cocoon. In the kitchen he found a tall girl with straight, black, shoulder-length hair prepping a breakfast shake in a blender. She wore blue jeans, sandals and a loose-fitting natural cotton shirt unbuttoned deep into her cleavage. She grinned at the sight of him. Her lips were thin, and her smile was broad, and when she really smiled, her lower lip curled down to give a glimpse of how she appeared as a little girl. But what struck Jonathan the most were her eyes – dark eyes, almost as black as her hair.

"Here you go. This ought to take the edge off." She offered him some coffee in a huge ceramic mug. Steam wafted above it as she handed it to him.

"Thanks, this smells great." Jonathan walked to an enormous window in the dining room. It seemed a frame for the mountains to the east, a giant painting continuously changing with sunlight and seasons.

"This is our favorite view," Georgia said, wiping fruit juice from her hands and joining him to share the view.

"How long have you been with Tarris?"

"Oh, about a year. We met at a bar in Taos."

"That's great that you're so..." he stopped, suddenly realizing he had set himself up.

"What," she said, smiling at catching him, "that a woman like me can love a paraplegic?"

"Well, no...I didn't mean it that way."

"It's okay," she laughed. "Tarris can be very persuasive when he wants to be. And besides," she leaned over, as if confiding a secret, "don't let that chair fool you. Not everything is off line below the belt with Tarris." She smiled broadly again and returned to the kitchen.

Jonathan turned back to the view, embarrassed that his first conversation with her was a little awkward.

"Tarris told me a lot about you," she said.

Jonathan choked on the coffee in his mouth.

She looked up from the sink. "Don't worry, Mr. Telekinetic, your secret is safe with us."

"Oh, great, so you know, too."

"Hey," she stopped prepping and turned to face him. "Don't worry. I'm very open to this kind of thing. So is Tarris. You're safe here with us. Stay as long as you want. Here, let me refill you." She came over and took his mug. When their hands touched, an energy passed between them almost like a static discharge.

"Oh!" she said, almost dropping the mug. "I hate this dry air sometimes. The static can build up so much. Watch it with Tarris and that darn chair. It can almost stop your heart." She took his cup back to the kitchen to refill it.

"So, you've met Georgia. Wasn't I right?" Tarris beamed as he motored his way from the back porch to Georgia. She bent down and gave him a long, passionate kiss. "God, I love this girl!" He slapped her butt as she passed him with her shake on the way to the hall. Tarris winked at Jonathan. "Is that fine or what?"

Jonathan watched her for a second before turning back to the mountains. "Do you think the Agency really exists?" he asked Tarris, who was now standing up with his chair and making some toast.

With all the skill of a gymnast, Tarris went from countertop to cabinet, "walking" almost without effort. One of his foot pads caught in the grout of the tiled floor. "Goddamn this floor. I'm going to change it out when the residuals come in from my next game. What did you ask? Oh, the Agency, right. I don't know for sure. But if you ask some folks out here, they'll tell you it does."

"If they're so secret," Jonathan asked, looking over to the kitchen, "how do you get in touch with them?"

"I wouldn't worry about that; they'll probably get in touch with you." Tarris pointed the knife he was using at Jonathan to emphasize that last word.

Jonathan recoiled – both at the knife and at the thought that he was possibly being watched. It unnerved him, and Tarris could tell.

"Hey, Jonathan, if they do exist, at least you're not alone. Maybe they can teach you how to harness your abilities. Put it to good use for mankind and all that kinda stuff." He crunched down on his toast and leaned against the counter like he still had use of his legs.

"Well, one thing's for sure," Jonathan said. "My life has changed forever."

"I'll tell you what," Tarris responded, as he joined Jonathan at the window, "I know that story, buddy."

Contact...17

DOC Martin's was a Taos institution. Even with its 21st century urban transformation, Taos still had little pieces of history. Doc Martin's was the place for a drink with friends and a great meal for less than four hundred bucks, and it had been that way for nearly two centuries. Much of the original building was still a working hotel. But if you were a local and had the credit, Saturday night was the night at Doc's. You could bet on the best local music, and all your friends would be there, whether you wanted to see them or not.

Jonathan, Tarris and Georgia squeezed their way to the bar. People didn't seem to notice Tarris's "walking" chair, or if they did, they were cool enough not to stare or ask questions. Taos still retained a touch of the Old West. People here left you alone.

"I know what you two want!" the bartender said, pointing at Tarris and Georgia. "But I'm clueless about him. What'll it be, friend?"

"Scotch, house blend is fine. With ice, no water, please," Jonathan said, taking an elbow in the ribs from a large Indian with a three-foot ponytail.

"I'm so sorry," the big Indian said in a deep voice. His skin was the color of rich coffee, and his eyes nearly black. Deep age lines radiated from their corners and deepened when he smiled. "My name is Whitehorse, Jacob Whitehorse. And you?"

"Jonathan Kortel."

"Are you new to Taos?" He eyed him seriously.

"Visiting some friends just outside the city."

"Well, welcome to Taos, Mr. Kortel. I hope you have a good stay." He turned and resumed his conversation with another tall Indian, who looked over the shoulder of Jacob Whitehorse at Jonathan. Jonathan smiled and took his drink from Tarris. Georgia was busy hunting down a table.

"You certainly are lucky, Tarris. She seems very nice," Jonathan said when Georgia waved to them from across the room.

"Yeah, I lucked out on this one. I just hope I can make her happy."

Jonathan and Tarris settled at the table while Georgia summoned a waiter.

Jonathan watched the regulars of Doc's go about their business. Families chattered and laughed in the large booths. Men shook hands and bellied up to the bar. Couples cuddled by the fireplace. The two Indians stayed at the bar. Every so often, one or the other would glance in his direction. It began to put Jonathan's netdar up.

"Hey, Tarris. Who are the two big guys at the bar?"

"They're gamblers," Georgia cut in. "They come up from Los Alamos every other weekend."

"Oh. The one with the ponytail seems nice enough. He introduced himself to me at the bar."

"Yeah," Georgia said, "he can't play blackjack to save his life."

They ordered from the specials. It was real food. Not bioenhanced. Jonathan was looking forward to some local cuisine, and he wished Hector was there to share it. He took a long drink from his Scotch.

By the time their food arrived, Doc's was in full swing. The band had set up, and the dance floor was cleared. It was a small group. The lead guitarist was a rotund little man dressed in vintage cowboy ware. His hat was huge compared to the rest of his body, and his thick glasses were an unusual touch, considering the need for eyewear had gone out with the silicon chip. His vest was embroidered in lariat type that read "Riders of the Purple Sage." The bassist was a tall, pretty older woman whose rugged looks matched her jeans. But the oddest of the crew was the blind piano player. She was dressed in an authentic period dress from the 1800s. It was a dress you'd imagine your great-great-great-great-grandmother wearing to the ice cream social. The food, Jonathan noted, was excellent, with subtle flavors a bioprogrammer would envy.

They finished their meals and waited for the band to start. It opened with "Boot Scootin' Boogie." Jonathan noticed that the two big Indians were gone. He looked over at Tarris, who was looking at Georgia.

"Baby, this is our song," Tarris said, taking her hand.

"Come on, lover," Georgia grinned. "Let's show Taos what you can do." She stood up, took his hand and came around the table. He backed away, engaged the chair's systems and stood up to meet her face with his. He winked at Jonathan.

Jonathan watched them swing to the vintage 20th-century tune with such ease that it was hard to tell that Tarris even had a disability. He smiled as they passed, scootin' across the old wooden floor.

"May we join you?" a deep voice from behind Jonathan asked.

Jonathan turned to see the two big Indians looking down at him. Their large presence gave him a start, and only Jacob Whitehorse was smiling.

"Sure," Jonathan said, "have a seat. And your name is?" Jonathan extended his hand to the silent Indian, who said nothing and didn't return the offer of the handshake.

"Please excuse my friend," Whitehorse said. "He is very shy around crowds. Jonathan, I can call you Jonathan, can't I?" Whitehorse asked.

Jonathan nodded. The silent one didn't strike him as the shy type.

"Let me be blunt, Jonathan. We know who and what you are." A cold chill ran down Jonathan's spine. "But before you get up, we're not the Agency. You know about the Agency?"

Jonathan nodded.

"Then you should know we're not like them. If you're interested in preserving some semblance to your life, you'll meet us at this address tomorrow morning at ten o'clock." He handed him a card, and they both rose to leave.

"Oh, and Jonathan," Whitehorse added. "If you don't show, we can't be responsible for how your life will turn out." He leaned down, his hulking face in shadow from the stage lights. "Think of Tamara, Jonathan....I know you don't want to lose her." He straightened and followed the silent one out the front door.

Tarris and Georgia stumbled to the table laughing. They had been on their third song when he had pulled her from the dance floor.

"How you doing, buddy, having fun yet?" he asked breathlessly. Then Tarris sat so in sync with his chair's transformation that it appeared as if it were part of him.

"Doing great..." Jonathan lied, still staring at the front door.

"Are you sure?" Tarris pressed, following in the direction of his stare.

"Oh yeah." Jonathan tore his eyes from the door. "You two look like you're having a blast. You really are adept with that chair. It's amazing! Don't you get tired with all the implants?"

"Yeah, I get tired. It's tough on the body to walk in this thing." He patted Georgia's knee. "I mean, it doesn't make me a Fred Astaire, but it gets me around."

"It does more than that," Georgia said, winking.

They all laughed. But Jonathan wasn't listening. The words of Jacob Whitehorse kept resounding in his mind. All he could think of was the meeting tomorrow, and the answers it might bring.

The pueblo...18

THE air was crisp, and the swirling wind twisted the steam from Jonathan's coffee into little tornadoes that disappeared as fast as they rose. He stood on Tarris's back porch looking east to the mountains, now silhouetted in their predawn colors of purple and blue. As a lone hawk rode the quickly heating thermals high above his head, Jonathan wondered what the day might bring. He closed his eyes and thought of Tamara. A crack appeared in the kiva next to him.

"May I join you?" Georgia asked, interrupting the morning quiet.

Jonathan smiled as she came up to his side.

"Beautiful, aren't they?" she asked, referring to the mountains.

"Yes, they are." He took a long sip from his coffee.

"Did you bring that with you?" she asked, gesturing to his cup.

"You don't mind? It's my own special blend."

"No, I'm not a purist. Biofoods are fine, I think."

The sun exploded over the mountaintops, flooding the New Mexican land with bright, overexposed color. Jonathan and Georgia diverted their eyes from its intensity. The wind whipped her hair across his face. He looked into her dark, almost pupilless eyes. She was naturally pretty, and a smile crossed his face when he thought how Tarris had seemed so happy with her.

"What?..." she asked, questioning his look.

"Oh, nothing....You happy with Tarris?"

"Yes," she said, turning back to the view, "he's a good man."

"Yeah, he is."

"You are too, you know." She stepped between Jonathan and the sunrise, pulled her hair off her face and looked deep into his eyes. "You know, you're not like the rest of humanity. You're different, Jonathan Kortel. You're not even like the others that are like you. You know that now, don't you? You're more powerful than they ever could hope to be..."

"Now that's a damn sunrise!" Tarris exclaimed, rolling onto the porch. Jonathan started to say something, but Georgia stopped him and greeted her lover with a kiss.

"I can see why you're out here," Jonathan said. "This land is," he glanced over to Georgia, "powerful."

"Man, I tell you, you can't beat it," Tarris laughed. "It never ceases to amaze me."

"Hey, I'm gonna go into Taos this morning. Do you all need anything?" Jonathan asked.

"Let me go with you," Tarris cut in. "I'll show you around!"

"No thanks. I need a little 'me time,' you understand. I just want to roam around, maybe go out to the Pueblo."

"Come on, baby," Georgia said to Tarris. "I'll cook us a big breakfast. Let's see what the big-time biochef thinks of our special 'Tres Piedras' omelets." She laughed and flipped up the handles of Tarris's chair.

Jonathan watched her begin to wheel Tarris like he was in an old-fashioned wheelchair. It looked oddly affectionate, like it was their special bonding thing – her pushing and him accepting. Tarris reached up and held her hand as they went into the house.

~

For more than 500 years, Taos Pueblo had been one of the oldest working pueblos in New America. What was once a tourist trap in the latter 20th century had been returned to its original purpose through a change in the elders.

Jonathan drove slowly as he approached the entrance. Two large Indian men in contemporary clothes stopped Jonathan by lowering their military issue Light-Force weapons and letting the ends of the barrels rest on the hood of his car. Their mirrored sunglasses reflected the car and 180 degrees of the scene behind it. One with a red bandanna approached the car's window. He tapped the glass with the end of his weapon.

Jonathan lowered the window. "I'm here to meet with Jacob Whitehorse."

The bandanna Indian didn't respond. He waved to his partner to let Jonathan pass.

Jonathan slowly pulled into the Pueblo. The people in the plaza moved out of the way, ignoring him as if he and his car didn't exist. The square was large and filled with men, women and children going about their affairs. The whole scene was like stepping back through time. Some people were in native dress, while others wore modern business bioware. Children played on front stoops with their netpad game units, and old men sat together in what little shade the sparse trees supplied. Jonathan crept along, searching for some indication of where he should go, when, suddenly, a tall Indian appeared at the hood of the car. Jonathan slammed the brake system, kicking up a dust cloud. When it settled, Jacob Whitehorse was smiling from the front of the car.

"Welcome, Jonathan," he said. "I'm so glad you chose to come." He opened the door for him and took his keys. A young Indian boy jumped into the driver's seat.

"Don't worry," Whitehorse said. He pointed to a shaded spot under a set of two trees. "He'll just park your car over there."

Jonathan didn't say a word.

"This was a very smart move on your part," Whitehorse continued, putting his large hand on Jonathan's shoulder. "There are many people who want to meet you."

Whitehorse led Jonathan through the maze of Pueblo streets. Ducking under a low archway, he brought him to a small courtyard where about a dozen people were milling around. They were of various ethnicity: some were Indian, some black, others white or Hispanic. The courtyard grew quiet at their appearance, and everyone turned to greet them. Jonathan scanned their faces and could feel compassion, almost as if they were family.

"Ladies and gentlemen," Whitehorse said in his deep voice, "this is Jonathan Kortel." No one responded, other than to continue smiling. He glanced at Jonathan. "These are your people, Jonathan. Welcome home."

A small Indian girl broke from the crowd and walked right up to within a foot of Jonathan. She didn't say anything for a moment. Then she slowly rose off the ground until she came face to face with him. Hovering in front of him, she kissed him on the cheek. "Welcome to Taos Pueblo, Mr. Kortel," she said in a soft voice. Then she turned in the air, spread her arms and floated back toward the group, giggling all the way.

A woman gently pushed her way forward to catch the little girl in her arms. It was Georgia.

She hesitantly smiled at Jonathan.

The people began to laugh a little, and Whitehorse motioned for Jonathan to go and meet them. He headed straight for Georgia. She set down the little girl, who scurried off behind the group, and met his quizzical eyes through her dark black bangs.

"Look," she said sheepishly, "this isn't what you think."

"And what do I think?" Jonathan said coolly. "Or are you one of those who already knows what I'm thinking?"

"No, no, come on now, don't be that way. These are good people. We're just like you, Jonathan. Well, sort of."

"Does Tarris know?" he pressed.

She turned away. Jonathan grabbed her arm. Quiet descended once again on the courtyard.

"Please don't tell me you were planted for me," he said angrily. Whitehorse looked up from a conversation.

"No, Jonathan," she said, though she would not meet his glare. "I love Tarris, really..."

Jonathan's look said he didn't buy it. He tightened his grip on her arm. Whitehorse stepped closer.

"Okay, okay! At first, yes, I was a set up. We knew of you and your tie with Tarris. We bet you'd come to him eventually." She tried to wriggle free. He firmed his grip. Whitehorse carefully began to make his way to them.

"Believe me, Jonathan," she quietly pleaded, "it wasn't supposed to turn out the way it did. I told you" – Jonathan pulled her close to his face – "Tarris is very persuasive."

Jonathan's grip was extreme. Georgia winced in agony. Whitehorse was nearly within reach of Jonathan when suddenly he shot 15 feet into the air. Jonathan looked up at the big Indian, who was now floating like a Macy's parade balloon. "This is between me and Georgia!"

"I know, Jonathan," Jacob yelled down, "but she's telling you the truth!"

Georgia was clawing at his grip with her free hand. "Please, Jonathan, I love Tarris with all my heart!" She broke down into tears.

Jonathan released her arm. Shocked at himself, he examined his hand like it had acted on its own. He took in the whole scene: Georgia rubbing her arm, glaring at him in awe and anger, Whitehorse dangling helplessly in the air, the crowd waiting in stunned silence for his next move.

Jonathan was overwhelmed. "I'm so sorry..." he blurted, and ran out of the courtyard.

Whitehorse fell to the ground, kicking and flailing.

"Go, Georgia! Get him!" he commanded, struggling to his feet. "We can't afford to lose him!"

Georgia immediately sprinted after him.

~

Jonathan tried to remember the way back, but the more frantically he searched, the more lost he became. "That's all I need is to join some stupid Indian cult," he swore under his breath. People stared at him as he ran past.

Running down an alley he hoped was the way out, he turned a corner and ran headlong into the chest of the silent Indian.

Jonathan fell back to the ground.

"Shit..." he said, picking himself up. The Indian didn't respond.

"Jonathan!" Georgia called from the end of the alley.

He turned and saw Georgia running toward him, clutching her arm.

"Jonathan! Come on!" She grabbed his hand and yanked him away from the large Indian, who lunged at them and just missed Jonathan's shirt.

Georgia pulled him through an archway and into the open square. "In the car!" she said.

"I don't have the keys!" he answered, sliding to the door.

An old Indian seated across from the car threw the keys at him. "Come back now," he said, revealing a toothless smile.

They jumped in, and Jonathan started the car and gunned it in reverse. Three old women scattered like cats.

"Sorry, sorry!" he said, as if they could actually hear him.

As they approached the gate, the two guards put their left hands to their ears, then looked up at the car.

"Jonathan! Stop!" Georgia screamed. "This isn't some movie!"

Jonathan looked at her and smiled.

The two Indians charged their Light-Force weapons and raised them at the car.

"Jonathan?!..." Georgia scrunched herself down in the seat.

Five feet from hitting the men and the gate, the two Indians were vaulted up and over the car, and the gates flew open, slamming hard against the adobe walls.

Jonathan grinned at Georgia and raised an eyebrow. Georgia looked at him through her dark bangs and smiled that smile.

~

"James, it looks like Mr. Kortel's first meeting with the Rogues did not go so well," said Jimbo's partner. He snapped the field optics shut and returned them to their case.

"Yeah," Jimbo said, tracking the car, "and it looks like our hero gets a new girl, too."

"Don't be so sure. If she is a true Rogue, her loyalty will be wherever Whitehorse wants it. I should know. I trained him."

He struggled to light another cigarette. Jimbo stepped over, stared at the lighter, mentally created a field flux wall just in front of it and blocked the wind.

"Thank you, James. I was just about to do that myself." He blew a perfect ring. "I am hungry. We should see what this city has to offer."

"What about them?" Jimbo asked, indicating the dust trail growing more distant from the Pueblo.

"Oh, we have time. She will work on him, tell him about the Rogues, talk down the Agency...you know, the usual. Jonathan will become enamored with the romantic vision of the Rogues, world peace and all. But if he is as smart as I think, he will catch on to Whitehorse soon enough." He blew another smoke ring and watched the dust cloud rise into the warm midday air.

"Yeah, well, what if he doesn't get enamored?"

"Then we have an easier time selling Mr. Kortel on the Agency."

"You got this all figured out, don't you?"

His partner kept watching the cloud.

"What if he isn't enamored with *us*?" Jimbo asked.

"Then, James, things might get a little ugly." His cigarette left his mouth, snuffed itself out and dropped to the ground. His arms remained folded.

The Rogues...19

THERE was no conversation on the trip back to the Interway. Jonathan's mind was thick with confusion. He struggled with his conflicting images of Georgia: the original "Tarris loving" one, and the new "Indian cult" version.

When he finally reached the Interway for the hour-long ride back to Tres Piedras, he broke the silence: "Were you ever going to tell him?"

"That depends," Georgia quietly started. "If you join us, then yes, he'll find out eventually. But if you choose not to, then I don't see the point. Why hurt him. Anyway, if you leave, I'm leaving the Rogues and staying with Tarris."

"You really do love him?" he asked, searching her face for signs of lying.

She hesitated. "Yes, I do. I know it's hard for you to believe, but you have to. I've come to love your friend very much. Whether you turn out to be The Infinite Tel or not, I'm staying with Tarris."

"The Infinite Tel? What the hell is that?"

"You don't know?" she asked, surprised.

"No!" he said, mimicking her surprise. "Come on, Georgia. I'm new to this game. You all are 'hovering' and 'floating' about, giving the hairy eyeball and saving villages. Hell, I'm just over here stopping light waves with my mind!"

Georgia looked at Jonathan in shock.

"Yeah, got you on that one. Whitehorse didn't tell you about that little episode, did he?"

"No," she said somberly.

"Stopped a Light-Force bioweapon beam within two inches of my girl..." he quit in midsentence, suddenly realizing that he had never referred to Tamara that way.

"Girlfriend, Jonathan?" Georgia finished.

"Yeah...girlfriend," he said and turned his attention to back to the Interway.

~

For 20 miles it was quiet.

"So, what's The Infinite Tel?" Jonathan asked, breaking the tension. "What do you all think I am? Some sort of Confucius or Mohammed or Buddha?" He looked over at her. "Or Christ?"

"No, nothing like that. But possibly that important," she answered.

"Oh yeah, I'm the Son of God," he said, and rolled his eyes.

"No, but your impact on man could be as long-lasting."

"You're serious about this stuff, aren't you?"

She nodded.

"Okay then, tell me about...what did you call them...the Rogues?"

Georgia spent the next 30 minutes explaining the splinter group that had broken away from the Agency more than 10 years ago. Some of the most talented Tels had become disillusioned with the direction of the Agency and had left to form an underground group dedicated to world peace. Their efforts had made a difference throughout South America and Asia.

"So how did the disenchanted end up in the Land of Enchantment?" Jonathan asked.

"Jacob Whitehorse."

"He's the head man? Tell me about him. Do Indians have more potential of being telekinetic than most?...You know, with their culture being so tied to the land and all?"

"Well, statistically, Potentials that are at least 70% Native American do exhibit abilities that are at Level 5 or higher. Now, whether that's because they're Native American, I don't know. What I do know is Jacob Whitehorse is a powerful Tel."

"Who came up with the concept of The Infinite Tel?"

"Jacob..." Jonathan said in unison with Georgia. "Right, got it. So what do you all do? Fight oppression, poverty, crime? Go where no man has gone before?" he mocked.

"We go where we're needed. There's a lot of work to be done in the world. If a small village in, say, Bogota needs help after a flood, we move in and give them a little nudge. Help recess the water or move large amounts of debris. You know, things like that. And we never reveal ourselves, ever!"

"That's admirable. I can buy into that," he said. "But where would I fit in?"

"You could help stop conflicts, or even a war. Maybe bring people to a bargaining table." She shifted in the seat to face him. "Think of it! You could reveal the Tel subculture to the rest of the world and possibly help usher in a new age for mankind." She reached over and touched his arm.

"Well, before you anoint me the new messiah, what are we going to do about Tarris?"

"I think it would be best if neither of us said anything until you decide. I don't want to lose him."

"Fair enough." He drove the rest of the way in silence, trying to sort out his next move.

~

"Look what I picked up in Taos!" Jonathan said to Tarris as Georgia stepped out of the car.

"Baby, where's the truck?" Tarris asked.

"It died in Taos."

"Shit. I'll go deal with it tomorrow." Tarris motored back into the house, and Georgia gave Jonathan the thumbs up.

After dinner, Tarris and Jonathan relaxed by the fire. The meal was good, but Jonathan thought the pesto could have used a little programming to punch the flavors. He took a long sip from his Scotch and thought about his conversation with Georgia. If the Rogues really were the telekinetic version of Green Peace, maybe it wouldn't hurt to join them. World peace. Saving lives. Who could argue with that? But revealing the Tel subculture seemed dangerous to him. Not much different, he reasoned, than the government revealing the evidence of aliens on earth.

He laughed into his Scotch.

"Are you all right?" Georgia asked from the kitchen.

"Yeah. My Scotch just went down the wrong way," he lied, wiping his chin.

Tarris had fallen asleep in his chair, and Georgia was peering into the refrigerator. "Darn, the milk is bad, and I wanted to make waffles for us in the morning."

"I'll go get some. There's a biomart in town, isn't there?"

"Biomart? Jonathan, please," she laughed.

"Okay, mart. Is there a mart?"

"Yes, it's just as you enter town, off to the right."

"Ok, I'll be back in a sec."

"Jonathan," she yelled and whispered at the same time. "Be careful."

"Now, don't worry. It's me – faster than a beam of speeding photons."

~

TP Mart was void of customers and, for that matter, counter help. Jonathan walked down the aisles of biodiapers, synthoil and flip-flops.

"Flip-flops," he mused. "I haven't seen these in years." He threw a pair of black ones in his basket. As he approached the checkout station, a small Hispanic man seemed to rise from beneath the counter.

"Sorry," the TP Mart clerk said, "I be cleaning under the sink."

Jonathan paid and left. The parking lot was oddly still. Then again, it was almost one in the morning. He stopped to soak up the New Mexican night sky. Its inky blackness was the perfect backdrop for the billions of stars the universe had on display. A shooting star sliced through the sky.

"I wonder if I'll ever stop one of those?" he pondered out loud.

"You might, if you're smart and do the right thing."

The deep voice of Jacob Whitehorse almost made Jonathan drop his bag.

Jonathan spun around. "Damn, Jacob, don't sneak up on me like that."

Jacob and his silent friend slowly walked out of the shadows. "Jonathan, has Georgia talked with you about us?" Jacob asked.

"Yes."

"Well?"

"Well, what? You want an answer like that? I just met you folks today, and it wasn't the best introduction I've ever had."

"Jonathan...we're not screwing around here," Whitehorse said.

"Okay, Jacob, easy. You wouldn't hurt your messiah, would you?" The Scotch was beginning to show itself.

A searing pain cut through Jonathan's skull. He collapsed to his hands and knees and writhed in pain on the warm dirt.

Whitehorse and the silent Indian walked up. "How funny is it now, Mr. Messiah?"

The silent Indian smiled.

"Oh, that's good, that's real good..." Jonathan said. The pain increased. He buried his head between his knees. "Oh my God!" he screamed. He rolled to his side and curled up into a fetal position.

"Should we intervene, sir?" Jimbo asked.

"No," his partner answered. "I know Whitehorse." He adjusted his field optics. "He will take him to the 'threshold' and hold him there to make his point."

"How do you know?"

"It is what I would do."

Jonathan was crying from the pain tearing at his mind. Whitehorse and the silent Indian just stood and watched.

"Jonathan, let us help you develop your skill. We can teach you how to harness it and put it to great use."

"Yeah, like jerking with people's brains, AUGH!" Jonathan curled more tightly as the pain reached the threshold point.

"If need be," Whitehorse said softly.

"Sir, he looks majorly screwed here," Jimbo said.

"Just wait, James. I think we are about to get a 'level test' from Mr. Kortel."

"Please, Jonathan, listen to reason!" Whitehorse demanded.

Jonathan suddenly stopped struggling, and Whitehorse and his companion bent down to check on him.

The silent one felt it first. He fell to one knee. His face went white. Whitehorse began to back away. The silent Indian lifted his head, his face twisted in agony. His mouth moved like he was crying, but there was no sound. Jonathan was still curled on the ground. The silent Indian took his head in both hands, and, to Whitehorse's horror, a small dent appeared on his forehead that slowly expanded. Blood poured from his nose. He collapsed without making a sound.

A muffled voice came up from the dirt: "Now who's screwing with who, Whitehorse?" Jonathan struggled to his feet.

"Now that's interesting," Jimbo said, not pulling his eyes from his field optics.

"Jonathan!" Whitehorse exclaimed. "I would have never gone that far!"

"No? I don't recall ever reading about Green Peace using pain threshold tricks to stop whaling. What did you do at the Agency, Whitehorse? Really?" Jonathan rubbed his head and staggered toward him.

Whitehorse backed away. "Jonathan, you've killed a man!" he said, changing the subject.

"He's not going to die," Jonathan answered. "Now, he might have one hell of a headache, but a little bioregeneration should do him fine. I'm not sure I'll be able to say the same for you."

Whitehorse grabbed his head and dropped to the ground.

Jonathan watched with contempt, as Whitehorse convulsed in the dirt. He calmly wiped his face with his sleeve.

In the distance, a dog began to howl.

~

"I think that will be quite enough, Jonathan," the senior Tel said. "Well done, well done." He was clapping his hands and smoking a cigarette, Jimbo in tow.

"Who are you?" Jonathan asked, retaining his mental grip on Whitehorse.

Jimbo cut in, "James McCarris, and this is my partner..."

"The Agency!" Jonathan interrupted, pointing his finger.

The senior Tel took a drag from his cigarette and motioned for Jonathan to release Whitehorse, who had slipped into unconsciousness. Jimbo was checking the silent Indian.

"This one's alive, but he's going to need a doctor...and fast," Jimbo said.

"No, he will be all right." His partner came over to examine the silent Indian's forehead. "Not bad, Jonathan. A front temporal compression, without severe damage to the brain or the sepra orbital arteries. Very impressive work." The senior Tel straightened. "I think I can help this man." Jimbo and Jonathan watched in amazement as the silent Indian's forehead returned to its natural shape.

"Lesson one: To damage or repair a victim, a Tel must have a complete, commanding knowledge of human anatomy and medical procedures. And you do not! You were lucky tonight, young man. You did well, but you were a millimeter away from severing the artery. He would have hemorrhaged and been dead in seconds." He put out his cigarette.

"So, who are you, the good guys?" Jonathan asked.

"That all depends on your point of view," Jimbo said.

"James is right, Jonathan. It is all a matter of point of view. Take Jacob here." He strolled over to Whitehorse. "He was my finest student – loyal, powerful and cunning. But he has one weakness. He sees the world as black and white."

"But isn't he...aren't they helping the underdog?" Jonathan asked.

"The underdog?" the senior Tel asked, turning to Jonathan. "Define the underdog. One man's militia for peace is another man's death squad for a government. A saved village today harbors terrorists tomorrow. Overthrow a regime and usher in another dictator. At one time this band of Rogues were some of our best, but now they meddle in the affairs of nations. They do not see the big picture. They are out of their league, and they should return to us. The world, Jonathan, is still a very dangerous place..." he walked back over to Jonathan and got right into his face, "...as you should know."

He walked away and lit another cigarette. The dog still could be faintly heard, his howl carried to them on the cool night wind.

"I do know," Jonathan said softly. The senior Tel's words hit him hard. He had always felt cheated out of his boyhood and truly wondered what it would have been like to have parents. Real parents. Parents who would have loved him and protected him.

"Listen, man," Jimbo said quietly. "There are no good guys or bad guys, just agendas. And you'll have to decide which agenda works for you."

"Jonathan," the senior Tel called out. He was standing about 20 feet away. He had his back to them and was looking up at the stars. "Do you want to make a difference?"

"Well, I don't know what I...hey!" Jonathan was abruptly lifted 70 feet into the air. "I don't like heights!"

Jimbo was caught off guard by his partner's theatrics.

"Listen to me, and listen well, Mr. Kortel!" the senior Tel yelled. "We need you and you need us!"

"Alright, Alright! I get the picture!"

"James, think fast," he said, releasing his control over Jonathan.

"Heyyy!"

Jonathan fell 60 feet before Jimbo mentally caught him. Hands on his hips, he shot a contemptuous look at his partner. Jonathan hung six feet off the ground, suspended face down like a puppet on invisible strings. The senior Tel slowly walked up to him. They were now face to face.

"We are not *screwing* around either, Jonathan." He took a long drag off his cigarette.

"What if I don't want to go with either of you..." Jonathan began, but he was stopped by a sharp pain in his shoulder. He grimaced in agony.

The senior Tel said nothing.

Jimbo looked away.

"What are you doing?!" Jonathan screamed, and panic filled his face. He felt the pain tear through his shoulder as his arm shifted of its own accord under his shirt.

"In plain English," the senior Tel said casually, "I am separating your arm from your shoulder." He leaned in closer. "And I could do a lot worse." Then as quickly as it began, the pain suddenly ceased. "We are not monsters, Jonathan, contrary to what you may think."

Jonathan glared back and began to prep for whatever he could bring forth. He was going to show this bastard what he was made of.

"Do not bother, Jonathan," the senior Tel bluffed. "You are strong, but inconsistent and untrained. I am a Level 8, very consistent, and very well trained."

The bluff worked; Jonathan backed off. The senior Tel gently lowered him to his feet.

"That was a little demonstration in control, on both of our parts." He acted as if he was about to walk away, when suddenly he spun on his heels and came back to within an inch of Jonathan's face. "I could kill you where you stand," he threatened. "You would never feel it, and no one would ever know who did it." He took the last drag off his cigarette and casually set off for the car.

Jimbo walked up to Jonathan with his hands in his pockets. "Think about it, man. He's a little over the top, but he makes a good point." And he made that click sound for emphasis.

~

The compound was quiet when Jonathan got out of the car. It was now three in the morning, and he was exhausted. He leaned against the hood and rubbed his shoulder.

The impact of his meetings with the Agency and the Rogues was soaking in. It was obvious to Jonathan that the Rogues, despite their "help the world" platform, were not what they seemed. Jacob Whitehorse had done a pretty thorough disinformation job on Georgia and probably the rest of the group. Jonathan thought it obvious that the big Indian's agenda was not world peace. To him, Whitehorse seemed borderline psycho, and he probably had his own agenda for the world that focused particularly on his place in it.

At least the Agency presented itself pretty straight up. They didn't hide their agenda; in fact, they reveled in it. And their view of the world did strike a deep chord within him.

The house was still, the living room empty. Jonathan crept to the freezer and got an icy gelpack for his throbbing head. He also washed down a fistful of bioprophin.

"Where've you been?" Georgia asked, appearing in the kitchen archway.

Jonathan turned, the gelpack covering half his face.

Georgia gasped. "What happened?"

"Like you don't know?" Jonathan cut back.

"No!" Georgia said, stepping toward him. She reached up to touch his head, but he pushed her hand away.

"Your fearless leader made a serious impression on me, literally."

"Jacob did this?"

Jonathan shot her a "cut the crap" look.

"What did he do to you?"

Jonathan studied her. From all indications, she truly was clueless to Whitehorse's ruthlessness.

"Well," he said, "let's just say Whitehorse has a different view of the world and the Rogues' role in it." He rubbed the gelpack across his forehead.

From where she stood, Georgia was backlit from the living room light, and Jonathan couldn't help noticing her naked frame through the robe.

"And I met the Agency boys, too," he said, dropping into one of the antique Mexican leather chairs by the big window.

"What were they like?" she asked, curling into the chair's identical twin across from him. The top of her robe fell open and she quickly gathered it about her, never taking her eyes off Jonathan.

"Well," Jonathan said, pretending not to notice, "they're government guys, real pros, and they present a compelling argument for joining the Agency. At least they don't mask their agenda, and they have a pretty realistic view of the world."

Jonathan closed his eyes and draped the gelpack over his face.

"Hey," she said, leaning over the table, "I know about Jacob Whitehorse. We all do. But you have to understand, he and the others like him are powerful men. You got a taste of that tonight. They're passionate about their beliefs. Yes, their methods may be a bit extreme at times, but their motives are genuine. And they truly believe you could be The Infinite Tel."

She settled back into the chair, her dark hair decorating her shoulders. In the light of the small lamp, she seemed prettier than Jonathan had ever seen her. She closed her eyes.

Jonathan didn't know whom to trust, and he wasn't about to buy Georgia's "Jacob Whitehorse is really a good guy" line.

"I know one thing for sure," he said. He pulled the gelpack from his face. "I'm too tired to pick my life's destiny right now. I'm going to bed. Good night, Georgia."

Georgia watched Jonathan as he slowly walked down the dark hallway. She sat quietly, hugging a large pillow, and contemplated Jonathan's plight. If he was The Infinite Tel, then he might choose neither the Rogues nor the Agency. He might choose to go it on his own and live life as he wished. If he really was as powerful as Whitehorse believed, there might be no way of swaying his decision.

But Georgia knew Whitehorse, and how volatile he had become. If Jonathan Kortel could be forced toward the Rogues, Jacob Whitehorse would find a way.

No matter the cost.

Destiny...20

HECTOR watched Marco, one of the line chefs, open a new shipment of hydrotank octopi from Australia. He checked out the manifest: Their genetic profiles were in order, but three of their 20 ink sacks had burst in shipping, which lined the crate with the new fluorescent, genetically altered ink. (Cooking the octopus in its own ink was such the rave in Japan.)

"*Caca!*" Marco declared. "This new distributor is an asshole! They packed these octopi like shit. Look at what we got to clean up, and it's eleven thirty!" Marco carefully lifted each one of the hydrotanks out and laid them on the prep table; they glowed green and yellow in his hands.

Hector didn't care.

Hector hadn't heard from Jonathan in four days, and for him not to show on a Monday without calling gave Hector the sense that something was terribly wrong. Four netmessages in as many days had gone unanswered. In the ten years he had known Jonathan, he had never just disappeared. Hector flipped his netphone around in his hand. He stared off into space.

Enrique couldn't miss the worry on his cousin's face.

He stopped chopping and walked over to his relation. "Are you gonna call him again?"

"I don't know. Why, what's the point? If he wanted to call, he would." He slammed his fist on the metal countertop. The kitchen came to a halt.

"Hey!" Enrique barked. "What are you *vatos* looking at, eh?!" and the men of Kitchen Kortel returned to their work.

"It's that damn dancer," Hector said, still staring. "She's jerking him around, I know it." He finally looked at his cousin. "This is crazy. Jonathan should have called by now. I bet she's twisting his head around. You know how he is when he gets into a chick; he can be led so easily. And those dancers, they're the worst. Believe me, I know!" Hector waved his finger to emphasize his point. "What time is it?"

"It's almost noon. Why?" Enrique asked.

Hector put his netphone down and began to strip off his apron.

"Cousin," Enrique warned, "this is not your affair!"

Hector didn't answer. He threw the apron into the prep sink.

Enrique knew him too well. When Hector got something into his head, it was practically impossible to get it out. Enrique stepped in front of him.

"I just want to see this girl and talk to her," Hector objected. He tried to inch his way past.

Enrique reluctantly stepped aside. "Just watch what you say. Jonathan's a big boy. He can look out for himself, eh?"

Hector grabbed his netphone and charged out of the kitchen. "Claire, I'll be back in a couple of hours," he said to the new hostess, and he stormed toward the front door.

Lost in the thought of getting tough with the dancer, Hector jerked the handle and carried the girl who had hold of the other side right into the restaurant. She stumbled and fell into Hector's large chest.

"I'm terribly sorry, please let me..." Hector started, but he suddenly realized who she was.

Tamara picked up her backpack.

"Aren't you Nicki from the club?" Hector asked, surprised. "I...I...thought you were with Jonathan. What are you doing here?"

"I haven't heard from him in days. That's why I'm here. I thought you all might know where he'd gone."

"Oh," Hector moaned, "this is not good. Not good at all. I thought you two...were..."

"Together?"

"Yes, you were, weren't you?"

"Yes, yes, we were. He hasn't told you, has he?"

"Told me what?!" Hector boomed.

Tamara brushed her hair off her face, and Hector could see the worry in her eyes. "I'm sorry...Nicki?..." he ventured.

"Actually, Tamara, Tamara Connor." She held out her hand. The big Mexican engulfed it in his own. For the first time he noted her real beauty, and was struck by its intensity.

"Please, come sit down." Hector led Tamara to a small two-top by the kitchen and motioned for Claire. "Would you like something to drink?" he asked.

"Water would be fine, thanks."

Hector sensed a presence about her. A maturity. Something intangible that calmed him. He took a deep breath. "What should Jonathan have told me, Tamara?"

Tamara gave Hector the whole story. She told him about the kit cab accident, the club, the reper and the Light-Force weapon. She also told him about Jonathan's message.

Hector absorbed the tale without a word. He honestly wasn't sure what *to* say. When she finished, he sipped his coffee and eyed her cautiously.

"You don't believe me." She began to get up from the table.

"Now, now...I didn't say that," Hector assured her. "But you have to admit, it's all a little out there."

Tamara took Hector's hand and leaned close to him. "Listen. Jonathan thinks the world of you. You're his family, his only family! That's why I came. I'm not blind. I can tell how you feel about me and what I do. You have to take what I say as true, because it is! I saw it all, Anari saw it all. She was standing right next to him. I wouldn't have come here if I didn't care for him like I do." Her voice began to quiver. "Jonathan and I have something. It's intense. I...look Hector, I have to find him. Where would he go if he needed to get it together, if he needed to really get some answers? Who would he turn to?"

"Well, me, quite frankly. The only other person I could think of would be Tarris. Tarris was like his brother. Hell, he was his brother!"

"Where is he, Hector? Do you know?"

"No," Hector said, rising from the table. "But I do know someone who would...hey?!"

Tamara was already halfway to the door.

~

"Max? Max?" Hector called.

"Good afternoon, Hector. How have you been?" Jonathan's front door unlatched. "And how are you, Miss Connor?"

"I'm fine, Max," Tamara answered, and they entered the loft.

"Max, do you have in your database an address or netaddress for Tarris. You know, his best friend from when he was a kid?"

"Yes," Max said.

"Please download the data into my netpad," Tamara instructed. She checked the address. "New Mexico..."

"Yeah, that's right," Hector cut in. "I remember now. He moved there after the accident."

"What accident?"

"Oh, this guy is a genius, but he took it bad in a biobike crash. It left him a paraplegic. The way Jonathan describes it, he was legally dead, but they brought him back. Too bad the bioregen didn't take all the way....Anyway, he moved to a little town outside of Santa Fe, or something like that....Hey, what happened here?" Hector asked, noticing the condition of the loft.

"I think this is Jonathan getting upset with a message I left."

"Shit, he was pissed," Hector said.

"No, not pissed, I think he was..." Tamara couldn't find the words.

"Hurt, Miss Connor," Max interrupted.

"What?" Tamara asked.

"Jonathan was hurt by the message, Miss Connor," Max corrected.

An uncomfortable silence settled between Tamara and Hector.

"Max," she finally asked, "there hasn't been anything on the net about...you know."

"Jonathan's death?" Max asked.

"Yes..." she answered.

There was a pause. Hector walked over and picked up the broken picture of himself and Jonathan deep-sea fishing.

"No, there has been no information of his death. But his debit chipcard was used at 12 different locations throughout New Mexico."

"Give me the last place he used his card," Hector ordered.

"TP Mart number 23, in Tres Piedras, New Mexico. Will there be anything else?"

"Please, Max," Tamara instructed, "download those locations to my pad."

"Will there be anything else?"

"No Max," she answered. "You've been a great help." She began to leave.

"Miss Connor?" Max asked, stopping them.

"Yeah, Max?" she asked in surprise.

There was another pause.

"Are you and Jonathan in love with each other?"

Tamara was caught totally off guard. It was a simple question and, coming from an artificial intelligence, had an innocent quality about it. It was the kind of question a child might ask a parent that instantly put life into perspective.

Hector turned and looked at Tamara.

For the first time in her life, Tamara felt something she had never had with a man. Comfort. Jonathan just felt right. He fit. Like no other man had ever fit into her life before. "I really don't know what Jonathan feels, Max," she answered. "But yes, Max...I believe I am."

"Thank you, Miss Connor, I'll add that to my database."

Hector smiled at her, and they left the loft.

~

It was almost one o'clock when Jonathan woke up. The house was quiet. Tarris and Georgia were gone. Jonathan entered the kitchen and saw a message flashing on the system panel of the refrigerator. He played the vid. It was Georgia.

"Good afternoon, you." It was odd to see her in a dress, Jonathan thought. "We're going into Taos to get the truck and do a little shopping. There's plenty of food and beers, so help yourself. You know where everything is. I know you had a rough night, so relax. Our casa es su casa. Oh, if you think about it, we feed the strays, and there's some dog food in the kitchen closet. Their bowls are outside." She leaned into the screen, which distorted her face and made her look 20 pounds heavier. "Be careful, Jonathan," she whispered. Then she suddenly pulled back, and the vid ended.

"Great," Jonathan quietly said to himself. "Beer for breakfast. Just what I need, a little hair of the dog."

Jonathan made a sandwich, opened a beer and stepped out onto the deck. The sun behind him filled the San Cristobal Mountains with rich, deep hues. The air was warm, and in the distance, a vintage Harley disrupted the New Mexican quiet with its patented two-cylinder growl.

He ate his sandwich and debated the words of Whitehorse and the Recruiters. If he was as powerful as Whitehorse believed, the Rogues were probably not equipped to train him. And if Whitehorse was as ruthless as he seemed, then Jonathan wanted no part of him. The Agency, on the other hand, had the infrastructure and ability the Rogues lacked. It also seemed that they had a better sense of how the world actually worked and would be better suited to deal with complex global politics. Then, though, there were the rumors of their death squads. It didn't surprise him that the Agency would have this kind of force. Governments for centuries have had elite forces that worked in secret, all in the name of "good," as defined by their particular doctrines. It was the thought of being a part of an organization that controlled whether a person lived or died that unnerved him.

Jonathan picked up his empty beer bottle and peered through the glass at the mountains. "It all depends on how you look at it," he said out loud.

Jonathan closed his eyes and listened to the wind. The sound was rough against his ears. No netphones, no pots or pans banging together, no netpad interfaces, no nightly specials to be programmed. Just wind.

And something licking his fingers.

"Hello there!" he said to the two stray dogs who had wandered up to sniff the new guy. He rubbed behind the ears of the bigger one. "I bet you want your dinners."

Jonathan went into the kitchen and brought back their food bag. The two strays yipped and jumped with anticipation, then attacked their bowls as Jonathan poured them generous portions.

Jonathan returned to his chair on the deck. His life over the last few weeks had changed so much. To discover that you're not as human as you thought would freak anyone. To also discover someone like Tamara and be forced to choose your future at the same time was almost more than he could take. He had come to New Mexico to see an old friend, someone who had always been there for him. Instead, he was introduced to his destiny by two factions of a secret world culture. Both good. Both bad.

What if he was The Infinite Tel?

What if he was destined to usher in a new phase of human development?

What if his future was not his choice?

Jonathan thought of his father and the book, the only item he had to connect him to the life that could have been...with them.

Jonathan was overwhelmed.

No father, no mother, no friend could tell him what to do. He was solo on this one, and what he decided now could possibly change the human landscape forever.

The two dogs came over and put their heads in his lap. Jonathan closed his eyes and listened to the wind.

Rustling in the sage...21

JONATHAN spun his netphone around in his hand. He was afraid to turn it on and discover that the world was looking for him. He knew there would be netmessages from Hector and Tamara. And he knew that eventually he would have to confront his other life.

He clicked it on. Twenty-two messages. Six from Hector. Ten netdirect mails selling everything from the latest hydrobiopaste programs to self-aware refrigerator units that could suggest menu designs or select waiter wardrobe – all without attitude. Three from BioFood Netzine, probably hyping its netvitorial on the fusion of food and biotech.

One from Tamara. He launched it.

"Hey, you," Tamara said in a low and careful voice. "How are you? I hope you're doing what you need to do. If there's anything I can do to make it easier, please...let me know. Ah, hey...look, I went to the loft...and got the message. Sorry, I just needed to see if you were all right. Your message was, well, I don't know what to say. I, I...I know we'll see each other soon. Jonathan, I don't want to lose you....Not now. Look, I'm worried, baby. I want you to be safe. I know you're going through a difficult time, but I know you'll come out of it." There was a long pause. "You're special, Jonathan. I know you know that now. I don't know what's happening to you, but whatever happens, I'll be there for you. Call me...when you're ready. Bye, lover."

The netmessages from Hector followed. He sounded worried. Even more, Jonathan could hear the fear in his voice. Jonathan launched Hector's netID. He was going back online.

"Jonathan!" Hector answered in his all-too-familiar booming voice. "Where the hell are you?"

"Hey, Hector, look, this has been a pretty rough couple of days. I'm not going to be back for a while. There's just a lot I have to sort out."

"I'm sure. Ah, Jonathan, you need to know, Tamara came by the restaurant. She told me everything."

"Everything?"

"Yes, my friend...everything. Are you all right? Do you know what's happening to you?"

"I'm fine, Hector, but to tell you the truth, it's getting a little scary. Look, it's probably not safe to talk on the net. You're going to have to trust me here. I seem to be gaining strength, if that's what you'd call it, every day. It's getting easier and easier to do things that were almost impossible only days ago. But to answer your question, so far, I'm all right."

"Is there anything I can do?"

"Yeah, keep this between you, me and Tamara, okay? I'm not sure how all this is going to end."

"Okay, Jonathan."

"Hector, look...ah, this could get ugly. I mean, there are people..." He stopped himself. "Let's just say there are those who aren't out for my well-being."

"Jonathan, take care and watch yourself, all right?"

"Hector?"

"Yes?"

"It was good partnering with you..."

There was a long silence.

"Shut up, Jonathan." Hector's voice cracked a bit. "Do what you need to do and get your ass back to this kitchen. We have art to make!"

"Okay, Hector. You take care."

"You too, Jonathan." The netline cut out.

Jonathan thought about calling Tamara, but the net was too volatile, and he didn't want to involve her and Nicole any more than he had to. He clicked off the phone and dropped it into his pocket. The two strays were competing for his attention.

His strength had been gaining every day, and his ability to control and focus was becoming more refined. There was always the threat that a passing thought might manifest itself, though. He had to temper his gift, or he would almost never use his hands. The simplest of things were becoming innate to him, and he had to catch himself or he'd expose his true nature. The Recruiter was right: control was vital to a Tel. Without it, life would be chaos. Even dangerous.

Jonathan glanced down at the two dogs. He stopped petting them and mentally lifted them up into the air. As they rose, they whimpered and struggled a little. He began to juggle them slowly 12 feet off the ground. Then he lifted a deck chair to join the two dogs in their aerial acrobatics. The dogs actually seemed to enjoy the spinning and swirling. Jonathan added the outdoor cooker and thought about adding his rental car.

He opened another beer. His netphone signaled.

Startled, because he was off line, Jonathan stopped juggling and let dogs, chair and cooker all hang in the air like some bizarre, living mobile. He connected to the net. Unknown name, unknown number.

"Nice juggling, slick, but pretty amateur for a Tel at your level."

"James?" Jonathan asked in shock.

"Come on, you can call me Jimbo – everyone else does. My partner and I were wondering if last night's little demo scared you a little. You know we didn't want to spook you, but sometimes we've got to improvise, and he's one for the high drama, know what I mean? Anyway, what are you doing right now, besides juggling pets and outdoor furniture?"

"How did you..."

"Launch your phone?"

"Yeah..."

"Jonathan, come on. If the Agency wants to connect with you, it will. You'd be surprised how easy it is to launch one of those netphones. Which one is yours again, a MitsuSony? Hell, those pieces of crap couldn't be secured even with a biowall. We'd still get through."

Jonathan searched the area for the two Recruiters. The dogs-and-cooker mobile was still hanging.

"Don't bother looking. We can see you, but you can't see us. Hey, the big dog looks seriously pissed."

Jonathan looked up to find the bigger dog growling, tired of the vertical playtime he had shared with the new guy. Jonathan returned them to earth, and they trotted off to the next handout.

"So," Jimbo started, his voice getting serious. "Are you ready to learn what you can really do?"

"Well, I..."

Jimbo's voice shifted to an authoritarian tone: "Jonathan! It's time to face the music. Whitehorse isn't your answer. You know that. He couldn't teleconnect if his ass depended on it. Listen to your gut! You've got the gift, and you've got it big! Whitehorse knows this, and that's why he wants you. You're a threat to him. He's one mean motherfucker, and he's not going to let you just walk over to our side, if you know what I mean. Come on, let us teach you. You'll be able to do things you never dreamed possible. Believe me, the Agency knows what it's doing, and it doesn't screw around. And you know what else?"

Jonathan didn't answer.

"You'll finally be with your own kind...and that alone's worth the price of admission."

"I'm listening..."

"Let's just have dinner and talk. No games, no demos and definitely no tricks."

Jonathan rubbed his shoulder.

"Where, Jimbo?"

"Let's meet tonight at The Sage, up on Kit Carson Road, say around seven o'clock?"

"Yeah, that's sounds fine, and hey, Jimbo...just you, not your partner. All right?"

"That's cool, Jonathan. Just me. I'll see you there at seven. And Jonathan, this is a smart move. Trust me on this." Jimbo disconnected.

The netphone hung in front of Jonathan as he leaned back in the chair. The clouds were beginning to build over the mountains, and the wind had picked up again.

As Jonathan finished his beer, his mind wandered back to Hawaii. If he thought hard enough, he could dredge up the fragments of memories from his childhood. The time he started opening his Christmas presents before his mother and father were up. The look on his father's face when he wandered into their bedroom and found them kissing and hugging each other naked. And there were the many trips to the ocean. Hawaii was one of the most beautiful places on earth until the event. Jonathan could still feel the cool water and the power of the surf when he and his father would snorkel the reefs near their home. He could almost taste the salt on his tongue.

The pain rose in his throat, and Jonathan swallowed hard. "It's times like this I could really use you, dad," he said out loud, staring at the netphone that would never connect him to his father in spite of his ten-dollar-a-minute family plan.

There was a rustle in the sage.

About 10 feet from the deck, Jonathan saw a small image appear. Like a holovid from some bad museum exhibit, its translucent surface floated between the sage bushes and played a clip through for about a minute, then repeated itself.

It was his father on the beach.

Jonathan leaned forward, transfixed as he watched his memory play out dimensionally on the New Mexican landscape. The clip shifted, and a new image ran. His father and mother were walking down the path that led from their lab to the main house. They walked and talked, though Jonathan could hear no sound. His mother was dressed in the clothes she always wore to conduct their research: a tight, sleeveless black shirt with khaki knee-length pants worn low on her thin hips. Her chrome belt buckle sported the vintage reclining naked girl like a mud flap from some antique truck. His father wore one of his flower-print bioshirts – with blooms that actually moved as you walked – and shorts that had a dozen small pockets for carrying anything, even though he never did. Both of them had on their white lab coats – just to make them feel like real scientists, they used to say. As they drew near the main house, his mother looked up at Jonathan and winked.

Jonathan slowly began to cry.

"Oh, mother..." he said quietly.

The ground began to shake. Jonathan's beer rattled its way off the chair. A crack appeared in the soil, starting at the deck and ripping toward the image. It widened and swallowed up every sage bush in its path.

Again the ground shook, this time more violently. Another fissure opened up that ran from the deck to the fence at the back of the property. Another split opened and another, until there were 10 fissures radiating from the deck, with Jonathan as the hub.

Jonathan, with his head in his hands, cried out to his dead parents. "Oh, I miss you, I miss you!" he wailed.

The cooker exploded, sending metal and plastic flying through the air like tiny missiles.

Jonathan jumped to his feet and looked up into the vast expanse of the southwestern sky. "Fuck you, God!" he screamed. "Fuck you!"

The mesquite tree near the deck burst into flames, the needles of fire rising 20 feet into the air.

"Come on," Jonathan yelled to the sky. "You've done this all to me. First you kill my parents, then you make me inhuman! And just as I discover that I will probably never relate to people again, you put in front of me a girl..." Jonathan fell back into the chair sobbing, "...a girl I connect with like no one I've ever known. And to top it all off..."

He closed his eyes.

The mesquite tree flamed out.

"...I think I'm in love with her."

There was another rustle in the sage.

The image had shifted. Now Jonathan watched as his parents sat at their breakfast table, eating what looked like lunch. His mom talks with her mouth full, again with no sound, while his dad reads a netpad. He raises his glass to take a drink, but suddenly they both jerk their heads as if startled by something outside the window above the sink. There's a flash from outside. His parents lift their arms to cover their faces. The image goes to white.

Jonathan's netphone signaled again. Unknown name, unknown number.

"Hello?" Jonathan asked tentatively.

"Hi..." a little voice said.

"Nicole."

The netphone was silent.

"Jonathan, are you there?"

An icy feeling ran through his nerves.

"Yes, Jacob, I'm here."

"Jonathan, Nicole is such a pretty little girl..."

"If you hurt her in any way..."

"Your display last night was impressive, but you caught me off guard." Whitehorse's voice was low and stern. "I can assure you that won't happen again."

"How's your associate, Whitehorse?"

There was a long pause.

"He'll be fine, as soon as they take him off life support."

Jonathan cracked a small smile.

"Jonathan, I am a man who is used to getting what he wants. And I want to have a meeting, just you and me. Tel to Tel. With no telekinetics. And Nicole is my...shall we say, insurance that you'll show?"

"Yes, Whitehorse, I'll show."

"Good. Then meet me at the Pueblo at eleven o'clock tonight. Oh, and Jonathan?"

"Yes, Whitehorse?"

"Don't bring those Agency boys. Do I make myself...clear?"

Jonathan could hear Nicole whimpering in the background. "Yeah, Whitehorse, you're coming in loud and clear."

The line cut off.

The image had disappeared.

~

"Did you hear all that?" the senior Tel asked Jimbo.

Jimbo nodded.

"I told you Whitehorse was a man of means," his partner said, pulling the biomicrotransceiver from his ear.

Through his field optics, Jimbo watched Jonathan get up and walk back into the house. "He's getting stronger almost by the hour," Jimbo said. He refocused on the cracks left in the earth by Jonathan's emotional rage. "That's one hell of a telekinetic display, and what's up with that mental holoprojection manifestation thing? Man, this boy just keeps on surprising us. I've never seen anything like that!"

"Nor have I. All the more reason to convince him, James. And I know you will."

"I'll do my best, sir."

"You will have to, James, because I know Jacob Whitehorse," his partner said, walking up to Jimbo's side. "He will kill that little girl if he does not get Jonathan's loyalty."

"And how do you know that?"

"Because if I were in Whitehorse's place..." the senior Tel turned and looked at Jimbo, "...I would kill her, too."

Showtime...22

PASSING the mirror in the bedroom, Jonathan stopped and checked out what he saw. He saw a man who had changed so much in the last few weeks. This one had to be perfect. There was no room for error – not with Nicole's life on the line. He tightened his gut and held it.

"I'm not the superhero type," he said under his breath.

"I don't know about that," Georgia said from the doorway, her arms folded.

Jonathan turned around as Georgia walked up to him.

"You're more powerful than a locomotive, faster than a speeding bullet, if there were bullets anymore..."

"But I can't leap over tall buildings."

"How do you know? Have you tried yet?"

"The tallest building in Tres Piedras is only two stories."

Georgia laughed.

Jonathan had told Tarris and Georgia about the meetings with Jimbo and Whitehorse, but he hadn't said anything about Nicole. He knew Georgia didn't have any knowledge of Nicole, because when he tested her, she acted as if Whitehorse had been humbled by Jonathan's display. In her eyes, everything was above board, and Whitehorse just wanted to talk.

Humbled my ass, thought Jonathan. Whitehorse had been embarrassed, and he was out to get even. If Jonathan was going to get Nicole back, he might need to recruit the Recruiters.

"You look nice," Georgia said. She brushed off some lint from his sweater and let her hand rest on his shoulder.

Jonathan turned and reached for his netpad on the table across the room. It flew over, but not into his hand.

Georgia handed it to him. "Good luck," she said and kissed him on the cheek.

Surprised, Jonathan looked into her dark eyes. She began to lean closer, her mouth slightly open, but she stopped herself and stepped back, brushing the hair off of her face.

"Thanks," Jonathan said. He pretended not to notice what might have happened.

Georgia, embarrassed, smiled and rushed out of the room.

~

The Sage was quiet, and Jonathan found Jimbo at the bar. Jimbo's tall lanky frame seemed almost too big for the barstool, and his wavy red hair made him look younger than he probably was. He had his back to the door.

"Hello, Jonathan," Jimbo said without turning around.

"James," Jonathan replied cautiously. He climbed onto the barstool next to him.

"Join me?" Jimbo asked, raising his glass.

"Sure."

Jimbo glanced at the bartender, never uttering a word. The bartender looked over suddenly and walked the length of the bar to where they sat.

"Yes, sir, may I help you?" the bartender asked, confused.

"Yes, I'll take an Oban, with ice, no water," Jonathan said and turned his attention to Jimbo, who was still looking straight ahead into the bar mirror.

"Do all you Agency guys wield your ability so freely?" Jonathan asked.

"You ever try getting a bartender's attention in New York?" Jimbo shot back.

There was an awkward silence.

The bartender returned with Jonathan's drink.

More awkward silence.

"You advanced Tels sure like your Scotch," Jimbo finally said.

"Excuse me?"

"You and my partner. You both like Scotch, with ice, no water. It's just funny, that's all." Jimbo slammed back his beer.

"Are you not the same level as your partner?"

"Shit no. He's the highest testing Tel ever. Me? I'm a lowly Level 5. But I think I could get to a Level 6, maybe even seven."

The bartender returned with two plates of food. "A steak for the gentleman," he said, handing one to Jimbo. "And the rainbow trout for his friend."

"Good guess, James," Jonathan said.

"We know a lot about you. It was one of the only things on the menu I'd thought you'd like." Jimbo cut into his steak.

"So tell me, James. What will happen to my life if I go with the Agency?"

"Well," Jimbo began, wiping his chin, "first you'll relocate to D.C. We'll probably get you a nice place, maybe in Georgetown. Then you'll be introduced to the director and his agents, blah, blah, blah.

"But here's the deal, Jonathan. You are one special Tel." He turned for the first time to face him. "We don't know if we can really teach you anything. Hell, do you have any idea what level you are?"

Jonathan shook his head.

"You, my friend, are at least a Level 8, probably a Level 9. You're stronger than my partner. And like I said, he's the hardest working Tel in show business." Jimbo made that click sound and dug into his mashed potatoes.

"Now don't get me wrong, we can get you all professionaled-up," he continued between forkfuls of potatoes. "You know, teach you control, focus, balance and timing. Make it so your talent is like second nature. But this FTL shit, wow, now that's off the charts, mister. You're definitely in another league. Hell, you're on another planet!" He ordered another beer.

"FTL?" Jonathan asked.

"Faster Than Light? Come on, don't give me that 'I didn't know I did that' routine. You created a grav field strong enough to stop a Light-Force bioweapon dead in its main discharge cycle. You're redefining the laws of physics, Jonathan, and that's way beyond all of us." He leaned over to Jonathan. "And you know you did it too, am I right?"

"Yeah..." Jonathan acknowledged slowly.

"Yeah, I'm damn right," Jimbo said, and he took a gulp from his fresh beer.

"Yes, James, but back to my life. What will my life be like from now on?"

Jimbo stuffed another bite of steak into his mouth, wiped his lips, put the napkin on his plate and turned on the barstool to face Jonathan. He grabbed his beer.

"We don't really know," he said seriously. "You're a whole new animal, Jonathan. You could be The Infinite Tel. But at the very least, you're the next phase, the next evolutionary step for us...for humans." Jimbo took a sip of his beer. "Look man, it's like I said before. There are no good guys or bad guys, just agendas. Our agenda is for you to be what you're meant to be. But we don't know what that is yet, and you don't either. We will, though. It takes time, and it takes the resources only the Agency can provide. Do you really think Whitehorse has the capabilities to develop a Tel of your caliber? Get real. The Rogues at best are a bunch of dysfunctional, mid-level Tels led by a bipolar psycho Indian. Now there's an organization I want to be with." Jimbo finished his beer.

"There's something you should know..." Jonathan began.

"Nicole? Already ahead of you, boss. Whitehorse is certifiable, that's for sure. He'll kill Tamara's kid as sure as I drank that beer. You need to play this out smart, Jonathan. Does Tamara know yet?"

"I don't know. She hasn't called me since her last netmessage, and I've checked, but she's off-line."

"That's odd. She must be in transit, and that means she's probably heading here. Does she know about Tarris?"

"No, but my loft's HDI system knows everything, and she has access to him...I mean it."

"Yeah, it's easy to trace you on the net through your biochip-card incep points. If she's a good mother, she's called her kid and hasn't gotten an answer, so she's probably beginning to get worried. But I doubt she's jumped to the conclusion of kidnapping, or that she's tied your situation to not getting an answer at her grandma's."

"Oh my God, I forgot about her...you don't think..."

"I doubt it. Whitehorse is a psycho, but he's not stupid. Quite the contrary, this man knows his shit. He should: my partner taught him everything he knows. You've got to understand, secrecy is way too important to us. The less people involved, the less of a containment issue you have. He probably STMN'd her. She just lost some memory, that's all. But she'll have one hell of a headache." Jimbo laughed under his breath.

"Yeah, how has that worked? The only organization I know that can keep a secret is the Mafia. And you're telling me you've done it for over a hundred years?"

"Oh, it's not that tough, really. It's a combination of disinformation and containment."

"What type of disinformation?"

"Remember all that UFO crap? You know, Area 51, or whatever it was, and all that shit back at the turn of the century? Hell, it almost became a religion. That was us....It was a perfect dis job. Notice how no one ever got a real great photo of anything? And like hundreds of people would see a huge craft, then it would all just die down? Funny, wasn't it? You see, Jonathan, after World War Two, our kind came onto the scene and freaked everyone out. They thought we would be the super race – take man to the stars. But back then, we crashed more than we flew. Remember the flying saucer crash in 1952 or ,53 and the 'alien bodies'? Those were kids. The first real strong Tels back then were kids. And that space shuttle blow up...what was the name?"

"You mean Challenger?" Jonathan said, surprised.

"Yeah, that's it. Man, we screwed that up. That event alone set the Agency back 20 years. Remember the Kennedys?"

"Ah come on, the Agency didn't kill the Kennedys, did it?"

"Nah, not all of them. John was mob, but Bobby, so I've heard, was us. Total coincidence with that guy with the two same names....What were they...Turhan something? I can't remember. But I heard we fried Bobby about a second before the other guy shot him. Lucky for Bobby, he probably never felt a thing. I don't know about John Jr., I think that was all him."

"Why Bobby?"

"I was told he was a real ball buster and was going to shut the Agency down. Something about budgets and all. That's when the Agency went into shadow..."

"Shadow?"

"Yeah, it's our slang for how we exist. Back then, very few in government knew about us. Now...*nobody* knows. And the Level 8's keep it that way."

"Mind displacement?"

"You've been reading up. I bet that's Tarris, right?"

"Yeah. He gave me a textbook to read."

"Hah!" Jimbo laughed sarcastically. "It's probably giving you only a millionth of what we're really about. But come with us, and you'll see for yourself. Look,

Jonathan, this is a no-brainer here. You can go with the Rogues, but I mean, really, mentally moving logs to free a river in some bug-infested rain forest? You're basically a telekinetic beaver. Now that's exciting, eh? Besides, I doubt Whitehorse wants you to do good around the world. My guess is he's got bigger plans for you. Plans that probably involve changing around some governments." Jimbo motioned as if he were about to let Jonathan in on the world's biggest secret. "Jonathan, you need to know: Whitehorse is very, very dangerous. He'll do whatever it takes." He leaned closer. "Whatever."

Jimbo leaned back on his stool and took a big swig from his beer.

"What about Nicole and Tamara?" Jonathan asked.

"Yeah, well, we wish you hadn't connected with her. We were almost ready to contact you. But, no matter," Jimbo said, climbing off the stool. "We've got to get her back and keep Tamara safe. And that's a commitment from the Agency. Think of it as a show of good faith." Jimbo stuck out his hand.

"Yeah, but Whitehorse said..." Jonathan started.

"We already know what he said, and we won't be there...will we?" Jimbo winked at Jonathan.

As Jonathan saw it, he had no choice. His inexperience left him vulnerable, and the Agency knew how to deal with ruthlessly dangerous men such as Whitehorse. Plus, he didn't want any harm to come to Nicole or Tamara. Jimbo seemed like a good "company man," but Jonathan was still not sure of the true intentions of the Agency.

Jonathan reached for Jimbo's hand, and a static discharge leaped between them before their fingers met.

"Good move, Mr. Kortel, welcome to the Agency," Jimbo said, shaking his hand. He pulled Jonathan closer and looked right into his eyes. "If this is going to work, you need to do it our way....Are we clear on this?"

Jonathan nodded.

"Good," Jimbo said firmly. "Now, let's go get that little girl."

~

The Pueblo was dark. Jonathan's car headlights flooded the entrance, and the two guards were conspicuously absent. The gates were wide open.

Jonathan drove slowly into the plaza area. No one else was in sight. A large bonfire roared in the center of the plaza, and the Pueblo's adobe walls were awash in deep contrasts of orange, yellow and black that danced across the uneven surfaces. As the shadows moved in sync with the flames, it gave the Pueblo a Dali-like feel. It gave Jonathan the creeps.

When Jonathan pulled around the fire, Jacob Whitehorse stepped from the dark shadows into the path of the car.

Nicole was in his arms.

Jonathan engaged the braking system, and the car stopped amid a small dust cloud.

Whitehorse stood his ground. He wasn't smiling this time.

"Well, Whitehorse," Jonathan said as he closed the car door. "I'm here. Now give me the little girl."

Whitehorse just stood there, silently tracking Jonathan's every move. Nicole looked scared. She reached her hand toward Jonathan.

"We had a deal, Whitehorse." At Jonathan's first step, six Indians emerged from the shadows, each one carrying an M-21 Tactical Light-Force biorifle. They flanked him three and three.

"Yes," Whitehorse said, "we had a deal. But I need your assurance. No telekinetics, and I'll just hold onto little Miss Connor here as security."

Jonathan spun slowly around to size up each Indian.

"Oh, I know you're FTL against one bioweapon, but I seriously doubt you can duplicate that against six. Are we getting the picture here, Jonathan?"

"Okay, Whitehorse, I'm getting the picture. Now let's talk."

Whitehorse walked inside the circle of men. "How was your dinner with James? Did he feed you the company line?"

"I suppose," Jonathan said, not taking his eyes off Whitehorse.

"And you bought into it, didn't you?" Whitehorse accused, circling Jonathan.

"Well, they do have a compelling argument."

"Did he tell you about their 'special units?' About the men and women trained to be assassins, to do covert ops across the world?"

"Well, no, we never..."

"And I'm sure he didn't tell you about the other world 'Agencies' and their men and women, and their death units? I think not!"

Nicole began to squirm.

"And he obviously never said a thing about the deaths that take place when different Agencies with different agendas run up against each other. Well let me tell you something..." Whitehorse stopped circling and stood right in front of him. "...I know a little about death."

Nicole was beginning to cry.

"The Agency that Jimbo so eloquently described to you killed my wife." He was now inches from Jonathan's face. "And the man who ordered her assignment is James's partner."

The light from the fire painted Whitehorse's face in harsh contrasts. Jonathan saw the years of bitter hatred stored in his eyes, and he knew then that Nicole's life was in grave danger. As Whitehorse walked away, Nicole looked back over his shoulder at Jonathan. Tears were running down her cheeks.

"What do you want, Whitehorse? You want me to join you in your quest for world peace? Or is there another agenda here? Tell me!"

Whitehorse quickly turned. Nicole screamed.

"Of course I do!" he yelled. The six Indians charged their bioweapons; their collective whine echoed through the Pueblo.

"You're a Level 10, Jonathan. Don't you see that?! Together, we can bring balance back to the world and correct years of oppression. I can give my people justice from the goddamn white man!" The glow from the fire gave Whitehorse a demonic look. "Jonathan, you can usher in a new beginning for mankind! You're the next step! The Agency knows this. That's why they've been watching you, testing you. Remember the cab accident? That was a test. And guess who administered that test?"

Whitehorse began heading toward Jonathan. "The same man who sent my wife to her death, almost sent Tamara to hers."

He was three feet from him.

"Jonathan," he bellowed. "Open your eyes! The world is not what it seems. These men, these...Recruiters, are nothing more than henchmen for an organization that answers to no one. It's unchecked and unpoliced. It can do whatever it pleases...." He drew less than a foot from Jonathan. "...It can kill whoever it wants, and no one is held responsible."

"Yeah, well you might be right," Jonathan said while Whitehorse walked away from him. "But you're holding a little girl who should really be in the arms of her mother."

Whitehorse shook his head, his back still to him. "Ohhh Jonathan. I was afraid you would say something stupid like that." He slowly turned, and Jonathan saw he wasn't holding Nicole anymore. She was suspended about a foot away from him, kicking her legs and crying uncontrollably. Whitehorse had his hands in his pockets and looked fairly relaxed – for a homicidal psychopath.

Jonathan didn't dare move.

"You know," Whitehorse said in low voice, "I could crush her little brain in seconds." He narrowed his eyes at Jonathan.

"Go to hell, Whitehorse," Jonathan quietly uttered, and Whitehorse jerked forward like he'd been punched in the back. His face registered shock, his mouth flew open, and his arms and legs were outstretched like something was tearing his limbs from his body. He began to rise off the ground, and a gurgling noise was coming from his throat.

At the same instant, Nicole flew away from Whitehorse, over Jonathan's head and out of the circle of Indians. She screamed all the way.

Surprised to see their leader seemingly floating away, the Indians leveled their bioweapons at Jonathan's head. His vision turned to colors, then twinkling, then swirling. A symphony of tones filled his mind.

He went into phase.

Six bioweapons discharging filled the plaza with light like midday in Taos.

Jonathan, his arms outstretched, hovered a foot off the ground. His eyes were opened wide and staring up at Whitehorse. The six Indians were held tight in his imaging field: their bioweapons caught in mid-discharge with motionless beams of light protruding from their guns.

Jimbo and his partner calmly walked into the circle. Nicole was in Jimbo's arms.

The senior Tel walked up to Jonathan.

"You know, Jonathan, you have a dilemma here. If you relax your imaging, the bioweapons will discharge, killing both of us. I can keep Jacob up there for some time. But how long can you hold these weapons in check?"

He took a drag off his cigarette. A drop of blood fell, landing on the top of the senior Tel's shoe. Another drop fell to the dirt.

"You could move yourself out of the circle," he continued. "But there is Law Number 5: a Tel cannot move himself. Gravitational displacement does not work in reverse, but obviously you again are proving our laws and levels are mistaken. You are hovering right now, so you must be able to move yourself! Do it, Jonathan!"

He walked around to face Jonathan. Jimbo slowly backed out of the circle.

"I'm going to stay in the middle until you move yourself out. Now do it!"

Jonathan lowered his head to view the senior Tel.

"You used a contraction," Jonathan said hoarsely, and he rose about seven feet and floated backwards out of the circle.

The senior Tel smiled and followed.

As soon as Jonathan's feet touched the ground, the six bioweapons finished their discharge. Foolishly, Whitehorse's men had lined up directly across from each other, and they weren't faster than light.

Jimbo buried Nicole's head from the sight.

There was no sound. No screams. Just the creation of six small puddles of biomatter where each man had stood.

The senior Tel lit another cigarette.

Jonathan collapsed to the ground. Wiping the blood from his nose, he looked up at Whitehorse, who was still suspended about 20 feet in the air.

"What are you going to do with him?" Jonathan asked.

The senior Tel turned and looked up almost forgetfully at Whitehorse. He walked back into the center of the ring of former Indians, and Whitehorse began a descent that stopped about seven feet off the ground.

"Jacob, can you hear me?" the senior Tel called up to him between drags. "Jacob?" he asked again. He didn't get a verbal response. Instead, the senior Tel suddenly reached for his throat as his cigarette dropped to the ground. Jacob Whitehorse fell to earth, landing on his hands and feet.

Jimbo, who had handed Nicole to Jonathan, began to rush to his partner's aid, but the senior Tel waved him off as he fell to one knee.

There was panic in Jimbo's eyes.

Whitehorse regained his composure while the senior Tel struggled for air. "I've waited a long time for this, Zvara," Whitehorse said, circling the senior Tel.

Jimbo's face betrayed his shock at hearing that name.

"What's the matter?" Jonathan asked. "Don't you know who he is?"

"He told me he was someone else, but Whitehorse just called him Zvara!" Jimbo whispered. "Armando Zvara's kind of an urban myth in the Agency. We were told he was dead. Damn, this is too much."

Jonathan and Jimbo watched as the two Level 8's completely focused on each other and began round one of their telekinetic heavyweight bout. But in this ring, the stakes were much higher.

Jonathan tried to intervene but was too weak from displacing six bioweapons.

"Don't try, Jonathan. You're in no condition to help Zvara."

"Is there anything we can do?" Jonathan asked.

"No, their field strengths will be too strong, at least for me."

"Can you call in reinforcements?"

Jimbo looked tersely at Jonathan. "We're not the damn army. This looks like it's between Whitehorse and Cas...I mean, Zvara."

Whitehorse stepped closer. Zvara looked up at him, his eyes partially rolled back from the lack of oxygen. Suddenly, Whitehorse was thrown to the ground as if he had been kicked in the chest. He rolled to his side coughing and spitting blood. The dust gently settled around him.

Zvara was now on his feet. "Jacob," he coughed, wiping the sweat from his brow. "Do you really think you can take me on?"

Zvara doubled over, grabbing at his stomach. He groaned in agony and dropped to his knees. He vomited in the dirt.

"Shit," Jimbo whispered, "this doesn't look good. We need an exit plan – and fast."

"Why isn't Zvara winning?" Jonathan whispered back. Nicole turned her head and clung tightly to Jonathan's neck. He had never held her before, and a strangely protective instinct welled inside him.

"I don't know. He should be kicking Whitehorse's ass right about now. Come on!" Jimbo began pushing them toward the car.

"Where are you going, James?" Whitehorse asked, his attention drawn to their movement. "Don't you want to see your partner here die...oh, ohhh my God!!" Whitehorse screamed in midsentence and stumbled backwards, reaching for his face.

Armando Zvara was coughing as he rose to his feet. He wiped the bile from his mouth.

"And I have waited a long time for this, Jacob," Zvara said, stumbling toward him.

Jimbo grabbed Jonathan's shoulder: "Hold on." They stood next to the car and expectantly waited for Zvara to demonstrate why he was the highest testing Tel ever.

Whitehorse seemed frozen, his hands clutching his face. Thick, red blood oozed between his fingers.

"I should have..." Zvara started, but he stopped and raised his head as if to peer into the New Mexican night sky.

A shooting star passed overhead.

Whitehorse lowered his hands. His dark eyes reflected the orange radiance of the fire, and his blood was smeared in streaks across his face. The big Indian was now in warrior mode.

Zvara's arms were outstretched from his shoulders, and he began to rise off the ground. Whitehorse glared as Zvara slowly rose 10 feet and rotated horizontally onto his back. Whitehorse was about to crucify the killer of his wife on a cross only his mind could see.

The color had drained from Jimbo's face.

"It's over," he said quietly. "Let's get the hell out of here."

Jonathan handed Nicole to Jimbo and climbed into the pilot's seat. Jimbo took the passenger side and held her tightly against his chest. Whitehorse paid no attention.

They sped toward the main gate, and Jimbo turned in his seat to look back into the plaza. Through the dust raised in their wake, he could see Whitehorse laughing at his partner, who hung Christ-like in the air.

Whitehorse had positioned him over the fire.

Escape...23

ɪᴛ was four in the morning when Jimbo, Jonathan and Nicole finally entered Tarris's compound. The ride back had been quiet. Neither man wanted to relive the events of the night. Jimbo broke the silence for barely 20 minutes to tell Jonathan about the Agency legend, Zvara.

As a child entering the Agency, Armando Zvara had shown great promise, possibly the potential to ascend to the unthinkable status of Level 9. He grew in strength as he grew in age. Taking on the tough assignments, he demonstrated an uncanny ability to adapt and reconfigure his grav field to match, or better, whatever or whoever was in his way.

He became the ultimate weapon.

It was only a matter of time before the Agency put its prodigy to work. Zvara was dispatched throughout the world, correcting issues and delivering the Agency's own special brand of justice. All in the name of good.

Zvara rose through the ranks and created for himself a status that teetered on the edge of myth. He became the youngest Director the Agency ever had and soon gained control of the world's most secret organization. No one challenged him. No one, that is, until a big Indian from the desert southwest began finishing assignments before the assigned Tels could.

Jacob Whitehorse thought he'd shake things up at the Agency. Armando Zvara was intrigued with this *rogue* Tel.

Their partnership became the stuff of legend. They dominated the Tel world for nearly a decade, but then the collaboration crumbled. Zvara made a fatal mistake with the big Indian from the desert. He fell in love with his wife.

The affair lasted nearly three years. But when Zvara demanded that she choose between him and Whitehorse, he failed to foresee the dire consequences of her choice. Wrought with jealousy and blinded by power, Zvara directed Whitehorse to a dangerous assignment. Only Zvara knew how dangerous it really was. But the result was not the death of Whitehorse.

It was of his wife.

The loss of his soulmate changed Whitehorse. He began questioning Agency policy, refusing directives, and challenging Zvara's power. He turned his back on the Agency and went underground, creating an alternative group for Tels who were fed up with the Agency's agenda. He named this new group after the nickname Zvara had given him so many years ago.

For his part, Zvara was chastised for such reckless use of power. He was stripped of his title and demoted to the Recruiter Division of the Agency. In the wake of the incident, the world's most powerful organization also adopted a new form of management for itself. It would never be headed by one person again.

Jimbo pulled the rental up to the house and flooded the front porch with light. The door swung open, and Tamara and Georgia stepped out with Tarris rolling behind them. Tamara ran toward Jimbo, who was holding Nicole.

"Oh, my God!" she said, shocked to see her child in the middle of New Mexico. "What are you doing with Nicki?!"

"It's a long story, baby, but thank this guy here," Jonathan said, motioning to Jimbo. "He got her out of danger."

Tamara gathered Nicole into her arms and kissed her on the forehead. She looked over to Jonathan. "Oh, baby..." She hugged and kissed him, then suddenly stopped.

"Grannie..." she said with fear in her voice.

"Go ahead and call her Tamara," Jimbo said. "But I'll bet she's okay – a little in pain probably – but okay."

Tamara instantly pulled out her netphone. Georgia, arms folded, stood silently. Jonathan looked over at her.

"What happened?" Tarris demanded.

"I'll tell you what," Jonathan answered, eyes still on Georgia. "Right now, I'd give anything to be just a simple, powerless man. You can have this telekinesis crap."

"We thought you'd be back hours ago," Tarris said.

"Well, sir," Jimbo cut in. "We had a little business to take care of."

"Oh, I'm sorry everyone," Jonathan said. "This is James McCarris. He's with the Agency."

"Ma'am," Jimbo said, shaking Georgia's hand.

"Oh, thank you, James," Tamara said and snapped her netphone shut. "Grannie's okay. She doesn't remember a thing." She stepped over and hugged him. Nicole giggled for the first time.

"Yes, ma'am. It was our obligation to Jonathan to get your daughter back. She's a real pretty little girl." Jimbo's Southern drawl was thicker than usual, and he tickled Nicole under her chin. "Your grandmother will be all right, little one." He looked down at his transwatch. "Jonathan, we need to get out of this state as soon as we can. Tarris, do you know when the first flights start taking off from Albuquerque?"

"Ummm, the earliest I've ever seen is a five o'clock. I think it's a Nations Air into Daley or O'Hare. I can't remember which."

"No problem, I'll confirm that. Okay, Jonathan, get packing," Jimbo said, going professional. "And Tarris, do you have any weapons, bio or conventional?"

Tarris smiled and stood up with his chair. "Follow me, Mr. McCarris."

Jimbo pulled out his netphone, amazed by Tarris's walking chair, and followed him back behind one of the metal buildings.

Georgia stopped Jonathan as he headed toward the house with Tamara. "So, you're going with the Agency?"

"Hey, baby," Jonathan said, "give me a moment, please." Tamara read his look. She took Nicole's hand and continued into the house.

The light of dawn was beginning to fill the sky as Georgia and Jonathan stood alone in the compound's courtyard.

"Look, Georgia," he finally said. "I don't know what Whitehorse has said to you, but that man is out-of-control crazy. What I saw last night confirmed to me that the Rogues are way too under the netdar for me. And you should really think twice about staying with them. At least get rid of Whitehorse. Like I said, he's evil on a stick."

"We've had discussions about just that, but we're split as a group. I told you before, if you went with the Agency, I would leave the Rogues and stay with Tarris." She looked down, then toward the house. "Tamara seems like a nice girl....It's...just..."

"Just what, Georgia?"

Her dark hair blew across her face, and he stepped closer.

"Since I've met you...I..." She turned away. Jonathan pulled her around to face him. "Look," he said quietly, "I feel it, too. You and I are Tels. We probably have more in common with each other than Tamara and I, or even you and Tarris." He stopped and looked into her eyes. "Don't get me wrong..." He hesitated. "Another time or place, yeah, I'd be after you in a heartbeat. But not now."

He ran a finger down the side of her face, pulling her hair aside. "I would love to kiss you right now," he continued. "But that would be wrong. Way wrong."

Jonathan touched her on the lips with his finger, and a static discharge passed between them. He turned and walked into the house.

~

Tarris led Jimbo to the second building from the house, maneuvering almost effortlessly around rocks and sage bushes. The flimsy metal building was Tarris's workshop, where he built the modifications to his chair. The room was large and contained work tables, computers, biofabrication equipment and an 8-foot flat, liquid crystal TVid screen. Tarris moved one of the work tables aside to expose a large metal floor locker with an integrated systems lock. He transformed downward into a standard chair and began the sequence for unlocking the case. The system hummed and whined until the lock tripped. The lid slowly raised, and Tarris smiled at Jimbo.

Jimbo was viewing an impressive array of weaponry. A 20th-century M-16 lay on top of the pile, with the rest a mix of bio hand-held weapons and three Hitachi/Wesson Light-Force biorifles.

"Wow, now you're talking." Jimbo said, kneeling to examine the various weapons. "Tarris, you old survivalist. I'm glad you call me friend."

"You just never know," Tarris said proudly.

"No, you don't, and today we're gonna need most of these. Do you mind?" Jimbo asked, pointing to the antique M-16. He picked it up reverently, like he was handling a delicate glass sculpture. "Yeah..." He lifted the gun to his shoulder. "Now this is what I'm talking about. This here's a weapon."

"Damn near perfect shape, too." Tarris said. "But for my money, give me a Light-Force any day." He reached in and brought out a Beretta Light-Force Hand-Held. The contrast between its chrome and flat-grey surfaces made the weapon appear almost toylike, but anyone who had witnessed its bioshifting results knew that it was anything but. He stuffed it into his coat pocket.

Jimbo set the M-16 down and lifted out the three biorifles. "One for each of us," he said. He pocketed a Beretta for good measure.

~

Jonathan busily packed. He told Tamara about the Rogues, the Agency and the ordeal at the Pueblo. Tamara quietly listened as she washed up Nicole. Tamara was dressed in her mannish way: work boots, baggy rip-stop pants with four large pockets down each leg and a vinyl T-shirt. Jonathan packed the last case and watched her with Nicole. He had not seen her much as a mother, and the contrast to how he had seen her in Liquid Courage was, well...beautiful, he thought.

Tamara could feel his stare and turned around, brushing her curls off her face. "What?...Why are you smiling?"

"I'm sorry. I rambled on about myself, and you're listening so patiently, and it hits me. What you're doing. It's so real. I've just never really seen you...you know...in action."

"In action?"

"As a mother. It's okay, I find it quite wonderful, actually. You seem to be a natural. So...happy."

Tamara smiled and resumed washing Nicole.

~

Tarris closed the lid and reinitialized the locking sequence. Jimbo had picked up the biorifles and was heading for the door.

"Where's your partner?" Tarris asked.

Jimbo's hand froze on the doorknob, his back to Tarris. "When we left, he was still fighting Whitehorse in the middle of the plaza."

"And?" Tarris pressed.

"I doubt he won," Jimbo said gravely and opened the door. He trotted over to Jonathan's rental car.

"Hold on," Tarris said. "I wouldn't take that piece of shit. Come over here." He started "walking" toward the third metal building. When he reached it, he put his hand in his pocket, and the large front door began to open, revealing an antique 2035 Hummer with full off-road setup and desert military paint job.

Jimbo smiled for the first time that night.

"Now this will get us to Albuquerque," Tarris said proudly, "any way we want." He pushed the controller in his pocket again, and the Hummer turned over, producing the odd multipitched hum of a dozen different retrofitted aftermarket engine parts grinding together. The lights came on and flooded the area with bright yellow and white lights.

The Hummer rolled out of the building and right up to Jimbo, who was standing with the bioweapons in his arms. "Sweet..." he said.

Jonathan, Tamara, Nicole and Georgia emerged from the house.

"Tarris, are you sure this thing will get us there?" Georgia asked over the noise of the engine.

"Baby, this will get you anywhere. Stow the gear and let's get going. We haven't much time."

Tarris climbed into the pilot's seat, with Georgia in shotgun.

Tamara and Nicole sat in the middle of the rear seat with Jonathan and Jimbo flanking them, biorifles ready on the floor. Georgia checked her weapon's system pad, then turned back to Jonathan.

"Ever discharged one of these?"

"Honestly, no," he answered. "But I'm a quick learner."

"I'll show you," Tamara said. She lifted the Hitachi/Wesson off the floor, flipped it around and began the precheck on the system pad. The whine stopped everyone cold.

"Tamara!" Tarris yelled. "What are you doing?"

"Relax, everyone, it's not loading. It's charging. See?" She flipped it again, with the system pad facing out. "This yellow light is standby, not load. And besides, this isn't the right pitch. The loading sequence is just a little higher, listen."

She pressed a pad sequence and the weapon began loading, its whine just slightly higher. She quickly shut it down to standby and spun it around in one hand so that the butt end faced Jonathan. Everyone in the Hummer collectively turned and looked at her. "Hey," she said, "picked it up in Nevada." She winked at Jonathan. Nicole giggled.

~

They charged out of the mountains riding an empty Interway as the sun was cresting over the mountaintops, sending golden rays streaking across the peaks. The tension in the Hummer was thick. Whitehorse was a seriously resourceful man, and they all assumed he would try to stop them before they got out of New Mexico.

Jimbo was working his netphone. "...Bill, don't give me any crap, we're in a situation here," he barked. "...I know that most of the team is in the Middle East....I know that, too....Put Berger on." There was a long pause. "Berger, why the hell didn't you tell me my partner was Zvara?...Oh, right, like that's gonna help the situation....Ah, I don't know....No, he waved us off. Besides, you know my level parameters....I doubt it, sir....Yes, sir...Yes, sir...Thank you, sir, that will help a lot." He clicked off his netphone and looked out the window.

They all bounced in sync as the Hummer sped toward Albuquerque.

~

"That's odd," Jimbo said, finally breaking the silence.

"What's that?" Georgia asked.

"I would have bet you that Whitehorse would have showed by now. We're almost to the airport."

"I think you spoke too soon, Jimbo," Tarris said. He pointed to the rear vidscreen. About 200 yards back, a pair of car lights approached them at a high rate of speed.

"Showtime..." Jimbo said, still looking out the window.

The car kept gaining. Tarris pushed the antique to its limits, but even with his retrofittings, the Hummer could only do 120 mph max, and he was already pushing it on the flat stretches.

"Everyone ready?" Jimbo asked.

They all nodded. Jonathan looked at Tamara and handed her back the biorifle. "Here, looks like you know how to use it better than I do. Give me your hand-held."

Tamara took the Hitachi/Wesson and handed Jonathan the Beretta. "Give me the window," she said and they crawled over each other in the cramped cabin. She settled in, reviewed the system pad and propped the Hitachi/Wesson between her legs. "Cocked and locked."

Jimbo and Tarris laughed.

Jonathan was now next to Nicole. She looked up, and he brushed the hair off her face. When he glanced up, he caught Georgia staring at him.

"Here they come!" Tarris said.

"Be sharp, everyone!" Jimbo ordered.

The car pulled right up to their bumper, held for a moment, then jerked to the side lane and flew past, chewing up the road ahead of them.

"I don't get this," Jimbo said, frustrated. "Where's Whitehorse?"

"This doesn't feel right," Tarris agreed.

"Maybe," Georgia said, "he got what he needed when he dealt with your partner."

Jimbo shot her a look.

~

"Welcome to Georgia O'Keefe International airport, please state your airline, flight number and departure or arrival time," the simvoice said through the netradio of the Hummer.

"Nations Air, 1213, departure, six thirty," Tarris answered.

"Thank you. Please follow the signs to terminal 3, Gate 17. Have a nice flight."

Tarris pulled up to the curb, and the Hummer released some steam from under the hood. They hid the weapons under the mats and climbed out. One baggage handler grabbed their gear as Jimbo handed another his netpad.

"Four through to Chi town," the first said. "Now isn't she precious." He tickled Nicole in the belly; she grinned and buried her face in Tamara's neck.

"Just give me your eyes right here, everyone," the second handler said. He raised his handheld WAA scanner and processed their retinas. "Thank you, you're all checked through to Daley/Chicago. Have a safe flight."

Jimbo took the handler's netpad and entered in his tip.

"Thank you, sir!" he said with a tip of his hat.

"Well, buddy," Tarris said to Jonathan, "not quite the relaxing time off you were looking for, eh?"

Jonathan put down his carry-on and walked over to his friend. "Nah, I guess not." Jonathan gazed awkwardly at his shoes like he couldn't think of the right thing to say. "Thanks for everything, Tarris," he finally settled on. "You be safe...and take care of that lady."

"Listen, Jonny, we may not see each other for a long time, so good luck, little brother. I hope you find what you're looking for." Tarris glanced at Tamara and Nicole, then back to Jonathan and smiled.

Jonathan grabbed his friend and hugged him. They shook hands, and Tarris "walked" to the Hummer and climbed in.

Georgia stood there quietly with her arms folded.

Jonathan motioned to Tamara and Jimbo to go on. "I'll catch up with you at security, okay?"

Jimbo nodded and led Tamara through the huge sliding glass doors into the terminal.

"You take care of him, you understand me," Jonathan said.

Georgia didn't answer. She walked up and took his hands. A plane passed overhead as she came up to his ear. "My love goes with you, Jonathan. Please be careful." She kissed him on the cheek, turned and crawled up into the Hummer. She lowered the window.

"Go save the world for us, will you, little buddy!" Tarris laughed from the pilot's seat.

Georgia silently mouthed "goodbye." And smiled that smile.

Dear God...24

THE huge Airbus was crowded with ski tourists and business types. Because of their last-minute reservations, Jonathan, Jimbo and Tamara were assigned seats in the back of the plane on the first level near the workout gym. Jonathan stowed his bag while Jimbo took his seat in front of Nicole and Tamara. Nicole stretched her arms and reached for Jonathan. He picked her up and placed her in his lap. Tamara smiled.

"I think she likes me," he declared.

"I think you're cool," Nicole said in her little voice.

Tamara began to laugh. Jonathan, surprised, was infected by it and broke out laughing for the first time in several days. The release felt good.

An elderly lady across the aisle with her head buried in a vidbook shot them a look.

Jimbo clicked his netphone off and turned around to face Jonathan. "Okay, we're all set. There'll be a car waiting for us when we land in Chicago to take you to your apartments...or wherever you need to go....Hey, what's so funny?"

"Nothing, James. You had to be there," Jonathan said. He and Tamara froze for a second, exchanged looks, and burst out laughing again.

Nicole smiled at Jimbo. "I think you're cool, too."

"Ladies and gentlemen, this is your first officer Mike Mathews, and sitting next to me in the captain's chair is Jackson Stoval. We've been cleared for vert takeoff and we'd like to ask the flight attendants to finish preparing the cabins for an early departure from New Mexico. You folks in the gym: get your last mile in, we'll be lifting off in approximately 10 minutes."

Jonathan leaned back into the seat and finally began to relax while the flight attendants scurried up and down the aisles, prepping the different cabins for takeoff.

He reached over and gently squeezed Tamara's hand. She squeezed back.

The lights dimmed as the holojectors lowered from their various ports in the cabin and began the preflight holovid. Thirty life-size, holojected flight attendants began explaining the safety procedures and emergency escape routes. A lone flight attendant came up the aisle, spot-checking different passengers. Her face eerily merged with the holoattendants when she walked through each holojection.

She stopped at Jonathan's seat. "What a darling little girl. You two must be very proud." She continued down the aisle, and Tamara squeezed his hand tighter.

"Ladies and gentlemen, this is your first officer again. We've been cleared for vert takeoff, and we'd like to ask the flight attendants to please take their jump seats."

The lights dimmed further, and the plane's turbines started up. Their rhythmic hum built to an apogee as the plane was moved backwards out onto the tarmac. Jerking to a halt, the muffled sounds of the ground crew's disengagements traveled down the fuselage, each station uncoupling from the huge aircraft from front to back. There was a moment of quiet where the sense of activity, either in the plane or on the tarmac, disappeared. Then the turbines roared to life. The plane vibrated, shuddered and began to lift vertically into the early morning sky.

It hovered briefly at 300 feet to receive air space clearance from O'Keefe tower; its engines droned deeply, fighting the winds pouring down off the mountains. Then the plane rotated on its center axis, pointed its nose up slightly and began the transition from vertical to horizontal flight. Without spilling a single first-class drink, it slowly edged forward, headed toward the mountaintops and the airspace of the Midwest.

"Ladies and gentlemen, we've completed our transition sequence and begun our flight to Chicago's Richard J. Daley Airport. Our computer puts us in on time, even though we've had a head start out of Albuquerque, we've got a head wind which should eat up any extra time we gained. We'll be climbing over the mountains and might get a little chop, so I'm going to ask that the flight attendants please remain in their jump seats until it's safe to move about the cabins. Thank you."

Four large turbines shifted from the low tone of vertical takeoff to the high-pitched whine of horizontal flight. The plane's angle of attack increased, and Jonathan clicked his seat out of takeoff position. He leaned back into its body fitting fabric – not as nice as the first-class's biofitting seats. They would mold to the passenger's frame, but as far as Jonathan was concerned, anything that would help him sleep was perfect.

He closed his eyes.

The TVid screens in the headrests glowed up, and NNN came on.

"Good morning. Yesterday in the former Hawaiian Islands, scientists believe that they've detected a shift in the..."

Tamara reached over and touched Jonathan's arm. He kept watching and patted her hand at his shoulder.

"Don't worry, baby. I'm not going to get all emotional on you. I've been watching this stuff for years now. I learned to tune it out a long time ago."

The plane buffeted a bit as it neared the mountains. Both Jimbo's and Jonathan's TVid screens suddenly went blue, then a flight attendant appeared on the screen.

"Mr. McCarris? Mr. Kortel?" she asked in a serious tone. "You both have an emergency netcall. Shall I put it through?"

They nodded, surprised. The flight attendant was replaced with a commercial about the latest biodiaper. Jimbo turned around and looked seriously at Jonathan through the gap in the seats. The netphones in their arm rests buzzed, and they slowly picked them up in unison.

"Relaxed, gentlemen?" asked Jacob Whitehorse.

Jimbo's hand began to tremble. Jonathan's heart began to race.

"It's too bad you all left so early last night. Armando and I talked over old times and had a few laughs. Didn't we, old friend?"

There was a long pause.

"James?..." Zvara's voice was weak and broken.

Shocked, Jimbo could barely speak. "Are...are you all right, sir?"

"Forget about me, James, your job is to get Jonathan..."

"Enough!" Whitehorse interrupted. "Jonathan, you really should have come with me. I'm so surprised..."

"Whitehorse!" Jonathan pleaded. "You're out of control. I'm not worth the deaths that have happened already. Don't kill Zvara, please. I'm not the Infinite whatever you call it, believe me. Jimbo says I'm probably just a Level 8, but that's it! Please don't kill anymore. I'm not worth it!"

"Oh, but you are, Jonathan. James isn't telling you the truth, are you, James?"

Jimbo was silent.

"I thought so. James, did you tell him about the results of the GDRD test, or the Field level tests, or the Grav Reflux data?"

Jimbo still didn't respond.

"The Agency," Whitehorse said in disgust. "They're no better than we are." He paused. "I've waited a long time for you, Jonathan. You may not know it now, but you have the potential for great things. To take our kind beyond anything we have ever imagined. I believe you are The Infinite Tel, and I know the Agency does, too. I'll give you one more opportunity. Come with me, and we'll change the world!"

A quiet hiss from the net connection filled their ears.

"Jonathan?"

"No, Whitehorse...I won't."

Whitehorse sighed. "Look at that little darling Nicole for me, will you?"

Jonathan complied, unsure what Whitehorse was up to.

"Now, take a look at your beautiful girlfriend."

Jonathan did, although he felt a gnawing unease.

"Look at those lovely blond curls that fall so delicately over her face. And her lips...they're so full. And her eyes, look into her eyes, Jonathan. What do you see?"

Tamara sensed his gaze. She turned from the window and met his stare. She smiled softly.

"I...I see *love*, Whitehorse."

"Then enjoy that love, Jonathan Kortel, because it will be the last thing you will ever see!" The netline cut out.

Jimbo jumped to his feet so fast he hit his head on the storage bin. He spun around to face Jonathan.

"Sir, you must take your seat," the flight attendant scolded from the TVid screen. "We're still climbing over the mountains!"

"Jonathan!" There was absolute panic in Jimbo's voice. "Jonathan!" People around them began to turn and take notice.

"James, easy, easy, we're on our way. Whitehorse can't..." Jonathan stopped dead in midsentence, suddenly realizing what he was saying.

"Dear God..." Jonathan said to himself. "He wouldn't."

"The hell he wouldn't," Jimbo replied.

Tamara's eyes widened. She had figured out what they where talking about. "No!...Oh no! Not my baby!" She scooped up Nicole and held her to her chest.

"Sir, please!" the flight attendant yelled from the TVid screen. "If you don't sit down, I'll have someone physically restrain you. Now take your seat immediately!"

Jimbo spun back around to face the screen. "Lady, if you don't get me the captain right now, there won't be a seat left to take!"

Her face turned white, and the screen went blank. The cabin became oddly quiet. Then it hit.

Jimbo was just stepping into the aisle when the Tactical Short Range Bioweapon tore through the plane's fuselage. The TSRB was an efficient, shoulder-launched surface-to-air missile capable of bringing down anything from a unmanned drone to a Nations Airbus and its 520 tons of metals, electronics and plastics. Not to mention its 652 manifest head count of human cargo. The TSRB engaged its target not by exploding, but by releasing a biomatrix warhead at the point of impact. In this case, the point of impact was just behind the first-class cabin, near the number one lavatory.

At 7:03:03 a.m. Mountain Daylight Time, Nations Air Flight 1213 heavy, ascending out of Albuquerque, New Mexico, to 60,000 feet would have declared an air emergency. But the captain, along with his crew, the two levels of first-class, the forward galleys, and the numbers one and two lavatories were gone.

The front quarter of the plane had been sheared off.

The warhead's biomatrix was glowing bright green as it traveled around the bulkhead from the point of impact. It was only a matter of seconds before it would consume the entire frame and tear the aircraft apart, raining bits of plane and human across the arid landscape.

To Jonathan, everything appeared a grotesque slow-motion ballet. Metal, plastic and pieces of first-class passengers flew through the cabin, riding the 400-mph wave of bitter cold air that rushed into the now-open cabin.

The haunting death screams of the remaining 500-odd passengers and crew faded from his hearing. The wall of air punched him in the face, slamming him back against his seat. Simultaneously, he watched in horror as Jimbo was lifted and flung down the aisle, followed closely by a lower part of an arm that still held the pretakeoff cocktail reserved for first-class passengers.

Jonathan slowly turned to Tamara. Her face was contorted as bits of plane flew between them carried by the savage rush of air. She wasn't holding Nicole anymore.

An overwhelming heat took over his body. He burned from the inside out with such intensity it made him want to tear his skin from his body like an old shirt. His vision violently shifted to vivid, swirling colors that exploded across his field of view. It shifted to white. A pure, smooth, blinding white. The music followed, but this time it didn't fill only his mind.

It filled his soul.

Like a million angels singing, the chorus reached its crescendo. The music consumed his entire being.

And subsumed it into what seemed like eternity.

~

Jonathan's vision returned, and what he saw was beyond his comprehension. The cabin, the passengers, the debris – the whole plane itself – were frozen as if the horrific moment had been captured in a photo. A hideously lit and gruesomely staged image. Jonathan had opened his eyes to a nightmare no one should see. The plane was tilted down and to the right, caught in Jonathan's telekinetic gravitational suspension field, 10,234 feet above the earth.

He stood and hit his head on a woman's purse. Its contents spilled in a spray pattern that hung in the air. The woman herself was caught in midair above the seats in a bizarre gymnasticlike position just a few rows ahead of her purse.

He turned to check Tamara. She was caught in a silent scream, her tears motionless like little crystals, her hair pulled straight out by a wind he could no longer feel. Behind Tamara, in the arms of a large businessman, he saw Nicole. She had flown six rows before she stopped, her face almost touching the man's stomach. One of her little arms was bent behind her and her leg was caught in mid-kick. He was looking down, as if preparing to wrap his big arms around her.

Jonathan slowly turned back to the aisle, afraid of what he would see. About twelve rows back, Jimbo was suspended upside down, his left arm touching the floor and his feet almost touching the upper bulkhead. Shock was written on his face. He was entangled with a flight attendant whose nose was a spray of blood from his 400-mph elbow. The force of the impact had lifted her out of her shoes.

Jonathan began to traverse his way up the aisle, heading for the front of the plane. He ducked in and out of wreckage, gingerly stepping over people and contorting his way through, trying not to disturb any part of the motionless carnage. The air was freezing in the huge gaping maw that had been the first quarter of the plane. Jonathan inched his way to the edge of the torn fuselage. He looked down through the tangle of wires and fiber optic cables, down through the wispy clouds to the mountaintops a mile below.

He jerked back with fear, stumbling into a passenger in the front row of remaining seats. Her feet and ankles had been consumed by the biomatrix. Startled, he jumped off her and fell into the aisle. The whole row was in various states of debiolization.

Jonathan scrambled to his feet and noticed for the first time how the biomatrix worked. It first consumed everything in its immediate strike zone, then fingered out through the electronics of the massive aircraft. Its bright green glow had traveled along cables and wires like needles shooting toward the back of the plane.

Jonathan began making his way back to his seat. He entered the back cabin, but the closer he came to his row, the stranger he felt. He noticed someone in his seat, or, more accurately, suspended slightly above his seat in a half-sitting, half-standing position.

It was himself.

Jonathan tried to hurry down the aisle but, like a dream, his way kept getting blocked by debris he couldn't seem to clear fast enough. He stumbled to his seat and looked down at himself. He was almost standing up – his head and eyes rolled back, his arms outstretched from his sides. A small amount of blood was coming out his nose and being pushed back across his cheek by the phantom wind. Jonathan reached down and touched the top of his head. It was hot, almost too hot to touch. He felt suddenly qualmish and threw up into the aisle. The shock of the scene began to sink in. Wiping his chin, he couldn't take his eyes off of himself.

The plane violently jerked to the left and knocked him to the floor. From his hands and knees, he saw blood start pouring from the nose of himself in the seat. His own nose hurt. He put his hand to his face and came away with blood on his fingers. He stood up, his legs unsteady. The blood rushed from his head. Faintly, he grabbed for the edge of a seat to steady himself.

Again his vision shifted, and the choir of angels resumed their chorus. This time, though, it seemed to come from outside the plane.

From the clouds themselves.

It's a miracle...25

"**HOW** do you feel?" Tamara asked Jimbo.

"I'll be okay. My elbow is sore, and I think I cracked a rib. I can't really tell without my equipment, and I don't feel like digging through the belly of this plane right now to find it. You think he's going to be all right?" he asked, gesturing toward Jonathan, who was wrapped in a blanket, asleep in the shadow of the plane's gigantic wing on a cushion pulled from one of the sleeper cabins.

The massive Airbus rested on its belly in the middle of a valley on the eastern slope of the Sangre de Cristos. It lay in the warm sun like a huge silver snake that had been decapitated. The cockpit and first-class cabin had been cleanly sheared off by the TSRB's impact. At the severed front, brightly colored fiber optic biocables and hydraulic tubing dangled in the wind like techno entrails on a giant metal carcass. Hundreds of people milled about. Some were helping older passengers, while others just sat in shock. Families huddled together and tended to their children; individuals collected into small groups. The flight attendants who had survived were organizing people as best they could or calming those who were panicking. Given the enormity of the event, most people were rather calm, considering they had just been through what all collectively agreed was a miracle.

Five doctors who had been on board were tending to the injured and helping identify the dead. One of them approached Jimbo, who was sitting on the ground cradling his broken rib.

"How you doing, son?"

"I'm all right, but how's our friend there doing, doc?" Jimbo asked, pointing to Jonathan.

"I don't know. He appears to be in some kind of coma. I can't really tell without my BMP. He seems generally okay. No broken bones. He had some blood loss from his nose hemorrhaging, but besides being unconscious, he's fine."

"Hey, doc, could you use some standard netpads and some scanner equipment?"

"Hell yes. You a doctor?"

"No, but if you go through the cargo area, look for three silver cases and bring them here. They'll have what you need to help these people out."

The doctor called over one of his colleagues, and they ran to the front of the plane.

"Tamara, help me up please." Jimbo said.

She gave him her hand, and they walked over to Jonathan. Nicole was sitting next to him.

"He's not woke up yet, Mommy."

"Don't worry, baby, he will. I promise." She bent down and stroked his forehead.

"I still can't believe it," Jimbo said. "He's beyond what we ever thought humans could achieve." He lifted his face to the wing looming over them. "This is unbelievable. He moved this plane out of the air, down at least a mile to the ground, and held a grav field so vast...it's...unthinka..." Overwhelmed, Jimbo reached for Tamara as the consequence of Jonathan's telekinetic power sunk in.

"James, are you all right?" Tamara asked. She jumped to her feet to steady him.

"Yeah, it's all just a bit much, I guess. Whitehorse was right. He is the next step for our kind. He could be the next evolutionary path."

Both looked down at him.

"You really love him, don't you?" he questioned.

She smiled. "With all my heart, James. And you know what's funny? I really can't tell you why. But I know I do...I *feel* it."

"Can you handle this, Tamara?" He waved at the airplane. "This is some powerful shit here."

"I'm a tough girl, James, I can handle it."

"That's not the question. Most non-Tels eventually leave their Tel lovers because...well, you know. It's just too different. They can't relate. You understand? And Jonathan's a new human, for God's sake. This is all new ground; we're into uncharted territory here."

"She can handle it," Jonathan said roughly. He sat up and coughed.

"Hey, you, we thought we'd lost you," Tamara said, kneeling down beside him.

"What happened. Did we crash?"

Tamara looked up at Jimbo.

"What, what's going on?..." Jonathan said. "Oh, you got to be kidding me. Did I do this?" He leaned back onto the cushion.

Jimbo knelt down. "Yeah," he said, patting his shoulder. "I'm afraid you did this all by yourself."

Jonathan moaned. "I thought it was a dream."

"Tell me about it. Tell me about this *dream*," Jimbo pressed.

"Obviously it wasn't, because I remember all of it – the passing through the clouds, the landing. But there was a part that was really weird, I mean weirder than this weird." He briefly glanced at the plane. "It was right after I went into phase. I thought I came out of it, but everything – the plane, the people – everything was suspended, except me...or least part of me. I mean, there were two of me, one sitting in the seat and me, walking through the plane...up in the air." He pointed to the sky. "Everything was held in my grav field displacement. Then I, the one walking

through the plane, went into phase again and...oh, I can't explain it. My head hurts."
He curled into a ball under the blanket.

"Baby, it's okay. We believe you," Tamara consoled. "I mean after this, I'll believe
anything."

Nicole patted him through the blanket.

Jonathan slowly pulled the blanket off his face. "Hey, how many are, you know..."

"Dead?" Jimbo asked.

Jonathan nodded.

"The count seems to be right around 150. That's all of first-class, the flight crew
and some people who were caught early in the biomatrix." He motioned to 13 bodies
covered in blankets by the tail of the plane. Jimbo leaned closer. "You saved over 500
lives, Jonathan. Keep that in your mind when the reality of this situation gets to be
too much for you. It's one of the only things that's keeping me from breaking down
right here." Jimbo's voice cracked, and his eyes welled with tears.

"Oh, James," Tamara said, putting her arm around him.

Jonathan grabbed Jimbo's arm. "Hey, man," Jonathan said. "This was a rough
thing to go through. I know what you're feeling. We all do." He looked to the
mountains. "You wouldn't believe what I saw up there..."

"Are these them, young man?" the doctor asked, walking up with the three silver
cases under his arms.

"What?...Oh, great," Jimbo said, composing himself. He stood to greet them.
"Just set them down right here."

Jimbo knelt beside them and went through the unlocking sequence on their
system pads. The cases hissed, and their lids rose in sync with each other.

The doctor looked down into the array of proprietary biotechnology. In all his
years in medicine, he had never seen this type of equipment before. "Now, what do
you do exactly?"

Jimbo hesitated. "I work in government, sir. Let's just leave it at that, shall we?"

Jimbo carefully fished through the different devices, pulling out five small
netpads, half the size of standard ones, and two Kyosera hand-held netlink
medscanners. Each piece was nestled in its own cocoon of biofiber foam. When Jimbo
lifted out a piece of equipment, the living foam reset back to the default shape of a
circle or square. When he placed an item back, the foam's memory would reconform
to the specific parameters of the equipment's shape.

"Here you go, sir," Jimbo said. "These should help with your diagnosis and
treatments."

The doctor looked over the different devices. He hesitated. "Son, ah...these are
a little out of my league."

Jimbo looked to Jonathan and raised an eyebrow.

"No problem. Come on, I'll work with you and get you familiar with them." He
grabbed a netphone from the case, pocketed it and walked off with the doctor. The
three silver cases slowly closed, hissing together as they locked down.

~

Jonathan sat up and surveyed the area. "How long have we been down?" he asked.

"About an hour," Tamara replied.

"It won't be long before help arrives. A big plane like this doesn't just drop off the netdar without O'Keefe, the NAA, NORAD and God knows who else tracking it. And I'm sure they won't believe what they'll find out here."

"Most of the passengers are saying it was a miracle. That God intervened."

Jonathan rubbed his head. "Well, this god has a splitting headache. Help me up, please, baby?" Tamara helped Jonathan to his feet. Nicole hugged his leg.

A booming voice came from behind them. "Where's that little girl I caught?" The large businessman who had caught Nicole came walking up. He laughed as Nicole hid behind Jonathan's leg. "How's she doing?"

"As well as can be expected," Tamara said.

"I see you're up and around," he said, looking at Jonathan. "Name's Marshall, Calvin Marshall." He extended his hand.

"Jonathan. I guess you've already met Tamara."

"Yes, and Nicole, too."

"I can't thank you enough for saving her life," Tamara said.

"Aw, it was no problem. Like I said earlier, when I came to, she was lying there in my lap, and we were already on the ground, for heaven sakes. It's the darndest thing I've ever seen. Gives me the willies just thinking about it. Well, I just wanted to see how she's doing. You all have a beautiful child there."

He left to join a large group of people collecting their baggage from the plane's cargo hold.

Tamara laughed a little under her breath.

Jonathan shook his head. "This 'you've got a beautiful kid' routine is getting just a little weird."

Nicole never let go of his leg.

~

Jimbo left the doctors on their own and returned. He clicked his netphone off as he approached. "The Agency says they're going to send a private plane out for us. It'll meet us at O'Keefe." He gingerly rubbed his broken rib. "There are probably 500 netphones on this flight, and each one of them has called somebody about the 'miracle' landing. The news of this crash is all over the net. Hell, I think half these people are on their netphones right now doing interviews."

"Yeah, they're all going for their fifteen minutes," Jonathan agreed.

"No doubt," Jimbo said. "And they've dispatched a damn army to rescue us. They'll probably be here within the hour. What's funny is there aren't any reports of the missile. Nothing on the newsnet about this plane being hit. They're all saying it was a catastrophic structural failure. I know we have masking technology for missiles and planes, but that's real 'black' stuff. How Whitehorse got hold of that kind of weaponry is beyond me."

Jonathan walked over to the three equipment cases that sat innocently in the bright New Mexican sun. Their smooth silver skins were void of any visible seams, and their simple design gave no hint to the powerful technology stored inside them. Jimbo quietly stepped up behind him.

"All this for me?" Jonathan asked, still looking down at the cases.

"Oh yeah," Jimbo replied, clearly uncomfortable with the question. "For you, only our best."

Both Tels stood silently as the wind swirled dust around their feet. "Jonathan," Jimbo finally said, "what Whitehorse told you up there was partially true, and I'm sorry." He hesitated. "Zvara and I did hold back some data results, but not because we were trying to trick you or something. It's...just..."

"Just what, James?"

"Look, man, right now you're developing at an alarming rate. I won't get into details here, but you need to know that you're probably leaving Level 8. Hell, I know you've left that level." He waved his arms around at the plane. "I mean, come on – landing a 400-ton airplane, stopping a Light-Force....Oh, yeah, we see this kind of stuff all the time at the Agency. Seriously, Jonathan, you're scaring me a little here. I don't know where you're going to level off. I wish your field hadn't been so huge up there. Otherwise, my equipment could have taken readings during your phase. But you held *everything* in field. I'm surprised you didn't bring down a damn satellite along with this plane."

Jonathan broke into a smile.

"Don't get any smart-ass ideas, mister. You're strong, but you're not *that* strong. I'm drawing the line. And don't even think about one of the space stations."

"James, do you really think..."

"Listen, Jonathan," Jimbo said, stepping closer. "I like you. I like Tamara. Hell, I even like Nicole, and I'm not into kids. But there's something else you need to know." He leaned in and looked Jonathan right in the eyes. "If you do go...you know, 'critical' on me, I have my orders."

"Critical?" Jonathan questioned seriously.

"Yeah. Some Tels who develop too fast for their bodies to handle go what we call 'critical.' During their phases, they can literally fry. Or implode. I've even read of some who exploded. You, my friend, get hot when you phase. Real hot..."

"I know. When I was outside myself, I touched the top of my head...my other head, and it was burning up."

"That's what I'm talking about. It's like a fever. Except this is the mother of all fevers."

"Why doesn't it cause injury, like brain damage?"

"That's something we don't know too much about. There haven't been many cases, and certainly nothing like you. It's like I told your girlfriend, we're in uncharted territory here. Until we get you back and get our teams on you, I'm flying by the seat of my pants." He looked up at the big engine looming overhead and shook his head.

"So, James," Jonathan asked gravely. "What *are* your orders?"

Jimbo hesitated and turned away. "It all depends. If you look like you're going to hurt yourself, I'm tranq'n you. If you look like you're going to hurt someone else...someone innocent, I'm going to tranq you then, too."

"And what if my power gets out of hand, like dangerously beyond my own control?" Jonathan pressed. "What then?"

Jimbo sighed and knelt by the biggest of the three cases. He worked its system pad, and the lid slowly opened. Moving aside a shelf, he reached in and pulled out a small gunlike device. Its chrome surface reflected the midday sun, and Jonathan noticed two tiny buttons: one red and one green.

"Then," Jimbo said, standing up, "I use this."

"And what is that?" Jonathan asked tentatively.

"A TGD-1200 Field Matter Disrupter. Custom-made, one of a kind." Jimbo spun it around in his hand.

"In layman's terms?"

Jimbo hesitated. "A death ray."

There was a long silence. The wind began to pick up.

"If I have to use this," Jimbo whispered, going serious on him, "you'll probably be begging me to."

He returned the TGD-1200 to its compartment in the big silver case. The biofoam shifted to match its shape and swallowed it like gray quicksand. Jimbo stood, and they silently watched the lid slowly close. It made a hissing sound, indicating it was locked down and secured.

The wind began to blow harder around them. Jimbo walked away to join Tamara and Nicole, who had retrieved their baggage and were now sitting on the cushion playing one of Tarris's netgames together. Wearing the biosensory headgear that had made Tarris so famous, Tamara and Nicole laughed as they raced each other in the virtual Net Grand Prix.

Jonathan hadn't moved.

His attention was held captive by the bright silver case. Jimbo's words echoed in his mind while he stood quietly in the valley of the mountains named for the Blood of Christ.

Crossing...26

THE lights gradually came up. Jonathan leaned back into his favorite chair; its biofabric cradled his telekinetically exhausted body. It was almost midnight, and he was glad to be home in the loft. In the last five days, he had gotten 18 hours of sleep, and he had taxed his telekinetic prowess to its limits. Having tossed men about like garbage, put another in a coma, stopped not one, but six Light-Force bioweapons, grav-fluxed his own body out of a deadly situation, halted a biomatrix warhead, and brought down a 520-ton airliner from 11,000 feet (saving over 500 lives), Jonathan Kortel did what most people do after a tough week.

He poured himself a drink.

Putting the glass to his forehead, he let its cool moisture spread over his tired brow. His mind was off-line.

What he had hoped would be an enlightening visit to an old and dear friend turned out to be quite literally a living nightmare. He closed his eyes and recalled the events of the last week. How ironic, he bemusedly observed, to have almost died so horrifically in the land of enchantment.

The Scotch burned his throat with every swallow.

The sheer stress of his telekinetic phases had strained his body to its limits. The extreme heat he experienced during each phase had left his muscles aching, while the nasal hemorrhage had made his throat dry and sore. He hadn't shaved or showered, and his skin had taken on a pasty appearance, like he had been ill for a month. Worse, his head ached continuously like a migraine caught in some torturously vicious repeat loop. In short, Jonathan Kortel felt like shit, and he was seriously considering taking Tamara and Nicole and dropping out of sight for about 30 years.

He drifted into sleep.

~

"Jonathan."

The loft's system waited.

"Jonathan, excuse me, but you have a netcall."

He coughed. "Yeah...Max...what time is it?"

"It's three thirty in the morning, sir, and you have a netcall from Miss Connor."

"Oh, put it through please...and no visual."

"Jonathan, I can't sleep..."

"Nicole, honey," Jonathan said, surprised, "where's your mommy?"

"She's asleep with Teddy Boo, but I had a bad dream."

"Honey, it'll be okay. You're safe now. Be a good girl and go crawl in bed with your mommy and Teddy Roo..."

"Teddy Boo..."

"Yeah, Boo, Teddy Boo...just crawl back to bed and snuggle with your mommy. Sweet dreams, you, okay?"

"Okay, night night." The line cut out.

"I wish I was Teddy Boo," Jonathan said. He sat in the dark of the living room, gazing out the large windows at the Chicago skyline and the lake beyond. Lights twinkled through the city heat that radiated from the concrete 30 stories below. It all looked so foreign. What had been familiar only days ago now seemed distant, almost alienlike, as if he had landed on another planet whose populace had nothing in common with him. If the events of the last week had taught him anything, it was that he was not like anyone else. He wasn't even like any other Tel. But what he was, or what he would become, was as elusive to him as the good night's rest he so desperately desired.

He began to fall asleep, again.

~

"Jonathan."

There was a pause as the system waited.

"Jonathan, excuse me, but you have a netcall..."

"Yeah...Max...what time is it this time?"

"It's six thirty in the morning, sir, and you have a netcall from a James McCarris."

"Yeah...okay. Put it through."

"Jonathan, I hope I'm not...man, whoa, you look like crap..." Jimbo said from the six-foot TVid screen.

"Thanks, Jimbo. I was hoping for a little rest here. Why are you calling so early?"

"Well, a couple of things. One, I'm packing up and heading for Washington. I gotta debrief, do my reports and get things prepped for you. Two, our sources tell us that Whitehorse has gone underground, which doesn't surprise me. The Rogues can scatter pretty easily and reassemble whenever and wherever they want. But having Whitehorse missing means it isn't safe for you....Hey, are you falling asleep?"

"No, no..." Jonathan said sleepily. "Please, I'm listening."

"And third..." Jimbo hesitated.

"What?" Jonathan demanded.

"Have you tried Tarris or Georgia lately?"

"All I've tried is to get some sleep. Why, what's up?"

"I don't know. I've called, thinking Georgia might know where Whitehorse is, but there's no answer, and they haven't returned any of my netmessages. Isn't that a little odd?"

"Not really. Tarris is one for keeping to himself. It wouldn't surprise me if he didn't connect, especially after a week like we've had."

"Yeah, I know, but it's me...my number. I would think they would try and connect, especially after an incident like the plane, wouldn't you?"

"Tarris is a weird guy. Don't get me wrong, I love him like a brother, but I bet Georgia probably has broached the Rogue subject with him. And that, more than likely, didn't go down too well. Plus, he's reclusive. I mean, look at that compound where they live. And we know he's not a big fan of the government. James...you are the government, after all. Nah, I wouldn't get too worried yet. I'm not." Jonathan let his eyes close again.

"Maybe you're right." The lid hissed shut on the last of his equipment cases. "I'll give them a try later. It's just that my seventh sense is picking something up on them. You know what I mean?...Jonathan? Jonathan!"

"Yeah, boss...I'm here," he said, jerking back from half-sleep.

"Can I ask you a personal question?"

"Sure, why not."

"What are you going to do with Tamara?" he quietly asked.

"What do you mean?"

"Well, you know she really cares for you. I mean, I think she's pretty much in love with you."

"Yeah, I know. So?"

"I've never heard you say that."

Jonathan kept his eyes closed and sunk deeper into the chair.

"Listen," Jimbo said, "if I've struck a nerve here..."

"No, no, it's not that. It's just...how can I put this?" Jonathan rubbed the sleep from his eyes. "Only a couple of weeks ago, I was normal. I had a business, a life, friends, a couple of girls I was seeing and..."

"And what?" Jimbo folded a shirt.

"And I was...human." Jonathan opened his eyes.

An awkward silence fell over their conversation. Jimbo stopped packing his clothes, faced the lens and moved to the middle of the apartment that had been the base of operations for him and Zvara. Jonathan, struggling for words, stared out the loft's big windows at the sun cresting over the top of the skyline.

"Then..." Jonathan said finally, "...I met Tamara..."

Jimbo folded his arms.

"...and I stopped a Light-Force weapon," he continued, his voice cracking a little.

Jimbo's TVid image didn't change.

Jonathan stared at the sunrise.

"Hey, James?" he asked, still staring.

"Yeah, man, what is it?"

Jonathan hesitated and then looked directly into the TVid screen. "What's happening to me?" A lump came up in his throat.

Jimbo moved closer to the lens. "You're 'crossing' man...that's all," His face filled the screen.

Jonathan leaned forward toward the TVid. "Crossing?"

"Yeah, it's the moment when a Potential finally realizes what they are...*really* realizes. I've seen it happen a hundred times. That's one reason why I'm here — to help you get through this."

"Yeah, but this is different. I'm different."

"You wouldn't believe how many times I've heard that. But you know something?"

"What?"

"This time, you're right. You are different, Jonathan. You're the most different thing...person...whatever, to hit this planet since...since..." Jimbo was caught in his own analogy.

"Since what, James?"

"Since...I don't know...Christ himself, probably." Jimbo was looking down, his arms still folded tightly across his chest.

Jonathan closed his eyes and leaned back into the chair; its memory quickly reshaped to accept his body.

"Hey, look, I'm not saying you're the Second Coming. I'm just saying that your presence could have a great impact on mankind. I mean, Jonathan...wake up. You're doing things that we thought could never be done."

Clearly uncomfortable with the subject, Jimbo swept his hair back off his forehead. He sat down on the edge of the bed. "Jonathan, this is one of the most difficult times a Tel faces. The crossing is considered to be almost a sacred time. It's not like we don robes and chant, but you're entering a brotherhood of sorts. There are very few of us, really. When you consider the total population, we're just a drop in the bucket. But, you, my friend..." Jimbo walked back toward the lens, filling the screen. "...you are the most important drop ever."

Jonathan kept his eyes closed.

"Hey, how do you feel?" Jimbo asked sincerely.

"Like shit."

"You've been through a lot in the last couple of days. But don't let this crossing stuff get to you too much. Now get some rest, okay? I'll call you when I get into Washington." Jimbo returned to his packing.

"Oh, hey," he said, coming back before the call could end. "You never answered my question."

Jonathan's eyes remained closed. "I know, Jimbo. Talk to you later."

The TVid screen cutout.

Jonathan opened his eyes and looked around. The early morning sun was beginning to flood the living room. His service had cleaned the loft, and only the emptiness left by the destroyed items gave any clue to the telekinetic fit he had thrown. Many of the most precious objects that had defined his life were gone. One of the pieces that had survived was a folk art crucifix he had purchased on a visit to Hector and his family in what was now called Old Mexico.

He raised his arm, and the cross flew across the living room and into his waiting hand. He studied its rough wooden surface. His fingers glided gently across the hand-carved Christ. His head was tilted to one side, and his expression was sad. The artisan had carved away the minimal amount to perfectly capture the moment of the Savior's death.

Jonathan contemplated its meaning.

"I'm no Christ..." he said. His eyes slowly closed, and as he slipped back into sleep, the cross slid out of his hand and dropped gently to the floor.

Point of difference...27

GEORGIA bit into the carrot, which snapped hard in her mouth. She watched the stray dogs wolf down their evening dinner and glanced over to the TVid screen, debating whether she should call or not. She had never seen Tarris so angry. It was almost like he had become another man.

Since Jonathan had decided to go with the Agency, Georgia intended to keep her promise of leaving the Rogues, but not without coming clean with Tarris. On the way back from O'Keefe International, she had told him everything about her association with the Rogues. Needless to say, it hadn't gone over as well as she had hoped.

~

Tarris was enraged. No matter how hard Georgia tried to explain her feelings for him, all he heard was that she had been a plant and that their relationship had been a fabrication for Jacob Whitehorse's agenda.

Driving back to Tres Piedras like a madman, he twice almost crashed the Hummer, and his silence hung in the cabin like a rotting carcass. Roaring into the compound, Tarris skidded up to the front door of the main house and demanded that she get out. Then he drove around to the back of his workshop and began loading up the Hummer.

He also called her a whore.

Georgia was in the bedroom by the time Tarris came "walking" in. He stormed through the house gathering things into a large canvas bag. Walking into the bedroom, he ignored her and headed straight to the dresser, yanking open the top drawer so hard that it flew out of his hands and crashed to the floor. He dug through its contents until he found what he needed. Tarris, who had been clean since the accident, was going to take a ride.

Georgia watched in fear as he scooped up the small plastic bag of biodrug, stuffed it in his coat pocket and stormed out. Clambering up into the Hummer, he glared at her as she stood at the front door. He spat on the ground and drove off just as the sun dipped below the mountains that loaned their name to the town.

~

Georgia took a bite off the carrot and looked again at the TVid screen. Jonathan's netnumber was on the monitor, ready to log in. Tarris had been gone almost three hours. She took another bite, hesitated, and pressed the send button.

His image came on the screen. "Morning, Georgia, what's up?"

"I'm sorry, Jonathan, I didn't mean to wake you..."

"That's okay, it seems to be the in thing to do today. What time is it?"

"It's seven thirty here, so it's eight thirty where you are. Were you sleeping?"

"Yeah....So what's the matter? You look worried. I know James has been trying to get ahold of you. Are you all right?"

Georgia, folding her arms, teared up and looked away from the screen.

"Georgia?" Jonathan sat up. "What's the matter?"

Georgia waved off the question without a response.

"Hey, come on, talk to me." Jonathan had slid to the edge of the ottoman, which made his image fill the screen.

Georgia looked back. Tears were running down her face. "I told Tarris about my involvement with the Rogues," she said between sniffles.

"I figured you would. Did you tell him...everything?"

"Yes..."

"And he went biothermal, didn't he?"

Georgia nodded and burst into tears. A vase holding a fresh bouquet of desert flowers exploded behind her.

"Easy there, girl," Jonathan soothed. "Cry anymore and you could destroy that shack you live in. Believe me, I speak from experience."

Georgia grinned through her tears.

"Now, what's going on?"

"Tarris just went crazy. He wouldn't listen to me. He really feels like our relationship was just a ruse to get you to come out. And then he packed up and stormed out of here, to God knows where. And...he..."

"He what?"

"He called me a whore and spit at me."

Jonathan scooted closer. Georgia turned around and looked at the remains of the vase.

"It was a risk you had to take. Ignorance is bliss, as they say, but I think you can never go wrong with honesty. He would have eventually found out, and it's best he heard it from you, not someone else."

Georgia had calmed down and was quietly listening.

"Besides, he does have a point. I mean, I know that you grew to care for him, but would you have ever gotten together if the situation was different?...You know, more of a natural beginning and not mapped out by Whitehorse?"

Georgia nervously averted her eyes.

"If I know Tarris, he's probably run off to a hole somewhere to get his head straight, and he'll be back....What's wrong now?"

Georgia pensively folded her arms and moved into the corner of the room.

"Georgia?..." Jonathan pressed.

"He...he took something else."

Jonathan knew what that "something else" was.

"How much did he take?"

"Not much. I didn't even know he had any. I'm worried, Jonathan. You know how he gets when he's riding. He's so unpredictable...."

"Hey, did you take the weapons out of the truck?"

"No..." Georgia said slowly. "Oh, God, this isn't good."

"No, it's not. You don't think he would try to go after Whitehorse, do you?"

"I don't see how. He wouldn't know where to look after the plane crash. And I assume that was you?"

Jonathan sheepishly nodded.

"God, Jonathan, you're unbelievable. It's all over the net. The TVid news shows are calling it a miracle, an act of...are you okay?"

"I don't really want to talk about it right now, if you don't mind."

Georgia nodded knowingly. "Like I was saying, after news of the plane, most of the Rogues wondered if it had been Whitehorse. But we're still not sure how..."

"Biowarhead. Jimbo thinks it was delivered on some kind of masked missile...real Black Op stuff. Do you know how Whitehorse could have gotten hold of that kind of weaponry?"

"Whitehorse made a lot of friends when he was in the Agency, and I think he's maintained many of those relationships since he started the Rogues. Most were in the military."

"That explains a lot right there."

"This is going to split the Rogues up. Whitehorse had become way too militant for most of the members, and I think there was going to be some action taken against him. But now it doesn't matter. He's disappeared, and nobody knows where he's gone."

"James's sources say he's gone into hiding, whatever that means. You wouldn't know where that is, would you?"

"I can't think of any place right now. There were a few who were pretty loyal to his cause. But they've disappeared too. They could be anywhere. If I hear of anything, I'll call you or Jimbo."

"Yeah, that would be good. I don't like having this crazy, psycho Indian on the loose. I feel like I should be looking over my shoulder all the damn time."

"Jonathan, if you can bring down a plane, you can handle Whitehorse."

"I wish it were that easy."

"You know something else?" Georgia stared blankly at the TVid. "There's a part of me that's relieved...that I told him."

Jonathan's image blipped a little from the satellite connection. When it cleared, he was smiling.

"What?" she asked.

"Oh, nothing..."

"What, Jonathan."

"Well...it's nothing..."

"Come on. Don't play games with me."

"It's just...you know, sometimes you look so....No, wait, I can't...I've got to go, so call me if you hear from Tarris, or if you hear anything about Whitehorse, okay? You take care." Jonathan quickly cut the line.

Georgia took the last bite out of the carrot and slowly smiled.

~

It had been almost a week since Jonathan had returned. A week of preparation, reflection and the occasional dodge of overzealous reporters trying to make their careers with the plane "crash" of the century. On his list of things to get done, one task stood out above them all as the one he was least looking forward to.

Jonathan cautiously opened the door to the restaurant, knowing that his unexpected appearance would set the kitchen off like a bomb.

A new hostess greeted him. "Welcome to Kortel's, table for one, sir?" she asked.

"Sure...table for one, thanks," he said, testing out the new girl. Her clothes said she was a professional, with a contemporary edge. She led him to a two-top near the front. The waiters almost gave away his scam, but he silenced them with a finger to his lips.

"Here you are, sir. Will this be all right?"

"No, I was hoping for something in the back, something a little more removed."

"Ah, no problem, let me see..." She led him through the busy restaurant to a secluded table near the bar.

"Would this be okay, sir?"

"Actually," he said, continuing his scam, "I was wondering if you could set me up in the hallway...by the bathrooms? I'm very private you know." He acted paranoid, constantly looking about.

"Ah...yes, well...whatever the gentleman would like. I'll have one of the busboys set up a table. Just give me a moment....Would you like to sit at the bar?" She gestured for him to sit.

"Oh, I can't! It's too exposed, much too exposed...I'll just stand right here if that's okay with you," he said, playing it up for all it was worth.

"Very good, sir. I'll be right back to set up your table." She put the netpad to her chest and turned on her heels right into a small group of wait staff gathered behind her. They all broke out laughing.

"Whatever you're laughing at...it's not very funny!" she sternly scolded them.

They all struggled to control themselves. "What? What's going on?"

"Hey, everyone, she's right!" Jonathan said firmly. The staff jumped to attention. "If a customer wants to dine alone...in private, then at Kortel's we certainly don't laugh at him. We make it happen. Right...ah, what's your name?"

"Kimball, and you are?..." she said, turning to face him.

"Jonathan, Jonathan Kortel." He extended his hand and stifled a laugh.

"Oh, sir, I'm so sorry. I didn't know. They said you might not be back for several weeks." She whipped around and lunged at the staff. They recoiled, laughing, and some snapped their bar rags at her.

"Okay you all, back to work!" Hector's booming voice announced, and the staff scattered like cats back to their stations.

"Jonathan!" He grabbed him by the shoulders. "We thought you'd be gone awhile." He leaned in, his voice going soft. "How are you?"

"I'm fine, Hector, but who is the new hostess? Man, where did you get her?" He watched her walk back to the front of the restaurant.

"Ah, yes. That lovely thing is Enrique's cousin, Kimball. She's not a bad hostess, I might add."

"Hell, we'll get repeat from the businessmen alone with her. Forget the food."

Hector looked over his partner closely. "Jonathan," he confided in a low tone, "you look tired, my friend, even a little sick. Are you all right?"

"I'm all right, really. But it's been a long week. It wasn't the trip I was hoping for. Say, Hector," he put his arm around him, "I came in because I wanted to talk with you. Can Enrique or Marco close up tonight?"

"Sure, Marco can. Let me clean up, and we'll go."

"Great. Let's go to the Blind Monkey for a drink."

Jonathan entered the kitchen to a round of high-fives from the men who turned his bioprogramming into reality. The air was saturated with the pungent smells of cilantro and curry. And as he walked around laughing, talking and spot-checking the cuisine, melancholia descended upon him that took him by surprise. In the eyes of the men who had been so much of his life for the last five years, he saw something that he had never really taken the time to notice before.

Love.

They shared a love that men have for one another when they come through a difficult time together, when they share an accomplishment and look back proudly at what they have done. Such was the feeling Jonathan shared with the men of Kitchen Kortel. At the same time, though, he felt like a stranger in his own house. He looked at the crew he had come to call family and felt the same way he had in the loft when he had looked out over the city: an overwhelming sense that his life, the life he had shared with these men, the life he had created with Hector, and the life he could have had with Tamara, was coming to an end.

Jimbo was right.

He was "crossing," and there was nothing to stop it. It was as inevitable as death, and Jonathan was beginning to accept the harsh reality of who he was. Or, more accurately, what he wasn't. Because to Jonathan, that was the point of difference.

In his mind, he wasn't human anymore.

~

"Look what the cat dragged in!" Deaka announced.

"Hey, Deaka," Jonathan said.

"A little early for you two. Are you guys drinking or are you gracing us with eating?"

She slid her netpad down the front of her jeans. Deaka had always given them a little grief, but she couldn't deny that she was slightly envious. Here were two of the hottest young Turks in the city's restaurant scene, and they chose her bar to hang. Deaka, though she never would admit it, also was flattered.

"Nah, we're just drinking, Deaka," Hector answered, and they walked past her and into the bar.

The Blind Monkey was slow, and it was easy to find a seat. While Jonathan and Hector pulled in their stools, the bartender was already pouring their favorite drinks.

Hector licked the salt from the rim of his glass and turned to face Jonathan.

"So, my friend, what is on your mind, eh?"

Jonathan took a long, slow sip of Scotch.

"Hector," he started, "have you ever had an epiphany?"

"Well, if you consider my first divorce, yes. Why?"

"My friend, I have had one hell of an epiphany."

"Is it Tamara? She seems like a sweet girl but..."

"No, it's not her. It's something else....Something that's a little hard to describe." Seeking comfort in his Scotch, Jonathan took another long drink. "I'm not really sure where to begin," he said wiping his mouth.

For the next hour, Hector sat in silence as Jonathan told him everything, from his childhood to the incident with the plane. At times it was hard for Jonathan to talk, especially about the crossing and its life-changing ramifications.

Hector intently listened. The concept was remarkable, and the revelation that a hidden society of new humans had been evolving for the last 150 years was almost too much to believe.

He ordered a double shot when Jonathan finished. The bartender placed the tequila on the bar.

"Well?" Jonathan asked.

"It's all...so..." Hector stammered.

"Unbelievable?"

"Well, quite frankly, yes! I didn't believe Tamara when she told me. I mean, you have to admit this all sounds like some bad sci-fi vid."

Jonathan read the skepticism in Hector's voice. Jimbo had warned him not to say anything. Non-Tels won't believe or accept the news, he had told him. Especially relatives and close friends. "You don't believe me, do you?"

Hector shrugged.

Jimbo also said not to give any demos.

Jonathan looked to the back of the bar where the bottles of liquor sat stacked in neat rows. He waited for the bartender to turn his back, then raised his left hand in front of Hector's face. A bottle of vodka flew into it; Hector almost jumped off his stool. Jonathan released the bottle, and it floated back to its place on the shelf.

Hector slammed his tequila.

"Now, are you getting the picture?" Jonathan asked with a smile.

"Jonathan, this is a miracle!" He crossed himself and looked to the ceiling.

"Hey, whoa, it's not a miracle. It's a combination of gravity displacement, genetics, evolution and mind control. Along with a few hundred other factors that I'm going to learn about at the Agency. You see, we're..."

"We're?" Hector interrupted.

"Sorry...we're called Tels. It's short for telekinetics. What I was going to say was that we're like lighting rods. We're conduits to channel gravity and alter its properties, though I'm not sure how yet. Hopefully, the Agency is going to teach me."

Jonathan noticed that his close friend had inched back on his stool, and he could sense that Hector was wrestling with his feelings for Jonathan the old friend and his fear of Jonathan the telekinetic. He could also sense something else. It was the last of Jimbo's warnings: the alienation of friends and family. He was probably going to lose Hector as a friend.

Hector was staring blankly into the mirror behind the bar.

"Are you scared of me, Hector?"

"No, no...it's just that this is all so...so...weird. One day you're my partner and friend....The next, you're...you're..."

"I'm what, Hector?"

Hector almost had to force himself to look at Jonathan. He took a deep breath before continuing. "You're not like us...I'm mean you are, but you're not. Know what I mean?" He stared straight ahead into the mirror again.

"Believe me," Jonathan said, "I know what you mean. I've been wrestling with this for the last couple of weeks now, and it's still pretty weird for me, too. Look, Hector," Jonathan pulled his stool closer, "I don't want to give up what we have here. This is a great partnership. I couldn't ask for a better organic chef than Hector Ruez – or a better friend. But I know what I am now, and I've got to see where this will take me. I've been given a great gift, and I owe it to myself to discover my potential."

Hector couldn't face his friend.

"Hector, it's me, *Jonathan*. I'm still the same. I haven't changed that much..."

"But you *will*."

"Hector!" Jonathan said as he grabbed the big Mexican by the shoulder and spun him on his stool. "I'm not going to let our friendship just...just slip away because I'm different. I'm not really sure if I'm going to stay with the Agency. Yes, I want to see what they have to offer, and yes, I'm going to use their help to keep Tamara and Nicole safe. But I'm not going to disappear behind some virt wall that develops because I'm a Tel and you're not!" Jonathan's voice had risen to the point that some of the people around the bar began to take notice.

Hector studied Jonathan's face. "Jonathan," he said finally, "I haven't come this far with you just to abandon a friendship that's endured the things we've had to deal with. If you need to go and discover who you are or what you are, then I'll be behind you all the way. And so will the kitchen. We're not going away just cause you're gone for awhile. We have your programs on file. Hell, we haven't even gotten to half of them yet. The restaurant is called Kortel's, not Ruez's, and there's a reason for that."

Jonathan heard what Hector was saying, but he knew that Jimbo was right. Their relationship would never be the same again.

"When are you going?" Hector asked.

"Soon. There's something I have to take care of before I go..."

"Jonathan?..." Hector began.

Jonathan knew what was coming.

"...What about Tamara?...What are you going to do about her?"

He didn't answer, instead checking his netwatch. "I've got to go, Hector, I'll see you tomorrow." He stepped off the stool and walked toward the front of the Blind Monkey.

"Do you love her?" Hector called after him.

Jonathan stopped but didn't look back. "Good night, Hector." He headed for the exit.

Guess I do...28

ANARI checked her netpad for the current tally on her tables. She had the Den and its clients choreographed to her own unique rhythm. These poor marks wouldn't know that they had been part of her show until they checked their chipcard netstatements the next morning. By then, Anari would be surfing the next wave of horny businessmen, whose expectations for Liquid Courage were as high as their multinational corporate spending limits.

Anari was in the zone, and it wasn't even midnight.

As she hustled the six-top full of Canadian medtronic salesmen, she saw two tall, older marks walk in and stand impatiently, like they were waiting for their luggage at O'Hare.

Perfect, she thought, *first-timers.*

"Would you gentlemen like a booth tonight?" she screamed over the vicious sounds of RageOn, a black market sampling from the Russian underground.

The two marks nodded. Anari led them through the smoky darkness to a secluded booth set back from the main stage. Their tailored biofabric suits were the finest Rome could produce, and as the two men sat, the suits reset to the tailor's preprogrammed settings, purging any wrinkles and giving the fabric a crisp, new appearance.

These boys smelled of money, and Anari was out to break her own record. "And what would you gentlemen like this evening, for drinks and the ladiesss?" She hung on the "S" like a snake.

"I would like a vodka martini, dirty...*very* dirty," the taller one answered as he stared at Anari.

The other mark was caught up with the dancer on the main stage. He didn't look over.

"Make that two..." the taller one added, and he ran his finger down her arm.

"Yes, I think I know just the martini for you, sir."

Anari turned to go. Without warning, the taller one grabbed her arm, which startled her because the clientele in the Den were usually prescreened, and any display of aggression toward the wait staff, even as little as grabbing an arm, was strictly forbidden.

"Sir?!" Anari demanded.

The taller one smiled a smile that had been cultivated through years of official practice and pulled Anari into the table. He reached across her chest, slightly grazing her nipples, and took her netpad from her belt. Without letting go, he entered a gratuity that not only set a new record for Anari, but raised the bar beyond what she would achieve for probably the next 20 years.

Anari looked down at the amount and almost wet her latex. "Sir! Thank you, sir!" He let go and let out a laugh that competed with RageOn for air time.

Power Dicks, she thought. Men who got off roughing up women, then making it all right in their minds by buying back their actions with guilt money. She hadn't seen guys like this in a long time, but that was fine with her: what you had to put up with usually didn't justify the reward. These two had set a new standard, though. Anari was ready to play.

"Two dirty martinis coming right up."

She headed for the bar, quickly calculating her total for the evening. When she got to the drink station, she tapped her best friend on the shoulder and nodded toward the booth with the two older marks.

Tamara cut off the Japanese netjournalist she had been hustling for over an hour and spun her barstool in the direction of Anari's nod.

"Power Dicks," Anari said into her ear. It was all she needed to say. Tamara knew these types and could play with the best of them. This single mom had been around a few times, and a couple of insecure high-threads with a passion for demeaning women didn't phase her at all.

New Mexico was a week behind her, and it had taken Anari that long to convince her to get back to work. Yes, she had been through some rough shit, Anari had lectured. And yes, it had been life changing. But sitting around her apartment wasn't going to pay the bills. Or get Jonathan to call back.

Tamara pulled the front of her dress down a little and walked her best "take me" walk over to their booth. Both men watched her approach with the cool of players who had been in the game for quite a while. Tamara slid next to the tall one, while never letting her attention fall from the other.

"You gentlemen look like you could use a little company. Do you mind if I join you?" she cooed, wrapping herself around the taller one's arm.

He smiled and nodded and looked at his friend, who leaned on the table and grinned.

Anari arrived and presented their martinis along with Tamara's drink, which she had left at the bar, compliments of Nippon NetNews. She winked at Tamara and left the booth.

"I propose a toast," Tamara declared.

"To what?" the taller one asked.

"To living large and loving long." She raised her glass. "My name is Nicki, what's yours?" She extended her hand to him.

He leaned back into the booth and shifted his attention to the girl on the main stage. He sipped his martini, holding the glass like this was one of a thousand cocktail parties he had attended. "Oh, now...Nicki...that's such an appropriate stage name. I should have guessed." He laughed under his breath, not looking at her, and pulled the olive off its swizzle stick. His white teeth glowed in the black light of the Den.

Puzzled, Tamara began to take a drink. The other Power Dick hadn't said a word; in fact, she now noticed, he hadn't even touched his martini yet.

"Oh, I'm so sorry, let me introduce myself," the talkative one said, holding his glass out and casually looking at it like he was inspecting for flaws. "My name is Jacob Whitehorse."

Tamara's drink never made it to her lips. The glass slipped from her hand, but Whitehorse caught it with his mind. As the drink hung suspended in front of her, he grabbed her body and held it tightly, like a vice.

He was still inspecting his drink.

Caught in Whitehorse's telekinetic grip, she sat there unable to move. He allowed her to blink and breathe, but nothing else. To her, it was as if every major muscle group had been paralyzed. Her nerves, on the other hand, were fully functional. If she had been able, Tamara would have been trembling.

Whitehorse leaned close, and she could see his years chiseled deeply into his skin.

"Tamara," he said, looking straight into her eyes, "you look so pretty tonight. I can see why Jonathan is attracted to you." He ran his fingertips down the edge of her face, lightly parting her hair with his index finger.

"You know," he continued, "our Mr. Kortel has made a poor decision – not only for himself, but for you as well."

He sat back and leisurely finished his martini.

"I'm so sorry to bring you into this, but Jonathan leaves me no choice, really. You see, your boyfriend is quite extraordinary. He's the next step, you know. I'd venture to say he's not really that human anymore." Whitehorse put down his empty glass. "What's it like," he said, running his finger down her jawline, "to make love to someone who isn't human?" He leaned in so close that she could smell the gin on his breath, and his demeanor instantly changed. "Do you really think, Tamara, that a Tel like him will stay with a *whore* like you?"

He sunk back into the booth and again watched the dancer on the main stage. Tamara could see him with her peripheral vision. He sensed her attention and slowly grinned.

"The Agency will change him. Mark my words, young lady. The Jonathan Kortel you know won't exist a year from now. The Agency is not a family show, regardless of what they tell you. They'll change him so subtly you won't know it's happening until it's too late."

Whitehorse reached into his coat pocket and pulled out a small Light-Force handgun. Smaller than the one the reper had used. Probably the smallest bioweapon Tamara had ever seen.

"We're going to leave the club now, Tamara, and when I release you, I want you to act perfectly normal. You're a good actress. I'm sure you've done it all your life."

Tamara felt her muscles relax, like a painless cramp had instantly disappeared.

"My dear, you're trembling," he said.

"Please, Mr. Whitehorse..."

"I said act normal, and that means shutting up!"

Tamara felt a pressure on her throat as if an invisible hand was beginning to choke her. She gagged from the pain.

"Now get up and lead us out of here. And don't worry about the other employees. We'll take care of them, believe me." Whitehorse charged the weapon.

All of them slowly rose from the booth and started toward the exit. In the dark, smoky environment of the Den, their actions hardly appeared out of place, except Anari didn't have her car this evening, and her ride was now walking out of the club.

"Hey, Nicki," she said, catching up to them. "Are you just showing these gentlemen to the..."

Anari stopped in midsentence when Whitehorse's partner turned and looked at her. A blank expression washed over her face, and she stood motionless while her drink tray crashed to the carpet.

As they walked out into the main club, Tamara looked back and saw Anari collapse to the floor. The Den's gigantic door slowly closed on the scene.

"Don't worry about your friend," Whitehorse said. "You should be worrying about yourself." He jabbed the Light-Force hard into her ribs.

Liquid Courage was cranking, due in part to the free publicity it had gained from the wild rumors of a paranormal who had saved a dancer's life, even though no one could confirm or deny the event. They slowly pushed their way through the crowd of parafreaks and Liquid regulars, and Whitehorse became increasingly more agitated.

"How can you work among this waste of humanity?" he whispered into Tamara's ear.

They walked past the main bar toward the entrance to the club. Suddenly, Whitehorse jerked Tamara to a halt. His grip on her arm tightened so much she grimaced from the pain. Whitehorse turned to his silent partner and motioned to the entrance with his head. His partner smiled. Tamara, being a foot shorter than the two Indians, couldn't see what they were looking at.

"This is more perfect than I could have planned," Whitehorse said. He smiled at Tamara. "Your boyfriend is here."

Jonathan stood at the entrance talking to Joshua. The crowd around the bar thinned and left Whitehorse, his partner and Tamara exposed.

Whitehorse pressed the Light-Force even tighter against Tamara's back. "Let's all smile when Jonathan looks over, shall we?" he announced. His partner laughed a little under his breath.

Jonathan ended his conversation with Joshua and began to walk toward the Den. He took in the circus of Liquid Courage and wondered if he would ever get used to it. He hadn't returned Tamara's net calls, partly because he had been busy preparing to go to Washington and partly because he didn't know what to do next. Jimbo's words kept playing in his head, and strangely, they made sense. But he had never met a girl who affected him like Tamara, and no matter how hard he tried to rationalize it, his heart kept getting in the way.

His eyes swept the club to the main bar where he saw Whitehorse, his partner and Tamara. They were smiling at him in a freakish sort of way. Jonathan froze and locked eyes with Whitehorse. Both of his fists instinctively clenched as he prepared to phase. Whitehorse slowly shook his head and stroked Tamara's hair. Jonathan backed down, and Whitehorse dropped his smile. He noticed that Whitehorse's right hand had never left Tamara's back. He stepped toward them, but Whitehorse jammed the Light-Force against her spine, jerking her forward. She shook her head at Jonathan. He stopped again. A drunken frat kid bumped into him and kept walking.

Whitehorse leaned down to Tamara. "Is there anywhere in this godforsaken place where we can talk privately?"

"Yes," she answered, "but it's back through the Den."

"All right, let's go." Whitehorse motioned for Jonathan to move toward the Den. He moved past, and Whitehorse and Tamara fell in behind him. The silent Indian trailed.

The Den had a long line of marks waiting to get in.

"I'm going to need some incentive to get us back in," Tamara said. "You have any Liquid cash?"

Whitehorse answered by pushing the tip of the Light-Force between two of her ribs. They bypassed the line and confronted the vampiresque doorman.

"Nicki," the doorman sneered. "You're back so soon, but you'll have to wait just like the rest."

Tamara grabbed the vamp's balls through his thin nylon pants and squeezed, her thumb pressing hard against his scrotum.

The doorman jumped and sneered at Tamara. "Ohhh," he moaned. "I didn't know you wanted to play."

Tamara squeezed even harder. "I want into the Den, Kastor, and I want in right now!"

"Well, dear, you'll have to...augh!"

Tamara's thumbnail began to draw blood. "If I had wanted to play, Kastor, I would have ripped these off of you."

The door slowly started to open.

"Well *done*, Miss Connor," Whitehorse said, and they entered the Den.

~

Anari was propped on a barstool with an icegel at her head. She saw Tamara first and started to approach, but Tamara stopped her with a raised eyebrow. Whitehorse,

Jonathan and the silent Indian filed in close behind. Jonathan glanced over as they walked through the Den; his look said it all.

Anari, streetie that she was, read the moment instantly. She hopped off the stool and headed for the main offices of Liquid Courage.

Tamara led them past the Den's main stage toward the kitchen, but before she reached the back hallway, she stopped at a set of glass doors whose thick curtains deadened the sounds coming from the Den. She swiped her chipcard, and the doors clicked open. They stepped out onto a large balcony 40 stories above the pavement. The wind whipped at their legs.

Whitehorse pushed Tamara into the center of the balcony and followed with the Light-Force still leveled at her. He grabbed her arm and walked her over the edge of the balcony, which was surrounded by a waist-high wall.

"Lovely view," he said, casually tilting his head to see the street below. Tamara betrayed no emotion at all.

Jonathan emerged, a Light-Force trained against his back by Whitehorse's partner.

"Now, Jonathan, before you get any brilliant ideas about being faster than these weapons, let me remind you that the butt of this Light-Force is directly touching your dear girlfriend's back. You might be FTL, but you're not that fast. She'll be biomatter faster that you can create a field flux to stop it. And, by the way, I've already developed a grav field around the two of us."

A huge clay planter in the far corner of the balcony flew at Whitehorse so fast that it hit his grav field in a blur. Tamara ducked involuntarily, but Whitehorse calmly stood his ground, never flinching. It bounced off the grav field and over the edge of the balcony, where it stopped in midair and hung waiting to fall.

"That's the spirit, Jonathan!" Whitehorse laughed. "But we can't forget the innocent people of Chicago. That would cause quite a mess when it impacted the sidewalk."

The huge planter floated back over their heads and settled into its corner across the deck. Whitehorse watched it all the way and then turned his attention back to Jonathan.

"Look, Whitehorse," Jonathan pleaded, "this is between you and me, not her. Let her go, and you can take me wherever you want. You want to go back to New Mexico, fine. Africa? Fine. I don't care. Just let her go!"

"Always the chivalrous one, aren't we, Jonathan? What high drama! No, I think I need to hold on to your pretty little whore here for just a little longer."

Whitehorse stepped around Tamara and raised the Light-Force to the side of her head. He jammed it so hard that Tamara's head was shoved at a right angle. She winced at the pain.

Suddenly the balcony door flew open. Anari charged out with a military issue Walther PPKLF. She hit a combat stance with both hands cupping the Light-Force, its light tip pointed directly at the head of the silent Indian.

He spun around to use Jonathan as a shield. Jonathan felt the Light-Force dig into his back.

"Don't be a hero, Kortel," the Indian whispered and pushed the Light-Force deeper into his kidneys.

"Drop your weapon," Anari screamed at Whitehorse, "or I turn Cochise here into biomatter!"

A deep rumbling drowned out the noise of the city, and the building began to shake. The tower's structural skeleton creaked and cracked as it fought against the earthquake that affected only one square block of Chicago real estate. Everyone on the balcony was thrown about like rag dolls; everyone except Jonathan, who was in phase, floating just slightly off the floor.

He was staring directly at Whitehorse.

Anari hardly lost her balance or her bead on the head of the silent Indian. He stumbled and fell to one side of Jonathan. A bright flash of light caught everyone off guard. The earthquake stopped.

Whitehorse regained his footing and his grip on Tamara as Jonathan touched down into the puddle of biomatter that had been Whitehorse's partner.

Anari shifted her attention and her sights onto Whitehorse. "Drop...your...gun. Now!" she yelled.

Whitehorse glared fiercely at Anari. His face had the look of death as he trained his hauntingly dark eyes at her.

"I don't think so, bitch," he said viciously.

Anari was lifted off the balcony so fast she didn't have time to discharge her weapon. Her body was a blur as she headed for Wacker Drive. Her scream faded and was replaced by the howl of the wind off of Lake Michigan.

Tamara gasped as she watched her dearest friend thrown to her death like a football. Jonathan tried to grab her as she went over the edge, but he was coming out of phase and didn't have enough reaction speed to match Whitehorse.

"An eye for an eye, eh, Jonathan?" Whitehorse chuckled.

Tamara was sobbing into her hands.

~

James McCarris had a hunch, and like all good Southern boys, he bet on his hunches. And Jimbo was betting that Whitehorse would come after Tamara.

When he pulled to the top level of the parking garage next to the tower where Liquid Courage occupied the 43rd floor, he was hoping that his hunch was wrong. But as he stepped from his car, he heard what seemed to be the screeching of a brake system in need of new synthfluid. It wasn't coming from the street, though. It was coming from above. He looked up the side of the tower and saw the wriggling figure of a small woman hurtling toward the parking garage pavement.

He went into phase.

Pushing his Tel level to its limits, he caught her at the 21st floor and slowed her free-fall to a crawl. She stopped struggling and leaned back in a sitting position for the rest of the way down. She barely bent her knees when she touched the cement.

"Hey, are you all right?" Jimbo asked, running over to where she had landed.

Anari stood in the harsh mercury vapor light, her arms folded tightly across her chest. Her lower jaw jittered in sync with her shaking.

"Hey, hey...it's okay now," he said, consoling the pretty little Asian girl.

She still couldn't reply and shook even more.

"You're safe now. I'm not going to hurt you. Let me introduce myself," he said putting his hand to her shoulder. "My name is James, James McCarris."

Anari instantly stopped shaking and pulled back, pointing at him. "Jimbo!" she exclaimed.

"How the hell do you know that?" he asked, dumfounded.

"Come on," Anari yelled, grabbing his arm. "They're still up there!"

She jerked him along as they ran toward the parking garage elevators. Jimbo wiped some blood from under his nose and smiled as he ran with her. His hunch had paid off.

~

Jonathan, still coming out of phase, couldn't help Anari as she plunged to her death. He pulled himself away from the scene and faced Whitehorse, who had returned the Light-Force weapon to Tamara's temple. "I'm going to kill you, Whitehorse," he said, wiping the blood from his nose, "if it's the last thing I do on this earth!"

"Well, cowboy, it might be," Whitehorse replied. He mentally lifted Tamara up and over the edge of the balcony, dangling her 430 feet above Chicago.

Drained from the telekinetic earthquake he had induced, Jonathan struggled into phase. He weakly punched at Whitehorse, knocking him slightly to one side. Whitehorse grav fluxed a narrow field directly into Jonathan's chest, slamming him hard against the deck. His blood splattered across his hands as his head impacted the wood surface.

"Don't even *think* about phasing against me," Whitehorse uttered. He let Tamara drop 5 feet.

Tamara jerked to a halt like she had landed on an invisible table; her arms and legs flailed helplessly as her hair blew violently about her face. "Oh God, Jonathan," she screamed from her telekinetic purgatory. "Please don't let me die!"

Her tears fell into the abyss.

Jonathan stumbled to the wall and reached desperately for her.

"I won't let you die!"

He looked back at Whitehorse, who stood there smiling as his ponytail whipped in the wind. His Light-Force pointed directly at Jonathan.

"Little telekinetic dilemma?" Whitehorse mocked.

Jonathan's attention vacillated between Tamara and Whitehorse, desperately searching for an opportunity to strike.

"I'd say so!" Whitehorse gloated. "Sure, I lowered my grav field to be able to discharge this weapon, but..." He raised his hand and pointed at Tamara. "...I also control the fate of your lovely girlfriend.

"So here's the test, Jonathan. I'm going to fire at you with this Light-Force, a weapon I know you can stop, but I'm also going to release your girlfriend 40 stories to her death. You can't save her and yourself. Once you're in phase for one, you can't prevent the other. Save her and you die, or save yourself, and she dies."

He raised the weapon. "Jonathan...the choice is yours."

Jonathan's vision instantly went to white, but he couldn't distinguish whether the cause was the Light-Force or his own entry into phase.

The nanosecond of flash filled an eternity.

Jonathan's vision returned, pure white giving way to blurry shapes of varying contrasts. The scene on the balcony came back into focus, and he could see the beam from the Light-Force weapon suspended about 10 inches from the muzzle. Whitehorse was frozen in the pose he held before Jonathan had gone into phase. His ponytail was sticking straight out from the side of his head, and his mouth was caught on the last word he had said.

Jonathan slowly turned to look at Tamara. All he could see was the Chicago skyline.

"Noooo!"

He lunged at the balcony wall and looked down on the fate of his lover. There, five stories below, was Tamara facing down, her arms and legs spread-eagled like a skydiver. She was slowly rising back toward the balcony.

"I can't let a Level 10 lose his girlfriend to a Level 8," Jimbo said. He pulled a toothpick from his mouth. "I would *never* hear the end of it."

"Jimbo!" Jonathan yelled. He turned to find the Tel and Anari walking toward him from the balcony door.

Jimbo pointed to Whitehorse. "Don't forget your flux field, Mr. I'mthemostpowerfulTelever," he said, half grinning. "That Light-Force is still in a state of discharge!"

Jonathan again focused his attention on Whitehorse, who was still suspended in his flux field.

Tamara appeared above the balcony wall and gently settled onto the deck. Too shocked to speak, she rushed toward Jonathan with her arms outspread.

"Easy, chicky" Anari cautioned, "he still has that Indian in...in..."

"...a Level 10 Grav Field Flux Suspension," Jimbo helpfully finished with a smile.

Anari eyed the Southerner and returned his smile.

"Can you hold him much longer?" Jimbo asked.

"Just for a minute or more," Jonathan said. Blood was dripping from his nostrils. "Anari, do you still have that Light-Force?"

"Absofuckinglutely!" She pulled the weapon from the crotch of her pants.

"Put it on him while I get into position." Jonathan stepped to the side of

Whitehorse's hand that held the Light-Force. "Cover your eyes, everyone, this might be bright."

He released Whitehorse. The Light-Force finished its discharge. The beam flashed out over the city and harmlessly dissipated. Jonathan snatched the weapon from Whitehorse's hand and jammed it into his ribs.

"I know *you're* not FTL, Whitehorse..." Jonathan whispered into his ear. "...so don't even *think* of going telekinetic on me."

The sun was beginning to break over Lake Michigan. Whitehorse turned and looked at Jonathan through its rays and, for a second, Jonathan thought that the big Indian from the Southwest was going to give in. Whitehorse's face seemed spotlighted as the sun crept between the buildings.

He smiled evil as his answer. "You don't have the balls, white man."

Jonathan felt a sharp pain drill down into his mind from Whitehorse's telekinetic invasion.

The flash from the Light-Force filled the balcony faster than the sun could rise.

~

Everyone except Jonathan had been caught off guard by the discharge, and they rubbed their eyes in a desperate attempt to soothe their retinas. He surveyed his temporarily blinded friends and lowered the weapon.

"You all okay over there?" he asked.

"Oh yeah, we'll all being doing great," Jimbo said, blindly waving in what he thought was Jonathan's direction, "in about a fricking hour!"

Jonathan didn't say a word as he reflectively watched a beam of light slowly pass over the puddle of biomatter that, only a moment earlier, had been Jacob Whitehorse.

"Guess I do..." he answered to the puddle, and he raised his face to the morning sun as it crested over the city.

Containment...29

THE elevator was viscid with silence as they rode down to the parking garage floor. Jimbo was conspicuously beside Anari, who, in turn, was leaning on the Southerner for physical, if not mental, support. Jonathan held Tamara and gently kissed the top of her head. She had her eyes closed and was hugging him tightly across his chest.

Tamara's emotions were surprisingly calm, but her mind was racing. In the last week, she had had her child kidnapped, her best friend and herself almost killed, and had been through enough life experiences to fill at least 20 lives.

All because of the man she was now hugging.

She wrestled with the reality that the one she had fallen in love with might be more than she could handle, and Jimbo's comments about the statistical inevitability of their relationship ending because she was not a Tel cut deeply into her heart. All her life, she had never played by the rules. She had always done it her way. *Why should I start now*, she thought. She squeezed him even tighter.

At the 23rd floor the doors slid open, and a cleaning woman began to enter. Stopping, she looked over each one of them, raised her eyebrows and gingerly stepped back out of the elevator. The doors slowly closed.

~

When the elevator finally reached the parking level, they all piled out and began walking toward their cars.

All except Anari. "Ah, I need a ride here."

"Oh, sweetie, I'm so sorry," Tamara said. "Come on, I'll take you home."

"Hey," Jimbo offered, "I can take you home....If that's okay?"

Anari smiled at him.

Jimbo put his arm around her and whispered into her ear, "I have to talk to Jonathan for a second. I'm on the top level. It's a silver MicrosoftFord."

Anari began walking up the ramp to the upper level, then turned back and graced everyone with a shit-eating grin.

"Excuse me, Tamara," Jimbo said in a serious tone that made her uneasy. "I need to talk to Jonathan for a bit."

"It's all right, baby," Jonathan reassured her. "I'll meet you back at the loft." He kissed her on the cheek. She looked over to Jimbo, then back to Jonathan and tilted her head with that "is everything okay?" kind of look. He smiled and gestured toward her car. She turned and slowly walked away, not letting her fingers fall away from his hand until the last second.

Both men watched Tamara get into her car and drive down the ramp. They waited as another car drove past.

"You know, Jonathan, you *crossed* up there," Jimbo said, turning to face him. Jonathan didn't answer or meet his gaze.

"I guess I won't be needing this any more."

Jimbo handed him the tattered Melville novel. Jonathan pondered the only tangible evidence that he had ever had a father and quietly pocketed the small book. For a moment, both Tels remained silent.

"You know," Jimbo said somberly, "I have a serious containment issue here."

"I know," Jonathan answered, still looking away.

"I'm going to have to bring in a Level 8 to handle all the erasing," Jimbo warned.

"Everyone?" Jonathan asked.

Jimbo flicked his toothpick. "Everyone."

Jonathan finally looked at him. "If you want me to come to the Agency, you don't do Tamara and Nicole."

Jimbo didn't say a word. He just smiled and headed for the upper level ramp.

"Do you understand, me?" Jonathan called out.

"Good night, Jonathan, and get some rest...." Jimbo kept walking. "...You're going to need it."

At peace...30

JONATHAN felt himself falling.

He jerked back from the dream. Opening his eyes, the pitch black of the bedroom was disorienting, and his clothes were drenched in sweat. He rolled over to find empty indentations in the pillows. "Oh no..." he quietly said to himself. "Max, where is Tamara?"

"Miss Connor is on the main balcony, sir."

"Thank God," he whispered, and he looked over to the clock. 11:28 p.m.

~

Jonathan walked down the stairs into the loft's unlit living room and saw Tamara silhouetted through the sheer curtains, which were billowing in the warm night wind. She was leaning on the balcony railing, looking out over the city.

"I don't think I can go out onto another balcony for a long time," he said, smiling at her from the large glass door.

She didn't respond.

"Hey, you, what's the matter?" he asked. He walked up and leaned on the railing next to her.

Tamara still remained silent.

He put his arms around her, and her curly hair flicked at his face. They stood there and listened to the hum of the city.

"Look, baby," he softly began, "I'm sorry. Real sorry. I...I just reacted..."

"...shhh," she said, putting her finger to his lips. "James explained it all to me. Don't worry, I understand. You didn't have any control over the choice. The instinct to save yourself overpowers any other drive. Like James said. You're strong, Jonathan Kortel, but not that strong...*yet*."

"Yeah, but I should have..."

"...saved yourself first, then dealt with me." She stroked the side of his face. "No, it's not that Jonathan....It's just that you've nev..."

Jonathan put his finger to her lips. "...shhh," he said, pulling her tightly into his arms. "I love you so much, Tamara. I...I just had to let go of a lot of things first."

As they kissed, he felt a cold feeling pass over his heart, and he was suddenly gripped by the realization of what this moment might be.

The last thing that she would remember of him.

Tamara pulled back to see her lover's eyes. "You know I can't stay. I've got Nicki tonight."

Jonathan was dying inside. He wanted to tell her...to *warn* her. It took all of his willpower not to break down and reveal Jimbo's plan. But he didn't. He just nodded and remained silent.

He knew that Jimbo was right.

SECOND PLACE ForeWord Magazine's Book of the Year
FINALIST for Science Fiction Independent Publishers Book Awards.

"It's a **HIGHLY ORIGINAL** novel set in the near future and **IT MOVES AT LIGHT-NING SPEED**....The **ENSUING ACTION IS BIZARRE** enough to read like something straight out of *The X-Files*."   ~ *Steve Powers, Dallas Morning News*

Book 2

SOULWARE

Originally published in 2005

The beginning...31

THE Blind Monkey was busy for 10:30 in the morning.

Jonathan waited for the next available booth.

Sammy, the morning host, motioned for him to take one of the six-tops by the window. Sliding into the booth, he looked out at the corner where he had first realized what he was. The kit cab test had been ruthless, he thought, but it did set the stage for his true development.

He thought of Zvara.

The girl in the booth in front of him turned around. "Excuse me," she asked, "but can I have your ketchup?"

"Sure..." Jonathan said, not paying attention. He was still preoccupied with thoughts of the senior Tel and all that had happened over the last few weeks.

"Thanks," she said.

The voice was familiar. A tingle shot through Jonathan's nervous system.

He looked up.

It was Tamara.

Jonathan's heart collapsed with the cold realization that Jimbo had already started. His throat tightened, and tears began to form at the edges of his eyes. Nausea started to build in his stomach, and he clenched his jaw.

He had lost his parents.

He had lost his childhood.

He had lost his humanity.

And now, he had lost his love.

She turned back and looked at him. "Have we met?"

Every nerve cell and every ounce of his strength strained against his desire to tell her what they had had. What they had shared. What they had been.

"No..." he barely uttered.

She smiled, and her eyes disappeared into little slits. His mind instantly went back to the club. To the Den. To the first time he had seen her smile.

"Funny, you seem so familiar. Well, thanks." She turned her back to him.

A small tear rolled down Jonathan's cheek as a small head rose from behind the edge of Tamara's booth. Little Nicole looked at him and giggled.

Jonathan wanted to tear his heart from his chest, and at his level, he could have easily done it. He ran from the booth, out of the Blind Monkey and onto the busy sidewalk. His mind, his body and his soul ached beyond his capacity to control. He wanted to vomit.

Wildly looking about, he focused his rage on a netphone booth, which instantly exploded. People screamed and scattered around him as plexiglass and metal rained on the crowded sidewalk. He turned his attention to a biomeal cart, and it blew up, sending plastic, condiments and biopaste spattering violently against storefronts and cars.

He was consumed by his loss.

Jonathan ran down the sidewalk, tears and mucus dripping from his face. Everything in his wake either shattered or exploded. His heart pounded erratically his chest.

In his anguish, Jonathan turned into an alley, leaving the crowded sidewalk in chaos from his telekinetic rage. He pushed and kicked at piles of trash, almost slipping on an bright yellow rain slicker that had spilled from a large wet box. Suddenly in the corner of the alley, a translucent image appeared. It floated eerily between an old rusted recycle can and a broken TVid screen.

Jonathan froze in midstep.

It was another memory fragment of his parents. They were standing in their Hawaiian backyard, the beach and ocean visible through the palm trees. They faced forward as if they were looking directly at him. His father was dressed in his favorite Hawaiian shirt, and his mother had on her lab coat and the belt that she loved so much.

Startled, Jonathan gasped and fell back into the wet box of old clothes. He watched his mother, with his father's arm around her, blow him a kiss. He buried his head in his hands and began to sob. Then the image shifted. His mother was saying something to him.

"*We love you,*" she silently mouthed.

A gentle rain began to fall.

Jonathan looked up and let the cool drops hit his face. *My life is just beginning,* he thought.

But as the world's most powerful telekinetic leaned forward and looked back at his parents and the past with which he had finally made peace, a strange calm fell over him.

He thought of his future.

Jonathan Kortel had finally crossed. And he wasn't afraid anymore of his destiny.

Idi v pizdu... 1

JONATHAN Kortel quietly sipped kapustnyak in his favorite booth, the three-quarter-circle one in the rear corner of the VIP section.

Nikita's was one of Moscow's oldest nightclubs – nothing fancy, but hell, what was fancy in Russia these days? Mainly, it was dark, quiet, and Jonathan felt a kind of kinship to its spavined black vinyl marked by a hundred years of patched tears and embedded effluvium. He had passed many a good time in this booth. He often thought that the owners should put up a small plaque in his honor. Lord knows he had spent enough digirubles to warrant it. Best of all, it was right under the VJ's cage. Just reach up and pass her some extra credits, and she would stream whatever you wanted. That's why he had always requested it. Asking was merely a formality, though. As soon as he called, they knew what he wanted.

And who he wanted.

But the best part about Nikita's? No one would bother him. Nikita's was deep in the heart of one of the world's darkest cities, and Jonathan could bury himself in the booth with the glow from the table candle as his only light. In a remote corner of the club.

Far from the world.

Far from the Agency.

He looked into his soup at the flecks of pork and fat and garlic. This was not biofood; this was real food from the old Russia, the Russia that had seen a hundred invaders since its birth in the ninth century. A flood of memories came swimming back in the bowl.

In a prior life he had been a successful programming chef, riding the crest of a revolution that had washed over all of humanity. The Biolution had changed life forever and had made the world a different place – a dangerous place, some felt. The fusion of organic peptides and nanobiotics had swept away all the old issues of bandwidth. Entire industries were changed virtually overnight. The Net was everywhere, which meant the world was in your pocket like it had never been before.

But tonight, Jonathan Kortel was off line. Maybe permanently, if things could go his way.

He sensed the three Russian Tels the second they entered. He didn't know how he could sense others like himself; he just could. It was like a scent he could smell in his mind. These were big Russians. Powerful. Probably from their equivalent of the New America Agency. They were simply known as the *u'ebitsche*. The Freaks.

They turned down the collars of their thick gray overcoats while they calmly walked past Zoya, the door girl. Fresh snow fell from their shoulders and melted into the warm, plush carpet that had covered the floor of the restaurant for five decades. They passed the main stage and its caviar bar, where the Moscow elite hungrily dug in and knocked down its precious vodka. They passed the VIP doorman, who stood oddly motionless, staring blankly into a world only he could see. The Siberian cowboys refused to meet the gaze of any patron, so focused were they on their target. They knew exactly whom they wanted and where he could be found. The club became coldly silent, as if Stalin himself had walked in and taken a table.

Jonathan meticulously separated the pork from the fat. The Russian Tels stopped at the narrow entrance of his booth. The tops of their coats were now soaked by the melted snow, and a wide trail of wet footprints followed them from the front door. Like trees from the frozen Siberian forests, they stood planted, watching Jonathan calmly slurp the sauerkraut off his spoon. These men were like the country itself: massive, cold, and as emotionally frozen as a Murmansk river.

Jonathan scooped another spoonful.

"*Govorite li vy po russki?*" the middle one asked. The creases in his cheeks deepened as a smile crept across his face.

Jonathan didn't grace him with his attention. He continued to eat his soup.

"I would think not," the Russian said, now in perfect English. "We have heard a lot about you, Comrade Kortel. I quite frankly thought you were nothing more than disinformation from your Agency, but I can see that you are real *and* quite human."

The one on the left grunted under his breath with what could have been taken as a laugh.

"Is it true, Jonathan..." he said as he leaned forward until Jonathan could smell his acrid breath. "I can call you Jonathan, can't I?..."

Jonathan took another spoonful.

"...that you're *faster* than light?"

A noodle slapped Jonathan's upper lip as he sucked it down.

The Russians looked at each other, then back to Jonathan. "*Idi na huy!*" [*Go to hell (penis)*: a mild insult] the one on the left exclaimed.

"He's nothing but a *pedik!*" (a male who is used as a female in prison) said the one on the right, and they started to laugh.

"*Idi v pizdu* [*Go to hell (vagina)*: a worse insult]," Jonathan said apathetically. He ripped off a hunk of bread to wipe his bowl clean.

The Russians stopped laughing. Their expressions turned deadly serious. The muffled pitch of black-market, handheld Light-Force bioweapons collectively whined under their dense wool coats.

"No," the one in the center replied, *"you* go to hell!" And with the grace of Bolshoi dancers, all three drew in sync.

The light from their weapons' discharges exploded like an antique flash photograph and captured on the retinas of the patrons every terrible detail of the dank Moscow nightclub.

Jonathan calmly wiped his mouth with the linen napkin, leaned back against the cool vinyl and casually took in his would-be assassins. The beams of matter-shifting light protruded about four feet from each gun muzzle, suspended motionless. They emitted no sound and glowed white hot. He calmly leaned forward and lit a cigarette from the end of one of the beams.

"Now," Jonathan said, smiling around the cigarette. "Who did you say was going to hell?" He exhaled smoke into the face of the center assassin and settled back into the comfort of the booth.

The big Russian's eyes were wide with fear. "Forgive us–" He choked on the rest of his sentence.

Jonathan took another drag and sighed. He had grown weary of challenges. If someone had told him two years ago that the strange little "episodes" that had riddled his former life were just manifestations of his true telekinetic nature, he would have thrown them from his restaurant. But when someone finally did tell him, he didn't do a thing. Because ever since the Agency had approached him, he had been in denial of the truth. He was a Tel, and perhaps the most powerful one ever.

Jonathan slid gingerly out of the booth, knowing all too well the deadly nature of the Light-Force beams. One touch and he would be reduced to a biological puddle, hardly distinguishable from the puddles of water left by the Russian Tels' march through the club.

As he made his way through the tables of Muscovites, he felt their stares burn deep into his soul. Being a Tel meant living in the world of rumor – that aberrant space between headlines and copy. He had become part of a secret family that had grown weary of a world consumed with petty conflicts and global egos. Still tolerant of human limitations, yet having no patience for their arrogant view of life, the Tels had come to look upon their human brethren with an admixture of pity and disdain, and Jonathan had become their point man, whether he wanted the role or not. But tonight, all he had wanted was a bowl of soup. With a side of solitude.

He neared Zoya, who stood next to the receptionist booth with his coat draped across her arm. She was the classic Slavic beauty: tall, solid, and with enough intelligence to cut someone off at the knees. They didn't exchange a word while he slid his arms into the sleeves and hiked the heavy garment onto his shoulders. When she stepped back, the coat's living fabric sequenced to the preset protocols of his body grid. It wrapped tightly at the neck, cuffs and legs, creating a personal cocoon against the harsh winter night. He took her netpad from her hand, entered his tip for the evening and watched as she read the amount. She slowly lifted her eyes and smiled a wide, red grin. He returned a slight smile and began to leave.

Knowing he had a serious "containment issue" at Nikita's, Jonathan stopped short of the front door and turned to the room of hardened Russians. They were all staring at him with the same dead expression inculcated by a culture that had seen it all. Every Tel knew that the key to their joint survival was complete and utter secrecy. Jonathan looked over to the three assassins still held in his grav field and knew he had serious breach. There was only one thing to do. He quietly slipped into phase.

As Jonathan came out of phase, his vision changed from white to a blur of color and, finally, into focus. He looked around at the 60 or so patrons and staff draped in various ways over chairs, or in crumpled heaps on the dense red carpet. All had been put into deep telekinetic sleep, and all would wake with a wicked headache and not remember the last five to nine hours of their lives. The three assassins' bioweapons had completed their discharge, the impact coming where he had sat just moments before. The center of the damaged booth was now a gooey, disfigured blob of congealing wood, horsehair and vinyl. It hissed as it slowly dripped and spread across the floor.

I'm going to miss that booth, he thought.

Zoya had fallen where she stood. He lifted her body and gently placed her in an overstuffed wingback. He brushed the hair off her forehead. His hands never left his pockets. He finished his cigarette.

Jonathan bent and softly kissed the top of her head, then passed the back of his hand down the side of her cheek. He let the tip of his finger stop gently at the edge of her mouth. *"Do svidaniya,"* he said reflectively.

When he approached the antiquated front door, he stopped and let his hand slide over its worn surface of knots and grain. It was real wood, from an actual tree, probably felled in the forests near Moscow more than 200 years ago.

Only in Russia, he thought.

The winter wind hit his face like a thousand tiny needles. The gale had whittled the snowflakes to ice, and even the high-tech thermo biofabric of his overcoat couldn't stop the brutal Arctic wind.

He had ordered a bowl of soup. What had come was a helping of grief for a life lived in shadow. He'd had his fill of it for two years, moving from one black assignment to another, shuttling between bleak apartments in a country that had never really crawled out of the collapse of Communism. His world now was a far cry from his prior life. It had its own rules, its own agendas and its own judgments. He had been warned that it would change him, but he had jumped into it anyway, arrogantly dismissing the possibility that *he* could be changed. He turned his face from the bitter wind and headed back to a cold and empty hotel bed. His netphone hummed deep inside his overcoat, and his nerves, even after all this time, still flinched from the knowledge of what that vibration meant. He let it hum through its answer sequence.

Jonathan Kortel was off-line.

"Screw the Agency," he said to himself, and hailed the first cab that could move out of the busy Moscow traffic and get to his side of the street.

The life left behind...2

"MR. KORTEL?...Mr. Kortel?!"

Jonathan, his seat still trying to vibrate him gently awake, snapped back from a deep, thick sleep to see the flight attendant's face in his sleep station's vidscreen.

"I'm so sorry to disturb you," she chirped, "but you have a vidcall. Would you like to take it, or shall I have them call back after you freshen up a bit?"

"No, no. That's okay. I'll take it," he said, clearing his throat. His bed finished transforming to its seat configuration and settled into place.

The flight attendant smiled, and her image was replaced with the logo of Nations Air. Then James McCarris appeared, his slim face pressed to the edges of the small screen. "Ahh, did I wake you? Sorry, man. I can call back..."

"No, don't worry, James. I needed to get up. I think they're about to serve dinner anyway. What's up?"

"Well, for one thing, the unit director wants a debrief on Paris as soon as you get in tomorrow."

"Shit, James, can't it wait till Monday?..." Suddenly, the gigantic transcontinental Airbus jerked to one side and threw Jonathan against the bulkhead. "What the hell?..."

James's face instantly was replaced with the flight attendant's, her smile calm and bright. "Please take your seats, ladies and gentlemen. We're experiencing a little turbulence. We should be out of it shortly. And for you folks exercising on the second level, please stop what you're doing and take an available seat until we enter clear air. Thank you."

With the Biolution, the giant modern commercial airliner had become more of an airborne mall at 48,000 feet. Flight control, thrust and stabilization were now a fine art. Planes didn't fly, they slipped through the air, and to experience a bump, much less a jolt that knocked you against your seat, had been almost unheard of for 30 years.

James's face returned. "Everything okay there?"

Jonathan cautiously surveyed the cabin. "Yeah...yeah, I think we're okay." He slowly turned in his seat and faced the vidscreen. Both Tels were silent, remembering a similar jolt that had ended in tragedy.

Jonathan settled back into his seat, its living fabric nestling him in First Class luxury as it recalled the memory of his frame. "Now, what were you saying?"

"Oh right, there was one other thing..." James hesitated.

"Yeah?" Jonathan pressed.

"...we found Tarris."

Jonathan stared into the inky blackness of the airspace high above the Atlantic. They were slicing through the boundary zone between the atmosphere and the edge of outer space, high above the weather that wrapped the earth in a blanket of sporadic turmoil. Even though the need for a crew to fly the huge aircraft had vanished over 20 years ago, it was comforting to Jonathan that a human was still required in the cockpit. His thoughts drifted...

Tarris had been more than just a boyhood friend: He had been a brother figure and, many times, a father figure.

When the first wave of the Biolution hit, it took with it certain industries that had been the foundation of the world's economy. When the ability to create synthetic oil and its thousands of byproducts became a reality, the need to pump the planet dry of what was once its most important resource dried up. So, too, did the power of the Arab world. Checkmated in a global chess match, the Middle East never saw it coming. The resulting demotion in world ranking had pushed radical elements of the Arab world to show the infidels one last demonstration of anger. But this was not going to be your average terrorist act. Sadder than the World Trade towers, deadlier than the Jerusalem incident, more heinous than the Olympics of 2044, the detonation of an untested biothermonuclear weapon not only obliterated the Hawaiian Islands, it robbed Jonathan of a childhood and the parents who would have shared it.

Tarris had not been the best surrogate brother or father, but he always had been there when Jonathan needed him. Growing up parentless in the Midwest had left a scar on Jonathan's soul, and Tarris had filled the void when questions about life, or love, had overwhelmed him. Years later, when the inevitable realization of his telekinetic nature had overthrown his orderly life, Jonathan had sought out his old boyhood friend.

Tarris had introduced Jonathan to the urban myth of the Tels and their secret culture. He also had unknowingly set into motion a sequence of events that drew Jonathan into a battle between two rival Tel leaders. Like telekinetic Mafia dons, Jacob Whitehorse and Armando Zvara fought their own personal battle, with Jonathan as the prize. Each knew that Jonathan might be the next step for their kind, but each had his own agenda and his own view of where Jonathan fit into the Tel world order.

Whitehorse had been the founder of the Rogues, a radical group that had left the Agency to pursue a platform of helping their human cousins throughout the world. They secretly intervened when necessary – helping the downtrodden on the world stage. Whitehorse had used Tarris to get to Jonathan, and in doing so, he had leveraged the love of Tarris's life.

Always the good Rogue, Georgia dutifully took the assignment, but didn't foresee that she would fall in love with Tarris, the man she had been sent to set up. When the plan to bring Jonathan into the Rogues via Tarris turned into Jacob Whitehorse's personal vendetta against Armando Zvara, things turned deadly. Whitehorse was blinded by his hatred for the Agency and vowed that if he couldn't have Jonathan, no one would. Arrogantly, he had underestimated Jonathan's telekinetic potential, and in a desperate attempt to force his decision, Whitehorse had threatened the only thing that mattered in Jonathan's life: the woman he loved.

Pushed by a series of deadly events and driven by fear for his girlfriend, Jonathan had unleashed a telekinetic ability the Tel world had never seen before. With the death of Whitehorse at Jonathan's hand, the stage had been set for him to "cross over" to the cold hard reality of what he was.

When Jonathan chose to join the Agency, Georgia felt it was time to come clean with Tarris, her lover. It didn't go exactly as she had planned. Tarris felt betrayed by the only woman he had ever truly loved – a woman who had overlooked the fact that he was paraplegic and loved him for who he was. Crushed by the deception, Tarris left Georgia. He disappeared, leaving behind his life as one of the top independent developers of biogames. He left his beloved compound in the New Mexican desert and never looked back.

To his lover.

Or his boyhood friend.

"Jonathan? Hey Jonathan, are you with me?" James asked from the vidscreen.

"Yeah." He stared out the window. "Is he...all right?"

"Not really, unless you think being strung out on Jack is all right."

Devil's Jack was the biodrug of choice for heavy riders. Tarris had battled with addiction all his life. He had stayed clean for many years, until the truth about his lover   tipped the scales.

"Is he bad off, James?" He already knew the answer.

"Yeah, well...I guess he's surviving. I mean, he's living off his royalties. Man, he's buried himself really deep. You know it's taken us a year to find him. This guy is so good he's firewalled himself into oblivion. He made it so hard to trace his money flow, we gave up for a while. Shit, he should come work for us!"

Jonathan kept staring.

"Well, I'll let you go. Enjoy your dinner, and we'll see ya when you get back." James made a click sound with his mouth and the vidscreen cut out.

"Later, James," Jonathan said to the blank screen. He never heard the answer to his question.

~

The flight attendants began to prepare the First Class cabin for dinner. Jonathan had ordered the salmon and was interested to see how the biofood would be prepared. As a former programmer, chef and proprietor, he was always curious how other chefs worked. When the attendant served his dinner, the presentation and the smell seemed strangely familiar. The texture and flavor combinations had been programmed to his specific genetic requests, but as he ate, there was a palatable *deja vu*. He motioned to one of the flight attendants.

"Yes, sir. Is there a problem?" The attendant squatted down in the aisle to meet his eyes.

"This dinner is excellent. Do you know who the chefs are, or what programs they may be using? I'm very curious. The flavors are so unique."

"I don't know, sir, but I can certainly ask the head steward. He probably knows." The attendant hurried toward the forward galley.

Jonathan continued to enjoy his dinner, savoring the salmon and the delicate hint of saffron in the rice.

"This flight's dinners have been prepared in our Chicago facilities, sir," the attendant said on his return. "I was told that we are featuring dishes from different Chicago restaurants. I believe yours is from..." (he pulled a napkin from his pocket) "...oh, yes...Kortel's. I've never been there, but I've heard the food is fabulous. Is that the information you were wanting?"

Jonathan went numb. He quietly pushed the dinner forward, picked up his merlot, and turned his attention out the window. It was Saffron Salmon from kitchen Kortel. It was his old partner's recipe.

~

The lights dimmed throughout the cabin as the flight attendants collected the empty dinner trays. Jonathan sipped his wine while the plane slipped through the night. His thoughts drifted back to his old restaurant and friend.

And to the life he had left behind.

Good night...3

JONATHAN clicked off the vidscreen, folded it tight and returned it to its compartment in the seat in front of him. Throughout the cabin, most of the individual lights were turned off as the First-Class passengers slept off their sherry-glazed ducks and crème brûlées. He couldn't sleep. Only two lights – along with a woman's across the aisle from him – were on. Younger than most trans First-Classers, she had taken her seat back in Orly. He had noticed her immediately, and couldn't help occasionally glancing over. With her curly blonde hair and tall frame, she reminded him of someone he had once been very close to – someone who had changed his life. He watched intently as she engaged in something most people had given up years ago, a ritual that had disappeared with the postal service and land-based telephone. She appeared to be writing a letter.

Abruptly, she put down her pen and turned in his direction. Like a schoolboy caught in class, Jonathan quickly shifted his attention to the window. After a few moments, he slyly glanced back and found she had returned to the business of writing. She turned to fish something out of her purse, and her elbow knocked her antique pen off the tray table. Jonathan considered mentally catching it, but instead, he decided to pick it up with his hand and introduce himself.

"Excuse me," he said, sliding over, "you dropped your pen." He had snatched it before it could roll under the foot of the snoring passenger behind her.

She met his advance with quiet, cool blue eyes that disappeared into slits when she smiled. Her curly hair fell over her forehead. "Thank you," she said with an unfamiliar accent. She took the pen while tucking her hair behind the edge of her ear. "I've lost a million things on these huge planes."

"I can relate. I've lost a ton of things, too. It looked like a beautiful antique, and I thought you might miss it. Besides..." He glanced at her writings, then back to her. She met his look with the beginnings of a wary smile. "...it would be a shame for you not to finish your...letter?"

She completed her smile and clicked the pen's cartridge into place. Her fingers grazed the paper. "Poetry, actually."

"Really? Poetry?"

"What? You find it odd that I?—"

"No, no. Nothing like that. I think I'm more...I mean, I thought it might be, you know, something personal."

She began to laugh.

"What? What did I say?"

She looked over, her eyes slivers of blue framed by the most perfect complexion. She covered her mouth as if she were ashamed of laughter. *"Hvordan yndig, deres flurting med meg,"* she said more to herself than to him.

"Hvorfor ikke? Det er ikke daglig de møter en vakker, intelligent kvinne," he replied.

Her laughter waned, and he was again looking into her crystalline blue eyes.

"Thank you," she said cautiously, her English returning. "Where did you learn Norwegian?"

"My work demands that I know a number of languages." He held her gaze just long enough, remembering a similar face and a similar look. His smile fell away, and he began to slide back to his seat.

"Excuse me," she said, "are you all right?"

"Hmm?" he questioned. "Yeah, it's nothing. It's just that you remind me of...ah, I'm sorry to have disturbed you." He resumed his sliding.

"Who...*is* she?" she softly questioned.

He stopped. "Excuse me?" he asked, slowly looking back.

"You know, who is she?... Who did I remind you of?" She sported an intuitive half smile.

Jonathan sheepishly grinned, embarrassed at having been so obvious. He leaned on the armrest of his seat. He stroked the hair he had let grow under his chin. "Was I that obvious?"

"Well...no. I mean, I could just tell..." She smiled nervously, like she was trapped in a conversation she might not want to have.

"I'm sorry if I embarrassed you."

"No, not at all...please, tell me about her."

"Nah, it's boring—"

"No, please," she pressed.

Jonathan's attention was caught by a cute little girl playing with a toy horse in an aisle seat two rows ahead of him. His mind flashed back to the last moments he had with Tamara – the girl who had taught him how to let go of his pain – and her daughter, Nicole, playing at their feet in the restaurant where she and Jonathan had talked, and laughed, and decided to let their walls down. Possibly, even, to love one another. The thought of her crashed against his heart.

"Although," he said reflectively, still staring at the little girl, "I sure did love her." He glanced back.

They sat staring at one another, as when two strangers acknowledge the same feeling toward something with a laugh or nod of the head. Jonathan sensed, momentarily, a shared feeling. A shared pain. That she had also lost someone. Someone important. Someone she had loved.

"Tell me about her," the stranger urged again.

"Well..." Jonathan hesitated. "No. No I can't. It's a very complex story, and one that I can't really go into."

"You can with me."

Jonathan's look questioned her.

Her smile returned. "It's all right. People talk to me every day...it's part of my job...to listen to people."

"Are you a psychologist or something?"

"I've studied psychology, but I'm not a psychologist. I'm in the priesthood, actually."

Jonathan felt himself staring.

"What," she asked, "are you that surprised?"

"No, no, it's just...that..."

"That a priest can't be pretty?" Her grin returned.

"No...I mean, maybe...wait..."

She began to laugh, and Jonathan joined her.

"I'm sorry," Jonathan said, "I didn't mean to be offensive."

"Don't worry, I get this more than I care to admit."

"So what, ah...faith are you?"

"Catholic," she replied with an edge of pride.

"That's right...that was passed last year."

"It's been a long time coming, and our new Holy Father has a more progressive point of view than his predecessors."

"But you're Norwegian...I thought Norway was mainly Protestant."

"There're a few of us in Norway, probably more than you think."

"Say, um, how did you get?..." He pointed to her seat.

"They had overbooked, and this was the only seat left."

"Really? Well then, I guess congratulations are in order for your ordination."

"Oh, I'm not a priest yet. I've just been ordained into the Transitional Diaconate. I have another six months of studies to complete before I'm ordained into the Permanent Diaconate. But thank you. Now, weren't you going to tell me about this woman I remind you of?"

Jonathan was already feeling the fatigue from his Paris assignment. He hadn't talked with anyone about Tamara since the last time he had seen her – at their breakfast spot two years prior, where he saw firsthand how brutal the Agency could be.

"All right then," he said, letting his guard down. "But will you have a drink with me, or is that not allowed?"

She smiled and nodded. "Obviously you haven't been around many Catholics."

~

The huge plane was quiet as most of its 800 passengers slept or read. He told her about the life he had led in Chicago, his partner at the restaurant, and the girl who had entered his life and shown him what it was to love. He told this complete stranger about Tamara's life as a single mom and about little Nicole, an exact miniature of her mother. He remarked to the stranger that she had eyes similar to Tamara's, which went to slits when she smiled. He had loved that trait. She blushed at the comparison.

He continued to tell how they had met, and how most people hadn't understood why he was so drawn to her. Why neither of them could explain their deep, passionate need for each other. Beyond just sex. Even beyond love. Their feelings had been almost instinctual. He also explained what Tamara did. She was a dancer, and not your Broadway kind, either. Tamara was the kind that preyed on the insecurities of men and women and parted them with their credit faster than their netbanks could transfer the funds. Even with her high marks in art history, she couldn't escape the lure of easy money. Combined with the need to care for her child, it kept pushing her back into a life she despised. He didn't even get into the Nevada thing – that she had turned tricks at an age when most girls were worrying if their major was going to get them a decent job. Even though they had both known that it would probably never work out, they had gone for it nonetheless. They both had let go of their bags and jumped aboard a relationship that was sure to become a train wreck.

"Why did it end?" she asked.

"Because..." But Jonathan caught himself. He had never told anyone before about his true nature. He hesitated and took a large drink of Scotch.

"Because why?" she pressed.

"Because I discovered something about myself, and it changed my life." He couldn't meet her eyes.

"Oh, it can't be that bad," she offered. "You seem pretty normal to me."

Hardly, Jonathan thought. He glanced up and met her questioning look. "I shouldn't really say any more. I'm sorry to have taken up so much of your time." He turned away, but felt her hand at his shoulder. He slowly faced her and was met again by her eyes. This time they were filled with a profound care.

"Is there something you'd like to...confess?" Her voice was quieter and had a taken on a more serious tone.

Jonathan smiled slightly. "No, it's nothing like that. Don't get me wrong, I've done some questionable things....It's kind of required in my world now. But why my relationship with Tamara ended is, well...you wouldn't believe me even if I told you."

"It's not about whether I believe you, it's about whether God will forgive you." Her look seemed to cut to his soul. She leaned over and said, "And He *will.*"

"Thank you, I'm sure He will. But what I discovered about myself has nothing to do with sin....It's a little, ah, out there."

She politely folded her hands. "Please, go on."

There was something about her sincerity that caught him off guard. *What the hell*, he thought, *she'll never believe me.* "Okay." Jonathan took a large gulp from his drink and faced her. "I'm telekinetic," he said, and the sensation of relief rippled though his being.

The stranger just stared at Jonathan for a second, then her expression changed, like the temperature in her body had suddenly fallen 20 degrees. "I see," she said, nodding her head in a professional manner.

Jonathan pensively pulled at the patch of hair under his chin. "I told you it was out there."

"I have to admit, I've heard some strange things before, but this does qualify as one of the stranger. Who else have you told?"

Jonathan laughed slightly to himself. "You don't understand...there's a lot of us out there. Possibly a couple of thousand–" Jonathan stopped himself, knowing he was seriously breaching Tel protocol.

"What's the matter?" she questioned.

"It's weird," he said. "I've never explained it before, I mean...we're not supposed to."

She gave him that look again. "Remember, this is between me, you and God. What we discuss here is in complete confidence."

Jonathan didn't know whether it was the fatigue or the third Scotch, but the idea of divulging the Tel world to this woman seemed the perfect panacea for a life lived in secret. "I'm not sure where to begin," he said.

"Well," she replied, settling back against her seat, "why not start at the beginning."

He thought for a moment. "We call ourselves Tels....It's short for telekinetics, and we were discovered at the end of the old war – you know, World War II. Back then, they thought we had developed from the extreme conditions of that conflict, which is partly true. Humans have been evolving for thousands of years. But with us, the race took a left turn, so to speak. For some reason, nature decided to click on this ability, probably driven through stress, like the soldiers experienced in battle. It's adrenaline, you see, that triggers the effect, as we call it."

"So...what is this *effect*?" There was a new edge of skepticism in her voice.

"We can manipulate gravity. We're like lighting rods – conduits, if you will, for gravity to flow through. But it's our minds that can alter its properties. Imagine if you could isolate and displace the gravity around, say, a car. Then that car would begin to levitate off the ground. And say you could also control, with pinpoint accuracy, the force within the field of displacement. Then you could move that car around like a toy. Now, not all Tels can do the same thing. There are 10 different levels for the various degrees of strength. Most Tels are between 4 and 6. Some never make it beyond 3 – they can't move much more than a suitcase. But at Level 8, our highest level, they can do some amazing things."

"So, what happened to the Tels after the war?"

"The major governments created departments for us. Sort of safe harbors for the early ones. It also gave the scientists an opportunity to study the effect. As our population grew, so did the size and complexity of the different departments around the world. They kept us a secret...I mean a deep secret. Nobody knew. In America, the early ones were kept at a remote Air Force base in the Southwest. As the level strength grew, we became more of a threat than a experiment, but this is where it gets a little gray for me. I think one thing led to another, and a decision was made between the world departments to go underground. I won't bore you with how they did that, but today, we number around just under a thousand worldwide."

"What level are you?" she inquired.

Jonathan paused. "Me? Uhmm, I'm a little different."

She raise an eyebrow.

"Yeah, it appears that I don't fit the mold. You see, when the Recruiters–"

"Recruiters?"

"It's how we're discovered. They're a special team. Recruiters will go and study a Potential, what we call a person with the gift..."

She scrunched her face, confused.

"Sorry, the ability. Anyway, they'll study Potentials for a month, a year, however long it takes to confirm they have the gift. Then they'll extract them from society. The age of the Potential dictates the method of extraction. Young ones just...disappear. With older people, they fake something – kidnapping, dying in an accident, whatever–"

"You mean to tell me that you just take a baby from its mother?!" she said on the verge of outrage.

"No! No! Nothing like that. It's thoroughly discussed with the parents before extraction. I mean, you've got to admit, there's no way someone with an ability like ours can function in regular society. Some have tried, but it never works. They always come back–"

"But what about the secrecy thing?" she questioned. "Don't these parents now know about the Tels?"

Jonathan apprehensively looked away.

"What?..." she pressed.

"A high level Tel can also...*impair* a person."

Her look questioned him again.

"Erase their memory, either in fragments or all of it. How do you think we just collectively disappeared one day?"

The stranger sunk back into her seat, staring ahead. Jonathan took a slow sip of his Scotch.

"You never answered–"

"Nine. I'm a Level 9, or so they think," he replied, not looking her in the eye.

"So," she said, "how were *you* extracted?"

Jonathan grinned. "Oh, I found religion."

She started to laugh.

"What? What's so funny?"

"Nothing...religion, that's all. It's just funny."

Jonathan started laughing also. "Yeah, I'm *supposedly* in Nepal right now, at a temple."

"At a...temple?!" She burst out laughing.

He laughed with her. "Well," he said, sharing the moment, "there's more if you're interested—"

"Interested? Why yes," she encouraged. "Please, go on."

"When I was discovered, I guess I was something of an anomaly. The Agency, the New American organization – the one I belong to now – their Recruiters really wanted me. But so did the Rogues. They're sort of a splinter group. A bunch of high-levels from the Agency who got fed up with all the protocol and agenda this, agenda that, and took off to form their own group. Anyway, things got a little ugly. I won't go into all of it right now, but trust me, it got to a dangerous point, involving my best friend, my old business partner and..." His voice trailed off as a memory surfaced like a body that had spent days underwater.

"Are you okay?" she asked tentatively.

"Hmm? Yeah. Just remembering..."

She gasped. "Tamara!" she said, realizing the inevitable conclusion.

"Yeah," he said, nodding, "Tamara."

"Did they?... "

"They did. She, along with everyone else, had to be erased."

The stranger's look softened, as if she actually were buying his tale.

"It's okay...really. It was for the best." He sipped his drink. "So," he proclaimed, cutting the edge off the somber moment, "what do think of my bizarre little story?!"

The stranger, her resolve returning, took a gulp from her wine and went with his lead. "Honestly, I think you're in need of some professional help. This is a little out of my league. I really should get back to my writing." She started to pull the antique pen nervously from her purse.

"Whoa there. Easy. Just a minute, come on now." He motioned for her to stop.

The stranger tentatively returned the pen to her purse. "Please," she whispered from across the aisle, "I'm still in seminary...I'm very new to all this, and I'm feeling very uncomfortable. I know that what you've told me seems very real to you, but with the proper help, I'm sure you'd be able to work out whatever it is you need...to work out....Look, maybe it would be best that I move my seat." She began to collect her things.

"Well, if you're going to move," he warned, "you'd better be careful. We might enter some unexpected turbulence." Suddenly, the plane seemed to jerk.

She stopped what she was doing and looked at him gravely. "You didn't just do that...did you?"

Jonathan kept facing forward, calmly sipping his Scotch.

"Oh, that was good. That was funny! You really had me going there..." She laughed nervously.

The plane bounced.

She grabbed her wine before it tipped and trained him with a look of utter disbelief. The color had drained from her face.

Jonathan glanced over and raised an eyebrow.

She slammed the rest of her wine.

"Go ahead and blink," he whispered as he leaned across the aisle. "When you do, I'll move the plane, just a little. It'll appear to the pilot like a little rough air."

She pulled back with a "Yeah, right" look on her face.

"Come on, it's okay. I'm not joking. Really, try it."

Determination came over her face. Challenging him, she leaned into the aisle and met his gaze for 20 seconds, then blinked.

The plane again bounced. Her smile disappeared. She sat back into her seat and glared.

"Sir?" Jonathan said to a flight attendant with a chuckle, "I think she'll have another!"

The stranger wasn't laughing.

"Ah, come on. That was funny! You've got to admit. The look on your face was priceless."

"Did you...did you just really do that?" she asked.

Jonathan nodded with a sudden seriousness.

Her expression shifted like this news had hit somewhere near the foundation of her faith.

The flight attendant placed another merlot in front of her. After he left, it rose off the tray. "Oh, good Lord!" she yelled and grabbed the drink.

"Shhh. Easy. It's okay." He glanced at the attendant, who had shot them a look. "Let's not make this an event, all right." He glanced about the cabin to see if anyone else had noticed.

The stranger looked away.

"Hey, don't be scared," he reassured. "We're not here to hurt or do anything bad."

"You talk like you're not human...like you're something else. You are human, aren't you?"

Jonathan hesitated for a moment. "Technically yes, we're human. But in some ways, we're very different. For one, some of our genetic code is different. The resequencing that..." He stopped. He had never explained the science behind their gift. He wasn't sure if he really understood it himself. He could tell he was about to lose her. He smiled. "Look, this isn't coming out right. Let's just say that yes, we're human, but we're developing into something else. Something more *advanced*." He leaned forward, as if he were about to tell her the most important secret ever, and whispered, "We believe that it could be the next step for humanity. Who knows the possibilities?"

The stranger pulled back in her seat, and Jonathan could see fear in her eyes. He had seen it before with Hector, his friend and partner in his restaurant in Chicago. When Jonathan had told him of who he was, what he had become, he could tell that a chasm opened up – himself on one side, and Hector on the other.

It happened to all Tels.

The stranger lowered her head and stared at her wine. "I think I really should move now," she barely managed.

"I don't even know your name," Jonathan said, just realizing it.

The stranger regarded him painfully. Jonathan could sense she was grappling with this new revelation, and it appeared to be testing her faith. "Oh, my name?" she questioned. "Heavens, I can't believe we never introduced ourselves to each other. I'm sorry, my name is Freja—" She froze.

Jonathan leaned back against the seat and studied her eyes. He had never looked so closely into the eyes of someone he was about to erase. He took a slow sip from his drink. The stranger sat motionless, like a holoimage stuck on pause – her mouth caught in the middle of her first name, Frejasomething. It didn't matter. When she woke up, she would find herself in her seat with a glass of wine, figuring she probably had drank too much. She would attribute the headache to the tannins.

Jonathan leaned forward and began his "surgery." He narrowed a grav field to the width of a needle and began applying pressure to the part of her brain that directs short-term memory, and he watched her eyes for any signs of his invasion. They didn't vacillate or dilate. They remained motionless. Quiet. Clear. Blue.

When he finished, he slowly released her, and as she came out of his mental grip, her eye muscles shut in response to the telekinetic sleep he had induced. He caught her head before it hit the tray table and turned her face gently to one side. He neatly arranged her hair. His hands were still swirling the ice in his glass.

"Is she okay?" the young flight attendant inquired.

"Oh yeah. Just a little too much – you know." He made a motion like he was slamming down an imaginary drink.

The attendant smiled, turned off her light and continued down the aisle.

Jonathan turned his attention to the window and the blackness of the sky. A twinge of guilt cut through him. He thought about her reaction, when she pushed back from him in fear. He glanced down at his netwatch.

11:14:58 pm GMT. Habit. He was supposed to have called in an hour ago.

"Screw the Agency..." he said under his breath...and yawned. His seat sensed the change in 127 of the 200 different anatomical aspects it was programmed to monitor and began shifting into sleep mode. He leaned back while it reconfigured into a bed. He looked over to the stranger, who was quietly sleeping with her head on the tray table.

"Good night, Mother Freja," he whispered. "Sweet dreams."

Jeffrey and Cyril...4

"HERE you go, Mr. Kortel," the driver said, piloting the MicrosoftFord out of traffic and up to the curb.

"Thanks, Mazza. This is good right here." Jonathan patted the young Tel on the shoulder. "More training today?" The car opened his door, and he stepped to the curb.

"Yes, sir. Hopefully moving a level by the end of this year."

Jonathan leaned in through the passenger window. "I wish you the best, man. I know you'll do well in the displacement field tests."

"Thank you, sir!" Mazza said, smiling, and he raised his right hand as if to high-five. But when Jonathan raised his left, their hands never touched. The Tels met each other halfway with their grav field, a mental high five. Jonathan liked the kid. He was 18 years old and, like himself, an orphan. They had that special connection. Nothing weird – just a connection. Like their high five.

"Hey, Mr. Kortel?" Mazza asked, catching Jonathan before he pulled out of the window.

"Mazza, I've told you a billion times, call me Jonathan. What's up?"

"How was...Paris?" His expression went serious.

Jonathan knew why he had asked. Paris had been a "dirty" assignment, one that meant having to displace a person.

"No, Mazza," he said coolly. "I didn't dis anyone."

Mazza nodded his head knowingly. "Yeah, I knew you were a little apprehensive."

Jonathan leaned into the window. "I didn't know you were telepathic–"

"Well...sir...I...I didn't mean to imply that...that you were...ah–"

Jonathan mentally grabbed the boy by the neck and pulled him gently toward him. Mazza instantly shut up. Jonathan glared into Mazza's eyes and smiled, then released him with a jerk and pulled out of the window. "Oh, by the way," he said with a glance back, "you were right. I was apprehensive." He smiled and saw the young Tel was visibly shaken. "You little shit, you're going to be good. You've got a keen sense about you. Work that seventh sense, man. It'll come in handy someday."

Mazza smiled with relief.

"Hey," Jonathan assured, "I'm just messing with you. Remember, you need to be ready...for anything. It's a tough world out here, and we seem to be the only ones who can get anything done these days. Know what I'm talking about?"

"You're right about that," Mazza said with the confidence that he had scored big with (if the rumors were true) the most powerful Tel ever.

Jonathan glanced up at the tall metal letters throwing their backlit argon blue at the top of the building. His pant legs whipped about in the wind. *Citenikelet Investments.* He snickered. Some thought they were a Finnish or Dutch firm, while others thought the name was just one of those trendy non-meaning marketing words, arrived at through thousands of dollars by "branding doctors" from the turn of the last century. It was more like a private joke of the New American Tel founders, who knew that they could move through the world's information net undisturbed as an investment firm. They had learned a long time ago that the basis for the world's rhythms was its global financial dealings. Its wars, famines, government overthrows – all driven by the ebb and flow of money and, ultimately, the power that accompanied it. Like some globalwide peristalsis, money moved power through cultures. In New America, *Citenikelet* closely monitored the wave.

In the early 1960s, when the imminent confrontation between the world Tel agencies and their respective governments loomed, the Tel leadership decided that the best course of action was not conflict, but complete disappearance. By erasing any evidence of their existence, both physical and mental, the Tels and their culture vanished as if they had never existed. Now they would live without the fear of reprisal and develop their culture in secret, away from their human cousins, who, by the mid-1960s, were dangerously close to wiping themselves off the face of the earth. The Tel leadership watched from the shadows a world locked in global struggle, until it became increasingly clear that a paradigm shift had taken place in human evolution. Once considered only random mutations, the Tels soon realized their true purpose: to save humans from themselves.

During the late 1960s, they organized into various legitimate corporations. In Europe, they were a food conglomerate. In Russia, they were into manufacturing. And in America, they were an investment firm. From these platforms, the Tels needled out and infiltrated all aspects of society. By strategically placing their people in key positions, they could exercise their own unique influence, hidden puppeteers reshaping a world that was hell-bent on destroying itself.

The first assertion of Tel influence impacted the world in 1963, with the changing of Khrushchev's mind about the nuclear missiles in Cuba. Deftly executed by the Russian Tel agency, it averted what could have been the third and final World War. Like their space agency counterparts, the Russian Tels had beaten the Americans to the world stage. But by the early 1980s, the American Agency discovered that the real money wasn't in political power changing. It was in the corporate sector.

At the beginning of the 21st century, many of America's high-tech corporations had ridden out the wave of the Internet revolution and were desperately searching for the next big "discovery" that would catapult their industries out of a floundering world economy. Many companies had built their fortunes on the backs of cheap brainlabor from India, who at the time still held the virtue of an education in high esteem. The American Agency had also ridden the wave of the Internet, investing wisely and creating a war chest that could, if necessary, sustain them through the lean, post-boom years. The American Tels, acting through their investment front company, began researching thousands of small start-ups, that, like decades before, had been the catalyst for the digital revolution. They discovered a small Indian bio-tech firm that was researching a bizarre concept about a new branch of science that could bridge the world of chemistry and technology – where living cells would be programmed to inject insulin into a diabetic's bloodstream or be incorporated into a bandage that would analyze an injury and heal the wound. Injected into a soldier, they even could detect when a toxin or agent was released. Taking a chance, the American Tels invested heavily in the firm and, after a period, became its sole funding source. Years of clinical trials and failures went by until e a researcher named Majit Singh developed the first fully functioning, living biochip. Its early processing power was close to a billion times faster than conventional chips. Thus was born (what the TVid pundits termed) the Biolution, with a *Citenikelet* front company owning all the patents.

For nearly 150 years, the Tel world had orchestrated its influence over a planet that was preoccupied with breast size and music videos. The Tel world was stable and hidden, which led them to believe they transcended any "outer world" laws or politics. Level 8's had set the standard and brought a sense of hierarchy and order. That is, until Jonathan Kortel came onto the scene with his faster-than-light field imaging, powerful enough to move 500-ton commercial airliners like model toys. With the arrival of a Level 9, the ground rules shifted, and the Agency might have had something it never possessed before – something that would allow it to manipulate the world order even further.

A weapon.

"Good morning, Jonathan," the receptionist beamed from behind the desk.

"Morning, Tessa. Is he in?"

"Oh yes, and he has Jeffrey with him."

"And how is Jeffrey?"

"He's in one of *those* moods. If I were you, Jonathan," she grinned knowingly, "I'd keep your field up."

"Greaaat. All I need are those two on my ass," he said to himself as he walked past a sea of biocubes, their human occupants busily jacked into the world's financial markets.

"Hey, Jules, how's the Global 200?" Jonathan yelled.

"Like a bull," the young associate answered, pulling the netgear from his face.

"And the Pac 50?"

"Like crap."

"Really?"

"You should know," Jules replied with a smile. "You tanked it last month." He wiped his brow and replaced his netgear; its fiber optic implants clicked in sync as they reestablished their connections.

"No shit," Jonathan said to himself. *Just a little influence on the right person,* he thought, *can always move market attitudes in your favor.* He turned the corner to the elevator bank and offered his eye to the retina reader. "Twentieth floor."

"Yes, Jonathan," it responded in its feminine metallic voice. "And how are you this morning?"

He didn't answer. He had grown tired of responding to public AI's, with their widely reported "collective netconscience," as if they really cared how you were.

~

The 20th floor was one grotesquely giant office: Takeda and Trumble's private sanctuary, appointed beyond anything that could remotely pass for civilized taste.

"Good morning, gentlemen," Jonathan said.

"Good morning," Trumble replied, not looking up from his netpad.

Takeda, silhouetted against the morning sun, didn't respond. There was an awkward silence while he stood at the huge bank of windows that ran the length of the floor. Without changing the direction of his gaze, he reached back, and Trumble's netpad flew into his gloved grip.

"Really, Cyril," Trumble scoffed.

Takeda reviewed the data, his back still to the room. Jonathan stood at the landing, his hands calmly in his pants pockets. Trumble sat at a long, steel-legged couch, his arms folded in disgust. More awkward silence.

The HVAC system engaged, and a rushing softly emitted from the wall vents. Trumble cleared his throat. "Today. And take off those silly gloves. You look like some Hong Kong drag fag."

Takeda released the netpad. It floated to Jonathan, who caught it about two feet in front of him. He spun it in the air so that he could view the screen. He played with a chip card in his pocket.

"Excellent work in Paris," Takeda finally said. He turned and walked to the center of the room. "And I wear these gloves because I hate the discharge effect, Jeffrey. You *know* that."

Trumble waived him off.

"Thank you, Cyril," Jonathan replied.

"Are you *comfortable* with the...results?" Trumble asked Jonathan.

Jonathan mentally moved the netpad back to Trumble, who was still waiting for a reply. He caught the tiny device with a casually outstretched hand.

Jonathan knew what the question really meant. "No," he cautiously replied. "I'm not."

"I don't blame you," Takeda said, "but I'm sure it was a last resort. Or so you said."

"The labor talks went as planned, but one of the French minister's bodyguards...let's just say he confronted me. I'm sorry that I overreacted."

"Yes, well...that was unfortunate," Takeda lamented, sitting down at his massive desk. "Control is one of our most important strengths. Maybe we've pushed you too much. After all, you're young, and you're still getting your mental legs as it were, yes?"

"Yes, quite," the older Tel agreed. "I remember when I was on assignment—"

"Jeffrey, *please*," Takeda snapped. "Don't start with that, *thank you*."

Trumble waived him off again.

"Sovann?" Takeda asked into the air.

A holoimage of an Asian woman appeared on Takeda's desk. "Yes, sir?"

"Make a note, please, to pay off the mortgage on the home of a...Jeffrey, what *was* that guard's name?"

"Mmm...oh, yes," Jeffrey began. "Le Flure. Lieutenant Henri Le Flure. It's all in file PS24563—"

"Yes, yes, I know that! Sovann, it's all in case number PS2456326. Tell them to make it appear to be a loan payoff to his family...from insurance, you know, like we did for that other case, the Jordanian fellow. I doubt his family will argue against it. Thank you, dear." The image vanished.

"Always the generous one," Trumble said, standing to leave.

"We may be serious about our business," Takeda declared, "but we're not without morals. Let's not forget that."

Jonathan just smiled.

Both Takeda and Trumble were Level 8's, and very adept at precise field movements. They had run the American Agency, along with the board of Overseers, for a decade. Trumble had been the first Level 8 to display tendencies toward Level 9. But the exercises had always fatigued the Brit, and his potential was never realized. When the two met almost 30 years ago, it was like a telekinetic firestorm. Had it not been for the partnership of Armando Zvara and Jacob Whitehorse, they could have been the longest governing Tels the Agency had ever known.

Twenty years ago, Zvara and Whitehorse were young Turks whose brand of telekinetics swept the Agency elite off their grav fields. They displayed an uncanny ability to second-guess situations and deliver remarkable solutions. Zvara advanced faster, and became the youngest Tel ever to be named head of the Agency. Over the years, though, the acquisition of power proved to be the undoing of Zvara. As well, he had developed an interest in something equally undoing – a love for Whitehorse's wife.

"Jonathan, please take some time for yourself, will you?" Trumble straightened his tie and eyed him like a father. "We have great plans for you."

"Thank you, sir," Jonathan acknowledged with a slight smile. He entered the open elevator and spun back to the room. "Gentlemen," he said with a tilt of his head, and the doors closed.

The HVAC system ended its cycle, conspicuously draining the room of sound. Takeda didn't respond. He sat quietly behind his desk and pulled at the tight, black micropore around his fingers. He intently stared at the closed elevator doors.

"If he discovers his true strength," Trumble sighed, "he will be beyond us."

Takeda cracked his knuckles.

Now I've got you...5

"**FINALLY**..." Kaya said softly to herself.

She leaned back in her chair and pulled her wavy black hair into a makeshift ponytail. The steady glow of her netport was her only light. She was tired. Worn by the search. For more than a year she had hunted, but not like her ancestors. She hadn't crawled through the prairie grasses of the American Southwest like her great-great-great-grandfather. Her hunt had been through the gigaquads of data that coursed through the world's information net like water through the rivers of her ancestral lands. She hadn't had much to go on: a rumor, a comment. It had all started with a netcall in the middle of the night, a message that pierced her heart like an arrow hitting its mark.

"Your father is dead."

Like her parents before her, Kaya's genetics had separated her from the general population. She had inherited the gift, but had disappointed her father by treading a different path. She had chosen a life outside of the culture and away from him. She had wanted just to be normal.

Kaya stared at the vidscreen with tempered relish. Here was the data she had spent hundreds of hours tracking down. She had hacked her way through multiple firewalls and deeply encrypted telenet security portals of the world's most secretive culture, and now that she had finally broken through, it was as though she had parted the thicket to view an open field – her prey before her, defenseless and unaware. She leaned forward, narrowing her eyes and clenching her jaw as the image of her father's killer quivered on her vidscreen in pixelated glory.

"Now I've got you," she said in the quiet darkness of the room. Then, like her ancestors before her who drew their bows and released death, Kaya Whitehorse clicked the download button.

Wondering...6

JONATHAN mused where he should go. He had never been to New Rio, with its Carnaval and its contest between *escolas de samba*. He had read that the *Cristo Redentor's* new location was even more breathtaking. Higher up. Closer to God.

"Stop on four."

The elevator slowed to a crawl, then halted. "Fourth floor, Jonathan."

As he walked through the open environment, people didn't look up; they just followed him with their eyes. Feigning preoccupation, they tracked him, sizing him up – judging him against what they had heard and what they now perceived. Jonathan rarely stepped onto the fourth floor. Conversations there stopped as he walked past, but it didn't really bother him. He had become used to it. Here on the fourth, people could at least pretend not to notice him.

He passed the ring of outer offices that encircled the pit of netcubes like a Roman amphitheater. In the pit were the new Tels, who hustled in the world markets during the mornings and trained for their levels in the afternoons. Like a giant financial commune, everyone started in the pit. Jonathan had been the only exception.

Approaching the row of Recruiter offices, he slowed as he passed Armando Zvara's. It was sequestered in the corner, silent and sepulchral, and still as Zvara had left it when he and James McCarris had departed for assignment more than two years ago.

Jonathan stepped into the doorway of James's office. "Jimbo," as he preferred, was at his netport slashing someone to his knees. Jonathan leaned against the door frame and folded his arms. A young woman patiently waited in one of the side chairs while Jimbo ranted. Her back was to the door. He smiled at Jimbo, motioned toward the girl and mouthed, "Should I come back?"

Jimbo, still in the the thick of his argument, shook his head. "...that situation is going to be a big bucket of assholes....I don't care, just get it done!" He clicked off the netport. "Jonathan, come on in." He gestured toward the girl. "Look who's coming back to the fold."

The young woman turned in the chair, and her dark, shoulder-length hair fell over her face. She brushed it back and smiled a smile that Jonathan hadn't seen in a long time. He missed that smile.

"Georgia..." he said, and a warmth moved across his heart. "What are you doing here?"

She stood, and her smile grew to the point that her bottom lip curled down in a way that revealed what she might have looked like as a little girl. Her dark, nearly black eyes locked onto his as she wrapped her arms around him and pulled him close. They held for a moment, the air about her redolent with a fusion of rosemary and clary sage. It filled his mind with short little memory trips. He breathed her in; she gently kissed him on the cheek.

"Jonathan," she said, leaning back from their hug. "It's so good to see you." Her hand went to his face.

"God, Georgia, you look great. What...what are you doing here?"

"Coming back to the fold," Jimbo said.

"Oh?" Jonathan questioned tightly. "And what brought this on?"

"She's seen the error of her ways," Jimbo said, cutting her off before she could answer.

"I came back because I was asked." She shot Jimbo a look and curtly smiled.

"Hey, don't blame me. You can stay with the Rogues if you want," Jimbo said, folding his arms. "But, come on, if you—"

"*Really want to make a difference, you can't do it from some compound in New Mexico.* Yes, James, you told me. But if you must know," her voice went soft and serious, "I do want to make a difference in the world. And after Whitehorse, the Rogues have been fractured, at best. No, it's time I got off my butt and started doing something. You know...give a little back. We've been given a great gift, after all."

The men exchanged glances.

"So, Jonathan," Jimbo said, "what can I do you for?"

"I'm thinking about taking some time off, and I wanted to ask you about that place you went to on vacation. You know...the island, in the Caribbean, with that beach house..." He snapped his fingers. "Come on, what's the name again?"

"Tortola?"

"Yeah, that's it. You said it was heaven on earth."

"It's the best. You have got to go! Georgia, you ever been?"

"No, no I haven't. Look guys, I have to run, but Jonathan, call me...please. I want to catch up. My number's in the system now."

Jimbo, ever the Southern gentleman, stood. Georgia hugged Jonathan again. "Please call me," she whispered in his ear. She squeezed his arm and stepped back. Jonathan let his right hand glide down her arm till their hands met. They held for a second, then she hurried away.

"You tell her about Tarris?" Jonathan asked, watching her hurry through the pit.

"Hell, no. I don't think she wants to know, to tell you the truth."

"She still looks great," he said without taking his eyes from her. "And by the way, thanks for finding Tarris. I know that was a pain in the ass for you."

"It wasn't, really," Jimbo assured. "Just more of a challenge figuring out his net patterns. He is one cagey *hombre*."

"That's for damn sure," Jonathan said. "You're still not going to erase him, right?"

"No, don't worry. He's way too screwed up to be any threat," Jimbo said, stretching. "Besides, if we closed in, he'd probably just lose us."

"No shit," Jonathan replied and intently watched Georgia step into an elevator.

"Hey, man, what are you thinking?" Jimbo asked.

"Oh, nothing..."

"Bullshit. I know you, Kortel. You're thinking about how great she looks, and how you'd like to get some of that."

"To be honest," he said, still staring at the spot in front of the elevator, "I was thinking about the last time I saw her...at the airport in Albuquerque."

"And?"

"And how she and I had this connection thing going." He glanced at Jimbo, who was looking at him with half a smile working. "What are you looking at?"

"A *connection* thing?"

Jonathan waved him off. "Give it a rest. I was with Tam at the time. We never did anything–"

"But?"

Jonathan reflected back to the time he had met Georgia. There *had* been something special between them. He had felt it from the moment he first met her. But he cared too much for Tarris, and would have never done anything to hurt him...or Tamara. "But what?"

"*But*," Jimbo said now in full smile, "now that it's been close to two years since she and Tarris were together, and with Tam–"

Jonathan shot him a harsh look that said, "don't go there."

Jimbo nodded and his smile quickly disappeared. "I think you get my drift."

"I get your drift. It's just..."

"Jonathan, come on. I saw how she looked at you. What's done is done. She and Tarris have been split longer than most marriages. Let it go and ask her out. You need to get laid. Besides, when did you get all full of morals?"

Jonathan sighed. "Maybe I will. Hey, you wanna grab a drink after the meeting this afternoon?"

Jimbo nodded and said yes, as well as one could in the course of a yawn, then intently returned to reading his file.

"What's got you so interested there, another strong Potential?"

Jimbo leaned back and pointed to his screen. "This one's a 10-year-old boy in Lawton, Oklahoma, who had been so frightened by the artillery practice at Fort Sill that he lifted one of the old projectile-firing howitzers from five miles away and threw it like a damn football. Or, at least, that's the rumor running around."

Jonathan whistled. "They're getting stronger younger, aren't they?" He began to leave, but paused and turned back. "Say, James. Where are they going to assign Georgia?"

"Hmm?" he questioned. "Oh, she's going to be a Recruiter."

"Really? And who's she going to be under?"

Jimbo, his attention apparently still in Oklahoma, only grinned.

~

"Bar of Chocolate" was one of Washington's most fashionable restaurants. Housed in an old candy factory, the turn-of-the-century building had been retrofitted for the huge bandwidth requirements of bio-tech interface cooking. Its new owners had removed much of the original processing equipment and created multilevel "personal food environments" where patrons could dine from practically anywhere in the restaurant and always have a spectacular view of the Potomac.

Jimbo and Jonathan secured a small table in the corner of the outside patio and cooled their eyes in the urban flow. The air was relatively warm for spring, and the late afternoon sun cut long shafts of light through the area. Being Friday, the sidewalks were filled with freshly released office types. These biped symbols of corporate sovereignty wore their blackest of blacks and descended into the "Chewy Nougat Center": the huge bar inside the restaurant. Here, they could drink and smoke and hunt for the lifemate – or, at least, nightmare – of their dreams. A girl in a tight biotex jumpsuit strolled past Jonathan's table. The living pattern of leopard spots undulated as if the suit were the skin of a real cat. The accuracy of detail wasn't as important as the perception, because most people didn't know the difference. The leopard, along with about a thousand other endangered species, had gone the way of the dodo. Given the kind of light upon her, the effect was eerily real, like a sick genetic experiment gone horribly wrong. Still, the whole package was oddly erotic.

"Now there's some split-tail," Jimbo noted. He took another swig from his beer.

Jonathan shot him a look.

"Hey," Jimbo said, "I can't help how I was brought up."

"I know, you're just a good ol' country boy." Jonathan sipped his drink. "I wonder what kind of work *she's* doing tonight?"

Both men keenly watched as she preened for the crowd, but just before she reached the front doors of the restaurant, she stumbled backward like she had slammed into an invisible wall. Her purse spilled onto the sidewalk, and she almost fell off her heels. She quickly pulled herself together and gathered the essentials of her life – netpad, lip enhancer, various credit and debit chips – back into the purse, and her spots, which had retreated from the trauma into one giant black island in a sea of orange, cautiously began to shift back into pattern.

Jimbo laughed into his beer.

"Did you do that?" Jonathan asked.

"I couldn't resist. I was hopin' to set one of those bad boys free."

"You're such an asshole."

"That I am, Jonathan. And proud of it." He laughed with an air of pride that seemed rooted in some deep history of Southern justification.

"So tell me about this place you rented," Jonathan inquired. "It's on the west side of the island?"

"Yeah, it's a killer house, man. All tricked out. Owned by some Texan – you know the type. The artwork alone was worth the trip. They rent it for damn near nothing, considering you're on the ocean and you get a maid, a cook and a driver. You've got to go, Jonathan. And if you can, take a girl. Man, it's the best place on earth for a little fun in the sun, if you know what I mean."

"I hear that. So, it's right on the beach?" he asked, reflectively sipping his Scotch. Jimbo nodded.

"Sounds like the place. I'm due some major R&R. That Paris assignment was screwed. Real screwed."

Suddenly, a high-pitched snap echoed about the small shopping canyon. Jonathan looked across the plaza and saw installers hoisting a giant KFBC sign up the front of an old brick building. The snap echoed again.

Jonathan followed the cabling up to the top of the hoist and saw its multistrand interlacing unthreading at the coupling near the roof. The safety wires, which should have been taut, had way too much slack. Another snap echoed. One of the installers on the street desperately began waving people off, but at this last snap, the sign broke free. The giant annijection face of Colonel Sanders started to fall, still smiling and selling the accolades of simfried, cloned chicken as it scraped down the front of the building in a spray of electric gold sparks. The leading edge caught a windowsill and crumpled, which splintered the sign into large, jagged fragments. Plastic and metal showered the crowded sidewalk. The force of the impact caused the trailing edge of the sign to fall away from the building, and the street-level installer frantically began shoving people out of the way. The safety cables snapped with two loud cracks. The installers gave up and ran. A woman screamed.

In the single moment that it had taken for the situation to spiral out of control, Jonathan had begun to go into phase, but a waiter, spinning at the scream, fell into his lap and broke his concentration. Pushing him, Jonathan jerked his attention back to the street and was startled by what he saw. Like a bizarre post-modern sculpture, the sign and its splintered fragments had slowed to a crawl above the plaza. Jonathan whipped around in his chair.

"Nice catch, slick," Jimbo said with a grin.

"I thought you caught it," Jonathan said, surprised.

Jimbo's grin instantly disappeared. He jumped to his feet and pointed to the plaza. "Look!"

Jonathan spun around. "What the hell?!" he said, and watched in horror as the sign resumed its freefall. The plaza instantly fell into chaos. People scattered in panic, screaming and stumbling. In a situation like this, the protocols of containment demanded that a Tel deal with the people first; finesse dropped out of the equation. Jimbo instantly phased and telekinetically hurled people out of the impact zone, their legs continuing to kick as if they were on solid ground. Some landed in merciless heaps, while others just kept running. The sign slammed into the pavement, transforming a thousand pounds of annijection plastics and metal into hundreds of pieces of jagged, high-velocity shrapnel. Jonathan tried desperately to envelop the spray pattern and prevent its radius from expanding, but the trajectory angles were vastly too complex to calculate in the milliseconds it took for the sign to disintegrate. Several of the deadly pieces evaded his field and sprayed omnidirectionally across the crowded sidewalks, each shard carrying with it a little element of the Colonel's promotional enthusiasm. Jimbo caught a 10-inch, delta-shaped slice of the Colonel's left cheek inches from the back of a woman's head. It dropped harmlessly to the ground. Jonathan deflected three shards comprising most of the beard and tie as they flew in formation toward an Asian family who struggled with a baby carrier. Diligently, Jimbo and Jonathan stopped as many of the pieces as they could, despite the randomness of their sorties of mutilation about the shopping canyon. One sliced through the shoulder of a boy, sending him to his knees in screams of agony. Another carved a perfect triangle from the calf of a man eating at a biomeal cart. He retched as he collapsed from pain.

While the dust settled, Jimbo and Jonathan stood motionless in a sea of hysteria. Jonathan snapped back from phase and turned to congratulate his friend. A high-pitched whipping sound dopplered into the threshold of his hearing.

He shoved Jimbo out of the way.

The multi-pointed fragment careened through the air and halted between them, right where Jimbo's head had been. For a second it hung motionless, a hideous example of their premature celebration, then it dropped to the ground and splintered the Colonel's right eye into a triptych that winked sickeningly back at them.

Both Tels took their eyes from the Colonel's and slowly looked at each other.

"Thanks..." Jimbo said, still in shock from what might have been.

"I-I didn't stop it," Jonathan acknowledged.

Jimbo frantically pulled out his netpad and began to sweep the area for who – or what – had stopped the fragment from plowing through his head.

"What are you reading?" Jonathan anxiously asked.

Jimbo didn't say anything and continued scanning.

"James?!"

"Got it...no, wait, yeah, no...wait. Damn!" He slapped the netpad against his fist. "I had 'em, but then the sigs just dropped to zero. I mean gone. They never drop like that. There's always some background res floatin' around."

Jonathan searched the area for anyone who might appear out of place. The panic in the canyon began to subside.

"You don't dis gravity at the levs I saw and not leave at least a little res," Jimbo said. He tapped the netpad against his fist. They both slowly sank into their chairs. *This*, Jonathan conjectured, *had been at least a Level 7 effort*. The heavy sign, falling at a high rate of speed, along with its vertical force – not to mention the erratic spray pattern of fragments – made for a challenging telekinetic field displacement.

"No," Jimbo said, still tapping his pad, "something's not right here...not right at all."

Jonathan watched the crowd build around the debris. The installers busily scurried about and gathered pieces to haul away in their truck. Some people had rushed to the aid of the few who had been struck down. The faint screams of sirens began to fill the air. Soon, the whole area would be swarming with EMS, police and local netnews TVid trucks, their junior reporters all jockeying for the unique paranormal angle to their 10:00 filler segment.

Jonathan picked up his drink, now more water than Scotch, and gulped it down. There had been no bulletins issued about any foreign Tels in Washington, and he seriously doubted any Level 7 Rogues would just wander into the nation's co-capital without being detected. Besides, he should have sensed the Tel's displacement a mile away. He watched the cleanup and wondered. Jimbo kept tapping his netpad.

There are plans in place...7

"**STOP.** Play back my last sentence."

"So, in conclusion, the transfer of 32 million shares will balance the portfolio in favor of the acquisition. I am not concerned..."

"Stop. Change that to: will balance the portfolio *toward* the possibility of acquisition. Resume."

"...that this transfer will signal a change in direction. Rather, it will strengthen our position and allow us to guide the future of the company more easily. If acquisition occurs, then, to the victor go the spoils. Please call me when you have had time to discuss this with your board. Take care and give my best to Leigh. Yours truly, Cyril."

"Good. Send that at 3:30 this morning with the usual protocols."

"Yes, sir. Will there be anything else?"

"Yes, resume the concerto...no, wait. Play something Mozart...mmm, ah, no. Play Pachelbel, the Kanon-Albinoni. Yes, yes, that will be excellent." Cyril Takeda leaned back. The oily water and bubbles swallowed him up to the neck. He mentally reached for his wine. The adagio began.

It was almost nine o'clock in the evening, and Takeda was beginning to relax. He glanced at the TVid, with its split screen of PREM and Kuwaiti Exchanges, and clicked it off. He was sick of the markets. He needed to languish, if even for an hour, in the sanctuary of his own thoughts. No netcalls. No decisions. No interruptions. He slowly closed his eyes.

~

"Cyril?..."

The adagio was playing.

"Cyril?!"

"In here."

Trumble threw his overcoat onto the bed, reconsidered and outstretched his hand. The coat flew back, and he hung it in a cavernous room the two of them called a closet.

"I had the most dreadful evening. Three long, boring hours with Ortiez and Toliver. Those Senate subcommittee boys can be the worst," he lamented. He entered the 1,000-square-foot master bath. The 500-gallon tub was the focal point of the room. It rose from the floor entombed in a marble platform, and was practically a Mayan altar with its eight-foot palm trees and natural rock waterfall. "I believe we made an impression on them, though."

Takeda didn't look up, apparently lost in the bouquet of his wine. "Did you convince them of our urgency?"

"Yes."

"And will they now vote their...conscience?"

"Oh, I'm *sure* they will."

Takeda laughed.

"As I was saying, those Senate subcommittee boys...God, is this what we pay for? They're a joke. All they're concerned about is their damn reelection." Trumble yanked at his tie, and it slapped out of the collar. "We need to move out of this town. Somewhere quiet—"

"Like Nice?"

"Possibly. I was thinking more tropical. There's that island we were looking to buy. I believe it's still available—"

"*Please*, Jeffrey. Don't start with that again. You know how I hate the bugs." Takeda disappeared under the bubbles.

Exhausted, Trumble eschewed his upbringing and threw his clothes into a pile at the base of the TVid. He began studying his face in the large vanity mirror that hung in the middle of the dressing area. On the other side of the room, a long white robe left its hook. As it floated, its arms and body filled with the rush of air, creating the eerie appearance that a ghost had donned the robe and was sneaking up on Trumble. He reached back his arms, and the robe gently slipped onto his body. He tied its thick sash around his waist and resumed his study of the mole that had competed for attention on his face for the last 30 years.

Takeda's head broke the surface of the water. "Why don't you just get that thing removed? They've had the technology for, oh, I don't know...200 *years*."

Trumble didn't answer. Takeda rolled his eyes and slipped back under.

"Cyril, I'm worried."

"What?!" Takeda asked, bobbing amid the islands of bubbles and wiping the foam from his face. "What are you worried about now?"

Trumble hesitated. "Jonathan."

Takeda nodded knowingly.

"He's a smart, ambitious boy," Trumble continued. "He's going to discover his true nature soon. We can't hide it from him forever. He is, after all, our future, and it would be in our best interest to nurture that potential. Am I right?"

"Does he still believe his plane incident was...*unique?*"

"As far as I know he still thinks that it was an Extreme Condition Situation, and he hasn't reproduced that kind of grav intensity again, either in the lab or in the field. At least...not yet."

Takeda eyed Trumble. "How's his training going? Are they still holding him at level?"

"Yes, yes, they are," Trumble said. He tore himself away from the mirror. "But all it's going to take is an assignment where another ECS comes up and he'll begin to develop again. And this time, we're not going to be able to contain him. Look at what he did to that French security man. My God, all he did was look at the poor fellow, and his head practically imploded."

"Oh, Jeffrey," Takeda said, "so he overgrav'd. It's a natural reaction—"

"Piss off, Cyril. There's nothing natural about it. The boy's becoming downright unstable. You know that! Remember the bus in San Francisco? It was one of the worse containment issues we've ever had to deal with. My God, I think we still are! I swear, sometimes you defend him like he's your own damn son." Trumble returned to his mole.

"Jeffrey, you know we must protect Jonathan from himself. But don't worry ..." He took a sip from his wine. "...if Jonathan does begin to develop again, there are plans in place. You know that...Jeffrey?..."

Trumble didn't respond.

"Is that...*jealousy* I'm sensing?"

Trumble continued to analyze his mole.

"Jeffrey Trumble, are you—"

"You're not telepathic, Cyril."

"*Jeffrey?*"

"No, I'm bloody well not!" Trumble reluctantly faced his partner.

Cyril Takeda rose out of the water like a leviathan standing up into the clouds. Large clumps of bubbles began to rise and hover around his body. He smiled a slow, devilish grin.

"My God, Cyril," Trumble mused. "What's on your mind, hmm?"

Takeda stretched out his arms. "Come here, *lover.*"

Jeffrey Trumble smiled as the robe slipped off his body and glided back to its hook.

I owe you one...8

JONATHAN approached his Georgetown walk-up.

"Are you going to need a ride when you leave on your vacation?" Mazza yelled from the driver's side window.

"What? Oh, yeah. Sure...I'll call you."

"You okay there, Mr. Kortel?"

"Yeah, Mazza, I'm okay."

"Still thinking about the sign?"

"Yeah. There's something about it that bothers me..." He turned back to the car.

Mazza, his arms folded, was leaning out the window. "It's 'cause you didn't pick up on the other Tel before the grav field was created, isn't it?"

Jonathan thought for a moment. "You're right, I should have picked up on it. And what really disturbs me is that this was a Level 7 display. We haven't had any Level 7's in D.C. for months. I mean, it was a powerful grav flux, and James didn't even capture it with his netpad. I don't get it."

"Could be a Rogue, or maybe the *u'ebitsche*."

"Nah. They wouldn't enter the D.C. Zone. That's way too ballsy. No, this was something else." He looked quizzically at Mazza.

"An Indie?" Mazza asked, raising his thick, Baltic eyebrows.

"That's what I'm thinking."

Mazza whistled.

Indies were advanced Potentials who not only recognized their ability, but thought they could master it on their own. They came around only once in a lifetime, and of the 11 known Indies in the history of the Tel world, just one had even survived. The Tel ability was an efficacious addiction, and without proper training and guidance, the sheer intoxication of it could quickly spiral someone into deep trouble. Some were injured or killed in reckless, self-induced level tests. For others, the tremendous stress of overuse debilitated their bodies to the point of death, or, worse yet, left them sucking their meals through a tube the rest of their lives. The only person to have lived a "normal" life never really developed to her full potential. By the time she was discovered, she was in her late 50s, and had so many psychological scars from dealing with her ability – which kept her on the fringe of society all of her life – that it had been impossible to integrate her into the Tel culture.

If this had been a true Indie display, as Jonathan feared, it was imperative for the Agency to find this person before he or she caused irreparable damage. Even worse than someone being hurt, the Tel culture could be widely exposed, and the containment issue would grow exponentially with each passing day.

Jonathan shrugged off his thoughts. "Well, it's not my problem. It's James's now. I'm on vacation. Good night, Mazza. I'll call you when I know when I'm leaving."

He watched Mazza drive off and began walking up the steps. As he approached the landing, a searing pain shot through his head like a needle piercing his skull. The intensity drove him to one knee. He clutched his forehead and almost vomited over the side of the stairs. Then, as fast as it had appeared, the pain vanished, leaving a thick, gritty sensation, as if a chemical had been released and was spreading into every recess of his brain. He slowly stood up, shaking from the voracity and suddenness. He wiped a little sweat from his brow and tried to swallow, but found his throat dry and raw. He reached for the doorknob, but his vision was blurred. A strange sensation of seasickness was creeping through his body. He gingerly sat on the top step and cradled his head in his hands. He had been warned that as he developed he might experience sudden and severe headaches.

After a minute, the sensations passed, and his vision returned. Collecting himself, he entered his home and slowly walked down the hallway toward the kitchen, only to stop twice as the sensations returned and briefly held him in a state of *mal de mer*.

"Lights, Max," he ordered. He stumbled to the refrigerator.

"Jonathan, is there something wrong? Are you ill?"

"No, Max, I've just been thinking too hard."

"Sir?"

"I'm just having another reaction...probably from those grav exercises I did before Paris." He collapsed onto a stool and leaned heavily on the counter. "Water, Max. Cold, with ice." A glass slid into view in the front of the refrigerator, and the plexi door moved aside. He put the cold drink to his forehead and quietly sat as the condensation numbed the residual pain.

"Do you need your medication?"

"No, Max, it's passed." He swept the glass from side to side. "Do I have any messages, here or at the loft in Chicago?"

"Yes, sir. Here you have one net message from James McCarris, one from SATVid Plus, one from Georgia–"

"Stop. One from Georgia?"

"Yes."

Jonathan sipped the water and closed his eyes. "She leave a message?"

"No."

"An ID?"

"Yes."

"Recall it."

He placed an ice cube to his temple. Georgia's holoimage appeared on the countertop.

"Hello, Jonathan...hey, what's wrong?"

"Oh, nothing. Just a bad headache. I saw that you called, but you didn't leave a message."

"I didn't want to bother you."

"You're never bothering me, Georgia, you know that. What's up?"

"I was wondering if you..." she hesitated, "...wanted to have dinner...tonight?"

The pain all but disappeared. He opened his eyes. "Yes...yes, that would be great. What are you hungry for?"

"I'm new here. I have no idea where to go in D.C."

"Are you up for high energy, or quiet conversation?"

"Maybe a little of both."

"I know just the place." He popped the ice cube in his mouth.

~

The bar in the Chewy Nougat Center was circular and seemed to have no visible means for the bartenders to enter or exit. Yet, they appeared and disappeared as if choreographed with the driving beat of the club's music. People shimmered around the bar like a mass of neon tetras, edging in and out of the hot shafts of light that cut from floor to ceiling. Standing out conspicuously were the Net Keepers, an androgenous government army of tech masters who kept the world's T-12 lines in order. Their silver, Czech-made Micro-Night Shades, which kept them continuously jacked to the net, reflected the shafts of light and sent prismatic ovals fluttering about the dark room. Peppered into the throng were the Potomac People, the new symbol of power in Washington. Sporting jaunty yellow bow ties, they looked tragically lost against the midtier business types scaling the walls of corporate dominance, where bioaugmentation wasn't a luxury, it was a rite of passage. This legion of narcissism perched their manufactured beauty strategically at the bar, where they flaunted their surgeons' visions of the perfect human much as one might have sported a fur or a diamond a century earlier. Their casual perfection reflected an amalgam of interpretations, all desperate followers of a constantly shifting "ideal" paraded in the faces and bodies that populated the popular media.

Jonathan observed it all from the comfort of a booth he had secured with a little Tel influence. He rarely called upon his ability to obtain something as inconsequential as a good table, but tonight was special. She was special.

He spied Georgia swimming through the teeming sea of black, her tall, thin frame effortlessly parting the full-length trenchcoats and drably patterned knee shirts popularized by the German netbands. Her mock turtleneck pullover was the color of an old school bus. Its ribbed stitchwork gave the appearance of an old silicon circuit board. Her thigh-high boots were made from the finest genetically grown eel, and they made her appear taller. He watched her as she searched the bar. She wasn't looking for him, she was sensing for him. He had thrown up a field wall around himself, just to make it interesting. He let her circle twice, then dropped the field. She instantly turned in his direction and caught his stare through the crowd. She smiled and wagged her finger.

Strutting up to his booth, she stopped and put her hands on her hips. "Very funny, Mr. Kortel."

"Just testing," he replied. He leaned over and kissed her cheek.

"This is a great place," she said, settling into the booth. "Do you come here a lot?"

"Yes. As a matter of fact, James and I were here yesterday and a really strange thing happened—"

"Drinks, food, candy or oxygen?" the holowaiter asked, suddenly appearing.

"Ah, Oban. No water, just lots of ice, thanks," Jonathan answered.

"I'll have a vodka tonic. House is fine, thank you very much." Georgia studied the pixelated holoimage that glowed its simgirl likeness in the darkness of the bar. Its manga eyes bright and spread wide, each cast its own curved rectangle of phony light reflection. Its spiked pink hair reverberated as the raster lines twitched every 3,000 cycles. Vintage.

A human waitress passed through the image, disrupting the connection. "Thanks, Kasis!" it snipped in a shrill electric voice that reminded Jonathan of old Japanese anime. "Okay, one house vodka-t and one Oban, no H20. Solid." Suddenly it was gone, and the booth darkened.

Georgia shook her head.

"Hey," Jonathan said, "you wanted a little high energy and a—"

"Oh, if you want food or whatever, just press the big red button there," the holowaiter said, suddenly reappearing and pointing across the booth. It disappeared without a sound.

"Well," Jonathan exclaimed, still staring at the space formerly occupied by the holowaiter. "Hungry?"

"Yes, I am. Let's see what the Chewy Nougat has in the way of some dinner." Georgia pressed the red button, and two holomenus appeared in the center of their table. She tentatively touched hers, and it flipped through its pages. "So, mister big-time biochef, what do you recommend?"

"*Former* big-time biochef," Jonathan said. He smiled at her through the holomenus. "I like the burgers. They're big, dumb and..." he leaned forward, "...taste like they're damn real."

"Really? How do they manage that?"

"It's in the programming. But how they get their ground beef texture is beyond me. It's very impressive work."

Kasis slid up to their booth. She smiled tersely as she reached through the holomenus and placed their drinks in front of them. "Enjoy," she quipped, turning back toward the bar while spinning her tray with her index finger. She stepped off the platform and was swallowed by the fray.

"Friendly here, aren't they?" Georgia said sarcastically, and she took a sip from her drink.

"Yeah, but you can't beat the show."

Jonathan and Georgia settled back, each studying the other. "It's good..." they both said simultaneously. They laughed.

"Go ahead," he said.

"It's really good to see you, Jonathan. It's been too long." She focused on him with a presence that he didn't recall ever seeing from her.

"You, too. You look so, so..."

"Healthy?"

"Yeah, healthy. What have you been doing?"

"It's what I haven't been doing." She pensively swizzled her drink's ice with a finger. "I haven't been with Tarris, for one."

"I wondered about that. What happened, you know...after he left?"

"I just laid low. After he disappeared, I stayed on at the compound, but only for a few weeks. I got a place closer to Taos. It was a lot easier to get to and from the casino."

"Why'd you leave?"

Georgia reflected. "Too many memories."

"Yeah, well. I know what that's about," he said, remembering.

"I heard about Tam—"

"All right," interrupted the holowaiter, "do we know what we'll be having tonight, or do you need a little more time?"

"Yes," Jonathan said. "We'll both have the burger. Hers will be dry, prepared well-done, and mine will have everything, medium-well."

"Good choices!" the holowaiter exclaimed, and its pixels blurred to nothing.

"You remembered," Georgia affectionately said, leaning onto the table.

Jonathan moved closer. He remembered the feeling they had shared when he said goodbye to her at Tarris's compound. They took long, slow sips.

"I heard about Tamara," she said tentatively. "I'm sorry that had to happen."

Jonathan's attention shifted to a young couple at another booth. They were kissing. "Me, too," he said softly.

"It's a shame they had to erase her—"

Jonathan motioned for her to stop and shook his head. "Let's not go there, if that's all right?"

Georgia smiled. "Sure. I'm sorry to have brought it up."

"No, no...it's all right. I'm over it now. It's just..." He searched his drink as if it contained his answer. Georgia took his hand. "Never mind," he said. He gently squeezed her fingers. "So!" he declared, pulling away from her. "You're going to be working with James?"

"Yes, this ought to be interesting." She brushed some hair off her face. "How's he doing these days?"

"Still basically the same ol' Jimbo, but he's changed some." He ruminated on the crowd around the bar. "We all have."

"Kasis will be right out with your food. Do we need a refill, hmm?" the holowaiter asked.

Startled, they both nodded without looking up.

"Oh, sorry. Bad timing." The booth darkened again.

~

Kasis brought their food and another round. While they ate, Jonathan told Georgia about his time at the Agency. He talked in depth about the training she could expect – and about the politics that drove the world's most secretive culture.

"God, Jonathan. It sounds like they've been keeping you busy. Have you had any time off?"

"As a matter of fact, no. But I'm going to take some time here in the next couple of days. I'm thinking of going to Tortola. Know anything about it?–" Suddenly, the same sharp pain that he had experienced on his steps sliced through his head. "Oh, shit," he groaned, grabbing at his temples.

"Jonathan?" Georgia asked, alarmed.

The pain intensified. It drilled down into the core of his brain and embedded itself deep within his mind. "My...my medication," he said, trying to retrieve it from his inside coat pocket. He began to slip into unconsciousness. He slumped forward onto the table, but was violently thrown back against the booth.

"Oh, Jesus, Jonathan!" Georgia jumped to her feet but was instantly slammed back against the booth and held firmly in place. She watched in horror as Jonathan's eyes rolled back and blood ran from his nose over his mouth and chin. He went limp and began to slide onto his side.

Georgia instantly went into phase and created a field flux wall around the booth. Struggling to his side, she could feel the attacking grav field punching against her telekinetic strength. She propped Jonathan up, wiping at the blood with a napkin and stuffing his nostrils in a desperate attempt to stop the flow.

"So," the holowaiter declared, "how's the food?" Its glow was wavering from the gravitational distortion and filled the booth with a nightmarish cerulean hue. "Oh!" it said, glaring down at them, "gotta go!"

Jonathan was now leaning heavily against Georgia's shoulder. She wrapped her arm around him and began slapping at his cheek. "Jonathan, don't leave me," she pleaded firmly. "Come on, come on. Don't go under!"

He slowly surfaced. The pain had ebbed, but he was disoriented and struggling to breathe. "Oh, shit," he coughed, straightening. "What happened?"

Georgia felt the grav pressure evanesce off of her field. "I don't know, but let's get the hell out of here," she said into his ear and helped him out of the booth. Keeping her guard up, she scanned the bar with her netpad for anyone or anything that might appear out of the norm.

"Be careful," Jonathan said above the pounding beat of the music. "They might triangulate on us."

She shot him a look, and quickly reshaped her field to plow through the crowd around the bar. "How are you doing?" she asked as they crept along. Her grav field shoved people aside like the bow of a boat carving through an ice flow.

"Better," he answered hoarsely.

"You have any strength yet?"

"Some."

"Good," she said, slipping into professional mode, "we might need it."

They emerged from the crowd and headed toward the front doors. "Everything all right here?" the holowaiter asked, suddenly blocking their path.

"Will you please get the hell out of here!" Georgia said. She expanded her field and disrupted the image's connection.

"Bitch!" the holowaiter shrieked. Its pixels dispersed into a cloud of electronic vapor.

Leading Jonathan out of the bar and toward the parking area she asked, "Did you drive?"

"No...no I didn't." He straightened and tried to collect himself.

"Let me take you home." She handed the valet her chip card.

Jonathan swept back his hair and wiped at the blood that had spread over his shirt. He noticed Georgia's sweater was stained as well. "Sorry about your clothes."

"Hey, don't worry. Let's get you home and cleaned up." She kept scanning the parking area for anything unusual. "I don't feel safe exposed out here in the open."

"That was pretty fast phasing you did in there," he said. "I owe you one."

The valet pulled Georgia's car around, and they climbed in. She pulled into the Interway traffic, while Jonathan dug the medication out of his coat pocket. He placed the small pneumatic infuser to his neck and clicked the injector. It made a short hiss sound. He settled back against the seat, finally able to relax.

"Jonathan, what happened back there?" Georgia asked.

"Just give me a moment, please, while the medication takes effect." He folded his arms across his chest and closed his eyes. The cabin fell silent as the car sped through the narrow Georgetown streets.

"I didn't know you were that strong," Jonathan said, breaking the silence. "I mean, that sure felt like a Level 7 grav field you put out. I thought you were only a Level 6." He kept his eyes shut. "It takes something seriously major to jump a level like you did."

Georgia, her attention focused on the road, didn't respond. "Two levels...actually," she finally said, just above a whisper.

I want you...9

THE task lights in the kitchen intensified and brought the richness of the marble countertops into full detail. Jonathan sat on a stool, his head having a viscid feeling, as if someone had poured a bag of Polycrete into his skull to slowly harden.

Georgia went to the refrigerator.

"*Deja vu...*" he said to himself.

"What?" she questioned from inside the freezer.

"Oh, nothing." He rubbed his temples.

"What did you mean back in the bar when you said 'they might triangulate on us'?"

"I've had migraines all my life, but lately, I've been getting these monster ones. The guys in the lab say it's normal, especially with all the exercises they've been putting me through. That infuser has some drug that's supposed to neutralize the effects, but it doesn't feel like it's doing shit tonight."

Georgia placed a cold gelpack against his forehead. "There, how's that feel?" Jonathan closed his eyes and forced a smile.

"I'll take that as a 'Thank you, Georgia, that feels sooo good!'" She stepped back and folded her arms. "You haven't answered my question."

"Tonight didn't feel like one of those migraines. It felt different...like we were–"

"Being attacked?" Georgia said with an edge of sarcasm. She wiped at his chin and neck with a warm towel.

"That's just the Rogue in you talking." Jonathan tilted his head back and pulled the gelpack over his eyes. "No. It felt more like being...tested."

"That didn't feel like any test to me. Here, let me get you some water." Georgia turned back toward the refrigerator.

Jonathan gently grabbed her arm. "Hey," he said, his eyes still covered. She stepped between his knees. He let the gelpack fall from his eyes into his lap. He placed it on the counter. She was conspicuously averting his look. "*Two* levels?" he questioned. He reached for her other shoulder.

Georgia sheepishly smiled that smile. "A girl's gotta do what a girl's gotta do."

He softly brushed some hair behind her ear and let his finger follow the line of her jaw. He held his touch at the bottom of her chin. Her smile fell away, and they instinctively leaned toward each other.

"Jonathan," Max interrupted, "you have a netcall."

"Who is it?" Jonathan snapped, reluctant to release the spell of nature.

"James McCarris."

His eyes met hers. Her grin returned.

"Okay...but no visual." He leaned back and put his finger to his lips.

"Jonathan?"

"Hey, James, what's up?" He folded his arms. Georgia walked around the counter.

"I've got that info on Tortola you wanted. It should be in your netmail."

"Great, thanks. I'll let you know what I decide."

"Hey, Jonathan?"

"Yeah?"

There was a pause. "You don't mind...you know, having Georgia working with me...do you?"

Jonathan glanced over to Georgia, who was leaning on the counter. She smiled and shrugged. "What do you mean?" he replied.

"I always sensed that there might have been something... you know...between you two—"

"James," Jonathan interrupted, "don't worry. I don't have any issues with Georgia working with you. I think she's a great lady. And no, there's nothing between us, okay?"

"All right, thanks...I just wanted to make sure. I'll catch up with you tomorrow. Good night."

"See ya, James." Jonathan shook his head, hopped off the stool and headed around the counter. "That guy, I'll tell you, he can be the biggest—"

Georgia, her back to him, was removing her blood-stained top. "No offense," she said, pulling the bright yellow sweater over her head, "but I want to get to this blood before it sets." Her long black hair fell across her shoulders. "Now..." she slowly turned to face him, "...where were we?"

Jonathan gathered her to himself. He unhooked her bra and let it slide gently off her breasts. He kissed her neck and savored her perfume. "That stain," he exhaled, "will just have to wait."

~

A candle's flicker sent hypnotic streaks of mikado and maize to dance upon the dark walls. Jonathan lay on his side watching a small bead of sweat slide down Georgia's back. He leaned over and let it roll onto his tongue. He had tasted her and wanted more.

Georgia shuddered. "God," she whispered, rolling to face him, "don't get me started again." She reached for the edge of his jaw and let her fingers glide down its line. Then she dragged her finger down his chest and over his stomach, until she found what she wanted, and squeezed slowly, letting her nails dig to the border of pleasure.

Jonathan moaned and softly kissed her. "You know," he said, "I've thought about you."

"Me, too," Georgia whispered. "I often wondered, you know, where you were, what you might be doing." Her fingers went to his chest and playfully entwined themselves in the hair he had at the top of his sternum. "You're getting gray."

"The hell I am," he said, looking down. "I'm only 31."

"Made you look." She laughed.

He reached over and pinched her nipple.

"Ouch," she giggled, "not fair."

"Ha! Made you...say...ah...ouch, or something..."

Georgia rolled her eyes.

"That didn't work, did it?"

"No," she said, falling back against the pillows, "but nice try, Mr. World's Most Powerful Tel." She rubbed at her breast.

Jonathan lost his grin and sat up.

She ran her hand down his back. "Hey...what's the matter?"

He didn't answer.

"What? Tell me."

"Remember me telling you this afternoon about James and I seeing something weird?"

"Yes, why?...What happened?"

"It's bugging me. I mean, we're outside the Bar of Chocolate having a drink, just watching the world, when this huge sign they're putting up across the street snaps free from its guides and falls. This is a huge sign. It's got to weigh at least half a ton." He rubbed his face at the memory. "And just as I phase to catch it, it stops, just for a second, like it's in a grav field...I mean, it had to be in one." He turned and faced her. "I thought James had caught it, but he thought I had. Then it crashes, and all hell breaks loose. I mean, we jumped into a Situation 6 mode so fast....There's pieces flying all over the place. It's a really screwed up ECS. And just when we think we've caught them all, this fragment flies right for James. I shove him out of the way, and the damn thing freezes right in front of our faces! James gets his pad out and scans practically the entire eastern seaboard, but it doesn't show a damn thing."

"My God. Do you think it was the Rogues?"

Jonathan shrugged.

"Russians?"

"Nah...it was *weird*."

Georgia sat up. "An Indie?" she asked quietly.

Jonathan didn't answer.

"Shit..." she softly exclaimed.

"Yeah. That's what I thought, too," he said. "Until tonight."

They both watched the candle slowly die, bringing the frantic dance of the shadows to a quiet and serene halt. The flame hissed into oblivion when it drowned in its own wax. A thin line of smoke rose from the charred wick.

Jonathan thought back to the bar. "What happened tonight?" he asked the fresh blackness.

"I think someone was after you."

"Maybe," he said. He picked at the dried blood inside his nose. "Welcome to my world."

"What? You mean this has happened before?"

"Yeah, sure. I've been challenged...oh, I don't know, a dozen times now? I had one last week...in Paris."

"God, Jonathan." She sat up behind him and wrapped her arms around his chest. "Have you been hurt?"

"Nah, I'm always too fast for them. It's kind of unfair." He swept his fingers through his hair. "Until tonight, that is."

Georgia hesitated. "You know, tonight sure felt like a Rogue move."

"Really?"

"Yes." She nestled her chin on his shoulder. "At least two. One for me, and one to get you."

"And a third for good measure?"

"Possibly..."

"And you know what's really weird about all this? I should've sensed them coming."

"Don't be too hard on yourself. I felt a lot of displacement in that bar. There were a lot people and energies moving around. They just caught us off guard. Are you going to report it?"

"I usually don't report the ones that happen on my time."

Georgia pulled his head around to face hers and frowned.

"Look," he said. He wrapped his arm around her waist. "There are a lot of reports to fill out, not to mention the debrief. Besides, I'm on vacation."

"At least go and get checked out. Please...*for me?*"

"Okay. If it makes you feel any better, I'll go in and have Franks run some tests...just to make sure." Jonathan pulled back and looked at her through the darkness. He could barely make her out. The slight bump at the bridge of her nose. The silhouette of her thick black hair. The little cleft at the base of her chin. Georgia leaned close to his face. He could feel her breath against his lips.

"Come here," she whispered with all the seriousness of a woman who was used to getting what she wanted. She leaned closer, her lips grazing his. "I want you," she barely uttered and gently pulled him back down onto the bed.

Using trust... 10

JAMES McCarris wasn't a big man. It wasn't his size that intimidated people; it was his demeanor. James was the kind of man who could get things done without the added influence of height or muscle. He wore his 5-foot-11, 195 pounds like guys who were 6-10, 280, and he usually did it smiling. Like an alien in a sci-fi vid who grinned at an expendable extra while its tail was sneaking up from behind, James McCarris could smooth talk anyone into thinking he was becoming their new best friend. He was a true Southerner. From the real South. The "Old South." And if you said you were from the South in New America, you could mean the Yucatan. And James McCarris wasn't from Old Mexico, he was from Savannah – where men still rose to their feet when a lady entered a room. That's why he asked most people to call him Jimbo.

Glancing about Takeda's office, his eyes darted from the desk to the painting to the sofa and back to the desk. He shifted his weight back to his left foot. He passed his fingers through his wavy red hair, thinking that this time it would be perfect.

"James!" Takeda said as he entered the room. "Please, have a seat." His black-gloved hand gestured like a claw at one of the oversized chairs in front of the desk where he ran the Agency.

Jimbo knew not to lean back. Anyone who did ended up looking like a child in the huge chair – their legs off the floor and body sunk into the soft, overstuffed cushion. Just the way Takeda planned it.

"How are the Recruiters these days?" Takeda asked.

Jimbo's back straightened at the simple question. He knew Takeda never asked simple questions. "Doing well, thank you, sir," he replied with no hint of the suspicion that was welling inside him.

"James, relax. This is not an inquiry. The Recruiter Unit is one of the most important divisions we have. And, I must say, since you've taken charge, people are *very* pleased."

"Thank you, sir."

Takeda leaned back into his chair and intently studied the Southerner. "I've finally read your report....We are sorry for the deception about Zvara, but it was at his request. Too much history, you know," he said with a smirk. He leaned forward and moved a file pad to its correct position on the desk. "We paid for the surgery."

Jimbo grinned just a little.

"You have to admit," Takeda continued while he pulled at his gloves and glanced out the windows, "learning under him did have its rewards, did it not?"

"Yes, sir. It did."

"There, I knew it. Well, he's gone. Such a pity. He was a bit..." he trained his attention on Jimbo, "...unbalanced."

"A bit."

The room fell silent as Takeda scrutinized Jimbo's bright blue eyes. Jimbo didn't flinch.

"James," Takeda said, abruptly standing. He walked to the windows and stared out over the Potomac. The morning sun defined the river with glittering ripples that lacerated the reflection of the trees on the Virginia side. "I need to discuss something that's a bit...*sensitive.*" He placed his hands behind his back. "Jonathan Kortel is very important to us, and I'm sure you would agree that his well-being is essential to this organization. We all like Jonathan very much, and we don't want any unwanted influences distracting him from his studies, do we?"

"No, sir."

Takeda paused for a moment as he took in the view. "Would you say you're *friends* with him?"

"Uh, yes," Jimbo replied, on edge from the odd line of questioning. "I got to know him during my assignment, especially when he crossed. I think we've become fairly close."

"And would you say he *trusts* you?"

Jimbo hesitated. "Yes...yes, I think he does."

"Good," Takeda said, never looking away from the window, "because we might need to use some of that trust."

Jimbo's back straightened even more.

Maybe another time...11

"...**NINETY**-three, ninety-four, ninety-five, ninety-six, ninety-seven, ninety-eight, ninety-nine...one hundred."

Jonathan relaxed onto his back, his knees up and his ankles tucked tight against his butt. He looked at the foundation cracks that ran like gray rivers from the subcontinent of the ceiling to the shores where the walls met the molding. NNN was clicked in, its morning news anchors droning on about regen'd pork and the recent FDA findings that it could cause colon cancer in cloned lab mice. They segued to the next news segment: "...those poor mice. Isn't it a shame, CeCe? In other news, scientists have discovered a shift in the biodegeneration curve that has been occurring in the former Hawaiian Islands–"

"Off!"

The vidscreen instantly cut to black.

Jonathan put his fingers to his wrist. *Pulse rate was good,* he thought, and sat up.

"Sir," Max said, "your car is here."

~

Jonathan threw his gear bag hard into the backseat and followed it, landing on his side. The car shut its door.

"Mazza, this is one beautiful day!"

"Ah...yes, sir. It is," an unexpected voice said from the front seat.

A jolt like liquid electricity shot through Jonathan's nerves. He sat up. "You're not Mazza! What's going on? They didn't tell me about a driver change!"

The carbon-smoked, ballistic-proof window behind the driver slipped down into the divider wall, which forced the rate of time inside the car to accommodate its slow, even speed. A girl with long, curly dark hair turned and acknowledged Jonathan. "Good morning, Mr. Kortel. My name is Sasha Kuntar. Mazza has been reassigned.

I believe he's moving up."

Jonathan cautiously studied her. She was foreign, but with a look he couldn't process. Her sharp cheekbones set off a pair of dark green eyes – the kind Jimbo called "bedroom eyes." Her hair was curly – not in an ethnic, tangled sort of way, just curly. Maybe Italian, or possibly Arabic. "Let me see your pad...Sasha," he asked warily.

She passed him her netpad. It floated through the opening and stopped, suspended in front of his face.

He carefully studied her file. "Okay...okay, thanks." He leaned back against his bag. "And I like to keep the window down....You know, that elitist crap. I hate that."

The car glided through the morning traffic, and Jonathan caught a reflection of Sasha in the nav screen. She was staring at him intently.

"Sorry about back there," he said.

"Sir?"

Her face appeared on his vidscreen. She looked pretty, to him, in spite of the distortion. "My swearing...I apologize if that offended you."

Sasha nodded, and a slow smile spread across her face. She shifted her attention back to the road, and the screen cut out.

When they went over Key Bridge, he caught her staring again. He leaned forward into the window and folded his arms. He could smell her bath rinse, or whatever she used. It was citrusy, but not heavy, with a sexy edge to it. "So," he asked, watching the road out the front window, "what have they said?"

"Sir?"

"Call me Jonathan, please." He patted her shoulder and felt her muscle under the light mesh of her coat. She was hard and athletic. "I'm just asking because I've caught you looking more at me than the road."

"Well," she hesitated, "come on. I mean, you're Jonathan Kortel. Everyone knows about you." She turned to look at him and smiled. A sensor buzzed.

"Ah...the road?" he said, gesturing.

"Sorry." She jerked the toggle and the car vaulted back into position. "You are just a little intimidating."

"But...?"

"But you're not what I thought."

"Oh? What'd you expect?"

"I don't know exactly. You're more...more," she looked back again, this time keeping the car fixed in position. "Sweet."

Surprised, Jonathan pulled back. "Sweet?..."

"Okay. Bad word choice. How 'bout...gentle?"

Jonathan's expression questioned her again.

"This is not how I wanted this to go." She slapped the top of the toggle.

"It's all right, Sasha...I think I know what you're driving at." He laughed. "I bet you thought I'd be this big hairy asshole kind of guy, all tough and full of himself – right?"

"Well..."

"Hey, look," he rested his chin on his arm, "I'm pretty new to this stuff, too. I'm still trying to get my level strength under control. In fact, that's my training on Mondays, Wednesdays and–"

"Fridays," she finished. She glanced at him out of the corner of her eye. "I know your complete schedule. But I thought you were on vacation."

"Yeah, I haven't figured out where to go yet. So in the meantime, I thought I'd get in a session with Franks. That's why I called the service."

She nodded, keeping her attention on the road. An awkward quiet filled the cabin.

"So," he asked, breaking the silence, "where are you from?"

"Around..."

"Around where?"

"I'm a military brat. We moved around a lot. My father did real special ops stuff. I didn't really know him well."

"What was he? Army NetForce?"

"You could say that. He was all over. Always off doing something he couldn't talk about. You know how dads get..." She suddenly caught herself. "Oh, sir. I'm...I'm so sorry. I–"

"Don't worry, it's all right. I'm used to it, really. I appreciate the thought, though." The cabin fell silent again, as Jonathan leaned back against the seat and watched the Virginia landscape rush by.

~

They left the Interway, and Sasha resumed control and piloted the car down some rural roads to the satellite campus of *Citenikelet Investments*. Tracked since they entered Virginia, when they approached the campus, their displacement signatures identified them to the Agency's system, and the gates opened automatically. Their signatures were like fingerprints, displacing gravity and registering a pattern as unique as a voiceprint or a DNA sequence. Sasha drove to the main testing lab and pulled the car around the back.

"You've been studying up on me," Jonathan said. He collected his gear bag and stepped from the car.

"I don't blame you," she replied. "I'm sure you get tired of all the attention."

"It gets a bit much, the staring and all."

"I'll see you in three hours. Have a good session." The car shut its door, and Sasha drove off.

Jonathan approached the lab, or "gym," as everyone called it. Its name seemed appropriate, given that the mental exercises that took place in it were as strenuous as anything performed in a physical workout. The equipment was definitely not your typical health club, though. Reading his dis sig, the doors slid open.

Ashton Franks had been an Agency man for most of his life. He was one of the only Level 8's teaching Advanced Field-Flux Technique, and since Jonathan's arrival at the Agency, they had gotten along almost like father and son. Franks looked up from behind a biomed scanner, his handlebar moustache seeming whiter than usual. "G'day to ya, Jonathan!" the Aussie bellowed.

"Ashton," Jonathan replied. "Did you get my message...about running some tests this morning?"

"Oh, my dear boy. We're...ah, off-line for a bit," he said awkwardly.

"You weren't when I scheduled in."

"Right, yes...well. We've had a bit of a snafu in the systems...ah, the field harmonics and such," he answered nervously. "We can't test our star pupil without the harmonics in calibration, now can we?"

Jonathan looked around, and upraised faces quickly disappeared into work stations. "Yeah...right, Ashton. No, we can't." He scrutinized the senior Tel. "Maybe I'll go try the Grav Center."

"Right, then," Franks said. "Come back when we're up and running. G'day to ya." He wiped the bottom of his moustache with the back of his hand and went back to calibrating the scanner.

~

When Jonathan entered the Grav Center, he found that it was booked for the day, which seemed odd, because the system had shown that it was available from 10:00 to 12:00. Again, he received a conspicuously nervous reception from the center's director. Resigned that the morning was a bust, he called Sasha. Her image came up on the netpad's vidscreen. She was working out at the Training Center.

"How's your testing going?" she asked, breathless. She appeared to be biking through a lush countryside in one of the Center's virt booths.

"It's not."

She frowned while she peddled furiously. "What happened, Franks spill his coffee in one of the TCV panels?"

"Just some systems glitch. How's...ah, where are you?"

"I've programmed a beautiful day here in France. You should join me."

"Nah, I think I'll just head back home. How much longer do you have...I mean, I wouldn't want to interrupt the *Tour de France*."

"About another 30 minutes," she said, crouching down to enter a steep curve. "But I can bring the car around immediately if you'd–"

"No, please...finish up. I'll meet you up there."

Sasha looked over, smiled, then raised her butt and bore down on the pedals.

~

Jonathan slowly approached Sasha's virt booth and began watching her on the monitor. It displayed the occupant in the context of the program, and he intently followed her through a series of sharp curves. Her body leaned and shifted in perfect sync with the bike.

"She's an excellent rider," said a voice from the equipment. Probably the guy monitoring the virt booth.

"Yes, she is," Jonathan answered, not taking his attention from the monitor.

"You want me to shut the program down, Mr. Kortel?"

"No...no, that's okay. Let her finish."

"You know, you could step in."

"While it's running? That would be way out of line."

"Not for Sasha....She's tough. She can take it."

Jonathan hesitated. "Well...I really shouldn't."

"Come on, let's have some fun." The seal to the inner service door broke with a hiss, and Jonathan hesitantly stooped through the service hatch.

Entering a running virtbooth was like stepping into another reality. Jonathan emerged beside a rural country road near the outskirts of a small French village. "Where are we?" he asked casually, knowing that without a holosuit, he would be a disorienting visual for Sasha. The holoimage of the village began passing through him.

To Sasha, it appeared that he suddenly materialized in the tall grass that skirted the road and sped right along with her. In reality, though, he was standing on a 50-foot by 50-foot virt-holo grid. "What?!..." she yelled, startled by his sudden appearance.

He gave a sheepish little wave.

Sasha slammed on the brakes. "Shit!" she exclaimed. The bike jerked to the right and slid into the gravel shoulder. Her front wheel dug into a large hole, which catapulted her over the handlebars. Her legs flew over her head as the bike cartwheeled down an embankment. Jonathan telekinetically caught her in midflip and held her motionless above the pavement. He had grav'd all of her except her head.

"This is not funny!" she screamed, suspended upside down.

Jonathan was laughing.

"Off program!" she ordered. The holosystem shut down with a mechanical groan, exposing the room's true appearance.

"Oh, that was good," Jonathan said, still laughing.

Sasha just glared at him from her telekinetic purgatory.

"Lighten up, for God's sake," he said. He stepped over to her. "You're the one who applied the front brakes."

"Let me down!" she ordered sternly.

"Oh, I don't know. You look kind of cute all sprawled out, with your legs going every which way." He turned his head to mimic hers. Sasha's hair was a spray of curls, and her back was arched to the point that it looked almost disjointed. "Damn, you're flexible!"

"Jonathan," she said, calming. "Please...this hurts."

"Oh, sorry." He gently lowered her and released the grav field just as she touched the grid's surface.

Sasha collected herself while the biofabric of her holosuit reshaped to the preset contour specs of her body. Jonathan watched the fabric move across her frame like a snake's skin.

"There," she said, adjusting her breasts, "that feels a lot better." She looked up and caught him watching.

"What?" He knew full well what her look meant.

Sasha put her hands on her hips. "Enjoying the view?"

"Well, now that you mention it—" Suddenly, Jonathan felt what seemed like an invisible fist punch him, just hard enough, in the stomach. He instantly flexed, but the suddenness had caught him off guard, and he stumbled back.

A slow smile crossed Sasha's face.

"Cute," he said, coughing. "I'll admit, I deserved that."

She slowly walked over and folded her arms. "Yes, you did."

"Nice focus," Jonathan said, straightening. "Your field flux was as tight as I've ever felt. What level are you again?"

"Oh, I'm just a...ah, Level...4," she said, helping him to his feet.

"That's funny," he said. He tucked his shirt back into the front of his pants. "I barely sensed your displacement before you phased. How did you manage that little trick?"

"It's, ah, something I kinda worked out on my own," she replied, clearly disturbed by the question. "I'll bring the car around." She hurried from the booth.

~

The cabin was quiet as the car skimmed along the road's surface: The only sounds were the systems interface clicks that broke the silence every five miles as the car dialogued with the vast Interway network of the D.C. Zone grid.

"Hey," Jonathan said, "I'm sorry for startling you in the virt booth." He watched Sasha's reflection in the front nav screen.

His vidscreen flashed to life; her face filled most of it. "I shouldn't have punched you," she replied.

"No." He turned his attention out the window. "I deserved it." Clicks followed by sharp processing sounds emitted from the dash panel. Jonathan gingerly rubbed his stomach.

Sasha moved out of traffic and pulled onto his street, piloting the car to the curb in front of his home. The car opened the back door.

Jonathan threw his gear bag onto the sidewalk and crawled out of the backseat. He motioned for her to lower the window. It slid down to slowly reveal her face: her hair, still in a wild state from the bike accident, her eyes, bright with life, her mouth, deep dimples on each side. She smiled with a look that asked, "Yes?"

"You were right, you know," he said, hefting his gear bag.

"What do you mean?"

"I should have joined you for the ride."

Her smile returned. "Another time."

He nodded in agreement and began up the stairs, but turned back to catch the argon window raising. It stopped, and all Jonathan could see were Sasha's eyes and hair. "Say–" he began.

"I'm 24-7," she interrupted. "Call the service if you need a ride anywhere." Her eyes squinted slightly, a suggestion of a smile. For a second, they took in each other.

"Take care, Sasha."

The squint again. "I will, thank you."

The window resumed its journey. A wide-angle reflection of his brownstone and the darkening sky above replaced her face. There was a sucking sound as the window slipped tightly into the frame that rimmed the driver's door. A light rain began to fall.

A message from the past...12

JONATHAN fell into his favorite chair and eased back; its memory cradled his body as a thousand times before. Rain drew tiny streaks down the antique panes of glass, and as he looked through the 200-year-old windows, he wondered about the people and families that might have been in the room.

"Sir," Max said, "you received two messages while you were gone."

"Play back," Jonathan replied through a stretch.

Georgia's image appeared on the coffee table. She was holocaptured from the waist up and was in a thick robe with a tall collar that seemed to swallow her head. "Morning," she said while she vigorously tugged her hair. "You've got me using towels now – it's a nice change to the microdryers. I'm meeting with James at three o'clock, but I wanted to see if you were interested in connecting tonight, maybe for dinner?" She stopped rubbing and stepped closer, her image swelling in the fixed frame setting of the holo projection's parameters. She lowered her chin and smiled that smile. "Call me." Her image disappeared.

"God, you're sexy," Jonathan said under his breath. "Next message."

"Yes, sir. It is audio only."

That's odd, he thought.

A gray static, like a distant antique cell phone connection, filled the room. *"Jonathan...this is a warning."* The unidentified male voice was low and measured. *"You can not trust anyone. The Agency is not out for your best interests. They will suppress your growth. They fear you. Your potential is vast, beyond anything ever imagined. You owe it to the world to reach your true level."* There was a pause as the static ramped up and flooded the room again. *"Be careful, and remember...trust no one."* The message cut out, leaving a steady hiss.

Jonathan shot upright in the chair. "Max, what's the ID origin on this transmission?!"

"Unknown, sir."

"Is it traceable?"

"No. It was encrypted and had a multi-fragmented band dispersion rate. Its origin code degraded point three milliseconds after connection."

"Play it again."

Jonathan listened to the message a dozen more times. With each playback, the voice seemed familiar, but he couldn't place where he might have met the man or heard the voice. A crack of thunder rippled through the neighborhood, and the rain began to pelt the windowpanes in waves. Jonathan leaned back into the chair and carefully listened to the stranger's voice, trying to distill its inflection, cadence and rhythm. He thought back through all the people he had met over the last two years and desperately tried to remember their faces and voices. He moved to the edge of the chair, searching his memories for any indicator or trait that would expose the messenger.

"Max, play the first two sentences again."

Max dutifully complied.

"Isolate the second sentence."

Jonathan closed his eyes. *"You can not trust anyone..."*

"Isolate the words 'can not.'"

As Max replayed the words, Jonathan strained at every syllable, even listening to the space in between the words for any clue to their origin. The voice was serious, and devoid of emotion.

Or contractions.

Jonathan opened his eyes as realization hit his soul. "Zvara..." he said quietly to himself, and a rumble of thunder rattled the panes of glass in their 200-year-old frames.

It appears that way from the data...13

"YOU haven't touched your soup."

"Hmm?" he responded, still staring into his bowl of lobster bisque.

"Your soup," Georgia repeated. She pointed with her knife. "You haven't touched it." She put another forkful of Caesar salad to the test.

Jonathan shrugged.

"What is it? What's troubling you so?" Her face was lit softly by the candlelight, which set her cleft in a deeper shadow and gave her a slightly mannish appearance.

He met her question, hesitantly began to speak, but went back to stirring.

"Jonathan, please. Talk to me. I haven't seen or heard from you in days–"

"I don't know who to trust," he blurted. The stirring continued.

"What?..."

Jonathan sorrowfully looked up.

Georgia shrugged questioningly. "What are you talking about? You can trust me. Jonathan, come on, of all the people–"

"I received a message a few days ago."

Georgia's demeanor shifted. A seriousness came over her and she leaned back into her seat.

Jonathan rubbed his face and likewise sat back. He breathed a heavy sigh. "I could barely make out the message, it was so encrypted and distorted. But it was clear enough. It said that the Agency is suppressing my growth....That, that they're afraid of me. That my potential is vast, and I owe it to the *world* to reach my potential."

Georgia listened intently and took a sip of wine.

"Why would it say the world and not the *Tel* world?"

"I don't know....Maybe you're reading too much into it."

"And it said to trust no one."

"Hey," she said, "you can trust me."

"Guess who sent it," he said gravely.

She shrugged again.

"Zvara."

Georgia's eyes flared. She flinched as if a cold chill had run down her spine. "Jonathan," she gasped, "are you sure? I...I thought he was dead."

"Apparently not. I'd do a voiceprint comparison, but I don't have a vid of him to compare it to. Only the Agency does, and that's restricted, even to me. Hell, I've spent the last two days searching the archives trying to find one."

"Couldn't you request a sample?"

"Under what pretense? No, that would draw a lot of attention. I think they track my movements....It's something I've always suspected since I arrived."

"They wouldn't me. I could–"

"No!" he said, biting off her words. "No, no way. I'm not going to get you involved."

"Jonathan," Georgia reached over and took his hand, "I've been involved ever since Taos."

Jonathan smiled at this and gathered her hand into his. "It means a lot to me that you say that," he said softly, "but really, I don't want you to get hurt."

She read his anguish. "There's more, isn't there?"

"Yeah. Over the last few months, I've noticed this weird energy when I step into a room, more so than the usual looks. This seems..." he struggled for words, "...calculated."

"How so?"

"Like just the other day, the system said that Franks was available, but when I show up for those tests – the ones you wanted me to get – suddenly he's shut down. Says there's a system glitch, and he acts all nervous. Real odd. So I go over to the Grav Center, and it's closed, and I get the same funny reaction from the Center's director as I got from Franks...and I considered Franks a close friend." He pensively swirled the wine in his glass. "It's been like this for the last two or three months. Then I get this message saying not to trust anyone, and I'm being suppressed." He let go of Georgia's hand and retreated into the corner of his chair. "And these headaches are getting worse." He reached for his wine.

"Come on now, don't go all paranoid on me. Let's do some digging and see if this message is the real thing. Let me snoop around. They're not going to watch me. James has me doing grunt work, just to get familiar with the systems and procedures. It's real desk stuff. I can do some hacking, and they'll never know what happened."

Jonathan frowned from the top of his wine glass.

"The Rogues weren't just do-gooders. I was a pretty damn good hacker when I needed to be."

"All right," Jonathan conceded, leaning onto the table, "but *be careful*."

"Oh, don't worry about me," Georgia said slyly. She leaned close to his face. "I'm a big girl. I can watch out for myself."

"Oh, you are, are you?" He slid his finger down the front of her lips. She bit his finger and licked the tip of it.

He smiled. "Oh, yeah...I bet you are."

~

Georgia deftly navigated the Agency's massive information grid, hopping from node to node with the care and agility of a cat burglar sliding from one windowsill to another. Hacking the Agency's network meant patiently unlocking the heavily walled security structures of the system's bioprocessing molecular supercomputers. Georgia knew she'd never get further than the outer layers, but that was as far as she needed. Information such as a vid of Zvara resided in the shallows, which were heavily protected but not invulnerable. Anything deeper would require the expertise that came only with age and a history of time served in a correctional institution. To traverse the virtual domain of the Terra-Cray platform, Georgia was required to carefully encrypt her digital footprints. Such encryption made her travel through the domain slow and arduous. She masked her sojourn as data retrieval for the Recruiter Unit, which allowed her to enter and exit sensitive files virtually without question. She found Zvara's file buried deep inside a case area that would have been caked with dust in the physical world. Untying the string of code like a safecracker in an aged celluloid gangster film, she broke through the firewall and entered the file.

Before her was the life of one of the most celebrated Tels in history. It was all there: the impoverished childhood; the rural family background; and the original Recruiter notes, complete with data analysis and real-time grav readings – even a detailed account of his faked death, arranged by the Agency when he had turned 16. The extensive file confirmed Armando Zvara had been a prodigy and, until Jonathan, the most powerful Tel ever, as well as the most feared.

Lost in the fog of forgotten information, Georgia suddenly felt the breath of someone directly behind her on her neck. She ripped off the virt headset, almost taking a clump of hair with it. It hissed and whined as the fiber optic connections tore loose from their jacks. She spun around as the face housing separated into its standby components.

"Jesus, James," she exclaimed, and pulled her hair off her face. "You scared me half to death!"

Jimbo straightened and folded his arms. "Why's your vidscreen off?"

"I assumed the data you requested was sensitive."

"Not really." His eyes searched her face.

"I'm sorry. Have I breached protocol?" She smiled that smile.

Jimbo relaxed. "No, it's just odd." Suddenly, he reached across her and clicked the screen to life.

Georgia whipped around and watched the vidscreen pixel up; she prayed she had been quick enough to the download. Her nerves shivered like they had life of their own. The first page of a bio on a Potential that Jimbo had requested appeared.

"See," he said, placing his hands on her shoulders, "this is a kid out of Mexico

City. We think he might have the gift, but the preliminary data says he's probably just a Displacer. Definitely nothing special..." he leaned down behind her ear, "...*or sensitive.*" He squeezed her shoulders, and his fingers dug deep into her collarbones. "Don't worry; the data you're retrieving is your basic background crap. I'm going to run to a meeting." The headset levitated off the table and floated into her lap.

"Is this a hint?" she asked.

He smiled. "I'll see you later."

Georgia quickly reviewed the data transmission after he left. Zvara's file was now nestled deep inside Max's core, and the transmission stream had been successfully encrypted. Finally able to breathe a sigh of relief, she leaned back in her chair and wondered if Zvara had really sent the message. She bit at her thumbnail as she stared at the blank vidscreen. *If Zvara was alive,* she wondered, *what was he up to, and why now?* She gingerly rubbed at her collarbones.

~

"Were you able to retrieve his file?" Jonathan anxiously asked the holoimage.

"Oh, you bet," Georgia confidently replied. "Once I'd sequenced the code structure for the preliminary levels, it was like a house of cards."

"Now I know why you're so good in the casinos."

"That's right," she said smugly.

"Did anybody notice you in the system?"

"Jonathan, *please.* I've been breaking code since before you knew what a grav field was. You'll find it in a folder named Zman, inside Max's base function area. It's pretty interesting. I think I got most of it before James interrupted me."

"What?! He doesn't suspect anything, does he?"

"No. I sweet-talked through it. He thinks I'm the good little Agency girl."

"Don't underestimate him. He's dumb like a fox."

"Don't worry. Ten years with the Rogues taught me a lot." She stepped closer, and her image grew in the holoframe. "Hey," she said coyly, "what are you doing later?"

Jonathan smiled, knowing what that look meant. "Oh, I don't know. What did you have in mind?"

"I was thinking a little drink, a little dinner." She smiled that smile.

"Okay, okay, I'm getting the picture." He chuckled. "Sure...I'd like that very much. I'll see you, when? Seven?"

"I was thinking..." she grinned again, "...now?"

"Jeez, Georgia, don't you have work to finish?"

"I'm almost done, and James isn't coming back."

"All right, I'll see you in two hours."

Georgia giggled devilishly, and her image vanished.

"That girl is going to wear me out," Jonathan mused. He reclined and folded his hands behind his head. "Max, you'll find a new file near your base functions."

"The Zman file? Yes, sir. I have it."

"Good. Display it and make sure your security grid is as tight as it can be. I don't want you scanned by any third parties."

"Yes, sir."

Max displayed the extensive holochive, and for the next hour, Jonathan intently scanned Zvara's file. The psychotic so often portrayed in cocktail party discourse emerged from the data stripped of his myth. As he studied further, Jonathan began to distill a clearer picture of the infamous Tel, learning more about the man and his tortured life.

"Max, this is fascinating...I never realized his early childhood was so violent. I have a whole new concept of this guy. He's not really the devil that his mythos makes him out. He's more of...a..."

"Victim?" Max offered, with all the emotion an artificial bioconstruct could deliver.

Jonathan knew that Max was an intuitive AI, designed to evolve beyond the sum total of its programming, but the answer was still brutally accurate. "Yes, Max. A victim is exactly what I was thinking."

"It appears that way from the data," Max continued without prompt.

Jonathan read on. Much of the holochive he already knew. Zvara was a legend, and most of his life had been covered in his Intro classes. It was no secret that the Agency leaders had pushed Zvara from an early age. Believing that he could ascend to a Level 9, they had driven Zvara relentlessly. There were even rumors that Zvara had been augmented. Yet as Jonathan skimmed the vast holochive, he sensed that there were elements missing. Certain areas seemed fragmented, with subtle gaps that appeared to have been altered or smoothed over. He studied the files, and diligently searched for a pattern to the incongruities.

After an exhaustive hour, he gave up and retrieved one of the many interviews with Zvara. "Max, compare the voiceprint from the audio net message I received to the voice track in this vid from the Zvara file." Jonathan relaxed against the chair and began watching the interview. It looked like it must have been conducted sometime during Zvara's last year as head of the Agency. Gone were Zvara's youthful grin and boundless energy. The man in this vid looked old and tired, more like the Zvara Jonathan had met two years prior, even with all the surgery. He studied the great Tel and wondered...

"I have finished comparing the two voiceprints," Max announced.

Jonathan froze the vid, catching Zvara just as he turned to the camera. "Are the two from the same person?"

"Inconclusive," Max replied. "There is too much degradation in the net message to accurately evaluate. There is a 26.7 percent match rate on 234 evaluation points."

Jonathan toyed with the small patch of hair under his lower lip and figured that if Zvara were alive, he would know more about what the Agency might be doing to him than anyone else. The image of Zvara looked out from the vid. His mouth was caught in a stern half-frown, but it was his eyes that made Jonathan flinch. They had an intensity that was penetrating, and as Jonathan looked into them, he began to feel a strange kind of kinship with the man many had called the Master.

"Sir?" Max questioned, which brought Jonathan back to the moment. "Do you suspect the Agency might be doing to you what it did to Zvara?"

Jonathan grinned with the profound clarity of the simple question. "If you mean are they pushing me to be some kind of supertel, then, yes, Max...I believe they are." He rubbed at his temples. "Max, how did you arrive at that conclusion?"

"Because..." there was a slight pause as the bioconstruct expanded again beyond its sum total, "...the trend represented by the data bears out this conclusion."

Must you...14

"ARE you sure?"

"Her encryption codes were difficult to break, but by tracing her inception points, we're fairly certain of the download path."

Takeda reflectively stroked his thin beard; its white tip barely touched the top of his vest. "What do you think, Jeffrey?"

"He's probably just curious. Jonathan is an intelligent young man. I'm sure he's just trying to understand his future. After all, Zvara *is* the closest thing to a contemporary that he has."

"Had," Takeda corrected.

"Yes, quite." Trumble cleared his throat. "I wouldn't be too concerned. There's nothing in the file that pertains to the augmentations, is there?" He glared at Jimbo suspiciously, his eyes grossly distorted through the lenses of his antique glasses.

"No," Jimbo answered cautiously. "Not that I'm aware of."

"And what about this girl?" Trumble asked.

"She's harmless," Jimbo replied.

"She won't be too much of a *distraction?*"

"Doubtful. If anything, she'll probably do him some good."

"Well then," Takeda declared, "if you two aren't worried, then I'm not. Thank you, James."

Jimbo headed to the waiting elevator.

"James?"

He spun on his heels at Takeda's beckon. "Sir?"

Takeda leaned on his desk, sinuously weaving his obsidian-esque fingers together. Like an assassin focusing on his mark, he rested his index fingers on the front of his upper lip and trained his gaze intently at Jimbo. "You are *sure* about the file...aren't you?"

Jimbo instantly felt the incision of Takeda's telekinetic force. It burrowed deep into his mind, which created an odd sensation that wasn't quite pain, but definitely not pleasure. He secretly fought the reflex to blink because the acknowledgement of Takeda's presence would destroy any status he had in the eyes of the Agency leader. "Yes, sir," he assured, falsely calm; "I'm certain."

Like removing a hat two sizes too small, Jimbo felt Takeda release his mind. The suddenness caught him off guard, and he jerked back onto his heels. He tightened every muscle he had and strained to stop his movement.

Takeda's eyes flared slightly.

"Thank you, James," Trumble said. "Keep up the good work."

When the elevator doors shut, Trumble removed his glasses in disgust. "Really, Cyril! Must you be *so* theatrical?"

"We have to keep them honest, Jeffrey." A thin smile spread across his face.

Trumble rolled his eyes.

A beautiful day...15

JONATHAN and Sasha approached Virt Booth 12. It was early, and the training center was vacant of the usual student crowd engaged in everything from the practical application of telekinetic quantum dynamics to recreational fly-fishing in the foothills of Aconcagua.

"Hey, Kreet," Sasha said into the panel to the left of the booth's door, "do you have my program loaded?"

"You are locked *and* loaded, Miss Sasha."

"Killer. Thanks, Kreet." She threw a glance at Jonathan. "Are you ready to get after it, Mr. Kortel?"

Jonathan's grin said "bring it on," and he yanked the handle to open the door. A click followed by a series of little pops accompanied his pull and the door glided effortlessly, its true weight disguised by a movement that resembled viscous fluid.

Entering a holobooth was like stepping into a coral reef, minus the water or distortion that came with navigating a thick haze of pollution. The booth's holo-optics were composed of 300 million biocones that covered every square inch of surface. With each step that Jonathan and Sasha took, the living optics quivered in slow-motion ripples that mimicked the surface of a shallow gray puddle.

Sasha cautiously put her bike down while Jonathan stepped to her side and gingerly positioned his bike between them.

"I realize once the program is running, we jump all over this stuff," he said, strapping on his helmet, "but it still unnerves me to walk on it when it's in this state."

"I know," Sasha agreed. She adjusted her gloves. "It's like we're intruding on their space. Even though I know they're not sentient, it still creeps me."

They paused as their virt headgear analyzed the contours of their heads and began conforming.

"Augh!" Sasha exclaimed. "I wish my helmet was back from service. These off-the-shelf models never get my shape right." She started blindly, fiddling with the headgear's control panel.

"Here, let me help you," Jonathan said.

"Back off!" She pushed his hand away. "I can handle it."

"You're in a mood this morning. If you weren't so rough on your equipment, your helmet wouldn't be in service."

"Really, Jonathan?" she replied sarcastically. "I didn't know that."

"Oh, come on," he said; "lighten up." He situated himself on his bike and threw a challenging look to her. "So, Miss Kuntar, are you ready for a little ass-kicking?"

Sasha positioned herself for holostart. "The real question is, are *you*?" She snapped her optic visor into place.

Even though Jonathan had been in virt booths a hundred times, holostart still unsettled him a bit.

"Hit it, Kreet!" Sasha yelled.

The booth droned for a second, as if some unseen force was exhorting it to do what it didn't desire. Then the grid exploded with the input surge that fed the holosignal to the biocones at a trillion gigaflops per second. They were enveloped in an intarsia of virtual dimension.

New York City.

"What the hell is this!" Jonathan yelled over the noise and confusion of Central Park North. His bike teetered at the edge of a littered malodorous gutter. A bright yellow cab laid on its horn behind him.

"Bite me!" Sasha yelled at the driver.

"Bite...me?"

"It's slang from the period."

"And what period is this?!"

"New York City, late 20th century!"

"Why?!"

"No shit!"

"What?!" Jonathan exclaimed over a police car that rounded the corner with siren screaming.

Sasha hopped to the ground. She shuffled toward Jonathan and grabbed his shoulder, supporting him as he balanced on his bike. "No Biolution!" she said into the side of his headgear. "No Interway or network hubs. These people knew how to move. They fought the traffic. It was like a game to them!"

"What people?!"

"Messengers!" A screech of tires from a FedEx truck sliced the air. "Bike messengers!"

Jonathan now noticed how the booth's matrix had interfaced with their virtsuits. Sasha was wearing period clothing for a spring day in New York, probably the late 1980s. Her short pants were made from some organic material – denim, Jonathan thought it was called – and her sleeveless shirt sported the letter "I," a cartoonish heart, and the letters "NYC" running across her chest. Sasha also wore a backpack, like the kind Jonathan had seen in old paper magazines. It was filled with an assortment of cardboard tubes.

Sasha answered the question in his eyes. "This was their uniform, I think."

Jonathan dismounted his bike to look himself over. He was wearing long, faded blue pants that were frayed at the bottom and made of the same material as Sasha's cutoff shorts. His right knee protruded from a tattered square hole. The patch for it hung by a few threads and flapped erratically in the brisk, chilly wind. His left pant leg was rolled up past his ankle, and the program also had created a hooded garment of soft, thick fabric. It had long sleeves and thin drawstrings that dangled from two holes on either side of the neck. On its front was a graphic lightning bolt that bisected the letters AC on the left and DC on the right.

"AC, DC?...What am I, an electrical engineer?" he asked.

"I don't know," Sasha replied. "Maybe."

"I look like a 'streeter,'" Jonathan declared. He noticed another large hole in the seat of the pants. No detail overlooked, he now sported bright red underwear.

"Homeloss, actually," Sasha said.

"Homeloss?"

"Yeah. They were called homeloss people. They lost their homes in the weird 20th-century economy. That's why they became bike messengers."

Jonathan shrugged. "Works for me."

The cabby blared his horn again, this time holding it down. Sasha spun and angrily gestured with three fingers under her right eye.

"Sasha," Jonathan said, laughing; "he's not going to be programmed to know what that means. You need to get in the spirit of the times!" He turned and flipped the driver off.

Sasha laughed and joined him, gesturing at the driver. "Bite me!" she yelled.

Jonathan straddled his bike. "It's actually 'fuck you,' but nice try." He felt at the pack on his back. "Let me guess, we've got to deliver these somewhere, right?"

"Right," Sasha said. "And the first one there wins."

"Where's there?"

"You know Manhattan?"

"Yeah," Jonathan said, looking around at the canyon of buildings.

"You know where the Daimler Building is?"

"You mean the old Chrysler? Yeah, sure."

"That's *there*." Sasha swung her leg over her crossbar and began teetering in place. Jonathan followed.

"Ready?!" she yelled.

Jonathan nodded.

The cabby laid on his horn again, and Sasha took off toward the entrance of the park.

"Fuck you!" Jonathan yelled at the cab. He snapped his optic visor into place and sped off after her.

Without the controls and safeties of post-Biolution transportation, 20th-century New York traffic, with its unpredictability, made for a formidable challenge. As they jammed through the streets, Sasha maintained her lead, darting and swerving to avoid the onslaught of pedestrians, delivery trucks and the errant car door (which would open to release yet another obstacle into their agonistic game). Sasha jumped a curb and dove through a curtain of cucumber-colored slickers. She rounded a corner wearing one of them for headgear. Jonathan followed, almost slamming into one of New York City's finest. "Hey, you!" the holojection cop said. "Watch it, you damn kids!" It was now obvious that Sasha had programmed an array of elaborate obstacles so perfectly integrated into the program that distinguishing them from the base scene was virtually impossible. And all of them, Jonathan figured, accomplished without a stochastic subroutine.

Sasha cut a hard left and nearly clipped a Yellow Cab (its driver yelled something only known in the Sudan) and sped into Central Park. With Jonathan drafting tightly behind her, they flew like one against the traffic of East Park Drive. Jonathan barely maintained his position as Sasha weaved in and out of the in-line skaters and joggers. The holoprogram was so accurate that the people actually reacted to them. At the Lawn, Jonathan shot around her and hugged her left side. She looked over, smiled, and slammed into his bike. He wagged his finger at her and sprinted ahead. She closed in on him and deftly rubbed her front tire against his back tire. Jonathan tapped his brakes and ejected her from his bike. They jockeyed like this for a hundred yards, one testing the other. Suddenly Sasha surged ahead, but Jonathan quickly gained and rode up beside her. He stuck his tongue out at her. She answered. A small orange disk abruptly entered Jonathan's peripheral vision. It appeared to sail right along with him before it ricocheted off his helmet and caused him to almost lose control.

"Shit!" he exclaimed.

"That was a freebie!" Sasha yelled. She angled toward the Boat House.

"I think you mean Frisbee." He laughed at her destruction of the period vernacular.

"What?!"

"Frisbee...that was a Frisbee!"

"How do *you* know?!" Sasha asked.

Jonathan's humor began to wane. "Because," he said, slowing his bike, "I had one as a kid." He left the street and rode into the grass.

Sasha, still at full clip, looked over her shoulder and saw Jonathan hop from his bike. She braked to a crawl, turned, and rode back to Jonathan. She jumped from her bike and let it continue riderless until it crashed with a little semicircle twist flip. She peeled off her headgear, and its couplings hissed in protest. "What are you doing? We're only halfway through!"

Jonathan, his bike on the ground next to him, back tire still spinning, was staring into a small grove of dogwoods.

"Ah, Jonathan?" Sasha badgered, hands on her hips.

Jonathan kept staring. "It's so weird..." he said under his breath.

"Not really. I was beating your ass!"

Solemn and distant, he kept his attention on the trees. "Why?" he said more to them than to her.

"Why what?" she asked sternly.

Without word, Jonathan pointed. Sasha followed his finger and recoiled at the sight. There, at the base of the thickest trunk, was a three-dimensional image that floated a foot off the grass. It gently quivered like a bedsheet hanging in a light breeze. The eerie image portrayed a boy and a man playing catch with a Frisbee. The setting was tropical, with a glimpse of a beach between the palms in the background. The boy laughed as he caught the Frisbee, and the man ran over and tackled him. They fell, laughing and rolling. It stopped and replayed.

Sasha intently watched it three times. "What the hell is that?" she asked. "Do we have a glitch in the system?"

"No," Jonathan said somberly, "we don't."

"And just how would you know?"

"Because," Jonathan said, pointing to the boy in the image, "that's me."

"What?!..." Sasha exclaimed.

Jonathan finally turned to Sasha with a quizzical, sorrowful voice: "Why do these happen?" he asked.

Sasha, hearing his anguish, was at a loss for words. "I, I...didn't know, I–"

Jonathan gestured for her to stop. "It's all right," he said. "My mind creates these images. They're like a manifestation of my subconscience....I don't know how, though. And no one knows about them – except James, that is, and now you."

"Jesus, Jonathan. I had no idea. This is incred–"

A flock of birds overhead startled them, their squawks muffled by the distance. Jonathan and Sasha watched them circle for a moment, then smiled to each other. There was no need to say how wonderful it was to see a flock of birds – again.

Sasha gasped. "Jonathan, it's gone!"

"I know."

Sasha's hair whipped in the wind. Jonathan parted it from her face. She took his hand. Jonathan circled his other hand around her waist and pulled her closer. Sasha slowly reached to touch his face.

"Coming through!" An out-of-control in-line skater screamed and careened toward them. Sasha and Jonathan jumped apart just in time for the girl to tumble between them.

"Sorry! Sorry!" the blader said, picking herself up. She tiptoed out of the grass and rejoined a pack that was blading *en masse* down East Park Drive.

"Well," Jonathan said, looking about and trying not to acknowledge what might have happened, "it's certainly a beautiful day here in New York..."

Sasha reached for his arm. Jonathan resisted, but finally acquiesced to her overt show of caring.

"Jonathan," Sasha said quietly, "is there something you need to talk about?"

He looked away, but she pulled his face around. He painfully nodded, took her hand from his face and gently kissed the top of it. "Thank you," he said, not taking his eyes from hers.

She returned the gesture with a soft smile.

"Come on," Jonathan urged. He tugged her toward her bike. "Last one to the Chrysler has to buy lunch."

Sasha held her ground, pulling him back in midtug. "Tell me..." she began, but hesitated.

Jonathan questioned her.

"Please tell me," she continued, "about...Hawaii."

Jonathan smiled at her request. "Yeah, sure, that would be nice. Besides," he said, walking back to her, "I was going to beat you anyway."

Sasha playfully punched him in the stomach. The squawks from the flock were louder now, and the two of them lifted their faces in awe as the birds descended into a clearing 20 feet from them. For a brief moment, it felt as if they were actually in New York.

Before the Biolution. Before the Terror Years.

~

The door to the virt booth shut with an odd little "clunk," not the expected sound from a door that held a quarter ton of bioholo processing packs and nearly three miles of fiber optics.

"Thanks, Kreet," Sasha said.

"*No problemo*, Miss Sasha. You guys have a good time?"

Jonathan grinned at Sasha.

"Yeah, Kreet," she answered. A smile crossed her face. "We had a nice time in New York."

"Most people do. We'll catch ya on the return."

Jonathan and Sasha rolled their bikes into one of the large storage lockers that took up most of one side of the staging area. They were quiet as they hung their headgear, and he could sense an awkward energy between them. Sasha stepped behind the translucent wall of the women's dressing area, but just as Jonathan rounded the wall to the men's area, a sharp pain carved between his two main frontal lobes. The sensation was excruciating, like a lobotomy performed with no anesthesia. He crumpled to the floor.

Lying on his side, Jonathan looked through the gap between the floor and the bottom of the wall. He could see Sasha's figure through the translucent divider wriggling out of her holosuit. He tried to speak, but the sheer intensity of the pain gripped him in a state of paralysis. He could only manage garbled, choked sounds as he clawed at the wall. He caved. A small puddle of drool formed on the floor and spread toward his cheek. His toes began to curl.

"Jonathan," Sasha said flippantly, "since I was kicking your butt in there, I think we can conclude that you'll be buying lunch today. Agreed?"

Jonathan could barely move his eyes to watch Sasha's backlit image against the scrim wall. With every ounce of strength he could rally, Jonathan forced his throat open and made a noise that sounded vaguely like gargling.

Her figure stopped undressing and turned. "Jonathan?"

He couldn't muster the strength to answer.

Sasha's figure moved to the edge of the wall, and she poked her head around the corner. "Jonathan, are you listening?..."

Jonathan's arm had dropped into the space between the two dressing rooms. His hand lay palm up; his fingers twitched in spasm as nerves misfired throughout his body.

"Jonathan!" She ran around the wall and knelt beside him. "Oh, my God, what's happening?!" she said in quiet panic, and pulled him off the floor and into her arms.

Curled tightly from convulsion, Jonathan's arms had bent so that his elbows almost touched, and his hands had contorted in on themselves. His brow and hair were soaked. He couldn't turn his head, but his eyes were still able to move in their sockets. He looked up at her like an infant in its mother's arms.

She swept his hair from his forehead, but when she touched him, the grip of the seizure abated.

"Oh, shit," Jonathan moaned. He coughed and spat. He turned away from her, but Sasha kept touching him as he crawled out of her arms. He curled up on the floor, shaking and clutching his head. He began to cough uncontrollably.

"Please," Sasha urged, "let me call a med team."

"No!" Jonathan exclaimed between coughs. "I-I'll be fine. Just...just give me a moment." His breathing returned to normal and he began to regain his composure. He quietly lay on the floor while Sasha stroked his head.

"Hey," she said softly, "look at me, please."

"I...I really shouldn't."

"Why?" she tenderly questioned.

"Because," he said with an odd little sound that came across more like a cough than a laugh, "you don't have on a top."

Sasha quickly examined herself. In her instinctive reaction, she had rushed to his aid topless; the holosuit peeled halfway down to her hips. She quickly covered her breasts with folded arms. "Excuse me, I, ah, need to finish getting dressed." She rose to her feet. "Are you going to be okay for a second?"

He nodded, still averting his eyes.

Sasha returned to her dressing area.

Jonathan said, "Don't be embarrassed. You're beautiful. Very beautiful."

Sasha paused just behind the wall and grinned to herself.

Jonathan closed his eyes and curled his body tighter. With his brain throbbing and his mind filling with suspicion and fear, he gingerly laid his head on the floor. All he could think about was the Zvara holochive with its haunting glimpse of a proleptic future. Overwhelmed, he silently began to rock.

Patience...16

JACOB Whitehorse had taught his only child that patience was the virtue of a great hunter. In the late summer of her 12th year, he brought young Kaya to his ancestral homelands of the Southwest, where, for eight weeks, he educated her on her Indian heritage.

Kaya learned to survive in the harsh New Mexican environment, living off the rugged land that, for the most part, hadn't changed since her ancestors roamed it more than 300 years ago. She grew to admire her father as he instructed her in the "old ways" of their people. During the days, they hunted for mule deer and black-tailed jackrabbit, and she discovered that the depth of a paw print, the angle of a broken branch or the direction of a blood trail could help track prey. At the end of each day, they built their camp wherever their hunt had taken them. When night fell, her father passed on their people's language and lore, and often, before Kaya slipped into sleep under the expanse of the New Mexican sky, she wondered about the Indian children and how they survived such a hard life. She learned to understand her father's passion for preserving their people's teachings, and by the end of their trip, she was fiercely proud of her heritage. She also could fell a deer at 50 paces.

The instrument panel of Kaya's vehicle suddenly chattered as the system conducted its routine dialogue with the D.C. Zone Interway. "All connections are secure and operational," it said, snapping her back from the memory. The car idled with barely a hint of vibration on the quiet street. Kaya settled against the pilot's seat and watched her prey ascend the stairs of his Georgetown walk-up.

She was always struck by Jonathan Kortel's physical appearance. He wasn't particularly tall or strong in stature (although his gait revealed that he worked out). He had a youthful look, but not in a "baby face" way. Many considered him handsome, though much of this was born, Kaya suspected, from his dry wit and natural charm – in truth, there wasn't anything really special about Jonathan Kortel at all. And this, more than anything else, is what enraged Kaya. She often wondered how a man like this could have killed a legend like Jacob Whitehorse.

She intently watched Jonathan unlock his front door. Every part of her being wanted to lash out, and it took all of her strength not to jump from the car and level her weapon. She rehearsed the words of her father: *Patience, Kaya. Practice the art of deception. Track your prey until it thinks you're no longer following it...then strike.*

Jonathan Kortel began to enter his residence, but turned as if he had heard her thoughts. He keenly surveyed the street; the dim porch light slid across his face so that Kaya could make out his eyes. He looked pained somehow, his posture sullen. "This is the Infinite Tel?" she mused in the quiet of the cabin.

Not for long, she thought.

Another urban myth...17

GEORGIA stirred. She wrapped her arm around Jonathan's chest and ran her fingers through his chest hair. The room was quiet, and the light from the neighbor's porch came through a sliver of space between the old shutters that covered the windows in Jonathan's bedroom. She scooted tighter against him, and her eyes moved into the path of light that cut through the dark room. She twitched.

"What is it?" Jonathan whispered.

"Nothing. Just that light again."

"I'm tired of that light." He focused and created a narrow grav corridor that traced the light beam back to its source. He didn't need to phase for something like that. In his first year at the Agency, his training and development had refined his ability to the point that a small exercise like breaking glass four houses away was no more difficult than blinking.

It shattered, and a dog began to bark.

"You want me to shut the dog up, too?"

"No, please don't," Georgia whispered. She squeezed him tighter and kissed the back of his neck.

Jonathan could feel her breath against his skin. He pulled his knees in, tightening his fetal position. He shuddered and coughed lightly.

"Are you all right?" Georgia asked.

"Yeah, I'm fine."

"You've been quiet all night, and you hardly touched your dinner."

"I'm okay, really."

"How was your ride today with...what's her name? Your new driver?"

"Sasha?"

"Yeah, her. How was it? Did you win?"

Jonathan hesitated and coughed again. "No...no I didn't."

A few moments passed, and all Jonathan could hear was his own breathing. Georgia sat up on her elbow and leaned into his ear. "What are you thinking?" she asked with a slight huskiness that Jonathan found sexy. Very sexy.

"You really want to know?"

"Yesss," she said in a way that sounded special, like it belonged only to him.

"I was thinking about Zvara...his life. About how I have so much in common with him—"

"I was thinking of getting more of his file," Georgia said, stepping on his thought. "There was another section I couldn't retrieve. It had a ton of security around it, but I think with a little effort I could break through. I'm curious about what's inside it."

Jonathan rolled over. "Please don't. You've already risked way too much exposure. I can't let you risk yourself any further."

"Shhh," she whispered, silencing him with her finger. "I know the risks, and I'm willing to take them. If Zvara's message is true, then the more we find out about him, the more you'll understand about what the Agency might have planned for you." She kissed him. "Besides, I'm not in this just for you. I'm in this for *us*."

Jonathan searched her face. "Is there an...*us*?"

She leaned in close and licked the tip of his upper lip. "I'd like to think so."

Jonathan gently crawled on top of her. She spread her legs to let him nestle against her hips. Her skin was warm, and she smelled of sex and sweat and need. "I can't promise you anything," he tenderly whispered.

Georgia put her arms around his neck and smiled that smile. "I know. But tonight, just love me...even if it's for a few hours." She wrapped her legs tightly around his waist.

~

Jonathan sat at the kitchen counter and watched the national netnews. The talking heads were deep into an enter-tainment segment about the new fashions from Milan. The supermodels stood like perfect statues as their individual platforms hovered about the exhibition hall. Holographic projections of the clothes quick-cut between detail vids of the various collections, all choreographed to the biting fused rhythms of Middle East core and New American electronica. Jonathan tentatively sipped coffee and paid scant attention to the segment. Georgia was devouring a bowl of fruit and yogurt.

"Max," she said, "what is the life date for these strawberries?"

"Approximately 3.8 days for optimum flavor, with a 1.3 day window of spoilage on either side. The current strawberries are at 2.4 days for optimum flavor."

She questioningly glanced at Jonathan.

"Welcome to the big city, New Mexico girl." He began to cough.

"Are you sure you're all right?"

"Yeah, I just pushed it too hard yesterday with Sasha." "If you haven't been training for that kind of thing, you can't just go into one of those booths and expect to win. She's a ripped little lady..."

"You've met?"

"I met her at the training center. She's pretty cute," Georgia said. She waited to see if he'd rise to the bait.

"I guess," Jonathan said, borrowing his disinterest from the news segment. "She's too ethnic for me."

Georgia pinched his side. "I'm not *too ethnic*, am I?"

"No." Jonathan batted her hand away and hopped off the stool. He slid behind her, wrapped his arms around her waist and kissed her neck. "You're just right."

Georgia reached up with one hand and stroked him behind his head while she took another spoonful. "What are you going to do today?" she asked through a mouthful of breakfast.

"I'm now officially on vacation, winging my way to sunny Tortola," Jonathan said sarcastically. "At least that's what I've told James."

"What about Sasha?"

"I think she's cool. She's too concerned with her classes to care if I'm on vacation or not."

"She's a little old for a driver, isn't she?"

"A little. She told me that they discovered her later than most."

Georgia nodded and glanced at her watch. "I've got to go. James wants my opinion on the new Potential files by noon."

"Oooh, so he's asking for your opinion now, eh?"

She winked. "Yes, he is. I'm advancing quite fast in the Unit."

"Very impressive, young lady."

"Why, thank you, Mr. Kortel." She bounded toward the garage.

"Hey," Jonathan yelled after her. "Meet you at the Nougat tonight?"

"Yeah...call me," Georgia called from the hallway and slammed the door to the garage.

Jonathan turned back to the TVid to find the netnews had moved on to a science segment. A field reporter was doing a remote from the deck of a ship somewhere in the middle of an ocean. The wind kicked at his coat and blew his hair to one side, which exposed an odd, pre-Biolution era comb-over. The color of the sky was a deep, almost artificial blue. Probably done in post. He pointed to the horizon. "There, 60 miles away, is the start of the Hazard Zone, and beyond that, the former Hawaiian Islands—"

"Shall I turn the TVid off, sir?" Max inquired.

"No, let's see what this is about." Jonathan propped himself back on the stool. "Louder, please."

"Scientists now believe that the biodegeneration of matter that has been taking place since that fateful day 16 years ago has stopped. A research team from the French Oceanic Institute believes that the rate of decay has slowed to an almost imperceptible pace. It appears that, for all intents and purposes, the Hawaiian Islands have stopped merging their matter. This means that scientists may soon physically enter the Hazard Zone for the first time since the event. Who knows what they'll find? With a target date for entry just a few weeks away, the whole world waits in anticipation for the first look at ground zero. For this reporter, it won't be soon enough. I, like thousands of others, lost relatives in the event, and we hope finally to have closure on a terrible chapter for humanity. This is Reynard Moskowitz reporting from the Safe Zone in the Pacific Ocean."

"Off, Max." Jonathan sat and stared at the now blank TVid. Moments passed. He didn't move.

"Are you all right, sir?" Max questioned.

He didn't answer.

"Sir?–"

"Yeah, Max...I'm okay. Don't worry."

"I am not programmed to worry, sir. Just observe changes in body temperature, eye capillary dilation, motor movement–"

"Thank you, Max...for your observation."

"Certainly, sir. Are you leaving this morning?"

"Yes, I'm going out."

"Shall I call the car service?"

"No, I'm going to work out, then walk over to Arturo's and have some lunch."

"Yes, sir."

Jonathan's mind was back in Hawaii.

"Are you worried, sir?"

"Hmm? What, Max?"

"Are you worried, sir, at what will be found at ground zero?"

He smiled at the AI's intuitive question. "No, Max. Not really. I imagine there won't be much to find."

"What if they do?"

"Do what?"

"Find something, sir."

"Well then," he said, rising from the counter, "we'll have to deal with it as it comes, won't we?"

"Actually, sir," Max continued, "only you will."

~

Arturo's was slow, and Jonathan found himself enjoying the outdoor cafe almost alone. A young couple laughed and kissed at a small table near the back of the patio. He relaxed against his chair and let the warm midday sun pour over his face. He could feel it heating his skin, and he removed his sunglasses to enjoy its full effect. The shadows along the street were black, as if light itself couldn't escape from them. By contrast, the areas lit by the sun glowed with the intensity of a billion-K spot. A "Santa Fe sun," as Tarris used to call it. He had just finished his sandwich and was gulping down the last of his tea when he saw Jimbo step from a shop across the street. He was in dark shadow, but Jonathan could spot that red hair a mile away. He began to wave, but a small, pretty woman also stepped from the shop and joined him on the sidewalk. Her hair was pulled back with dark, oversized sunglasses balanced delicately on top.

"Well, well," Jonathan said, "ol' James finally has himself a girlfriend." He watched the woman take Jimbo's arm, and as she shifted a large shopping bag to her other hand, her face entered a shaft of sunlight that cut a path between two buildings. Jonathan slowly lowered his hand as the shock of whom he saw began to wrap itself around his soul. There, in the edge of the midday light like a detached fragment from a nightmare, was Anari – Tamara's best friend.

For a second, Jonathan truly thought he was hallucinating, or that the combination of sun and shadow was only making the woman with Jimbo look like Anari. But as she came fully into the light, the cold truth that Anari was truly standing across the street hit him like a discharge from a Light-Force. He fell back against the chair, his breath caught in his throat. He quickly shoved on his sunglasses and rushed into the restaurant, where he stood at the window, frozen – seized by the cruelty that was unfolding before him. He watched them walk, arm-in-arm, down the sidewalk – Anari laughing, Jimbo bending down every step or two to say something in her ear. They stopped, and Jimbo passionately kissed her before entering another shop.

Jonathan's heart collapsed. His mind struggled to process what he had witnessed. He had always thought that Anari, along with Hector, his former staff at the restaurant, Tamara and her child had been purged of any memory of him. He had allowed the Agency to wipe away part of his past, only to discover that the man he called "friend" had lied to him for his own gain. While the brutal realization that he had been a pawn sunk in, he thought of the warning in the mysterious net message. He had given up so much for the Agency: his life, his past, his love. And when he watched Jimbo tenderly kiss Anari, his pain and hurt began to transform into a new emotion.

A case of 10-year-old Barossa Shiraz exploded behind him.

~

Georgia took a deep breath and warily eyed her netport. The last time she had invaded the Agency's system, it had taken all of her skill just to retrieve the basic file on Zvara. Now she was contemplating a hacking that really required someone who did it for a living. She hesitated ...

... and snapped her optic visor into place to enter the Terra-Cray landscape. Stealthily retracing her steps back to Zvara's file, she found everything as it had been. The system's protocols had not been altered, and travel through the domain went smoothly. Too smoothly, she felt. The security codes encapsulating the second file on Zvara proved complex, and after 20 minutes of hacking, she grew nervous. All good hackers knew that the longer the stay, the more likely you pay, and Georgia felt she had spent 15 minutes more than she should have. Just a few bits of data from breaking through, Georgia struggled with the last string of code that would unravel the security subroutine that guarded Zvara's file. Again, she crawled within a megabyte of success, but the code resequenced itself like a drug-resistant, recombinant biological virus. Frustrated and defeated, Georgia noticed a subtle shift in the system to the left of her virtual field of vision. Someone else was hacking the same area – and closing fast on her. Georgia panicked. She wouldn't have time to back out and encrypt her exit path. The hacker's data stream flooded the area, and Georgia could only watch as it entwined itself around the last data sequence she had been hacking.

Astonished, she noticed that the intruder was not preventing her from entering Zvara's file. It was helping her.

She watched, awestruck, as the hacker's data stream resequenced the last bit of code and released the file. Immediately, the hacker's data began to dissipate until only a few bits of data were left from the original stream. They reformed into the words: YOU ONLY HAVE 10 MINUTES.

Georgia instantly dove into the file and began rifling through the volumes of data. Frantically, she caught only glimpses of Zvara's life. An email from one doctor to another expressing concern over inordinate cranial pressure. A memo to Trumble about cost overruns. Grav tests with field ranges 10 times that of a "normal" Level 8. Then a file, which appeared to have had extra security, caught her attention. Its content proved rich, and as she scanned from netmails to meeting summaries to confidential memos, a pattern began to form. Neural tests just before Zvara had assumed leadership of the Agency revealed a tremendous surge in his neurological activity. Surgical notes from a doctor's personal log detailed a series of cranial explorations: its three-dimensional holorecord indicated an experimental implant of bionanoware technology directly into Zvara's cerebral cortex. A handwritten note next flashed by; its rudimentary characteristics stood out like a wrongly struck note amid the symphony of statistical data. It was addressed to Jeffrey Trumble:

Jeffrey,

You are the only one I have left who will listen without
malice. I wish to meet with you and the board to discuss my
future. I know I am in no position to dictate terms, but my
dedication to our culture and way of life should outweigh
any protests that you may have to field. I leave my fate
in your hands.

Your friend always,
Armando

Georgia continued to scan. If she understood everything correctly, the procedures on Zvara only confirmed her suspicions about the Agency. They also imparted an ominous feeling that Jonathan might soon (if not already) be subject to the same desires that drove the Agency to conduct its first experiments a decade earlier. Engrossed in the data, Georgia suddenly noticed that the 10-minute deadline was rapidly approaching.

Along with the system's security constructs. *00:03:16...*

The virtual domain was easy enough to navigate, but its security measures were some of the best ever designed. Georgia didn't see them coming: she felt them. Any good hacker could sense their presence a nodal point away. Like disfigured ripples in the sea of information, the security sentries could be sensed by the subtle shift of data flow left in the wake of their movement. Agency sentries roamed the vast Terra-Cray network, digital white blood cells that sought and attacked any intruders in the bloodstream of information.

00:02:32...

Georgia sensed their imminence and immediately executed her exit strategy. She quickly downloaded as much of Zvara's file as she could, then bounded from level to level, all the while encrypting her path to confuse the constructs.

00:01:46...

She entered the exit path to the outer layer, but found it blocked by a sentry application. Instantly, she veered off, hitching onto a stream of transfer data. It dragged her to a flow she recognized as a path to the entry hub. She surfed it wildly, executing sharp cutbacks and shifts to keep herself in the swiftest current.

00:00:46...

Passing through the final layer, she emerged at the base level of the system and exited through her inception point. She ripped off her netgear and threw it on the desk. Her hair was saturated. She shook her head in a futile attempt to shake away her nerves with the sweat.

00:00:08.

Georgia leaned back and reviewed her path on the vidscreen. As far as she could tell, the system's sentries never drew close enough to sample her data. She was free and clear. Breathing a sigh of relief, she began to shut down her portal when suddenly her vidscreen shifted color. Her path architecture was replaced with a black screen and a simple two-word message that, in an odd way, gave her a feeling of accomplishment. "GOOD LUCK" glowed for a second in a bright green sans serif, then slowly faded into the inky blackness.

~

Jonathan tracked Georgia as she made her way through the current of people around the bar. Her gait was fast, and she didn't display her usual posture of confidence. Even after she had caught her first glimpse of him, she didn't smile. Instead, she only made eye contact, then nervously looked away. Something, he sensed, was seriously wrong.

Georgia slid into the booth, wadded her raincoat and slammed it against the wall. She ran her fingers through her wet hair, put her elbows on the table and folded her hands. She looked out over the crowd. Then finally to him.

Jonathan swirled the ice in his drink and studied the emotion in her eyes. She averted his stare.

"Well?" he questioned, his voice cool and void of its usual soft timbre. "What is it? What's the matter?"

"Oh, Jonathan. I...I–"

"You went back in, didn't you?"

She hesitated, then nodded.

"I asked you not to! It's too damn dangerous. You're taking way too big a risk. It's not worth it."

"It was," Georgia said firmly.

"What? What did you find?"

She hesitated again, then reached across the table and took his hands.

Jonathan could feel her fear. "What did you learn?" he asked gravely.

"I was able to hack into the other file, but I didn't do it alone."

He winced questioningly.

"I got within a few strings of data, but I couldn't untie the last security sequence, until this other hacker charged in and finished it for me." She pulled away and folded her arms tightly across her chest. "It was Zvara, I know it!" Her leg began nervously jittering.

"And?..." Jonathan pressed. His voice had an edge that pushed Georgia against the vinyl booth.

"And I discovered something." She couldn't face his glare.

Jonathan mentally pulled her face around. Her eyes widened with shock at his abrupt display. "What did you learn?" he asked sternly.

Georgia, experiencing for the first time the rawness of Jonathan's telekinetic power, sunk back against the booth. "This other file," she nervously continued, "was full of data that detailed experiments they had performed on Zvara."

"Go on!"

"You know when Zvara began his rise within the Agency, just before they made him director?"

"And?!"

"The reason he surpassed Whitehorse was that the Agency had conducted some experiments..." She looked away. Both legs jittered in sync.

"What *kind*?!" Jonathan demanded. His impatience boiled over in a primal display of rage that spun Georgia's head so forcefully she yelped. Unaware that his thoughts had become manifest, he dragged her over the table.

"They implanted some kind of bionanoware!" she exclaimed, her eyes flush with fear. "Jonathan! My neck...my God, you're hurting me!"

Suddenly realizing, he recoiled at his own actions. Georgia fell back, her knees slamming against the bottom of the table. Her face went blank as she vigorously rubbed at her neck.

Jonathan was stunned. He began to apologize but saw in her eyes that the damage had been done. "Goddamnit!" he raged. He jumped from the booth.

"No, Jonathan! Wait!"

Too late. He already had charged into the crowd, telekinetically shoving people aside, their drinks ripped from their hands by the field disruption. Georgia leaped from the booth like her legs were hydraulic and pushed through the dense mass, trying to keep within his wake; but the crowd, collectively connected to the Net and seemingly oblivious to Jonathan's telekinetics, closed in as soon as he passed and continued dancing like one thick, undulating being. Frustrated, Georgia focused and created a grav field corridor that not only slammed through the dancers, but caught Jonathan off guard. She spun him around and yanked him back so fast his feet dragged on the tips of his toes. She caught him by his lapels. He was shocked at her aggression.

"Don't you ever do that to me again!" she growled, pulling him tight to her face.

"Georgia, look...I'm—"

"Shut up and listen. I went back in because I care for you, Jonathan Kortel. You might think of me as just some sex buddy, but to me..." He felt her grav field relax, and his feet slowly lowered to the floor. "...it's more than that. Lord knows why — after tonight." She released her grip from his lapels and began to straighten the wrinkles she had caused. "I must be the craziest girl on the—"

"No," Jonathan said, grabbing her hands, "no, you're not. Quite the opposite. You're the best thing that's happened to me since..." He looked down, caught in his own analogy.

"Since...*Tamara?*" Georgia tersely finished.

Embarrassed, Jonathan nodded. "I'm sorry. That didn't come out the way I wanted it to."

"You're damn right it didn't! You know what your problem is, Kortel?" She leaned in close. "You need to just let go!" And she shoved him away.

"Georgia, come on! Wait!" Jonathan pleaded, but she was already halfway to the door. "Damn it!" he said, and chased after her. He caught up and grabbed her arm. "What about these people? They saw us phase!"

Georgia glared back into the bar. "Screw them. These people are so jacked, they don't know what reality they're in." She pushed her way past Jonathan and stormed toward the parking lot.

They tensely walked in silence through the cool night air, Georgia a few steps ahead of Jonathan. She marched up to the car; its doors slowly opened. She stopped and waited for him to reach the passenger's side. Shooting him a deadly look over the top of the car, she said, "Those people back there? They could use a new urban myth!" She climbed into the pilot's seat. Her hands flew over the instruments. The door slammed behind her.

Alone with his thoughts...18

THE room was draped with a thick blackness, the kind of blackness that masked depth and scale. Jonathan sat on his bed, solemn. He thought about what Georgia had told him, about Zvara and the experiments. He looked at the empty side of the bed, sheets still tucked crisply into the frame.

He would sleep alone, his thoughts his only companion.

The ride to his home from Bar of Chocolate had been quiet. Jonathan hadn't said a word, partly from embarrassment, but mostly from the anger that was building again inside him. Just before they had turned down his street, Georgia broke the silence to tell him that if he wanted to know more about Zvara, the data had been transferred to Max. She didn't know exactly what she had retrieved, just that she had grabbed as much as she could. Jonathan had appeared calm, but a maelstrom raged inside, fueled by the revelations about experiments upon Zvara. Georgia's anger seemed absolute, and she hadn't even asked about what he had discovered. She had just pulled the car up to his house and quietly let his door open onto the sidewalk.

He stared into the blackness, her words replaying in his head. The Agency had conducted bioimplant experiments on Zvara. Had they done so on him? The pieces all fell into place: the cool reactions he had been receiving from key people on the staff, the crippling headaches that struck out of nowhere, and now, the discovery that his friend had been deceiving him. Like a tattoo on his soul, the words from the message kept running through his mind.

Trust no one.

"Max, run the file you received today on Zvara."

A holojection materialized at the foot of his bed. He scanned its volumes of fragmented telekinetic data, beginning with the childhood grav tests and field exercises. The file bore out the rumors that Zvara had been extremely powerful early on, and it appeared the Agency had pushed the young Tel to his limits. Jonathan read through the teen years, with Zvara's prodigal angst in full documentation. Then he entered a period labeled only as the "project" years – Zvara's early 30s – when the Agency tested its theories on level acceleration. The concept was to enhance Zvara's power a hundredfold by interfacing fledgling bionanoware technology into the part of the brain from which it was believed the Tels derived their telekinetic ability. Twenty surgical procedures were performed on him, three of which almost resulted in his death, and for a short time, the bioenhancements showed promise. Zvara started to display an immense power range, able to move massive objects on an obscene scale. But not without a price. His brain started to show signs of swelling, and the telekinetic stress began to devastate his neural system. Thereafter, the Agency's scientific elite abandoned the project. They tried to remove the technology, but the implants had integrated so completely into his brain tissue that removal would have left him a vegetable.

Having ridden a power curve that thrust him to the top of the Agency, Zvara had been the youngest leader the Tel world had ever known. But with the failure of the experiments and the crippling effects of the bioenhancements, Armando Zvara had been left a broken man. Now the poster child for the Agency's failure in producing the Infinite Tel, Zvara's pride drove him to a final conclusion. He approached the governing board and requested that his death be faked, his appearance altered and his identity changed, for he wished to live his life free of the stigma that would have followed him the rest of his days.

"Off!"

The room slipped again into blackness.

The flat bedsheets greeted him with all the comfort of a plague. He moved through the path of light from the neighbor's porch. Its 100 watts of irritation burned itself onto the backs of his retinas. He quickly shot a grav wave up the beam to shatter the light, which sent Toto into a fit that seemed to loop after every fifth howl. His anger grew like a fever, and in a paroxysm of rage, he trained his imaging in the direction of the barking.

A silence settled egregiously over the neighborhood. Jonathan was returned to staring into blackness.

They know everything...19

HE cautiously approached the lab. At this hour the hallway was at 20 percent illumination, where it would remain for another three hours until 5:30 a.m. Ashton Franks usually arrived at his lab around 6:30, giving Jonathan a decent window to find some answers. Wearing the illegal signature displacer was uncomfortable enough, but telling the cab driver to let him off two miles away infused the whole act with a sense of melodrama that felt like he was in one of those spy arcade virt booths he and Tarris used to play in when they were kids. Jonathan felt a twinge of pain begin to attack the base of his skull. He reflexively pulled the infuser from his pocket, placed it to his neck, and pulled the trigger.

Franks's door appeared no different than the others on this floor, with its unassuming, brushed-metal surface and industrially designed handle – the kind that revealed no locking mechanism yet probably contained more security technology than most vaults. It did, though, have one glaring contrast: the light suffusing its small frosted-glass window. Jonathan tried the handle. It unlatched with a high-pitched click. The room was dark, except for a lone antique table lamp that spotlighted a netport station on the main counter. Finding the door unlocked, his senses were on point. He scanned the room with his netpad. Nothing.

Relaxing, Jonathan entered the code to lock the door, walked to the counter and spun the netport around. On the screen was a series of field tests, and as Jonathan scanned them, he saw ranges like nothing he could have imagined. He read the name on the tests. His name.

A cold chill spiked through his nervous system. The room grew oddly still.

"Impressive stats," said a disembodied voice.

"Thanks...Sasha?"

Sasha stepped to the counter, grazing the edge of the lamplight. The fluorescent glow cast a sallow hue across her chest and set her stomach in dark shadow. Her low-cut pants exposed an antique navel ring, and Jonathan could barely see the tip of what appeared to be a dragon's tail biotattoo escaping over the top of her belt. The rest of the dragon couldn't be far below. She had stopped short of the circle of light, which kissed her lower lip as she talked.

"Really," she continued, her voice barely above a whisper, "these are scary. The APT's, the Grav Dis...they're all off the charts." Sasha flexed her stomach. The dragon's tail flicked and disappeared.

"I hadn't seen these," Jonathan said, casually gesturing to the screen. "Now I know why."

Sasha, still partially in shadow, reached to spin the netport around. Jonathan grabbed her arm, clamped down with the force of an eagle's talon and pinned her wrist to the countertop. He leaned into the light to reveal the breadth of his anger. "What the hell are you doing here?"

"The same as you, I suppose," Sasha said without a hint of recognition to his action.

Jonathan tightened his grip. The dragon's tail flicked into view. "Don't bullshi–"

"I'm not," Sasha said, cutting him off with an air of confidence. "If I'm going to work for you, I want to know all I can..." she leaned into the light "...about the Infinite Tel."

"That's not for public knowledge."

"Now who's bullshitting?"

Jonathan felt a razor's edge slice across his knuckles. He looked down, but there was nothing there. Suddenly, a thin line of blood appeared. He released Sasha's arm and examined his hand. His blood looked almost black in the anemic harshness of the light. The dragon's head appeared over the top of Sasha's belt. It smiled and spit a flame of fire arcing across her stomach. She flexed her stomach and the dragon disappeared into the front of her pants, just above her left pocket.

"Neat trick," Jonathan said. He examined his hand. "Where'd you learn this one?"

"I've been around," Sasha coolly replied. She rounded the counter and took his hand. "Now, that didn't hurt...did it?" She tenderly rubbed the blood away with her thumb. Her eyes were fully dilated, and Jonathan sensed something more than desire behind them. She guided his hand to her hip, tucking his fingers into the top of her pants. "Shut up, Mr. Kortel..." she whispered. She grabbed the back of his neck and pulled his ear to her mouth. "...You wanna find my dragon?" Her breath was warm against his ear, and he could smell a faint tinge of honey emanating from her skin. She was riding.

Jonathan dug his hand deep down the side of her hip and slid it to the front of her pants. He gently kissed the side of her neck. Sasha let out a soft gasp as his fingers explored the dragon's lair.

"Oh, God," she moaned and turned her back to him. Her top's design was slit up the back, exposing much of her muscular body. Three small tattoos – Rembrandt self-portraits, each from a different period of his life and perfect in every detail – appeared just above the top of her low-cut pants. Jonathan stopped.

"Whoa," he said, pulling back to admire the workmanship.

"What's the matter," Sasha purred, "not into the classics?"

Jonathan slowly smiled and met her salacious look. "Not really. I'm more of a...*modernist.*"

Sasha spread her legs comfortably and leaned onto the counter with her elbows. "Don't worry," she said into the expanse of the lab, "just give them a second....I think you'll like the next showing."

Jonathan watched in amazement as the three masterpieces transformed into a triptych by the late-20th century artist Roy Lichtenstein. Again, the biotattoos had captured every brush stroke of the pop icon's famous masterwork depicting a stylized paper-era comic, its World War II hero exclaiming his hatred for the Nazis.

Sasha lowered her head to spill her hair across the countertop. "More *your* taste?" She arched her hips slightly.

Jonathan grabbed her hips and pulled her against him. He leaned down to kiss her neck, but jerked away, startled, as the dragon leaped across her back. It slowed just enough to turn its head and wink at him before it danced back to its den.

"If I didn't know any better," he said, "I'd say you're trying to seduce me."

Her eyes almost slits, Sasha turned and smiled sex at him.

Jonathan bent down to her ear and whispered, "There was a time when I would have been very tempted by this, not to mention we're taking quite a risk–" Suddenly, Jonathan felt the heat of her telekinetic presence at the gates of his mind. She had scaled his ego and was descending into his id. A burning sensation nestled at the base of his neocortex. He became aroused faster and harder than he had ever experienced before. He was pressing like steel against the warmth of her inner thighs. Jonathan moaned as the sensation intensified and hovered deliciously between pain and pleasure. He collapsed onto her back, letting his forehead rest between her shoulder blades.

"Who ever said we needed to get physical? *Besides,*" Sasha sarcastically whispered, "it's time you started taking some risks–" She froze in midsentence and gasped.

Jonathan raised his head off her back. "Tag," he whispered, "you're it."

Sasha opened her mouth to speak, but Jonathan silenced her with the palm of his hand. He gestured for her to be quiet. A tiny drop of sweat fell from his forehead and landed on the countertop. She licked it off.

The door handle to the lab clicked.

Jonathan quickly motioned for them to hide in one of the huge service lockers. They slipped into the nearest one, cramming between three rollaway carts piled high with diagnostic scanners and grav flux readers. Sasha yipped as her back pressed against a cold metal cart handle. Jonathan quietly closed the locker's door. The latch echoed around the lab.

Ashton Franks was whistling loudly as he pushed a lengthy equipment cart into the lab. The lights came up when the system read his grav sig.

"Oh, shit!" Sasha whispered. "Our sig displacers, they're on the counter!"

"Shh," Jonathan said.

Through the locker's mesh, they anxiously watched while Franks wheeled the cart to the lab's center counter and began to unload small brown boxes. Abruptly, the whistling stopped. He stared at the displacers for a second, then the netport caught his attention. He slowly stepped to it and read what was on the screen. Momentarily his eyes darted between both. He twisted around, his steely eyes keenly searching until they landed on a locker at the opposite side of the lab. He began to approach it cautiously.

"Looking for something?" Jonathan asked. He walked up to the counter.

Franks jerked around, stumbling into the cart he had wheeled in. There was fear in his eyes. "Oh, Jonathan!" he said, putting his hand to his chest, "you gave me quite a start."

Sasha scrunched down, watching.

"Getting in a little early this morning, aren't we?" Jonathan said. His hand glided over the top of the netport.

Franks's eyes shifted to it. "Just getting, ah...head start. You know, end of the quarter and all."

Jonathan coldly studied the Aussie. He spun the netport around and glanced at the screen.

"So...ah...Jonathan, what brings you to my lab so early? Wanting to get a jum–"

"When were you going to share your data with me, Ashton?" Jonathan coolly asked, his attention still focused on the netport screen.

"My boy, I'm not sure what the devil you're ta–"

"Don't screw with me, Franks." He snapped the netport shut.

"Look...Jonathan...let me expl–"

"Three percent increase in APT Waves? A thousand times the field size of a Level 8?" Jonathan slowly began to step toward the Aussie. "Over a million CTU movements in a second?!" He pinned the Aussie against the cart, his face only inches away.

"Jonathan, please...I can–"

"My God, Ashton. What else do you know? How strong am I?"

"Listen to me," Franks began, his demeanor suddenly shifting from his usual outback hickness to a cold, deadly seriousness. "You don't know what you're dealing with here."

"I don't think *you* know what you're dealing with." And Jonathan telekinetically grabbed Franks's throat and began lifting him off his heels. He field fluxed his arms tight to his body.

The Level 8 Tel balanced helplessly on the edge of his toes, gasping for air. "Jonathan," he groaned, "all I know is...AUGH!"

Jonathan folded his arms and lifted Franks a foot off the floor, hanging him like a freshly hooked salmon. "What else do you know, Ashton!"

"Jonathan!" Sasha yelled, "please don't!" She ran to his side and grabbed his arm.

Franks fell to the floor and desperately struggled for air. "Jonathan!" he said, coughing and spitting. "Just hear me out, for Godsakes!"

Jonathan shook off Sasha's grip and stepped over the Aussie. "To think," he said angrily, "I actually thought of you like a father."

"Please, listen to me," Franks pleaded in an attempt to cut through Jonathan's loathing. He rubbed at his throat. "I only do APT and field testing." He looked up in awe. "But there is someone who might help you."

"Who?"

"Shoalburg." He coughed violently. "He invented the nanogenetic implant."

Jonathan calmed and knelt down. "What the hell is going on? Why am I being kept in the dark?" Sasha stepped up and placed her hand on his shoulder.

"I don't know, son," Franks answered. "There are rumors, but they're only rumors."

"What, what are they?!" Jonathan asked. He seized Franks's wrist. Sasha squeezed his shoulder, and he relaxed his grip.

"I wish I could tell you more," Franks confessed, "but they're holding everyone to a limited knowledge parameter."

"Am I being made into some kind of a weapon?"

"That is the general theory floating around."

With Sasha's help, Jonathan lifted Franks to his feet. The senior Tel straightened his shirt and brushed back his white hair. "You haven't introduced me," Franks said, his eyes on Sasha as she nervously adjusted her top.

"Ashton Franks, Sasha Kuntar. Sasha is a Greener and assigned as my driver."

Franks stuck out his hand, and she tentatively shook it. "Don't be too embarrassed, young lady," he assured. "I have two grown daughters. It's nothing I haven't seen before, you know."

Sasha sheepishly smiled.

"Ah, Ashton...I'm sorry for–" Jonathan began.

Franks raised his hand to cut him off. Like a father consoling a son, he took Jonathan by the shoulders. "I understand." He looked him over. "I wish I could help you more, but there's really nothing this ol' dingo can do. I'm afraid you're on your own." He smiled, stepped back and folded his arms. "Now, you two," he said, pointing at the counter, "get those displacer units on before you forget and walk out of their field range."

Franks stood by as they put on their units. Jonathan turned and faced the Aussie. They warily eyed each other.

"Remember to tighten your focus, my boy, *before* you enter the shift threshold," Franks said. He winked at Sasha. "Less pain, you know."

Jonathan knowingly nodded.

Franks closed his eyes.

"Jonathan," Sasha said. "Do you have to?"

"He most certainly does, young lady," Franks answered, opening one eye. "Get on with it, my boy."

Jonathan began to focus, but hesitated.

"Damn it, son," Franks exclaimed, "just be done with it!"

Jonathan phased.

Franks flinched, gasped and collapsed. Jonathan tried to grab him, but his head bounced like it had landed on an invisible pillow.

"Nice trick...a grav bubble," Jonathan said. He turned to Sasha, who grinned slightly.

"Is he in pain?" she asked.

Jonathan looked at him, his head now nestled in the comfort of field displacement. "No," he said with a hint of disgust.

Franks' heavy breathing began to fill the room.

Goodbye, Jonathan...20

"**SIR,** you have a netcall."

Jonathan stopped drying his hair. "Yeah, Max. Who is it?" He threw the towel onto a chair.

"Georgia, sir."

"Put it through." Georgia's holoimage appeared at the foot of the bed. "Morning," Jonathan said somberly.

"Good morning," Georgia said. There was an uneasy pause. "Jonathan...I'm sorry about what happened in the bar."

"No," he said. He tightened the towel around his waist and stepped to the edge of the bed. Her holoimage quivered as the steam from the shower wafted through it. "Don't apologize. It's me who should. I know what I did was unforgivable. It's...it's just...look, I'm in a real weird place right now. I...I just overreacted, and I'm sorry. I hope I didn't hurt you."

Georgia shook her head slightly. Her eyes locked on his as she stared out from the holojection. "I've been assigned."

"Oh?" he said, surprised. "Where?"

"A small town in Wisconsin...it's called DePerre. There's a little 8-year-old boy who's shown some Level 4 tendencies."

"That's pretty young for a Level 4."

"Yeah," Georgia said, sighing. She nervously shifted her weight. "It should be very interesting. There hasn't been this strong a Potential, at this age, in about 10 years. I'm kind of flattered that he wants me to take it on. It'll be my first assignment."

"Who's going with you?"

"James gave me Rolo."

"He's good. You can learn a lot from a guy like that." He eyed the door to the bathroom. "I guess congratulations are in order."

Georgia bit her lower lip. "Thanks," she replied with no emotion. "Jonathan, about last night..." She cut herself off and pulled some hair from her face, tucking it behind an ear. "It's probably a good thing that I go out on assignment right now...you know?"

Jonathan hesitated for a second, then nodded.

She smiled weakly, and the holoimage dissolved.

"Who was that?" Sasha asked, emerging from the bathroom wrapped in one of Jonathan's towels.

"Just catching up on some messages from my property in Chicago."

"You okay?" She walked to the edge of the bed and ran her fingers through his wet hair.

"Yeah, I'm all right."

"Good," she whispered, and licked his ear. She walked toward the bathroom, but as she neared the door, she let the towel fall to the floor. The dragon on her back acted startled, like a naked cartoon character that had suddenly been exposed. He looked at Jonathan, quickly crossed his legs and covered his body with his arms, then pranced around her side to the comfort of his cave.

"You know," she said, half turning, "I think we need to finish what we started last night in the lab." A flame of bright yellow tattoo fire shot around her waist.

"There's nothing to finish," he said. He coolly looked at her like boring sculpture. The towel floated up to her hand. "Get dressed..." he said flatly.

She awkwardly gathered the towel around her with a look that sheepishly questioned his request.

"You're taking me to the airport."

I got your back...21

CARTER Shoalburg was considered the best biosurgeon in the Agency's network — some felt in the Tel world. He had conducted experiments that, fully practiced in the "outer world," would have probably won him the Gates Prize. His microsurgical techniques had revolutionized biosurgery, but many of his true achievements could never be fully unveiled to humanity without risking the exposure of the Tel culture. His heritage both empowered and frustrated him, such that if it had been up to him, he would have unmasked their world years ago. His drive was legendary, bordering on manic. And those who worked with him could attest that without his immense capacity for discipline, he might easily have been committed. Outbursts and rants were routine. And even though the occasional nurse would run from the OR sobbing as a result of one of his tantrums, no one would dispute that tolerance and patience were the only ways to deal with the Agency's resident genius, because Carter Shoalburg was handicapped. He had been born deaf, dumb and blind.

"Good night, doctor."

Shoalburg looked up, which itself was a miracle considering his mind could only "see" what was being fed to his brain from the ocular implants that occupied his once-empty sockets.

"Good night," he said in the even timbre imparted by the nanotechnology that ringed his underdeveloped vocal cords. "I'll see you in the morning, then?"

The nurse looked into Shoalburg's eyes. Even though she had worked with him for more than a decade, she was still unnerved by his eyes. At first glance they appeared real enough, but with time one noticed their androidian quality. Their movement was slightly off, as if with every glance they were processing billions and billions of photons to create his field of vision. She constantly had to remind herself — they were.

"Yes, Carter," she answered affectionately. Carter Shoalburg was 43, yet his insecurity was like that of a 12-year-old. He knew she'd be back, yet he still had to ask. "I'll see you in the morning," she said on her way out.

As soon as the door clicked shut, Shoalburg reached for the direct netlink connectors that had been retrofitted for him. He deftly plucked out his ocular implants and laid them in their special case, its living foam swallowing them like gray quicksand. The ocular implants were more for other people's convenience than his. They worked well enough, processing the same trillions of details as organic human eyes, but compared to the neural connectors that fed his brain the vastness of the world's information net, they might as well have been porcelain.

Having a brilliant mind trapped in a useless body propelled Shoalburg to achievement. In his early 20s, he invented the first genetic nanoimplants. The Biolution had fostered the technology, but his handicap inspired its development, and the secretive Tel culture allowed the experiments that the legal and moral agendas of the outer world never would have sanctioned.

By his early 30s, he had refined the technology and had persuaded the Tel elite to allow for a "leakage" (the calculated release of technology) into the outer world. Soon, his technology revolutionized how medicine dealt with the severely handicapped and rocketed to fame the operatives who had introduced it. It also filled the Agency's coffers with profits from the various publicly traded front companies that had launched the technology. By the time most medical students were just beginning to pay off their loans, Carter Shoalburg had changed the face of medicine. He had risked his own life by experimenting on the only subject he knew he could trust. He was the prime example of his own achievements – seeing, hearing and speaking, all with the aid of a technology that some had scoffed at as flotsam from science fiction. At his age, he should have been at the top of his career, but the Tel culture held him in frustrated obscurity. With the profiteering from his genius fueling the fires of his bitterness, Carter Shoalburg was not the model company man.

He gently slipped the net connectors into place.

Integration into the world's information net would have jolted other nervous systems into epileptic seizure, but for Shoalburg and the miles of nanoneural connections that threaded throughout his body, it was like tuning in to the evening news. In the virtually limitless dimension of cyberspace, Shoalburg was truly himself. His lack of organic senses meant nothing here. A physical presence was useless; what mattered was the organ that had always served him well – his brain. The Biolution and its swell of technology meant there wasn't anything in the real world that couldn't be done faster and safer in the virtual. For Shoalburg, it was the perfect laboratory. He raised his head in the direction of the door, connector cables dangling from the modified headgear like techno dreadlocks.

The handle clicked.

"Pretty late for a visit, isn't it...Mr. Kortel?"

"How'd you know it was me?"

Shoalburg tapped at his ear and smiled.

"Oh, yeah" Jonathan said. "Better hearing than a dog."

"A bat...actually. And when you spent that month in our lab, I learned your walk. So," he nonchalantly added, "were you going to tell me why you're wearing a sig displacer?"

"How did you?..."

Shoalburg tapped under one of the chrome net connectors in his eye socket.

"Right...the system."

"*The* system," Shoalburg affirmed. He leaned back and tracked Jonathan around the lab.

Jonathan pulled out his netpad and punched in a sequence of numbers. "Can you see me now, Carter?"

"Yes, yes. There you are. Smile..." Shoalburg pointed to the upper corner of the lab.

Jonathan turned and searched for the camera. A fly landed on a light sconce. "Where is it?"

Shoalburg pointed to the sconce. The fly buzzed off and landed on a cabinet.

"The sconce? That's pretty obvious."

Shoalburg laughed a little, then pointed to the cabinet.

"The fly?" Jonathan questioned, slowly stepping toward it.

"Kind of gives a new meaning to the old phrase, doesn't it?"

Jonathan reached for it, but it flew off into a dark part of the lab. "So," he said, turning back to Shoalburg, "how do I look?"

"Like you could use a haircut."

Jonathan smiled. "Hey, check into the main system. Am I showing up there?"

Shoalburg paused as he moved through the Net. "Nope. You're invisible to the main system. I can see you here in the lab, but they can't."

Jonathan intently studied the chrome connectors where Shoalburg's eyes should have been. "Say, Carter," he asked, "can you ever see...like us?"

"You mean in dimension and color? Sure," Shoalburg said. He pointed to the ocular implant's case. "These implants give me an almost perfect representation of the world – maybe a little richer in color, that's all. And, I'll never have to regen when I get old. Now, what's on your mind, Jonathan? You didn't come all the way to California to play spy and talk about my handicaps."

"That's true," Jonathan said, nodding. He pulled a chair beside Shoalburg. "Tell me, Carter, what do know about bionano implants?"

"I'm the father of it. You know that."

"What about for the brain?"

Shoalburg shrugged. "Depends. Neural sensory augmentation, no problem. Making someone a genius," he smiled, "that's got to be mother nature all the way."

"Okay, not a genius. But how about stronger..." Jonathan leaned closer, "...in *level*?"

Shoalburg shrugged again. "That's touchy territory, Jonny. They experimented with it before my work came onto the scene–" He stopped himself.

"I know about Zvara," Jonathan said softly.

Shoalburg nodded. "Well, who do you think tried to extract that technology out of Zvara's head? God, what a butcher job that was." He laughed. "No, if you're thinking about asking me to–"

"No, Carter. I'm not." Jonathan tensely rubbed his hands together. An uneasy quiet filled the lab.

"Jonny. What's wrong? You in some kind of trouble?"

"No. Nothing like that, at least...not yet."

Shoalburg frowned. He quickly turned to Jonathan, the connector cables whipping around and slapping into the counter's edge. "Awww, man...they didn't try nanogenetics on you, did they?"

"I don't know," Jonathan said coolly. "Did they?"

"Only one way to find out." Shoalburg rose from his chair. "Lets hook you up." He began to walk away, but was yanked back by the tether of cables. His rotund little frame bounced to the counter. "Damn! Excuse me, Jonny. You may not want to watch this."

"I've seen worse." Jonathan watched in fascination as Shoalburg carefully removed the net connectors from his eye sockets. "Doesn't that hurt?" he asked.

"What, these?" Shoalburg questioned. He rolled the two units around lazily in his hand and they clanked together. He clumsily set them on the counter. "I've done this so many times, it's as painless as removing a hat."

Shoalburg gingerly searched for the box that contained his ocular implants, and Jonathan saw for the first time the great scientist as he truly was. He reached over and guided Shoalburg's pudgy hands to the case.

"Thank you," Shoalbug said. He slipped the units in and faced Jonathan. "You *do* need a haircut."

Shoalburg walked to an area of the lab that looked more like an operating room than a science station. He patted the platform. "Hop up here and let's have a look at you."

Jonathan climbed up and began to lean back. Shoalburg swung a large, articulated armature into position over him. "Don't worry, this is totally painless," he said with a sly grin. The armature came to rest just above Jonathan's chest. Its sinuous tip whined as it sequenced though a set of three ominous heads.

Jonathan shot up.

"Easy there, I'm just kidding," Shoalburg said, pushing him back down. "Just be still for a second while I scan you." He shoved aside some carts that cluttered the lab and stepped behind a small console. "Now, don't move."

The 12 seconds it took for the scan seemed like 12 years to Jonathan. Shoalburg emerged from behind the console and stepped to the platform, his eyes glued to the screen that hung behind Jonathan's head. He intently watched the data cascade down the screen.

"Well, I'll be damned..." Shoalburg said softly.

"What?!" Jonathan shot up again.

Shoalburg's ocular implants shifted alienly in his direction. Jonathan could have sworn he heard them click into place. He swung his legs over the edge of the platform and sat there staring. "Well?" he finally asked.

"Hold on, I'm checking this out," Shoalburg said, his attention glued to the screen at the scan station. He leaned on his elbows and diligently studied the images. He whistled to himself. "Damn, this is some good work."

Stunned, Jonathan didn't answer. He hopped off the platform and paced the floor. Finally, he asked, "How bad is it?"

"That all depends on your point of view," Shoalburg said, still studying the data. "If you don't mind not being completely organic anymore, it's no big deal. But if you do..." he slowly trained his implants on him, "then you have a ton of bionanoware growing in your head that's been genetically coded especially for Mr. Jonathan Kortel." He leaned toward Jonathan. "And you may not want to yank it out of there." Shoalburg blinked in a mechanical sort of way, like the act was more for show than reflex, and began walking over to another console. "It's not that bad, really."

"What?..." Jonathan asked, still grappling with the reality of his situation.

"Having implants. I've had them most of my adult life. I couldn't function without them. And there are a million people out there with my technology in them, all living happy, normal lives." He tapped in a sequence code at the station. "Roll that net connector cart over, will you?"

Jonathan wheeled the cart to Shoalburg.

"The only problem in your case, Jonny," he said, removing his implants, "is that me, and the other hundred million or so handicapped people who have my nanoware, know *why* we have it." He slipped the connectors into his eye sockets. "You don't."

"There's a rumor going around saying this stuff's supposed to make me into some sort of weapon."

"Possibly. They tried to make Zvara one." Shoalburg paused for effect. "After they'd tried to make him the 'Infinite Tel.'"

"What do you know about this Infinite Tel?"

"That whole business was started by Jacob Whitehorse.... You know about him and Zvara, don't you?"

Jonathan winced. "More than I ever want to."

"Right. So when Whitehorse left and started the Rogues, he was on a quest of sorts – to find the Infinite Tel. A real Don Quixote thing." Shoalburg suddenly jerked to attention. "Hey, what the...aughhh!"

"What's the matter?" Jonathan asked, stepping to him.

"Nothing. Sometimes you run into data that's real hard to process, even with all my implants." Shoalburg stood quietly motionless as he filtered the stream coming off the Net.

"So, what about the Infinite Tel?" Jonathan pressed.

"Hmm? Oh, yeah...sorry. The Infinite Tel supposedly can not only manipulate gravity, but alter matter as well." He abruptly faced Jonathan, the connector cables wildly following his motion. "I'll believe that when I see it." He smiled again. Suddenly, Shoalburg's teeth clenched and he jerked forward, almost into Jonathan's arms. "Oh, God! That hurt!"

"What happened?"

"I was retrieving some data from the Agency's archives when I got hit with what felt like a predator stream." He rubbed at his head and sat down in the station's chair. "Man, I haven't felt that in years."

Jonathan sat next to him and put his hand on his shoulder. "Carter...tell me the truth. What am I?"

"Whoever did this to you did a hell of a job. This was no amateur procedure like they did on Zvara. Yours was done by a seasoned biosurgeon." He reflected for a moment and said, "I'll bet it was Adrian."

Shoalburg stood and pulled down a screen that was hanging above the console. "Now, let's see if you're a weapon, shall we?" He scrolled through the data faster than Jonathan could manage, pausing every second or two, then plowing ahead. "Aha, see these?" He waited for Jonathan to catch up. "These can control your vision center...and, and those?" he said, enthusiastically pointing. "They can control your motor functions. But I don't understand how they would make you more powerful....Here!" He nudged Jonathan, barely able to contain himself. "These can increase the flow of adrenaline into your system. It's the same thinking they had with Zvara, but that backfired when his brain started to swell." He rubbed at his temple.

"Maybe you should get out of the Net for a while," Jonathan said.

"No! No, that's okay. I can stay in here forever. Listen, if they've found a way to control the swelling and the residual side effects, you might well be on your way to being Mr. I.T. But if they haven't, who knows what this stuff will do." Shoalburg shrugged. "Beats me." He leaned back in the chair and folded his arms. "As a package, this stuff could have been intended for a number of things. Level enhancement. Sensory enhancement. Yeah...they could be prepping you for power. You'd be one helluva weapon. At your advanced level, you could wreak some havoc." He sighed. "In any case, I can't tell with this equipment. I need a nanogenetic reader, and not this one." He slapped at the console. "This is out of date, and what they've put into your head is quite advanced. It's breakthrough stuff, for sure." Shoalburg paused, then asked, "Are you experiencing any light flashes, headaches, that sort of thing?"

Jonathan slowly nodded.

"The technology is growing. They give you anything for the pain?"

Jonathan reached into his coat pocket and showed Shoalburg the pneumatic infuser.

"Typical," Shoalburg said, shaking his head. "That drug's nothing more than a masker. But watch yourself, you can get addicted to that shit. Over time, your body's going to grow tolerant of its masking effects, so get ready for more pain....I'm afraid it's going to get worse before it gets better."

Jonathan sighed. "Carter, is there anyone in the system who could help me find out exactly what I've got?" He tapped the side of his head.

"Except for the people who did it? Nah. I'm your best bet. Besides, you'd be taking a big risk...I assume you're doing this covertly?"

"Yeah. They think I'm on vacation. And those who did know, don't." Jonathan winked at Shoalburg.

"You Level 8's and your erasing....Oh, excuse me, Level 9. Or is it higher?"

"Hell, I don't know. I've been kept in the dark so much, I have no idea anymore." Jonathan leaned forward and put his head in his hands.

"Jonny," Shoalburg said, reaching over and patting his arm, "what do you want...really?"

Jonathan looked up mournfully, then smiled. "You know, you're the first person who's asked me that. Seems like everyone else just wants a piece of me...."

"I remember when the rumors of your discovery came out. Man, it tore through our world like wildfire! You're supposed to be the one, you know."

"One, what?"

"The one to reveal us...you know, to the outer world. Come on, from what I've heard, nobody's going to mess with you. You're way too advanced."

"But they're not teaching me, Carter...I'm mean they are, but they aren't. They take me to a certain level, then slam on the brakes. And if I want to go further, it's virtually impossible. They hold me at arm's length. It's driving me crazy!" Jonathan jumped up and kicked his chair into the lab.

Shoalburg sat quietly facing forward as Jonathan paced about the room. Finally, he started to chuckle.

"What so funny?" Jonathan asked.

"Oh, nothing. It's just that you and I are a lot alike, you know."

"How's that?"

"We're both freaks."

Jonathan stopped.

Shoalburg kept staring into cyberspace. "The Agency doesn't want us, yet at the same time, they need us." He finally turned in Jonathan's direction. "I make them money...*lots* of money. Plus, they know I'd go biothermal if they tried to mess with me." He smiled. "I can do a lot of damage if I want to." He tapped at the connectors. "But you? You're in your own league, Jonny boy. Something's up. They're hiding it from you, and I'm afraid you're going to have to go to the top to get your answers."

"Takeda and Trumble?"

"The dynamic duo themselves. God, what a freak show. How we let them stay in power is beyond me." Shoalburg stretched his arms above his head. "Looks like you got a bit of a road ahead of you."

"What do you mean?"

"Well, you can't just walk up to those guys and ask, 'Excuse me, what the heck are you doing to me?' They'll be prepped, you can bank on that."

"Bank on that...on what?" Jonathan questioned.

"It's an old expression. One my grandfather used to use. When there were banks, they were perceived as secure. It's where you kept your money...when there was paper money. Get it? Banked on?"

Jonathan nodded hesitantly.

"Never mind. Just be smart about Takeda and Trumble. They know their stuff. And don't let that fatherly routine of theirs fool you. They're ruthless bastards."

Jonathan put his hand on Shoalburg's shoulder. "Thanks, Doc. You've always helped me when I needed it."

Shoalburg gingerly reached for Jonathan's hand and patted it. "Us freaks got to stick together."

Jonathan laughed. "Hey, Carter?"

"Yes, sir?"

"If I need you, can I...ah, depend on you?"

Carter looked in Jonathan's direction and smiled. "Of course you can. I got your back."

"My back?"

Shoalburg shook his head.

"Let me guess, another old term...from your grandfather?"

Shoalburg smiled.

"It means...you'll watch out for me?"

"Close," Shoalburg replied. "It's old military speak. More like, I'll protect you...while you walk point."

Jonathan smiled in approval. "I may need it, Carter."

"Don't worry," Shoalburg said, removing the connector units. He closed his eyelids as he fumbled for his ocular implants. He slipped them in, blinked several times, and then faced Jonathan. "I'll be there for you."

"I know, Carter," Jonathan replied. "I know."

Did you get your answer?...22

REAGAN International Airport was choked with Beltway insiders, middle-aged Japanese tourists and Hare Krishnas, who had made a recent comeback once they ditched the robes and finger cymbals. The new breed of devotees had donned a more approachable style, which included contemporary clothing and a bit more hair. They had kept the ritual of chanting, though, and their mantra reverberated in Jonathan's head 20 gates after he had passed them.

Jonathan picked his way through the masses like a salmon fighting upstream. He looked at his netwatch for no special reason, a habit brought on by being part of an organization that prided itself on precision.

Fatigued by the flight from California, he slowly shuffled along the conveyor walk, trapped between a young Hispanic family and a few government types. He was preoccupied with the technology that was currently entwining itself around his cortex. Even though he sensed no evidence of its presence, he had an odd, nagging feeling, as if an imperceptible headache had taken permanent residence and was oscillating somewhere near the base of his skull. He felt for the infuser in his coat pocket, but quickly fought off the urge.

The young mother began straightening the sullen posture of her little girl, who fought every attempt at correction. She finally swatted the child on her butt, and the girl gave out a yelp that snapped Jonathan back to reality. The little girl looked up at him as tears ran down her face. Jonathan began to grin, but a bolt of sharp, jagged pain carved a path through the back of his skull. Startled at its severity, he lurched forward and almost dropped his bag. The little girl ducked behind her mother's leg. The pain struck again, this time with twice the intensity. This second invasion dropped Jonathan to his knees, but when he landed, the pain instantly vanished. The government types, still busy on their netphones, never looked over. Relieved, he stood, but the moment his head cleared the edge of the conveyor's handrail wall, the pain struck again. Jonathan landed heavily on the moving floor, and the pain disappeared. Instead of standing again, Jonathan grabbed his bag and started to crawl down the moving sidewalk on his hands and knees. The little Hispanic girl giggled as he passed. People nonchalantly stepped aside, still engrossed in their netphones as if a man crawling along were an everyday occurrence at Reagan.

Jonathan emerged from the conveyor and the pain struck again, though not as crippling. He struggled to his feet and bolted toward one of the exits.

Sasha, you better be on time, he thought.

Running into a crowded area where several large hallways converged, he felt a force upon his body that slowed his momentum as if the ground beneath his feet had suddenly adopted the gravity of Jupiter. At the same time, his back was lacerated with a sensation like a thousand tiny knives, and the pain in his head became almost unbearable. Jonathan lost his grip on his bag as his nervous system began to shut down. He felt himself scream, but heard no sound. He forced his head around and could see through breaks in the forest of people a figure at the end of one of the hallways. The man stood motionless, watching him collapse to the floor.

Jonathan sensed he was about to pass out. Desperate, he resorted to something he rarely did in public; he created a field flux corridor and directed it right at the figure. As the corridor traveled the length of the long hallway, it punched a path through the crowd and sent luggage and people careening to both sides. It struck the mysterious figure and held him like a giant fist. The forces on Jonathan's body vanished. He slowly began to stand, but was hit again with the same savage pain to his head. *Always in twos,* he thought.

A second dark figure stepped into view just at the edge of the flux corridor that held the first. He slowly crossed his arms.

Jonathan sent another flux corridor down the hallway. It seized the new figure like the other, almost knocking him off his feet. Jonathan's pain instantly vanished.

Tired of playing a game that brought him down to the level of an 8, Jonathan prepared to do something he had done only once. Risking major exposure and possible harm to himself, he phased and reversed his own grav field. The time before he had slowly moved himself a distance of about 12 feet. This hallway was more than 100 feet long. He only had a few seconds to execute the move before the two at the end of the hallway recovered. He instantly phased, betting their file on him didn't contain one of his talents.

Launched like an Olympic long jumper, Jonathan sailed down his flux corridor, legs leading and arms trailing. He landed, with a slight step, two feet from his antagonists. He mentally grabbed them and yanked them off their feet. "Bonhiem? Lewis?" he said quizzically, looking them over. "They sent you two?"

Both of the Agency men were in a state of awe. They had never seen a Tel move himself through the air before.

"Not in your files, gentlemen?" Jonathan asked.

"N-no!" Lewis exclaimed. "There's nothing about...what you just did!"

"My God..." Bonhiem said, "...it's *true.*"

Jonathan slowly lowered them. Some of the people who had witnessed his feat were approaching them, pointing and talking, while others were on their netphones.

And the chaos from Jonathan's flux corridor was beginning to draw attention. Suddenly, security alarms went off.

"Gotta go, boys," Jonathan said. He stepped away from them. "You know I have to do this."

Both men meekly nodded, then crumpled to the floor. Jonathan sprinted for the exit, projecting a field corridor that crashed through the crowd; but just as he was about to plow his field into the exit doors, his back was again riddled with the same sharp, hideous pain. He fell to the floor in convulsion. *Triangulation*, he figured.

With the security alarms blaring, people screaming, and his body slowly going into meltdown, Jonathan breached Tel protocol and cast a broad displacement field. He prayed that he'd hit his mark. The innocent people would just have to become what his grandfather referred to as "collateral damage."

He went into phase. The gravitational disruption flowed like a sound wave in water. It enveloped everything in its path: people, suitcases, trash cans, news kiosks – everything that wasn't welded, bolted or chained down within 100 feet of Jonathan's hypothalamus was displaced by the disruption. He watched, detached, as everything caught in the wave's path lost its gravitational integrity and floated briefly like some kind of gruesome, public water ballet. As the wave passed, anything affected dropped to the floor, which, depending how high it had floated, could be a harsh fall. Jonathan's heart sank as he watched a teenage girl float to the top of a hallway ceiling, only to drop violently like a puppet whose strings had been cut. His pain and convulsions vanished as the wave passed down a wide corridor that led to the Nations Air terminal.

He had only seconds before security would descend upon him. Jonathan sent a powerful grav field toward the exit. The narrowly focused field slammed against the ridged doors, which were now in auto lockdown. They vibrated, shuddered, and exploded, sending plexi shards, metal and glass spraying over the passenger loading area outside. He phased himself through the spray of debris and landed in the middle of the street, crunching and sliding on the remains of the shattered doors. He was searching desperately for Sasha's limo when he felt his head yanked to his right.

"Jonathan! Over here!"

Forced to look in the direction of the yell, Jonathan saw Sasha standing up through the sunroof of the limo. She was in one of the inner lanes, stuck in a sargasso of traffic.

Suddenly, the blare of a horn, followed by the screech of six air brakes locking in sequence, cut the air with a deafening shrill. Jonathan twisted around to find a two-ton *You-Go/We-Park* bus skidding uncontrollably toward him. The huge vehicle began severely listing as its back end jackknifed. To Jonathan, everything instantly slowed: the bus, skidding at him in a cranked-down celebration of the chaos theory, and Sasha, waving creepily at him in a slow-motion, frantic sort of way.

"*Jonathan!*" Her scream had an unnatural, guttural edge.

He phased over the cars to land in a sprawl on the limo's roof.

"Holy shit!" Sasha exclaimed. "How did you do tha–"

"Just drive!" Jonathan yelled.

Sasha shot down into the pilot's seat while Jonathan crawled through the sunroof and into the back. "GO! GO NOW!" he screamed, landing on the floor of the limo.

Sasha jumped the sidewalk and swerved into the outer lanes.

"Mask us before they read the car's ID!"

"I'm way ahead of that!" Sasha yelled. She gunned the limo into the Interway, weaved through the late-night traffic and barely missed the rear bumper of a recycle hauler.

"So," she asked sternly, her image appearing on the screen in the back, "where am I taking you?"

Jonathan sat pensively as the car glided along.

"Ah...yes? An answer, today—"

"I'm thinking!" Jonathan barked. "We can't go back to my house."

"Can't come to mine," Sasha added sternly. "They'll have it all secured up, too."

Jonathan shrugged. "I...I'm out of ideas here..."

"I know!" Sasha blurted. She jerked the toggle and the car veered sharply over six lanes, barely making the exit ramp. Jonathan was thrown against the door, his legs hitting the roof of the cabin.

"Sorry," she said from the rear screen, "but I just remembered a place that might be safe."

"Might be?!" Jonathan questioned, straightening.

"You got any better ideas?"

"All right, fair enough." He caught her staring. A grin had spread across her face. "What...what the hell's so funny?" he demanded.

"Nothing. It's...just..."

"Just what?" There was a raw seriousness in his voice.

Sasha's grin was replaced with a soft look of concern. "You really are what they say you are."

Jonathan turned away and wiped the blood from his upper lip. "I guess."

"You're meant for great things. You know that, don't you?"

Jonathan didn't answer. He stared out the window while his hand searched his pocket for the infuser.

~

They were enveloped in a part of the city where Jonathan had never been, and by the look of it, neither had anyone else for the last 20 years. Old warehouses crowded gutted bodegas; exposed retrofittings undulated in the night wind like mechanical cilia.

Sasha piloted the limo down a narrow alley, swerving around trash and splashing through puddles, which struck Jonathan as odd, since it hadn't rained for a few days. She pulled up to a loading dock that looked like the last thing to have left it probably ran on gasoline. A single mercury lamp surreally flooded the area with the kind of harsh yellow light that could burn through the epidermis and create a sickly pale translucency that revealed every vein in its bluish glory. The whole scene reeked of decay and urine, the kind of stench that was tasted more than smelled.

Sasha got out and smiled over the top of the limo. "Here we are," she said.

Jonathan stepped into a puddle that didn't respond like water. "Charming," he said as he inspected the underside of his boot.

Sasha hiked herself onto the loading dock and approached a small panel to the left of a giant rusted roll door. The panel had protruding buttons that reminded Jonathan of the old telephone in his grandfather's house. She tapped in a number.

"Yeah?" a scratchy voice asked from the speaker.

"Is Kreet there?" Sasha yelled at the panel.

"Yeah..."

"Can I talk with him?"

"Guess so..."

There was a long pause. Sasha nervously grinned at Jonathan.

"This is Kreet."

"Kreet, hey, it's Sasha."

"Miss Sasha. To what do I owe the honor?"

"Listen Kreet, I need your help. I need a place to crash."

"Well now, Miss Sasha, that's going to cost—"

"Don't screw with me, Kreet. This is serious....I've got *him* with me."

The speaker went dead for a second. Its paper cone crackled, "Jesus..."

A buzzer echoed from somewhere inside the platform, and the roll door started to rise.

~

The elevator jerked to a halt and threw Sasha into Jonathan's side. He grabbed her to steady both of them. She affectionately squeezed his arm. The cage door opened onto a large room that had been segmented into six living areas by crates, prefab packing grids, bubble pack and anything else that could serve as a wall. The room in front of them looked like a kind of kitchen, and there were four people milling about. All heads turned when they emerged from the darkness of the elevator. One guy, startled by Jonathan's presence, dropped his cup of coffee.

"Welcome, Miss Sasha," said a little man, his voice casually Bostonian. He was leaning against a concrete column and wearing a bright red scarf that wrapped his neck twice before it spilled down his side into a small pile on the floor behind him. Its biofabric slithered a vaguely erotic scene of a dancing woman who Jonathan swore winked at him every time he moved.

"Thanks for taking us in, Kreet," Sasha said.

Kreet didn't respond. He studied Jonathan. The others slowly rose to their feet.

"So this is Jonathan Kortel," Kreet said. He began walking toward them; his scarf deftly avoided his feet. "Welcome to the hotel Kreet."

"Thanks," Jonathan said. He reached to shake his hand.

"Nooo, sir," Kreet replied, his hand still buried deep in the large pockets of his canvas jump pants. "No offense, boss (it sounded like *bass* to Jonathan), but I'll bet the electro-jump from a guy like you could light this place up for a week." There were snickers all around. "Here." A can of beer flew into his hand from the counter. He offered it to Jonathan.

"Thanks," Jonathan said. "I think I will." The can floated over to his outstretched hand.

"What kind of hotel is this?" Sasha demanded.

"I know. You only drink white wine," Kreet said evasively.

A paper cup floated to Sasha and hung in front of her. "Thanks," she said, taking it.

"It's not every day that we have such an honored guest," Kreet said. "Let me introduce you to my roommates. Jonathan Kortel, this is Rocket...." He pointed to a gangly boy of about 20 with long, bright red curls that spiraled down the sides of his head. "This is Bixx...." A thin X-ray of a girl – maybe 17 – bowed her head. "And this is Sanjiv." An older Indian man smiled, his white teeth a glaring contrast to his almost black skin.

"Ah...hello everyone," Jonathan said hesitantly.

"Mister Kortel?" It came out more like *Meester Korvel,* and had a Slavic edge to it. The X-ray girl had cautiously raised her hand.

"Not now, Bixx, it's late," Kreet scolded.

"No, it's all right," Jonathan said. "Yeah, Bixx. What's your question?"

She hesitated. "Is it true?...You know..."

Jonathan looked to Sasha for help. She shrugged. "Know what?" he questioned.

Bixx hesitated again. "That you're...faster than light?"

Jonathan smiled, slightly embarrassed. "Yeah, Bixx...it's true."

Rocket whistled. "I told you!" he said to Sanjiv. "You owe me big time!"

Jonathan took a swig from his beer.

The room fell into a silence that seemed impenetrable.

"Daaamn..." Kreet eventually said under his breath. "You're bending time."

"If it's okay with you all," Jonathan said, "I'm pretty tired. I'd really like to get some sleep." He glanced at Sasha and took another swig.

"You can have my room. I'll sleep on the couch," Kreet said. He looked at Sasha. "It's a *big* couch."

"Nice try Kreet, but...ah..." There was a sudden awkwardness in Sasha's voice.

"I'm sure Kreet won't mind us doubling up...would you?" Jonathan interrupted.

"Ah...no, no please," Kreet said, bowing. "My shit-hole, your shit-hole."

~

Jonathan leaned back against a poor excuse for a pillow, but a T-shirt stuffed with underwear would have done, considering that he felt like crap. Anything that was soft and could cradle his aching head was just fine with him. Sasha pulled off her top; the dragon was nowhere to be found.

"Why do they live like this?" Jonathan asked.

"You mean, Kreet?" Sasha replied. She slipped on what a century earlier would have been called a Guinea-T.

"Yeah. They're all Tels. They can live better than this. I don't get it."

Sasha crawled onto the old futon. "They want to live like this."

Jonathan frowned and downed the dregs of his beer.

"Did it ever occur to you that just because the Agency takes you under its wing doesn't mean that you'll like it?"

"Yes, but—"

"But nothing," Sasha said. "Tels come from all walks of life. The Agency hasn't found a pattern that explains the shift, so...some people just can't adapt to a new way of life." She cuddled up to him and wrapped herself against his side. "Not everyone was successful like you." She nestled her head on his chest.

Clearly uncomfortable with her show of affection, Jonathan started to push her aside, but she rucked her leg over his hips and squeezed even tighter. He watched as she slowly rose and fell with his breathing. "Hey, ah...Sasha. About the night in the lab...look, don't get me wrong, that was...ah, intense, but I need to focus right now. I can't...Oh, how can I put this without digging a hole here?...I'm not sure it would be good if we got, you know...close. I mean, we're already kind of close...I guess what I'm trying to say is, there are some things I've got to take care of....Important things. And I'm not sure how it's all going to turn out. I don't want you to get hurt. Understand? Sasha?..." He felt her gentle snoring through his chest. He chuckled and gently kissed the top of her head.

~

In the dark quiet of the kitchen, a low industrial hum emanated from deep within the building and filled the floor with the kind of vibration that, once felt, was hard not to notice. Jonathan had sensed it through the futon, and it had kept him in a state of quasi-sleep for the better part of the night. Having opened every cabinet in search of a clean glass, he wiped out a bowl, leaned against the counter and waited for the gray liquid coming from the faucet to begin resembling something close to water. The pain at the base of his neck turned cold as he felt, more than heard, what sounded like the loading sequence of a Light-Force weapon. The water became clear.

"That's an older model, isn't it?" Jonathan asked into the darkness behind his back.

There was no answer.

"I'll bet it's a Hitachi 2300 — the old ones with that field imager that takes forever to recycle."

Quiet blackness.

"You know, if I wasn't such a nice guy, I'd explode your heart right now...*Kreet*."

"How'd you know it was me?"

Jonathan slowly turned around. "Just a little Tel intuition." He folded his arms and relaxed against the counter. He could barely make out Kreet's figure in the dim light of the kitchen. Kreet had an old-style Light-Force leveled directly at him. "Kreet," he said, "what do you hope to accomplish with this stunt?"

"Just a little test for Mr. Big Time," Kreet said mockingly.

"I told you earlier that I'm FTL. You're going to gain noth—"

"Shut up...just shut up!" Kreet exclaimed. "How do we know you're not just bullshitting us? Hmm? We've seen guys like you before – waltzing in all full of yourselves and boasting about your high levels of power." His voice jumped an octave. "People like Rocket and Bixx and me – we don't come from any fancy backgrounds. We come from the streets. We work our asses off just to get noticed for a level jump. But you, you just appear out of nowhere and land right at the top."

Jonathan shifted his weight and put his hands in his pockets. "I don't get this, Kreet. What do you have against me? I haven't done anything to affect whether you jump or not....Hell, I don't even interface with your area of the Agency."

Kreet laughed. "The Agency's like any other corporation. It's designed to keep people like us – the ones who really get things done – in their place. It's guys like you who make it impossible for us to get anywhere in our world. You should know better," Kreet's voice was filling with anger. "You just go with the flow, as long as it fits your needs. You never came up through the ranks. Ever drive a car, Kortel? Or put in a year straight in the Pit?"

Jonathan didn't answer.

"Thought so. You get all the breaks. You get the best assignments, the best instruction....You even get the best women...."

"Ohhh," Jonathan said softly, "so that's what this is really about." He peered into the darkness at Kreet's silhouetted figure. "This is about Sasha....You've got a bone for Sasha, don't you." He started to laugh under his breath.

"Shut the hell up, Kortel."

"Easy, tough guy. You ever discharged one of those? It's not a toy, you know."

"I've discharged more of these than you ever will."

"Well then," Jonathan said, stepping away from the counter and folding his arms across his chest, "what's stopping you?"

Kreet didn't answer.

"Come on, Kreet. If I'm not as fast as the rumors say, then there'll be one less fancy Tel for you to deal with." He took a step toward him. "Then again, if I am FTL..." He took another step. "...you'll just have to find out what happens...won't you?"

Kreet still didn't answer.

"What's the matter? You said yourself you've shot more Light-Forces than I ever will. Go for it!"

The low hum from the building suddenly shut off. The room fell into a thick, tense silence.

"Hey, Kreet, some of us are trying to get some sleep..." Yawning, Sanjiv suddenly appeared in the room. He hit the lights.

The flash from the weapon split the air like a silent lightning bolt had erupted in the loft. Sanjiv jumped back so hard he slammed into a concrete pillar. Sasha, in her bare feet, ran from the bedroom and skidded to a halt beside Jonathan. Bixx sheepishly peered around the wall of the kitchen, and gasped as she gazed at the bizarre scene captured like a photograph.

"Oh...my...God," Sanjiv uttered.

In the center of the kitchen was Kreet, suspended four feet in the air. His long scarf cascaded to the floor and looked oddly like a tether that kept him from floating away. Hovering just out of his hand was the old Light-Force gun, its white needle of laser light extruding from its silver barrel. His legs were caught in sort of a half scissor kick, the look on his face sheer terror. The whole scene reminded Jonathan of a trick from the old kids' magic show he used to watch on the Retro Channel. He took a long, slow sip from the bowl.

"What the hell is going on here?" Sasha demanded. She began to approach Kreet, who looked like a sculpture in the full light of the kitchen.

"I wouldn't get too close there," Jonathan warned. He took another drink.

"Oh, my God," Sanjiv repeated. "This is unbelievable!"

Sasha walked back to Jonathan and patted him gently on the chest. "Let him go," she said.

"Better move first," Jonathan warned. "That's an old gun, and there's no telling what its discharge will do."

Everyone shuffled behind one of the freestanding walls that divided the kitchen from Sanjiv's area.

"Will it be loud?" Bixx asked shyly.

Jonathan just smiled.

With a flash, Kreet dropped to the floor while his weapon completed its discharge. The beam went directly into one of the cabinets, debiolizing it into a liquid state that resembled melting plastic. It dripped and oozed over the dishes piled in the sink.

Kreet struggled to his feet, entangled in his scarf, as Jonathan stepped from behind the wall. He mentally seized Kreet, raised him off the floor and held him tight, though he allowed his head to be free. Jonathan circled Kreet, eyeing him with contempt. The others cautiously stepped into the kitchen. Unconsciously, they stopped at the edge of the light that illuminated Kreet like a theater spot.

"So," Jonathan said as he came around to face him, "did you get your answer?"

A large dark spot appeared at Kreet's crotch. "Jonathan...sir, please...I...I never meant for it to go off. I-I was just fooling around—"

Jonathan motioned for the young Tel to stop. "Don't say any more, just listen. If you weren't Sasha's friend and helping us right now..." Kreet began to choke. Sasha started to protest, but Jonathan shot her a look. Bixx gasped slightly. "...you would have been facing God before you knew what hit you." Kreet choked for air when

Jonathan released his throat. "Let this be a lesson to you. Don't screw around with things you're not ready for." He stepped up and glared into Kreet's face. "Make myself clear?"

Kreet nodded. Sweat dripped off his forehead.

Jonathan walked over to the counter and picked up his bowl. "I'm tired," he said with his back to the room. "I'm going to bed." He swirled what little water was left and downed it in one gulp. He quietly placed the bowl on the counter and stepped through the makeshift curtain into the bedroom.

Kreet fell to the floor gagging and coughing.

I'm on my own...23

BIXX was seated at the kitchen table quietly eating while Sanjiv scrambled eggs in a small metal bowl. Rocket was in the shower enthusiastically singing to himself, oblivious to whatever key the song might have been before he wrapped his lips around it. Kreet, his back to the curtain of his bedroom, reverently sipped his coffee and stared blankly across the table. His scarf hung neatly on the back of his chair, the dancing woman replaced with a serene pastoral image of the Swiss Alps, clouds cycling lazily through its peaks. The air was filled with the kind of tension that revealed itself in stilted conversations or awkward pauses. It hovered over them like a living thing.

Jonathan pulled the curtain aside and emerged from the bedroom. All movement instantly stopped, and the room fell into an even deeper quiet. He surveyed the kitchen and felt the tension like a sunburn on his soul. Rocket's voice sliced the air in a futile attempt at a high note, then cracked a bit as he struggled with the range. Kreet winced and spilled coffee over the tops of his knuckles. Bixx began to giggle.

"Does he always do that?" Jonathan asked to no one in particular.

"What, sing in the shower?" Sanjiv questioned. His attention was clearly focused on pouring the precise amount of milk into the bowl.

"If that's what you call it," Jonathan answered. He stepped over to the pot of coffee, poured a cup and listened to Rocket's rendition of *Crying Train*, the last major hit from Nympho Scooter Pie. He hadn't heard the song in years. It had been one of Tarris's favorites – one they used to listen to when they took Tarris's dad's car out on midnight joy rides. With Tarris high on Jack and Nympho blaring from the car's Muzak system, they would tear across the back roads of the Midwest Interway with all the car's protocols disengaged. To Jonathan, it seemed a lifetime ago.

"He does that every time," Sanjiv said. "Drives us crazy." He poured the raw eggs and milk into an old-fashioned skillet, which hovered above an antique open-flame burner. The eggs crackled when they hit the pan.

"Could be worse," Kreet said. "At least he sings good songs." Bixx giggled into her bowl of cereal.

The shower shut off and sent a low rumble through the floor's exposed piping. Rocket rounded the partition wrapped in a large green towel. He was drying his hair with a microdryer, its high-pitched whine barely audible.

"What?" he asked as all eyes landed on him. Bixx giggled again. His eyes met Jonathan's, and he clicked the dryer off.

"You like Nympho?" Jonathan asked.

"Ah, sure...I guess." Rocket averted Jonathan's gaze and took a seat at the kitchen table. He grabbed a banana, peeled it back and took a bite that practically vanquished the whole fruit. Everyone kept staring.

"What?" Rocket asked, barely managing the word with his mouth so full of banana. Bixx began to laugh, and everyone broke out.

"Aw, screw you all," Rocket exclaimed. He stormed out of the kitchen and headed to the sanctuary of his cubicle.

"Oh, Rocket, come on..." Bixx called and bounded after him.

The chorus of *Crying Train* kept looping in Jonathan's mind, and he began to think about Tarris. He missed his friend. To Jonathan, he was the only one he could trust – really trust. But now he was strung out, forced back into addiction by the same people Jonathan was growing to loathe. He kept thinking of Jimbo's words to him on his flight back from France, "We found Tarris."

"Hey...Sanjiv," Jonathan said pensively, "you're a techno-guy, right?"

"Systems specialist, to be exact," Sanjiv replied, vigilantly watching his eggs. "Why do you ask?" The skillet left its position above the flame and floated to the table. It tilted to slide the eggs onto a plate, then moved to the sink, where it settled into a large bowl of dirty water that hissed violently and sent steam and the smell of burnt eggs and curry into the room.

"I need to retrofit something. It's kind of...well..."

"Off the netdar?" Kreet offered, finally giving Jonathan his attention.

"Yeah..." Jonathan replied, looking down at him, "...*off* the netdar."

"What do you need?" Sanjiv asked.

"I need a sig displacer that can mask for any platform or system."

Sanjiv and Kreet exchanged glances, and looked in the direction of Rocket's area.

"What?" Jonathan asked. "Rocket knows this kind of stuff?"

"No," Sanjiv replied. He smiled at Kreet. "Bixx does."

~

Jonathan watched Bixx diligently pore over the sig displacer. She hummed as she worked, testing and retesting – calibrating the sensitive device to mask Jonathan in any platform's environment.

Sanjiv leaned in to Jonathan's ear. "Don't let that innocent act fool you," he whispered. "She can do things I still can't figure out."

Bixx giggled in her little-girl voice, her hands not skipping a beat as they danced over the displacer.

"How's she doing?" Sasha asked, coming to Jonathan's side.

"Hell if I know," he replied. "I got lost after she tore down the drive board."

Bixx giggled again. She scanned the displacer for a tenth time and flipped up her headgear. "There!" she declared. The connections hissed from uncoupling. "You should be able to walk into a session of the Joint Chiefs and not be detected." She proudly handed Jonathan the displacer.

He held the unit up and inspected it like he knew what he was doing.

"Let's test it," Bixx said with a girlishly sly grin. She snatched the displacer from him. "Rocket!" she declared, suddenly taking charge. "Let's jack this in and see what we see."

"Let's hope we *don't* see," Rocket said. He pulled his headgear over his face, and his hair protruded through the straps in a patchwork of clownish red clumps.

Bixx clipped the sig displacer to her belt and stepped into the middle of the room. "Rocket, are you online?"

"Yeah, baby."

"Well? What *don't* you see?"

"I don't see you!"

"Good. Now scan through the different platforms and tell me what the ranges are...if there are any."

Rocket dutifully scanned through the various platforms that were used by the Agency and most any other network.

"Well?..." she demanded impatiently.

"Hold on! I'm not a genius like you."

Bixx shied. "Sorry," she said.

"Not a damn thing," Rocket announced. "Baby, you're a genius!"

Bixx clapped with glee and looked to Jonathan for approval. She slipped off the displacer and mentally passed it to him.

"Thank you, Bixx. This is extraordinary work." Jonathan collected the device as it floated into his hands.

"I'm glad she's on our side," Sanjiv said, chuckling.

Bixx just grinned.

"Why does a Tel at your level need a sig displacer?" Kreet asked. His voice carried an edge of accusation.

A silence descended on the group like a thick blanket of seriousness. Jonathan leveled his gaze at Kreet. "I have some...*unfinished* business to take care of. Why?"

Kreet stepped back reflexively. "I...I didn't mean anything. We won't tell anyone, honestly!"

Jonathan slowly eyed the whole group.

"Please don't!" Bixx blurted, and she covered her face. Rocket slowly lifted the eye trodes of his virt headgear. Sanjiv folded his arms tightly across his body and stared at the ground.

Sasha stepped over to Jonathan. "You don't need to," she whispered. "They're not going to say anything."

"All right then," Jonathan said to the group. "Let's just keep this between us...shall we?" He pulled the blanket aside and stepped into the bedroom.

The tension lifted as a collective sigh went through the group. "Excuse me," Sanjiv said, "I need to use the bathroom." He hurried out.

Bixx began whimpering into her hands, and Rocket came to her side. "Don't worry, baby," he said in an attempt to comfort her. He shot a sad look at Sasha.

Sasha stormed toward the bedroom. She mentally whipped the blanket aside, almost tearing it from its hooks, and found Jonathan packing his gear bag with relaxed precision.

"You were really going to do it, weren't you?" she questioned sternly.

Jonathan straightened but kept his back to her. He stood for a moment, then sighed. "I'm not in a position to trust anyone."

"These people just gave you a place to hide."

"*These people* have no interest in my well-being—"

"They're the backbone of the Tel world," she said, angrily biting off his words. "Think, Jonathan! They just altered a sig displacer, possibly jeopardizing their futures! They're not doing it out of some sense of duty. These are smart, ambitious people. They've been given a gift that's alienated them from the rest of the world, and they just want the same thing we all do. And guess who they think might lead them out of this absurd secrecy all of us exist in?!"

Jonathan turned and severely regarded her. "You done?" he asked.

"I don't know why I'm—" Sasha cut herself off and scoffed.

"You know," Jonathan said, his voice turgid with aggression, "it would be nice if just *once*, someone would think of my situation." He stepped closer. "I'm the one who has all the mystery technology growing in his head! I'm the one who's lost practically everyone who was ever important to me!" He was almost touching her face. "*I'm* the one who has everything to *lose* here."

Sasha could feel his rage. It was like heat against her skin.

"I should go back out there and erase all of them!" he declared, pointing to the curtain. "It would be for their own good." He turned and resumed packing his gear bag.

Sasha folded her arms and trained her attention at his back.

Jonathan flinched in midfold and angrily spun around, but his arms slapped to his sides and his body went rigid.

Sasha walked up and stopped inches from his face. "Those people are *my* friends," she growled.

Jonathan's look of surprise dissolved into a steely mask of anger. Sasha felt her windpipe begin to constrict, as if invisible hands had wrapped around her neck. She gagged and slowly dropped to her knees. "I know, Sasha," Jonathan said quietly. He knelt and took her face in his hands. "That's why I didn't erase them." His face softened, and he gently released her throat. She let out a small gasp. "Please don't ever test me again. I don't like being forced to demonstrate my level...especially with someone I like." He softly kissed her forehead, stood and walked to the curtain.

"Jonathan," she said hoarsely.

He stopped, but didn't respond.

"Let me go with you. I can help you...."

Sasha suddenly felt herself being lifted to her feet.

"From now on, I'm on my own," Jonathan said. He stared at the floor, and his shoulders slumped. "Hell," he lamented, "I'm not sure if what I'm going to do will even work..."

He turned to look at her, and for the first time Sasha saw in his face something she had never seen before.

Fear.

She began to speak, but Jonathan motioned for her to stop. His demeanor hardened, and, without looking, he reached back, and the gear bag flew into his outstretched hand. The curtain flew open.

"Sasha, please remember..." Jonathan hesitated, then shook the thought away. He hiked the gear bag onto his shoulder. "Goodbye," he said coldly, and quickly stepped from the room.

I don't really know...24

JIMBO pensively studied the data stream.

His netphone hummed, and he glanced at the ID. "Hi, baby," he answered. "Why are you calling so late?"

"Oh, I don't know," Anari replied. "I was getting off from the club early, and I'd thought I'd call and leave you a good-night message. But you picked up."

"I can cut off and let you call back."

"No, I'm glad you answered. Although, I wish I could see you when I call. So why are you working late?"

"Just reviewing some field results from one of our latest assignments. Nothing special. A lady in New York had shown some ability, but she turned out to be nothing much at all...just a Displacer. And you know I don't want you visually calling 'in system.' It's just safer that way."

"I know, I know. Too bad about the woman. A trip to New York would've been fun."

"Don't get your hopes up on this one. This lady's more talk than anything else." He shifted to a new file and a new data stream.

"Say, Jimmy..." Anari's voice was tentative. "Have you heard from Jonathan?"

"Hmm?" he questioned, his mind lost in the flux parameters of a new Potential in Idaho. "What'd you say?"

"Have you heard anything from Jonathan?"

"No. He's on vacation. He went to that island where you and I went last year. Why?"

"No reason..."

Jimbo looked up from the netport. "Bull. I can hear it in your voice."

There was a pause. "I had lunch today...with Tamara—"

"Anari, I've warned you about that! You're only going to frustrate yourself and possibly hurt Tamara in the process. Is she still having those dreams?"

A longer pause followed. "No," she said. "I don't think so."

"You don't think so, or you don't *know* so?"

"We didn't really talk about it. She hasn't mentioned them for a long time."

"Good, because if they start up again, I'm going to have to send out a Level 8–"

"Jimmy, please don't. You people have put her through enough all ready. Just let her have her life–"

"Anari!"

"Okay! Okay!"

"Look, baby, this is my job. Hell, it's my life. We have to protect ourselves. I took a huge risk with you. My God, if the Agency found out I let you go – free and unerased – I'd...I'd..."

"You'd *what?*"

"I'd be screwed for sure," Jimbo said, his voice rising. "It would be erase city. Nothing left. A clean, goddamn slate for ol' Jimbo."

No response.

"You don't want that, now...do you?"

More silence.

"*Anari?*"

"No! Of course I don't. It's just that...well, it's so hard to see Tamara sometimes, you know, knowing what she was...what she and Jonathan had together."

"What they had was never going to work out."

"You don't know that!"

"Oh, sure. A hooker into 'riding' with a guy like Jonathan Kortel?"

"She doesn't trick anymore, and she hasn't ridden in years. That was a cheap shot!"

"Okay, I'll give her that," he said, backing off a bit. "But you've got to admit, it would have never worked out...*never*."

"I've seen it happen."

"Where, in a romance vid?"

"No. Katrina married that doctor–"

"Yeah, after he promised to augment her."

There was a long pause, and Jimbo resumed his study.

"It was different between them," Anari said quietly. "You know that."

Resolved, Jimbo slowly shut his netport. "I know," he said, rubbing at his temples. "They did have something special."

"And you people took it away!"

"*Us* people had to take it away! Jonathan is special, Anari. I've told you a million damn times. We did what we had to do. End of story!"

Anari began to cry silently.

"Oh, baby...please don't..."

"You never saw them...how they looked at each other. We all saw it. They really...were..."

"Were what?"

"In love...true love." A sob escaped, and she gave in to it. "A love where their backgrounds didn't matter to them."

"That doesn't exist, Anari. It's only in the vids."

"They had it, Jimmy. You should have seen it....It was...beautiful."

"Look, Jonathan Kortel thinks too much with his other head. Maybe Tamara isn't your typical dirty girl, but believe me, they would have never lasted. He would have dumped her as soon as he got bored with her. Come on, think about it, what could a girl like Tamara Connor offer a guy like Kortel? They come from two totally different worlds. I know you've said she's been working on her degree, but even after she gets it, she'll still be an ex-prostitute – smarter maybe, but still a prostitute. We probably did him a favor by erasing her. Breaking up is such a pain in the ass anyway."

Solemnity fell over their conversation.

"I gotta get back to work," Jimbo finally said. "Are you going to be all right?"

"Yes..." Anari said coolly.

"Okay, then. Good night, baby."

"Yeah, sure..."

The netline abruptly severed.

"Jesus, what a bitch," he said into the empty room. He clicked to the next file.

Jimbo's screen filled with the image of Shirley Valentine, a Northern California medium who had claimed on a local TVid talk show that she was telekinetic and telepathic. A month earlier, Jimbo had dispatched two Recruiters to investigate her claims and discovered that she was as telekinetic as the average Shih Tzu. Shirley was mostly a media hype, and strictly out for the money. People like her were often left to continue with their sideshows. The Tel world had learned that allowing charlatans to amuse the masses only reinforced the notion that telekinetics was the stuff of tabloid journalism. It provided a simple and effective deflection to a relentless issue, as well as a great source of amusement to many in the Tel world. And when someone did come around who was a true Potential, he or she never lasted long enough in the public spotlight to do any damage.

Scrolling further only revealed more boring documentation. Jimbo leaned back and stretched. Glancing at his watch, he pulled the netport closer and dove into the last file. Lost in concentration, he never heard the latch move on the outer office door.

The hum of the netport drive filled the void as the HVAC system reached the optimal temperature and shut off. The drive whined and whirred, processing teraquads of data for Jimbo to study. The desk lamp buzzed just under an audible range.

"Working late tonight?"

Jimbo almost jumped out of his chair. "Shit! Jonathan, you scared the crap out of me!" He snapped the netport shut. "What the hell are you doing here? You're supposed to be in Tortola!"

"Yeah, I know. But a funny thing happened to me on the way to the islands." Jonathan slowly paced the office and glared at Jimbo with gelid disdain.

"Oh yeah...what happened?" Jimbo's senses were sharply alert due to the system's failure to announce Jonathan's approach.

"I was having lunch the other day, and I saw the weirdest thing." Jonathan stopped and leaned against a cabinet. "There I was, sitting outside, taking in the afternoon...actually thinking about Tortola..."

Jimbo apprehensively shifted in his chair.

"...when I looked across the street, and guess what I saw?"

Jimbo shifted again. "I don't know...what did you see? Where were you?"

Jonathan stepped to Jimbo's desk and leaned on it with all the burden of his anger on display. "I was at *Arturo's*...James."

Confused, Jimbo didn't respond. He carefully studied Jonathan's emotional state and nervously smiled. "Yeah...so?"

"Oh, come on, *Jimbo*..."

Jimbo's nerves shot to attention. Jonathan never called him that. Ever.

"Man, what's up?" Jimbo asked, testing.

"You don't know what I'm talking about?" Jonathan asked mockingly.

"No...I don't."

Jonathan shook his head. He began to laugh a little under his breath. "Goddamn you," he said more to himself than to Jimbo.

"Jonathan...hey, what's the matter? Oh *shit*–" Suddenly, Jimbo's tongue was yanked from his mouth almost to the point of tearing. His body rose over his desk, and his arms slapped tightly to his sides. His legs flailed madly, sending his chair slamming against the windowsill behind him. As his tongue led his body's slow forward movement, blood began to drip from the sides of his mouth. Jonathan was still staring at the desk, his arms tightly folded as if this action was causing him pain, too. He finally looked up and regarded Jimbo with callous hatred. "You goddamn, son of a bitch," he said.

Jimbo came to a halt, his eyes on level with Jonathan's. His tongue was stretched to its anatomical limit, and blood poured from his mouth. Tears streamed down his cheeks, and his eyes were filled with terror.

Jonathan didn't say a word. He just stared into his former friend's eyes and searched for a reason. "What's the matter," he asked, "Tel got your tongue?"

Jimbo tried desperately to speak.

"Let me answer that for you with another rhetorical question." Jonathan leaned forward till he almost touched Jimbo's tongue. "How's *Anari*?"

Jimbo frantically began to groan.

"Yeah, thought that might shake you up a little." Jonathan leaned back against the cabinet to watch Jimbo squirm in his telekinetic grip. "How long did you really think you'd get away with that one?"

Suddenly, the window behind Jimbo's desk exploded into a spray of fragments. The bits of glass stopped in midair, then slowly collected together into a shape that to Jonathan resembled one of those old disco balls he had once seen in a New York dance club. It glittered in the night air reflecting the lights from the campus's buildings. Jimbo tried to look back at it. Jonathan released his tongue.

"Shit!" was all Jimbo could manage at first. He coughed and spit blood, speckling the top of his desk and netport. "Jonathan," he eventually gasped, his tongue swollen, "let me explain!"

"Explain what?" Jonathan asked. "That you're a selfish, manipulative bastard?"

Jimbo began to slowly back toward the open windows. "Jonathan," he yelled, "what the hell are you doing?!"

Jonathan didn't answer and followed Jimbo to the window.

Jimbo continued floating out of the office until he stopped eight feet outside the window. He futilely wriggled within Jonathan's hold as he hung 20 stories above the campus. One of his feet kicked the ball of glass fragments, but it didn't move.

Jonathan stepped to the window and folded his arms. He eyed the Southerner whom he dangled in the night breeze. The hatred had left, replaced with a deeper emotion, one that took him by surprise. Tears welled at the corners of his eyes.

"Why?!" Jonathan demanded. "Why did you do it?!"

"We had to!" Jimbo pleaded. "There was no other choice!" He coughed and watched his blood fall 200 feet to the pavement.

"But there was a choice when it came to Anari!" Jonathan exclaimed. "Sure, you can screw me over, but yourself – that's different!"

"Jonathan, it wasn't like that! You've got to believe me!"

"I really want to, James, really. From the bottom of my heart, I want to believe that your reasoning has some...some viable purpose – something I'm not seeing." He looked at him wildly. "Well?!" he screamed. "Does it?!"

Jimbo, knowing he was caught, couldn't respond. Resolved to his fate, he stopped fighting and relaxed.

"That's what I thought," Jonathan said in disgust. He slammed his fist on the sill.

"Jonathan!" Jimbo cried from his purgatory. "Let me explain."

"Yeah, I'm listening."

"Man," Jimbo started, "when you came on the scene, it rocked our world..."

Jonathan rolled his eyes.

"...no, really! Listen to me. Jonathan, you gotta understand...." His voice dropped to a serious register. "...You're like nothing we've ever seen. You're off the charts."

"How far off?"

Jimbo hesitated. "That's classified, man. Really, I have no idea." He fell about three feet, and jerked to a halt. "NO! Shit...goddamn it, Jonathan, listen to me! I'm not bullshitting you! Only Takeda and Trumble know. Everyone else is too fragmented. We only gather parts of the puzzle, but they have the big picture!"

"Tell me, James, what else is going on?! What other things are being conveniently kept from me?"

Jimbo shrugged. "What do you mean?"

"Was that KFBC sign an accident?"

Jimbo reluctantly nodded. "All right, Jonathan. Look...do you really think all your training takes place in a classroom? Don't be so naive! How else are we going to test you?"

"God, James, people could have died!"

"No! No, not with you there! Besides, it's a calculated risk—"

"And the bus in San Francisco?"

Jimbo looked away. "I..I don't know about that one. But..." he looked back to Jonathan "... the French guard was."

Jonathan fell back. "James," he said, aghast, "I killed him."

"Like I said, man...a *calculated* risk."

Jonathan fell into despair with the realization that he couldn't be sure of anything. What had been a test, and what had been real? He stepped to the window and deathly eyed the Southerner. His despair morphed into something more deadly.

"What about Anari, James?"

"Yeah," he acknowledged, "I screwed that up big time. But you gotta understand, I was lonely...SHIT!" Jimbo had fallen another four feet. "OHHH! Man! Don't do that!"

Jonathan raised him slowly to his eye level. "Just tell me *why*."

"Buddy, pal, friend...you've been there! Haven't you?"

Jonathan didn't grace him with an answer.

"All right," Jimbo said, coughing. Blood dripped from his mouth. "What can I say? When I first saw her...I...I just wanted her, all right! Can't a guy just want a girl that bad?!"

Jonathan dropped his glare. "Yeah, James..." he said, reflecting on what he had with Tamara, "...a guy can."

"Then you understand!" Jimbo said, desperately reaching for rapport.

"You know what I *understand*, James?" Jonathan leveled a savage glare at Jimbo. "That it's about damn time I started living my life."

Jimbo's heart palpitated. The wind punched his face. "Look, Jonathan, I'll do whatever you want!" he exclaimed in panic. "I'll even erase Anari!" Jonathan's eyes narrowed, and Jimbo knew he had only minutes, maybe seconds, left. "Jesus, Jonathan, please, you're on the system right now! They're recording this....They'll hunt you down!"

"We are?" Jonathan asked mockingly. He pulled his netpad from his pocket and opened his coat to reveal the grav sig displacer strapped on his belt. He smiled. "To the system, I'm not here." He glanced at his netpad. "And according to this, your section of this building is experiencing some..." he looked back at Jimbo with a hint of pleasure "...technical difficulties."

Reverting to his Southern Baptist roots, Jimbo closed his eyes and began to recite the 23rd Psalm.

Jonathan leaned out of the window. "Don't worry," he said, not hiding his disdain, "I'm not going to kill you..."

Jimbo pitifully stopped in midverse.

"...I'm going to do something *a lot worse*."

Jimbo gasped. "How far back?!"

Jonathan's eyes narrowed more. "I don't really know..."

The life drained from Jimbo's face. "No, *please*!–"

Instantly, Jimbo's body stiffened, as if it were in some kind of cataleptic lockdown. Jonathan phased and focused his rage, wiping the Southerner's memory from his being. He gave no thought to precision or accuracy; he was out to get even.

In the brisk night wind, Jonathan stood at the window with detached numbness and observed Jimbo convulse. Like a marionette in the hands of a child, his body shook spasmodically. Spittle built at the corners of his mouth and his eyes rolled back in their sockets. Jonathan had cast an unusually broad erase field, which might wipe away 30 or more years of life. He didn't know. He didn't care. The man in front of him had taken away all that had been dear to him, and as Jonathan figured it, the law of karma had caught up to James McCarris.

Jimbo's body gave one final, violent jerk, then caved. His head fell forward, and a mixture of vomit and blood gushed from his mouth. The wind whipped his red hair about.

Jonathan stepped back as he brought Jimbo's limp bulk through the window and into the office. He slowly lowered him to the floor, almost reverently settling him onto the tile. He looked down at the man he had once called friend and reflected on the night they first met.

"What happened to you?" he asked.

Jonathan knelt and checked Jimbo's breathing. It was labored, but steady. And as he studied the inert body, he was overcome with an odd mixture of emotions. Jonathan actually still cared for James McCarris – even pitied him. He couldn't really fault him for thinking with his dick rather than his heart; he had done it himself more than he cared to admit. But to Jonathan, Jimbo had come to represent his whole Agency experience and, unfortunately, had also become the recipient of his wrath. He thought of Tamara and began to break down, but rapidly quelled the emotion. Jimbo wasn't the only metaphor for his pain, and there was still more karmic justice to dispense.

Jonathan slowly rose and reviewed his netpad. The office remained off-line to the system, but not for much longer. He shot a glance at the shattered window frame, and the ball of glass fragments glided into the room. They settled onto the floor in a small pile by Jimbo's feet. Edges of the shards caught the light from the desk lamp and reflected hot shapes of light about the room. Jonathan began to leave, but he glanced back at Jimbo quietly sleeping off his telekinetic judgment. He had no idea what would be left of Jimbo's memory. Nor did he care.

His path became clear...25

THE limo splashed through fresh puddles left behind by a front that had passed
through the D.C. Zone, and the sky was littered with broken clouds that marked the
approach of another line of storms. A deep rumble of thunder echoed like a backdrop
on the stage of the dark East Coast night. Jonathan piloted through the streets, his
mind, his soul, his whole being consumed by a deep, almost instinctual rage. With
his motivation fluxing between need and revenge, the Jonathan Kortel who had
entered the Agency full of hope and trust had now descended to a primal state of
mind. All that was dear to him had been ripped from his life. He had nothing to lose,
because in his mind, there was nothing left to lose. His thoughts were a spastic
collage, hyper-jumping between the images that represented the life he had loved
and the life he now had. Living in a cold reality of bitterness was not what he had
expected from his life, but if this was the hand he was dealt, so be it. He had crossed
this threshold of anguish before, but this time he had a strange sense of renewal, of
cleansing. This fresh bitterness slipped on his soul like a finely tailored suit, and for
the first time in his life, Jonathan Kortel felt justified in wearing it.

He punched in an ID sequence on the limo's netport, and Carter Shoalburg's
image appeared. He was crowded into a small council station; his chrome net
connectors reflected the light from a small lamp.

"Carter, are you picking up my sig?" Jonathan asked.

"Negative, Jonny. I'm deep in, and you're nowhere to be found."

"Good. When I get closer, I may need your help....Are you still up for this?"

"Hell, yeah!" Shoalburg said. "Don't worry about me. You just watch yourself,
you hear me?"

"Thanks, Carter, I'll owe you one."

"You'll owe me nothing, Jonny," Shoalburg said sincerely. "I just hope you get
your answers." He paused, his image frozen on the screen like a mutated humanoid
bug. Shoalburg's blank expression gave nothing away, but Jonathan could sense that
the famous Tel had something on his mind.

"What are you thinking?"

Shoalburg hesitated. "Be careful. These two are ruthless sons of bitches. Believe me, I know."

"I appreciate that, but I'm not worried. I know you've got my back."

Shoalburg smiled and tapped the side of his headgear. His image cut out.

~

Jonathan parked the limo a few blocks from the downtown *Citenikelet* building. It was one of the few street spaces left in D.C. A light rain began to fall as he walked down the sidewalk that led to the loading dock area. Stopping just short of the entrance, he checked his netpad for the vid readouts from the building's security grid. Shoalburg had effectively masked him from the security cameras, and the modified sig displacer was working perfectly. "Thanks, Bixx," he said quietly, and pocketed the netpad. The collar of his coat sensed the rain and tightened slightly around his neck.

It was 2:00 in the morning, and there wasn't a soul around. The wind from the storm had kicked up, swirling dust and trash into little tornadoes that Jonathan disrupted. The rain intensified. Water began rolling down the ramp of the loading dock in waves, and droplets pelted the back of his coat with a relentlessly manic syncopation. He ducked under the platform's overhang, and his coat's biofabric mesh expanded and shifted to its "dry out" setting. He approached the set of doors that led to the lobby level.

"Carter," he asked into his netpad, "can you unlock these doors?"

The center door clicked twice.

"Like that?" Carter said with a cocky smile from the pad's tiny screen.

The hallways were dim from the repressed lighting, and Jonathan's boots squished unforgivingly against the freshly polished travertine. He approached the main elevator banks and stopped. He cautiously peered around a corner. The lobby of *Citenikelet Investments* presented itself in a vaguely Greek motif. The main foyer was ringed by ten massive Corinthian columns that rose five stories from the lobby floor, and with its severe lighting reflecting harshly off of every surface, it seemed to have been designed to give visitors the impression that they had just entered the gates of heaven. Two stories above the lobby floor, the firm's holovid promo was still projecting its 30-foot-tall corporate hype. A guard would have been dwarfed in the cavernous expanse, but suspiciously, the security station was deserted.

That's weird, Jonathan thought. He clicked his netpad to life and whispered, "Where's the lobby guard?"

No response.

"Carter?" he asked, looking down at the pad.

The screen's pixelated static greeted him with the coldness of a New England winter.

"Carter?" There was a trace of panic in his voice. "I need the elevator!" His nerves jumped on edge with the realization that he was utterly and completely solo. He glanced at his watch: 2:21:06 a.m. With only about an hour left of masking time and Shoalburg out of the equation, what little safety net he thought he had was gone. The loss might mean his presence had been detected, but it also could be just a signal disruption caused by the building's complex web of interlink hubs. His heart began to race. He glanced back down the hallway to the loading dock, to the false comfort of a life to which he knew he could never return. He shifted his attention back to the remarkably simple oak doors that distinguished the private elevator car to the penthouse. His heart pounded erratically against his chest. His breathing was shallow and rapid. It was now or never. All that Jonathan was – all that he would be – had come down to this moment.

A memory came into his mind and tugged at his heart like an insistent child on the pant leg of a parent. He thought of the last time he had seen his mother and father alive. And his path became clear.

The monkeys kept staring...26

JONATHAN'S access to the private elevator's security codes had vanished with Shoalburg's signal, and with his limited masking time, he couldn't even consider the 70 flights of stairs. He keenly trained his telekinetic force at the beautifully hand-carved elevator doors and began to pry them apart.

Takeda and Trumble weren't casual with security. They knew their positions within the Tel world were fragile at best, so Jonathan figured the entrance to their private car would be heavily reinforced. He phased and focused a tight field against the doors. The thick oak veneer began to splinter, which revealed a honeycombed titanium skeleton. He focused more tightly, and the doors started to give. Blood began to run from his nose.

The titanium doors buckled and compressed like sponges to expose an opulence reserved for the privileged few. Jonathan sprinted into the cab's burled wood luxury, slamming into one of its fabric walls. Polynesian hand-carved monkeys glared at him from perches above the cab's leather floor. He frantically searched for the elevator's emergency door, running his fingers along the ceiling trim until he found the release catch. It was cleverly disguised in the rope molding. He clicked it and jettisoned the door onto the elevator's roof. Peering up through the escape hatch, he could see the elevator shaft rising the height of the building. At every floor were emergency lights, demarcating the perfect path to the penthouse.

Jonathan stepped directly under the opening, pressed his arms to his sides, looked up and quickly slipped into phase.

The monkeys kept staring.

Mother...27

CYRIL Takeda poured himself another sherry. The squeak of the cork being replaced severed the living room's calm just as the concerto started. Jeffrey Trumble looked over his reading glasses and frowned.

The Burton of Kendal chimed once. 2:30 a.m.

As the second movement ended, the solo of German violinist Mansford Drural began. His artistry was legendary, and this particular movement always left Takeda melancholy. He threw back his sherry and slammed the glass onto the bar. Trumble looked over again, glanced at his watch and sighed. They never heard the initial cracking of the stress on the striations in the wood.

Mansford Drural reached the apex of his tenuto.

The two wooden doors of the penthouse elevator blew so completely free of their frames that they flew into the room like cardboard. One slammed into the Burton of Kendal and obliterated its 18th-century mahogany body. Its master painted arch dial went sailing across the room and shattered against a Queen Anne desk. The other door carved a deep rut to the subfloor of the living room and skidded to rest at the foot of Trumble's ottoman. It bunched his grandmother's Victorian rug into an accordioned mass of ornate cadmium flower patterns.

Jonathan slowly floated up from the dark shaft and through the shattered door frame.

"Good evening, Jonathan," Trumble said, casually considering him through the distortion of his lenses. He delicately removed the glasses and folded them away into the breast pocket of his robe. "We've been expecting you."

"It's morning, actually, Jeffrey," Takeda corrected. He generously poured himself another drink.

Trumble waived him off.

"You know, Jonathan," Takeda said; "you could have just asked for the access codes. There was no need for theatrics."

"Grandmum would be heartbroken to see her rug this way," Trumble said.

Jonathan glided into the center of the living room and landed gently in the middle of the gouge left by the elevator door. His knees bent slightly as he settled down. He viciously eyed the two Tels.

"So, my boy. What can we do for...augghh!" Trumble desperately reached for his throat.

"Jonnnathaaan..." Takeda sang, wagging his finger.

Seething, Jonathan focused on Takeda.

"Manners, Jonathan," Takeda said disappointedly. "Haven't we taught you anything?"

Jonathan released Trumble, who gasped for air.

"You *know* why I'm here," Jonathan said in a low, measured voice.

"My God," Trumble said. He rubbed his throat. "Is that any way to treat your elders?—"

Jonathan's glare cut him off. "What's in my head?...*Asshole*."

Trumble cautiously shot Takeda a questioning look, then turned back to Jonathan. "Well, my boy," he began, "that's not really for you to, hughhh—" Trumble let out a gasp as his body seized. His back arched and his hands shot straight to his sides. Motionless in the large chair, he sat like an old-style mannequin in a bathware display. He started to vibrate, slowly at first, but picking up speed until he was violently shaking. His eyes rolled back into his head: first his right, then his left. Foam curdled at the edges of his mouth and began splattering about.

"*Release* him!" Takeda screamed.

"I asked a question," Jonathan demanded.

Cyril Takeda took a step forward. "You," he said coldly, "are in no goddamn position to bargain."

Trumble's body was now a blur.

Suddenly, Jonathan's vision shifted and the room's darkness became blacker, as if he had just donned a pair of solar goggles. The darkness shifted again, and what little edges of blurred light his eyes previously picked out of the black vanished. Jonathan was instantly gripped with shock as the realization hit: He was completely blind.

Trumble stopped shaking, but the residual force threw him out of the chair like a rag doll. He landed in an unconscious heap on his grandmother's rug. His arms flapped limply to his sides, coming to rest in contorted positions.

Panicked, Jonathan stumbled back. He caught his foot on the edge of the gouge left by the door and fell to the floor.

"I think *you're* the one who's *screwed*," Takeda commented.

Jonathan's hearing quickly faded. All he could sense was the soft, rhythmic swoosh of his own blood as it pulsed through his now-useless ear canals. He felt his throat go numb. He tried to speak, but he couldn't form a sound. He was cripplingly void of all his senses.

Takeda trained his attention on Trumble's body. It slowly rose off the rug, floated to the couch and gently settled onto the soft cushions of the heirloom. Trumble's arms folded themselves across his chest.

Radically disoriented, Jonathan groped across the floor on his hands and knees. His fingers caught in the gouge, and he fell to his face. His chin struck the polished hardwood with a crack.

Takeda sighed loudly.

At that moment, Jonathan's senses mysteriously returned. Startled, he squinted at the sudden reintroduction of light to his brain.

Takeda came and stood over him. "How does it feel," he asked, "to be defenseless?"

Jonathan crawled to face him. His chin swollen and bleeding, he tried, still squinting, to look up at the Agency leader.

"If you think I'm bluffing..." Takeda said just above a whisper. A sharp, deep pain instantly gripped Jonathan's chest, and a throbbing shot down his arm. He frantically clawed at his shirt, gasping for air. "...here's a little glimpse of *eternity*."

As if a switch had been thrown, Jonathan's heart abruptly stopped. He collapsed backwards, landing with his legs bent underneath him and his arms out to his sides. He felt his organs begin to relax inside his body, and his eyes focused on the ornate vine pattern carved into the woodwork of the living room's ceiling. He gasped and took his last breath.

"Mother..." he softly exhaled.

His vision faded to white.

You are destined...28

CRASHING.
Hard.
Like a thousand body bags slamming to the ground.
A screech...no, a squawk.
Wind. A sound like chimes.
Heat. Burning, but not.
Light. Intense brightness.
Trying the eyes.
"Shit..."
Standing. Vibration in the feet.
Feet. Sunk into...wet.

Jonathan cautiously opened his eyes. There was a rushing sound, as if the air itself were being drained away. Then everything repeated itself, but not as before: He now had a sense of where he was.

A beach.

The waves crashed, and Jonathan's vision returned, but the color seemed muted, like a faded photo from the past. The ocean's green, the sky's blue, the sand's silver – all *distended* somehow. The beach stretched to the horizon on either side. He looked down at feet buried in the sand, warm between his toes. He turned, but the physical sense of turning was missing. A forest of palm trees rose behind him and ran the length of the beach as far as he could see.

He had an urge to walk down the beach, but something inside him prodded him to head toward the palms. As the ground rose, his legs responded, but with a leaden detachment. He entered the forest and pushed his way through the undergrowth. It was slow going at first, but as he made his way, the trees began to thin. Looking up, he saw the sunlight cutting through the canopy of fronds, and he began feeling shafts of warmth with each step. Time had seemed to pass. A minute? An hour? A lifetime?

He didn't know. And strangely, he didn't care.

He emerged onto a large grassy area where beds of flowers, infant palms and a bench – sitting in the center of a concrete circle – all greeted him with a vague sense of purpose. He stepped forward. His foot struck an object. Startled, he looked down. It was a child's toy. He picked up the little red truck and spun its front wheels. It made a familiar sound. A sweet sound. A haunting sound.

His bottom lip began to quiver. The warmth he had enjoyed surrendered to a cold that seemed for him and him alone. He knew where he was.

Hawaii.

His heart pounded while he desperately searched the yard. It continued to rise, past beds of roses and heather, to a house. Jonathan realized it was his parents' house. Then he saw the pale green door that led to the kitchen, to milk and cookies, to the waist of his mother, where he had buried his face when he wanted the world to vanish. Jonathan ran as fast as he could, occasionally stumbling, but feeling no pain of his toe being stubbed or his ankle rolling over. He stopped short of the threshold and paused to take in the home. His fingers ran over flaking paint and loose-fitting hardware, and he stepped into the kitchen and found everything in its place. A search of the house unearthed tangible memories of a life he had experienced too briefly, but had longed for his entire life. The only thing missing was his parents.

If I'm dead, he thought, *then surely this is hell.*

Suddenly, Jonathan's mind began to fill with a strange sense of doubt, as if his lucid self were rising to the conscious surface – a hint of reality that beckoned for his attention. He ran back down the hill and plunged into the forest. He fought through the palms, the sounds of the beach growing more intense until he glimpsed it through the maze of trunks. He stopped, barely at the edge of the beach, hidden (he hoped) at the lip of its density.

A figure was on the beach. It was a woman.

She faced the horizon, her feet at the perfect point where a wave lost its momentum and fell back to rejoin the sea. She turned. Jonathan recognized her. He fell to his knees and started to weep. "Mother..." he said, again the child he had been. He started to wail, letting go of all that had held him for so many years.

His mother spread her arms. Jonathan burst from the palms. He didn't care if he was dead. He didn't care if this was hell. He just wanted to hold her.

As he got closer, he could see that she was dressed as he had last seen her, more than 20 years ago at the Honolulu airport. She wore her crisp, white lab coat and khaki short pants. She even wore her favorite belt with its silver buckle of the stylized naked woman, the one that had adorned the mudflaps of old trucks. She had loved that belt.

Painfully prudent thoughts gripped his rational self, and he stopped just out of arm's length. He fought the emotional urge to hug her, to kiss her, to simply nuzzle her face, and smell her lab coat and soak in all the comfort her arms could bring. One more time.

"Mother...what's happening?" His mouth formed the words, but he hadn't heard a sound. Was it in his mind? He didn't really know.

"Don't be afraid, darling," his mother assured. Even though she had moved, he didn't have the sense that she had. She was now barely a foot from him.

"Am I...dead?" he asked. He searched her face, which he noticed had no visible signs of age – the soft crow's feet that he remembered from their final embrace were gone. Her brow was void of the concentration lines that her profession had etched over the years. Her face, in fact, was smooth, almost like a Kabuki dancer – ageless as well as genderless.

She smiled, and Jonathan's heart filled with an awing sense of love that seemed to radiate throughout his body.

"Mother," he softly asked, "what should I do?"

"You are destined for a different passage, son."

Behind her, Jonathan could see dark, featureless figures moving in and out of the surf's mist. They were beckoning to him. He shifted his attention back to her. "I've missed you so much..."

She brought her hand to his face, touching it tenderly with the tips of her fingers. "It's not your time," she whispered, and knowingly smiled.

Jonathan looked into her eyes and suddenly felt his whole being – the sum of all that he was – rush through them and into her soul.

His vision dissolved to black.

You might know him...   29

"**HAVE** a nice trip?" Takeda asked.

Jonathan, his clothes drenched with sweat, gasped for air while his heart came back on line. Takeda was glowering over him.

"You've been gone for five seconds," he mused. He straightened and walked back to the bar to pour another sherry. "I believe your original question was 'What's in my head?'" He raised his glass in mock toast, "Only the best," and threw back his drink.

"Why?" Jonathan said roughly. He rubbed at his chest and started to cough violently.

"Why?" Takeda retorted. He wiped his mouth with the sleeve of his robe. "Because you're very, very special, Jonathan. In fact, you're one of a kind. Oh, we've had powerful Tels before," he placed his gloved right hand into the pocket of his robe, "but never anything like you."

Jonathan began to rise, and was instantly jerked into a standing position. His arms were held tight against his body by a force that felt eerily like it was coming from inside him.

Takeda chuckled.

"What will this technology do to me?" Jonathan asked. "Am I...a weapon?"

Takeda hesitated and smiled. "Let's start with the first question, shall we?" He calmly walked over to him. "The genetically tailored bionanoware that we implanted is currently integrating with your cerebral cortex, brain stem, cerebellum...basically, everything from your neck up. In time, the nanoware will spread and fully merge with your central nervous system. It's intelligent nanoware, Jonathan. Or as the lab boys affectionately call it, *soul*ware."

Jonathan flinched.

"Oh, it won't be painful..."

"Tell that to Zvara."

"Zvara," Takeda said, "was an experiment, nothing more." He resumed pacing. "Currently, the nanoware can control most of your base functions...sight, hearing, speech. Or motor control, such as you're experiencing right now. But soon it will be able to augment your higher functions, as well. Thought, reason...the like."

"And my gift?" Jonathan questioned.

Takeda stopped and eyed him. "Especially your gift."

"Now the second question," Jonathan said. "Why?"

Takeda slowly smiled. "Lights!" The living room lights dimmed to 10 percent of their illumination. "Jonathan," Takeda said out of the darkness, "do you know how powerful you are?"

"No...not really."

"You are, without a doubt, the most powerful Tel ever to exist."

"How powerful?" Jonathan thought he sensed Takeda smiling through the darkness.

"I thought you'd ask. Stream file Kortel 0005!"

A 10-foot by 10-foot holojection instantly appeared in front of Jonathan. Its lucent glow highlighted every exposed edge and gave the room a dated look, like a celluloid silent he had seen in history vids. The feed began to stream. Test after test, case study after case study, the file was an endless torrent of telekinetic data. The grav results, APT waves, field flux levels – all beyond normal parameters. For several minutes, Jonathan scanned the massive holochive. It became almost overwhelming. Takeda stood motionless, warily studying his reactions.

Halfway through, Jonathan began to formulate the complete picture. His level strength was immense, and if he read correctly, his ability bordered on evolutional. He was, he concluded, more than just a Tel.

He was something new altogether.

"God..." he said under his breath.

"Not quite yet, Jonathan, but who knows?" Takeda said flippantly. "Keep reading. I think you'll find the last part *very* interesting."

The streaming came to a file marked "SECURED" and stopped.

"Release!" Takeda ordered. "Voice authorization: Takeda alpha."

The file launched, and Jonathan began scanning through its abstruse gravity charts and quantum mechanics computations. After a minute, he looked at Takeda who had been intently watching him. "I...I don't get it. This stuff is way over my head."

Takeda grinned and motioned excitedly for him to keep reading. He was almost gleeful with the anticipation of what Jonathan would find.

Jonathan continued to read the rest of the file. Just before the last page streamed, he gasped. "Stop!" he ordered. The file froze. "Prior page!" It sequenced back.

Takeda started to chuckle.

"Holy ssshit!" Jonathan exclaimed just above a whisper.

"Holy shit is right," Takeda said smugly.

"This can't be. This is impossible!"

"Oh, it's not only possible," Takeda came closer, "it's *quantifiable*!" He stepped between the holojection and Jonathan, his silhouette rimmed with a glow that gave him a transcendental presence. "Before you came to us, you brought down a 500-ton airliner that had been partially torn apart by a Tactical Short Range Bioweapon. The warhead of that missile contained a biogenetic agent. When you field fluxed, you altered the molecular properties of that agent."

"But James told me that his equipment hadn't recorded anything," Jonathan argued.

"James lied," Takeda said. "And by the way, you were a bit excessive, don't you think?"

"How bad is he?"

Takeda shrugged nonchalantly. "He's eating intravenously right now. We might recover some of his memories....It's hard to say."

Jonathan looked away.

"These results are unassailable," Takeda continued. "You have altered matter at the molecular level!"

"You haven't answered my second question," Jonathan said.

Takeda paused. "Control," he said with such casualness that what he had said barely registered with Jonathan.

"Excuse me?"

"You're not a weapon, Jonathan. Our world has no need for anything like that. Our arsenal is built on influence – financial, political, it doesn't matter, as long as it serves our needs. Do you really think we would let someone like you do anything to disrupt the order that we've been building for the last hundred years? We could have revealed ourselves years ago, but what would that have accomplished?" Takeda paused as if inviting Jonathan to answer. "Probably the destruction of our kind. If we reveal, our human cousins will fear us and eventually hunt us down like animals. Jonathan, who do you think has been saving man from himself? If it hadn't been for our influence, this world would have been a charred, dead planet 50 years ago. We've been controlling the dynamics of mankind ever since we went under. Who do you think influenced the decision for Khrushchev to turn those warships around in 1962? Who stopped the freighter in New York harbor 12 years ago? Who prevented the space stations from colliding last year?" He was now inches from Jonathan's face. "The Tels."

"What about Hawaii?" Jonathan asked gravely.

Takeda's demeanor suddenly shifted, and Jonathan could tell he had struck some kind of Machiavellian nerve in the Agency leader. "Jonathan, Hawaii was...a *calculated* action."

Jonathan thought he felt his heart stop again.

Takeda cautiously stepped back, his hands still in the pockets of his robe. "You must try and understand," he said with all the solemnity of a father consoling a child, "with Hawaii, we...oh, how can I put this?...*let* it happen, more than made it happen."

Stunned, Jonathan glared at Takeda. It was almost too much to comprehend.

"Now, Jonathan," Takeda said, "before you make any rash moves..." He took his right hand from his pocket and showed off a small device. It caught the light from the holojection and glowed a steely blue against Takeda's black glove. "I still control you." His fingers closed around it. "I know you don't understand it now, but, someday, perhaps you will. Hawaii, Jonathan, *has* changed the world. It has put into motion more security measures than a thousand interventions."

"You murdered a million people!" Jonathan said, hardly restraining his rage.

"And by doing so," Takeda said, "there are finally in place safeguards to prevent atrocities of unimaginable scale! No war could have accomplished this!" He was pacing again. "Such a war would have cost more lives and caused more sorrow, not to mention risking the complete annihilation of this planet! We live here, too, Jonathan, and we certainly can't trust *them* to take care of it." Takeda faced the holojection and spread his arms wide. "Look at you, Jonathan! You're the next step!" He spun on his heels to face him. "With your power, there's no limit to what we could do! New technology! New advances!" He stepped closer. "My God, you might even take us to the stars!"

"Cyril," Jonathan said with loathing, "I would rather die than help you."

Takeda slowly folded his arms and tapped the controller on his lower lip. "Don't be so melodramatic," he said with all the weight of his power. "You need to start thinking about the big picture – and *your* place in it."

Jonathan began to sense an extreme heat building inside his body. It started spreading into every cell, radiating from the center of his chest to his extremities. He felt like he was being cooked alive. He tried to phase, but the ability, which had become second instinct to him, had vanished.

Takeda looked down his nose. "Come on, Jonathan. Don't waste your life. We don't know when another one like you will come around again."

Sweat came from Jonathan's every pore; his body desperately tried to extinguish the heat that was consuming him. He was shaking, even in Takeda's telekinetic grip.

"Go...to...hell...Takeda," he barely managed.

Takeda sadly shook his head, and with a sigh that summed his frustration, he pressed a small green button on the controller.

The heat instantly intensified, surging toward Jonathan's head. His lungs felt filled with a fire that was licking at the back of his throat. "Oh my God!" he screamed. Takeda, his finger poised on the green button, gave him a "had enough?" look.

Suddenly, the room exploded with a vision-crushing flash. Takeda was thrown off his feet like he had been slammed by an invisible truck. The controller flipped end-over-end out of Jonathan's field of vision. The heat, and Takeda's telekinetic grip, abated, and Jonathan collapsed to the floor. The flash, he realized, had been a Light-Force.

Takeda was visibly shaken. He began to stand, but was struck again with another blast. At each discharge, the beams deflected off the field wall he had induced and struck the ceiling in bright explosions. Its wood and fabric turned into gooey upside-down puddles that dripped and hissed as they struck the floor.

A numinous figure slowly approached with each successive cratering of the ceiling. Jonathan's eyes were partially blinded by the Light-Force's discharges, which rendered it impossible for him to distinguish the attacker in the dark room. Then the silhouetted form walked into the glow of the holojection, and his nerves spiked.

"Jesus, Takeda!" Georgia exclaimed. She fired off another round into his field. "Won't you just die!" She glanced at Jonathan. "You look like shit."

"Nice to see you, too," Jonathan said, coughing and wiping the sweat from his face.

Takeda was pressed flat against the floor as Georgia let off one more round. This discharge slammed his head violently against the wood, creating a horrific gash that ran the length of his face. Suddenly, her handheld Beretta began to whine down, and in a manner that resembled a ballet move, she flung it over the bar while pulling from behind her back a weapon Jonathan had never seen before. Its matte black surface was featureless and seemed to absorb the holojection light. To Jonathan, it appeared she was holding a shadow.

Seeing his opening, Takeda grav'd and caught Georgia before she had time to fire the weapon. He lifted her off the floor and spread arms and legs out in his own version of a telekinetic crucifixion. Jonathan tried to phase, but was slammed to the floor by Takeda's unyielding wrath. Something in his arm snapped.

"You're not the only one with nanoware!" Takeda raged. Blood poured down his face. He glared at Georgia, and her limbs began to stretch to the boundary of their structural integrity. Jonathan watched in disbelief as Georgia's left arm acquiesced to Takeda's will and slowly started to separate from her body. Blood spurted from her shoulder joint as the skin and muscle began to shred. She screamed an inhuman sound, like some wild animal being torn apart.

In the horror of the moment, Jonathan felt a strange sense of clarity press upon the edge of his mind. The bionanoware gestating deep in his neural system had reached its first stage of development. Reflexively, the telekinetic ability that had so long dominated his thoughts slipped away to join the rest of his body's autonomic functions. In its place came a new, more powerful ability: one that fed off his heritage and expanded his Tel perception. It was like a cataract being removed from his mind's eye.

Jonathan simply thought about being free of Takeda's grip, and the field wall that had kept him pressed to the floor vanished. He looked at Georgia, just milliseconds from tearing apart, and his mind almost occluded from the torrent of memories that jammed his consciousness. His heart went out to her. Instantly, the telekinetic force lacerating Georgia disappeared. Takeda fell onto his back, while Georgia crumpled to the floor.

A new pain moved through Jonathan's body. Its recondite wake trailed a neural sensation that seemed strangely inorganic — more technical in nature. Like an electronic digital signature, it pulsed with an androidlike rhythm. Jonathan desperately tried to grasp what was happening to him. It seemed that phasing was not part of the equation anymore, and thought — or even emotion — could become manifest. He looked at his hands. They were shaking in sync with this new pain. Suddenly, there was a deep, almost subsonic rumble behind him, but the sound seemed compressed, like a miniature clap of thunder. Then Jonathan felt a thin edge of biting cold air whoosh past his head.

Takeda groaned.

Jonathan torqued in his direction and recoiled in awe. In the dim light of the holojection, Takeda was wearing a look of complete surprise. He was on his knees and appeared to be in a queer state of being, like his body was out of focus. Jonathan rubbed his eyes, thinking them affected by the extreme heat. But when he looked again, the Agency leader seemed to be morphing, becoming...transparent.

Takeda was beginning to look like a medical hologram. He sorrowfully examined himself, and gingerly stuck his fingers *into* his chest. He grinned at Jonathan with a childish look that asked, "Isn't this amazing?" But his expression changed as he registered the horror of his imminent death. His form quivered for a second, and in the time it takes for a heart to beat, his matter delicately dispersed into a fine vapor that glittered blue and pink in the glow of the holojection. His black gloves dropped silently to the floor.

Jonathan heard behind him a small click. It cut through the numbness of his shock and filled the room with a soft, audible hum that barely registered at the threshold of his hearing. A leather sole scuffed into position, accepting a shift in weight. He turned to find Georgia, her left arm barely hanging at her side, in the quiet glow of the holojection. She was holding the shadow weapon.

"Georgia!" Jonathan exclaimed. Every muscle in his telekinetically exhausted body collectively relaxed as she stepped fully into the light. "Oh, God, am I glad you're—"

"I've always hated that name," Georgia said with a strange monotone to her voice. She slowly stepped toward him. The weapon remained raised.

"Georgia?..."

Georgia kneeled down and cringed when the fingers of her shattered arm met the floor. The tip of the weapon's barrel came to rest inches from Jonathan's nose. She studied him with a detached severity. "You're not the only one who's lost someone they loved," she said finally. "I, too, lost someone dear to me." She stood and leveled the weapon directly at his face. The edges of its black housing were devoid of any reflections. "You might know him," she said, grimacing from the movement. "His name was Jacob Whitehorse."

A harsh sensation tore through Jonathan's nerves like shards of jagged glass. He peered into Georgia's eyes, but found they held no memory of him, and as he searched her face, he suddenly realized these eyes were identical to some he had looked into once before – on a balcony in Chicago, a long time ago. They had the same pupilless feature. The same intense black. The same intense hate.

"Georgia, please..."

"*My* name," she said, with a surge of power and pride, "is Kaya Whitehorse!"

The humming stopped...   30

CAREFUL to keep the shadow weapon trained at Jonathan's head, Kaya Whitehorse took a few steps back. She clicked a button at the tip of the trigger. The humming rose an octave.

"Georgia...I...I mean Kaya. Please!" Jonathan pleaded. "It was self-defense! Your father forced me—"

"Forced you? What a joke!" she exclaimed. "My father offered you your future. Your *true* future! But no, you had to choose the Agency. And look what that got you." She smiled smugly. "What's it like being a puppet?"

"You should know," Jonathan said coolly.

Kaya Whitehorse's eyes narrowed. "For the record, I *loved* Tarris." She relaxed and let out a snicker that seemed to define her disgust at a bad memory she had kept locked away. "You know, my father really believed that you were the one to lead us out of this absurd existence, and he was willing to do anything for your—"

"Like kill anyone who got in his way?"

She hesitated. "If needed."

"What about us?" Jonathan asked, trying to connect with the woman he had known.

Kaya Whitehorse's eyes softened as she regarded him with what seemed to Jonathan a glint of compassion, but they quickly narrowed with resolve again. "Oh, don't worry, baby," she mused, "you were a damn good screw. But like most male Tels, you're easy to lead around." She began to laugh.

"You know I'm faster than light."

Her laugh dissolved. She stood like a warrior at the end of a long and arduous hunt. "This is a Matter-Force weapon, Jonathan, and unless you're the Infinite Tel, this ought to do to you what it did to ol' Cyril there." She flicked the barrel toward the gloves. "You know," she said with a sigh, "I am sorry you miss your parents so much." She leveled the Matter-Force rifle at his chest. "Maybe there's something I can do about that."

The humming stopped.

Kaya Whitehorse discharged the shadow weapon: its spatial-altering wave radiated directly into Jonathan's chest. The ebony wake consumed any light, and the recoil knocked her to the floor, screaming, her left arm spinning to rest somewhere in the middle of the room.

Jonathan instinctually phased, and his vision detonated into a bright field of white. His mind, his soul, his whole being flooded with beautiful, brilliant music of ten thousand upon ten thousand angels in full chorus. Still on his knees, Jonathan spread his arms to receive the Matter-Force wave like a miscreant accepting God's love. The wave slammed into his sternum and began to curl and spread in two equal directions along an invisible path that arched back upon itself directed by the curves of his outstretched arms. Within a nanosecond, it appeared he was hugging a giant oil-filled bubble, which continued to grow until it enveloped Kaya Whitehorse. Her figure wriggled and deformed as the bubble washed over her. Then the Matter-Force wave collapsed upon itself and crushed Kaya, along with all matter within, into subatomic oblivion.

Her death scream echoed in Jonathan's mind.

Jonathan collapsed to his hands and knees. A sharp tingling ricocheted throughout his body, and his head throbbed from the spatial-altering trauma. His vision slowly clarified. Disoriented and shaking from paroxysm, he surveyed the room. The holojection seemed to be the only thing moving. Jeffrey Trumble lay motionless on the couch, and both Takeda and Kaya Whitehorse were gone. He collapsed onto his side and threw up. His netpad spilled from his pocket. He clicked it on, and Carter Shoalburg's face pixeled up on the tiny vidscreen.

"Carter," he said weakly, "I think I need a little help here..." He felt himself starting to go under.

"Hold on, man," Shoalburg said. "Some friends of yours are heading your way."

Jonathan tried to focus on Shoalburg's tiny image, but his vision was too blurred. "Thanks, Carter," he said.

Shoalburg smiled. "I told you I'd have your back."

The netpad slipped from his fingers. *It's done,* he thought. But even as he wavered on the edge of consciousness, Jonathan Kortel felt a foreboding sense of doubt crawl into bed with his soul. With one last glance around the room, his attention came to rest on the holochive, its brutal data still quivering in the center of the room.

He smiled, then carefully wiped the vomit from his mouth. "Off program," he uttered, and quietly passed out.

I know him pretty well...31

JONATHAN awoke to a blurry, whitish-green light that was obliterating his field of vision. A black silhouette of a head eclipsed the light and appeared to grow as Jonathan's eyes began to focus.

"Kreet?..." he asked, his voice cracking a bit.

"Who'd you think you'd see?" Kreet replied. "God?"

"The thought had occurred to me," Jonathan quipped. He tried to sit up, reached to rub his eyes and noticed the biomed regeneration unit that cradled his arm.

"Easy there, killer. Just lay back down," Kreet said. "You're in no shape to be getting up."

"What...what happened?" Jonathan asked hoarsely.

"Your forearm took the brunt of the fall, fracturing your ulna in two places," a familiar voice replied. Kreet stepped aside to reveal Sasha, who was sitting on the edge of the table next to him. She was wearing a black sleeveless T-shirt, military rip pants and dull gray work boots. Rocket and Bixx stood behind her. She smiled affectionately. "How are you feeling?"

"Okay, all things considered," Jonathan said. "Hey, who did my arm? This looks like a pretty high-end unit."

Sasha motioned behind him, and Sanjiv stepped to the table.

"I thought you were a systems specialist," Jonathan said.

"You never asked what kind!" Sanjiv replied with a laugh.

"Hey...ah...can I have a moment with Jonathan?" Sasha asked the group.

They nodded knowingly and shuffled out of the makeshift medical area. Sasha hopped off the table and came up to Jonathan's side. She took his hand. Jonathan began to speak, but stopped himself. She smiled and pulled his hand to her face, holding it tight against her cheek. "I'm glad you're all right," she said. She kissed the back of it, and her expression changed. She placed his hand at his side. "I have something for you." She hesitantly removed an old PDA from her pocket. "I'm supposed to give this to you now."

Sasha helped Jonathan sit up. He took the small pad, and she stepped back in a gesture that gave the perception of privacy. He clicked it on. The bearded face of Armando Zvara appeared on the tiny LCD screen. Jonathan had never seen him smile.

"Hello, Jonathan," Zvara's image said. "If you are seeing me, then more than likely, Trumble or Takeda, possibly both, are dead. And, I would venture to say...you know what you are now." He paused and pulled at his beard. "This will be a difficult time for you. You are now a fugitive in the Tel world, and you will not be able to stay in New America. Time is critical, so you must act fast." He cleared his throat. "I sent Sasha to assist with your crossing in any way that she could."

Jonathan glanced at Sasha, who nervously pulled stray hair from her face.

"Now, I know you are probably thinking that you had already crossed when you killed Jacob Whitehorse on that balcony in Chicago. That is what the Agency wanted you to think. Your real crossing, Jonathan, could only come when you fully knew what you were. And now that you do, it is time for you to develop into what you are destined to be. But not yet. First, you will have to...disappear for a while. There are Tels in Russia who will help you with this – you will have to trust them. Sasha has all the file work and identity protocols that you will need. When the time is right, we will contact you." Zvara pondered his next thought. "Jonathan, let me be frank here....I do not know if you will ever be able to come back to New America again. It is hard to say at this time what the fallout from this situation will be. We will monitor it and try to keep you informed. And, Jonathan..." Zvara's voice became grave, "...I do not need to remind you that you are still human and quite killable. So watch your back, keep your field up, and good luck." The image cut out.

Jonathan sat quietly staring at the blank screen.

"Are you all right?" Sasha asked.

Jonathan shifted uneasily on the table. "Yeah," he said softly, "I'm all right."

Sasha handed him a small envelope. "Here's your new ID card, itinerary and travel passcard. And also a chip with software to teach you to speak Russian....We think it will be able to dialog with your nanoware. There's a series of words that will automatically create the interface. If not, there's a vid for backup, along with all your contacts." She gingerly removed a tiny device from her pants pocket. "This is for you. Hang onto it. You never know when you might need it."

It was the controller.

Jonathan cautiously took it and the envelope. "I want to go through San Francisco," he said solemnly.

Sasha smiled tenderly. "I knew you would. It's already been arranged."

"Hey," Jonathan said, grabbing her hand and gently pulling her close, "how well do you know Zvara?"

"Oh...I know him pretty well." She kissed him softly on the cheek.

"Really?" he questioned, pulling away. "How?"

Sasha hesitated slightly. "Because," she said with an intuitive grin, "he's my father."

Blanket of the night...32

A lone seagull rode a current of air as the Pacific Ocean released its might against the jagged rocks of Point Reyes. The wind blew hard against Jonathan's face, and he could taste the salt on his lips after each relentless gust. He looked to the edge of the world at the sun starting to slip beneath the horizon, its dying rays of gold and yellow extending between the breaks of a storm building a hundred miles out to sea. Lost in his thoughts, he watched the sun disappear completely, never noticing the blanket of night being pulled over the earth.

He turned and slowly walked to the memorial. The small acreage in the Point Reyes National Park seemed a fitting place, since it was one of the nation's westernmost points. It, along with three other locations, had been put to a national netvote, and five years after the event, the International Memorial for the Victims of Hawaii opened its doors to anyone who wanted to pray or reflect or say goodbye.

Jonathan, as he had done once before with thousands of other relatives of survivors, entered the Great Hall and approached the small kiosk. Its simple design had a quiet dignity that was apropos to its patient wait for the next visitors to use its gigantic database to help their healing. He entered his parents' IDs, then looked around the hall at the 360-degree holojection that had been taken by the Freedom 10 Space Station only days before the event.

The kiosk chimed. "As a courtesy to the survivors," a pleasant, yet authoritative female systems voice announced, "will anyone who is not a family member please leave the Great Hall at this time. The doors will automatically close in three minutes. Thank you for your cooperation." An elderly Japanese couple sadly glanced at Jonathan, bowed, and quietly left the hall.

Jonathan sat on the large wooden bench in the middle of the expanse. The kiosk chimed again, signaling the closing of the hall's doors. The lights dimmed. The Freedom 10 holojection disappeared, and Jonathan found himself alone in the memorial whose curved walls camouflaged any concept of depth or space in cavernous darkness.

A moment of silence for the dead.

His parents appeared in a huge holojection that floated 20 feet in front of him. Jonathan had opted for the simpler memorial, though he could have had their images morphed into an introduction where they said "hello" and "we love you" or some other absurd beginning. He always felt that his parents talking back to him from the grave was horrific, at best. He just wanted to remember them as they were: Jonathan Sr. and Sarah Kortel, career scientists, father and mother of Jonathan Jr. He quietly watched their lives played out through family pictures, home vids and any public records that might have captured them. Having been a fairly high-profile scientific couple, their careers came to public attention every now and then, and the memorial tribute producers had spared no expense in their research. He had to admit they had done a pretty good job of capturing, as far as he could remember, the essence of his parents. The music and the editing had all been designed to pluck the heartstrings without being too morose, or too over the top. The producers also had strategically placed another moment of reflection at the end of the program. After his parents' memorial finished, Jonathan quietly wept in the darkness.

The lights came up and the doors slowly opened, and the Freedom 10 image went back to reminding the generations how the Hawaiian Islands once looked.

~

Jonathan slowly returned to the spot at the cliff. He looked to the southwest, where the islands used to be. He picked up a small clump of dirt. The wind was now gusting, whipping his hair and forcing the seagulls to tack erratically in the air.

"Goodbye, Mom...goodbye, Dad," he said into the wind.

He recited the Lord's Prayer and stood quietly with his thoughts while the dirt filtered through his fingers. The seagulls squawked, and the ocean continued its relentless bombardment while the world was tucked in for the night.

Do the right thing...33

ANARI sat at the VIP bar and rested her chin in her hand. It was a Thursday night, and Liquid Courage was suspiciously vacant of the automotive conventioneers who wore their paunches like badges of honor. They had descended upon Chicago for two weeks of dealing, drinking and any other kind of devilment overweight, fortyish salesmen could get themselves into. A lone dancer slithered apathetically across the stage; the sequins at her crotch refracted little rainbows about the dark room.

"Who in the hell did her tits?!" Anari asked.

"Karmenowski," the bar back said with a knowing grin.

"I should have guessed," she declared. "He should be shot for that aug job. Those things look absurd."

"You can take the girl out of the country..." the bar back started.

"That's so sad," Anari said. "She's going to regret those in about 10 years."

"Maybe she'll be screwing another doctor by then," the bar back offered and laughed.

The door to VIP slowly opened, which wasn't an odd occurrence in itself, but Anari knew that the doorman was on break, and nobody got into VIP without being checked by him first. It didn't matter how important you were...nobody just *walked* in.

The man wore a high-end biocoat still wet from the evening's light snowfall. She contemplated calling security, but figured what the hell: the night was a bust, and she needed to pay the rent. She followed him at a distance, watching the living coat reform into its dry-out setting. *Money,* she thought. He slipped it off and chose a dark booth against the back wall. He kept his face out of the narrow spotlight that judiciously illuminated the top of the table.

"Neat trick," Anari said as she slid beside the booth.

"Pardon?" the man asked.

"Opening the doors to VIP...neat trick, because they're voiceprint controlled, you know. Was there a doorman out front?"

"No."

"Then how'd you open them?"

The man hesitated. "I have my ways," he said dryly.

"Well, usually I'd have to ask you to go see the doorman, but since we're dead and all..." she leaned on the table, trying to get a better look at him. He retreated into the darkness of the booth. "...I guess we'll make this our little secret, okay?"

"Thank you," he replied.

"So," she asked softly, "what are we drinking tonight?"

"Oban, with ice, no water, please."

She paused for a second before punching in the order.

"Something wrong?" the man inquired.

"No, no..." Anari said, and she quickly headed for the bar.

~

"Anything the matter?" the bartender questioned.

"Hmm?" Anari asked, staring into space.

"Anything the *matter*?" He handed her the drink.

"No, nothing. I was just remembering something..."

Anari walked back to the booth. The man hadn't moved. "One Oban, with ice, no water," she said, presenting the drink. "Do you live here, or are you in town with the convention?"

"I used to live here, but I'm in for...business."

"Cool. Are you going to stay with us long?" she asked in an effort to make conversation to relieve the boredom.

The man hesitated again. "I don't know..."

Anari thought she detected a touch of sadness in his voice. There was an awkward pause, the kind two strangers share when they realize that their conversation is really nothing more than forced small talk.

"Well then, I'll come back and check on you in a little bit." She began to leave the table.

"Anari..." the stranger beckoned.

She stopped in midstep. "How do you know my real name?" she asked, charging back to the booth.

"It's me, Anari," the man said tenderly. "Jonathan." He leaned forward, and the spotlight flooded his face in harsh contrasts. He had aged a bit, but the sharp angles of his jawline still announced his boyish charm.

Anari almost dropped her tray. Her legs started to buckle. "J-Jonathan...I...I–"

"It's okay, Anari. I know you haven't been erased. James told me everything...before the–" He stopped and smiled. "Please...sit with me?"

Anari composed herself. "Sure," she said. She cautiously settled into the booth, careful to keep a fair distance between them. She studied him for a moment. "Oh, Jonathan," she finally said, "it's so good to see you again." Tears welled in her eyes.

"Anari, please don't cry..."

"I'm not even sure why I am," she said.

"Mia?" her voice pin interrupted, "are you going to be there a while?"

"Give me a minute, will you Trev?!"

"I'm cool to that, baby. I'll send Tissy. She needs the scratch."

"Sorry," Anari said, focusing on Jonathan.

"Hey, if you gotta go..."

Anari scooted over and hugged him. "No," she said into his chest, "I can hang for as long as you want."

Jonathan returned her hug, but it was restrained, and Anari could sense it.

"How've you been?" he questioned. He took a sip from his drink.

"I'm all right. Just working and living...you know the drill." Anari pulled back and folded her arms tightly across her chest.

"Anari," Jonathan said, "when was the last time you heard from James?"

"Oh, God, I don't know...at least two years ago. Since I was a secret, I never knew what to expect. Our relationship was pretty strange, you know, with your culture such a secret and all. Then one day, Jimmy just quit calling. I kind of figured he got tired of all the sneaking around. For a long time I was always looking over my shoulder...thinking he'd send someone to erase me. But after a couple of months I quit worrying. I guess he just got busy and forgot about me." She noticed Jonathan seemed to react to this comment, but she couldn't figure why. She looked painfully at him. "Did he ever say anything to you...about me?"

Jonathan struggled for an answer. "There was an accident," he replied flatly. "His memory was...ah...damaged."

"Oh no," Anari said softly. Tears came into her eyes again.

"In a sense he did forget you, along with about 27 years of memories. They say with time he may recover close to 60 percent of them, but they never really know what a Tel will remember until the recovery process is over."

"When will that be?" Anari asked between sniffles.

"It's hard to say..."

Anari forced a smile. "Well, it's been a long time now....Maybe someday he'll remember me."

"Maybe he will."

Anari wiped her nose with a cocktail napkin. "Jonathan, why are you here?" She already suspected the answer.

Jonathan's demeanor changed, and he leaned back against the booth. "I think you already know the answer to that question, don't you?"

"Oh, Jonathan, don't do this...don't try. She's moved on. She's got a new life and a new job. She's not the same Tamara you knew." A seriousness came over Anari. "Especially after what the Agency did to her."

"I'm not with the Agency anymore. I haven't been for some time now."

"What happened?" Anari said with surprise. "Where have you been?"

"It's a long story..."

"Are you in some kind of trouble?"

Jonathan sighed. "Yeah, you could say that."

"Jonathan, what happened? What did you do?"

"Let's just say that I'm not the golden boy in the Tel world any more, and keep it at that."

"Okay," Anari said, nodding, "but you're all right, aren't you?"

"For the moment," he said gravely.

They both became silent. Anari's thoughts drifted to Tamara. "She's done well for herself," she finally said.

"I'm so glad to hear that," Jonathan replied. He smiled. "Tell me about her....What's she doing, and how's Nicki?"

"Oh, Jonathan, Nicki's so big now. She's got her mother's body for sure, with those long legs and all. You should see her..." Anari caught herself and quickly turned away.

"That's why I'm here, Anari...to see Tamara."

She hesitated, then looked back.

"Anari, what? What is it?"

"It's...it's just that you two had such a love for each other. Everyone saw it. It was different....It was...true."

Jonathan concentrated on his drink and took a big gulp. He leaned against the booth and watched a lone dancer shuffle about the stage to a retro tune that sounded like Desperate Sense. "If you really believe that, Anari, then let me just try. If we had it once, we might be able to have it again."

"It doesn't work that way, Jonathan, you know that–"

"It might."

Anari looked at him, confused. "What are you saying?"

Jonathan pensively swirled his ice. "There's something you need to know. I'm not going to get into the technical details, but basically, when a Level 8 erases a person, most of the time it takes. There's full erasure and that's that. But once in a while, an erasure doesn't take fully. Now, this varies from person to person, but there can be 'leftover' memories still present in the person's mind. Depending how much is left over, a Level 8 may have to go back and finish the job. But that gets tricky. Erasing a person who has already had the procedure can be dangerous, even fatal."

"So that's why Jimmy never wanted to do it on Tamara!"

"What?!" Jonathan exclaimed. He grabbed her shoulder.

"Ever since the procedure, she's not been the same girl. I mean, she is...it's just that..."

"What, Anari? Just what?"

"She's...sadder, that's all. Nothing manic, just sadder. Like she's in a state of being perpetually bummed, which is weird, because the way I understood the procedure, it shouldn't change her personality....Should it?"

"No, no it shouldn't. It only destroys memory, nothing else." Jonathan leaned back, thinking. "Anari, is there anything about her that seems odd, like headaches or sleeplessness?"

"Well, there's the dreams–"

"Dreams....What kind of dreams?"

"Strange ones, real disjointed. She says they've really affected her...and I think her love life, too."

"Why's she say that?"

"I'm not sure. She closes up when I try to help. It's like she's embarrassed or something." Anari processed her last statement. "Oh my God, Jonathan!" She put her hands over her mouth. "They're about you! Her dreams!"

Jonathan didn't respond. He sat against the booth with his eyes shut.

"One way leftover memories come forward is through dreams," he said, his eyes still closed. "They're sometimes called repressed dreams." He leaned forward and looked at Anari. "In this case, though, it's not the mind suppressing a trauma or something. It's more of a leakage, due to the procedure not taking fully."

Anari sat quietly contemplating. "What do you think?"

"I think that if there's a chance in hell of getting back some of my life, I'm going to take it. I haven't come this far, and risked this much, not to at least see if there's anything left between us." He leveled his gaze at her. "And if you have any compassion for us, you'll tell me where she is."

"Do you think that's fair?–"

"Fair?!" he blurted. His drink shattered and sprayed Scotch and glass across the table.

Anari jumped back against the booth. "Easy, Jonathan. I'm just saying, would it be right?"

"I'm sorry," Jonathan said. He wiped away the ice and glass with his napkin.

Anari noticed that some of the ice appeared to shift – the melted water separating from the Scotch and reforming into tiny cubes.

Can't be, she thought. *Must be the light.*

"I...I just have to see if there's any possibility," Jonathan continued. "I don't think I could live with myself if I didn't at least try."

Anari could see the intense pain and torment in Jonathan's eyes. She also knew that her friend had never been the same since the procedure, and every time she saw Tamara, it cut into her heart a little bit more. Anari reached over and stopped Jonathan from wiping off the table. She took his hands in hers.

"Hey..." she tenderly began. Jonathan stoically looked at her, trying not to display what his eyes already revealed. "Give me your netpad." Anari entered Tamara's work address and handed it back, but as Jonathan took it, she held on and shot him a firm look.

"Don't worry," he said. "I'm not going to force it if it's not right. I would never do anything to hurt her."

Anari smiled. "I know you'll do the right thing, Jonathan." She leaned over and kissed him on the cheek.

I don't really know...34

A cold winter wind blew up Michigan Avenue and slammed hard against the broad shoulders of the city by the lake. Its citizens, as they had for hundreds of years, braced themselves for the onslaught of frozen nose hair, sordid gray snow, and relentless overcast from what meteorologists affectionately called "the lake effect."

Jonathan watched this world go by from the cozy warmth of the coffee shop booth he had occupied for the better part of the afternoon.

"Need a refill, hon?" the waitress asked. She stood expressionless with her right hand on her hip, her left hand dangling an antique coffeepot like she had a million of them to spare. Her makeup appeared to have been applied with an acetylene torch, and probably not since her last raving. The topiary that was her hair had assumed a shape that could only be grown on a steady diet of biogel and electric shock.

"Hmm?" Jonathan asked, prying himself away from the scene outside.

"Coffee?" Her eyebrow slowly raised.

"No thanks," he replied.

"Suit yourself." She sauntered back behind the counter; her hair bounced in sync with her steps.

Jonathan glanced at his watch. 4:45:34 p.m. He gathered his coat and walked to the counter.

"What, you're leaving us so soon?" the waitress asked sarcastically. "And just when we were getting to know each other." She handed Jonathan her netpad. He punched in his tip and handed it back. She raised her eyebrow again, and her mouth stopped chewing on what was left of a straw. "Mister," she exclaimed, "you only had a couple cups of coffee!"

"For taking up your booth for so long."

"Honey, come back and stay as long as you want!"

He smiled and pulled on his coat. It cycled through the presets for the harsh environment it was about to encounter.

"Damn, that's a fancy coat! Say, what are you, government or sumthin'?" She gave him the once-over.

"Something..." he said bluntly, and the collar of his coat tightened slightly around his neck.

~

Jonathan quickly crossed the street, bracing himself against the hard, driving wind. He slipped between the CitiCabs and CitiCars and tentatively approached the gallery. When he reached for the door handle, he noticed his hand shake a little. He couldn't tell if it was nerves or the bionanoware, though he wasn't sure if there was a difference anymore.

The gallery was quiet, only two other people looking at the art. A young girl, who was wrapped so tightly in winter clothes that it was impossible to tell where her neck ended and her head began, studied a giant holographic tampon. It dripped blood that splattered into a puddle on the floor, then went in reverse so that the blood flew back onto the tampon.

Jonathan drew beside her. "Interesting," he commented.

"It's called 'Life's a Bitch,' by the artist Koe-9," the girl said without taking her eyes from it.

"Hmm," he mused, pretending to care. He walked from piece to piece, diligently studying the assortment of paintings, holojections and three-dimensional sculptures as if he might truly buy one. He rounded the corner of a wall that displayed the torn remnants of a hundred T-shirts like the one Sasha had worn in their virt-booth bike ride, and stopped when he saw the back of Tamara. She was discussing the works with an elderly man who had an air about him like he could buy out the whole place. Jonathan quickly averted his face and started reading the vidbrief on the T-shirt piece.

Who Cares, by Albert Foster Milton Glaser.

"Do you like it?"

A wave of metallic cold swelled through Jonathan as his heart processed the sound of Tamara's voice. "Yes," he said. He turned face to face with the woman he loved and was struck at how little she had changed. Slightly older, a bit more weight, and definitely dressed more conservatively. What hadn't changed, though, were her eyes. Their crystalline blueness cut to his heart, just as they had when he had first met her.

"We'll be closing soon," Tamara said in a crisp, professional manner, "but I still have a lot of research to do. Please feel free to browse the work." She started to walk away. "Oh, I'm sorry. I'm Nicole, and you are?..." She extended her hand.

"Jonathan." He reached for her hand, and an arc of static jumped between them.

"Oh," she exclaimed, "I'm so sorry! We keep it so dry in here – for the protection of the work, you know." They held for a second, and she contemplated him like a piece in a portfolio.

"Is there something wrong?" Jonathan asked.

"No, not at all. It's just that you look...familiar, that's all. Do you live in the city?"

He smiled again. "No, I'm just visiting."

"Well, I'll be over here if you have any questions." She gestured to a small desk at the back of the gallery.

Jonathan noticed her diploma on the wall. "You have a master's," he said.

"Why yes," Tamara said, slightly put off. "At The Pudder Gallery, all associates are required to have at least an MFA."

"I'm sorry," Jonathan said, clearly embarrassed. "I didn't mean to sound so surprised."

"It's all right. I've worked hard for it, and I'm probably a little touchy about it." She curtly smiled and left for her desk.

~

While the elderly man closed the door behind him, Jonathan stepped away from the tampon holosculpture and slowly approached Tamara's desk.

"You sure like our little sculpture," she said, keeping her attention firmly on her netport. She tried to restrain her amusement.

Jonathan watched as she assiduously went about her research. *She did it,* he thought. Pulled herself out of a life that would have dragged most others down a path of addiction or tragedy – and usually both. He affectionately studied her, and his heart filled with a strange mix of pride and relief. Although he would never have admitted it, he was always fearful that her life might turn for the worse. But here she was, accomplished, independent, and more beautiful than he had ever remembered.

Tamara sensed his stare. "I can make a great deal on it for you," she said half laughing. She glanced up and read his look, as she had a hundred times before, and did that thing with her head where she tilted it to one side and gave a tender, questioning expression.

"It's interesting, but I'm not sure where I'd put it. I am, though, curious about these...in here." Jonathan motioned to a small room off the main gallery.

Tamara smiled in response. She rose and walked briskly toward the room. As he followed, Jonathan watched her stride and remembered.

Tamara and Jonathan entered the tiny gallery, and the spotlights brightened to highlight three paintings that hung conspicuously alone on the wall. The halogens bathed the paintings' surfaces in a cool light and created dark tapestries of highlight and shadow in the texture of the oils. Tamara and Jonathan stood for a moment and studied the lone figure that dominated each canvas.

"What do you think?" Tamara asked, considering the middle one.

Jonathan didn't answer. It felt so good to be close to her and hear her voice and smell her presence once again. He closed his eyes and took her in.

"Well?..." she pressed.

"They're..." Jonathan hesitated "...sad."

Tamara scrutinized Jonathan from the corner of her eye as he leaned in to read the artist bio. He got as far as the name – and stopped.

"These are yours," he said, unable to conceal his surprise.

"Yes," Tamara said, giving him her full attention, "they are."

Jonathan pulled back and settled on the third painting. A dark, faceless man looked mournfully through layers of vermillion and indigo and coal.

He gasped under his breath.

"These," Tamara continued, shifting into professional mode and gesturing casually to the middle painting, "are actually from some–"

"Dreams," Jonathan blurted.

Tamara's arm hung in midgesture as if held by a puppeteer's string. "Why, yes!" she said, her eyes wide with astonishment. "I painted these from my dreams. How did you know that?" Her arm slowly lowered.

"Just a lucky guess," Jonathan said. He tore his attention from the paintings to find her intently staring at him. Her eyes searched his face as if it held the antitoxin to her pain. Their intensity startled him, and he reflexively stepped back. Tamara cocked her head again and gave him that look. It cut through to his soul.

"Tam..." he started, but her netphone hummed, and she pulled it from her pocket.

"Excuse me...will you?" She stepped away, still staring at him in puzzlement.

Jonathan intently studied the figure in the paintings. There, in violent strokes, was Tamara's anguish. While his eyes passed over the complex interplay of color and form, he listened–

"...I'll be right home, honey, I'm just finishing up with a customer....No, no, remember, Michael is taking us to dinner tonight....No, he's the one you said you liked....Yes, dear, Mommy likes him, too....Now wash up and be ready when I get home....I love you, too. I'll see you in a few minutes. Bye-bye." She snapped her netphone shut and returned to Jonathan. "I'm sorry. Now, what were you about to say?"

Jonathan glanced back at her eyes, which had lost their curiosity and returned to a cool professionalism. A simple sense of peace washed over him.

"Nothing," he answered softly.

"Well, you certainly have an eye for art," Tamara said. She headed back to her desk. Jonathan slowly followed. "You're the first person to have picked up on the fact that I painted those from my dreams." She pulled a small card from her drawer and handed it to him. The heat from his fingers triggered the gallery's holopromotional. Tamara's image appeared in the center of the card. She was standing in the middle of the gallery in a crisp suit, then walking through the art, all the while explaining the virtues of investing with the Pudder Gallery.

He watched for a moment, then quietly pocketed her.

"They're a bit silly, but they do the job quite effectively, don't you think?" she said. She folded her hands in a businesslike manner.

Jonathan barely smiled.

"Now, if you make up your mind on my paintings or anything else you've seen," she turned and coyly smiled to the tampon holosculpture and back, "just ask for me."

Jonathan thought for a second. "I will, Miss?..."

"Connor," she said, extending her hand. "Nicole Connor."

He took her hand with both of his, and for the second they held, he desperately fought for balance between what his heart said was true and what his soul knew was right. He turned to leave, but as he approached the door, she called to him. "Are you staying long in Chicago?"

The simple question stopped Jonathan and held him like the Ice Age had returned and spread across his heart. He hadn't really thought past coming to the gallery. "I...I don't really know," he managed. He couldn't face her. He smiled to himself, opened the door and joined the rest of Chicago in battling a typical Midwestern storm on a typical Midwestern night.

WINNER ForeWord Magazine's Book of the Year

"...**A RIVETING SCIENCE FICTION** novel bt a gifted author..."

~ Midwest Book Review

"...**HIGHLY ORIGINAL**...Mr. Black has quite an imagination
and puts it to good use..." *~ John Strange, The City Wide Web*

Book 3

NEXUS POINT

Originally published in 2007

How 'bout that beer?   1

THE Elbow Room was the kind of bar that accepted its clientele like an old whore: as long as your credit was clean, you were welcomed. Bixx usually liked being at the Room, but right now there were a billion other places she'd rather be.

Rocket folded his arms angrily across his chest. "The guy is not coming."

"He is," Kreet said, "trust me. And if you say that again—"

"Will you two *please* shut up!" Bixx slammed her beer onto the table and a dollop of its head backflipped onto Rocket's fries.

"So much for my genetically tailored taste." Rocket watched the foam spread over the remnants of his "Mico's Special."

"If you believe all that biofood crap," Kreet said. "Besides, you're almost done with these." He reached over with his fork and harpooned the largest fry in the basket. "I don't taste anything different," he mumbled between chews.

"God, Kreet, how old are you?" Sanjiv asked.

"He's 22, though you'd never know it," Bixx said dryly. "And Kreet, you couldn't tell anyway. Those French fries have been prepared to Rocket's genetic profile.... Only he can taste the difference. The resequencing protocols they use today are light years past what they had five years ago."

"Thank you, Miss Genius, for enlightening us." Kreet kicked back the last of his beer.

Rocket took Bixx's hand and his forefinger stroked her knuckles. It was his special sign of affection, reserved for moments when he felt her feelings might have been bruised. She had come to appreciate its meaning, but more often than not it was unwarranted.

"Don't let Kreet bust you," Rocket said. He squeezed her hand. "You're smarter than all of us combined.... You can't help it that your pretty little head is so full of data."

Besides being overly protective, Rocket could say things that didn't come out quite the way he wanted. This was an aspect of his personality that Bixx didn't appreciate. She shot him a harsh look.

"So, Kreet," Sanjiv said, "tell me again: how did you make the connection with Kortel?"

Kreet smiled over the rim of his beer and placed the glass on the table. "I didn't," he answered. He wiped his mouth with the back of his hand.

Sanjiv blinked. "Then how did you?—"

"Kortel was brought to me...sort of. I had this guy approach me last month. He said he'd heard of my concept and could help me deliver it." Suddenly Kreet's glass slid toward the half-filled pitcher, ran around the bowl of mixed nuts and parked itself between two empty glasses.

The others stared at Kreet.

"What?" he asked.

"Man, are you that stupid?" Rocket said. "We're in public."

"Screw the normals," Kreet replied. "What's the sense of having this power if I can't use it now and then? Nobody saw it anyway."

"You've got a lot to learn, Kreet," Sanjiv said. "Our gift isn't something to take for granted."

"Thanks *dad*, I'll remember that when I get to be your age."

Sanjiv scanned the table for sympathetic eyes. "You see, everybody? This is the reason I moved out."

"Kreet, give it a rest," Bixx said. "Now tell us, who was this guy who contacted you?" She was always skeptical of Kreet's schemes. They were notorious for being void of detail and full of shit.

"He wouldn't say. Said it would expose him too much."

"So, you just went along with whatever he said?"

Kreet leveled a cold glare. "He had incept points...with the matching responder data."

"Did Kortel answer?" Sanjiv asked.

Kreet swung his attitude around. "No. But do you really think a guy like him would leave an answer?"

"So basically you have no idea if he's going to show or not?" Bixx asked.

Kreet hesitated. "If you're wanting some kind of confirmation, I don't have one. So, no, I don't know for sure if he's showing. But this guy had *Russian* responder data. Do you know how hard that is to get?"

"Of course I do," Bixx said. "Remember, I'm from Moscow?" Even though she hadn't been back to Russia for over two years, Bixx knew that Kreet's contact had to be very jacked to have that kind of information. At least, she'd never known anyone like this. Sure, you could get most anything on the Russian black net, but nothing approaching what this guy was offering. Kreet could be a real asshole sometimes, but she had to admit that the little shit could always find an angle. Still, she was tired of his constant dissing, and was seriously thinking about breaching Tel protocol and giving Kreet a headache he wouldn't forget.

"Funny thing about this guy," Kreet said. "He didn't look well. I mean, it wasn't like he was sick or something – more like he had been through some kind of brain trauma."

"Why do you say that?" Sanjiv asked.

"Because he had this face twitch, and sometimes he'd lose his focus. Said he'd been in an accident. And I could tell that part of his hair and scalp had been regen'd."

"How could you tell that?" Rocket asked.

"Because he had red hair like yours, and a small part of it didn't match perfectly. It was right here." Kreet pointed to the top right side of his head, just past his hairline.

"Prefrontal cortex," Bixx said.

"So?" Kreet asked.

"Memory, dumbass."

Sanjiv whistled.

"He was a Tel, right?" Rocket asked.

"No, he was a normal," Kreet said sarcastically. "And he knew right where Jonathan Kortel was, imagine that."

"Screw off you little—"

"Enough!" Bixx yelled. Her glass of beer exploded. It radiated outward to a 2-foot diameter, then froze in midspray before it collapsed to half its size. The sphere of beer and glass shards moved slowly around Bixx's arm and past the edge of the table, where it fell and splattered across the the Elbow's scarred wooden floor.

They held their positions, as if all their atoms had locked down.

"Ah, sorry guys," Bixx said.

Rocket leaned into her ear. "Easy, baby," he whispered. "Let's get it under control, okay?" He squeezed her hand, this time to the point of pain.

"I'm not going to say this again," Sanjiv said sternly. "All of you have to get control of your displacement fields...especially in public. I can't always be here to stop things from getting out of control." A small drop of blood was hanging from Sanjiv's nostril. He quickly wiped it away with a napkin.

"I'm sorry," Bixx said, "but you two" – she motioned to Kreet and Rocket – "have got to cool this bullshit between you.... It just pisses me off."

Rocket began to protest, but Bixx raised her hand and silenced him.

"Look, don't you guys get it?" she said. "I'll bet this guy who approached Kreet has been erased before, and he's had restoration surgery to the area of the brain that controls recent memory. The Agency doesn't do that for just anyone. This guy is, or was, a major player."

"Well," Sanjiv said, "whoever he is, he gave Kreet the right incepts." He pointed past the table to the front of the bar. "Look who just walked in."

Bixx turned and watched Jonathan Kortel walk through the crowded bar with the ease of a man who knew his power. It wasn't an arrogant swagger, just a gait that had a strength to it she couldn't define. It was like he knew fate had dealt him a strong hand, but he hadn't made peace with it yet. To look at him now, dressed in a simple black T-shirt, jeans and a pair of work boots – Russian-made by the looks of them – she would have never guessed that he was the most powerful telekinetic in their culture. The rumor was that he was faster than the speed of light. Since their gift was based on the mind's ability to manipulate gravity, that meant Jonathan Kortel, in theory, could bend time.

Even though she and the others had worked with him before, Bixx was still struck at how unassuming he appeared. He was basically average in height, build and looks, although there was a kind of gritty handsomeness about him that came more from the way he carried himself than his physical features. His calm expression didn't waver as he approached their table.

"Jonathan," Kreet said as he stood, which was odd to Bixx, since Kreet rarely showed respect to anyone. By default, Kreet had always been their group's leader, but Bixx figured he must still be gun-shy because of Kortel's "lesson" two years prior. Kreet had challenged Kortel, and had ended up on the losing end of his anger. Everyone at the table followed Kreet's lead.

Kortel, mindful of his unusual discharge effect, didn't offer his hand. He acknowledged Kreet with a nod, then met everyone's face with a slight smile. He stopped at Bixx. Rocket nudged her foot under the table.

"Hello, Bixx," he said.

Bixx choked a little on her spit. Her hello came out more like, *hell no*, colored by more of her Russian accent than she liked. It always surfaced when she was nervous.

Kreet rolled his eyes.

"You've cut your hair since the last time I saw you," Kortel noted. "It looks good on you."

"Thank you," Bixx said. "You look, ah...good too."

Kortel smiled past the moment's awkwardness and gestured for everyone to sit.

Bixx took her seat, mentally chastising herself for being so nervous. Rocket affectionately patted her knee under the table, but the gesture didn't help much.

Kreet had gone to some lengths to assemble the old group. Bixx and Rocket still lived in the warehouse space they had once all shared, but Kreet and Sanjiv had moved out, complaining they couldn't take the other anymore. The only one missing from the gang that had helped Kortel seek his revenge on their Agency's leadership was Sasha. The scuttle Bixx had heard was that Sasha and Kortel had had a baby, but she never put much credence in that story. Kortel didn't seem the type who would have allowed something like that to happen. Besides, Kortel had been a fugitive for the last two years, moving from safe house to safe house throughout the Russian Tel network. He had taken a big risk coming back to New America, and an even bigger one to meet with them. Kreet must have laid down some good bullshit to get him to the table. Or maybe it had been something more important, because in truth, nothing Kreet could have said would have brought Kortel out of hiding. As Kortel took his seat, Bixx wondered what that might have been.

Kreet gestured to the pitcher in front of him. "Would you like a beer?"

"No, thanks." Kortel shot a quick glance over his shoulder, and Bixx got the sense that he was checking his surroundings. His view wasn't spooked – just a cool, professional assessment that appeared ingrained, almost instinctive. He brought his attention around and planted it on Kreet, who flinched reflexively.

"Thanks for entertaining my request, Jonathan," Kreet said. "I hope you like this bar. When you said you wanted to meet in public, I figured this place was as good as any."

"That's okay, Kreet. I owe you guys my life." He smiled at Sanjiv when he said this. "The bar's fine. I don't like meeting in private....You never know what to expect, and things can get *difficult* sometimes." He glanced about again. "So," he said, relaxing somewhat and eyeing the set-up of beers, "what's on your mind?"

"It's like I said in my message. We have an idea that we think demands your attention. Oh, and thanks for clearing that channel. You were hard enough to find without the Russians running interference."

Kortel's eyes narrowed, and the worry lines at the sides of his temples deepened.

Kreet continued. "There are a lot of us who think it's time for a...a change."

"A change?" Kortel repeated.

"Yeah, you know. A change...in leadership."

"I think we just had one a few years ago, didn't we?" He laughed slightly, but instantly quelled it. His lean face hardened, and his attention focused on Kreet again.

"No doubt. The Agency is still trying to put the pieces together after your, ah, adjusting of its structure."

Bixx reflected on the events of two years ago. She couldn't really blame Kortel for seeking revenge on their Agency's leadership. In their quest to create a supertel, Jeffrey Trumble and Cyril Takeda had conducted covert experiments on Kortel that could have disabled or even killed him. It wasn't a secret that the two leaders had become dangerous with their judgments; yet in spite of the evidence that showed Kortel had acted in self-defense, most of the Tel world believed he had gone too far. The deaths of Trumble and Takeda had sent the New American Agency into a freefall, and Kortel into exile. He was still considered unstable and dangerous, although looking at him across the table, Bixx thought that the man who many felt was the next step in evolution was beginning to look older than his years.

"Well, Kreet, lay it out...what's this shift you want?"

Kreet searched his friends' faces. "We're sick of our existence," he said flatly.

Kortel's face didn't register the statement. He casually folded his arms.

"And there's a lot of us throughout the culture that feel the same way," Kreet said.

Kortel sniffed slightly, like he was fighting back the start of a summer cold.

"Look, we don't mind being Tels. What we mind is the secrecy." Kreet leaned forward. "We want to come out."

Kortel cleared his throat. "Impossible. We've been under since the 1950s. You can't just spring the knowledge of our existence on the outer world. For one, you'd never get all the other Agencies to go along. Hell, good luck finding the Pac Rim guys. And the Arabs? After Hawaii, they're so buried, they'll never come out of the desert."

"Not with the right advance team."

Kortel shook his head. "Kreet, this idea of yours is too dangerous. You know the score. If the Tel culture came out of hiding, the normals would hunt us down...and I'd bet the general public would probably never hear about it." He pushed back from the table, clearly done with the meeting.

"There is a way," Kreet declared.

"Look, I've seen the data. If we came out, the world would freak, and we'd either be hunted or worshipped. In either case, the model's conclusions always end up the same: a tougher life than we have now. And you know something? What we have isn't really that bad. We already have influence over most of the world. If we came out, we'd lose all of that. No, your idea is flat-out stupid."

Bixx's heart sank. She looked at Rocket and could tell he was crushed, too. When this was over, she was going to personally kick Kreet's ass. He should have explained the concept further instead of jumping right to the end.

"It's not my idea," Kreet said.

Kortel eyed him. "It's still too dangerous." There was a sharp edge of frustration in his voice, and Bixx was beginning to wonder if those bulletins about Kortel were true.

"What if I said the leader of the advance team would be someone as powerful as you?"

Kortel quickly stood, his anger now on full display. "Kreet, you're really trying my patience. I took a big gamble meeting with you. Who is this person?"

Kreet met Kortel's glare. "Zvara."

The anger in Kortel's face fell away. Bixx could tell Kreet's declaration had hit him like a Light-Force weapon. He slowly sank into his chair.

The bar was filled with the usual noise of the end of a work week, but around their table, a silence had descended that seemed custom-made for the moment. A cold shiver spiked through Bixx's nerves.

"Now," Kreet said, as the pitcher of beer and a fresh glass floated into his hands. "How 'bout that beer?"

Summertime. 2

JONATHAN Kortel awoke to the muffled turbine blast of a police gunship executing a vertical liftoff. As it slowly rose past his hotel window, it filled the bedroom with a chaotic strobe of red and blue lights. Thank God D.C. still prohibited the cops from turning on their sirens before they reached a thousand feet. The room fell back into a patchwork of deep shadows, and an odious tinge of spent fuel flooded his nostrils. Kortel could hear the transition blast as the craft cleared the roofline, followed by its sirens Dopplering away as it turned north and headed toward the main part of the city. When his eyes adjusted, he found himself on the bed, still dressed. He couldn't remember coming back to the room, but there was much he couldn't remember lately...this being one of the minor items.

He walked into the bathroom. Its lights greeted him, slowly intensifying like he had taken the stage for an audience of one.

"Water, please. Cool."

Clean water had become such a commodity in the D.C. Zone that even the cheapest hotels had regulator chips built into their faucets.

"Cooler, please." The flow chilled slightly, and Kortel splashed two cupped handfuls against his face. He filled for a third but stopped when he again noted a tremor in his left hand. He grabbed a towel and patted his face dry. Checking the mirror, he picked at the white flecks of cotton stuck in his stubble. No micro-dryers. "Cheap crappy hotel."

Then he remembered. Zvara. Sitting at the desk, he asked for the windows to lighten. It took a moment, but eventually they did, and as he gazed at the backside of his nation's co-capital, he thought about Kreet's idea. Or was it Zvara's? Did it matter? Hell yes.

Kreet, who was basically a kid, was dumb like a fox. But he could never pull off something as bold as coming out. There had been others who had tried, but they never got further than the back page of the tabloids. The Agency's disinformation machine made sure of that. And Kreet's source for the incepts sure sounded like James McCarris. The red hair, the tall build. But it was the regen'd scalp that nailed it for Kortel. He thought he had erased McCarris two years ago, but leave it to the Agency and their army of biosurgeons to put McCarris's memory back together again. At least some of it. Kortel seriously doubted that the Agency's biolab boys could have actually restored all of his memory (though it depended how much McCarris had backed up), but it didn't matter now. If McCarris had wanted to kill Kortel, he would have already done it. But why help Kreet? Maybe the biolab boys hadn't restored McCarris's memory.... Maybe they had just given him something new altogether.

He glanced at his watch. *1:32 a.m.*

Kreet's plan seemed too clean to have been conceived alone. The more Kortel thought about it, the more the Zvara connection made sense. Maybe Zvara had made contact with Kreet. Or at least someone close to Zvara had. Like an associate or a relative. Shit, of course.

Kortel reached across the table and grabbed his netpad. He tapped in coordinate numbers he hadn't thought of for a long time. The pad's tiny screen flared, and the NetTel logo faded in, danced out of view, and the word CONNECTED appeared in a trendy typeface Kortel had never seen. A young woman's dark face pixeled up. Her cropped tangle of thick ebony curls framed lustrous green eyes that blinked back at Kortel. Her full lips parted into a wary smile.

"Jonathan Kortel, we were wondering when you'd surface. I assume this is a secure transmission?"

"Hello, Sasha. It's been a long time. And yes, we're tight as tight can get." He passed the tip of his finger across her image, and the screen's organics quivered.

"You're looking good, at least what I can see of you."

Kortel placed the netpad on the desk. "Is that better?"

"A little. But nothing beats being there in person." Her smile widened.

"You've cut your hair. Seems it's the trend these days."

"Pardon, you broke up a little?"

"Your hair...it looks nice short."

"Yeah, it was time to cut it. My summer 'do, you know." She tentatively looked off camera, then back. "So, Jonathan, how have you been?" Her voice had shifted to a quieter tone, and the smile had contorted into a mask of tight concern.

"All right, considering my situation."

"We heard that you had reentered the country, direct from Moscow into Chicago?"

"Yeah, I had some unfinished business to take care of."

"That was very risky."

"It was worth it."

"And did you take care of your business?"

"You could say that."

An awkward silence fell between them, and Sasha glanced away again.

"Why are you in Washington?" she asked. "It's still not safe for you to be back in the country."

"You tell me."

Sasha's face screwed into a question. "I only know you're there, not why. Look,

Jonathan, we keep tabs on you, but we're not going to interfere. It's your choice if you want to take risks or not."

"That's comforting."

"You didn't answer my question."

"I met with your old gang."

"You mean Kreet and Rocket and everyone?"

"Just like old times. I think Kreet still holds a torch for you."

"Please, I just had dinner. Why were you meeting with them?"

"Kreet has a new plan for our culture to come out. Says he's assembling a front team that should be able to convince the other agencies. He wants me to be its number-two man."

Sasha shook her head; her curls fell across her face. She brushed them back with a swipe of her hand. "He's been dreaming this ever since I met him. Who does he have as the leader for this team?"

Kortel smiled for the first time. "Your father."

Sasha laughed nervously and folded her arms. "That's rich. How can he get a hold of him when I can't?"

Kortel shrugged. "Hard to say. I was kind of hoping you'd know something about all this."

Sasha shook her head again. "I wish I did. Believe me, I'd warn Dad about Kreet."

"Kreet says it was all your father's idea."

This statement seemed to make Sasha's face pale slightly, edging her already beautiful dark skin to a lighter shade of coffee. She bit her lip and looked off camera again.

"Oh, yeah, there's something else," Kortel said.

Sasha looked back, and there was tightness at the corners of her eyes.

"Seems I didn't erase James McCarris all that well."

"How do you know that?" she asked, her voice cracking a bit.

"'Cause I think he's the one working for your father. He gave Kreet my incept points. You and your father are the only two people who had them."

"Jonathan, I...I don't know what to say. Could your Russian contact have?—"

"No! There's no way Dmitri would have known. And even if he did, he would have never told anyone."

Silence settled over them again.

"Jonathan," Sasha said finally, "what can I do to help?"

Kortel sighed. "Find your dad for me, before Kreet takes this plan any further."

Sasha's image stared out from the screen, and Kortel flashed back to the first time he had met her father. Armando Zvara had ascended through the ranks of the Agency, attaining the head role at the unprecedented age of 34. His power level was legendary, speculated to be near 8 on a scale of 10. The leadership then, as they had with Kortel, tried to enhance Zvara's power level with bioaugmentation, but the experiments had failed. It had been rumored that he had requested a change of identity and appearance, and that he had assumed the role of a Recruiter. He was living a simpler life, until a file caught his attention and sent him on a trip to Chicago, where he discovered a young man whose telekinetic power surpassed even his.

"Jonathan?"

"Hmm?"

Sasha's eyes were staring from the screen. "Where did you go?"

"Oh, I was just remembering the first time I met your father...back when I ran my old restaurant."

Sasha smiled. "You know he thinks of you like a son."

Kortel thought for a moment. "Sasha, my mother and father disappeared with Hawaii." He rubbed his temple. "Still, it's a nice thought."

"So what are you going to do next? Go back to Russia?"

"No," he said, stretching, "I think I'm here for a while."

"That's a dangerous choice. You're not seriously considering Kreet's proposal are you?"

"That all depends."

"On what?"

"If your father's involved or not."

"Look, let me find my dad. You, on the other hand, should keep your head low. There're still those who were loyal to Trumble and Takeda who would like to see you erased...permanently." Sasha hesitated. "I was wondering..." she looked down, as if her next question caused her pain. She raised her eyes. "How are you feeling? Have the side effects gotten any better?"

Kortel glanced at his left hand. "Some days are worse than others. But overall it's not bad."

"That's not what I asked—"

"Sasha...concentrate on finding your dad, okay?"

She nodded, then asked, "And you, what are you going to do?"

Kortel hesitated. "Go find an old friend."

Sasha's face filled with worry. "You're not going to—"

"Sasha! This is my life, remember? I'm sick of hiding. Besides, maybe it's time we did come out."

Sasha sighed heavily. She stared for a second. "Promise me you'll be careful?"

Kortel grinned. "It's good to see you again, Sasha."

She smiled hesitantly, and the connection ended.

The lights of the D.C. Zone wavered in the thermals of the torrid summer night. In the distance, dark smoke rose like a nebula between two office towers, the latest gang act that made up the background for local news. Kortel looked down at his left hand. It had begun to spasm again. He was getting used to different parts of his body acting of their own volition. This month, it had been his left hand. Six months ago, his right thigh, which had a bad tendency to twitch violently when he had made love to Reza. Probably why she never returned his messages. He reached for his jacket draped over the back of the chair. Digging through its inside breast pocket, he fished out the pneumatic infuser. He turned the tiny device over in his hand and clicked it on. A barely audible hum reflected off the window's ballistic plexi as it sequenced through its presets. He raised the infuser to his neck and released 10 ccs of justification.

And exhaled.

The sound of the device hitting the parquet echoed somewhere at the edge of his hearing. He rubbed at the injection point, feeling for the welt that always came.

"Music, please. Low volume. Jazz. Smooth. Miles Davis if you have it." He coughed slightly and tasted the metallic bitterness that had become his friend.

The room obeyed with Davis's rendition of *Summertime* from *Porgy and Bess*— one of his favorites from the mid 20th century. The weight behind his eyes grew, and the lights of the Zone blurred even more.

To old friends. 3

THE instrument panel of Kortel's rental chattered as it dialogued with the vast Interway network of the Southwest. Kortel had given up trying to figure out how to turn off the audio feature. The vehicle exited the four-lane grid and slipped onto a feeder road that paralleled the artery for roughly a mile. The panel chattered again, and the system disengaged from the Interway link.

"You are leaving the Interway; manual control has been engaged," a silky female voice declared. Probably created from some bioengineer's wet dream and selected by the previous user. Salesman.

Kortel drove the rental down the feeder and into the parking area of a store that had seen better centuries. It looked like the TP Mart Corporation had barely retrofitted the place to modern standards. A vestige of prehistoric corporate culture still hung from a pole near the road. The sign was riddled with rusted dents that Kortel concluded had come from a time when people could actually carry a projectile-firing weapon. The image of a winged horse was still visible in its center, and the word MOBIL hung below on its own appendage. Kortel parked in the first available space, slipping between a classic ethanol burner and one of the new Familiagons advertised on the Net. *Big Enough for Everyone Important to You* was its tagline. Kortel thought it didn't look any bigger than his rental, but what did he know? He didn't have kids or a family.

An old man sat on the store's front porch next to a big white metal box with two chrome doors on the front. He was leaning against the wall, balancing in an oddly constructed canvas chair. His work shirt looked as if it hadn't seen a hydromat for a decade, and his sleeves were rolled tight above the elbows. Dust was caked like icing over the bottoms of his khaki pants and boots. Through the filtered lens of Kortel's optics, the guy could have been right out of a Dorothea Lang photo. Kortel glanced over his shoulder at the small island of sage and rusting metal columns near the feeder road. The geezer laughed.

"Pumps," he said. He cleared his throat and spat.

"Excuse me?" Kortel asked.

The old man laughed again. "Pumps. Gas pumps."

"Yeah, I know."

"Before the damn Biolution." He spat again.

Kortel shut the door to his rental, and its organics hissed into their dormant settings. He walked over to the old man, who was eyeing him from under the tattered rim of a long-billed cap. The same winged horse logo was stitched in faded pink on its brim. Kortel figured it had been bright red once.

"If you're thirsty," he said, "we got sodas, beer, even Hydrolike. We ain't got much biofood, if you're into that." He gave Kortel the once-over. "You look like you would be."

"Thanks," Kortel said. "But what I really need are some directions."

"Nice glasses. Those Sori Wear?"

"Yeah."

"They dialogue with your netpad?"

"Of course."

"Then why don't they tell you where to go?"

"Because..." Kortel said. He removed the optics and slipped them into the breast pocket of his shirt. "Where I'm going is a little out of the way." He had to squint now to see the old man.

"New Mexico isn't out of the way *enough*?"

"It is, but I'm going somewhere pretty remote."

"Where you're standing is about as remote as it gets."

"Right." Kortel was growing impatient.

"Where're you headed?" the old man asked.

"Chaco Canyon."

"Bitch to get to."

"I'm actually going to a place near there, by the north side of the park."

Another spit, deep and full of mucus. "Nothin' there except rattlers and jackrabbits, and not much of either."

Kortel nodded. "My pad says to take 509 north from San Mateo, then west on 9. But that's where it gets confusing."

"You'll need to take 57 up through the park. After that, you're on your own."

"Thanks." Kortel started walking toward the store's entrance.

"What's out there?"

"A friend, I hope." Kortel pulled the screen door open.

"You serious?"

"He's a bit of a loner." An elderly Native American woman shuffled out of the store. She was wrapped in a brightly colored shawl, even though the store's thermometer registered nearly 90 degrees. Kortel held the door for her.

"You'll need more than that rental."

Kortel sighed and walked back. The screen door shut with a crack. "Let me guess," he said, shielding his eyes from the bright New Mexico sun. "You've got the perfect car for the trip, right?"

The old man hocked another loogie, then grinned with all the teeth he had left.

~

Kortel glanced at the clock in the dash. *7:57 p.m.* Its dial was cracked and faded to the point that if the sun hit it just right, Kortel had to practically lean out the window to read it. He hadn't driven a pre-Interway truck since his uncle's back in Carbondale. That was 17 years ago. What the old man had rented him had probably been top of the line in the middle of the previous century. It was a Ford Super Duty supposedly retrofitted to run on ethanol, but it didn't smell like it. With the windows down, it smelled faintly like driving through a giant fart. Maybe it ran on methanol. The geezer had given him four extra cans full of whatever it used and said he might need them "just in case." In case of what, Kortel wondered. They rattled together, bungeed as tight as he could get them against the back of the cab.

~

It had been 20 minutes since Kortel had exited the boundary of the national park, and he was still headed north, sort of. He had left Highway 57 two cigarettes back and was now on the remains of a dirt road that reminded him of the paths his uncle had driven when he was checking natural gas wells for the government. Since Kortel hadn't driven a manual much, he found it hard to keep the wheels in line with the ruts. He glanced at his netpad, but it had gone off-line an hour ago after it bounced against the dash when the Super Duty hit a large hole.

Kortel was driving on instinct. The land looked familiar, but he had only been here once, and that was years ago when his friend had moved to New Mexico to "concentrate on his priorities." The turnoff still had the little sign with the carved marijuana leaves, but time had weathered it so that they could barely be made out. The ruts emptied onto another two-lane paved road. He didn't remember this.

"What the hell?" Kortel glanced at his netpad.

The truck's compass seemed to be working; it indicated the two-laner ran due east and west.

"Go west, young man." Kortel swung the Super Duty onto the road and headed toward the sunset, which was beginning to explode under a line of dark clouds on the horizon. He slipped on the Soris and set them for max. Their optics set up a faux eclipse spot that tracked with both the movement of the truck and his head. Occasionally it would lag, and the sun would form a corona to the side of it, but the Soris's filters adjusted and kept the glare to a minimum. After about 20 miles of nothing but sage and scrub oak, Kortel saw the lights of a building off to the right.

The last rays of the sunset were dying as he parked the Super Duty in front of *Deuces Wild, New Mexico's Hottest VidSlots.* Kortel seriously doubted that Deuces had been wild anytime in the last 20 years, but what the hell: he was lost, tired, and maybe due for a change of luck.

Deuces was the kind of relic that had vanished along with the landline and postal service. Gambling had become the exclusive domain of the big multinationals, and to find a casino with pre-holo vidslots was, well, quaint. Making his way past the watchful gaze of the gift shop girl, Kortel entered a carpeted room packed with vidslot machines. They were all playing a different theme, and the room's low ceiling and wood paneling made them blend into a hideous white noise that was probably 10 decibels above code. The carpet crunched under his boots with a texture brewed from thousands of parties, and it had an effluvium that Kortel swore he could feel on his skin. He found the bar and pulled up a stool. The bartender actually asked, "What'll it be?"

"Oban, over ice, please," Kortel answered.

"One J&B coming up."

Kortel was too beat to argue. Besides, this Native American was as big as the Super Duty, and Kortel didn't want to get sideways with him. The last time he had pissed off an Indian, his whole life changed, and people got killed. He took a sip of the J&B and winced.

"How's the drink?" the guy asked.

Swallowing, Kortel gave a reluctant thumbs-up.

The guy forced a grin, then lumbered to the other end of the bar. It was a classic: long, wooden, a huge mirror, and ancient neon liquor signs that either barely flickered hints of their products' former glory or else hung forlornly in darkness. The guy walked up to the other bartender, who had his back turned to talk to a semi-cute girl with rooster-spiked hair. Kortel felt a presence at his side.

"Reading?"

He turned to find a slightly heavier, older version of his high school girlfriend. He knew this girl couldn't be her, but the resemblance was still enough to make him choke a little on his drink. The girl wore bright pink lipstick with a hue that shifted as she moved, and her dress was a cheap off-the-rack type that filled the Trump Marts. His girlfriend had died in his senior year, but if she had lived, Kortel thought she might have looked like this girl.

"Excuse me?" he asked.

"I asked if you were *needing*...service?"

"Well, I, uh..." Kortel had never been propositioned so overtly before. "Look, all I need is this drink right now."

The pink lips smiled. "Not *that* kind of service. Net service!" She produced a tiny version of his netpad. It looked like it could have come out of a box of Japanese candy, all chrome and glittery in her palm. "It's cheap, easy and never gets affected by the dust." Her voice came across squeaky, like an old door.

Kortel eyed the pad.

"Aw, come on," she said, now with an edge of British Cockney. "I'll throw in global service! You'll even be able to connect to any of the Freedoms."

The resemblance to his high school girlfriend was eerie, and Kortel felt a little something pass over his heart.

"Okay," he said, facing her. "But what's the catch?"

"No catch," she said. "I swipe your credit chip, you get a week's worth of service. How long you gonna be in the area?"

"Good question. I'm trying to find an old friend, but I'm not having any luck."

"Well then, why not call him?" The pink lips broke into a big toothy grin that, unlike his high school girlfriend's, exposed too much gum.

As dumb as it sounded, what she was offering was probably the best thing he could do. With his netpad down, he was, as far as communications went, stranded. He didn't need to connect to any of the space stations, but the global service might come in handy.

Kortel fished for his chip-card and handed it to her. She placed the phone on the bar and swiped his card down a slot in its side. The little device lay dormant for a second, then blinked and buzzed to life. Miss Pink Lips clapped.

"Killer!" she said, and stuck her hand out. "Welcome to the Arroyo Network."

Kortel hesitated, then shook her hand. No discharge effect. "So what's your commission?" he asked, gingerly picking up the chrome rectangle with his thumb and forefinger. He placed it in his palm and it unfolded like a deconstructing origami.

Miss Pink Lips smiled again, this time showing off the little cracks that heavy smokers have around the edges of their mouths. Kortel thought she looked too young for that. But then again, maybe not in a place like Deuces.

"Fifty percent of gross, anything I sell," she said proudly.

"And how's business?"

"Better than you'd think." And with that, she turned and sauntered toward the vidslots.

Kortel studied the phone's interface panel: pretty standard, and about five years out of date. He hesitated punching in his friend's number, because his buddy spooked easily, and in that case Kortel would never be able to find him. But he was out of luck, no matter what Deuces' drink coasters promised, so he entered the numbers and put the phone to his ear. Its whole body pulsated a green glow for several seconds before it chimed.

"Hello?" a voice answered, coming across with surprising clarity. He should go find Miss Pink Lips and thank her.

"Tarris?" Kortel asked.

"Jonny?!"

"Who else would have this number?"

"That's true, no shit. Where are you?"

"I'm in your neck of the mesa."

"You are?"

"Yeah. I'm north of the park, somewhere off of 57. It's a little shit-hole called Deuces Wild—"

"Damn!" Tarris said, and Kortel thought he heard it from his other ear, too. Weird. Like old stereo.

"Hey," Kortel said, "you don't have to scream in my ear."

"Hell I don't!" Again the stereo, but even more pronounced.

"Look, Tarris, I was wondering if—"

"Turn to the right, Jonny Boy!"

Kortel turned and saw that other bartender waving from the end of the bar. He had a similar phone to his ear.

"Tarris?!"

Tarris came walking up the bar. His smile was the best thing Kortel had seen all year. The biomedtronic implants that allowed him to walk were barely visible under his apron. Their micro-servos hummed slightly as he stopped in front of Kortel. He picked up the J&B and smelled. "Billy, shit!" he exclaimed. "Get the Oban for Christ's sake!"

The big Indian shrugged.

Tarris looked Kortel over. "You look like hell, but goddamnit, it's good to see you."

Billy set a bottle of Oban and two fresh glasses in front of Tarris.

"Good to see you, too," Kortel said.

Tarris smiled. "This is the good shit. We hold it back for special occasions." He poured generous shots for himself and Kortel, then raised his glass. "To old friends," he said.

They clinked glasses, and Kortel knocked back his shot.

"I see you've met Jen," Tarris said, pointing to the chrome rectangle.

"She's quite the little entrepreneur," Kortel said.

Tarris winked. "She's more than that, if you know what I mean."

Kortel didn't want to. The friend standing before him looked all right, but his youthful spirit was gone. And there was something raw about Tarris, as if his years of living on the edge had finally caught up with him. From the first time they met in grade school, Tarris had taken Kortel under his wing. When terrorists detonated an untested biothermonuclear bomb on the islands of Hawaii, over a million souls, including Kortel's parents, debiolized in less than 10 minutes. Kortel had been visiting his grandparents in the Midwest when "the Event," as the news analysis dubbed it, made him an instant orphan. Tarris had made growing up parentless more bearable, and Kortel had always been grateful.

"How the hell did you end up out here?" Tarris asked.

"I took the old road, but now it empties out onto a highway. I headed west until I got this urge to try my hand at the slots."

"Shit, not these." Tarris thumbed toward the vidslots. "The Indians have 'em so rigged, it's a surprise when anyone wins. But, really..." The wild ecstatic look was gone, and his voice now had a serious edge. "How did you find me?"

Kortel smiled. "I had Max do a probability run on where you might be hiding."

"Max is your loft's AI...back in Chicago?"

"Yes, and—"

"God, that thing is close to 10 years old by now. You need to upgrade it."

"Max has been. He's perfect for my needs. You want me to answer your question?"

Tarris motioned for him to continue.

"After all the shit that went down between you and Georgia, Max calculated there was a greater chance of you hiding out at your old Chaco lab than at any of the other holes you might crawl into."

"I'd like to see that program. You were always good at writing them."

"Still am," Kortel said. He sensed his friend's mood had changed.

Tarris took a long look down the bar. "Come on," he said in a low voice. "Let's go to my place and get our drink on."

Dragonfly. 4

BIXX wiped the steam from the bathroom mirror and sighed. Rocket told her once that she had the body of a dragonfly. Even though he had professed his love on many occasions, this single comment had wedged itself deep into her psyche. Steam began building again on the mirror, reducing her naked image to a patchwork of mottled cream. She wiped again, this time using the meat of her forearm, and stared at her 22-year-old body. Luckily she had been graced with her mother's Russian skin. Its porcelain sheen was a family trademark, but it also set off her delicate chest, which hadn't changed much, she felt, since her 12th birthday. Occasionally Bixx thought it would be nice to be able to wear certain clothes or flaunt her sexiness. And even though Rocket had declared that large breasts were overrated, she suspected he wouldn't complain if one day she came home with a pair of 34 C's. The Biolution had made changing your appearance as easy as changing your mind, but Bixx was a purist who didn't believe in augmentation. She was among a select few who chose to shun the perfection promised in the infomercials that littered the media landscape.

"Hey, Bixx?" Rocket yelled over a piercing guitar lick from the song *Crying Train*. He was somewhere in their cavernous loft, but she couldn't tell where.

Bixx leaned into the mirror. "Dragonfly?" she whispered. The steam began to blur her image again.

"Bixx? Shit!"

"What?" Bixx had half a mind to lock the door and never come out. She met his glare as he entered the bathroom.

"Girl, what is taking so long?" Rocket's expression suddenly shifted, and his eyes wandered across her body.

Bixx could tell that his frustration was sliding away. Although Rocket had been driving her nuts lately with his rants about how their kind should free themselves from their secret lives, she still loved that slide. "What are you looking at?" she asked playfully.

His eyes came to rest with hers. "Candy," he said. A mischievous smile began forming at the edges of his mouth.

Bixx pushed away from the counter and began to speak, but Rocket put a finger to her lips. He wrapped his hands around her waist and deftly lifted her onto the counter. Its surface was slick with heat and moisture. He knelt between her legs and the buckle of his belt passed down the curve of her inner thigh. She flinched from its metallic chill.

"Rocky," she said softly, "we can't—"

"Shhh," he replied. He was now cradling her buttocks with his palms, and his shoulders were gently persuading her inner thighs to part.

Bixx looked down at the top of his perpetual mop of red curls and felt Rocket raise her hips to his mouth like a chalice. "Rocket, come on—" She started surrendering, but quickly tightened and grabbed a tuft of red curls. She pried his head back, and he gazed up at her like he had been pulled from the frontier of a perfect dream.

"Hi there," she said, and smiled her little girl smile.

Rocket's brow furrowed.

"We can't," she said with all the sweetness she could muster.

The lines of his brow deepened.

"You know why..."

"Screw him," Rocket said. His warm breath tickled her.

She pulled him away, this time squeezing her thighs against the sides of his neck. "We'll have a date later. I promise."

Rocket nodded in resigned agreement and stood.

Bixx slid off the counter and turned to the mirror, where her image was clearing like a slow-focus camera shot. She felt the tip of Rocket's finger pass down the middle of her back.

"I miss you," he said. He was staring at her reflection, but past it at the same time.

"I miss you, too." Bixx caught his anguish in the mirror and sensed that empty feeling opening again, like a sinkhole for her soul.

"When are you going to be done with that project?" he asked.

Bixx hesitated. It was hard for her to leave her work behind.

Rocket came up behind her ear and whispered, "Even a computer genius needs a little release now and then."

"Hey, where is everybody?"

"Shit," Rocket said. "Kreet, we're in here. What do you want?" He leaned into Bixx's ear. "Did you have to invite him for the *whole* weekend?"

Bixx caught herself clenching her jaw. "He didn't have a place to stay," she said.

Rocket kissed her neck and whispered, "Then it's up to you to think of a way to get him out of here...for at least part of the night." He kissed her again and quietly slipped out of the bathroom.

Bixx studied her reflection. "Dragonfly," she whispered.

The sinkhole widened.

Another little bonus. 5

KORTEL fought back a yawn as the Oban washed over the ice of his fifth drink. He watched the amber liquor fill the glass with another round of liquid courage. *Liquid Courage*. A smile came to his face as he thought of better times.

Tarris wedged the cork back into the bottle and reverently nestled the 50-year-old Scotch between his thighs. With his leg implants turned off, he relaxed in his MotoTrak, which made him seem to Kortel more paraplegic than ever. His vigor, which usually dominated a room, had been replaced with a presence Kortel could only describe as aged.

"So," Tarris said, "Zvara's thinking it's time your kind came out from hiding?"

"Remember that club I told you about, back in Chicago?" Kortel mused, his attention firmly on swirling the cubes in his glass.

"Ah, yeah...the Liquid something—"

"Liquid Courage."

"Right. I remember it. Why?"

Kortel hesitated. "I went looking for Tam.... That's why I came back to the States."

"Jeez, man. Don't torture yourself like that. What's done is done."

Kortel took a long sip of his Scotch. It burned delicately, and he could feel its effects pushing his rational self aside. "I know," he muttered. "It's just—"

"Man, talk...you're not going anywhere, so spill it."

"I just wanted to know if she might remember me...remember us. So I met with Anari—"

"She was her best friend?"

"Yeah. Anari still works at Liquid Courage, and she filled me in on what had happened after the Agency performed a limited erase on Tam. She's done well. I was surprised when I saw her—"

"You didn't go see her, did you?"

Kortel nodded.

Tarris shook his head. "Man, you are out of control. You can't go doing that kind of shit. You could seriously mess her life up. Why'd you go do that?"

"Because when a person's memory is erased, especially if it's a partial erasure, sometimes it doesn't take all the way. There can be what's called leakage.... That's when fragments of memories surface, usually in dreams. And Anari told me about these dreams Tam was having. They're about a guy, and how she's so attracted to him, but she can never see his face."

Tarris's expression suggested he wasn't getting it. Or maybe it was just the Scotches.

"I think the guy in her dreams is me," Kortel said. "Anari mentioned these dreams had really affected Tam's life, especially when it came to men."

Tarris moved his chair closer. "Jonathan, listen to me. Take it from a guy who's lost more women than he can count. Don't do this to yourself. I know you love Tamara a lot, but you can't keep doing this to yourself...or her."

"Don't worry. When I finally saw her, I realized that I couldn't force my way back into her life, no matter how big of an opportunity there was. And believe me, there was. Walking away from her was the hardest thing I ever did."

"Well, it's like what my Japanese friend, Endo, says: When you fall in love with a comfort girl, you fall into hell." Tarris grinned. "It's only natural; these girls are wired to do that. I'll bet they're genetically altered to release some kind of megapheromone...one that puts you under their spell." Tarris emphasized this last point by waving his hands like some kind of magician. Then he activated his implants, stood, and walked zombielike around the room. "Yes, Mistress Tamara," he said, in a low monotone. "I am your slave." He staggered up to Kortel, eyes bulged and arms stretched. "Let me bang you, and I'll give you my condo, my car and my inheritance!"

Whether it was Tarris being a complete ass or the five Scotches, Kortel burst into such a hard laugh that his drink spilled over the side of his hand.

Tarris zombie-walked to the end of the couch and began humping it. "One million. Two million," he said, each emphasized with a clownlike thrust.

This brought Kortel almost to the edge of nausea. He couldn't remember the last time that laughing had brought tears to his eyes. He let his drink fall and desperately grabbed at his side.

"Three *million*!" Tarris yelled with another thrust.

Suddenly, an intense pain carved through the middle of Kortel's brain. The shock of it made him disoriented, and for a second he could see himself in the chair, as if he were floating up by one of the room's *vigas*. Then an inhuman sound erupted from his throat, and he was back in the chair. It felt like a scream, but it came out at a higher pitch and echoed off the tile floor. He looked at his left hand as it curled in on itself. The pain shot again to the base of his skull, and his hand tightened with such force that he thought it would snap from his wrist.

Tarris spun around at Kortel's scream. "Jonny!" he yelled, but the lamp on the table next to the couch exploded, knocking him into the MotoTrak.

"Tarris, in my coat!" Kortel could barely get the words out before another bolt of agony hit. His back arched, and the large bookcase by the picture window flew across the room. It barely missed Tarris before it slammed into the opposite wall, sending pieces of wood, paper and glass in all directions.

Tarris pulled himself into a standing position.

"My coat...pocket," Kortel managed. "The infuser."

Tarris looked madly about, then spotted the coat piled on a chair next to the fireplace.

Kortel pointed. "Get it now, before I–" Another wave crashed inside his head, and he fell out of the chair onto his hands and knees. He retched, and the sculpture awarded to Tarris for BioGame Programmer of the Year shattered in a violent spray of purple and green glass.

Tarris made it to the coat in four lunging steps. He dug out the infuser and charged over to Kortel.

"Switch it," Kortel said, forcing back another surge of nausea, "to the maximum dose. The yellow button...twice. Now, please!"

Tarris looked the infuser over and pressed the tiny yellow button. "Where?" he said, panicking.

Kortel held back the urge to vomit. "My neck," he said, between gasps. "Near the main artery." He pointed to the side of his neck.

Tarris pressed the infuser against Kortel's skin and pulled the trigger.

Kortel felt his heart instantly palpitate, and a chill gripped his body like he had been fast-dipped in a tank of ice water. The room's spatial integrity distorted, and his vision blurred. Clenching his jaw, he forced back another surge of nausea and waited for the next wave.

"Jonny," Tarris said, cautiously. "Is it working?"

Kortel couldn't answer. He held his position on his hands and knees, waiting. Slowly his heart returned to a normal rhythm, and he relaxed his jaw.

"Man, are you with me?" Tarris asked.

"Yeah," Kortel said hoarsely. "I think so."

Tarris straightened. "Damn," he said. "No more Oban for you."

"I doubt it was the Scotch."

Tarris helped Kortel into the chair. "Let me get you a cold towel," he said.

Kortel collapsed against the pillows. His mind was thick with disorientation, and the room was still a soft blur. There was a twinkling band of light moving across his vision. It appeared to be fading as the room came into focus.

"You want some water?" Tarris yelled from the bathroom.

Kortel cleared his throat. "Yeah...thanks."

Tarris returned and pressed a cool towel to Kortel's forehead. He handed him a glass of water.

Kortel took it with shaking hands and raised it to his mouth. As he drank, each gulp washed away the metallic taste and soothed his burning throat.

"What the hell was that all about?" Tarris asked, easing back into his MotoTrak. He warily eyed his drink on the table and shoved it aside.

"That," Kortel said, "is what the good doctor Shoalburg calls a little side effect."

"Damn, I'd hate to see a large one." Tarris twisted around and took account of the damage. "Aw shit," he said, spotting the empty shelf.

Kortel studied the fragments of the sculpture strewn across the floor. "I'm sorry. I know that meant a lot to you."

Tarris leaned back. "Screw it," he said. "It was only an award...I'll just have to win another one."

Kortel wiped his mouth with the towel and then placed it over the puddle of vomit. "Give me second," he said, "and I'll wipe this mess up."

"Don't worry about it," Tarris replied. "We got a lot to clean up." He gestured at what was left of the bookcase against the far side of the room. "Besides, I'm too drunk and tired to deal with this right now."

Kortel eased his head against one of the chair's cushions and closed his eyes. The ribbon of light was almost gone, but his head was throbbing so hard he could feel it in his teeth.

"Shit, Jonny," Tarris said, "how long have you been having these seizures?"

Kortel cracked open his eyelids. "I guess about a year. They started just after I settled in Russia."

Tarris whistled. "Man, you need to get that checked out. Whatever the Agency put in your head is probably growing. And by the look of it, you can't control it.... Can you?"

Kortel shrugged. "That's the other reason I came back," he said, eyes closed. "There was nobody in the Russian Tel organization who could help me. This shit—" (he tapped the side of his head) "is too advanced. I'm just a walking experiment."

"So who knows anything about this stuff? That Dr. Shoalburg guy you told me about? He's with the Agency, right?"

"Mr. Nanogenetics himself." Kortel opened his eyes to find the room in focus, but the color was off somehow. "He's a Tel, but a reluctant one. He's very hard core about going public. I'm supposed to meet with him in L.A."

"Maybe he can get you under control," Tarris said. "In the meantime, you should get some rest. You're welcome to stay here for as long as you want." Tarris eyed the infuser sitting on the table next to his drink. "So what's in this?" he asked with a nod to the device.

"A neurogenic cocktail the lab guys mixed up special for me after I complained about headaches. I didn't know at the time I had the tech in my head. I just thought I was getting headaches from all the tests they were having me do. Shoalburg says it's just a masker drug. It blocks the pain instead of fixing it. Whatever it does, I only have three infusers left. Each holds about 10 doses, so I'm hoping Shoalburg can make me some more...and maybe figure out what's happening so I can learn to control it."

Tarris's expression hardened. "Are you addicted to that shit?"

Kortel hesitated.

"Man, listen. I know about addiction." Tarris patted his legs. "Riding with Jack stung me good."

"So what if I am?" Kortel asked. "It's not like I've got a choice." He leaned forward. "I never asked to be telekinetic, or to be this powerful, and I sure as hell never asked for all this shit to be put in my head." Kortel rubbed his temples. "Tarris, I've done things...things I thought I'd never do."

"It can't be as bad as you think."

"It is, Tarris. I've killed people, and not just Trumble and Takeda."

Tarris reached over and rubbed Kortel's shoulder. "I know you better than anyone. If you did, I'm sure you had a damn good reason."

"There were these tests," Kortel mused. "They were public tests...of my telekinetic strength. I didn't know at the time they were tests; I just thought I was reacting to a random situation. One involved a bus, with kids..."

"Hey, Jonathan." Tarris had rolled closer, and Kortel noticed their knees were touching. "It's like I said before, what's done is done. You're right.... You never asked for that tech. But it's there now, and you're going to have to deal with it. You're never going back to your old life, so you might as well accept that you're in the major leagues now. Either you let shit happen to you, or you act first, and that means people might get killed. You have an extraordinarily powerful gift. It's also very dangerous...especially if it's getting out of control." Tarris leaned back into the MotoTrak. "You know, sometimes I wish I'd never told you about the Tels."

Kortel waved the comment off. "Their Recruiters would have found me eventually, especially with my level strength. It was only a matter of time."

Tarris stretched. "You're probably right," he said through a yawn. He looked around at Kortel's telekinetic damage. "Screw this shit," he said, more to himself. "We'll deal with this later." He stood. "Well, I don't know about you, but I'm ready for some Z's. Your little fit wore me out."

"How are those new implants working?" Kortel asked, gesturing at Tarris's legs.

Tarris looked down. "The new interface program I worked out is a hell of a lot better than that crap I had before. I fatigue less, and the delay time is imperceptible, at least to my brain, which isn't saying much." He laughed. "I've killed so many brain cells, the delay could be two minutes, and I wouldn't know the difference."

"You're walking great – better than I've ever seen you."

"Yeah, it took me almost a year to write the program, and another couple of months to trial the technology."

"Whatever you did, it works great – a lot better than your old implants. You can hardly tell you were ever in an accident."

"Thanks, man," Tarris said. "Coming from you, that's a big compliment."

Kortel lightly touched the towel with the tip of his boot, and a large brown spot grew under his foot. He shouldn't have had the chili. It was much worse the second time around.

"What are you thinking?" Tarris asked.

"I was thinking that if I don't get this tech either out of my head or under control, my life is going to be pretty screwed."

"Don't count yourself out. See what Shoalburg says and go from there. It's a 'one day at a time thing,' you know?"

Kortel nodded, but time was what he didn't have. When Shoalburg had examined him two years ago, he guessed the tech would continue its integration process for up to a year or more, and he couldn't say for sure what it might do after that. Shoalburg was the father of the technology, but much of what had been put in Kortel's head was beyond even him. Kortel was on borrowed time, and the episode tonight was minor compared to some he had experienced in Russia. If it hadn't been for Reza, he probably would have killed himself. She had comforted him during many of his worst episodes.

Kortel looked down at his left hand. There was a slight tremor. "Well," Tarris said through a yawn, "I'm out of here. I put all your stuff in the laundry room. The couch is probably your best bet to get a good night's sleep. That is, if you can handle the smell of puke."

"Thanks," Kortel said. "I don't have much of an issue with smell anymore. It's another little bonus from the tech."

Tarris regarded Kortel with the big brother look he always used. "It's weird," he said.

"What's weird?" Kortel replied.

"You and I...we're kind of alike now, you know?"

"How's that?"

"We're both damaged goods." Tarris smiled. "Hang in there, man. I'll see you in the morning." He turned and disappeared down the dark hallway.

Kortel looked at his left hand and clenched it into a tight fist. He knew it was only a matter of time before he would lose control altogether. The question was when. He began to extract himself out of the large chair, but collapsed onto his right arm. There was a sharp, rhythmic tingling that ran from his shoulder to his palm, and the disorientation had returned. Kortel remained on the side of his face for a moment and took long, slow breaths. When he finally sat up, he tried to shake off the sensation, but it wouldn't let go. He examined his hands, turning them over in the soft light, and found his right shaking in sync with his left.

"Great," he said into the quiet of the room. "Just great."

What a pity. 6

BIXX anxiously trained her attention to the rear of the club. The place wasn't too busy considering the time of night, and as gaps opened between groups of people she could see all the way to the bathrooms. They were easy to spot because of their door handles in the shape of question marks. They appeared to be carved out of a block of wood the size of a refrigerator, and since there was nothing else on the doors, it was a crapshoot which was which. Bixx had to keep reminding herself that this was the point – to get messed up, as if you weren't already at a club like *Up Yours*.

What the hell is taking him so long? Bixx was hoping to buy several hours alone with Rocket by dumping Kreet with some friends. Her plan was to introduce Kreet, have a drink, and sneak out to meet Rocket for a late dinner at Thai One On. But Kreet had gone to the bathroom 15 minutes ago, and there were no signs of him or her friends anywhere in the club.

She glanced at her watch. *9:36 p.m.* "Damn it–" There was a tap at her shoulder. "Hi there."

"Kreet! Where have you been?"

"Just hanging in the bathroom. I met these girls from Georgetown. They say they want to go grab sushi later. I got their numbers, but I don't recognize the prefix."

Bixx looked at his netpad. "New zone on the other side of the Potomac. They're too money for you."

Kreet shrugged. "So where're these friends of yours?"

Good question, Bixx thought. "To be honest, I have no idea." She did a 360 of the club. "I told them nine o'clock, but maybe they blew us off." Bitches. She pulled out her netpad and placed a call to one of them.

Kreet took her hands and gently closed the pad. The music had kicked up a notch. "Bixxy, you don't need to entertain me." His voice had a sweet edge to it. "If you want to go meet Rocket, it's okay. I understand." He smiled and relaxed his grip. "I really do appreciate you letting me stay at the loft."

For all his faults, Kreet could be a decent guy – sometimes. He wasn't really that bad looking, either. (Sometimes.) He was a little short, and he dressed a bit street for Bixx. Maybe it was the silly scarves he always wore. To her, they made him look like he was trying too hard, and the animatics he programmed into them were always over the top. The scarf tonight had some kind of Japanese Kabuki image with big yellow eyes that kept following Bixx whenever she moved. But what really unnerved her was what the Kabuki kept saying. With the club's music so loud, Bixx could hardly make it out: something about why Bixx should get wrapped up with it, and the next line was always too soft to hear, even when Bixx put her ear to the fabric. Knowing Kreet, it was probably something off color.

"Go on," Kreet said. "Have a good time with your boyfriend." He smiled. The Kabuki did the same.

Creepy, Bixx thought. "You sure you'll be okay?"

He grinned. "I think I'll go have some sushi."

Bixx gave Kreet a little hug (half expecting the Kabuki to bite her breast) and left him at the bar. On her way to the bathroom, she glanced over her shoulder and watched him walk over to two vapid blondes who towered at least a foot over him. She laughed.

The bathrooms at Up Yours were more like living rooms with stalls. Bixx never knew which question mark to pull, so she always went with the right one. Most women's bathrooms in Russia were on the right, so she figured it was the safe choice. The bathroom was surprisingly empty: just a couple of druggy club kids huddled on one of the couches. They were too engrossed in their netpads to notice Bixx – probably trying to hook up some Ride. Bixx knew. Six years ago she had been no different, but that was before an Agency Recruiter sat next to her late one night and explained that drugs weren't going to help her; her problem was unique, and she needed to be with her own kind. He even recounted the time she had moved her family's car without touching it. She had been across the yard when the car accidentally engaged the Interway and almost ran over her parents. They had been arguing and never saw it coming. That was back in Russia, and she had been barely 8. The fact that this guy knew intimate details from her early life hadn't surprised Bixx much, since anybody with enough digirubles could obtain information. The guy had been insistent, though, so like any good clubber she ran a bunch of attitude and told him to piss off. But when the couch they were on rose off the floor, Bixx figured the guy was onto something. Besides, he was pretty cute and offered a way out of the stupid life she had sunk into.

One of the club kids shot a harsh glance at Bixx and said something into another kid's ear. Then they sneered and collectively rose and left. Maybe Bixx had spooked them. Or maybe she just reminded them that you could get off the Ride if you wanted to badly enough. Addicts of Ride could always spot one another, even after they were clean. Bixx could never figure out what it was, except that there was something. Base. As if the drug could genetically alter an addict so that others could pick up on the need.

Bixx stretched out on one of the bigger couches and activated her netpad. Maybe Rocket would still be at the restaurant and would understand why she was running late. They all had lived with Kreet for the better part of two years, so he would know.

She hoped.

Rocket's image pixeled up. "Hey there," he said. His smile told Bixx things were cool. "Kreet being a pain in the ass?"

"As a matter of fact, no. He's actually being quite the gentleman." She laughed. "I think he knew that we wanted a date. Besides, he's already connected with some credit girls from the new zone across the river."

"What happened to Marley and Cid?"

"No-shows. It's okay. They would have blown Kreet off anyway, and I would have never heard the end of it."

"Well, get that pretty little butt of yours over here. I've already gone through an order of corn patties."

"Okay. Just let me get my face on, and I'll be there in 15 minutes. Love you. Bye."

Rocket licked his netpad's screen and his image cut out.

Bixx went to the mirror and dug in her bag for the new makeup enhancer she had bought. She was determined to make this a special night, so she had picked up a Jamma stick. They were very in, very expensive, and available only at the Jamma boutique on Pennsylvania. The girl at the counter told her that once it was applied, the base would keep changing color for a week, if she chose to leave it on that long. Bixx never kept any makeup on for longer than a few hours, but tonight was different. She owed Rocket, because he had been so patient with her long hours in the lab. Tonight was going to be her treat – and not just the dinner.

The lighting in the bathroom was dismal at best, but the makeup would know where to flow. The girl at the Jamma counter had scanned Bixx's contour and programmed the stick. All Bixx had to do was apply it in the right general area, and the makeup would do the rest. She didn't know how most people could stand having their makeup crawl over their faces each morning. She could barely keep from squirming every time she applied the stuff – and that was only for special occasions like tonight.

She anxiously raised the Jamma stick to her left cheek, and its tip quivered as it anticipated making contact with her skin. Suddenly, the bathroom door flew open and Bixx quickly set the stick next to her bag. She wasn't experienced applying the stuff and didn't need a bunch of club kids gawking and making fun of her. She thought she heard the stick make a sound, like a sigh. *Maybe it was just switching off.*

Into the bathroom strolled a pasty, taut woman in a pair of heels so tall that Bixx thought she needed a step stool to climb into them. She wore her shiny black hair in a high, tight cone that jutted out at an unnatural angle. It made her head resemble an alien creature in an old scary sci-fi vid Bixx had watched late one night on the Classics channel. The woman walked around the bathroom, sizing Bixx up like a lioness. Bixx tracked her in the mirror. This woman had the Bitch Chic act cold, and Bixx knew all about their kind. They were always at clubs like Up Yours, and they loved to pick a fight. It was the drug they took that made them so aggressive. The woman stopped directly behind Bixx.

"Got a hot date tonight?" she asked. Her accent was familiar, but Bixx couldn't place it.

Still facing the mirror, Bixx shifted to one side so she could see all of the woman's reflection. "Yeah, I do. Is that okay with you?"

The woman smiled, and the open-weaved pattern of her fishnet outfit instantly shifted into a shiny black bodysuit. Bixx noted a slight glimmer during the change.

"Does your boyfriend like you wearing Jamma?" she asked.

Bixx turned and faced her. "For the record, he usually likes me wearing Jamma...and *nothing* else."

The woman reacted as if this declaration amused her. "I bet he would...Olga."

A spike of raw cold shot through Bixx. "How do you know my name?"

"I know all about you...Bixx. Isn't that what you call yourself these days?" The woman's smile disappeared.

This was getting very weird. Nobody knew her real name, not even Rocket. Bixx had always hated the name Olga. It didn't have any family tie and was so utterly... Soviet. Bixx looked at the door, wondering if she could grab her bag and make it out before things got any weirder. She'd probably have to leave the Jamma. Too bad; it had cost her a week's credits.

"How's your work at the lab going?" the woman asked.

The situation had moved into the serious range. Only an Agency Tel would know about her work at the lab.

"What part of the Agency are you with?" Bixx asked.

The smile returned. "I'm not with *your* Agency."

Bixx took a cautious step back and bumped into the counter.

"In fact," the woman said, "I'm not even one of your kind."

Shit. The woman was a normal, but how could that be? Tels were a secret society; even Bixx's parents hadn't known. They thought she had been killed in a car accident. The Russian Tel Agency had made sure of that. It was the best way, or so she had been told.

"I heard you had a meeting the other day with a certain telekinetic we all know," the woman said. "How is Mr. Kortel?"

Bixx wasn't sure how to play this. Whoever this woman was, she might know about Kortel and Kreet's plan. Straight up seemed to be the best course. "He's okay," she answered.

The woman widened her stance and put her hands on her hips. "You wouldn't happen to know where he's staying in D.C., would you? He's probably wearing a signature displacer, since we can't locate him anywhere."

"No I don't," Bixx lied. "But it doesn't matter because he said he was leaving the city. And before you ask, I have no idea where he went." At least that part was true.

The woman reached into a pocket on her leg, and the bodysuit rippled slightly. There was no pocket a moment ago, but suddenly it was there on the woman's quad. She removed an international credit chip-card. It was carbon black and appeared like an extension of her hand. The woman leveled it at Bixx, its edge disappearing at the perfect angle. "Are you sure you don't know where he was headed?"

Now Bixx was getting pissed. Bribery had become a fine art in Russia, and Bixx hated it. She decided it was time to show this normal who was in charge. "I told you the truth," she said, and produced a high-level grav field.

The woman's arms instantly slapped against her sides, and her body went rigid from the gravitational pressure. The chip-card flew out of her hand and was caught in the field. It hung motionless about a foot in front of the woman.

"Who do you work for," Bixx asked. "And how do you know my real name?" She had secured most of the woman's body, but had allowed her head to be free.

The woman didn't answer.

Bixx mentally lifted her off the floor and tightened her telekinetic grip. The woman gasped slightly.

"Are you going to answer me?–"

"Marcus," the woman called out. "I could use a little help here."

"What's the matter, love?" a disembodied male voice answered from one of the stalls. "Did a Level 4 get the best of you?" It was a distinctly British accent.

"Obviously she's not a Level 4," the woman replied, "or I wouldn't be floating off the floor!"

"You know they have little metal containers mounted to the walls in here. I don't think pubs have those back home. What do you suppose they're for?"

"Shut up and get the hell out here," the women said, trying to squirm in Bixx's field.

The toilet flushed in the middle stall. A man emerged wearing the same black bodysuit as the woman, but its cut was more masculine. His hair was slicked back against his head like plastic, which seemed to work with his thick features. He wore 'trodes over his eyes. *Jacked*, Bixx thought. He stepped over to the woman and looked up.

"Either our research is wrong," the Brit said, "or Olga here has advanced quite a bit since leaving Russia." He directed his attention to Bixx and smiled a set of perfectly crafted white teeth.

Bixx was on the edge of panic. She was totally clueless who these two were and why they wanted her. Sure, she had been in the meeting with Kortel, but she didn't really care if their kind came out or not. She tried to maintain her grav field, but was already pushing her telekinetic strength.

"How long are you planning to hold her?" he asked.

She didn't know what to say. "Well, I, ah–"

Suddenly Bixx was flying over the counter. She slammed into the mirror, and her head smacked against the base of a light sconce. She crumpled into the sink. The force of the impact almost caused her to throw up. Stunned, Bixx felt the back of her head and came away with blood on her fingers. She looked into the large mirror on the other side of the room and saw her reflection. A thin streak of blood ran from the base of the sconce to the top of her head. Her heart felt like it was coming out of her throat.

The woman had fallen onto her hands and knees, and she was picking the chip-card off of the floor. "Marcus," she said, straightening, "I distinctly said not to be rough." The wrinkles in her suit slithered away. "I'm already dealing with one lawsuit."

The Brit, ignoring her, strolled over to Bixx like he was about to ask her to dance. He smiled. More perfect teeth. "My colleague here is a normal," he said, gesturing. "I'm different. You're supposed to be a Level 4, but you held that grav field for..." he referenced his watch, "...two minutes. Not bad. You're probably a Level 5 now."

"Please," Bixx said. Her throat was tight and raw. "I don't know anything about—"

"Just hold her while I go talk to the scarf kid," the woman said, slipping the chip-card back into the invisible pocket. She shook her head at the mess. "Jesus."

"Yes, ma'am," the Brit said. He watched the woman leave and then got in Bixx's face. "You never answered her question," he said, pointing to the bathroom door.

Bixx felt herself yanked forward, as if invisible hands had grabbed the front of her sweater. She was inches from the Brit's face.

"Time to learn," he said.

He hurled Bixx against the mirror again, this time with such force that she bit her tongue. The room went out of focus, then came back. She looked past the Brit and into the other mirror. There was a new streak next to the first one. Bixx wanted to cry, but the shock of the moment wouldn't let her. All she could do was lie there and shake uncontrollably. Her crotch felt wet, and there was a faint smell of urine. The Brit leaned in.

"What a pity," he said, casually. "You've gone and smashed your Jamma stick."

Bixx looked down and saw the stick in three pieces next to her bag. Its brightly colored makeup had escaped and was halfway up the side of the wall.

"Bet that set you back a couple of quid," he said, now practically touching her nose.

Bixx could smell his breath. Gin.

The woman was at the door. "I can't find the kid with the scarf fetish."

The Brit turned and eyed her. "He's probably getting drunk at the main bar with Tolly and Brie. He's a bloody dolt, that one is."

Bixx's vision began to blur. There was a tingling at her temples. She tried to focus on the makeup as it inched its way up the tile. It disappeared into the HVAC vent just as everything went black.

Say hello. 7

KORTEL poured himself a coffee and stepped onto the porch. The morning sun had crested over the mountains and was flooding the small valley below with the quality of light for which New Mexico was famous. A dog barked in the distance.

A week had passed since Kortel had taken Tarris up on his offer to stay. He hadn't had another seizure since the first night, and the days had settled into a simple routine. He had breakfast with the sunrise, always sitting in the filtered shade of the blue cedars at the end of the porch. He spent the mornings walking the land around the compound, which was what Tarris called the architecturally arranged sections of an old 747 fuselage. The front quarter of the plane was partially embedded in a small mesa that ran along the edge of the property. Tarris made his bedroom in what had been the upper deck lounge, with the flight deck remodeled as a bathroom. On the ground level – which had been first class – was the kitchen and living room. Two sections from the middle of the plane sat at right angles to the nose, their bottom thirds sunk into the ground. They had been walled in on their ends; one served as Tarris's lab, the other his garage, which housed an antique, retrofitted Hummer along with various ATVs of his own design. Kortel always wondered how Tarris had gotten the sections to such a remote place – something about a favor being owed – but he had never asked for details.

Kortel spent most of his afternoons in the lab. Tarris had an on-again, off-again retainer with one of his former employers. EchoGame was a Pacific Rim conglomerate with its hands in everything from virt booths to holoporn. The gaming division was its brain trust, and Tarris had been its golden boy. But a decade ago all that ended on the night he mixed his love for drugs and motorcycles. Tarris was on retainer this month, and deep into developing a direct-link game that had promotional ties with a new action vid Kortel had only read about. It starred a new kind of virtual character whose name he couldn't pronounce. All Tarris could tell him was that it involved string-theory dynamics and was huge with kids 8 to 14.

In the evenings Kortel would prepare something: fish, steak, it didn't matter. It had been a long time since he had been in a kitchen that actually had modern conveniences. He enjoyed programming a meal again. Even grilling seemed refreshing. The nights were always capped off with a round of Scotch.

Tarris joined Kortel on the porch and took in a deep breath. "Helluva morning," he declared. His robe's sash whipped in the wind, and the servos in his hips complained as he shifted weight from one leg to the other.

"The best one yet," Kortel agreed. He took a long drink from his mug, turned from the sun and faced Tarris. His hair blew across his eyes. "So, what will it be for today? More modeling of the heroine?"

Tarris stood staring at the valley. "No," he said, finally. "I think we're going to dive into the background architecture. I'm not sure it's structured right, you know?"

Kortel nodded and returned to the view. The barking echoed off the land again. "Whose dog is that?"

Tarris shrugged. "Not sure. I just feed him when he comes around."

The barking intensified into sharp, repetitive yipes.

"Something's got him pissed off," Tarris said.

Then Kortel heard it. Or rather, he sensed it: the faint audible drone of aircraft engines. Distant. Coming over the high desert wind like a messenger. "Hear that?" he asked.

Tarris put an ear to the wind. "Yeah. Sounds like two."

Kortel listened. "One," he corrected, "with two engines."

Both men put their hands up to block the sun's glare. Kortel pointed first.

"There it is," he said, "over that tall peak."

Where the sky met the mountains, a plane skimmed through the morning clouds. Reduced by distance to a sliver of gold, it was thick in the middle and had two tampering appendages. The craft angled toward the compound, its engines barely discernable from the wind in Kortel's ears.

"You know anyone with their own personal jump jet?" he asked.

"CEO of EchoGame, but he'd never come out here." Tarris cupped both hands around his face and watched it approach. "There's no markings on it."

The jet banked and slowly circled the compound. Its mono-wing shape was more apparent as it came around.

"That's a shitload of money up there," Tarris said.

The jet slowed, leveled, and came to a stop near the north end of the property. It pivoted to face them and hovered about 100 feet off the tree line. Shadows from the clouds moved across the craft, dappling its skin with contrasts of gray and bright gold. A thin line of black bisected the fuselage horizontally from edge to edge. Probably the cockpit window.

"I've got something that could bring her down in a heartbeat," Tarris remarked.

"If we move," Kortel said, "my guess is we'd never make it to the back door."

Tarris cautiously lowered his hands. "They're here for you, aren't they?"

Kortel put his hands into the pockets of his jeans and felt the leftover dirt from a stump they dug up on Tuesday. "Not unless EchoGame's changed its policy on corporate travel." He kicked at an exposed nail in one of the deck's floorboards. "I knew it was only a matter of time."

"But you're wearing a sig displacer."

"No shit. But they've probably got a way around it."

"Can't you just throw up a grav wave or something and knock them out of the sky?"

"To move something like that fast enough to catch 'em off guard, I'd have to go into phase. I'm sure they're monitoring me right now, and I don't want to test their reaction time."

"But I thought you were faster than light."

Kortel sighed. "It doesn't work like that. I need motivation...to kick in the surge."

"This isn't enough motivation?"

"It has to be something radical," Kortel explained. "You can't alter that big a gravity field with just an idle threat. It's got to be severe. *Life*-threatening."

The jet began to move toward them, its engines now just slightly louder than before. It passed over their heads and disappeared behind the top of the lab. A large cloud of dust climbed into the sky, and the whine of the engines dropped an octave.

"Well," Tarris said, "what the hell do we do now?"

Kortel shrugged. "Go say hello?"

The dust kicked up from the jump jet's vertical thrusters was still settling as Kortel and Tarris rounded the east corner of the lab. Kortel could make out three figures standing about 10 feet in front of the nose. There wasn't a visible door, and the black line turned out to be the intake grill for the engines. At least that's what Kortel thought, because the only other apparent blemish on the craft was the windshield. It was gold, but a shade darker than the body. Kortel and Tarris stood their ground about 50 feet from the craft.

"I'll bet these are your people," Tarris said out of the corner of his mouth. "You go greet them."

Kortel laughed. "Pussy." He began walking toward the jet.

"All right, wait up."

The center figure was a large man with a shock of white through his dark gray hair. His face seemed fitted to his head, the skin unusually tight at the cheeks and jaw. He wore a black, formally tailored suit. It reflected the curved image of the fuselage, giving its dark fabric a golden hue. On his left was a small Asian woman in a deep blue jumpsuit. There were enough electronics across her outfit to be jacked into NORAD. Her hair was cut severely around her head, exposing her neck just above her ears. The cut apparently made it easier to wear the virtgear strapped to her head. She appeared to be the pilot. The guy to Mr. Shiny Suit's right was dressed like a garbage collector for a large European city. His coveralls were bright yellow and tucked neatly into a pair of black combat boots. He also had technology, but most of it was centered on his chest. His headgear spilled across his face, so Kortel couldn't make out the man's nationality. Or if "he" even was a he.

Kortel stopped about 20 feet from them. He put his hands in his pockets and felt for the dirt. Tarris stepped up to his side. His prosthetics were issuing an odd whining sound.

The suit and his associates slowly bowed.

The wind blew between them, and Kortel thought he saw the jump jet's skin quiver.

"Organic?" he said, finally.

The guy in the yellow coveralls turned to Mr. Shiny Suit. The pilot followed.

"Your jump jet," Kortel said. "It's mostly organic, right?"

"Yes," the pilot said crisply. "Micro-organics with a programmable titanium fuselage." There was a trace of an Asian accent...Korean, maybe?

"Bitchin'," Tarris said under his breath.

"Jonathan," the suit said, "how are you enjoying your vacation?" There was an air of sophistication in his voice, but it wasn't forced.

"Here, or the one in Russia?"

The suit smiled for the first time. "Here."

Kortel thought for a second. "The room service sucks, but the food's not bad."

The suit's smile faded. "It's time to become useful, Jonathan."

"I'll get useful on my own time," Kortel replied, and the jet began to rise slowly off the ground.

The pilot spun and watched it ascend.

"Is this the right way to say hello?" Tarris asked.

"It's a start," Kortel said.

The jet stopped and hung about 100 feet in the air. The pilot looked pissed.

"You're wasting your talent," the suit said.

Suddenly, Kortel felt numbness behind his left eye. It needled across his face and traveled down his neck. His throat began to constrict. The suit gestured to Mr. Coveralls, and the numbness stopped spreading. Kortel gasped slightly and fell to one knee.

"Jonny boy," Tarris said, "are you sure you want to play it like this?"

"Maybe...not," Kortel managed between gasps.

The jet quickly lowered and slammed to the ground, its hydraulics straining with the impact. Dirt flew, and the pilot scowled at Kortel.

The suit waved the dust from his face and cleared his throat. "I wouldn't test my patience, Jonathan. Or my client's." He walked over to Kortel and gestured again to Mr. Coveralls.

The numbness vanished, and Kortel gulped down a couple of breaths.

The suit helped him to his feet and dusted off his pant leg. "Now that we're past the one-upmanship," he grabbed Kortel's hand and shook it, "what a pleasure it is to finally meet you."

"Thanks, I guess," Kortel said, rubbing his throat. "Mr...?"

"St. John...Errol St. John." He turned to Tarris. "And you must be Tarris. My children have enjoyed your games for years. It's a pleasure." He offered his hand.

Tarris eyed it warily.

"Come now, Tarris, we're here just to talk with Jonathan. If we had wanted to cause harm, you would have never seen us coming." His hand was still extended.

Tarris cautiously took it. "Maybe," he said, and shot a sideways glance at Kortel, "but I got shit that can see right through stealth."

St. John pulled Tarris close and his expression went blank. "Not ours," he said seriously, and then his smile returned, bigger than before. "There, now we're friends."

"Who are you?" Kortel asked.

"All in good time." St. John eagerly surveyed the compound. "Well?" he said, wringing his hands. "Isn't it time for breakfast in this part of the world?"

Tarris turned to Kortel. "You're the chef here."

Kortel sighed. Obviously, St. John was a man of means, and whatever he was peddling, he wasn't going away until he made his case. Regardless, Kortel wasn't sure if he would have a choice in the matter. "Okay," he said, "I think I saw a dozen eggs in the refrigerator."

St. John's smile grew, and he motioned to his associates.

~

"Extraordinary, Tarris," St. John said from the living room. "How *did* you get all this out here?"

Kortel was in the kitchen inputting a Southwest *huevos* dish he used to prepare at his restaurant. It had been his partner's recipe, so it took him a moment to remember all the code combinations. He glanced at Tarris, who was washing a knife in the sink.

"It was flown here in parts. I scavenged what I wanted and sold the rest for scrap," Tarris said. "You'd be amazed at what you can sell on the black net these days."

Kortel finished inputting the recipe and began setting the table. St. John moved diligently through the room, as if taking account of every item, processing and storing whatever data he thought useful. The pilot and Mr. Coveralls remained by the door. St. John stopped at a wall that held many of Tarris's awards.

"Very impressive, Tarris," he said, examining the biogame interface patent. "I didn't know you invented the Opus Controller."

"How do you think I can afford all this?" Tarris said.

"I assumed it was the royalties from your games."

"No, what little I get of those goes to keep me walking."

St. John took a seat at the end of the table, and Kortel could feel his gaze. "You've been so quiet," St. John said. "Maybe we should have announced ourselves when we entered your country's airspace."

Kortel placed the last fork in St. John's setting. "This is your show. Maybe you should just get on with it."

St. John nodded and settled into his chair. "Jonathan, how many times has your life changed?"

Kortel leaned heavily on the back of a chair. "I don't get your question."

"Well, there was the death of your parents in Hawaii, the discovery of your gift, the loss of Tamara, the deception of Georgia, and the deaths of Trumble and Takeda...and that's not to speak of the technology now growing inside your head."

"Okay. Maybe a dozen times. I don't know. What's your point?"

St. John had done his homework, and it was beginning to creep Kortel out, especially his knowledge of Kortel's relationship with Tamara.

"What if you were to learn that the Tels were not the deep secret you thought they were...that they've been in collusion with certain non-Tel factions?"

Kortel shrugged. He always suspected that the Tels had contacts in select industries, so the revelation didn't surprise him much.

Tarris walked in with a basket of biscuits and a platter full of Kortel's egg dish. He set them down and took the seat at the other end of the table. Kortel sat in the middle chair, his attention locked on their new guest.

"Jonathan," St. John said, "the world your Agency has been defining for you is not what it seems. Yes, the Tels have been in control of things behind the scenes, but not without help."

"Are you a normal?" Tarris blurted.

St. John didn't acknowledge the question. Instead, he scooped a rather large portion of eggs onto his plate along with two biscuits.

"He is," Kortel said.

St. John smiled as he buttered a biscuit. "That ol' Tel instinct kicking in?" he asked, and took a large bite.

"Something like that."

St. John swallowed deliberately. "He's correct, Tarris. I'm a normal, and so are my associates."

The hair on the back of Kortel's neck stood up. He glanced over his shoulder at the pilot and Mr. Coveralls. They hadn't moved.

St. John wiped his mouth in a manner cultivated by years of fine dining. "You see, Jonathan, the Tels have been in association with my clients—"

"Who are your *clients*?" Tarris asked.

"They're a consortium."

"What kind of consortium?" Kortel asked.

St. John played with the patch of hair below his bottom lip. "Let's just say that, like the Tels, they have their hands in almost every aspect of life. Don't believe everything they teach you at that Agency of yours. Be assured, there are only a few outside of the Tel culture who know of your kind's existence. And even fewer who know about you, Jonathan...and your power."

This statement punched hard at what was left of Kortel's feelings of security. He had been told that the Tel culture was a secret, hidden by layers of front companies and years of disinformation. He also knew about their influence in various governments. But St. John was a normal and seemed to know all about the Tels and the New American Agency. He even knew about Kortel's history. And about Tamara. What other revelations were there? And if St. John's coveralled minion had the ability to tap into the implants in his brain, what else could he do? Suddenly, Kortel felt very exposed.

"The people I represent," St. John continued, "have been in association with your kind for over 50 years. They have what I would call a mutually beneficial arrangement. My clients exert influence that helps the Tels, and certain people within the Tel culture respond in kind. What's the phrase...you scratch my back, I scratch yours? It's really that simple. Good Lord," St. John said with a chuckle, "how do you think anything gets done in this world?"

"Get to the point," Kortel said.

"I'm here to present you with an offer."

Kortel bit into some eggshell. "What kind?"

St. John grinned sinuously around a forkful of *chorizo* and scrambled eggs, then chewed slowly as if the act were a calculated effort designed to bring the conversation to an excruciating pace. "My clients," he said finally, "want to wipe your slate clean, so to speak."

"I don't follow you."

"They want to help correct one of those changes we were talking about. You see, they have considerable influence within the circles that would like to...oh, how can I put this?... seek revenge for your handiwork against Trumble and Takeda?"

"And the catch?" Kortel asked.

St. John smiled again, and Kortel noticed an undignified amount of chorizo lodged between his teeth.

"There's always a catch, isn't there?" He wiped his mouth and tongued his teeth. "Life has a way of creating points and counterpoints. Action. Reaction. What's being offered is merely a reaction to your action."

The chorizo was gone.

"Poof, just like that?" Kortel asked, gesturing.

"Poof," St. John said, and he took a drink of his orange juice. His eyes never left Kortel's.

"I'd be damn sure about the ground rules," Tarris said.

"Let me make sure I understand this," Kortel said. "What you're offering, I mean, what your clients are offering, is a kind of immunity?" His attention went to St. John's shock of white hair. The guy was definitely a professional and obviously connected with a powerful group. But what kind? A corporation? A government?

St. John nodded. He had settled comfortably into his chair, his hands neatly folded across his lap. "That's correct," he said. "Total immunity."

"How can your clients guarantee that?" Tarris asked.

"At the moment, it's not important to know how, just that they can."

"You haven't answered my question," Kortel said.

"The catch," St. John said in a firm voice, "is simply this: for your immunity, you will be put on a retainer with my clients."

"To do what?"

St. John hesitated. "This and that...I really can't say at this time. It would be better if you met with them in person."

"This is bullshit," Kortel said, pushing away from the table.

"Before you go and erase us, Jonathan ..."

A pain shot through Kortel's head; he winced from its intensity.

"Consider the alternatives." St. John leaned onto the table, and Kortel noticed a large scar that started at the knuckles of his right hand and disappeared under the cuff of his suit. "Right now, your life is an abstraction. You're the greatest Tel ever, yet you're living as a fugitive hand to mouth. Jonathan, be reasonable." His voice was filled with earnest. "What do you have to lose? My clients aren't monsters – they're businessmen, just as you were once. This little demonstration is to remind you that you're vulnerable. They just wish to meet with you." St. John relaxed and leaned back in his chair. "Do you have a better option?" He motioned to Mr. Coveralls, and the pain disappeared.

"Okay," Kortel said, rubbing his temples, "new ground rule. No more making your point with pain. You don't need to keep reminding me that you've developed tech that can interface with my implants. I'm slightly more intelligent than a dog and can comprehend your intent without reinforcement."

Mr. Coveralls launched over the table and flew across the room, arms and legs flailing. He thwacked face-first against the bulkhead and fell to the floor in a tangle of yellow fabric and electronics. He groaned and tried to struggle to his feet, only to collapse onto his face. A small pool of blood spread from his cheek before he rose and floated toward the kitchen table, headgear hanging in pieces from his face.

Kortel maintained his focus on St. John. "Because," he continued, "if he uses that shit on me one more time–" Mr. Coveralls stopped above St. John, and a large drop of blood splattered across his plate.

St. John nodded tentatively. "You've made your point. There's no need for such drama. Please, put Mr. Kirasawa down and let's finish our talk."

Kortel moved Kirasawa toward the pilot and dropped him at her feet. She didn't react.

"What if I don't want to take you up on your offer?" Kortel asked.

St. John shrugged and took note of his right hand's fingernails. They were, like the rest of him, perfectly manicured. "Then your life will plod along as it has," he said, still regarding one of his cuticles. "One pathetic day after another. The greatest living Tel ever, wasting his life away. A wanted man, who will eventually meet his fate. If we can interface with your biotechnology," his eyes went to Kortel's, "just think who else can. No one really knows what it will do for your gift. If you don't meet with my clients, there will be others who will want to *persuade* you. And they won't be as forgiving as I am." St. John stood and adjusted his tie. "Take your time. When you come back from seeing Shoalburg," he eyed Kortel again, "call me with your decision." He produced an old-fashioned business card and stuck it into the remains of his scrambled eggs. It had his name and a coordinate number in a delicate serif typeface.

St. John turned and walked toward the pilot, who now had Kirasawa propped against her shoulder. "Delicious breakfast, Jonathan," he said. "So wonderfully regional. And good-bye, Tarris. Please don't try anything that shows your ignorance when we leave." He went up to the pilot and spoke into her ear. She nodded, and they all started to walk out the original first-class exit of the plane.

"Hey, wait a minute," Kortel said.

The pilot and Kirasawa shuffled through the exit. St. John stopped, but didn't turn back.

"How did you know where to find me?"

"A word of advice?" St. John looked over his shoulder. "Don't buy discount Net phones from strange girls in casinos. You never know what kind of service you'll get."

Heritage. 8

"**HEY,**" said a voice somewhere at the boundary of Bixx's consciousness, "I think she's coming out of it."

It sounded like Rocket, but she couldn't tell. She felt as if she were inside a dream – her mind soft, pliable, ready to liquefy and slide down the back of her throat.

"She's trying to open her eyes," the voice said, its tone rich with concern. It was Rocket.

Bixx felt someone approach and brush her arm. A smell wafted into her nose that made her flash back to summers at her family's farm and her grandfather fresh from the fields. It had been a thick odor that clung to his overalls.

"Should we keep her under?" she heard Rocket ask.

"No, it's time for her to wake up," another voice answered. This person sounded like Sanjiv.

Bixx felt someone gently squeeze her upper arm. "Hey you," Rocket whispered sweetly, "it's time to wake up." He was close to her face, and she could feel his breath on her cheek. Her mind went to the bathroom at Up Yours. The woman in the bodysuit. The Brit and his breath.

Gin.

"Nyet!" Bixx yelled, and opened her eyes to a stinging glare.

"Hey, hey. Easy there," Rocket said.

Bixx fought against the grip at her arm. Part of her knew it was Rocket, but another part could only see the Brit.

"Bixx, come on. It's me."

Another hand pressed at her shoulder. Rocket's face came out of the glare. Bixx focused on his eyes and stopped struggling. He looked scared.

"It's all right," Rocket said. "You're safe."

Bixx wrapped her arms around his neck and hugged him. She wanted to cry, but something instinctual was stopping her. Maybe it was her heritage. All Russian children were taught the history of their country: the struggles, the sacrifices, how the will of the Russian people was like a weapon, forcing back centuries of invaders. And now it was rising up like armor for her emotions. Rocket held Bixx and gingerly stroked her hair.

"It's okay," he whispered into her ear. "You're home, with me."

Bixx pulled away and felt the back of her head. A patch of hair had been shaved away, and a thick bandage covered the spot where she had hit the mirror. It was warm to the touch, and Bixx could feel a faint undulating under the film. She looked at Sanjiv.

"It's the nanomeds under the micropore's first layer," he explained. "They're, ah, eating the infection." He hesitated and smiled nervously. "They're in the wound glue."

Sanjiv wasn't a certified physician, but he knew a lot about medicine. Late one night during her first year in the warehouse when they were all living together, Bixx had overheard Kreet and Rocket talking in hushed tones. Something about Sanjiv and a lawsuit. She never heard the whole story but got the sense that something had happened that redirected Sanjiv's career path. Now he was a genetic researcher. And since it had never surfaced in any conversations, she never brought it up. Bixx fought the urge to scratch at the bandage.

"How did I get here?" she asked Rocket. The question sounded dumb even to her, but she really couldn't remember how she ended up in her bed.

"I waited at Thai One On for an hour," he said. "Then this girl called from your netpad. She said she found you passed out in a sink, and that a Bitch Chic had beaten you up. I blew every intersection to get to you, and when I got to the club, you were in one of the bathrooms, sitting on a couch with a towel full of ice to your head. Don't you remember any of this?"

Bixx didn't, which made her feel very weird. She pulled her legs close and hugged her knees. "No, I don't–"

"It's probably the drug I gave her," Sanjiv said. "It induces a deep sleep and sometimes causes a temporary loss of trauma-related memories. She might remember, but she might not."

"Can you tell us anything about your attacker?" Rocket asked.

"There were two," Bixx replied, and she proceeded to tell them everything she could remember about the bodysuit woman and the plastic-haired Brit. She explained how the woman wanted to know about their meeting with Kortel and where she could find him. Bixx even told Rocket that it all happened while she was putting on some Jamma, just for him, and that she was sorry for blowing their date.

"Shit," Rocket said, "that's the last thing I'm worried about. I'm just glad you didn't get killed. These two sound like they mean business. You're lucky you came away with only a scratch."

It didn't feel like a scratch to Bixx. She reached behind her head for the bandage.

"Don't disturb the wound," Sanjiv reiterated. "It won't heal if you start poking at it."

Bixx returned to hugging her knees. The nanomeds were beginning to itch like crazy.

"Let them do their job," Sanjiv said. "You're very lucky there was no concussion.

It should take a day or two for the wound to heal completely."

"We should have expected this," Rocket said. He was pacing their small bedroom, arms folded tightly across his chest. "Leave it to the Agency to send in some goons to shut Kreet's plan down."

"Rocket," Bixx said, "they told me they weren't from the Agency. They never said who they worked for, but I know the British guy was at least a Level 6." She began to reach for the wound, but stopped. "And there was something else.... The woman was a normal."

Rocket stopped, and Bixx could tell this hit him hard. He threw his hands up. "Shit, this isn't good. Kreet has gotten us into something stupid, I know it." His look went grave. "When's the last time you saw him?"

"I left him at the bar. When I was walking toward the bathrooms, I looked over my shoulder and saw him hitting on these two blondes–" Then Bixx remembered. The Brit's perfect smile. *What had he called Kreet...a bloody dolt?* "Rocket," she said, "you haven't heard from Kreet?"

"No."

"The woman asked the British guy about Kreet....She said she wanted to talk with him. The weird guy told her that he was with two girls. He called them by name, like he knew them."

"Shit," Rocket said to himself.

"Rocket," Bixx said, "how long have I been out?"

Rocket and Sanjiv exchanged tentative glances. "About a day and a half," Rocket said.

"Oh, my God," she said softly. "They might have erased Kreet by now." Then something began to rise inside Bixx. Hard. Guttural. She could feel her heritage pushing aside her anxiety and making a place for another emotion. "What was that guy's name?" she asked both Rocket and Sanjiv. "The one who got Kortel's incepts?"

Sanjiv thought for a moment. "McCarris!" he said. "James McCarris."

Bixx folded her arms, and her anger clicked into place. "Find him," she said, "and we'll find Kreet."

Serious as a heart attack. 9

KORTEL'S netpad chimed, yanking him from a dream he'd had before. He was sitting at an outdoor bar, somewhere in Northern California – the wine country, though he never understood how he knew this. His friend Carlton climbed onto the stool next to him and announced everything was fine, that Kortel shouldn't worry about him. The first time he had the dream was the week after Carlton had died of Netox, and although it had been more than seven years since his death, the dream still got to him.

Kortel wiped some sleep from his eye and read the salutation on his netpad's screen: *Get up. It's time for you to be great!*

"Hello?" he said blearily.

"Time to rise and shine."

Kortel read the time meter. *5:30 a.m.* "Shit, Sasha." He was having trouble focusing on her image. "It's 5:30 in the morning."

"Don't blame me. I didn't set the time for the meeting."

Kortel rolled back against the pillow and let the pad drop to his side.

"Hey, where did you go?"

"I'm still here," Kortel said to the ceiling.

"How's New Mexico?–"

"What meeting?"

"Didn't you get my message?"

"No, my pad's been off.... Hey, wait–" He grabbed the pad and brought it to his face. Its bandwidth meter was at full strength. "That's weird."

"I'm sorry, what did you say?" Sasha's hair was pulled up in a small ponytail. It set off her sharp cheekbones and bounced slightly when she spoke. "Stop moving your pad around; I can't see you."

"My pad...it was off-line, until...never mind. Now, what were you saying?"

"You have a meeting today."

"No I don't. I'm flying to L.A. this afternoon."

"We've canceled it."

"What? I need to see Shoalburg."

"First off, he won't be there. He's actually headed your way. Second, I did what you asked."

Kortel sat up. "He's headed where, and you did what?" He rubbed his neck, feeling for the injection bruise. Maybe two doses hadn't been a good idea last night.

"Will you wake up?! Shoalburg is landing in Albuquerque at 7:30 this morning."

"Why?"

"For the meeting. Will you focus?!"

"Hey, it's early. I'm still half asleep."

Sasha smiled.

"What?" Kortel asked.

"Your hair...It looks cute, that's all."

Kortel passed a hand through his hair. "Right, sure it does. And what did I ask you to do, again?"

"Find my dad."

"You did?"

Sasha nodded.

"What did he say?"

"Why don't you ask him yourself? You're meeting with him this morning."

~

Kortel had been driving for over an hour and now found himself traversing a narrow, rocky path. It had been years since he had driven a manually controlled vehicle, and never anything as archaic as Tarris's Hummer. It was hard to keep the huge vehicle away from the scrub sage. The path suddenly ended at an old metal gate that looked like it belonged on a ranch. There was a cattle guard in front of it, and the gate wasn't attached to any kind of fence, at least not within the last century. He put the Hummer in park and checked his position with his netpad. According to it, this was the point for the meeting. He confirmed the coordinates with the Hummer's SatNav and noted the time. *10:30 a.m.*

Sasha's instructions had brought Kortel to a remote area about an hour northwest of Tarris's compound. Tarris thought the coordinates would take him into the Navajo Indian Reservation, so he had given Kortel a handheld Light-Force. He said the Navajo were uptight about people on their land, now that 150 years of casino profit had transformed their lifestyle. The Light-Force was a low-power one, typical of early models, and Tarris had warned him to allow at least twice as much time for the loading sequence. Kortel glanced at it sitting in the drink holder of the center console, and hoped he wouldn't need it.

The land around him was pretty desolate, and the Hummer's SatNav indicated there was a drop-off about 200 yards past the gate. From all appearances, he was parked on top of a large mesa, but the Hummer's computer didn't have any information on the valley below. Kortel lowered the driver's side window and leaned back in his seat. A shaft of morning sun hit his face, so he pulled the visor down. A small holophoto fell into his lap, landing backside up. He turned it over, and a woman with long raven hair winked back. It was Georgia, Tarris's former lover.

It was a cheap print anyone with a holocamera could have made at home, and Kortel watched it cycle through her smile and wink. She had been captured from the waist up standing on a porch, but it wasn't at the Chaco compound; it was at Tarris's other home in Tres Piedras, probably at the height of their relationship. Her dark, almost black eyes followed Kortel.

"She was very beautiful," a raspy voice said over his left shoulder.

Kortel recoiled against the center console.

Armando Zvara's long, bearded face peered in from the window. It had been more than two years, but Kortel immediately recognized those sad green eyes.

"I'm sorry to have startled you."

Zvara took a step back, and Kortel noticed a slight awkwardness in his movement. The gray in his beard made him look old.

"It's okay; I was lost in a thought." Kortel wedged the holophoto under the butt of the Light-Force and concealed it with his coat before he stepped from the Hummer.

The last time Kortel had seen Zvara, Jacob Whitehorse had him telekinetically suspended over a fire like a rotisserie chicken. Whitehorse had wanted Kortel to join a group of loosely organized, disenfranchised Tels, but Zvara had wanted him for the Agency. At the time, Kortel wanted nothing to do with either, because things had gotten ugly between Zvara and Whitehorse – some old history about one screwing the other's wife. Both men had been top Recruiters, but Zvara had been made head of the Agency first. That, along with his wife's dalliance with Zvara, had sent Whitehorse over the edge.

"Do you ever think about her?" Zvara asked. He was leaner than Kortel remembered, and dressed in a blue work shirt, faded khakis and a pair of military boots. He looked rather ordinary, considering he was arguably one of the most powerful of their kind.

"Rarely," Kortel answered.

Zvara's expression challenged his assertion.

"Okay, sometimes I think about her. But it's weird."

"What do you mean?"

"To have known her as one person, then to find out she's somebody else, then having to kill her."

"But it was self-defense."

"Easy for you to say. You didn't see her die in front of you." The image of Georgia screaming as her molecular structure collapsed surfaced in Kortel's mind. That was the night that Georgia had revealed she was Whitehorse's daughter, that she had been fooling Kortel all along. She had played the part of Tarris's lover just to get close enough to kill Kortel. He had always rationalized that she had forced him to defend himself. A shiver cut through him.

"A hit from a Matter-Force can be an ugly way to die," Zvara remarked.

Kortel shot him a *no shit* look.

"She was just like her father."

"Crazy?"

Zvara's expression hardened. "Disturbed."

A hawk screeched above them, and both men watched it lazily ride the warm midday thermals.

"So," Kortel said, "are you really part of this plan to bring us out?"

"See that hawk?" Zvara said, still watching.

"Yeah."

"I think it is time our kind was free."

Zvara's contractionless speech pattern was a by-product of the tech the Agency had crammed into his head. Hearing it brought back a flood of memories for Kortel, and he found himself relating to the great Tel even more. He looked up again and watched the hawk glide over the top of a mesa and disappear behind its rim. "Do you think our culture could come out without repercussions?" Kortel asked.

"I think it depends on how it is handled."

"And you think Kreet is the man to do that?"

"No," Zvara said. "You are."

Kortel didn't know what to say.

Zvara gestured. "Walk with me?" he asked, and then started around the gate.

Kortel followed. "Is this the part where you bestow all your sagely wisdom on me?"

Zvara turned back. He had that look again. "No," he said, "this is the part where you grow some balls."

* * *

Kortel followed Zvara in silence along a tree-lined path that weaved down the side of the mesa. They approached what looked like an old military base, complete with long metal buildings and a tall barbed wire fence.

"What's this?" Kortel finally asked.

"Home," Zvara said.

The base was nestled near the north side of the valley. Much of it was overgrown with sagebrush, and when they drew closer, Kortel could see that many of the buildings were in various states of disrepair. Only a few looked like they had been restored.

They approached a gate, and two large men stepped into view, each brandishing a military-style Light-Force rifle. Their demeanor was all business. Zvara waved them off.

"How long have you been here?" Kortel asked.

"Since the night I last saw you, when Jacob had me compromised." The gate began to slowly open.

"I always wondered what happened to you. I thought you were dead that night.

But Whitehorse put you on that call...when we were on that plane, just before—" The words caught in Kortel's throat as he remembered the flight that he, James McCarris and Tamara took trying to escape Whitehorse's wrath. He flashed on the missile's impact and the resulting horror.

"Are you all right?" Zvara asked.

"Yeah, I'm okay." Kortel tried to shake off the memory of the plane breaking apart.

Zvara studied him. "You should be proud. You saved hundreds of lives and demonstrated the true power of your telekinetic strength."

"People died because of me—"

"More lived."

Kortel threw his attention to the slowly opening gate.

"Jacob thought I would be more useful alive," Zvara said after a moment. The gate finished opening, and Kortel followed Zvara into a maze of large shipping containers.

"After you killed Jacob," he continued, "what was left of the Rogues disbanded." They turned sideways and shuffled between some large self-sealing transport crates. Their third-world iconic hololabels kept saying hello to Kortel and telling him at which loading dock they should be staged. There was one icon whose character looked like an ancient *Samurai* warrior. It thrust its sword every time Kortel glanced at it, and after the third thrust, Kortel stopped ducking. Although he knew it was just projected light, it still creeped him out when the sword went past his temple.

"Only a few stayed behind," Zvara said. "They had no quarrel with me, so I was free to go." They emerged in front of a building that looked like it could have been a barrack. Its signage dated the installation from the time before America had merged with Mexico. This building was labeled number eight.

"So, what did you do?" Kortel asked.

"I stayed on. I was done with the Agency, and since most people believed me dead, it seemed fitting."

Kortel took account of the immediate area. There wasn't a person in sight – just sagebrush, packing crates and a row of three buildings, all standing on what had probably been the main street for the small base.

"These people needed a new leader," Zvara said. "Someone who could help them achieve what they wanted."

"What do they want?"

Zvara grabbed the handle to number eight's front door. "To be free."

Kortel followed Zvara into a small reception area.

"Good morning, sir!" a young boy said, quickly rising from behind an old military metal desk. He was Native American, and his bandanna had *Kick White Ass* in bold letters across its front.

Zvara gestured for the boy to sit, but the boy remained standing. He eyed Kortel with awe.

"Close your mouth, Billy," Zvara said.

The boy kept staring, and Zvara laughed.

"What?" Kortel asked.

"You are a legend around here," Zvara said. "Get used to it."

Kortel reluctantly acknowledged Billy with a slight grin.

Zvara led Kortel through the reception area and down a dark, narrow hallway lined with frosted glass doors. Dimpled shadows moved across the panes, and Kortel could hear muffled conversations as he passed.

Zvara stopped at the last door and knocked.

"Armando?" a distant voice asked from within.

"Yes," Zvara replied.

A shadow grew in the glass, then the lock clicked. The door opened, and a Hispanic man, probably in his 30s, greeted them. He gave a nod to Zvara; his eyes went to Kortel...and widened.

Zvara stepped into the room. "Alberto, this is–"

"Jonathan Kortel. Yes, I know...from the vids. I'm honored." The man thrust out his hand.

Kortel began to accept it, but an arc of static shot between them. The man jumped back.

"Sorry," Kortel said.

"I should have expected it," the man said, rubbing his palm.

The room was dark and crammed with electronics. Much of the equipment was post-Biolution organic, but some looked late 20th century. A large lab table dominated what little space remained in the center. Carter Shoalburg sat in the middle chair with two academic types flanking him.

"I think you know Dr. Shoalburg," Zvara said.

"Hey, doc," Kortel said. "It's good to see you again."

"It's always good to see," Shoalburg replied, edging his face into a shaft of light that illuminated the table. The two academics laughed, but the joke didn't register well with Kortel. It wasn't that he didn't understand Shoalburg's dry humor; it was simply that he felt more of a kinship with the famous scientist. After all, they both had tech running through their bodies. Shoalburg had invented the bionanogenetic technology that allowed people like Tarris to walk, or, as in the case of Shoalburg himself, to be able to hear, speak and see. Shoalburg's own need had been the mother of his invention, and its propagation into the mainstream had changed the lives of disabled people around the world.

"This is Dr. Robert Hammler." Zvara gestured to an unnaturally thin man on Shoalburg's left. "He is a normal, and one of the world's leading astrophysicists. He has taken a great risk to be here."

"Doctor Hammler," Kortel said.

"And this is Dr. Erin Richter," Zvara said of the other academic at the table. "You may be familiar with her work. Her pioneering theories on gravity are required study at the Agency. She, too, is a normal, and we are very pleased that she could join us. And you have already met my assistant, Alberto." Zvara shot a look at Kortel.

"What is the matter? Shocked to be in a meeting with people other than our kind?"

Kortel didn't realize his expression was so telling. St. John's revelations the day before were almost too much to process, yet here he was in a meeting with two prominent normals.

"Jonathan, are you all right?"

For a second, Kortel felt disoriented. "No…no, I'm not." He rubbed his temples and faced Zvara. "What the hell is going on here? I thought we were going to discuss how to reveal the Tels to the rest of the world. Carter I understand; he's wanted to do this for years. But what's with these two? The world's leading scientists on gravity and astrophysics? And where's Kreet?"

"I told you he wouldn't take this very well," Shoalburg remarked.

"Jonathan, we are here to talk about revealing our culture, but there is something else."

"Save it," Kortel said. "Whatever it is, I don't want to know about it." He shook his head. "What is it with you people? Can't anyone be straight with me? I came back because I thought there was a viable plan to bring our kind out—"

"I thought you said he was on board," Richter said to Shoalburg.

"Jonathan," Zvara said, "there is a plan."

"Shut the hell up. First, it's McCarris hunting me down for a bogus meeting with Kreet. Then, I'm approached by some shadow consortium that wants me to work for it to do God-knows-what. And guess what, they're all normals too."

Zvara exchanged tentative glances with Shoalburg and the academics.

"What, you're all surprised? Seems to me everybody knows about us."

"All right, Jonathan," Zvara said. "Yes. There are other normals who, ah…know of our existence."

"They do more than just know. I was told they've been doing business with Tels for years.... Right?"

This time Zvara and Shoalburg looked at each other. Shoalburg smirked and shook his head.

Kortel picked up on this. "Okay," he said, "you all can keep living in your little world, but I'm heading back to Russia. At least the Tels there are real."

"Jonathan—" Zvara said.

Kortel got in Zvara's face. "You don't get it, do you? I don't want to be famous, or powerful, or any other shit. I just want to be…I don't know…*free* of all of this!"

Zvara took his arm. "Please, Jonathan, just take a seat and I will explain everything."

"No!" Kortel jerked out of Zvara's grip. "Screw all this! I'm out of here." The room suddenly felt much smaller, and Kortel began to back up.

Zvara's assistant stepped up and took ahold of Kortel's other arm.

"Get the hell off me!" Kortel yelled. The man instantly flew back and slammed against a stack of electronics. Kortel could feel a residual grav wave bow out in front of him, probably from his anger. It shoved the table into Shoalburg's chest, as its leading edge contorted to the shape of the invisible wave. It deformed to about the center of the table and stopped.

The two academics quickly stood and backed away.

"Jonathan, control yourself!" Zvara said. "No one is here to harm you."

Kortel wasn't buying Zvara's concern. He quickly turned and reached for the door.

"For God's sake, don't leave!" Hammler exclaimed. "You could be our only hope!"

Kortel turned the knob.

"Please! I beg you. Hear us out." Hammler's voice was on the verge of panic.

Kortel leaned his forehead against the doorframe. There was a sharp pain rising in his brain, but he couldn't tell if it was the tech or just his world closing in on him.

"I sorry, Jonathan," Zvara said. "I should have explained to you the whole reason I asked you here."

"Shut up," Kortel said. "Just answer me this question: who's the 'our' in 'you could be our only hope'?"

A cold silence filled the room. "The world," Shoalburg replied matter-of-factly.

Kortel reluctantly turned. Hammler had a pleading look on his face, while Richter was absorbed with examining the deformed edge of the table. She gave a quizzical look, but behind her eyes there was something else; to Kortel, it looked like fear. Shoalburg was still sitting, his prosthetic eyes void of any emotion. Zvara had his hands thrust deep into the pockets of his khakis, and his assistant was out cold at the base of a 6-foot equipment stack.

"Carter," Kortel said, "you're the only guy I trust here." He pointed at Hammler. "Is he serious?"

Shoalburg blinked calmly. "Like a goddamn heart attack, Jonny."

Kortel was numb. Maybe St. John was right about his world being full of shit. And what *was* there for him in Russia, except bleak safe houses and a lifestyle that probably wasn't any better than what he'd have here?

"I told you," Zvara said with a fatherly edge to his voice.

"What?" Kortel said, resigned to the situation. "What did you tell me?"

Zvara smiled. "That this was the part where you would grow some balls."

Was. 10

"THAT'S him?" Rocket asked.

Sanjiv referenced his netpad. "His displacement signature matches what's on file."

"How did you get his sig data?" Bixx asked. She shifted her position, trying to get comfortable in Sanjiv's new Familiagon. The front seats seemed too close to the dash, but Sanjiv had assured her this was the "roomier" model. Big enough for everyone who was important to him, he had said. That was key, because Sanjiv had a huge family.

"A friend of mine got it for me," he said. "He works in records."

Bixx felt her butt going to sleep. She slipped out of her All-Terrains and propped her feet on the dash. Sanjiv shot her a harsh look, so she sat up in the seat and crossed her legs.

"He doesn't look all that special," Rocket said. He was in the back seat leaning over Bixx's shoulder. His breath tickled her earlobe. He reached across the console and snatched the last fry from her lunch.

Bixx peered out the tinted Familiagon's windshield at James McCarris, who sat comfortably at an outdoor cafe. His table had attenuated legs that seemed to merge with the tile of the porch. The whole four-top looked solid – dense, as if it had grown right out of the floor. But it hadn't, because she had seen McCarris slide the table out of a shaft of light. The cafe was part of Colonial Market and situated in one of its commons. The area was canyoned by other buildings, which by midafternoon would create a tapestry of light shafts that would creep through the area. Finding a calm spot to read or talk was usually a challenge, but it looked like McCarris had accomplished the task, because he had been quietly reading his netpad, uninterrupted, for the last hour.

"He was once the head of Recruiting," Sanjiv remarked. "Before Kortel erased him."

"Yeah," Rocket said, "I never understood why Kortel did that."

"The story I heard," Bixx said, "was that when they first discovered Kortel, he was running this upscale restaurant in Chicago."

"It was real good," Sanjiv agreed. "I ate there once, before he was discovered. All biofood and very chic. His genetic matching was award-winning."

"Anyway," Bixx said, "he was dating this prostitute—"

"What?!" Rocket interrupted.

"Yeah, a high-end one. What's your issue? I have a good friend back in Russia who put herself through grad school that way."

"Okay," Rocket said, "I'm sorry. No disrespect to that noble profession. So go on, Kortel's dating a skank, and?..."

Sanjiv snickered.

Bixx, still watching McCarris, flipped them both off. "Rumor was," she continued, "that he was completely into this girl. I've seen classified photos. She'd make a straight girl gay. She had a friend, an Asian, who was equally hot. McCarris had been assigned to bring Kortel in, but when he ordered the back-end erasing, he didn't do everyone."

"You're shitting me," Rocket said. "Who he'd leave clean, the prostitute?"

"No, the Asian. Seems they had a little thing going on the side. Kortel found out a couple of years later and went crazy. He scratched McCarris's brain all the way to his childhood. I heard that when they went in to do the restoration, he had the intelligence of a 5-year-old."

Rocket whistled. "Man, that's severe."

"Why? If I learned a Recruiter erased you, but had left one of your buddies clean so she could screw him, I'd go scratch her too. I guarantee you, when she woke up, she'd be looking for a diaper." Bixx put her feet back on the dash.

"I wonder how they built him back up?" Sanjiv mused. "I've never heard of anyone surviving that deep of an erasing."

Bixx shrugged. "One neuron at a time, I guess. I'm sure that guys like McCarris have their brains backed up. I would if I were at his level."

"Well, maybe," Rocket said. "But 5 years old? Come on, that's—"

"Hey," Sanjiv said, pointing. "He's leaving."

McCarris paid the waiter and began edging his way through the maze of patrons and tables.

"Come on," Bixx said, slipping back into her All-Terrains.

"Do you have a plan or something?" Sanjiv asked.

"Something," she answered.

Sanjiv shot Rocket a questioning look.

"I just do what I'm told," Rocket said. "She's in control here."

Sanjiv shook his head. "That's what I was afraid of."

"Shut up, you two!" Bixx said, tightening the straps of her All-Terrains. She jumped from the Familiagon and crossed the street, falling into step about 20 feet behind McCarris. She matched his casual pace and tried to blend in with the crowd. Sanjiv and Rocket fell in behind her.

McCarris strolled away from the mall's perimeter shops and headed toward one of its large parking garages.

"I don't like the feel of this," Bixx heard Sanjiv whisper to Rocket.

"There's three of us and one of him," she said over her shoulder.

"Yeah," Rocket said, "but his Tel strength is stronger than the three of us combined."

"Not anymore," Bixx said.

McCarris crossed Pennsylvania Avenue and began walking up the steep ramp of the parking garage. Bixx started to cross, but Rocket grabbed her arm and pulled her back onto the curb.

"Hold up," he said. His fingers were digging into her bicep, and Bixx knew she was about to get a lecture. "Do you know who you're dealing with here?"

Bixx pulled away and rubbed her arm. "I think I've got a lock on what this guy is about. Why?" She glanced over to the garage in time to see McCarris take one of the side ramps to the upper levels.

"Why? Because he's a Level 7!"

"I have it on good authority that James McCarris is, at best, a Level 3."

"And what 'authority' is that?" Sanjiv asked.

Bixx was losing what little patience she had. She got in Sanjiv's face. "Do you want to find Kreet?"

"Well, ah, yes...I do."

Bixx angrily pointed toward the garage. "Unless you've got a better plan, McCarris is our best hope of finding him!" She looked at Rocket.

"Baby," he said, "we don't know—"

"*Poshol nahuj!* I'll do it myself!" Bixx jumped from the curb and ran toward the garage, barely dodging two CitiCabs in the process. She could hear Rocket yelling at her, but she didn't stop. Something was pushing her, but it wasn't that she was particularly fond of Kreet – the little fart had gotten all of them into more trouble than she cared to remember. It was more about getting back at the latex bitch and the plastic-haired Brit. They had crossed the line with Bixx, and she was determined to get some revenge.

The ramp was deceiving, and about halfway up, the biomatrix of her All-Terrains shifted their soles' tread pattern to accommodate the grade. It was like having claws under her, and she opened her stride to catch up with McCarris. Bixx ran about 15 off-road miles a week, so she was used to her shoes thinking for themselves. The last she saw of McCarris, he was headed up the west ramp to the second level. It had only been about five minutes, so how far could he have gotten?

Bixx rounded the top of the circular ramp at full clip only to discover that it didn't lead to a parking level; it just kept going. Her thighs were beginning to complain.

Couldn't McCarris have taken the elevator?

She kept following the ramp as it curved upward until it finally emptied onto a parking level. All the vehicles were crammed two-high and looked like they were poured from the same vat as Sanjiv's Familiagon. Periwinkle blue seemed to be the color for this season. McCarris was nowhere in sight, and Bixx slowed to a trot. She craned her head to see over the vehicles, but there were too many, and with them stacked to the beams, she couldn't see the adjacent lanes.

"*Hooy na ny!*" Bixx's voice echoed off the old metal and cement surfaces. She stopped and gulped in some air. The soles of her All-Terrains shifted back to a walking tread, and the sensation made Bixx a little queasy, similar to what happened when she was stopped on a downtown lev and another tram slowly passed; it was a weird sense that she was moving, but she wasn't.

The parking area was strangely quiet, void of the typical tire screeches and impact warning signals. Bixx instinctually felt someone behind her. She turned. Nothing.

"Swearing isn't very ladylike."

The tread of the All-Terrains shifted to a climbing sole, and Bixx almost jumped onto the hood of an ugly green Familiagon. The imposing form of James McCarris loomed barely 15 feet behind her. He was backlit from a low-hanging mercury vapor lamp.

"But I have to admit," he continued, "when 'no fucking way' is said in Russian, it has kind of a sexy quality to it." He stepped forward, and his red hair caught the light from another lamp. He lit a cigarette and slowly exhaled the smoke upwards. "Where are your friends?"

Bixx hesitated and glanced over to the top of the ramp. She had run so fast, there was no way Sanjiv and Rocket could have kept up.

McCarris stepped closer and took a long drag. "Tell your Indian friend he needs to change the settings for the blackout filter on his van's windshield." The smoke lingered around his face. "It's not dark enough." He stepped closer. "You speak English?"

"Of course I do," Bixx said.

"Russian born?"

"Yes."

McCarris nodded, studying Bixx, then took another long drag. He wasn't at all what she had pictured. Not that she had a specific image in mind, it was just that he wasn't what she thought a guy who had been erased so badly should look like. He was taller than his photos suggested, and his red hair resembled Rocket's, though a deeper shade and not as curly. He seemed fit, his broad shoulders filling out the trim sport jacket he wore. For some reason, Bixx figured he'd be...well, scrawnier, like he had been bedridden or something.

"Am I what you thought?" he asked finally.

This caught Bixx off guard. "Pardon me?"

"Go ahead, get it over with. Take your vid, or whatever your friends put you up to." There was a frivolity to his voice, as if he sort of appreciated the attention. He blew three tiny smoke rings.

"Look," Bixx said. "I'm not here to—"

"Then why the hell are you following me?" McCarris's demeanor shifted, and his voice took on a hateful tone.

Suddenly Bixx felt all of her muscles lock down, and a crushing weight descended on her, as if gravity in her immediate space had tripled. She fought for a second, then dropped to her hands and knees.

McCarris stepped up and crushed out his cigarette inches from her right hand. He knelt. "When I was a Recruiter, bringing in Potentials, I used to feel like the weight of the world was on my shoulders. You ever have that feeling?"

Bixx struggled to raise her head and met his cold stare. There was emptiness in his eyes. She said, "I don't know what you're talking about."

"Oh, come on. You're not the first to try this. Because of my accident, I've become somewhat of an enigma in our culture. Kind of a phoenix." McCarris looked away for a second, then back. "No," he said, "more like Lazarus...back from the dead!"

The elevator at the other end of the level chimed. Bixx slowly moved her head in time to see the doors open. Rocket and Sanjiv stepped out. Rocket saw her first.

"Hey," he yelled, "what are you doing to her?!" There was a surprising amount of authority in his voice. He started charging toward them.

"The boyfriend?" McCarris asked. He stood and pulled another cigarette from his pocket.

At about 20 feet, Rocket froze in midstride. He rose into the air until his head almost hit one of the crossbeams. Sanjiv, who had been running behind, skidded to a stop.

McCarris lit the cigarette. His demeanor had calmed, and he lazily exhaled the smoke. Bixx felt the pressure lighten slightly. She could now move her head more easily; breathing, though, was still a bit of a challenge.

Rocket floated toward them, his face caught in a strange mix of shock and fear.

"Please don't hurt him," Bixx managed.

McCarris now seemed intensely focused on moving Rocket, which struck Bixx as odd, because even for a Level 3, moving something as small as Rocket's body should've been child's play.

Child's play.

Rocket's bright red hair was a spray of curls, and they bounced slightly as he settled onto the pavement. When his feet touched, he gasped and began coughing.

"Man," he said between gasps. "Your field strength...it's too tight. You were choking me." He continued coughing.

Bixx felt the pressure lighten again, but not enough to allow her to stand. Her lower back was beginning to ache, and her calves started to cramp.

"You put her up to this?" McCarris asked.

"Hell no," Rocket said. "Now release your grav field or I'll–"

"Or you'll what? Kick my ass?"

Bixx watched Sanjiv cautiously approach. He kept a safe distance and avoided eye contact. *Wimp.*

McCarris looked at Sanjiv. "Join the party, friend."

Sanjiv suddenly went stiff, then slid over to Rocket and slammed into him, almost knocking them both down.

"Okay, take it easy," Sanjiv said to McCarris.

"Come on," Rocket said, straightening. "Would you please release my girlfriend?"

The pressure on Bixx disappeared, and she collapsed onto her stomach. Rocket rushed to her side.

"Oh, my back," she exclaimed. Her left calf began to cramp. "Shit, my leg!" She rolled over and began desperately massaging her calf.

Rocket jumped to his feet and lunged at McCarris. "You asshole!" he screamed. He got within an arm's length of McCarris and froze.

McCarris didn't flinch. "Good ol' fashioned chivalry," he said. His attention went to Rocket's hair. "Nice color."

Suddenly the air around Rocket's body began to distort like a wall of water was washing over him. Bixx's ears popped. Then McCarris was thrown violently about 30 feet and crashed into the side of a small cargo van. At the same instant, Rocket yelled something unintelligible and stumbled forward, almost falling to his hands and knees.

"Damn, that was incredible," he said, looking himself over.

Bixx had never seen Rocket so angry, and definitely not that powerful. To break a grav field like that meant he must have jumped a level. In an odd way, the whole thing was kind of flattering.

Rocket turned to her and grinned. "You thought I'd never do something like that, did you?" he said.

Bixx smiled.

"Nice move," McCarris said. He was leaning against the cargo van and dusting off the arms of his coat. "Tight threshold, clean focus, and a hell of a punch."

Rocket faced McCarris. "You deserved that."

"Yeah, you're probably right." McCarris began to walk toward them, but doubled over and clutched his left knee. "Man, that smarts." He straightened and forced himself to walk.

"All she wanted was some information."

This stopped McCarris. "I thought you were out to get my image or something." He rubbed the side of his knee and continued hobbling.

Bixx stepped up to Rocket's side. "We came here to see if you knew anything about our friend Kreet."

"What's a Kreet?" McCarris asked. He limped over to a late-model silver Street Hugger.

"Back off now!" it commanded. "You have violated my security perimeter!"

"It's me, you piece of bioshit. ID: McCarris, James."

"My apologies, sir. Voice recognition confirmed."

Bixx thought she saw the color of its body redden slightly.

"Retard rental," McCarris explained while he sat on its hood. He began gingerly rubbing the side of his knee. "Now, who's this Kreet guy?"

"You gave Jonathan Kortel's incepts to him," Sanjiv said, finally doing something besides standing.

McCarris was now leaning heavily against the Hugger. He folded his arms tightly across his chest. "Oh, that guy. Always wore a scarf. Yeah, I remember him. He paid well. Had a big stupid plan to spring our kind out. So what's the problem? He get caught?"

"We don't know exactly," Bixx said, and she proceeded to tell McCarris about her encounter with the Brit and the woman.

At one point, McCarris's face went blank, like he either didn't buy that part of the story or he didn't understand its relevance to him. When Bixx finished, he just sat on the hood of the Hugger and stared forward.

"So," Bixx finished, "if you have any–"

McCarris raised his hand. "Hold on, I'm thinking...which is a little hard for me to do these days."

"Sorry."

McCarris sat there for what felt to Bixx like forever before sliding off the hood of the Hugger. He walked over with a slight limp, but less labored.

"I think I know one of these characters," he said. "I don't know who the woman is, but if your description of the guy is accurate, I think he's..." McCarris looked away, like he would find his answer among the Familiagons.

"What about him?" Bixx asked.

McCarris looked back, but acted like he was listening to something only he could hear. "He sure sounds like a guy I used to know," he said, finally. "But he can't be." His eyes lost focus again.

"Are you okay?" Sanjiv asked.

"Hmm, what? Oh, yeah... I'm okay, I guess. I mean, as okay as a guy can be given my condition."

"What is your condition, exactly?" Rocket asked.

McCarris's expression hardened, and Bixx thought he and Rocket would start in on each other again. But he relaxed and lit up another cigarette.

"I was told I was in a diagnostic accident." He made quote marks with his fingers, and the smoke from his cigarette formed little puffs that rose delicately into the air. "Hell, I don't know. When you lose most of your memory, you don't know what to believe. It's not like I had a choice in the matter. My brain got wiped pretty good...back to my childhood. At least I had that left." He took a long, thoughtful drag and exhaled. "I had my memory backed up, but they couldn't download all of it.... Something about a graying of the neural compatibility, so they did the next best thing."

"What was that?" Sanjiv asked.

"Connected me to my backup." He took another drag. "Via the Net. Bioimplants. They say I have enough tech in my head now to run a small city."

"That's why you looked like you were listening to something," Bixx said. "Just a minute ago, right?"

McCarris smiled and tapped the side of his head.

"You mean that some of your brain functions are being fed to you...right now?" Rocket asked.

"Kind of. It's not like my breathing or digestion is done for me – just some of the higher functions. You don't really use all of your brain anyway. When I need to access info or a skill I used to have, I just go online...in my head, sort of. It's complicated, but you get the idea." He laughed. "It's great for golf, and don't play chess with me. I'll kick your butt every time." He took another drag. "The only issue is storage. I gotta keep going back to the well."

"But what about this British guy?" Bixx asked. Her lower back twinged, and she rubbed at it with her knuckles.

McCarris's demeanor went serious, like a switch in him had been thrown. Maybe it had, Bixx realized.

"Right, the guy with the plastic hair. Well, that's got me puzzled. See, when I met him – about nine years ago – he was a corporate mercenary...a suit soldier. He did work for the Big Five, mostly around the Pacific Rim."

"So what has you puzzled?" Bixx asked.

"You said his grav wave, the one he hit you with, was a Level 6, right?"

"I think so. At least that's what it felt like." Bixx fought the urge to scratch at the bandage on the back of her head.

McCarris shook his head. "That's weird."

"What is?" Rocket asked.

"If this *is* the same guy, he didn't have that power when I met him..." McCarris's voice trailed off, and Bixx couldn't tell if he was thinking for himself or if he was being helped.

"Maybe he grew in level since you knew him," Sanjiv offered.

McCarris shook his head again. "No, you don't get it."

"What?" Rocket said. "Tels grow in strength all the time. You got a taste of that tonight, I'd say." He took Bixx's hand and gave a slight squeeze.

"I'm not talking about level strength."

"Then what are you talking about?" McCarris wasn't making any sense, and Bixx was beginning to think that his link with the Net was screwed up.

"This guy who attacked you, and probably took Kreet, shouldn't be able to do what he did." McCarris's voice was now filled with earnest. He threw his cigarette to the ground and got into Bixx's face. "The Suit Soldier came out of the SAS...*British Special Air Service*."

"Oh my God," Sanjiv said to himself.

Bixx was confused. She looked at Sanjiv then back to McCarris. "Okay, wait a minute. Does somebody want to explain this to me?"

Sanjiv cleared his throat. "If he was in the British military, he has to be a normal."

"Correction," McCarris said. "Was a normal."

Great. 11

KORTEL couldn't find any comfort in the faces across the table. Richter, Hammler, Zvara, even Shoalburg with those androidian eyes of his, were all looking at him as if he should say something profound. *Something profound?* he thought. *Hell, I'm still trying to get my head around what I just heard.*

Halfway through Richter's explanation, Kortel got lost when her holopresentation segued into the mathematics underpinning her theory. He started watching her lips. They reminded him of an old receptionist's of his, but fuller, and not so peaked. They puckered slightly when Richter said the word radiation, which she did about a hundred times. And the edges of her mouth curled into little dimples...just like Tamara's. He had loved that about Tamara and was beginning to enjoy it with Richter, who looked pretty damn good for nearly 50.

He leaned forward, and the bulb from the lamp above the table, which had been hidden by its shade, flared like a little sun. Even though he knew he shouldn't look at it, he did, and its glare burned into his vision. He rubbed his eyes and tried to will away the negative image of the bulb, along with the nightmare he had just heard.

"Are you all right?" Zvara asked.

Kortel leaned back and looked vacantly at him. The afterburn had died somewhat, replaced by a little crescent that floated in the center of his vision. He felt a headache coming on. "What kind of a question is that?" He couldn't think of anything better to say.

"Jonny, I know this is a lot to take in," Shoalburg said. "Hell, I work with this stuff, and it still takes me a while to absorb it all."

"I was with you until the part about extinguishing all life on the planet."

Richter gave a slight shrug. "It's just a theory," she said. "But, then again...the numbers don't lie."

The numbers. There was that math shit again. Kortel had a rudimentary knowledge of astrophysics, but this stuff, with its helioseismology data and CME stats, had his brain swimming. Richter had used more acronyms in her presentation than his Agency quantum grav teacher had in a whole year. It was the CME acronym – coronal mass ejection – that gave Kortel a particularly bad case of the willies. For the last decade, Richter had been tracking the eruptions of plasma on the sun's surface, which on a normal day kept the earth bathed in a steady, all-sustaining glow. But for the last eight months, there had been a disturbing amount of violent ejections that had bombarded the earth with ever-increasing amounts of radiation.

"I still don't get it," Kortel said. "Our sun has been cooking along for the last four billion years, and now its nuclear furnace is going to melt down? Why now?"

Richter exchanged an uneasy glance with Hammler.

"You see, it's quite simple," Hammler said. "Data from the NCAR's Coriolis 4 satellite confirms that the turbulence in the fraculae between the granules accounts for the disgorging of the mega CMEs."

Kortel felt his head beginning to throb. He rubbed the side of his temple.

"Umm...I think Mr. Kortel needs it explained in a more understandable way," Richter said. She grabbed her chair and walked around the table, careful not to touch its deformed edge. She sat, and her dark bangs fell across her forehead, revealing a look Kortel had sometimes glimpsed in women her age – that how-she-looked-when-she-was-20 look. The bangs also gave her a retro appearance that worked well with her biofabric cargo shorts and runner's warm-up top. When she approached, her shorts changed to the color of the aluminum chair, even matching the shadows that spilled across her legs. Kortel noticed that they were lean and muscular. Her quadriceps flexed as she settled in. He scooted his chair around and faced her. Up close, Richter had fine lines around her eyes – which Kortel had heard Tarris's mom call "crow's feet" – and a narrow white streak cut a path through her dark hair. Obviously, Richter had shunned the cultural pressure to bioaugment, which most people had done by the time they left high school.

"The sun isn't melting down," she explained, brushing back her hair. "It's actually doing the opposite. CMEs have been happening for millennia, and for the most part usually cause only minor disturbances such as power outages and communication disruptions.... It's the radiation that does it."

There was that word again. Kortel's attention was drawn to her lips. "I wouldn't call any of those minor," he said.

She grinned and her dimples reappeared. "Compared to what's going to happen, they are."

"*Might* happen," Hammler said. "It's still a theory."

Richter smiled curtly. Her eyes didn't leave Kortel. "Well, yes...it might happen. But as I said before, the numbers don't lie."

"What do you call this killer CME?" Kortel asked.

"A Tsunami Ejection," Shoalburg interjected, "but this one would be the mother of all ejections." He gave a nervous laugh, which no one else joined.

"Could it really do that much damage?" Kortel asked.

Richter gathered Kortel's hands into hers. The gesture caught him off guard, but for some reason he didn't resist. His attention went to her pale green eyes.

Richter leaned in. "Jonathan, what I'm telling you *will* happen. It's just a matter of time."

Her use of his first name came across with an intense intimacy, and her inflection on the word *will* hit Kortel somewhere near his survival instinct.

"If my calculations are accurate," she continued, "then within one, maybe two years, the earth will experience a coronal ejection on a level it's never seen before. When it arrives, it'll cause massive destruction in a matter of hours. It might even reduce the planet to a lifeless rock."

Kortel shuddered at this last statement. Although he tried to subtly slip from her hold, Richter pulled him back. There was strength to her grip, but it didn't feel like the result of the weight training she obviously did. It felt more like someone who was scared and didn't want to let go.

"I–" she began, but couldn't manage the rest. She nervously averted Kortel's gaze, and her grip fell away. The tough woman-in-charge who had just lectured Kortel about the possible end of the world had vanished. She folded her arms tightly across her chest; the reality of her numbers seemed to weigh heavily upon even her.

"Hey, come on," Kortel said, "it can't be as bad as–"

Richter's gaze cut him short. "I've been studying the sun for most of my adult life. You never think it could happen." She looked away again, struggling to find the words. "You're correct, you know.... The sun *has* been steadily burning for billions of years, but now I think something is changing." Richter composed herself and swallowed deeply. "Gravity," she said to herself.

"What's that?" Kortel asked.

The woman-in-charge had returned. "The earth is protected from CMEs by its gravitational field," she said. "But this kind of ejection will be too powerful. It will hit us with a southward magnetic orientation, the opposite of the earth's, and compress our protective magnetosphere. Its force will peel back the field lines like an onion and expose the planet to a radiation hit. It'll make Chernobyl look like a pinprick."

Kortel was stunned by this revelation. Chernobyl had been the worst nuclear accident in history. The plant had been partially shut down in the late 20th century by a similar, much smaller incident, but the recent energy crisis had forced the Russians to reopen it, supposedly safeguarded by new technology. Kortel was well aware that the term "new" was subject to debate in Russia. Today, a 100-mile radius around Chernobyl was still kept closed to human traffic.

Richter's intensity was beginning to make Kortel uncomfortable, and he shifted in his seat. The data from her research seemed plausible, but despite Hammler's insistence that her global destruction theory was weak, Richter's passion was carrying the day with Kortel. He could sense something about Richter's conviction that suggested she wasn't basing her theory on just the data. He also sensed the direction of her line of thought on gravity. "I'm not that powerful," he said.

"We don't know that yet, Jonny," Shoalburg countered. "You've demonstrated incredibly powerful grav fields. Hell, you're altering matter, for God's sake." He gestured at the deformed part of the table. "Hammler's right – you could be our only hope."

Kortel spun around. "Carter, you're talking about the earth! I could never produce a field that large!"

"You wouldn't do it alone," Shoalburg said. "You'd be the, ah, I don't know...what's the word?" He glanced at Hammler for help. "Lens?"

"Don't you see?" Zvara said. "It's your destiny.... It's why God gave you your gift."

Kortel felt nauseated, but at least he couldn't feel his headache anymore. He turned and faced Richter. She smiled thoughtfully with an expression that said, "Go ahead, ask the question."

Kortel hesitated. "What do you think, doctor?"

Richter took in a breath. "I don't know a lot about the technology in your head. That's Dr. Shoalburg's field of expertise. But from the technical data that I've seen on you, in theory, you have the potential. It's your... " She hesitated, and Kortel thought the woman-in-charge was vanishing again.

"The what?" he asked.

Richter nodded to herself, like she was doing some kind of mental bolstering. "I've read your, ah, psychological evaluations."

This hit Kortel squarely in his ego, as if he hadn't been hit with enough already. "And?"

"Let's just say that for this to work, we're going to have to work on your mental stability."

Kortel looked down and shook his head. It was almost impossible to wrap his brain around everything that had been handed to him over the last few days. And to make matters worse, now he was a neurotic asshole in need of therapy. He felt Richter stroke the side of his face: the touch comforting, familiar, like something borne on the wings of a memory. He raised his eyes to find Richter smiling.

"How do you feel?" Her voice suddenly put him at ease.

"Like a reluctant superhero in need of some self-actualization."

"Jonny, you've had enough life-altering presentations for one day," Shoalburg said, standing. "Come on. Let's get out of here and grab some dinner." He patted Kortel's shoulder and walked over to Zvara.

Kortel caught Richter staring at him. "Would you like to join us for dinner?" he asked her.

"Only if I'm not intruding."

He waved her comment off and stood. "Tag along. I'll have Carter show you one of his eyes. You'd appreciate its technology."

Kortel and Richter followed Zvara and Shoalburg out the door into the dark hallway. Her boots squeaked on the old linoleum as they walked along in silence. Closer now to her, Kortel could smell her bath wash – or whatever she was wearing. It was citrusy and had an expensive edge to it, like something from an exclusive African spa.

"Mikado," she said suddenly.

"I'm sorry?" Kortel asked.

"My body spray – it's called Mikado."

"How did you–"

"You were practically sniffing my hair."

Jesus. "I'm sorry," Kortel offered. "I-I don't know why–"

Richter laughed. "Don't worry. I'm not offended. I grew up with three brothers. There's not much that fazes me."

Down the long hallway, Kortel mentally chastised himself for being such an ass. He felt for the infuser in his pocket and fingered its reassuring shape. He caressed its trigger, fighting the urge to help himself to a dose. "Can I ask you another question?" He placed his hands behind his back.

"You can ask me anything, anytime," Richter said.

"How long will it take this CME to reach us?"

"A typical one takes two to three days to reach our magnetosphere."

"But I thought light from the sun took minutes."

"It does, but a Tsunami Ejection is different.... It's made of matter, not photons. Plus, we don't know how fast it will travel. It might take a day or less."

"At least you'll be able to detect this thing before it happens, and give me time to do whatever it is I'm going to do, right?"

Richter stopped and faced Kortel. Her expression suggested he wasn't going to like her answer.

"It doesn't work like that," she said gravely. "We can't accurately predict when an ejection will occur...yet. We could be hours, even days off. When it happens, you'll have to react instantly."

Richter quickly turned and continued walking. Kortel noticed her shorts had returned to their preset color of fatigue green. He watched her reach the end of the hallway and disappear into the harsh light of the lobby.

"Great," he said to himself. His headache had returned.

Media circus. 12

BIXX stared into her fresh beer and watched its head slowly dissipate. She never understood what the big deal was about getting the foam just right – to her, beer tasted the same, head or no head. Rocket and Sanjiv had indoctrinated her with the virtues of finding the perfect beer. For them, it was practically a religion.

"You need to start drinking...before it all dies," Rocket said, gesturing toward the foam.

"I know," Bixx said. "Before the head dips below the 1-inch mark." Beer, she had been informed, needs to be tapped with at least a 2-inch head in order to be considered a good draft. And to qualify as a perfect beer? Well, that was for the gods to decide.

"See," Sanjiv said, "she's learning."

Bixx raised her glass and proceeded to down the 16 ounces in one continuous gulp. It was a technique she had perfected in Russia, when she made 100 digirubles a night off of stupid freshmen by betting they couldn't beat her in a chugging contest. She'd just open her throat and let the beer flow. Most guys' gag reflex would end the competition before she had to finish her glass. Bixx had learned to relax her muscles and control the urge to puke. It had been a useful trick that had helped pay for her apartment during school.

"That's right, baby," Rocket said, sarcastically. "Go ahead and savor *every* drop."

Bixx shrugged. "Beer's beer. It all tastes the same to me. I drink for the effects." She turned to Sanjiv. "Wanna race?"

He shook his head. "No way."

Bixx let out a belch that caused the pool players to stop and turn.

"Excuse me," she called out.

"My, aren't we the lady," Rocket said. He scooted closer. "Why don't you order some food? That's your third one."

"*Yaytsa kuritsu ne uchat!*"

"What did she say?" Sanjiv asked.

"It's an old Russian saying," Rocket said. "I think it means: eggs cannot teach a hen, or something like that."

Bixx laughed. Rocket was always screwing up her language. "Do not give advice to someone who is more experienced than you." She raised her empty glass in salute. The beers were beginning to affect her, but she didn't care. Their encounter with McCarris had left her melancholy, but she couldn't put her finger on the reason. Sure, she was concerned for Kreet's well-being, but something else was unsettling her. Maybe it was the fact that for the last couple of weeks, Rocket and Sanjiv had been talking so much about the possibility of their culture revealing itself. Bixx never really cared if their kind came out or not, but all the talk had gotten her thinking. She wondered if this was how gays and lesbians had felt ages ago, before the Gender War and all the resulting legislation.

Rocket asked, "Bixxy, what's bothering you?"

"I don't know," she said, staring.

Sanjiv smiled. "I wouldn't worry about Kreet; he's a survivor."

"Besides," Rocket said, "McCarris promised he would do some digging on that British guy. Maybe he'll find something. He sure seems to be nicer than we figured, don't you think?"

"McCarris is just like all other senior Tels," Bixx said. "Memory or no memory, his loyalty will be to the Agency." She faced Rocket. "You think we'll ever come out?"

Rocket pondered the question for a second. "Honestly? I doubt it. Kreet's plan is cool and all, but I don't know. I can't imagine it coming together. I was surprised that he got Kortel to meet with us.... I guess everybody gets lucky now and then."

He thought for another second.

"No," he said, "it would be too difficult. Besides, there're too many higher-ups worldwide who would shut down any grassroot attempt. Kreet was right; Kortel was his ace." Rocket dropped his attention into his beer.

Suddenly, their holowaiter appeared. "Another round of Darrion's Ale?" it asked. "Genetically mapped for authentic taste." It was a tall, 20-something male, probably modeled from extensive focus groups where upwardly mobile women detailed to marketing experts their perfect man. He wasn't quite white or black, and as Bixx studied him, she concluded he wasn't quite anything. He appeared to be an amalgamation of every popular male star of the last five years. His eyes were a complete rip from Jordan Cash, the Australian action hero currently number one on the Net, and his cleft chin was from the sim star of a couple of years ago – Tora something – the one who had dominated all the war games. He was one virtual character Bixx could get pixeled with.

"I'll take another," she said.

Rocket rolled his eyes. "Hell, why not? Make it two."

"Make it three," Sanjiv chimed in.

The holowaiter batted his Jordan Cashes and disappeared.

"I think he likes you," Sanjiv said to Bixx.

"It's not a he, it's an it," Rocket corrected.

Bixx sighed. "It, he, who cares? I'd jack with him in a heart pound."

Rocket chuckled. "It's beat, baby. Heart *beat*."

"Vhatever." Bixx's accent was showing, which happened after a few beers. One more round, and Bixx was seriously considering taking on the big guy at the pool table in a game of Eight Ball.

Soon enough a waitress approached, carrying their drinks. "Here you go," she said. "Three cold ones from the best that Ireland has to offer." Bixx's head was turned toward the pool table, but she recognized the voice. Kara was a Tel who worked with Kreet, monitoring the virt booths at the Agency. She didn't hang with their gang, and the only time Bixx ever saw her was when she was working at the bar. Bixx had always wanted to know her better, but the timing never seemed right. Kara set the fresh beers down, then their empty glasses floated onto her tray.

"Watch it there," Rocket said to her.

Kara smiled. "In this place? I doubt anyone would even notice." She placed her tray on the table and slipped new coasters under each drink. "Have you guys seen Kreet? He wasn't at his station this last week."

Bixx, Rocket and Sanjiv exchanged glances.

"No," Sanjiv said, "we were hoping you might know something."

Kara shrugged. "He's done this before. I'm surprised they let him get away with it so much."

"Get away with what?" said a voice behind her.

"Kreet!" Bixx exclaimed.

"I was just telling them how much shit you get away with," Kara said while she grabbed her tray. "I knew you'd show up sooner or later. Just like a cat." She turned and walked away.

It took Bixx a second, but then she registered who the figures were behind Kreet. The tall-heeled woman stepped forward, and the Brit gave a little wave. Bixx sunk into the booth, her heart racing.

"Is that the guy?" Rocket whispered.

Bixx nodded.

Both Rocket and Sanjiv slowly stood. They didn't even acknowledge Kreet.

"You!" Rocket yelled, pointing at the Brit. "I'm going to fuck you up!"

"Whoa, easy, cowboy!" the woman said.

Sanjiv looked at Rocket sideways. "Remember what McCarris said.... He's powerful."

Kreet stepped up to Rocket and put his hands on his chest. "Stand down, Roc. These are my business associates."

Rocket glowered at him. "That asshole almost killed Bixx."

Kreet turned to the Brit. "You told me you only pushed her once."

"Right," the Brit said, flashing his perfect smile. "It was a little more than a push. Kind of a throw, I'd say." His attention went to Bixx. "Sorry, love. I got into the Ride that night, and that stuff gets me going. Hope you're okay and all. I know a good doctor–"

"Shut up!" the woman said. She turned to Bixx. "I am sorry, honey. Marcus here can get a little enthusiastic about his job. Ex-military, gung-ho and all, you know the type. Did he hurt you much?" She turned to the Brit. "You hurt her, didn't you?" She shook her head. "Good God."

Bixx didn't know how to respond. The whole scene was surreal: the woman standing there in those heels, her jumpsuit styled out in a crisp, businesslike manner. She wore a pair of heavy framed glasses, which meant she was jacked, because no one needed glasses anymore. Then there was the Brit, dressed in that same suit from the night in the bathroom. He was leaning against a chair, casually considering the decor of the bar. Bixx kept thinking about what McCarris had said about him, how he had once been a normal.

The woman gingerly touched the side of her glasses, and the lenses went dark. "Cindy, in the morning, get me the name of that doctor who did Jordan Cash's face, after the accident.... No, he's in L.A. How should I know? Look him up. No, keep this away from the front office.... And get me the folks in legal." She looked in Bixx's direction. "I don't think we have a problem, but you never know. We'll be back on Monday. Oh, and can you get me a reservation with Billie? My back is killing me. Thanks, you're a peach." The lenses became clear. She walked up to the table and folded her arms. "So these are them?" she asked Kreet.

"That's right," he said. "What do you think?"

The woman looked them over, and her lenses went dark again. "Cindy, get me a meeting with Tony on Wednesday.... I don't care if he's still in tech, get me a meeting." She pulled the glasses from her face and chewed on the end of an earpiece.

"Is everything okay?" Kreet asked.

The woman was studying Rocket. "I love this hair," she finally announced. "It's going to resonate with our demos beautifully." She turned her attention to Bixx. "And you, we'll fix the nose in post, but this whole Russian thing is perfect right now. The country is so out they're in again. And the waif look, ha! We haven't seen that for a hundred years. They'll eat this up in New York."

"Kreet!" Rocket yelled. "What the hell is going on?"

"Relax, mate," the Brit said. "Your life's about to change."

"Wait a minute," Bixx said to the woman, who was slipping her glasses back on. "Who are you?"

The woman didn't respond. She pulled from her pocket a tiny wafer of green glass and handed it to Bixx. As soon as Bixx placed it her palm, a tiny holojection began running through a montage of some of the biggest vids produced over the last 10 years. Full music came up while a voiceover declared the achievements of SecondSight Studios. Then the woman appeared, standing in Bixx's palm. She introduced herself as Megan Toffler, senior executive producer.

Bixx looked from the holo Toffler to the real Toffler. Things were getting weirder by the minute.

"The studio likes these," Toffler said. "I think they're too over the top, but they get the point across, don't you think?" Her lenses went dark, and she stepped away, barking orders to Cindy. The Brit followed.

"Kreet," Rocket said, "what have you gotten us into?"

Kreet smiled, and Bixx noticed for the first time the scarf he was wearing. On it was the famous Hollywood sign, cycling through an entire day, complete with time-lapse weather and a faint, cheesy soundtrack. She could barely hear a woman singing, but couldn't make out the lyrics.

"What have you told her?" Bixx asked. "If you've exposed us, I swear I'll break every bone–"

"She already knows everything," Kreet said. "Our culture, the levels. She even knows about the Agencies."

"How did she know all that?"

"She won't tell me. She wants to protect her sources. She originally wanted to do a vid on Kortel's life. I have no idea how she knows about him, but she does. *Everything.*"

"This is very dangerous!" Sanjiv said.

"No," Kreet said. "She wants to help us come out. She wants to make it a worldwide media event. It's about sell-through and cross-platform synergy."

"More like a media circus," Rocket said.

"She thinks it could be the biggest marketing event since the opening of the Disneyverse space station." Kreet looked at Rocket with a pleading expression. "I thought you, of all people, would understand this. You said it yourself: We can't do this by ourselves. Well, then, here's the opportunity, dropped right in our laps."

"There are 10 different Agencies around the world," Bixx said. "How are you going to get them all on board with this...*producer?*"

"Zvara's the man for that–"

"And how are you going to convince all the Tels around the world that this will work?"

"That's going to be my job."

"You already have this all worked out, don't you?" Rocket asked.

"Not everything, just the big-picture stuff. We have people who will–"

"You have *people?*" Sanjiv asked.

"Okay, Megan has people."

"You got shit without Kortel and Zvara," Rocket said.

Bixx was furious. "Kreet, we're a culture, not a product–"

"Culture is product," Toffler said, strutting back to their table. She was chewing on her frames again. "How many of your kind exist in the world?"

"Oh, I don't know," Bixx said. "Two, maybe three thousand."

Toffler smiled, and Bixx felt her stomach tighten.

"Young lady, I've created worldwide netcasts that involved hundreds of thousands of people. Uplink, downlink, transglobal feeds bounced off of the moon...you name it, I've done it. I think I can handle a few thousand outcasts." She turned to the Brit. "Did you check on our rooms in New York yet?"

"Yes," he said. "We're booked at The Thin, downtown."

"Oh, thank God. They have a wonderful spa. My blood could use an updating."

Toffler began to leave, but wheeled around. "We'll be in touch. Great to meet you all. Kreet, we'll be out front." She and the Brit walked through the bar like they owned it.

"I need you guys to do something for me," Kreet said.

"Let me guess," Sanjiv said. "Find Kortel for you, right?"

"Actually I was thinking Zvara, but find one and you'll find the other." Kreet looked at Bixx, and his expression softened. "I'm really sorry you got hurt. I had no idea. I was at the bar the night Megan approached me. She never said anything about what happened to you."

Bixx folded her arms. "I'm probably going to have a scar, you know."

"A small price to pay, considering what's at stake, don't you think?" Kreet read her look. "Come on, this will work. It's what we've wanted—"

"You've wanted," Bixx corrected.

"Okay, maybe, but think about it. No more hiding. No more false names or lying about our power." He faced the others. "Wouldn't it be nice to use what God gave you for a change, without having to keep it in check? You've always said you wanted to do good in the world. Maybe now you'll be able to. But we'll never know unless we try."

"Kreet..." Bixx bit off the rest of her thought and let her anger cool. There was no changing Kreet once he had his teeth sunk into an idea. "You be careful," she said resignedly. "I don't trust those two."

Kreet inched closer. "I will. Thanks for the thought."

As he turned to leave, Bixx caught a few lyrics from his scarf. It sounded like the lady was singing *That's Entertainment*, but she couldn't make out the rest.

Adios. 13

THERE was something about a New Mexico sunset that could lock up Kortel's attention for a good hour. He had seen his share of spectacular ones: Tortola, Hawaii, and a stretch of Trans-Russian Interway where during the summer the sun never quite set but rather skipped on the horizon before ascending again. But for Kortel, a New Mexico sunset set the standard by which all others were judged. And if he had his way, he'd package it and present it to every person from New York to Atlanta. God, he hated that sprawl. His netpad hummed inside his pocket, and he fought the urge to toss it into the creek bed that ran by the base.

Tarris's holographic figure appeared above the netpad's tiny screen. He had been captured from the waist up and was outside somewhere. "What are you doing?" he asked.

"Trying to enjoy one of your state's best assets," Kortel replied.

Tarris turned to his right. "Yeah, it looks like a beautiful one tonight."

"Where are you?" Kortel asked.

"I'm at my old compound near Tres Piedras. I'm doing a little cleaning before the real estate agent gets here tomorrow."

"So you're really going to sell it?"

Tarris looked to his right again and lingered on the sunset. Shades of orange and burnt yellow contoured his face. "Too many bad memories," he said, barely audible through the gusts of wind.

"You don't need two places anyway," Kortel said.

Tarris nodded in agreement. "So how's it going?"

Kortel placed the netpad on a large rock and rubbed his temples. "They're killing me, Tarris. Shoalburg and Richter have me doing all these extreme grav tests. And Shoalburg says he'll have to enhance my level past 10.... Says he's 'tweaking' the tech in my head to be more 'parallel,' whatever the hell that means."

"Isn't Richter the one who thinks you're unstable?"

"Yeah. She's got me in these therapy sessions twice a week with a guy from the Middle East. His last name sounds like you're hocking up a fur ball."

"Is he helping?"

Kortel shrugged. "I don't know. He says I have some kind of deep-rooted trauma from the deaths of my parents."

"Well...do you?"

"Sure, me and about a million other survivors of Hawaii. He says we're close to making a breakthrough, but it feels more like a breakdown." Kortel rubbed his temples harder.

"I have a therapist," Tarris offered. "He's a 12-year-old Tennessean who weighs about 750 milliliters."

Kortel burst out laughing, and he could hear his voice echo off the dry creek bed. "Shit, what I would give for an Oban right now."

"What? They have you off drinking?"

"It's all natural for Richter. Strictly juice and water."

"Screw that," Tarris said. "I can't cope without Mr. Daniel. He's my stabilizer, especially now that I'm not Riding."

Kortel turned his attention back to the sunset. Ashen clouds edged in purple and orange hung like heavenly flotsam on the lip of the horizon. He watched a hawk tack into the wind, then dive behind a row of ponderosa pines.

"How long have you been there?" Tarris asked.

It took Kortel a second to remember. "I don't know," he said. "Six, maybe seven weeks." He thought harder, trying to recall, but the days and nights had fallen into a tedious pattern of level testing, psychoanalysis and fitful sleep. He felt a burning behind his eyes. "Six, I think."

Tarris stepped closer, and his figure loomed within the constructs of the netpad's holoparameters. "How are you holding up?" His voice had the edge of a big brother, like when they were kids.

"Good, for the most part. But I'm having these dreams." Kortel was dying for a drink. "They're, ah...I don't know, just intense."

"And?"

Kortel watched a jackrabbit scamper through thick scrub sage, its form barely visible in the fading light. It cut four hard angles and disappeared over an embankment that led to the creek bed. "They're about Tamara," he said.

"And?"

"They're kind of sexual in nature, but kind of not."

"That figures. You're lonely."

"No, it's more than that. She's been on my mind lately."

"Quit torturing yourself. You've been down that road, and you made your decision. A good one, I might add."

Kortel glanced at the sunset again. Only a few fingers of light splayed on the horizon. Then he caught the glint of a metallic wing skimming the bottom of some dark, wispy clouds. It was gold and approached at a high rate of speed.

"Hell," he said to himself.

"What's the matter?" Tarris asked.

Kortel scooped up the netpad, clicked its imager for maximum zoom and pointed it in the direction of the craft. "Check it out," he said. "We've got company."

~

The only visible evidence of the jump jet's downward thrust was the slight distortion of air 30 feet below its fuselage. It had been motionless about a hundred feet above the creek bed for more than 20 minutes now. Its golden profile had been reduced to a sliver of black shadow as the evening sky gave way to night. Kortel removed the high-imaging field glasses from his eyes and stepped from the lab's bank of third-story windows.

"Tell me more about this St. John person," Shoalburg said. He pushed away from the console, but the tether of fiber optics connected to his eye implants didn't allow him to go very far. He twisted toward Kortel, and the optics slapped against the counter.

"It's like I told you," Kortel said. "He reps a consortium of companies that want me to work for them.... You know, dirty ops and crap like that. He stinks of big business and has a team of ex-Agency types who've figured a way to tap into my tech."

Shoalburg looked about, riding a wave of information only he could see. "I can't find a thing on this guy in the grid. If that's his real name, he plays under the netdar. I wouldn't worry about him interfacing with your tech. I've got this base so packaged, even the spy satellites can't see us. To them, we look like that old river bed out there."

"Then how did St. John know where to find me, assuming that is St. John out there?"

Shoalburg raised his eyebrows and looked more buglike to Kortel. "Good question."

"So where're Zvara and Richter?"

"They're in town," Hammler said, "but should be back any minute." He was busy across the room at another console and didn't seem particularly bothered by the presence of an unmarked aircraft hovering a thousand feet from the front gate of the base. Hammler had his attention buried in the latest data of Kortel's grav testing.

The door to the lab opened, and Zvara and Richter rushed in.

"Why did you not contact me about this?" Zvara asked Kortel.

"Because we didn't want to take a chance and breach the security grid," Shoalburg replied.

"Looks like it already is," Richter said, pointing to the image of the jump jet on Shoalburg's console vid screen.

Zvara picked up the field glasses and aimed them out the window toward the plane.

Kortel cleared his throat. "I think I know who that is out there."

"Errol St. John," Zvara said, still looking through the field glasses.

"Yeah, that's right. How'd you know?"

"Errol and I go back a few years...to my time as head of the Agency."

Kortel leaned against the counter and folded his arms. "Of course, I should have known."

"Jonny says he reps some conglomerates that want him on their credit roll," Shoalburg said.

Zvara slowly lowered the field glasses. He kept staring at the jet. "Mr. St. John does not work in the corporate sector," he said gravely. "He works on the fringe."

"You mean he's a freelancer?" Richter asked.

"No," Zvara replied. "He is a *consigliere*."

"A consi-who?" Kortel asked.

"A counselor," Shoalburg said. "But I'll bet this guy's more of a consultant. Nasty sons of bitches." He quickly turned in Richter's direction. "I'm sorry."

Richter waved it off, and then realized what she was doing. "No worries," she said to Shoalburg.

"You mean St. John works for the Mafia?" Kortel asked.

"Of a sort," Zvara said. "For decades the Tels have been in...oh, help me, Carter, what is the expression?"

"In bed?" Shoalburg offered.

"Yes, bed."

"I don't get it," Kortel said. "Why would we do that?"

"No other organization can keep a secret better than the Mafia. Even with our ability to erase minds, we always had leakage with our corporate clients. But with the Mafia, there was never this issue. And like us, they, too, live out of the mainstream. They help us, and we help them." Zvara faced Kortel. "I did not want this arrangement. I inherited it when I took control of the Agency, and believe me, I am not proud of it. I fought to end it, but you do not end something like this. When you get into bed with these people, you are in for life."

Kortel looked out the window. "Shit, it's gone!"

"Carter," Zvara said, "can you see where they went?"

Shoalburg sat motionless for a second. "They're masked. I can't find any trace of their presence."

Suddenly an explosion rocked the building. The lab's lights flickered, and Richter stumbled into Kortel's arms. They both went to the floor, along with Zvara, but Shoalburg clung to the counter. Hammler shrieked as he spilled from his chair. Then there were shouts, and the sound of boots running past the lab's door. The image of St. John pixeled up on Shoalburg's vid screen. Zvara frantically motioned for Kortel to crawl out of its imager's range. He did, quickly scooting around Richter and behind a lab station.

"Good evening, Armando!" St. John bellowed from the screen.

"Errol," Zvara said, struggling to his feet, "what did you just do?"

"Some of your men got a little excited by our presence."

"If you hurt anyone—"

"No one has been harmed, Armando. You know I don't work like that unless provoked. There is a vehicle, though, that won't be of much use to you now. And you can come out, Jonathan. I can see all of you, so there's no point in hiding."

There was a thunderous drone outside, and the glass in the old windows rattled in its panes. A dark, featureless form slowly lowered into view. Kortel could barely make out the jump jet's contour as it glided to a stop above the parking lot, slowly turned and faced the windows. Lights came on inside the cockpit, and Kortel could finally distinguish exactly where the windshield was on the jet. In the pilot's seat was the Asian, her interface gear strapped to her face like an articulated metal octopus. St. John was in the copilot's seat, bottom-lit in a red glow by the cockpit's instrumentation. He was grinning from ear to ear, but his skin remained smooth, as if defying nature to create any wrinkles.

"Jonathan," St. John said, "we need to talk...*now*."

Kortel shot a glance at Zvara, who motioned for him to come out from behind the station.

"He cannot be bought," Zvara said.

St. John chuckled. "What, are you his agent now?"

Richter and Shoalburg were standing in a dark corner to Zvara's right. Kortel looked at Richter. She smiled stoically, but he could see she was unnerved. Hammler was cowering behind his station. He looked terrified, and his eyes darted frantically between the jet, Kortel and Zvara.

"I am just a friend, Errol. That is all."

St. John's grin disappeared. "Doubtful."

"I'm not interested in working for organized crime," Kortel said. He and Zvara were now looking at St. John inside the cockpit, rather than his image on the vid screen.

St. John leveled his attention at them. "Armando, is that what you told them?" His smile came back, but it had a devilish look in the light of the cabin. "Jonathan, if you think I'm associated with the Mafia, you've been misinformed. The companies I represent are legitimate global enterprises."

"I don't care if they're part of the Pac 100," Kortel said, stepping to the window. "I'm not interested."

St. John leaned over to the pilot and said something into her ear. She nodded and the whine of the engines raised an octave. The jump jet began to pull back from the window.

"Armando," he said in a low tone, "I'm not leaving without Jonathan."

Zvara looked at Kortel knowingly, and then slowly closed his eyes.

Suddenly, the jump jet began to list to one side, its port wing coming dangerously close to the ground. Its engines roared, drowning out the audio feed to the lab, but Kortel could see St. John yelling at the pilot. The fiber optics attached to her interface gear swung madly about as she fought to get control.

"Zvara!" Kortel yelled. "Hang on, I'll join you!"

The jet violently recoiled, as if the force that had been causing it to tilt had instantly vanished. The craft rolled wildly and its starboard wing tip clipped the top of a light pole. The engines' thunderous whine cut the air as the pilot overcompensated.

"I have not gone into phase yet!" Zvara yelled.

Suddenly, the jet lurched at their building, its port wing rising toward the lab's large bank of windows.

"Look out!" Kortel screamed. "It's going to hit!–"

The jet's port wingtip tore through the wall of the building, hurling large chunks of cinder block into the lab. The leading edge of its gold biotitanium fuselage crashed into a scanning station, obliterating it in a spray of organics, metal and glass. The room's lights went out. Kortel instantly phased and launched himself at Zvara. He scooped the older Tel into his arms and landed, tumbling, behind a workstation.

"Jonathan!" Kortel barely heard Richter yell through the deafening sound of the jet's engines. He spun and saw Shoalburg on the floor. He was leaning against the wall, with Richter crouched next to him.

The wing began to exit, dragging parts of a desk and chair with it, but then it came jabbing back into the lab and slammed into the ceiling. The building shuddered as the body of the plane grazed the roof of the second story.

"It's Shoalburg!" Richter screamed through the chaos.

Kortel phased again and flew across the room. Richter's eyes were filled with awe as he landed in a skid next to her.

"My, God, it's true," she said.

"What's the matter with Carter? Shit!–"

The jet's wing was heading toward them. Kortel draped himself over Richter and Shoalburg and instantly created a grav field to protect them. The wing bounced off of it and plowed through the wall to their right. Shards of cinder block and wallboard rained over them, but the grav field acted like an unseen umbrella. Kortel watched the jet through the gouge in the wall as it moved away from their building, still pitching and rolling above the parking lot.

Richter stared at Kortel. "Thank you," she said.

Kortel just nodded. "What's the matter with Carter?"

"I think he was convulsing."

Shoalburg was still tethered to a remote interface pack that he held in his lap. Kortel watched his fingers dance across its control surface.

"Carter," he said, "are you okay?"

"It's really like one of those old vid arcades," he replied, scooting himself into a sitting position. "Once you get the hang of it, it's pretty fun. Watch this...." He pointed to the jet.

Kortel and Richter peered out though the gash in the wall. The plane was hovering about 50 feet above the parking lot when it suddenly started spinning like an old amusement ride: slowly at first, then gaining speed until it was hard to watch.

Kortel glanced from the interface pack to the 'trodes inside Shoalburg's eye sockets. "Carter, are you controlling that jet?"

"I am now. It was hard to figure out its computer's protocols. But once I did, it was surprisingly basic." He moved his head as if glancing around the lab. "Sorry for all the damage. The jet's core was tough to wrangle, and it put up quite a fight before I managed to disable it." His fingers danced again, and the jet slowed to a stop.

The door to the lab burst open, and three men rushed in. The beams from their flashlights cut erratic patterns through the dusty air.

"Mr. Zvara, are you all right?" one of them called out.

"I am, Louis," Zvara replied. He was kneeling next to Hammler, who was crumpled on the floor and bleeding from his head. "Get a med kit up here immediately."

"I thought you were convulsing," Richter said to Shoalburg.

"Nah, just some body English fighting the jet's AI core." Shoalburg looked in Kortel's direction. "What do you want me to do with St. John?"

"I've got an idea." Kortel rushed over to one of the active vid screens. It cast the room in hot edges of blues and greens. St. John's image was still projecting, although now his hair was tousled and his suit was torn at both shoulders. He was angrily shouting something, but the sound had been cut.

"Carter," Kortel said, "can you get back the audio?"

Shoalburg's fingers danced again.

"—if you don't release my jet," St. John yelled, "I'll—"

"You'll what?" Kortel asked as Zvara came to his side.

St. John passed a hand through his hair. "I never had any intent of taking you by force—"

"Right, and that blast earlier was just a warning shot?"

St. John tugged a bit at his suit's shoulders, but quickly gave up and settled into his seat. "Sometimes I have to emphasize my position," he said arrogantly. "Besides, your men gave me no choice."

"Errol," Zvara said, "I would say that you have made your point. I think it is time for you to leave now."

St. John started to protest, but Zvara motioned for Shoalburg to cut the audio. "Carter," he said, "can you program that jet to return to its point of origin?"

"Sure. It's just a reverse-out of its inbound flight parameters. Looks like they came out of a private airport just south of London."

"Then send them on their way, before they regain control of their craft."

Shoalburg took the interface pack into both hands and began programming. As he sat on the floor with his legs folded, humming to himself, he reminded Kortel of a kid with one of Tarris's original biogame units.

"Let me know when you're ready, Carter," he said, walking over to him. "I want to personally give St. John a little nudge."

Shoalburg looked up and smiled before he returned to his programming.

Kortel helped Richter to her feet.

"Your grav display was amazing," she said. "I didn't know you could reverse your polarity and move yourself like that. You were *flying*." She started to laugh.

"Done!" Shoalburg announced.

"Carter," Kortel said, "give me audio again."

"—my business associates won't tolerate this, Armando—"

"Mr. St. John," Kortel said, "if you ever come near me or any of my friends again, I won't be as nice as I'm about to be." Kortel motioned for the audio to be cut.

"What are you going to do, Jonny?" Shoalburg asked.

"Give him a kick in the ass. On my count, angle them for their flight home and engage their main engines. How's the air space around us?"

Shoalburg sat for a second. "We're all clear under 10,000 feet for 100 hundred miles in all directions...except south of us, of course, around Albuquerque."

"Good. Let's do it. Ready?"

Shoalburg nodded.

"Mark. Three, two, one."

The jump jet turned, and its nose angled toward the full moon rising just above the horizon. Its main engines engaged, but the jet remained in place. The jet began to shake as it fought the physics holding it captive.

"Jonny," Shoalburg said, "that fuselage can't take much of this stress. If you're going to let her rip, you better do it quick."

Kortel held the jet in a narrow grav field while its engines struggled to break free. A drop of blood slid down his upper lip.

Richter gasped. "Jonathan, don't." She started to approach him, but Zvara stopped her. "He knows what he is doing," he said. "And believe me, this is only a fraction of his capability."

Kortel felt another drop of blood slide, and he glanced at the vid screen. St. John was frantically strapping himself into the copilot's seat.

Shoalburg quickly stood. "*Jonny ...*"

"Now, Carter," Kortel said. "Kick in their afterburners."

Shoalburg passed his index finger over the upper corner of the interface's control pad, and flames shot from previously unseen exhaust outlets.

Kortel glanced at the vid screen. *Adios, asshole.*

The jump jet shot away from the base in a flash of orange and white. In the time it took for Kortel to exhale, it disappeared into a thin layer of clouds backlit by the glow of the full moon.

Kortel wiped away the blood from his lip. He examined it for a second between his fingers, and then rubbed it off on the side of his pants. *That's weird*, he thought. *I haven't bled like that in a long time.*

Richter came to his side. "Are you okay?"

"Oh, yeah. That's not that big of a deal to pull off. It's all in how you structure the grav field."

Zvara started chuckling.

Kortel turned. "I don't think I've ever heard you laugh before. What's so funny?"

"Nothing," Zvara said. "I just had a mental image of St. John cleaning out that cockpit."

"I hope he hurled into every nook and cranny on that plane," Shoalburg said.

Zvara approached Kortel. "You know this will not be the last time we see him."

"I know, but we'll be ready for him, right?" Kortel looked questionly from Zvara to Shoalburg to Richter. "Can I get a 'hell yes' here?"

"Jonathan, you have to understand something," Zvara said. "With these people, losing is not an option."

He knows everything. 14

MEGAN Toffler frowned behind the thick black frames of her Net glasses. "I thought you said she was good at this...a real natural."

"She is," Kreet said defensively. He leaned into Bixx's ear. "Bixxy, Megan has a six o'clock out of Dulles, and we need for you to start in *this* lifetime."

2:08 p.m. Bixx stared at the virtgear disc on the counter. Its inert presence could fool you into thinking it was just another of the inane tchotchkes collected from her travels that littered her workstation. Rocket had warned that one day she wouldn't be able to find her netgear amidst all the crap. *Maybe he was right. Maybe she should just dump it all into the waste can. And while she was at it, trash the virtdisc, too.* Bixx turned to eye Toffler. An eyebrow slowly rose over the top of the Net glasses.

Bixx let out a deep sigh. She loved being in the Net, but hated the way the new virtdiscs attacked your head. "Okay, let's get this over with." She spun and faced her workstation.

"That's my girl," said Kreet.

Bixx grabbed the disc and shoved her chair away from the station. The top edge of its lumbar support stabbed Kreet just above his crotch. He groaned and doubled over.

"Sorry," Bixx said, "I need a little room for this."

"Sure, right," Kreet managed. "Anything for a genius." He hobbled over to Toffler and parked himself on the counter of another workstation.

Bixx raised the disc to her forehead.

"Remember," Toffler said, "just locate Kortel. Don't try and collect any other data. I don't need to know what he's been eating or who he's been sleeping with. The less you gather, the less likely you'll expose yourself. The last thing we need is somebody getting to him first." She turned to Kreet. "She knows how to mask her movement, doesn't she?"

Bixx glared.

"She's the best," Kreet said.

This associate of Kreet's was beginning to piss Bixx off. With her marketing studies and genetigraphic mood charts, she had been into everyone's shit for the last two weeks. She had flown in three times from God knows where just on "dialogue" with Bixx, Rocket and Sanjiv about their "take" to approaching Kortel. Rocket finally lost it and suggested Toffler should let Bixx search for him, because she knew more about navigating the Net than all of Toffler's console jocks combined. Rocket's opinion of Bixx's ability was always flattering, but this compliment was a bit of a stretch, considering she only had a fundamental knowledge of nodal dynamics. But the door had been opened, and surprisingly, Toffler agreed.

Bixx hesitated, the virtdisc inches from her forehead.

"Today?" Kreet asked.

Even before Bixx placed the disc to her skin, its biomatrix sensed the impending union and released its interface tentacles. Bixx gritted her teeth while its fiber optics slithered across her face and neck, seeking the optimal points of contact. The last tentacle found the port at the base of Bixx's neck and clicked into place. Toffler, Kreet and the warehouse space melted away as the Net's vastness pixeled up in her vision.

"*Bliad*," she heard herself say before the Net completely engulfed her reality.

Bixx was now floating in what the Guardians for God labeled "the Devil's Playground." But for her, the Net was a gateway to an endless supply of information…and hope. As a little girl in St. Petersburg, she had often sneaked onto her father's old computer and explored the realm of cyberspace, although she never understood why it was called that. It was neither space nor cybernetic. After her parents had died in one of Russia's many mass transit accidents, Bixx had been shuttled through a maze of state structures. She luckily ended up in a *dyetskii dom*, a children's home for "educable" children. There, she begged the staff to let her log hours past the allotment mandated by the Ministry of Education. Around the age of 17, Agency Recruiters approached Bixx, and her life changed forever. She once tried to find out how they had discovered her, but she could never hack into the Agency's main grid. Nestled in the Tel culture, she continued studying the intricacies of the medium. When she learned of its history, she was amazed that the Net had been developed for something as archaic as email.

Suddenly, Toffler's image appeared, floating in front of her. She looked the same, except the lenses of her glasses were dark. The chaos of the Net swirled behind her to jarring effect.

"Hello, honey," Toffler said, her mouth and words out of sync. "I can't stay long. This netwear is a loaner from corporate, and it doesn't interface well with my chemistry. Gives me a hell of a headache." Her form jittered slightly, as if something had interrupted the feed. "I wanted to tell you that our boys lost Kortel a month ago outside of Albuquerque. I swear, ever since our country did this merger with Mexico, all those border states have gone Wild West on us. You might want to start there. Here are all the incepts we have from him." A menu box unfolded to the left of Toffler, and a series of inception codes cascaded down its screen.

"What's that one?" Bixx asked, pointing to the last code entry.

"Looks like startup protocol from a cheap credit phone. He must have bought one on the street, but I'm not sure why." Toffler shrugged. "Who knows? The more

I learn about this guy, the more I question the whole concept. Anyway, you go do whatever you Net folks do, and we'll chat when you come out. *Ciao.*" Her image vanished.

The Net always smelled to Bixx like long-chain monomers and lettuce. The plastic smell she could understand, but lettuce? That always creeped her out. It took Bixx a minute to get used to the rhythm of the Net. When Rocket asked her to describe it, she said it felt like an ocean of vegetable oil, the data like schools of neon fish on the Nature Channel, except there were trillions of them, and they were the size of your fingernail. Even this description paled in comparison to the real thing. Another aspect she could never get used to was the speed. The mass of data moved at an incredible rate, though it never looked blurred, at least not to Bixx. She could always capture individual bits if she focused hard enough; it was similar to looking at the spokes of a spinning wheel and catching a single spoke by blinking. One of her professors at the Agency said she had an "infinite perception," but Bixx just thought she was good at math. In the Net, the data seemed to speak to her. She couldn't explain it, and she never said anything in front of Sanjiv. He thought all her talk about nodal points and data textures was a bunch of crap. When Bixx suggested Sanjiv try the Net, he almost bit her head off, exclaiming he wouldn't be caught dead in there; besides, his body wasn't the right fit for a port connector. Bixx had to admit that only a small portion of the population had the correct "acceptance threshold" for porting. She had gotten her first one from an off-line vendor when she was at the orphanage. It was cheap and not very reliable. When she arrived at the Agency, its techies retrofitted her with a bioptic model custom-grown for her. They said it was more than she would ever need. One of the techs liked Bixx, and on her 18th birthday added a range booster to her port.

Bixx had learned practically everything she knew about the Net from her teachers at the Agency, especially her Construct professor, who taught her the finer points of nodal perception – or "listening," as he liked to call it. He told her that less than 1 percent of the people who worked in the Net had the gift, and that she should consider herself extremely blessed. Bixx had never considered herself extremely anything until Dr. Yanez had enlightened her to the subtle tones than ran underneath the data. "It's like rhythm," he had told her. "Either you hear it or you don't." Bixx had heard it all her life, but never knew what it was until Yanez taught her to open her mind and listen.

Bixx accessed a map port and jumped to the New Mexico grid. Toffler was right. It had become a little wild. Data around mega grids like New York had a certain essence about them. They were rich in texture and highly evolved technically. But the data streams in the New Mexico grid were a *mélange* of bio, digital and analog: everything from state-of-the-art bioptics to century-old T-lines. It was hard for Bixx to get a read on where to start. The incepts from Kortel's credit phone placed him in the north central part of the state. He had used the phone to make one call and buy a pack of cigarettes. But it was the call that caught Bixx's attention. It had an odd pattern, and the signal appeared to have looped in the grid, like Kortel had called someone within just a couple of feet of himself. The cigarette machine was leased to a corporation called Enchanted Entertainment, which had a gambling subsidiary named Deuces Wild. Bixx cross-referenced Deuce's address with the incepts from Kortel's credit phone. They matched.

Good, she thought. *At least I know where you were. Let's see if I can find where you are.*

Bixx started with the model number of the phone Kortel had called. It was difficult to trace, because it had been bought on the black net, which suggested that the person Kortel called lived off the grid. Since New Mexico was a haven for such people, trying to find this one might be impossible. But Bixx remembered a tip a friend at the orphanage had told her: most credit phones, like netpads, utilized the new living micro-engines, and almost all of these batteries where made in the new nation of Caribbeatan, specifically on the island of St. Lucia. Every battery had a genetic marker code. If Bixx could get the code, she could do some reverse indexing. She jumped to the Caribbeatan grid and easily located the battery company. After a little digging, she found the marker code. She then chased its history to an after-market refurbisher in Mexico City that resold to home-based companies throughout the Southwest. The one in the phone Kortel had called had been bought in Taos with a credit chip registered to a T. Finn.

Didn't Kortel have it out with Jacob Whitehorse in Taos? Bixx thought. She tried to recall the story. Wasn't there something about Whitehorse's daughter trying to kill Kortel? Hadn't she been married to a friend of his? A guy named Terry...Tarris? T...Tarris Finn.

Bixx quickly searched the Net for the name and found an extensive history on Tarris Finn. He was the inventor of the biosensory headgear that revolutionized the gaming industry and had developed many of the games Bixx had grown up on. He had battled a severe addiction to Ride and became a paraplegic after a bad accident. Then he dropped off the grid, settling onto property he had inherited outside of Tres Piedras, New Mexico. Bixx found its address, but it was up for sale and, according to the listing, not currently occupied.

What do I do now? Bixx glanced at the time code. *3:08 p.m.*

Most of Finn's data was untraceable. He definitely didn't want people finding him, and Bixx was out of ideas. She began to close the menu box when she heard a subtle droning beneath the data. It sounded like the old trains she had seen in museums in Russia — the type that ran on little black pellets. The drone sounded just like the trains when they were far away and heading toward you. Bixx closed her eyes and started to "listen." The image of Dr. Yanez came into her mind, along with his classroom and vast collection of music memorabilia. Maybe that's where she had gotten the bug to collect. Bixx listened while the drone increased, slowly at first, then building until she could feel it in her chest.

She opened her eyes on James McCarris, his form perfect in every detail.

Bixx let out a yelp. Her heart was racing. "What are you doing here?"

McCarris contemplated her for a second. "Playing chess. I was retrieving an old Bobby Fischer closing move when you entered my stream. I'm taking a bathroom break, but give me a minute, and I should finish this guy off." He winked. "I know it's cheating, but this guy's a jerk. I'll be right back." His image vanished.

The droning had been replaced with the Net's usual white noise, which always reminded Bixx of the murmuring in a theater just before a play started. For many Net people, this noise was too much of a distraction, but Bixx had learned to ignore it. That talent might have been her salvation, because if she couldn't tune it out, the idea of 5 billion people communicating all around her might be overwhelming. She floated and watched the textures resolve.

"Okay," McCarris said, his form suddenly appearing. "That went well."

"What did you end up doing?" Bixx asked.

"Do you play chess?"

Bixx shook her head.

"Then it wouldn't make any sense to you. Let's just say I checkmated his ass. And he deserved it."

Bixx shrugged. "If you say so."

"How did you get into my data stream? It has more security around it than most banks. It's my lifeline."

"I-I don't know. I just did."

McCarris studied her. "Are you one of those nodal readers? I've read about your kind. What do they call it?"

"Infinite perception."

"Yeah, that's it, I.P. So, what are you trying to perceive today?"

"Jonathan Kortel. Or where he is, to be precise."

McCarris's expression hardened. "Why?" he asked.

Bixx explained the whole story about Kreet, the Brit and Toffler. McCarris listened, nodding occasionally.

"Sounds ballsy," he said finally.

"I call it crazy," Bixx replied. "I could care less if we came out or not. I just have a bad feeling about it. Like once we do, our lives will be at risk."

"If there's one thing I've learned...or, ah, relearned, it's that people basically hate change."

"That's for sure," Bixx said.

"So this producer really thinks she can get Kortel and Zvara to go along?"

"That's what she says."

"Good luck with that. From what I know about Kortel, he's too wound up for something that big. Now, I know Zvara...well, sort of know him, at least what I've read. He's an idealist and would probably go along with the plan if he thought it could be pulled off." McCarris appeared to think for a moment, or possibly just retrieve more information. He nodded to himself. "Maybe this producer's onto something. Taking it prime time might be good. Anyway, did you find Kortel?"

"Not really–"

"You're in the right state. He always goes back to his friend Tarris Finn when things get bad."

"Yeah, so I've read. But Tarris's compound is up for sale...and he's not living in it."

"He's probably at his lab outside of Chaco Canyon."

"Do you know where it is?" Bixx asked.

"Well, kind of. When Zvara and I were assigned to bring Kortel in, we searched *everywhere*. Tarris's lab was one of the first places we went. It's in the case file, and I've got clearance. Hold on; this might take a minute." McCarris's image disappeared.

Bixx glanced at the time code. *3:46 p.m.* Something from behind tapped her shoulder.

"Shit!" Bixx said, spinning.

Toffler's staticky image smiled curtly. "How we doing?"

Bixx scowled. "Give me a few more minutes, and I'll have his location."

"Splendid." Toffler's image quivered and vanished.

"Here you go," McCarris said, appearing. A menu box unfolded next to him. It showed an address and some coordinates, then folded to the size of an old-fashioned envelope and glided into Bixx's hand before it dissolved. "That info's in your netgear's wetdrive now. Trash it as soon as you can. And we never had this conversation, *right?*"

Bixx nodded.

"Good girl. Now I've got to run." McCarris's image faded, but quickly returned. "Oh, I'm still working on the info on that Brit. I'll let you know what I find out." And he was gone.

The droning had returned, but it was fading. Bixx closed her eyes and listened. She had read once that a powerful stream like McCarris's was similar in concept to an old-style hologram. You could sample a tiny section anywhere along the flow and see everything carried by it at once. She wondered what kind of patterns and textures his stream would contain. She took a deep breath and focused her perception at the core of the droning. Then she let go, releasing herself into the mass of data that was James McCarris....

Instantly, the stream consumed her, digesting the almost infinite algorithms of her program like a digital reptile. Bixx frantically looked down at her form, but couldn't see it. She tried to pull away, but found she was caught in the riptide that was McCarris's life. Suddenly it all was there, every memory and thought, saturated in a thick torrent of emotion and pain. Bixx panicked and tried to rip at the virtgear disc, but her arms and hands were now phantom limbs. McCarris's life swirled around her. She tried to focus on individual elements, but the sheer volume was too much. Even when Bixx pinched her eyes closed, the data was still there.

She opened them to find herself floating outside of a building, several stories in the air. It was night, and Kortel stood at an open window, laughing.

"I'm not going to kill you," he called to her.

She remembered the story of how McCarris had used Kortel, and how Kortel had punished him for it. He had telekinetically suspended McCarris outside of his office window on the Agency campus and toyed with him until he had gotten the truth....

"I'm going to do something a lot worse," Kortel continued.

Bixx gasped, but it felt like someone had done it for her. A terrible fear gripped her. "How far back are you going to erase?" she heard herself ask. Again, she felt like a puppet through whom someone else was speaking. There was a perceptible lag before she heard her own voice.

Suddenly, the scene shifted. McCarris was now in the window. Kortel's eyes narrowed. "All the way," he said.

Kreet was pulling at the virtdisc, its tentacles stubbornly releasing their grip. "Stop screaming," he said. "Come on, you're okay." Toffler was next to him, her arms folded tightly across her chest.

Bixx sensed more than felt her lower lip quivering, as it had on frigid winter mornings in St. Petersburg. Her breathing came in gasps. She leaned back in her chair and stared at the virtdisc in Kreet's hand. Everything had a slight halo, and the color was off somehow.

"Jesus, girl," Kreet said. He placed the disc on the counter. "What the hell happened?"

"We have to get to New Mexico," Bixx said.

"Okay, but—"

"He lied about his memory loss.... He knows everything."

"Who lied...about what?"

"McCarris," she said, still staring. "I think he plans to kill Kortel."

Breakthrough. 15

KORTEL watched the psychiatrist enter something into his netpad. "Can we continue?" Kortel asked, his impatience building.

The portly man casually raised a finger and continued inputting. Barely a minute passed, but it could have been an hour to Kortel, who had already suffered through a long session.

"All right," the psychiatrist said, snapping his netpad shut. His dark brown eyes met Kortel's, which were bloodshot and seemed to carry all the anguish he had ever seen in his practice. "Let's move on to where we left off last time.... We were so close to a breakthrough."

Kortel sighed. *There was that word again.*

"Would you like to talk about something else?" the psychiatrist asked.

"No, it's just...."

"It's all right, Jonathan. Please, go ahead."

"Look, doc. It's not like I don't appreciate what you've been doing in these sessions. It's just that I've been through all this before."

The psychiatrist nodded. He referenced his netpad. "I gather you're referring to the Albers Mandate?"

A dead feeling began to rise in Kortel. His attention moved to the windows and the mountains beyond. A cloud formation that vaguely resembled the shape of a car he had owned in his third year of culinary school hung above the farthest peak. Shortly after the destruction of Hawaii, then-President Albers had decreed that all survivors of "the Event" should receive counseling for their grief. She brought the power of the government to bear and convened a panel of medical experts who were given the task of implementing the mandate. She had proclaimed it was necessary for the collective mental health of the nation. Kortel thought he had locked that time away, but Dr. Furball's questioning dredged it all up again. Now, the memories came rushing back on a wave of guilt and shame. He studied his right hand. His fingers twitched slightly. He rubbed them and watched the clouds shift the late afternoon light, as if God had slipped a filter across the sun.

The psychiatrist's eyes went to Kortel's hands, then to his netpad. He entered something. "Would you like to talk about that period of your life?" His voice was clinical and emotionless.

Numbness coursed through Kortel's body as he fought the urge to tell the doctor to piss off. But something was pushing him to spew out his angst. Gripped by the flood of memories, he stared out the windows. A bird flew past.

"Jonathan...are you all right?"

"I'm fine." Kortel leveled his attention at the psychiatrist. "One night, my grandfather came into my room. I was...I don't know, ten? Eleven? Does it really matter?"

The psychiatrist didn't respond.

"He said that my number had been drawn...that I was to begin my sessions. He said it would be good for me...set me straight."

"Did it?" the psychiatrist asked.

Kortel felt something shift in his brain, like his tech was advancing toward a new part of his nervous system. His heart began to race. He swallowed hard, and tightness wrapped around his throat. "I told those doctors everything they wanted to hear," he said. "They just sat there and listened."

The psychiatrist nodded and referenced his netpad again.

"They assured me I would be fine.... All I had to do was grieve. They said it was a natural function of the human spirit...that all victims went through it. They called it a disorder...post-trauma something."

"Yes," the psychiatrist said, "go on."

"I was only 10 years old!" Kortel tasted the salt of a tear at the corner of his mouth, and it startled him. His mind slipped back to the hot classroom. That summer, the Department of Intelligence had taken over an abandoned school and used it for processing survivors who lived in the Central Midwest zone. Like an assembly line, the doctors saw people around the clock. The team assigned to Kortel had informed him, rather casually and without remorse, that their primary job was to "cushion" him from the reality that his parents were dead. A boy his age wouldn't understand the consequences, a nurse assured him.

Something shifted again.

A bowl of fruit on a small table behind the psychiatrist exploded, sending bits of oranges and apples arching in all directions. A large chunk landed in the lap of the psychiatrist. He regarded it calmly and made another notation.

More memories quickly surfaced, one after another. Kortel could taste them at the back of his throat. They were bitter and acrid, like cognitive bile his body was trying to expel. "They said I would get over it," he continued. "That...that I was still young. That I would be able to recover with 'minimal damage.'"

"And?"

"They didn't know," Kortel said, feeling the salty echo of another tear.

The psychiatrist leaned forward, clearly puzzled at this statement. "What, Jonathan?... What didn't they know?"

The room blurred as the memories began to pile up at the door to Kortel's soul.

A voracious edge of pain tore through his mind. "I saw their photos," he said, wincing.

The psychiatrist's face screwed into question.

The team that had treated Kortel sat before him now, their faces heavy with the burden they had been assigned. One of them gestured. Kortel felt himself stand.

"Jonathan?" the psychiatrist asked.

Kortel glanced around the office, and its spartan furnishings seemed to morph into that room.... He was 10 again. "I saw them, sir," he heard himself say.

"You saw them?... *Who?*"

Kortel felt himself step forward, but the movement was vague and dreamlike. "I saw photos of my parents...as they were."

The psychiatrist shifted uncomfortably in his chair. "Do you mean *after* the Event?"

Kortel felt his lips moving, repeating what he had just said, but no sound came.

"How?" the psychiatrist demanded. "Those were highly classified!"

Kortel's attention ricocheted around the room until it landed on the bloodshot eyes of the doctor. He poured all of his pain into them. "I hacked into the government's database, into my parents' case file," he admitted. "I saw what happened to them, after they had debio..." He couldn't finish the word.

"You should have never seen those images!" the psychiatrist said. "They were...oh my God."

Kortel felt a scream emerge from his throat. All of his pain erupted in a guttural torrent of grief. "Mother! Father!" he screamed. He called out to them over and over until his throat was raw, the words coming out in hacks and coughs. He began hyperventilating as mucus and tears streamed down his face. It felt as if his body had been torn open and his guts were spilling. A hot spike of pain cut between Kortel's eyes. He screamed and stumbled into a chair. Suddenly, an intense white flash split the room.

As Kortel's eyes adjusted, he could make out only edges of detail. A brilliant glow roughly the size of a human floated by the windows. The psychiatrist was cowering in his chair, pointing the netpad toward the apparition. Like a small sun, the glowing mass floated about a foot off the tiled floor.

The psychiatrist swung his netpad at Kortel, then back to the apparition.

Kortel instinctively stepped toward it.

"No!" the psychiatrist ordered.

The apparition's shape quickly gained form. A head and extremities emerged, then eyes appeared, defining a face. Its pure light transformed into hair that spilled down the sides of its head, along with skin and clothes. The brilliance began to ebb, and it coalesced into a more discernable form.

It was a woman.

"Mother?" Kortel whispered.

The form's light flared slightly.

"Fantastic," Kortel heard the psychiatrist say.

The apparition's glow calmed, and the room fell into a greenish hue. Kortel could now make out the form of his mother: her dark shoulder-length hair, the lab coat and the ankle-length khakis. Even the belt she always wore when she worked in her lab – the one with the old mud flap image of the reclining naked girl set in chrome relief on the buckle.

The psychiatrist came up to Kortel's side. "Have you had these visions before?" The netpad had been put away.

Kortel felt dizzy and barely heard the question. "Yeah," he replied. "I've had three, maybe four of these."

"Amazing."

"Jonathan," the apparition said. Its voice was transparent, as though it had been reprocessed a dozen times over. It sounded to Kortel like it was coming to them at great risk. Maybe it was.

The psychiatrist gasped and took a step back. His attention vacillated between Kortel and the apparition. He quickly pulled his netpad from his coat and began scanning again.

Kortel approached it. "Yes, Mother?"

"You must release your father and me."

"But, Mother–"

The form extended its hand and put a finger to Kortel's lips. He felt an icy sensation at the point of contact, but didn't flinch. "You're very powerful, my son. Your destiny is before you. You can't live in the past anymore."

For a moment that felt like forever, Kortel teetered between shock and reverence. "Mother," he said, finally, "I...I miss you and Father so much."

The apparition's glow brightened. It took Kortel's face into its hands. "And we miss you." It passed a finger down his cheek, and he instinctually leaned into it.

"Jonathan, please," the form said, lifting Kortel's face by the chin. "You must let go of us and live your life."

Kortel's heart collapsed. He began to cry and sank to his knees. The apparition moved with him. It was close to his face now, and he could see its form was dissipating. It smiled.

"Remember, your father and I will always be here." It placed its hand against Kortel's chest.

"I love you," Kortel uttered.

"We love you," it mouthed before its form dispersed in a delicate mist of gray and pink and green.

Kortel remained motionless, staring at the floor. He felt something cold and delicate pass over the back of his neck. The psychiatrist knelt next to him.

"Are you all right?" he asked. He started to place his hand on Kortel's shoulder, but hesitated.

Kortel took a moment to find his voice. "Yes," he managed, still staring.

"Jonathan, I...I didn't realize the extent of your trauma. I would have never pushed you as I did. I'm truly sorry."

Kortel wiped the tears and mucus from his face with the sleeve of his shirt.

"Let me help you up," the psychiatrist said.

He took Kortel under the arm and helped him back into his chair. Kortel could feel the doctor's hands shaking. He leaned back and rubbed his temples.

The psychiatrist stepped to his desk and poured a glass of water from a metal decanter. "Here," he said, handing Kortel the glass, "this should help."

The cool water washed away the burning at the back of Kortel's throat. He emptied the glass in four vigorous gulps.

The psychiatrist sat in his chair. He clicked open his netpad and began entering data. His hands were still shaking.

An uneasy calm settled around them.

"Are you okay?" Kortel asked.

The doctor stopped inputting and raised his eyes. "I can't define what we just witnessed," he said. "Your ability to alter matter has developed to a point where your thoughts, even your memories can become manifest. I've never seen anything like this before. It's extraordinary."

"It might be extraordinary to you, doc, but it scares the hell out of me."

The psychiatrist contemplated Kortel's statement for a second. "It scares you because you don't understand what it means, and you haven't learned to control it. Once you have, the fear will be gone." He went back to his netpad.

"So, ah...was that the breakthrough you were looking for?" Kortel asked.

The psychiatrist looked up and snapped his netpad shut. He smiled, and his eyes seemed to have lost their sadness.

The best news. 16

BIXX was jolted from her sleep by the rental's inability to compensate for the rough road they traveled. The pothole must have been particularly deep, because her head smacked against Rocket's bony shoulder harder than the last dozen times. She'd been able to drift back to sleep after those, but this one definitely woke her up. She leaned forward and peered out the windshield. The van's argon beams cut through the New Mexico night with a precision that could only be found in German-grown vehicles. The road was empty, and the sky was darker than Bixx had ever seen. Kreet was driving and must have been plugged into his netpad, because he didn't notice her, and his fingers were tapping out a rhythm on top of the steering toggle. Toffler was passed out in the passenger's seat, her head mashed against the side window.

"Hey there," Rocket whispered, shifting to face her. His hair was pushed into a mass of red curls that spilled over the side of his headrest.

"What time is it?" Bixx asked.

"About 3."

Bixx peeked back over her seat into the van. Sanjiv was curled across the third row of seats, his jacket pulled up to his shoulders.

"Where's the Brit?" she asked. "You know, I don't even know his name."

"He's on the floor in the back, next to the equipment."

Bixx craned over her seat, but couldn't see him. She snuggled into the crook of Rocket's arm. "He gives me the creeps."

"I know what you mean.... He never says anything."

"Why does she keep him around?"

Rocket shrugged. "Insurance, I guess."

"What's insurance?"

"My dad told me it was a form of protection against anything bad, like an accident or something. You'd pay a company a lot of money just to protect you."

"Sounds like the Mob."

Rocket chuckled. "I think this was legal."

"So why does she need insurance?"

"I don't know. Some people just like to have others around.... They're paid to kiss ass, I guess."

"In Russia, we call people like that politicians." Bixx laughed. Rocket gave her a little hug.

"Can a guy get some sleep around here?" Sanjiv whispered between their headrests.

"Sorry," Bixx said.

"Where are we?"

Bixx tried to read the nav screen in the cabin's dim light. "I think we're about an hour from the casino."

The van hit a small bump, and the Brit coughed. Sanjiv's eyes widened. "I hope he doesn't wake up," he said. "I like him like this."

Bixx nodded. They all waited, but the cabin remained silent.

"I don't know why he came along," Sanjiv said. "He doesn't do crap except carry the equipment cases and fetch Toffler's iced Chai."

"You know how it is with Toffler," Rocket said. "It's not our place to question."

Sanjiv rolled his eyes. "I'm going back to sleep." He curled onto the seats and pulled his jacket over his head.

It had been more than a week since Bixx had sampled McCarris's data stream. She was certain that he was planning to erase Kortel, though it had taken a lot of convincing to get Sanjiv on board with her conclusion. He argued that the Net wasn't reliable, that studies had shown being jacked could alter your perception and change your reality. But it was Toffler who came to Bixx's defense. She said the Net was the new reality, and Sanjiv better get used to it. She cited the fact that there were hardly any human actors left anymore.... They had all been replaced with virtual ones. "Why waste your money with an untested actor," she declared, "when you could have classics like James Dean or Tirk Bradford." She said her company was in negotiations with the estate of a guy named Christopher Reeve for the rights to his likeness. Bixx didn't recognize the name, but Toffler assured her that he was pure money.

What really irked Bixx was that Toffler had taken five days just to get her act together. Something about her gear being so "on the edge" that Canadian customs didn't know what to do with it. Regardless, all Bixx knew was that more than a week had passed, and Kortel could be dead by now. Toffler said that for the sake of her career, he damn well better not be.

Another pothole pitched the rental, and Toffler snorted awake. She stretched and looked into the van, her Net glasses hanging around her neck.

"Morning," Rocket offered.

Toffler grinned and turned to Kreet. "Where are we?" she asked. He didn't acknowledge her, his fingers still drumming. She slapped his shoulder, Kreet jumped, and the van swerved slightly, throwing Bixx into Rocket's chest.

"What?" Kreet said loudly, obviously jamming to some kind of music.

Toffler reached over and clicked his netpad off. "I asked, 'Where are we?'"

Kreet referenced the nav screen. "Fifty-eight minutes from Deuces Wild." He pointed at it, as if to say, "Couldn't you have read that?"

Toffler stretched. "Right, I can get some more sleep." She propped her legs onto the dash, folded her arms and settled against the window.

The hum of the road filled the van.

"Oh, and by the way," Toffler said through a yawn, "his name is Marcus Nichols. And for the record, I pay him handsomely to kiss my ass."

~

"Are you sure this is where we can find him?" Kreet asked.

Bixx couldn't take her eyes off the woman's bright pink lips. They seemed plastic, almost stuck on like some terrible clown accessory. At least they matched the woman's hair, and there was something comforting about that.

The pink lips parted in a smile. "As far as I know, that's his address."

Bixx peered over Kreet's shoulder and read the coordinates on his netpad. She couldn't tell where the location was.

"Thank you," Toffler said.

"No problem. Since each of you bought service, it's the least I could do. Besides, I know Tarris, and he wouldn't mind the company. So, are you really going to do a documentary on him?" Bixx thought she caught a bit of Cockney in the woman's accent.

"That's correct. Look for it on the *Where Are They Now?* Channel."

The pink lips whistled. "Tarris is going to be so excited." She slipped her credit chip into her clutch. "Tootles," she said with a wave, and headed toward the vidslot room of Deuces.

"That was too easy," Kreet said. He tossed his credit phone into a trash can. Everyone else followed.

~

Kreet handed the field optics back to Toffler. "That's unbelievable," he said. Toffler passed them to Nichols. "What's your assessment?"

Nichols scanned Tarris's compound. "It's an old Boeing, all right. A 747. I'll bet they disassembled it and 'coptered it out here." He swept the length of the compound again, stopping once to zoom in. "Probably bought it on the black net. There's a junkyard for planes like this, probably somewhere out here. And I'd lay down a quid that it's wired to the gills." He handed the glasses back.

Bixx had never been to the desert Southwest. The sun was rising, and the air was crisp with a freshness she hadn't smelled since she and Rocket went to upstate New York to "decompress," as he called it. All she did was scratch herself raw from mosquito bites. Rocket had assured her New Mexico didn't have mosquitoes, but Bixx could swear she felt something biting her. She slapped her neck and checked for a welt. Nichols gave her a sideways glance.

"What do we do now?" Sanjiv asked the group.

Nichols retrieved one of Toffler's silver cases. He carefully laid it down and tapped a code across the interface panel. The case hissed and slowly opened. Inside were several devices nestled in green foam that looked like the putty Bixx had played with as a child. Nichols removed one of them, and the space it left started to fill back in, as if the foam were healing itself. With a sucking sound, the wound closed. Bixx was a techie and knew a lot about certain hardware, but the instrument Nichols held in front of him didn't look like any conventional scanner she'd ever seen.

"This Tarris Finn is a tricky little bugger," he said. "He's got this place tighter than my mum's purse." He scanned to his right and stopped. "What's this?" He clicked a button. "Smile everyone, we're being watched."

"Can you tell by who?" Toffler asked.

Nichols clicked again. "Hard to say, love. I can't get a fix on the point of origin. But I can say there's nobody home, if that helps."

"The place is empty?"

"Roger that. By the looks of it, I'd say they've been gone a long time.... More than a month probably."

"Damn it," Toffler said under her breath.

"What's the plan, boss?" Kreet asked.

Toffler shot him a look. "Since they know we're here, we wait. They'll come to us."

"We're not going to have to wait long," Rocket said, his attention focused behind them.

Bixx turned and saw two large men walking toward them through the scrub sage. Each held a military style Light-Force rifle, the butts tucked tightly into their armpits and the muzzles pointed down. One wore a bandanna and the other a wide-brimmed hat that was pinned to one side of the crown.

Nichols stepped toward the case, and the bandanna wearer dropped to one knee and raised his Light-Force. The other held his ground. Nichols stepped back, and the men resumed walking.

"I thought you said the place was empty," Toffler said to Nichols out of the side of her mouth.

"They must be wearing sig displacers or something. I can't be expected to read *everything*."

The men walked to within 20 feet and stopped. They stood silently. A hawk screeched in the distance, and a cold chill ran through Bixx. Finally, Wide Brim stepped forward. "This is private property," he said.

"Yes, we know," Toffler replied. She took a step, and Bandanna raised his weapon. "Easy there," she said. "We just want to talk with Mr. Finn."

"Why?"

"We're here to do a documentary on him. My name is Megan Toffler. I'm with SecondSight Studios. This is my crew."

"We weren't told about this," said Bandanna.

Toffler smiled. "Often, celebrities like Mr. Finn keep certain things from their staff. In this case, our pre-pro team tried on several occasions to confirm our arrival date with Mr. Finn. But, with all our busy schedules and flight arrangements, you know, things can fall through the cracks. I'm terribly sorry you weren't informed. Is Mr. Finn available? We'd be more than happy to wait."

The two men stood silently, and it occurred to Bixx that they were probably jacked and receiving instructions from whomever Nichols had spied watching them. A hawk screeched again, closer this time.

Wide Brim looked around, then nodded to himself. "Right," he said into the air. His attention came back to the group. "Mr. Finn knows all about the documentary and would be more than happy to grant you time. Please follow us back to your vehicle." Both men shouldered their Light-Forces and began walking in the direction of the rental.

Toffler and Kreet exchanged tentative glances before falling into line behind the two men. Nichols returned the scanner to the case, and the foam ate it like a sandwich. He gathered the case under his arm and trotted off to catch up with Toffler.

Sanjiv came up between Bixx and Rocket. "What documentary?" he asked.

"Toffler's just bullshitting to get us to Kortel," Rocket said.

"It doesn't make sense."

"What doesn't make sense?"

"Those guys...with the Light-Forces. Why does Finn need bodyguards?"

Bixx had been wondering the same thing. Something didn't feel right. If this was Finn's compound, why were these guys leading them back to the rental? "Yeah," she said, "something's wrong here. Why does he need them?"

"Insurance," Rocket replied, and gave her a little grin.

~

It had been over an hour since they had left Tarris's compound. The rental's nav put them somewhere northeast of Chaco Canyon, but exactly where was up for grabs. The two men drove an old-fashioned gas-guzzler called a Bronco LX. The LX Bixx got, but what the hell was a Bronco? For the last 30 minutes, they had been traveling a dirt road, and the rental's filter system was having a tough time with their dust. Bixx was beginning to taste it herself.

"Is anybody else getting a little nervous?" Sanjiv asked.

Toffler was on her Net glasses, "dealing" with New York. Kreet was jamming and driving, and Nichols was sleeping again.

"Not yet," Rocket said.

"I don't know enough to be nervous," Bixx said.

"Well, I don't like this," Sanjiv declared and angrily folded his arms.

The Bronco suddenly veered into a field filled with cactus and small rocks. Bixx could hear the rental's leveling system try to compensate for the terrain.

"Kreet, can you fix this?" Toffler asked as she bounced in her seat. "I'm in the middle of a conference call."

Kreet just looked at her and gunned it. The rental violently jerked, throwing Sanjiv against the back of his seat and sending Nichols into the equipment cases.

Bixx looked out the windshield and saw the back of the Bronco coming up fast through the dust. She punched Kreet's shoulder. "Look out!"

Kreet engaged the brakes, and everyone flew forward. The rental stopped inches from the Bronco's bumper. "The faster you get through it, the quicker it's over," he said as he switched off the rental's organics.

Sanjiv said earlier that New Mexico was called the Land of Enchantment, which, right now, Bixx was finding hard to believe. She watched the two men climb out of the Bronco, their Light-Forces glistening in the midday sun.

"Okay," Kreet said, "this is getting a little weird."

Sanjiv came up to Bixx's ear. "Now do you know enough to be nervous?"

Bixx nodded.

"Where are we?" Toffler asked.

"In the middle of nowhere with two rowdies with Light-Forces," Nichols replied.

Bixx flashed on a vintage movie about World War II, where German soldiers had marched Russians into a field and shot them. She tucked her knees against her chest and watched Bandanna approach Kreet's window. He tapped it with the muzzle of the Light-Force.

"We'll be walking the rest of the way," he said while the window slipped into the door. "Just take what you think is essential." He abruptly walked away.

"Marcus?" Toffler asked.

"Yes, love."

"If you had to, could you take these two out?"

"With my enhancements, I'm fast, but not faster than a Light-Force."

"Great," Sanjiv blurted.

"Come on," Kreet said. "We might as well gear up. What choice do we have?"

Bixx and Rocket stuffed what they would need into Rocket's backpack. Sanjiv, Toffler and Kreet had small duffle bags, but Nichols didn't have anything. He just carried the equipment. Maybe his stuff was buried somewhere inside the silver cases, Bixx figured, down in that living goo with all the tech gear.

They followed the men through a thicket of white-barked trees whose leaves fluttered delicately in the breeze. When they came to the edge of a drop-off, Bixx remarked that it was a tall hill. Sanjiv informed her that it was actually called an arroyo. Bixx asked if everything in the Southwest had more than one name. He looked at her like she was crazy.

They continued along a narrow path that angled down the side of a mesa to a dry riverbed. The sun was beginning to heat the landscape, and as they trudged across the dry clay, Bixx couldn't decide which was more obnoxious: the mosquitoes of up-state New York or the dust of New Mexico. They followed the riverbed for about a mile. As they rounded a bend, buildings began to appear, followed by a whole complex of old wooden-framed structures, complete with a high barbed wire fence.

"What the hell is this?" Toffler asked.

Nichols put his hand to his forehead to block the sun. "Looks like a military installation." He studied it more. "From the Old War, if I had to guess."

They approached a large gate guarded by more men brandishing Light-Forces. Wide Brim made a gesture, and the gate started to open.

"Stay together," he said to the group.

Bandanna exchanged nods with him and walked off.

They were led through a maze of tall shipping containers just like the ones Bixx's dad had off-loaded on the docks of St. Petersburg. No one said anything. Sanjiv kept glancing over his shoulder.

They followed Wide Brim across what looked like the main street of the installation and into one of the old buildings. Just inside was a lobby, of sorts, and a young boy seated behind a metal table. He also wore a bandanna. Bixx was beginning to suspect it was some kind of uniform. The kid snapped to attention. Wide Brim waved him off, as if it were embarrassing.

"Which room, Billy?" he asked.

"Twelve, Mr. Aarons."

"You can all drop your gear," Aarons announced. "It'll be secure here. Right, Billy?"

"Yes *sir*!"

Aarons laughed under his breath and motioned for them to follow.

Near the end of a long, dim hallway was a frosted glass door marked with a black 12 trimmed in gold. Aarons unlocked the door with an old-fashioned key and held it open for them.

As Bixx filed past, she brushed against Aarons. Something quivered under his shirt. Bioarmor.

The room had a metal table of the same style as the one the kid had sat behind, along with a several metal chairs with green vinyl seats. A light bulb attached to a wire hung above the table. Bixx stared. She hadn't seen a *glass* bulb on a wire since Russia.

"Wait here. Mr. Finn will be right with you." Aarons forced a grin and closed the door as he left.

"So far, so good," Toffler said, walking around the table.

"Are you kidding?" Sanjiv declared. "We're in the middle of who knows where, and you think everything is *good*. Where are we, and why do these guys have weapons?" He stormed around the table and got in Toffler's face. "What's this crap about a documentary on Finn? If you've gotten us into trouble–" Suddenly, Sanjiv's body went rigid. He hacked out the word "Shit," twisted around and slid into Nichols's outstretched hands.

Nichols pulled him close and smiled hideously. "Listen, mate. You're in the big show now. You gotta tighten up." On the word "up," he telekinetically raised Sanjiv into the air until his head disappeared into the rafters of the ceiling.

Toffler sighed. "Marcus, for the love of *God*, put him down."

"Yeah, Marcus, put him down," a voice said behind all of them.

Bixx turned to find Jonathan Kortel standing in the doorway. The light from the bulb cast him in sharp contrast. He looked bigger than Bixx remembered, though it might have been merely the shadows.

Nichols eyed him, still holding Sanjiv aloft.

Kortel's demeanor hardened. He stepped into the room and pointed at Sanjiv. "He's a friend of mine, Marcus. Put him down now." There was an inflection in Kortel's voice that cut through the room.

Nichols smiled coolly, and Sanjiv slowly lowered to the floor. "No harm done," he said, straightening out the wrinkles he'd made in Sanjiv's shirt. "Good as new."

Sanjiv adjusted his collar and threw back his shoulders. He glared at Nichols and walked over to Rocket's side.

A woman in a lab coat stepped into the room, followed by an older gentleman with a close-cropped beard. Then a rough character appeared. His hair was tousled, and he had a slight hunch. There was a whirring sound like tiny servos, and Bixx figured this was Tarris Finn. If she didn't know so much about him, she would have passed him off as just another of Aarons's men.

Toffler strutted around the table, and Bixx suddenly noticed the suit she had been wearing had changed style. She was still dressed in a professional manner, but it was sexier somehow. Her skirt was a little shorter, and her coat seemed to fit more tightly around her waist. Even her face looked slimmer, which is when Bixx noticed that her hair had changed style. It was now darker, shorter and curled delicately under one side of her jaw. She walked over to Kortel and stuck out her hand.

"Mr. Kortel, Megan Toffler, with SecondSight Studios."

Kortel regarded her hand. "Normally I'd accept your handshake, Ms. Toffler. But right now, given my conditioning, that could be a little dangerous."

Toffler looked at her hand like it was somehow offended. She cleared her throat. "On behalf of SecondSight Studios—"

"Pardon me, will you?" Kortel walked over to Sanjiv. "Are you okay?"

Sanjiv nodded, surprised. "I am, thank you."

Kortel scanned Rocket and Kreet before his attention landed on Bixx.

She smiled.

"It's good to see you all," Kortel said. "Come on, have a seat and tell me all about this vid you want to make. I assume it has something to do with your plan, Kreet, to bring us out?" Kortel glanced knowingly at the bearded guy.

"It does," Kreet said, taking a chair.

Bixx and the others sat. Nichols remained standing, though he had stepped back from the light that surrounded the table. This attracted Kortel's attention for a second. Tarris and the bearded man sat on either side of Kortel, but the lab woman stood behind him. This gave the appearance that she was protecting him, which seemed silly, considering his power.

"Our project has evolved since we last spoke," Kreet said. "I've had the fortune to become part of Ms. Toffler's business unit. Her group adds a certain dimension to the original concept."

"What is it that you add, exactly?" the bearded man asked. He had an accent that Bixx couldn't place.

"Sorry, everyone," Kortel said. "This is Armando Zvara."

"Whoa," Rocket said under his breath.

Bixx knew the legend, but never imagined she would actually meet the man in person.

"And this is Tarris Finn," Kortel said.

Tarris smiled and saluted with two fingers.

"And this lady behind me, you may have heard of.... This is Dr. Erin Richter."

"*The* Erin Richter?" Sanjiv asked.

Richter smiled. "In the flesh."

Bixx couldn't believe who she was looking at. Between Zvara and Kortel alone, there was more telekinetic power than most Agencies...at least according to the rumors. And Richter practically rewrote the book on gravitational theory.

Kortel gestured. "This is Bixx, Sanjiv, Rocket and Kreet. These folks helped me once." He glanced at Bixx. "Okay," he said, settling into his seat. "Armando had a question."

"What I add," Toffler said, standing, "is the global reach a concept like this requires in order to be successful. Here, let me show you what I mean." She produced another of those thin glass wafers, but this one was twice as big as her personal card, and it glowed bright orange in the harsh light. She placed it in the center of the table. "What I propose is a media event that would rival anything to date." At the word "date," a holographic presentation appeared. It took up most of the tabletop, and Bixx got a sense that from any angle, it would appear as if it were playing strictly for you. It quickly advanced through a montage of SecondSight history, then sequenced into a four-part plan for revealing the Tel culture, complete with projections about lifestyle issues and potential product-centric endorsement opportunities. It even contained a breakdown of which religions would be the most accepting of the Tels. Much of it went over Bixx's head, but Kortel studied it intently, only looking away occasionally to eye Nichols. When it ended, Toffler pocketed the card. The room grew quiet, and Bixx didn't know whether to clap or not.

Kortel chuckled to himself. "Ms. Toffler," he said, rubbing his forehead, "do you really make a living with this kind of stuff?"

"I have, Mr. Kortel, for over 20 years."

"I remember the Disneyverse opening."

"Most people do."

Kortel looked at Zvara and Tarris. They weren't smiling, which set Bixx on edge. She couldn't read Richter's reaction because her face was hidden in shadow. Toffler was still standing with her arms folded.

Kortel's expression became serious. "What you're proposing is very impressive." He leaned back in his chair and drummed the table with his fingers. "Unfortunately, something has come up that might, um, preempt this. I'll let Dr. Richter spell it out for you."

Richter stepped out from behind Kortel and took the only empty seat left. She motioned for Toffler to sit, which she did, reluctantly.

Richter's demeanor was grave, like she was about to tell them they had Netox or worse. "Do you all know what a solar flare is?" she asked.

Bixx looked at Rocket, then exchanged questioning glances with Kreet and Sanjiv. They all nodded.

"Good, then what I'm about to tell you shouldn't be that hard to understand." For the next 20 minutes, Bixx listened as Richter explained the deadly mechanics of a Tsunami Coronal Ejection. At one point, when she was describing what would happen to the earth's magnetosphere, Rocket gathered Bixx's hand into his under the table. She got a little lost with all the acronyms, but by the time Richter had finished, Bixx grasped the gist of the situation: Earth, in the very near future, was basically screwed.

A collective numbness settled over the table. Bixx could feel Rocket's hand shaking and saw in his face a fear she had never before seen. Sanjiv looked like he was about to cry, and Kreet leaned on the table with his head in his hands, staring at Richter. Toffler, on the other hand, didn't seem fazed by the pronouncement. In fact, she had an odd little smile on her face, as if this were the best news she had gotten all year.

Curtains. 17

KORTEL watched Richter explain the inevitable to Kreet and the group. Toffler was definitely the only professional in the group, but it was Marcus who gripped his attention. Even before Kortel had entered the room, the man's presence passed through him like an acid – burning and corrosive. And the displacement Marcus emitted lacked the integrity Kortel usually felt from other Tels. It was almost like the guy was bluffing his telekinetics, which didn't make sense. Either you had it or you didn't.

Richter started in on the results of the Tsunami Ejection on the magnetosphere, and Kortel caught Bixx flinching, like something had touched her under the table. He liked Bixx. She was smart, intuitive and, like him, an orphan. She looked thinner than the last time he had seen her, which wasn't good. It wasn't that she looked sickly; wiry was the word that came to mind. There was no doubting her toughness, either. Kortel had seen it displayed before and was amazed that so much power could come out of such a small body.

A spike of pain suddenly forged itself into Kortel's brain. With all the exercises he had been put through during the last month, headaches had become a regular feature. He shrugged it off.

Richter concluded her lecture on the end of the world, and Kortel waited for reactions. Both Rocket and Kreet appeared stunned, and Sanjiv was shaking his head. Bixx didn't show much of a reaction; she just kept looking from Richter to her boyfriend. It was the producer Kortel couldn't figure. She had a look on her face like she had just won a Peabody.

The pain struck again, this time deeper and more concentrated. Kortel fought the urge to wince. He grabbed his head. "Shit," he said, abandoning any manners.

Richter turned, alarmed. "Jonathan?"

"I told you," Tarris said to Zvara. "It's those damn APT tests."

The pain crashed through Kortel's nervous system. He shuddered from its intensity.

Richter scooted closer, her chair scraping across the old concrete. "Come on," she said in a low voice, "you're done here."

"I'm okay."

"The hell you are. I'm getting you into the med bay right now." Richter had the look she used when she wanted to ramp up the serious factor. She hung on every word now as if Kortel's life depended on it.

"Come on, doc."

More of the look.

Kortel studied Richter. She wasn't backing off. "Sure," he agreed, "let's go."

Toffler cleared her throat. "Mr. Kortel…"

"Ms. Toffler," Zvara said, standing, "Mr. Aarons will show you and your friends to your rooms."

Aarons had suddenly appeared in the doorway.

Kortel stood, his limbs feeling cold and disconnected. He leaned onto the table.

"Can you walk?" Richter asked, taking his arm.

Kortel nodded, but he knew the next few steps would be a bitch.

"Do you need any help?" Bixx asked.

The question, pure and genuine, hit home with Kortel. He turned, accepting Richter's support a little too much. Her fingers dug into his bicep.

"Not right now," he said, straightening. "But we will."

~

"You're pushing Jonathan too hard with the APT tests," Richter said.

Shoalburg was studying the med screen that hung above Kortel's head. It was angled such that Kortel couldn't read what was being displayed; he could only watch Shoalburg's eyes as they darted back and forth. The technology within them could process light a hundred times faster than organic eyes and feed it to the biochips inside his head. Only God knew what their processing power was. The movement of those eyes was beginning to make Kortel dizzy.

Shoalburg pointed at the screen. "This colored mass isn't the result of the APT tests…or anything else we're doing."

This clearly hit Richter hard. She folded her arms against her chest.

Kortel sat up and swung around to see what Shoalburg was referencing. An enhanced holoimage of his brain projected off the screen's surface. A tiny blue spot nestled among the textured pink layers of his neocortex. At the Agency, Kortel had taken several advanced classes on the brain and could read a medgram about as well as a doctor. Even though he didn't know what the spot was, he sensed that it wasn't good. "I see my tech's grown."

Shoalburg glanced at the screen, his eyes doing their dancing thing. "Yes, but not in the area of this mass."

"What do you mean?" Richter asked, walking up to Shoalburg's side. Her attention remained fixed on the screen.

The holoimage shifted to an extreme close-up of the mass while technical data ran down the left side. The streaming stopped, and a section of data enlarged. It moved through the close-up and became the center of focus.

"These numbers verify your tech is growing at a substantial rate everywhere except the area adjoining this mass," Shoalburg said.

"Is it slowing the tech's growth or stopping it?" Kortel asked.

"I think it's stopping it, but it looks like the tech just shifts around and continues developing."

"What's causing it?" Richter asked.

Shoalburg shrugged. "I don't know yet. It just showed up a day ago, and I've only had a couple of hours to analyze it. At first, I thought it was harmless – the result of the tech's growth.... You know, like the trail a snail leaves. But the data doesn't support that."

"What does it support?" Kortel asked.

The close-up shifted along with the highlighted data, and a new stream began to cascade down the screen. Then another data box detached and enlarged.

"The mass might be more like a by-product of the tech," Shoalburg said.

"What do you mean by a 'by-product'?" Richter asked.

"He means crap," Kortel said.

Richter looked from Kortel to Shoalburg. "You're kidding, right?"

"No," Shoalburg said, "Jonny's correct. The medical biotech used today is basically alive, though engineered not to create waste. But the tech in Jonny's head is radical, and I have no idea how it was engineered."

"Kind of makes you rethink the phrase 'shit-for-brains,'" Kortel said.

Either Richter and Shoalburg didn't get the humor, or the mass was more serious than Kortel thought. They continued studying the data and began talking to each other, their techno-speak far over Kortel's head.

"You want to let me in on the conversation?" he asked after another round of acronyms and nods.

Shoalburg started to speak, but Richter stopped him.

"I'm sorry," she said, "that was rude of us."

"That's okay," Kortel said. "Just tell me what you think it is."

"I need to study it more," Shoalburg said. "But the preliminary data shows that it could be doing a couple of different–"

"It could be harmless," Richter blurted.

"Possibly," Shoalburg said. "But not if this data is correct."

Kortel folded his arms, frustrated. "Get to the point."

Shoalburg motioned for him to look at the screen.

Kortel complied, and a chill shot down his spine. The blue spot was bigger. "Damn it," he said to himself.

"Now don't get all crazy about this," Shoalburg said. "It might be something that gets absorbed by your body."

"But that's not what the data suggests, *right*?"

The thing about Shoalburg's eyes was that they didn't reveal what he was thinking. Even though they were exceptionally realistic, they were not what Tarris's mother called windows to the soul. Kortel was looking into them now, trying to gauge how screwed his situation really was.

Shoalburg hesitated. "It's too early to say…. I need to run some tests to be certain."

"Carter, just get to the damn point!"

Suddenly the med screen exploded, spraying plastics and electric colored organics throughout the med bay. Shoalburg went to the floor covering his head, and Richter ducked behind the bay's scanner station.

A fine red mist dissipated around Kortel, as hot orange biocables quivered from the end of the screen's ruptured armature.

"Easy, Jonny," Shoalburg said, picking tiny elements of the screen out of his hair. Some of the holojection fragments still carried the complete image of Kortel's brain, creating a disturbing effect that resembled an installation Kortel had once seen in a Chicago gallery.

Richter slowly stood, brushing a bright green dust from her shoulders. She shook out her hair, and Kortel watched a dozen tiny holojections of his neocortex flutter gently to the floor.

"Sorry," he said.

Richter regarded him as a mother would a mischievous child. "We're going to work on that," she said, arranging her hair into a makeshift ponytail. She turned to Shoalburg. "What were you about to say before Jonathan had his little hissy fit?"

Shoalburg hesitated again, and Kortel seriously considered letting go of his anger and seeing what else might blow up. "*Carter…*"

"I really need to study the mass further, so I can rule out something."

"What's that?"

Shoalburg leveled his attention on Kortel, his eyes somehow revealing the graveness of the situation. "I think this new substance isn't stopping the tech," he said. "It's replacing it."

~

"Man, I didn't sneak this Oban in just for you to stare at," Tarris said. He propped his feet on the coffee table and settled back against the couch. "Time to go off-line," he declared, and clicked something on his lower back. The organics in his leg's servos hissed into their dormant setting. "Hell, yeah. That's what I'm talkin' about." He took a sip of his drink.

Kortel looked into his glass of Scotch wondering about the mass and what it might do. Would it replace the biotech and slowly take over his central nervous system? Maybe it would alter his DNA, and one morning he would wake to find he was something different. Shoalburg thought that it was the next phase of his tech and that he had never seen anything like it, which was pretty unnerving. Just as Kortel was wrapping his brain around his new responsibility for saving the world, now he had to deal with something that had the father of nanogenetics scratching his head. He looked into his drink again and knocked it back in one continuous gulp.

"Easy there." Tarris said.

"What do you think?" Kortel asked, staring into his empty glass.

"About what?"

"All this, you know...shit."

"You mean the stuff in your head?"

"No, I'm talking about the Tsunami Ejection, Kreet's plan, St. John...all of it. What the hell's going on?"

Tarris took another sip. "If you ask me, I think most of it is a bunch of bullshit."

Kortel grabbed the flask of Scotch off the table and poured himself another. "I don't think a cataclysmic solar flare is bullshit," he said, easing back against the bed's headboard.

"Richter's own calculations are spotty at best," Tarris said. "Is it possible? Sure. But there're too many factors that have to line up exactly right to produce the planet-destroying flare she's predicting. Now, damaging the atmosphere? Yeah, maybe. I'll give her that. But total annihilation? Puh-leez."

"And what about Kreet's plan?"

Tarris laughed. "Do you really think the other Tel Agencies are going to go along with it? Come on—" He waved it off. "There's no way in hell."

"Zvara's pretty powerful. He can wield a lot of influence."

"Zvara is old news. Besides, why would they?"

Kortel had to admit, Tarris was probably right. There wasn't really anything to gain from their kind going public, except a lot of grief. He took a long drink of his Scotch, and his thoughts went back to the new growth in his head.

"You think Shoalburg's right about this shit in my head?" he asked.

Tarris shrugged. "Take a wait and see. Carter's a smart guy; he'll figure it out." He pulled his now-inanimate legs off the table and propped them where he could lean on them. "You know what I think you should be worried about?" he said, swirling the Scotch in his glass.

"Let me guess...the price of biochip futures?"

Tarris grinned for a second before his demeanor tightened. "I'd be worried about this St. John character. You don't piss off the Mob and live to brag about it. Especially those Pac Rim tech boys. I've dealt a little with those sons of bitches. You don't say no to them. Mark my words – St. John will be back, and he won't be polite."

"He wasn't polite the last time we saw him."

"I know. That's why next time, we'll open a little can of good ol' fashioned whoop-ass on him." Tarris patted a small chrome briefcase next to his feet.

Kortel eyed it with suspicion. "I don't even want to know what's in there," he said.

Tarris laughed. "Just a little new-tech I've been working on, in case St. John or any other bastard wants to jack with you."

Kortel climbed off the bed and stretched. "I think I'm going to crash."

Tarris engaged the tech in his legs and grabbed the case. "Okay then," he said, standing.

Kortel hugged Tarris and could feel the tiny strips of processing packs that lined the sides of his spine. They were warm to the touch, and one of the packs moved under his fingers. He led Tarris to the door. "Thanks for the drink," he said. "And for listening."

"I'll always be there for you, Jonny.... You know that."

Tarris left, and Kortel locked the door.

Silly, he thought, securing a door that any Level 4 could rip apart with the simplest thought. He let the old-fashioned key slide from his fingers onto the nightstand. Its polished brass surface caught the light and reflected into his eye. Sitting on the bed, he wondered how the person who made the key had found the machine to make it. He pictured one of Aarons's men researching the Net and finding it in some forgotten corner of the country. He clicked his boots into their off setting and watched as they unwrapped from his feet like a flower in a time-lapse sequence. BioBoots were one of the few luxuries Kortel afforded himself. He settled back onto the bed and punched his pillow into the perfect shape. He didn't bother with the covers, because the base was vintage, right down to the lack of HVAC in any of the buildings. The screened window helped a little, but there was no wind to bring the cool New Mexico night air into the room.

Sleep was slow to come, and the distant howling of a coyote didn't help matters any. He tried to empty his mind, but Tarris's words kept cycling through his head.

What the hell, he thought through an especially big yawn. *Whatever happens,s happens.* He nestled his head into a soft groove in the pillow and let the world slip away.

Something cold at the side of his neck brought Kortel out of his dream. He had been watching Tamara as she worked in the gallery, wondering if she would notice him, but her face had been replaced by the room's darkness. The moon was up, back-lighting the sheer curtains that hung motionless on either side of the window. He tried to focus on them, but all he could see was milky forms.

"Don't even think about phasing," a voice whispered into his ear. It had an accent. Familiar.

British.

The coldness at the side of his neck was like ice now.

"Okay," Kortel replied.

The ice turned into a sharp pain, needlelike and deep.

"Time to go."

"Where?" Kortel managed, as whatever had been injected began its duties. He could feel it coursing through his system. His fingers were getting numb.

A small laugh. "Hell," the voice said, and the curtains blurred away.

Surprised. 18

SOMETHING brought Bixx out of her sleep. It usually didn't take much: a drop in temperature, a faint noise, even the slightest air movement. Ever since the orphanage, her sleep pattern had been altered. When she was a little girl, her parents had been proud that she could sleep through an entire night. Her mother used say "Our little Olga, such a young woman!" But at the orphanage, all that changed. Sleeping in a room filled with more than 100 children meant getting a full night's sleep was rare, at best. During her early years, she often woke in the middle of the night screaming for her mother and father. And when she grew older, she could hear the *moy angelochek* – little angels – crying out just as she had. Their high-pitched wails haunted her dreams. The orphanage never had enough "adult" beds or sheets, and Bixx's toes were always numb from pressing against the footboard's cold iron.

"I'm sorry; did I wake you?" It was Rocket's voice, cutting through the fog of her past.

"No," she said, sitting up, "not really." She began rubbing her toes.

"Dreaming?" he asked. His tall, blurred form stood by the window. Bixx's eyes adjusted to the dark, and she saw he was smiling.

"Yeah," she said, the word sticking in her throat.

"The orphanage?" The smile was gone.

Bixx couldn't answer.

Rocket left the window and came to the bed, a dark figure settling next to her. "It's okay," he whispered. "You're not there anymore." His fingers tenderly traced the line of her jaw.

"I know." A tear had formed at the edge of Bixx's eye. She could feel it building on the lip of her lashes. Usually she would wipe it and the pain away. But tonight, she fought the instinct and let it fall.

"Oh, baby." Rocket caught the tear against her cheek with his fingers. He leaned in and kissed her forehead. "You have nothing to be sorry about."

"Why are you up?" Bixx asked, changing the subject.

"I was hot. I went to open the window and ended up watching them take out the trash."

Bixx laughed a little. "Was it entertaining?"

Rocket clicked the light on his watch, casting his face and hair in a cerulean hue. "Best I could find at 3 in the morning."

There was a rustle of movement from outside. Bixx and Rocket went to the window and looked down into the street.

"See what I mean?" he said, gesturing.

"I wonder why they're doing it in the middle of the night?" Bixx watched a guard maneuver a hoverlift past the front gate to the back of a small transport truck. It was carrying a cargo container, the kind that filled the bellies of commuter jump jets. As the guard angled it onto the truck's lift, its metal surface caught the moonlight and sparked a reflection.

"Probably 'cause it's cooler at night," Rocket said.

The guard leaned on the container to rest as the lift rose to the level of the truck's bed.

"Kind of big for trash, don't you think?" Bixx asked.

"Not really," Rocket said. "The recycle containers we had at *Clone World* were about that size, and that place was 10 times bigger than this base."

"You worked at Clone World?"

"Yeah. When I was a kid, before they discovered me. I was a stocker, working hoverlifts." Rocket pointed out the window. "Bigger than that one. The kind you sit in."

Bixx giggled.

"What?" Rocket asked.

"I can't see you driving one of those. How old were you?"

"Sixteen."

"How'd you get around the labor laws?"

"My dad had a friend who got me the job."

"Ah-huh, sure...a *friend*."

"Shut up." Rocket playfully dragged Bixx from the window, and they fell onto the bed stifling their laughs. "You sure went to bed early," he said.

"I was really tired," Bixx replied. "Where'd the others end up?"

"Down the hall. They gave Toffler and her boy toy separate rooms, and put Sanjiv and Kreet in one room."

"Oh, God," Bixx said. "That's a big mistake."

"No shit. I bet Sanjiv doesn't survive the night. Kreet'll talk his ear off."

"They won't fight, will they?"

"Nah," Rocket said. "If Sanjiv gets pissed enough, he'll just knock his ass out."

"He's gotten that powerful?"

"I think so. He's moving up in level pretty quickly. It's getting harder to beat him in the grav tests."

"I'll make a note of that," Bixx said and rolled over onto her side. Rocket snuggled next to her, and they quickly assumed spooning positions. "Good night," she said.

Rocket didn't answer, but Bixx could feel him getting excited against her lower back.

"I'm not tired," Rocket whispered, then ran his tongue delicately down the side of her neck, ending with a soft kiss at the top of her shoulder.

"*Really.*"

Rocket laughed and pressed himself against her. "What was your first clue?"

Bixx rolled over and nestled into his arms. Rocket was rarely subtle about wanting to make love, but compared to her last boyfriend, he was downright shy.

"Hey, you," Rocket said tenderly. His look had an edge of little boy, as if he were surprised at how aroused he was. But his expression shifted, and Bixx sensed a seriousness filling him. He gathered her tightly into his arms.

"Tell me," she whispered. "What are you thinking?"

Rocket hesitated, his eyes searching her face. "How much I love you," he replied, and pulled her close.

A strange warmth wrapped around Bixx's heart, and another tear formed at the corner of her eye.

"I…I love you too," she replied.

Useless. 19

"TIME to rise and shine," the British voice said harshly into Kortel's ear. The effect was jarring.

Kortel coughed up some phlegm and spat on the floor. "What was your name again?" he asked.

"Nichols."

Kortel opened his eyes, fearing a bright welcome, but was greeted by a twilight of monochromatic shadows. A silhouetted figure stepped in front of him and knelt, his hulking form backlit by what little light there was.

"How is he?" another voice asked from somewhere deep in the room. Like Nichols, it carried a British accent, but older and with a film of tiredness overlaying it.

"Considering he's been packed in a crate for the last 12 hours, he looks pretty shipshape," Nichols said over his shoulder. Some light caught the rim of his ear, and a diamond stud winked at Kortel. Nichols stood and stepped into the folds of the blackness.

"Raise the lights to full level," the voice ordered.

The light in Kortel's immediate space brightened. The glare stung his eyes. He reached to rub them, but found his arms inoperable. They didn't feel asleep – more like puppet arms whose strings had been cut. Then he found his legs were also useless. Kortel fought the urge to panic as his eyes adjusted to the light.

"I should probably say it's good to see you again," the voice said. "But to be honest, the sight of you only brings back some very bad memories."

There was a high-pitched whirring, and Kortel thought he saw movement within the shadows. "Have we met?" he asked.

More whirring. "Oh yes." A cough, then a clearing of the throat. "Don't you remember?"

The whirring revved and two spiderlike arms emerged from the darkness, their sucker-pad feet catching the edge of Kortel's light. As they stepped, he could see the surface of their skin was a mesh composed of undulating metallic scales. A man appeared, his body integrated with a chair that was carried by four other legs – two on each side of the chair. He was older, maybe 70, his thin face expressionless. The chair seemed built of organic flex tubing, and the whole device looked like it could have crawled out of an Italian design annual. It whirred to a stop a few feet from Kortel.

"Still don't recognize me?" the man asked. His lips didn't move, yet his voice seemed to emanate from him.

Kortel's heart began to race. The whole scene felt like a twisted nightmare. "No," he said.

"Maybe I need to be closer – more in the light." The two front arms reached back and disengaged the chair with articulated fingers from inside their sucker pads. The chair and the man were brought forward, his knees stopping inches from Kortel's. "Is this better?" he asked.

Kortel tried to shake his head, but the muscles in his neck wouldn't respond. "I'm sorry," he said. "I still don't recognize you."

The man regarded Kortel with a sullen stare. "Come now, Jonathan. You should remember all the faces of the people you've killed...especially *this* one."

One of the man's eyebrows rose slightly before it sunk in. The lean face, the long nose, the thin lips. "My God," Kortel said. "Jeffrey?"

The edges of Jeffrey Trumble's lips turned up in a faint display of acknowledgement. The two front arms reversed their motion and locked the chair back into its original position. Trumble's face went back to hanging from his head.

You did quite the number on me. Trumble's disembodied voice was now inside Kortel's mind. Its tone was mournful and distant. *Clinically dead, the doctors said. But you know those chaps.... Occasionally they can be wrong.*

"How are you communicating with me?" Kortel asked.

Trumble's face remained blank. Tech to tech. *Unfortunately, I didn't retain much motor function, so normal speech is limited. But with you, I can communicate quite easily.*

"But how did you?–"

My body cooked for over a year in one of those ghastly German regeneration vats while the boys in the lab rebuilt part of my personality construct. I'd had the good sense to back myself up, but there were a few things I wanted to change. So while they worked on getting parts of my brain reconfigured, I spent my days at a spa in the south of France. A virtual purgatory, I'll admit, but it was a far cry from this wretched existence.

"How are you existing?"

Barely. I'm mostly integrated biotechnology. You, of all people, can relate to that concept. How do you like my chair? It's the latest from one of our R&D groups.

"Great if you want to scale an office tower."

It was designed for the military, but the lab boys made some modifications to accommodate my unique situation.

"Are you integrated?"

If you mean with the chair, yes. This is my life now, and I have you to thank for that.

"I recall that Takeda gave me no choice."

Cyril and I wanted nothing but the best for you. To think, I once thought of you as a son.

"I didn't need another father."

I think you did.

"Your policies killed my parents."

We let Hawaii happen to save millions of lives.

"At what cost?"

Someday you'll see that the husbandry of the world can't be left to the normals. If we did, they would eventually destroy it.

Kortel moved his eyes around the room. "I assume you're controlling me right now?"

A raucous laugh echoed inside Kortel's head. *Of course. We can't take any chances with you, Jonathan. You're way beyond us now. Tell me, has the partitioning begun?*

It took a minute for Kortel to register the question. "Do you mean the blue stuff?"

There was a pause, then a sound that resembled a laugh. *It would appear blue in a biomed scan.*

"Yeah, it has."

Right. Splendid. It took longer than we hoped, but what matters is that it's begun.

"What the hell will it do to me?" Kortel asked.

What it will do isn't important. What it will make you is.

"Okay, what will it make me?"

Another pause. *A god.*

Kortel figured if his body was off-line, maybe his mind wasn't, so he began to phase. His vision went to a swirl of color, followed by white.

"He's phasing," Nichols said from somewhere off to Kortel's right.

"Not to worry," Trumble replied, his voice suddenly outside of Kortel's head.

Kortel tried to create a grav wall around his immediate area and cut off Trumble's control.

"He's spiking," Nichols said, his voice rising.

A process that had become routine suddenly was a struggle. Kortel tried to erect a wall, but something was blocking his ability to form the field.

Jonathan, Trumble whispered from deep inside Kortel's mind, *it's useless to phase. Please, stop before you hurt yourself.*

Figuring that whatever was controlling him was being produced from Trumble's technology, Kortel brought all of his telekinetic strength forward and focused on the chair. Instantly one of its front legs began deforming. The meshing of the skin merged together and melted to the floor, exposing the technical skeleton of the arm. The skeleton then began liquefying, and the device lurched. A back leg slid forward and steadied it.

"Jesus, Mary and Joseph," Nichols said. "He's altering matter!"

Trumble laughed. "Wonderful, isn't it?"

Suddenly, a thunderous jolt of hot pain crashed through Kortel's body. It started at the base of his neck and plowed into his abdomen.

Jonathan, please. Trumble's voice beckoned like it could have been one of Kortel's own thoughts. *Fighting is useless.*

Kortel ignored the warning and concentrated as hard as he could on the chair. He felt a drop of blood leave his nose and slide over his upper lip. *It's time to waste you,* he thought.

I don't think so, Trumble replied, and the pain crashed again.

I know a way. 20

SUDDENLY, Bixx realized she was picking at a hangnail on her thumb and couldn't remember when she had started. It was a bad habit, one she had picked up at the orphanage, and Rocket always scolded her just like the nuns had. Twenty minutes earlier, Aarons had ordered her, Rocket, Sanjiv, Kreet and Toffler out of bed and marched them over to the building where they had been the day before. He didn't say why he had gotten them up so early, just that Zvara wanted to talk with them. Bixx figured it had something to do with Toffler, because she caught the brunt of Aarons's attention on the way over. Bixx couldn't make out what he had said to her, but she could tell it had upset Toffler. She had walked kind of slumped and with her head down.

Now they were all standing in the room with the one bulb. Rocket was on her right, the rest to her left. The only one from their group not present was the Brit, Marcus. Toffler looked gravely concerned, while Sanjiv just kept his attention focused on the tops of his shoes. Kreet, on the other hand, didn't seem too interested in what was going down. He just kept yawning and looking around.

Bixx glanced across the room at the stern faces of Zvara, Tarris and Richter. Tarris looked like he was about to climb over the table and kill the guy Aarons had brought in. The guy, Tony something, looked like he was about to shit in his pants.

"Go on," Aarons said. He slapped the back of Tony's head and almost knocked him out of his chair.

"It's like I said before." Tony looked from Aarons to Zvara. "It was a routine night. Totally by the book. We locked down the base and engaged the perimeter trip monitors."

"And you did not note anything unusual?" Zvara asked, his voice much deeper than the prior day.

Tony shook his head vigorously. "We had a couple of coyotes wander into Zone 4, but they just trotted through."

"Bullshit!" Tarris blurted.

Bixx flinched and drew blood from her hangnail. Rocket elbowed her, and she dropped her arms to her sides.

"Easy," Richter said, patting Tarris's shoulder. She was standing behind Zvara.

Tarris shrugged off her touch and pushed away from the table. "This is bullshit. Jonny's gone, and we don't know dick about where he is." He stood and began pacing behind Richter.

"Obviously, we have a mole," Zvara said. He motioned to Aarons. "Find this man and bring him to me. Then we will have our answer." He turned to Toffler. "And you have no idea where your assistant is?"

"No...sir," Toffler replied.

Zvara shook his head. "I assume you did a background check on this man Nichols?"

"Our HR department did. I didn't review their report."

Zvara waved the statement off. "No matter. This has been well thought out. I am sure his credentials were spotless."

The room fell into a desperate silence. Zvara rubbed the bridge of his nose.

"Sir?" Rocket said suddenly.

Zvara, Richter and Tarris looked over at once.

"Yes?" Zvara asked.

"I couldn't sleep last night, so I was looking out the window of our room, and..." Rocket hesitated.

"Go on," Zvara said, his voice gentler.

"I don't know if this means anything, but I watched this guard load what looked like recycle containers onto a truck."

"That's the week's trash pickup," Tony said. "It happens every Thursday night. It's totally routine. We contract it out to a local group."

"They think we're some kind of commune," Aarons said to Zvara. "It's the survivalist camp scenario we've been using for some time now. It's very effective in keeping the locals away."

Zvara sat up in his chair and leaned onto the table. "Did you see anything odd?" he asked.

Rocket thought for a moment.

"The containers were big," Bixx said, the words coming out almost as one.

"Yeah," Rocket said. "I used to work at Clone World, and theirs were half the size of these."

"We use the big ones to keep costs down," Tony said. He twisted to face Aarons. "That was the mandate from last month's—"

"Shut up," Aarons said and slapped the top of Tony's head again. The slight man spun back and grabbed the edge of the table.

Aarons turned his attention toward Bixx, his deep-set eyes taking her in with a kind of strange judgment. "Repeat what you just said," he ordered.

"Th-they were big."

"No! You said containers...plural, right?"

Aarons's look hardened, and Bixx froze. Her mind flashed on the headmaster of the orphanage, the night she had been caught showing off her budding telekinetic power to some of the other children. He had grabbed her by the hair and dragged her to his office. "You," he had said, slamming the door, "will not jeopardize the reputation of this institution. We've had your kind before. I know of people who will take you in.... You'll feel right at home with them."

"Hey, back off!" Rocket said to Aarons.

Aarons's attention locked onto Rocket. "Don't push me, son."

"There were three containers loaded last night," Bixx said.

Aarons's face scrunched into a question. He looked over to Zvara.

"Right," Richter said. "One for trash, one for Nichols and one for Jonathan."

"Mr. Aarons," Zvara said, his voice back to a deep timbre, "will you please bring me the man who loaded the trash last night?"

"That's Rodriguez." Tony said, his expression tightening with realization. "But he's in town seeing a...a doctor."

"Great," Tarris said, throwing his arms up. "We'll never see him again."

Zvara went back to rubbing the bridge of his nose.

~

Bixx stared into what the dining room whiteboard labeled Fiesta Casserole. It looked like something they had served at the orphanage, but darker and with green chunks of mystery vegetable that had a weird smell.

"What's a casserole?" she asked Rocket.

"Leftovers," he replied, his mouth full of the stuff. "All mixed together and given a fancy name." A little piece of the mystery vegetable landed next to Bixx's glass of tea.

"Say it," she said, "don't spit it."

"It's 'spray it,'" Rocket corrected. "Say it, don't *spray* it."

Bixx leaned into the plate and sniffed. "It looks like *kapustnyak*, but it doesn't smell like it." She picked up a larger piece of the mystery vegetable and examined it.

"It's a jalapeño," Rocket said. "They're sweet. Give it try."

Bixx took a bite and chewed. An acrid burning filled her mouth and quickly spread into every corner of her throat. The sides of her tongue then began to sting. She spit the gnawed piece of jalapeño onto her plate. Rocket laughed.

"Vhat the hell is that!" Bixx exclaimed. She grabbed her tea and took a large gulp.

"A little treat from old Mexico," Rocket said.

Bixx pushed the plate away. "Disgusting! That's worse than *kapustnyak*."

Rocket scooped another helping, and Bixx hit him in the shoulder. His spoon dropped from his hand, plopping Fiesta Casserole into his drink.

"Come on," he said, and began extracting chunks out of his tea. "I was just playing with you."

Bixx wiped her mouth and started on her salad. "I made this," she said, pointing with her fork. "I know what's in it, and there's no halapeenos."

"*Jalapeño*. It's Spanish for 'kick your ass.'"

"Vhatever."

"May I join you?" Richter asked, stepping up behind Rocket.

"Sure," he said, gesturing at the seat next to him.

Richter settled into the chair and began neatly arranging her tableware and napkin. Bixx watched as she arranged everything on her tray just as if there was a kind of mathematical logic at work. Richter finished by folding her napkin in thirds and gently placing it on her lap. She wove her long fingers together and bowed her head.

Bixx had never found a place for religion in her life and was always curious about people who practiced their faith openly. Rocket kicked her under the table and mouthed, *You're staring*.

Richter had ordered the chicken and rice, which Bixx eyed with envy. She cut the breast into perfect cubes, then used them to plow the rice onto her fork. She demurely chewed each bite with a determination Bixx had never before seen. It was like Richter's life depended on her ability to process the food before ingesting. The whole ritual had Bixx fascinated. Rocket kicked her in the shin.

As everyone continued to eat in silence, Bixx tried to watch Richter. Rocket caught her and raised a threatening eyebrow.

More silence.

"Do you pray often?" Bixx asked, finally.

Rocket slammed his fork down. "I'm sorry, doctor, Bixx is a little—"

"It's okay." Richter addressed Bixx directly. "I usually don't pray before a meal. But lately I have been," she said as if the realization had just hit her. She wiped her mouth and refolded her napkin.

"Why?" Bixx asked.

The question seemed to stump Richter for a second, but then she smiled. "It comforts me."

"How?"

Richter placed her fork next to her plate. "There are a lot of things I can control in this world," she said, folding her hands like she was going to pray again. "For everything else, I turn to God."

"But you put that food on that plate, not him...or her," Bixx said.

"God gave me the brain and the ability to create a life that brings food to my table." She gestured at her plate. "So, in a way, He has put the food there."

Religion had always been such an abstract concept to Bixx, but Richter's analogy had a certain logic that made sense to her.

"What about our telekinetics?" Rocket asked. "Is that God-given, or is it just a mutation...part of some evolutionary process?"

"Many scientists would probably say it's a mutation," Richter said. "I like to think of it as a gift."

"From God?" Bixx asked.

Richter nodded. "Yes...from God."

"Stuff I can't control," Bixx said, more to herself than Rocket or Richter.

"Do you pray?" Richter asked.

The question caught Bixx by surprise. "I, ah...don't know."

"What did you do before you went to bed at night, as a little girl?"

"I tucked the protein bar I took from dinner into the hole I had dug out in my mattress."

Rocket rolled his eyes. "Don't be so literal, Bixxy. She means did you pray before you went to bed. You know, on your knees, with your hands folded."

"*Nyet*. You had to be in bed before the alarm sounded. We never had time."

Richter leaned across the table and took Bixx's hand. The move startled Bixx, but for some reason, she didn't pull away.

"Bixx, dear," Richter said, "were you ever taught how to pray?"

Richter's hand was warm, and her long fingers came all the way past Bixx's wrist. Just like her mother's had.

Bixx paused for a moment, thinking back through the layers of memories. An image of her mother – tall, lean, her long hair a mass of delicate shades of blonde – unfolded in her mind. She had only vague recollections of her parents, their details having been eroded with each passing year. A montage of history, viewed from Bixx's young eyes, sequenced through her mind.

"I don't know," she said in almost a whisper. She felt Richter's hand gently squeeze hers. The touch was...comforting.

"Maybe someone just needs to teach you," Richter said as she pulled her hand back.

The action melted the image, and Bixx looked over to Rocket. He had that look, just as he had the night before when he had professed his love. He had taken her other hand, and she hadn't even noticed.

They all returned to eating, but Bixx didn't have much of an appetite. The conversation had her thinking, and besides, some of the leaves in her salad had black edges, and the thought of eating them made her stomach turn. She glanced at Richter, who appeared deep in thought.

"Do you pray before you go to bed at night?" Bixx asked.

Richter's attention was focused somewhere over Bixx's right shoulder. She didn't answer, but continued chewing.

"These days I seem to be praying a lot," she said finally.

"Why's that?" Rocket asked.

Richter went into her praying position, but instead of bowing her head, she rested her chin on her hands and stared forward.

"Doctor, is everything okay?" Bixx asked.

Richter closed her eyes. "The sun is becoming more active. There've been five massive flares just in the last three days."

"Is that why my netpad keeps dropping its connection?" Rocket asked.

"Most likely."

"Well, I'm sure it's not—"

"This is the start of the Tsunami cycle." Richter opened her eyes. "The readings are unmistakable."

"How long *is* the cycle?" Bixx asked.

Richter took in a long breath. "We don't know."

"Shit," Rocket said softly.

Richter looked painfully from Rocket to Bixx. "We have to find Jonathan. If we don't—" She bit off her words and went back to staring.

"I pray," Rocket suddenly interjected.

Richter chuckled and leaned back. "Then maybe God will hear you, because He sure doesn't seem to be hearing me."

Something in Richter's words clicked for Bixx. She pushed from the table and stood. "I'm not going to start yet," she declared.

"Oh, Bixx, honey," Richter said. "Praying isn't something you can just turn on or off."

"We have an old saying in my country. Praying is for the weak. If God gave me this brain, then He expects me to use it, right?"

"Well, yes...I suppose so."

"Then come on, I think I have a way to find Jonathan."

Not so black and white. 21

"**WHAT** do you think?" Tamara asked.

Kortel studied his wife's beautiful figure under the biofabric of the new dress. Its pattern slowly cycled from bright yellow roses to some kind of desert flower he had never heard of. Tamara knew all about it and had spent the better part of lunch explaining how important it had been to an Indian tribe called the Hopi. Kortel had only casually listened. All he knew was that the dress complemented Tamara's tall figure, hanging perfectly onto every curve. He watched intently as one of the Indian flowers delicately transformed into a rose across her left breast.

God, he loved her.

Tamara spun on the dressing room's platform, balancing on the ball of her foot like a ballerina. "I think this would be perfect to wear to little Jonathan's play, don't you?"

"I love you," Kortel said. "It'll be perfect."

Tamara's brow furrowed slightly. She trained her eyes on Kortel and smiled. "What did you say?"

"I said, 'I love it.'"

Her smile turned coy. "No, you said 'you,' not '*it*.'"

Kortel thought for a second. "I did?"

Tamara stepped down and walked over to Kortel, her eyes focused on him with a predatory hunger. She hiked the dress to her thighs, straddled him and settled on his lap. "Yes you did," she said, wrapping her arms around his neck.

"Okay...that's good, right?"

Tamara played with his hair, then her fingers traced the edge of his collar around to the front of his shirt. She began undoing his top button. Her eyes never wavered.

"Baby," Kortel said, suddenly embarrassed. "We're in public."

"I haven't heard you say you loved me for a long time."

Kortel thought back through their morning. He could have sworn he told her when she had stepped out of the shower. Hadn't he?

"I said I loved you this morning, when you were drying your hair."

Tamara started to undo the third button. "You never came back," she said, her eyes still locked on his.

"What do you mean?"

The tips of her fingers were now exploring the surface of his chest. "You never came back for me. You left me in Chicago. Nicole was so heartbroken."

"But...I didn't. We're here, together."

Suddenly Tamara's eyes went black, and Kortel felt himself falling, his whole existence draining into the depths of her pupils. She leaned in. "I waited a long time for you to return." She reared back and raised her arm, her hand clenched so tight her knuckles were white. "It's time to take what's mine!"

"Wait, I can explain!–"

Tamara punched Kortel's chest, the force knocking the air out of his lungs and pressing him hard against the flimsy chair. Her fist sunk into his skin. Kortel tried to scream, but the shock and the lack of air only fueled his panic. The pain was crushing. Bright red blood crawled up Tamara's arm like a living thing as she dug for her prize.

"Got it," she said with a grotesque smile.

Kortel watched in horror as Tamara removed his heart from the gaping wound below his sternum.

"It's mine," she declared, cupping the throbbing lump of muscle as if she were about to devour it.

"Shit, easy, mate!" Kortel heard somewhere from the edge of his consciousness. He opened his eyes to a dim figure kneeling by his bed. Something was holding him down, the pressure heavy against his chest.

"Don't scream again," the voice said. "You're hurting my ears."

"Nichols?" Kortel asked, his throat raw and dry.

"Who'd you expect, Trumble?"

The pressure on him released, and the room came into focus. Marcus Nichols stood and stepped back.

"Was that your field holding me down?" Kortel asked.

Nichols folded his arms. "Yeah."

"Nice pressure for a normal."

"Former normal."

Kortel sat up. He felt like he'd been hit by an interzone freight hauler.

"How do you feel?" Nichols asked.

"Like shit."

"What kind of shit?"

"Hell, I don't know.... Dog shit?"

Nichols smirked. "No, you don't understand. Do you feel cold or warm? Is it a sharp pain or an overall body ache?"

"What are you getting at? I just feel bad, that's all."

"It's important," Nichols said. "Certain pains mean certain things."

Kortel leaned against the wall behind his bed and took in the room. It was about the size of his grad school apartment and tastefully furnished with dark wood antiques. They looked like the real thing, but how would he know? He couldn't tell the difference between a priceless heirloom and one of those cheap vat-grown ones from Korea.

"Dull," he said, rubbing his forehead.

"What kind of dull?"

"A dull, overall body ache, emanating from my sella turcica, down to my phalanges."

"Piss off."

"Hey, you asked."

"Mr. Nichols?" Trumble's voice beckoned omnisciently in the room.

"Yes, sir?"

"How's Jonathan feeling?"

"Like shit," Kortel said into the air. "And don't ask what kind."

Wouldn't think of it, Trumble replied inside Kortel's mind. *Are you hungry?*

"What time is it?"

6:30...p.m.

"Where are we?"

We're in a suburb of the City of Lights.

Kortel took a deep breath. The air was sweet, and the mere act of taking it in made the top of his head tingle. "There're worst places to wake up in," he said. "What's for dinner?"

Chicken Paillardes with mustard cream and tarragon.

"Is it bioprepped?"

Heavens, no.

"What's the dress, black tie?" Kortel was still in the same clothes from Zvara's base.

I think you'll like what's hanging in the armoire. It's the latest fashion from Beijing.

Kortel rubbed some sleep from his eyes. He glanced at Nichols. "You joining us?"

"For what?"

"Dinner."

"No, thanks. I have some work to finish up. I'll let you get ready." He pointed at a dark, narrow hallway to Kortel's left. "The lav's that way. Nice shower with lots of hot water. The rationing hasn't affected Mr. Trumble, I guess." He opened the doors of the armoire and gestured. "And for you, the latest in fashion." He turned to leave. The door was made of a rough-cut wood that looked like it could have been carved during the 18th century. It appeared not to have a lock and creaked heavily as Nichols opened it.

"Isn't there any security?" Kortel asked.

Nichols turned back. "I know you, Kortel. You won't cause trouble."

"How do you know that?"

"Because you're curious about what Trumble has to offer. You're no dumbass, but you always take the easy way.... It's your pattern." The door clicked behind Nichols and echoed across the marble floor.

~

Don't you like your dinner?

"I do, but my throat is sore, and it's hard to swallow." Kortel took another bite, chewed, and washed the Chicken Paillardes down with a rich Cabernet Sauvignon. Its dark plum and cherry flavors lingered through a long finish. He had tasted better, so he decided it was probably manufactured. The tarragon sauce burned his throat. He took another sip.

Trumble's expressionless gaze blanketed him from across the table while the chair tried to feed him another spoonful of mandarin-colored paste. One arm fed as another quickly wiped his mouth. The whole scene reminded Kortel of Tarris's mom feeding his kid brother.

What do you think of the wine?

Kortel buried his nose inside the glass and inhaled. "Brazilian," he said, inspecting the last of its legs.

The napkin arm stopped in midwipe. *And?*

"There's a really good private label wine factory in Rio that can knock off anything on the planet. I met one of their programmers at a conference once. Cocky son of a bitch, but he knew his wines. I told him I could spot one of his by how it smelled."

Bravo, Jonathan. And the chicken?

"Oh, it's all right. I wouldn't have used so much tarragon, but what do I know? I've been out of the game for a while."

The arm finished its wipe and disappeared under the table, while another raised a glass of the Cab to Trumble's lips. The straw in the glass swished around the rim, but the arm deftly maneuvered the glass so that the straw stopped at the perfect point for Trumble to take a sip.

My palate was somewhat damaged. I now like foods prepared with a little more taste.

Kortel continued eating in silence, keeping his attention focused on his plate. He could feel Trumble studying him like some kind of experiment. *Maybe I am,* he thought.

In a sense, you are. But arguably, one of the greatest ever! Trumble's voice resonated deep inside Kortel's mind.

More silence.

Is Armando still fretting over the sun?

Stunned, Kortel slowly lowered his fork. "How the hell do you know that?"

I have people everywhere. Just because I don't run the Agency anymore doesn't mean I'm out of touch with what's going on in the Tel world. There were many people who owed Cyril and me, and believe me, I'll spend the rest of my life cashing in on those debts. Is Dr. Richter still predicting the end of the world?

"Yes. She thinks it's just around the corner."

Well, depending on your view of time and the universe, a thousand years could be interpreted as just around the corner. There are some scientists who believe that her theories are total rubbish. What do you think?

"How would I know who's right? I'm just a chef."

You're more than a—

Kortel slammed his fist on the table. Instantly two of the chair's arms appeared, forming an "x" in front of Trumble's face.

"Enough of this shit," Kortel said. "What do you want?"

The arms slowly retracted.

What if Dr. Richter is correct?

"What? I thought you said it was a bunch of rubbish."

I'm like you. I leave the big questions to be answered by the scientists. What's important to me is the potential of it happening.

"I don't follow you."

Fear, Jonathan, can be very useful. I plan on leveraging the world's fear of the Tsunami, but I'm going to need your help. You see, Cyril and I also made many enemies when we were in charge, and there are debts to be paid. Because of your intervention, they can't be paid so easily now. I know all about Armando's concept to stop the Tsunami, and in theory, it could work. When we implanted you, we wanted to create the Infinite Tel. But we never imagined a scenario like this. If Dr. Richter's calculations are correct, you will have to fulfill your destiny.

"Wait a minute. You want to do what Zvara is going to do?"

If you mean linking powerful Tels together to create a gravitational wall to protect the earth, you're correct.

"And your ass is in a crack with who knows who and you want me to join you, so you can blackmail them to get you off the hook?"

Blackmail is an oversimplification.

"Man, these must be some big debts you owe."

They are.

"So, you really think Zvara's plan will work?"

In truth, I'm in the rubbish camp. I believe the sun is stable, but Dr. Richter's data is very compelling. The problem with Armando's plan is that he doesn't have the power to do it. But I do. For me, it's a win-win.

"Why don't you just kill the people you owe? The Agency's been doing that for years."

You just don't kill off these types of people, Jonathan. The repercussions of their deaths would cause even bigger problems...for the culture and me. And I don't want to die a second time. If Dr. Richter is correct, then you and I will serve mankind like no one ever has. Either way, I get what I want.

"Why would I even consider this? It was you and Cyril who put all this tech into my head. I should waste you right here."

But you can't.

"I know, the great Jeffrey Trumble, master of all his domain. And now I've got this blue stuff." Kortel tapped the side of his head. "Mind telling me what it is?"

I would love to, but the technology you're referencing isn't part of ours. Why don't you ask your good friend Dr. Shoalburg? He should be able to answer that question.

"W-what do you mean by that? You talked before like it was a part of the original tech."

Trumble sighed. *You were always so naive. Cyril thought it was a weakness, but I felt it was one of your strengths. The world, Jonathan, is not all black and white....You should know that by now. Never underestimate Armando Zvara. He is a man of means and will do anything to get what he wants.*

Kortel couldn't process what he just heard. He looked down and found his right hand twitching violently.

You see, Jonathan, life is complex. If you view it as something less, you only set yourself up for more pain. Trumble's eyes went to Kortel's hand.

Kortel desperately tried to massage the spasms. "You didn't answer my question," he said, rubbing. "Why should I go with you? What's in it for me?"

For the first time that evening, Jeffrey Trumble's face seemed to relax. There was a slight smile at the edge of his mouth. *It's not what, Jonathan.... It's who.*

Kortel sat motionless. His attention went to the dining room door. The hallway that he took from his bedroom had been what, about 70 feet? It continued on for another 20 or so, but it dead-ended into a closed door. That was all he'd seen, except for that dark room he had woken up in the day before, and who knows where that was. He thought about making a break for it, but figured it would be a crapshoot. Besides, Trumble had control over his tech, and God knows what he'd do if Kortel tried to bolt. He looked back and found Trumble staring at him.

That was quite a dream you had earlier, or should I say nightmare?

Kortel felt the blood drain from his face. "How do you know what I dream?"

As your technology integrates, more of your body's functions become...oh, how can I put this? Manageable?

"Get out of my mind, or I'll—"

Or you'll what? You're not in control here, Jonathan. And if I were you, I'd listen to what I have to offer.

Kortel noticed his hand had stopped twitching. He leaned back in his chair. "Okay, fine. You're in control. So what did you mean before...it's not what, but who, or whatever? Dammit, just get to the point!"

The point, Jonathan, is that I can give you back what you thought was gone. Trumble paused. May I ask, do you think of her often?

"Think of who?" Then it struck Kortel. His dream. "Are you talking about Tamara?"

What if I told you I could restore parts of her memory – all of your moments together – without any trauma to her?

"You can't do that! It's impossible." Kortel was beginning to feel dizzy. Maybe Trumble was playing with his tech. Or maybe it was the revelation that Zvara and

Shoalburg had lied.

I'll have to call in one of those favors, but I'll need your help.

"It wouldn't be right.... You can't do that to her. She has a new life, and there's no place for me in it."

Life is too short, Jonathan. Isn't it about time you got something out of it?

Kortel grabbed the edge of the table; his fingers pulled at the white linen. The thought of having Tamara back in his life collided head-on with his rational self. "No," he said, "I won't let you."

A holojection suddenly appeared in the middle of the table. The image of Tamara, working at her desk in the art gallery, quivered above a shallow bowl of green apples. The holojection's depth seemed so real that Kortel for a microsecond actually felt he was inside the gallery. He watched in disbelief as Tamara stood and said hello to the camera.

"What the hell is this?"

Insurance, Jonathan. An old concept, to be sure, but one that works very well in this context. You remember James McCarris, don't you?

"Yes," Kortel said, cautiously.

I've employed James to keep an eye on Tamara...to make sure nothing bad happens to her. This is the feed from his optic nerve. Most of his brain functions are online. A slight laugh reverberated in Kortel's brain. *I called in one of the biggest favors owed to me to restore him.* There was another pause. *Look at her. Isn't she beautiful?*

Kortel was numb, and he knew it wasn't because of the technology. He watched Tamara show McCarris various works of art, gesturing and laughing as if they were old friends. Then they shook hands, and McCarris's eyes tracked Tamara through the open space of the gallery.

Why don't you go into the city for the weekend.... Get some clarity. I've arranged for you to stay at one of Paris's finest hotels. Eat, drink...get a massage. I know you'll make the right decision.

Tamara looked beautiful. Kortel couldn't take his eyes off of her, but as she stepped through a shaft of light, a shudder slashed through him. There, moving across her lean frame like a second skin, was the flowered dress he had seen in his dream.

Windows to the soul. 22

THE room in which Richter had dropped off Bixx wasn't like anything else on the base. Going through its doors was like stepping into another world, far away from New Mexico. Everything Bixx had seen up to this point was ancient, made of wood and retrofitted. Even the smell of the base was old; it reminded Bixx of her grandfather's farm, all musty and dry. But this room bore a faint technical edge, or at least what she pictured as such. Rocket had chosen to go back to their room — something about lunch not agreeing with him. Bixx had tried to get him to come, saying she needed his support, but he had just smiled and said, "You'll kick ass." Plus, he was in one of his moods, and she knew not to push it.

"Stay here for a second," Richter said. "Let me go talk to Shoalburg and see if they're ready." She briskly maneuvered through the maze of electronics towers until she disappeared around a large concrete column.

Bixx stood patiently near a row of lockers and surveyed the area. There were about a half-dozen lab techs busily going from workstation to workstation, their heads wrapped in the latest biointerface gear. The room was in the basement of the complex's centermost building. It had a raised floor, and the air was chilled, but not like a typical air-conditioned room. This was more like standing next to a refrigerator at a Grab and Go when some jerk had left the door open so that the cold air was rushing out. Bixx felt goose bumps raise on her arms, and she glanced down at her chest. She hadn't been blessed with her mother's shape, so she never worried about going braless, unless she was headed to someplace cold.

"Come on," Richter said, marching up. Her eyes went to Bixx's T-shirt. "Oh, honey, you're freezing in that skimpy thing. Here, put this on." She grabbed a sweater off a hook that was holding about dozen others. "They keep these around so people don't freeze to death."

The room was barely lit by the ambient light from the electronics, so Bixx kept close, following Richter around the concrete column like a shadow. They made their way through more computer stacks until they emerged into an open area that was brighter, though still cast in a green glow. Shoalburg was hunched at a small console, his interface cables tethered from his eye sockets like a techno umbilical. Zvara was sitting on a metal table at the edge of the light, tucked mostly in the shadows, while he pored over a netpad. Tarris was leaning against another console, moving a toothpick through its paces with all the determination of a surgeon.

Bixx stepped around Richter and instantly felt the stares of Tarris and Zvara. Shoalburg turned, and his interface cables slapped against the counter. An awkward silence settled around them.

Zvara finally said, "Dr. Richter says you have a way to find Jonathan." His tired eyes landed on Bixx with a palpable desperation.

"I-I think I do, sir," she said, the words coming out with more of her Russian accent than usual.

Richter nudged her. "Tell them what you told me."

Bixx hesitated.

Zvara sucked in a deep breath. "Would you like some water?"

"No, sir. Thank you."

"Bixx has a special way of negotiating the Net," Richter offered.

Zvara's brow furrowed.

Richter placed a hand on Bixx's shoulder. "Go ahead," she whispered.

Bixx proceeded to tell them why she and the others had come to New Mexico in the first place: how she had discovered James McCarris's cerebral Net feed and hacked its security skin. She told them how she had merged with his personality construct and discovered his hatred for Kortel, as well as his plan for revenge.

Everyone remained quiet when she finished. Shoalburg hadn't moved, and Tarris's toothpick was locked between his teeth.

"How long have you had this talent?" Zvara asked.

"Since the orphanage."

"And you really think that you can find Jonathan by tapping back into McCarris's stream?"

Bixx pulled the sweater tight across her chest and nodded.

Zvara folded his arms and thoughtfully tapped his netpad against his chin. He looked at Tarris. "What do you think?"

The toothpick disappeared, then reappeared at the opposite corner of Tarris's mouth. "We got dick right now." He pulled the toothpick from his lips and flicked it into the darkness. "I vote for letting her try. What the hell do we have to lose?"

"Carter?"

Shoalburg twisted in his chair and faced Zvara. His chrome interface connectors caught the light and flashed into Bixx's eyes. The effect was eerie, considering they were nestled where his eyes should have been.

"Her file says she displays an extraordinary amount of awareness when it comes to navigation, with elevated levels of primary and secondary tracing." He shrugged. "I agree with Tarris. We've nothing to lose."

"My *file*?" Bixx demanded.

Zvara set his netpad down and stood. His imposing figure caught the edge of the light and bathed him in a greenish hue. He focused on Bixx, and she felt goose bumps on her arm again. He walked up and put his hands in his pockets.

"There is no need for you to be upset," he said. "I like to know everything about whomever I am dealing with. And from what I have read, you are an extraordinary young girl."

Bixx felt herself blush. "Thank you, sir."

"Come," Zvara said, gesturing to the console where Tarris leaned. "I think you will like our equipment."

Tarris pushed away from the console and pulled a chair out all in the same movement, which was amazing to Bixx, given his disability. His motor movement was at times more fluid than that of a normal person, and she wondered if he had programmed the tech in his legs to be more graceful. Maybe he had downloaded the matrix of some famous ballet dancer or sports star. Was that even possible?

"Here you go," Tarris said, patting the chair's biofabric.

Bixx settled in and felt the chair mold to the contour of her body.

Shoalburg scooted across the area and bumped against the arm of her chair. Up close, his implants appeared the consistency of mercury. He looked at her as if he could see her, which she figured he could, but only in the context of the Net, and probably in a manner only he could process. He handed her a tiny wafer that seemed made from the same material as his implants.

"This is a new prototype interface I've been working on," he said proudly. "It'll enhance your connection."

Bixx turned the piece of tech over in her palm and thought she saw it quiver slightly. She looked from Richter to Zvara and back to Shoalburg, who was staring at her like a bug.

"Does it work like the regular ones?" she asked.

"Basically," Shoalburg said. "Just place it on your forehead and relax. It packs more of a hit than what you're used to."

Bixx raised the wafer to her forehead.

"Oh, and try and keep your tongue in the back of your mouth. One of our lab boys bit his the other day, and it bled for an hour."

The wafer felt like it was heating up between Bixx's fingers. She took a deep breath, moved her tongue back and closed her eyes.

The threshold jump was almost instantaneous. Bixx squirmed in her chair. The Net exploded onto her visual field with a profound intensity. She thought she heard herself gasp.

Are you okay? Shoalburg's voice was soft and somewhat reassuring. It penetrated the Net's vast white noise with total clarity.

"Yeah...I guess. This is amazing. The spatial acuity is beyond anything I've ever seen."

Shoalburg laughed. *I thought you'd like it. I'm going to back out of your field's parameters, but I'll be monitoring your travel. Just think of me as another conscience.*

Bixx nodded, and the action almost made her sick. It usually wasn't that important to remain still when in the Net, because the duality wasn't that harsh —

at least not for her. But Shoalburg's prototype was a billion times more real, and Bixx quickly learned that even the slightest movement could send her into a kind of dizziness shock. She felt something metal touch the side of her ankle. Again, the nausea.

Here's a bucket, in case you need to throw up.

Bixx almost nodded okay, but caught herself.

Oh, I forgot to mention: with my prototype, there's another threshold jump. Good luck.

"But—"

The second jump happened even faster than the first one. The suddenness startled Bixx, and she gripped the arms of the chair as if they would actually help her control the freefall. The Net shifted before her. She couldn't tell how; she just knew that it did. It now possessed such dimensional perfection, Bixx thought that if she reached out, she'd actually be able to touch one of the data streams.

Then something happened.

Usually when jacked, there was a sense of your "outer self." It would hover at the edge of your conscience, reminding you that the Net was just an illusion – a trick played on your cerebral pathways. But without warning, that presence, with all of its reassuring comfort, simply had dropped away.

To Bixx, it felt as if she were losing part of her essence, as if the fabric of her being was shredding and her soul might ooze out the tear. The metal bucket, the cool plastic of the chair's arms, even the seat's biofabric, which any other time she would have been a little squeamish about, vanished. Bixx found herself floating among the zettaflops of information without the lifeline she had taken for granted. A primal sense of panic began to rise in her, but she quickly engaged the breathing sequences she had been taught in her virt classes. The feeling subsided.

"Amazing," she whispered.

Bixx started emptying her mind and preparing to hunt for McCarris's data stream. Dr. Lee, her Advanced Virt professor at the Agency, had singled her out to teach her the art of *Listening with the Heart*. He had called her porous, but she never understood what he meant until years later. "You must listen for the chi," he had instructed. "Every person – every thing – has a life force. That chi is present in the Net. You must empty your mind and open your heart, even if the one you seek wants to harm you. Remember, you must show forgiveness before you can *listen*."

Bixx drifted effortlessly as she "listened" for the data flow she had felt previously. Soon, she caught the drone, then sensed its presence. She opened her eyes and saw McCarris's stream. Its distinctive signature had been imprinted onto her psyche so that she had no problem distinguishing it from other flows. Remembering her original encounter with McCarris's stream, Bixx performed another series of breathing exercises to relieve her fear. She closed her eyes, focused on the core of the drone and let go.

Bixx waited for the impact, but it never came. She opened her eyes to the river of data that was McCarris's life, but this time, there were no torrents of emotion. Instead, the streaks of informational light were displayed as an undulating mass of electric color. The other time she had entered McCarris's stream, Bixx's matrix became a "part" of it, but now she felt more like an observer. Gone was the feeling of chaos. Whether it was Shoalburg's interface or just her abilities, Bixx instinctively knew where to focus to find McCarris's chi. She pictured his gray-blue eyes and opened her mind.

Instantly the Net fell away, replaced by an oddly pedestrian scene. Bixx took a second to adjust, because the feeling of reality was so accurate that it scared her. It felt as if she were actually standing in a gallery opening, with people talking and laughing and milling about with fine-stemmed glasses of white wine. As she studied the scene, the depth of field and proportional range was astounding. People looked at her like she actually existed within their space. Suddenly, a hand came into her field of vision, but the sensation was that of her own hand. She glanced at its features and recoiled. It was a man's hand. Bixx instantly realized what had happened, but the shock was nonetheless frightening.

She was looking out the windows of McCarris's soul.

The initial jolt seemed to subside rather quickly, and Bixx began feeling comfortable with the arrangement. She wondered if Shoalburg's interface was making the situation more palatable for her brain to handle, because she was surprised at her lack of panic, and even more surprised at her curious desire to hang out and see what would happen.

It took a few moments to adjust to being a man. First, there was McCarris's height. He was at least a foot and a half taller than Bixx, and looking down at people was a bit disarming. Then there was the sheer bulk of his body, not to mention the obvious anatomical differences. Once, in a severely drunken state with two of her girlfriends, she had mused about what it would be like to have a penis, and now that she was in a situation to find out, she was completely repulsed by the idea. Studying the scene, Bixx had the feeling that if she let herself go, she might merge with McCarris's construct. A bald older man approached and smiled. He was about McCarris's height, barrel-chested and had a peculiar brown spot on his forehead.

"Are you enjoying the show?" he asked, his smile full of perfectly manufactured teeth.

"Yes, I am," McCarris answered. The sound of his voice had a slight reverberation, like feedback she had heard in old-time music vids.

"I'm Ryan Pudder, owner of the gallery."

The men chatted for a moment before Pudder moved on to another guest. McCarris shifted his attention to his left and began walking through the space. Bixx braced for a wave of nausea, but the movement felt queerly comfortable...almost too comfortable. His attention went from painting to painting. They were hideous works that looked to Bixx like someone had wiped his ass on the canvas. Thankfully, McCarris only lingered for a few seconds at each piece. Bixx felt someone tapping her shoulder. McCarris turned, and a pretty woman with short blonde hair was standing there with drinks in her hands.

"Mr. McCarris, I'm so glad you made it. You can't browse the gallery without a little libation, now can you?" The woman handed McCarris a glass of wine.

"Thank you," McCarris said, and immediately took a sip.

Bixx instantly felt the wine's coolness pass down her virtual throat, and she wondered if she could get drunk in this techno-schizophrenia.

"I wouldn't have missed this for the world," McCarris said. His Southern accent was more distinct now. He took another sip, and his attention went to the woman's breasts. She was wearing a low-cut flowered dress, and one of the weirdly shaped flowers changed into a rose. His gaze went back to her face. She had the prettiest blue eyes Bixx had ever seen – bright and full of life. She smiled and cocked her head, and Bixx felt something flush through McCarris's body. She became aware of his penis and fought back a yelp.

"See anything you like?" the woman asked.

McCarris leaned into the woman, and Bixx could smell her perfume. It was floral and complemented her appearance well.

"My real opinion?" McCarris asked.

The woman shyly nodded and smiled, then looked around to see if anyone was within earshot. She took another sip from her glass.

"I think it looks like a monkey did these," McCarris whispered.

The woman giggled into her wine. "Shhh," she said, wiping her chin with a small cocktail napkin. "The artist is right over there." She motioned discreetly to a tall Middle-Eastern man holding court in front of a particularly atrocious work.

McCarris and the woman laughed, and Bixx felt that flushing again. Their laughter waned, and both stared at each other for a moment.

"Say," McCarris said, "would you like to get some dinner after this?"

The woman smiled and glanced away. When she looked back, her eyes locked on McCarris, and Bixx felt something pass through his nervous body. It was a strange feeling: passionate, but darkly aggressive.

"Why, Mr. McCarris, are you asking me on a date?"

"Ms. Connor, we Southern boys don't call it a date. We call it a walk. And if there were a row of magnolias, I'd walk you among them."

"Well, you won't find any magnolia trees in Chicago, Mr. McCarris. But you can drive me to a nice restaurant."

"Consider it done."

The name Connor was so familiar to Bixx, but she couldn't place it. Pudder came up to Connor's side and whispered in her ear. Her face grew serious, and then she smiled at McCarris.

"Will you excuse me for a moment? My presence has been requested by the *artiste*." She rolled her eyes.

"Sure. I'll catch up with you later."

Connor smiled and tilted her head.

McCarris looked around and walked over to a secluded corner of the gallery. He pulled out a netpad, and Bixx intently noted the coordinates he tapped in. The NetCom logo pixeled up; the face of Marcus Nichols appeared, and a cold shiver cut through Bixx. She hoped McCarris hadn't felt it.

"How's it going?" Nichols asked.

"Swimmingly," McCarris replied.

"You gonna get some tonight?"

"Possibly."

Nichols smirked. "You're supposed to get close, not marry the bitch."

"Don't worry. I'm a professional. Tonight's for sport."

"Right. Report back in the morning."

"Make it the afternoon."

"Whatever." Nichols's image cut out.

"I've got good news," a voice said into Bixx's ear.

McCarris quickly pocketed the netpad and turned to find Connor standing there, her drink almost empty. "H-hey you," he said. "What happened to monkey boy?"

Connor glanced over her shoulder. "His assholiness is too busy pontificating about how great he is." She downed the rest of her wine and placed the empty glass on a serving cart.

"So what's the good news?" McCarris asked.

"Ryan's letting me leave early tonight. He says I deserve it.... After this week," Connor gave a nod to the artist, "that's an understatement." She wrapped her arm around McCarris's. "So, Southern boy, where are you taking me?"

"I know of a great little biofood place. Do you like bio?"

"Depends. What'd you have in mind?"

"It's called *Kortel's*. I've been there once, and it was excellent."

"*Tres chic*, Mr. McCarris. Isn't that the place where the owner just disappeared one day?"

Bixx felt a sudden rush of anger course through McCarris. The muscles of his neck, chest and arms tightened. "I read that he was killed. Some kind of tragic death."

"Oh, how terrible." Connor patted McCarris's arm, and the anger ebbed. "Let's go," she said, looking up with those beautiful eyes, "before monkey boy beckons, and I'm stuck here all night."

Strange that he would he take her to Kortel's old restaurant. And why did the name Connor nag at Bixx? She racked her brain, trying to remember the rumors she'd heard. Hadn't he fallen in love with some kind of high-end hooker once? Tammy? Tamara...

Tamara *Connor?*

As McCarris and Connor strolled toward the gallery's entrance, several guests stopped them to chat. Bixx decided it was a good time to back out of the limbo-state of piggybacking with McCarris, so she emptied her mind and pictured the Net outside of his stream. Again, like a cerebral magic trick, she found herself back in the Net, looking down at McCarris's flow.

Bixx had a great head for figures and immediately pictured the coordinate numbers McCarris had entered into his netpad. Nothing happened at first, and she began wondering if her ability was degrading, possibly because of limbic short-circuiting with Shoalburg's tech. But then the Net threw her a lateral, shifting everything into a hyper-blur that almost hurt physically.

When it finished, Bixx was staring at five delicate sans serif brass numbers attached to a richly lacquered wood door. The grain had been stained a dark glossy cherry so that the finish had an almost liquid appearance. The numbers, 22176, were washed in a spot of soft light. Above them, embedded in the door, was the unblinking eye of a vid lens, the kind used in ultra-high-end hotels. A man's fist came into view and rapped hard on the door, just below the numbers. Bixx flinched and thought she felt the tops of her knuckles tingle. A moment went by before the door slowly opened on Jonathan Kortel. He had a towel around his waist and looked as if he had just stepped out of a shower. Bixx almost peed her virtual pants.

"You told me you'd be ready," said the voice of Marcus Nichols. Bixx knew she was inside Nichols now, but how? Did he have the kind of tech to connect into?

"I fell asleep," Kortel replied. He turned, and Bixx watched him walk into a hotel suite that was bigger than most homes and lighted like a Japanese art vid. A bank of tall windows stretched the length of the cavernous space, and she could see the Paris skyline beyond. Its millions of lights blinked lazily through the thermals of a hot night.

Nichols said, "Jeffrey doesn't like to be kept waiting."

Kortel shot him a stern look and cinched the towel tighter. Bixx had only met him once, and he had definitely not been half naked. She was surprised at how ripped his body was and had barely begun to imagine what might be under the towel when Kortel turned and started drying his hair with it. Nichols's attention immediately went to the New Eiffel Tower, which was performing its famous light show. Bixx tried to will him to look back, but Nichols kept watching the Tower.

"Hurry it up," he said. Nichols's attention went back to where Kortel had been standing, but he had already gone down the hallway.

Damn.

"Ease up," Kortel yelled from somewhere deep in the suite. "You all need me a lot more than I need you." Bixx figured the bathroom was huge, because she could barely hear Kortel's voice.

"Asshole thinks he's so damn powerful," Nichols said to himself. Bixx could feel anger building in him, but it had an odd edge to it that felt like jealousy. Several tense minutes of silence went by. Nichols was clearly growing pissed. Bixx could almost taste his rage. More time passed, and he glanced at his watch.

"God*damn* it," he said under his breath. Nichols quickly stood and stormed toward the hallway. His vision had clearly narrowed; only the center was in focus now. The hallway was long and lined with large monochromes of sliced fruit that, at this scale, looked like studies of gothic medical experiments. Nichols entered the bathroom and swept his attention from side to side.

"Kortel, where the hell *are* you?" He searched the huge room, from the toilet area to the shower – which itself was nearly the size of Bixx and Rocket's apartment – to another large space that she guessed was for the super rich to have someone dress them, because it contained a little platform and three large mirrors. "Kortel?!" Nichols screamed again. Bixx felt adrenaline racing, but she couldn't distinguish whose it was.

"What the hell?" he said, looking wildly from side to side. Bixx could feel his rage mixing with panic.

Suddenly the door in front of Nichols blew open, sending its latticework splintering in all directions. Kortel was standing inside what looked like a linen closet, dressed in workout pants and running shoes. His head was cocked down, though he was looking forward under his brow. His hair had been combed, but his chest was still slick with moisture.

Bixx felt her throat begin to close as a pressure – like two giant hands – pushed Nichols back up the hallway. He tried to speak, but all that came out was gurgling as he frantically grabbed at his throat. Bixx felt herself floating backward and immediately realized that Nichols was horizontal as he sailed above the deep pile carpet of the hallway.

"I can bend time, you dumbass. What did you think I'd do?... Just let you push me around?"

Nichols gurgled an answer, which Bixx couldn't decipher. She figured it was probably some archaic Cockney expletive. They were now back in the main room, and Nichols's attention went to the skyline for a second.

"You can tell Trumble to–" Kortel grabbed his chest, and the pressure at Nichols's throat relaxed. Bixx felt a stabbing pain across her back as Nichols crashed onto a glass coffee table. His vision had shifted, and the room was cast in shades of deep red now, although Bixx knew this was his optic nerve changing, not the light in the room. A heat began rising in Nichols's body as he slowly got himself to his feet. Kortel was on his knees, clutching his chest.

Nichols wiped blood from his nose. "Oh, I've been waiting for this day," he said. "Get up, you piece of shit, and learn a lesson." Bixx could feel his muscles tighten as the heat increased.

It must be his tech engaging, she thought. *But how's he able to control Kortel?*

Kortel looked up like a wounded animal. He suddenly flew backward, slamming hard against a finely tailored cloth wall. He clutched wildly at the fabric, which tore and fell on top of him as he landed in a heap on the hardwood.

Nichols scrambled around a couch to see where he had landed, but when he looked down, Kortel wasn't there. Suddenly Nichols flew backward across the main room. He landed, twisted over a bar, and smashed into a row of liquor bottles and glasses. The whole scene remarkably resembled the night he had slammed Bixx against the mirror in that club's bathroom, but, thank God, without the full intensity. She felt she was sharing in Nichols's pain, but from a distance.

Nichols struggled to see over the bar, and when he stood, Bixx almost screamed at what she saw. Kortel was flying through the room, flat-out, his hands stretched in front of him like some comic vid character. She could feel Nichols's astonishment, and for a second, he froze.

Kortel flew right up and grabbed Nichols's throat, his thumbs digging into the esophagus. Only the whites of his eyes were showing, and Bixx, for the first time, felt fear run through Nichols's nervous system.

The grav pressure around Nichols's head was tremendous, and Bixx could feel his tech trying to counter it.

"Either I die, or you do," Nichols managed.

Bixx desperately tried to figure out how she could help, as Nichols's tech punched back at Kortel's telekinetic strength.

Nichols now had his hands at Kortel's throat, and the two Tels were locked together. Kortel slowly floated backward, dragging Nichols across the bar and into the room. He lifted the Brit off the floor and carried him up to the suite's tall ceiling. Nichols squirmed in his grip. Kortel released his hold, but Bixx could still feel the pressure at Nichols's throat.

He's formed a tight grav wave around him, Bixx thought.

Kortel spread his arms. Nichols began to lose oxygen. Suddenly, though, Bixx felt the heat of Nichols's tech build again, and both men slowly lowered onto the remains of the coffee table. The glass crunched under their feet.

"Give it up, Kortel." Nichols's voice was hoarse. "Your time has passed."

Bixx watched in horror as Kortel began to shake, slowly at first, then more violently.

"This is what you did to my father, you bastard," Nichols said. "How does it feel?"

Kortel had become almost a blur, and he had risen off the floor about a foot. Bixx started to freak. She knew she had to do something – and fast. She cleared her mind and thought of Nichols's tech. She knew what bioimplants looked like and pictured them in Nichols's brain, fused within the gray matter. She focused intently on the thought of them dying, turning black, and flushing out of his system.

Nichols screamed and grabbed his head.

Kortel collapsed to his hands and knees and looked up. His eyes rolled forward and narrowed.

Bixx could feel Nichols trying to engage his tech, so she concentrated on it dying. She knew she had to keep the pressure on, or he might get the best of Kortel again.

"I am *so* tired of you," Kortel said, blood pouring from his nose.

Panic was crashing in waves through Nichols. "W-What are you going to do?"

Kortel struggled to his feet and leveled his gaze. "What I should have done to your father."

"*No!*"

Bixx felt an intense grav field build around Nichols, but she kept her focus on his tech. The air around his body began to distort as the grav field grew. Kortel stepped back and casually raised his hand. Nichols rose off the broken glass, his legs and arms flailing.

Bixx sensed her connection with the Net was beginning to deteriorate, and she started to panic. The feeling was like being a kid again, hiding inside her parents' cramped and muffled laundry closet. But the thought of being trapped in Nichols's chi was infinitely more frightening.

"Time for you to go," Kortel said.

"Where?" Nichols asked, the sweat pouring from his armpits.

"Hell."

Kortel waved his hand, and the next thing Bixx felt was crashing backwards through one of the suite's large windows. She could feel the night wind hit Nichols's face, and through his eyes saw the lights of the *Arc de Triomphe*. They screamed in unison as his body began to flip and his feet arched over his back. While they fell, Bixx felt shards from the window tear flesh from his back and arms. He flipped through a spray of glass and blood and began tumbling forward again. The 22-story distance compressed at an unholy rate. Nichols instinctually put his hands out in a futile attempt to stop himself from hitting the pavement. Bixx felt a throbbing down her left arm. She knew his heart was beginning to fail. Complete and primordial fear tore through Bixx as the top of a green cafe umbrella rose toward them.

"Mother," Nichols said to himself.

A waiter looked up. His mouth formed an "O" as a tray of drinks slipped from his hand. The red star logo on top of the umbrella filled Bixx's vision.

Bixx opened her eyes to the faces of Zvara, Tarris and Shoalburg, who had replaced his eyes in his head. She was hyperventilating and covered with sweat. Zvara truly looked scared, and Tarris seemed pissed. Shoalburg had no expression – just the cool demeanor of a scientist.

"Oh my God! Oh my God!" Bixx yelled between gulps of air.

"Dear, it's all right," Bixx heard to her left. She turned to see Richter kneeling next to her chair.

Tear trails streaked Richter's face. She spread her arms. "Come here," she said, forcing a smile.

Bixx hesitated. She had been without a mother for so long that the thought of someone pretending made her guard go up. But something shifted in Bixx, and she dropped to her knees and fell into Richter's arms.

"It's all right," Richter whispered. She began rocking. "You didn't die."

Bixx began sobbing. Whether it was the near-death experience or the cumulative effect of every hell she had faced in her life, everything came out in a mournful cry into Richter's shoulder.

"Shhh," Richter said, patting Bixx's head.

While Bixx cried, fractured images flashed through her mind: Connor's eyes, Kortel's bloodied face...the waiter's shock.

"We lost your connection when you entered McCarris's stream," Zvara said.

"Then I regained the connection as you and Nichols went out the window," Shoalburg continued. "I-I'm sorry it took so long to get you out. I would have never let it go that far."

Bixx pulled away from Richter's embrace and turned to Shoalburg, her face awash in mucus and tears. She bunched the sleeve of the sweater and wiped her eyes. "Thanks for getting me out when you did. I...I don't know what would have happened if you hadn't."

Shoalburg exchanged tentative glances with Zvara and Richter. He smiled feebly. "Probably, ah...nothing. It's hard to say."

Zvara knelt to the right of Bixx's chair and placed his hand on hers. The gesture was oddly comforting. "When you are ready," he said gently, "you will need to tell us what happened in there."

Tarris flicked another toothpick into the darkness. "At least we know where Jonathan is, and that he's safe."

Bixx stood and faced him. "He's not safe," she said, wiping her checks with the other sleeve. "There's a guy named Jeffrey after him, and James McCarris is working for him."

"Jeffrey *Trumble?*" Zvara asked, his voice full of concern and unbelief.

The image of Connor hanging on McCarris's arm flashed across Bixx's mind. She remembered his comments about Kortel, and the hatred she felt from him.

Zvara slowly stood, the compassion wiped from his face. "Olga," he said gravely, "I think now is a good time to tell us what happened."

Trompe l'oeil. 23

KORTEL looked at his hands. They were shaking, and he couldn't decide if it was because his tech was free of Trumble's control or because he was scared.

Scared, he thought. *Damn scared.*

The humid night air filled the suite. When the HVAC engaged, Kortel glanced at the open window, or rather, the opening where the window had been, because all that was left was a metal frame bent toward the skyline – probably caused by the distortion wave from his grav field. He had maintained it on Nichols the entire time, and since Kortel hadn't kept a line of sight, it probably drove Nichols's body into the pavement. Kortel didn't want to think about what that might look like.

"Jesus," he said under his breath. But wasn't that the point, that he had kept his field on Nichols *all the way down*? Kortel wanted him to die. Horribly.

The sing-songy wail of a police gunship began dominating the congested street noise. Kortel knew it would only be a matter of minutes before Nichols's dive would be pixeled across every major news portal in Paris. He backed away from the window and headed to the bathroom, where he began gathering what little he had collected in the two days he had been in Trumble's grip: that Beijing fashion statement, a comb, some soap, three biobars and the top to a workout suit, compliments of the hotel's spa.

What the hell am I doing? Kortel threw the comb and soap into a corner, zipped on the workout top and pocketed the biobars. The suit's fabric compensated for the humid air when he ran back into the suite's living room.

The gunship's siren drew closer.

Kortel took a last glance out the window. He remembered the look on Nichols's face and something shot down his nerves. Turning to leave, there was a reflection of light in the remains of the coffee table. It was the screen on Nichols's netpad.

Thank you, God.

As Kortel lifted the pad out of the shards, two 60-million candlepower beams began sweeping the buildings across the street. At the down blast of the gunship's stabilizer engines, Kortel sprinted out of the suite. He ran the length of the hallway, passed the turbolifts and entered the stairwell. The *Napoléon* was an older hotel. Its fire stairs spiraled down an open center. Kortel looked down the 22-story drop and quickly calculated the distance. He climbed onto the railing, formed a grav wave corridor, and jumped.

The space between the stairs was so narrow that Kortel kept his arms tucked close to his sides. He had done a similar stunt once before, but that involved ascending 70 stories of the center of a very wide elevator shaft. Just before reaching the bottom, he increased the field and slowed his fall. The soles of the spa's cross-trainers shifted to their sports tread as he gently settled onto the concrete.

Kortel cracked opened the first floor exit door and found he was at the back of the lobby, close to a set of broad palms. He thought about pulling the suit's hood over his head, but figured that would draw attention. Given that a guest had just sailed out of the 22nd floor of one of Paris's finer hotels, he was struck at how calm the lobby was.

A manager type scurried about, and three policemen huddled next to a table with the biggest floral arrangement Kortel had ever seen. They seemed to be taking the whole event rather casually, as if this kind of thing happened all the time in Paris. The front of the hotel was walled with floor-to-ceiling windows, and he could see that the police were beginning to shut the street down. A large crime scene truck pulled to the curb.

Kortel folded the suit's hood back into its compartment and began walking casually across the lobby. He chose a path well around the police and hugged the wall opposite the registration desk. When he approached the hotel's entrance, the doorman tipped his hat and began pulling on one of the ornate doorknobs.

"*Arrêter, s'il vous plaît!*"

The doorman stopped in mid-pull and gave a sideways glance. Kortel turned slowly.

An officer, dressed in the traditional uniform of the *Police Nationale*, had stepped from the huddle and was gesturing sternly with his white-gloved hand. He wore a pair of police Net glasses, but they looked like they could have come from a boutique on the *Champs Elysées*.

"You are American?" he asked, walking toward Kortel.

"Yes, I am." Kortel had slipped into partial phase and was seriously considering sending a grav wave through the entire lobby. His vision was speckled with the swirling colors of the phase jump.

"Your name, please."

"Jonathan Kortel."

"You are a guest of the *Napoléon*?"

"A guest of a guest."

The officer eyed him. "Do you always jog at 2:30 in the morning, Mr. Kortel?" He flipped open his netpad, clicked through some files and muttered something in French.

"Only when I can't sleep."

"Jet lag?" the officer said helpfully, still working something on his pad. He suddenly looked up and stared forward, and Kortel sensed that information was being fed to him from his couture eyewear.

"*Oui, monsieur!*" The officer's attention shifted to Kortel. "Enjoy your run. And please be careful. The streets of Paris can be troublesome this time of night." He saluted crisply and walked off through the lobby.

Kortel stood down his phase.

The doorman smiled this time, and Kortel quickly walked to the hotel's cabstand. Another doorman, dressed in a tight-fitting black suit, consulted his netpad while he waved Kortel over.

"Where are you going?" he asked in a thick French accent.

Kortel froze. He had been so focused on getting out of the hotel that he hadn't considered his utter lack of credit or identification.

"A cab, *oui?*"

Suddenly, Nichols's netpad hummed inside one of the front pockets of the workout suit. Kortel removed the pad and flipped it open.

The doorman smiled tersely and walked away.

Tarris Finn grinned from the tiny screen. "*Bonjour*, dickhead!"

"How the hell?"

"Don't ask. It's way too complicated."

"But I just—"

"Threw Nichols out the window — we know. Now shut up and listen. We've got to get you out of there."

"Yeah, but the hotel's probably got me on—"

"No, they don't. We just hacked in, and you're off their grid. Did that Paris cop hassle you much?"

"Ah…he was about to, but he got called away."

Tarris smiled. "You're welcome."

Kortel felt the tension release from his shoulders. "Thanks. I owe you."

Tarris waved him off. "That's the least of your concerns. You've got to get back here right now."

"There's something I have to take care of first."

This statement sent Tarris into a little anxiety dance. "Man, the shit is hitting the stellar fan back here. Richter thinks the flare could come within the next two weeks. We need you—"

"I *have* to go to Chicago."

"We know all about McCarris stalking Tamara. What's Trumble blackmailing you for?"

Kortel didn't even want to know how Tarris had that information. "Some bullshit."

Tarris shook his head. "Man, that guy's a cockroach. I thought you took him out."

"He's connected in ways you wouldn't believe."

"Yeah, well, soon there won't be anything left to be connected with!"

"Tarris, just get me to Chicago. I promise I'll get back to New Mexico in time."

Tarris rolled his eyes. "I can't believe I'm negotiating for the survival of the planet."

"Tarris!" A distortion field formed off to Kortel's left and silently crushed in the side of a service van. "Look, Trumble knows all about the Tsunami. He doesn't think Richter's correct, but he's not taking any chances. He wants to do the same thing as Zvara, but on his own terms."

"And he knows he can't pull it off without you, so he's going to leverage Tamara."

Kortel nodded. "That's why I have to get to Chicago."

"Hold on." Tarris set his netpad down, and the screen shifted to a static image of black piping and bundles of zip-tied holocable. Kortel could barely hear him talking with Zvara. It sounded like they were getting into it.

A siren cut the air, and another crime scene truck sped past the cabstand. It skidded to a halt, and Kortel watched six personnel in orange HAZMAT gear jump out and begin unloading equipment. The screen shifted again, and Tarris's image reappeared. He looked worried. "Our time frame is critical, so we've got an idea," he said. "We can assume Trumble knows about Nichols's death and that he's contacted McCarris already. They probably think you're on your way to Chicago right now.... In fact, we'll make it look like you are."

"But–"

"Jonny, we don't have time! We have a way of getting to McCarris faster than you, so let us take care of him."

"How can you do that?"

"I can't get into it right now; just trust me."

That would be hard for Kortel. "I can't just...do nothing!"

"You won't." Tarris's voice was grave. "You're going to take out Trumble."

The words hit Kortel hard. Killing in self-defense was one thing, but murder was something he didn't want to consider. He stared past the screen at a *Napoléon* logo etched in the driveway's flagstone. Someone had ground a cigarette butt into the accent mark.

"Hey," Tarris said, "you with me on this?"

Kortel reluctantly nodded.

"That's my Jonny. Now, go to the hotel's trans counter. There'll be a rental waiting for you in your name. When you're done, contact us, and we'll get you back to New Mexico."

"How will I–"

Tarris's expression went critical. "You're the most powerful Tel ever. Just *make it happen*. If you don't, he will."

Kortel studied his friend's face and thought of Tamara. "I'm trusting you, Tarris."

Several disruption lines cut through the signal's picture, and Tarris reappeared. "I'm not going to let anything happen to her, I promise. Now get going. We don't have much time."

The image went to static.

~

"What would you like to hear, Mr. Kortel?"

Kortel thought for a moment. "Davis, Miles."

Haunting riffs from a concert early in Davis's career filled the cabin. It was a remixed version from his hard-bop period and was so clean that it could have been recorded yesterday.

Thanks to Tarris and Shoalburg, Kortel was navigating through a northern Paris suburb in a fancy rental. They had somehow managed to hack the bioencryption wall of Nichols's netpad to make it available for Kortel's use. They also had infused one of Kortel's old Net accounts with enough Euro Credit to last him a year. The vehicle was high-tech, even by Euro standards, and Nichols's pad had no problem porting with its navigation system. Kortel prayed that Nichols's last trip had been from Trumble's so that all he would have to do is retrace the route from the pad.

It was almost 5 in the morning, and the sky was beginning to fill with predawn light. Kortel intently studied the road, but his memory of the trip to the hotel was sketchy, at best.

The rental began speaking: "Mr. Kortel, you will be leaving the National French Interway System in one minute. Please prepare to take control of the vehicle."

Kortel gripped the steering toggle and began piloting. The nav system instructed him where to go and kept reminding him of inane things like the great savings he could expect if he would just take the time and apply for a credit rating. He fiddled with a couple of the control pads and tried to override the voiceover before he finally gave up and settled into guiding the rental through the narrow French streets.

"Mr. Kortel, please take a right at the next intersection. And did you know, you'll be eligible for a free upgrade in 53 kilometers?"

"Blow me."

"I'm sorry, please repeat the command."

Kortel slowed and turned as instructed. He was now on a dirt road, skirting a crumbling, vine-covered wall that looked like it could have been built before World War II. He drove for about a mile when the rental chirped again.

"Mr. Kortel, the next left will be the driveway entrance of the original departure point. If you're ending your trip with us, *avoir un grand jour*! Please leave your *Citroen Organique II* where it can be easily collected. *Bonjour!*"

Kortel debated whether he should park a few blocks away and be covert about the whole thing. But sneaking up on a guy like Trumble was absurd, and Kortel figured he had already been scanned and analyzed by the home's security system. It probably had produced a 10-point scenario on how to take him out seconds after recognizing Nichols wasn't piloting the rental.

"What the hell," he said, and angled the rental up to a large wooden gate that looked older than the wall. Kortel waited as the netpad dialogued with the vehicle's systems. After a moment, the gate slowly drew back, and he pulled forward into a small courtyard. The rental's hydraulics compensated for the loose gravel as he parked near a large poplar tree.

The house appeared harmless enough, much like all the other quaint homes in the town. Kortel removed the netpad and scanned the area for anything living. Nichols's pad was a basic corporate unit capable of complex tasks, though probably not powerful enough to penetrate fiber-reinforced walls. Kortel realized that even if he had an InterVision model, Trumble's place was probably so webbed up it wouldn't have mattered. Surprisingly, the pad revealed more detail than Kortel expected. He stepped from the rental and ran another sweep, but still caught no signs of anything living, human or otherwise.

The home's garage door was up. Kortel went and checked it out. It was bigger than it looked from the courtyard – able to hold four CityCars and maybe a couple of EuroPeds, if they were mounted under the cabinets. It looked like it had been swept recently, and all the shelves were empty. There was a solid door on the far wall. Kortel considered unlocking it, but decided not to chance it.

He returned to the courtyard and approached the back door. It had four panes of old rippled glass and no visible security devices. Kortel scanned again, with the same results. He wondered if the home's security was feeding disinformation to the netpad, making the place *appear* empty.

Pressing his face against the glass, Kortel could only make out blurred shapes. He passed the pad down the right side of the door. On the second pass, it clicked open, and he cautiously entered. Slipping into partial phase, he made his way through an empty mudroom and into a large modern kitchen. He stopped and scanned again. Still nothing.

On his previous "visit," most of his time had been spent in rooms beneath the main house, and he hadn't seen much of the first floor, except for the night Nichols had taken him to the hotel. They had gone out the front, so he had never seen the back of the house.

Kortel inspected the counters and found everything had been thoroughly cleaned. As he walked around a large butcher-block island, he began to consider that the readings were correct. He referenced the pad and saw that the hallway on the other side of the kitchen led to the front of the house. Following it, he came to a foyer that felt vaguely familiar. He tried to recall the night he went to the *Napoléon*, but all he could remember were fractured, meaningless images. Since it had been just two days ago, Kortel concluded that Nichols had probably jerked with his memory. The only thing that made any sense was a distant image of an ornate wooden door. If only he could remember.

"Damnit!"

In the room to his right, sitting in the middle of a large dining table, a lavish fruit bowl exploded. Hundreds of brightly colored plaster fragments sprayed about. One particularly large chunk from an orange smashed against one of the two doors in the room, causing it to quiver slightly. Perhaps it was a trick of the morning light, but Kortel figured it was more likely fatigue. He hadn't slept and was beginning to get that jittery feeling he used to get in Chicago after he had partied all night. He watched the door quiver again and realized it wasn't the light or his fatigue. Then the images aligned in his mind, and he remembered emerging from the basement into a large room with a fireplace and a table. A dining room. Nichols had led him through this room into the foyer.

Kortel approached the strange door. He ran his fingers across its surface and discovered it was actually an image – a kind of holographic *trompe l'oeil*, though extremely sophisticated in its production. He stepped back and focused a narrow grav wave directly at its center. The door's image began to degrade, then it went to static and vanished. Behind it was a reinforced metal door and frame. Kortel increased the field, and the whole thing crumpled like foil.

Now it all came rushing back. He descended the narrow stairs and began searching the corridors of the basement. Everywhere he looked had been scrubbed cleaned; even the bed where he had slept had been stripped and redressed. Kortel checked the armoire and found the rest of the Beijing casual wear.

Kortel stepped back into the main corridor and scanned again, but nothing registered. He stormed upstairs and searched the rest of the house, but found only the same meticulous cleaning effort in every room.

Kortel went back to the courtyard and climbed into the rental. He engaged its organics, ported the netpad and hit recall. Static filled the onboard com screen.

"Come on, Tarris. Connect."

He tried four more times, but was always greeted with pixilated snow. Maybe Tarris and Shoalburg's hacking had been compromised. He should have at least gotten a TransLink logo or a Network Error icon. Static meant the whole system had gone down, satellites and all. Or it was the netpad. He thought about testing it by calling the Pudder Gallery to warn Tamara, but what the hell would that accomplish?

Suddenly the netpad flashed an incoming tag: Unknown. He thought about letting it pass to vidmail, but he had nothing to lose now. He pulled the pad from the port and flipped it open. Trumble's stern face pixeled up.

"Jonathan." His lips didn't move. "You are truly amazing. Cyril felt that you would burn out someday, and we'd have to institutionalize you. But here you are, defying my technology and killing with reckless abandon. Tell me, when you threw my son out the window, was he still alive?"

Stunned, Kortel remembered the look on Nichols's face. "Yes," he said finally.

Trumble's eyes closed for a second, then slowly opened. "Marcus was discovered in Liverpool as an infant. Cyril begged me to take him in. He said it would strengthen our relationship." He paused. "Marcus never got beyond a Level 2, so we implanted him, much like we did you. He achieved a modest gain, but the boy was never satisfied. Then he became unruly. I guess the military did that to him. It was only in the last year that we came back together. He helped with my recovery. I will miss him."

"Look, Jeffrey. I'm sorry about what–"

"I know that you're headed to Chicago. What do you hope to accomplish? I've already instructed James to kill that whore of yours. Shall we call it an eye for an eye?"

Something pressed against Kortel's heart. "I thought we had a deal."

A small laugh answered him. "Deal's off."

Kortel felt nauseous. His throat was dry, and he tried to swallow. "Okay, Jeffrey. Let's—"

"I've never landed from the north before. You get such a lovely view of Lake Michigan."

The back of Kortel's neck prickled. "What are you doing *there?*"

"Just making sure my order is carried out. Tamara is a very beautiful woman, and I know how young men think."

At that moment, a part of Kortel gave way. Out near the liminal point of his rational self, the factors that governed reason and control reverted, exposing something mammalian. Raw.

"I don't know how you're jamming my technology," Trumble said, "but when I break through, I'll introduce you to hell."

A heat was building inside Kortel. It coursed through his body on a wave of primal anger. Every nerve was firing off a message of limitless strength. He could feel his technology metastasizing, and for the first time he embraced it.

"If she dies," he said. "You die."

Trumble's eyes narrowed. "I look forward to that. Again."

I won't let you. 24

"**WHAT** is *she* doing here?" Tarris asked.

Bixx looked at Rocket, who looked at Kreet.

"Ms. Toffler is here to document the proceedings," Kreet said, trying to sound important but failing miserably. Ever since teaming with Toffler, he had been running an attitude, and with Nichols gone, he had grown downright rude. He now addressed everyone as "people" and kept demanding that they act natural. They were creating a docu-drama, and he was the line producer, but the way Bixx saw it, the only thing he was producing was a lot of resentment.

Bixx watched Toffler angle close to Tarris. She was wearing the vid gear Nichols had carried in the chrome cases. She seemed to be going for one of those reaction shots she talked about incessantly. Bixx never understood all the terms Toffler used but figured she knew what she was doing. Toffler had spent the last couple of days creating what she called "master takes" and establishing shots. She told Bixx this was going to be her legacy piece, whatever that meant. Now she was practically sticking the fiber lens of the vid gear up Tarris's nose.

"Lady," he said, his voice threatening, "if you don't get that equipment out of my face, I'm going to cram it up your—"

"We're set to go, everyone!" Shoalburg announced.

"Excellent," Zvara said. He turned to Bixx. "Are you ready?"

Toffler angled into Bixx, who could feel the heat from the vid gear's lights on the side of her face.

"Ms. Toffler," Zvara said, "I have allowed you to document this because the world should know the real story behind stopping the Tsunami. But must you do this...what is it called?"

"Back story," Toffler said.

"Yes. Must you do this back story now?"

Toffler's eyes went to Zvara. "You told me you wanted to present the Tel culture in the best light. I think you said, 'Show the world we're not a threat.' The best way to do that is to document your struggle. It's compassion I'm going for. Real, raw, in-your-face material."

"No shit," Tarris said.

"I realize that," Zvara said, walking around Bixx. He placed his hands on her shoulders; their weight surprised her. "But what we are about to do here," he said, "is not what I had in mind."

Toffler clicked off the lights, peeled the vid gear from her head, and drew right up to Zvara's personal space. "If I can work this correctly," she said conspiratorially, "I can promise you an audience share in the billions. Everyone, and I mean everyone, will see this production. When I'm through editing, Jonathan Kortel will look like the second coming."

Zvara leaned into Toffler until she stepped back. "My dear woman," he said, offering a slight smile, "he might *be*."

Toffler grinned. "Even better. Religion is hot right now, and the world could use something new to worship."

"If we don't do this soon," Shoalburg said, "he might end up a martyr."

"All right, Ms. Toffler," Zvara said. "Continue, but be mindful that there are lives at stake."

"Don't worry," she said, grabbing the vid gear. "After five years in the China Wars, I think I can handle this."

Rocket knelt and took Bixx's hand. Zvara thought he might have to persuade her to go back in, but Bixx didn't need any convincing. Time was against them, and she was the only one who could find McCarris's stream. Still, having Rocket there made her feel safe.

"I'll be right over there," he said and pointed to Shoalburg's console. "All you have to do is find his stream. Once Shoalburg's synced, you can back out. Nobody's expecting you to do the dirty work, okay?"

Bixx's stomach was doing flips. The thought of reentering McCarris's body was tough enough, but doing it so that Shoalburg could cut his Net feed was making her physically ill. "You're not going to kill him, right?" she asked.

Rocket squeezed her hand. "No, baby, they're just going to shut off some of his base functions. Kind of like putting him in a coma." He placed Shoalburg's interface unit in her palm.

Bixx felt Zvara lean next to her ear. "It is time," he said, and patted her shoulder.

"Good," Kreet said. "Now remember, people, act natural."

"Kreet," Toffler said sternly, "would you please go back to my room and monitor the uplink."

"But—"

"Now!"

Kreet mumbled something and walked out of the lab.

"Is Kreet short for cretin?" Tarris asked.

Shoalburg laughed under his breath.

Bixx eyed the interface and raised it to her forehead.

"On my mark," Shoalburg said. "Three, two, one."

The interface's tentacles grabbed Bixx's head, and the room fell away. It had been just a few hours since she'd been yanked out of Nichols, and in that time Shoalburg said he had customized the unit for her. The phase jumps came instantly, and before Bixx could prep, the Net exploded onto her visual field.

You okay? Shoalburg asked inside her mind.

Of course not, Bixx thought. *You're going to kill him.*

We're not going to kill him, unless we absolutely have to.

Bixx felt herself gasp. *Y-you can hear my thoughts?*

See is more accurate. And for the last time, we're not going to kill him. I've made some adjustments to the interface unit, and we shouldn't lose communication like we did before.

Shouldn't?

Okay, won't. Now listen – the last incept we have for McCarris was at the restaurant, but we don't have anything after that. Something is interfering with our ability to track him. He took a Net call during dinner at Kortel's. The feed was untraceable, so I'm betting it was Trumble. I just...

What?

I just hope we're not too late. Now go do whatever it is you do. I'll tell you when to back out. Good luck.

Bixx felt Shoalburg's presence fade into the white noise. She tried to focus on McCarris's chi, but the images of falling with Nichols were still ricocheting about her mind.

Get it together.

Bixx closed her eyes and did a quick breathing exercise. It was hard to forgive someone like McCarris, but she had to if she was going to connect again. She tried to think of him as a victim of circumstance – a pawn. Almost immediately, she heard the distinctive droning of McCarris's stream, then the cerebral shift came, and her cognitive sense slipped away.

Bixx slowly opened her eyes and felt the surreal duality of being with McCarris again. He was in what looked like a small living room, and the lighting was low. The furniture was trendy; the kind Bixx had seen in vidzines for people who cared about style. From this point of view, she couldn't see anything that indicated whether he was at Tamara's apartment or some boutique hotel.

Okay, Dr. Shoalburg, she thought, *I've got you in.*

A moment went by.

Doctor?

Hold on. Shoalburg's presence felt distant, like an old memory. *I'm having trouble getting synced. Stay connected until I can get this worked out.*

Bixx's stomach began to flip again.

McCarris raised a drink to his mouth. She felt the burn of whiskey down her throat. Sensations were stronger this time.

"Come on out," McCarris said. "I won't bite."

"Just a second." It was Tamara. She sounded like she was in another room.

McCarris took another gulp; a cube of ice slid past his lips. He crunched down, and Bixx's teeth stung.

Tamara appeared at of one of the two doorways in the room, which drew McCarris's attention. She had changed out of the flowered dress – or maybe it had changed. The pattern was different. It was darker and made up of small black birds, and the "v" of the neck was much lower. Bixx noted that it looked higher off Tamara's knees than before.

"*Hello* there," McCarris said. "Aren't you a picture?" Bixx felt him getting excited.

Tamara smiled. "This feels much better."

"Here." McCarris picked up another drink off a small side table, but this one appeared to be vodka or gin. "I hope you like the way I made it."

Tamara took the glass and drank. Her eyebrows went up. "Oh, I usually like a little tonic with my vodka." She took another sip. "If I didn't know better, I'd say you're trying to get me drunk, Mr. McCarris."

"Who, me? I'm a gentleman. I would never take advantage of a lady." McCarris gestured to the couch, and they sat.

"Well, thank you for such a lovely dinner," Tamara said, settling in. "I haven't been to a restaurant like that in a long time."

McCarris faced her and rested his arm on the top of the couch. "Really?" he said. He swirled the ice in his drink. "I'm surprised a beautiful lady like yourself doesn't get taken to wonderful places all the time." He took a sip. "And you're welcome. It was my pleasure."

Tamara leaned in, and McCarris's attention went to her cleavage.

Pig.

"I'm afraid I don't have time for much dating. Between the gallery and Nicole, my life is pretty full."

McCarris passed a finger down the side of her face and guided a stray lock of hair away from her eye. "Maybe that's going to change," he said tenderly.

Tamara leaned into his gesture and looked up with those incredibly clear blue eyes. "I thought you weren't going to be in Chicago for very long."

"I'm thinking of changing my plans," he said, leaning in.

Tamara glanced away. "I'm sorry; I haven't done this in a long time." She looked back with a hint of sadness in her eyes.

Bixx was going crazy. It was like watching a bad slasher vid where the whole audience knew the girl was going to get it.

With their lips almost touching, McCarris gently took her chin with his fingers. "I told you before," he whispered, "I don't bite."

Bixx had kissed a girl once, on a dare and full of *Stolichnaya*. But as McCarris and Tamara's lips touched, she felt a disturbing aggression building behind his emotion. It was foreign, and she felt him succumbing to it.

Where the hell is Shoalburg?

Bixx couldn't take it anymore. As McCarris and Tamara kissed, she thought about jacking with his Net feed, but that was way out of her league. Then an idea hit her.

She screamed.

"Oh, shit," McCarris said, almost biting Tamara's lip.

Her eyes went big. "Are you all right?"

McCarris's vision blurred. "I-I don't know." He rubbed his temples for a second, then shook it off. "Now then," he said, and put his arm around Tamara, "where were we?"

"Are you sure you're okay?"

McCarris smiled. "Very."

When McCarris and Tamara began kissing, Bixx felt like screaming again. But something out near the edge of her mind stopped her. It was a dynamic presence that seemed to be closing on her parameters.

Finally. Dr. Shoalburg, is that you?

Suddenly Tamara and McCarris morphed, and Bixx was standing in a low mist of infinite whiteness.

"Vhat the hell?" She looked around, but there were no edges and distance was hard to judge. The mist seemed to extend forever. A rush of adrenaline crashed through her nerves. "Doctor, I need your help!"

An older man formed in front of her. He was tall and thin and dressed like he could have stepped out of one of the fashion vids always playing at the Nitz Salon on 23rd. His suit undulated between an aluminumlike herringbone and mossy green tweed. In the latter state, it seemed to absorb light.

"Who are you?" he asked. His voice was human, but with an electronic edge that sounded a bit like rushing waters.

Bixx didn't know if she should answer.

"I asked you a question." Now the man sounded like an avalanche, thundering and apocalyptic. He had a faint accent that Bixx couldn't place. She recoiled and covered her ears.

"Shut up!" she yelled.

Suddenly the man appeared hundreds of feet tall. His form took on the angular characteristics of an office tower. He looked down through the clouds of white mist. "Well?" he boomed.

Bixx had dealt with hackers before, and the giant routine was so last-century. She shifted her parameter settings and was instantly face to face with the asshole. "This is a secured link," she said, modulating her voice to sound menacing. "Who the hell are you?"

The man's surprise shifted, and his eyes filled with a kind of liquid fire. "Tell Armando he's wasting his time."

Instantly, Bixx found herself floating in the Net with McCarris's stream off to her right.

"Shoalburg, where are you?"

There was no reply.

What was it he had said? The call had come from Trumble? Bixx put it together and knew she had to get back into McCarris. She tried several times, but couldn't connect. She began to panic.

Shoalburg's voice came through without warning. *Bixx, can you hear me?*

"Yes, yes! I can."

Why aren't you connected to McCarris?

"I got pulled. I think by Trumble."

Oh my God. Have you tried to reconnect?

"Of course, but I can't. Something's blocking me."

Let me try and help—

Shoalburg's presence vanished.

"A-are you there?"

... this might work. Here... His voice crackled, then vanished.

"What? What might work?" Bixx felt a surge of energy. It struck at the base of her skull and needled through her nervous system. Suddenly, she was back in McCarris. The room was darker, and he and Tamara were still kissing, but now there was an intense passion about them.

The edge of McCarris's hand brushed against one of Tamara's breasts. He began kissing her neck. She moaned softly.

Aren't you a little young to be a voyeur?

It was Trumble.

Could two streams merge with another? Bixx's brain was spinning. *Get out of here!* she demanded.

There was an odd sound that resembled a laugh. *You're the trespasser. How did you hack into this proprietary wetware?*

Poshol k chortu! Bixx thought.

Again the laugh. *Young lady, I already live in hell.*

Tamara moaned loudly as McCarris gently bit one of her nipples through the fabric. The pattern of birds had migrated to the back of the dress, and the area where McCarris was kissing had become much darker.

They seem to be enjoying each other. Trumble's voice echoed in Bixx's mind. *It's a shame it all has to end.*

Not if I can help it, she thought.

I doubt you can.

McCarris's hand slid between Tamara's legs. Bixx could feel the soft cotton of her panties on his fingertips. His other hand had moved to the side of her neck; his thumb gently stroked the underline of her jaw. Her breathing grew deeper. Then there was a change in McCarris's feed. Something was coming down his cerebral stream and corrupting his parameters. Bixx could sense that his passion was being replaced with something dark and evil.

Both hands went to Tamara's throat. His thumbs dug in. She began to struggle, but he had shifted so that one of his knees was pressing against her stomach. She tried to cry out, but couldn't.

"Carter," Bixx said. "Please, please connect in!"

He can't help you now.

The more Tamara fought, the deeper McCarris dug his fingers. One of her legs thrashed and sent her drink careening off the coffee table. She was beating him about the face, but the insurgent data had numbed his ability to feel pain.

Trumble laughed.

Bixx screamed again, louder and harder than she ever had before. It came from somewhere deep and instinctual. A high-pitched, inhuman cry that seemed to carry all of her fear.

McCarris yelled and grabbed his head. Tamara connected her elbow square on his jaw and sent him tumbling backward. He landed on his side, and Bixx felt something small and hard in his pocket.

...out of there. I'm trying to get synced.... It was Shoalburg.

McCarris struggled to his feet and backed away.

Bixx screamed once more.

McCarris doubled over, knocking a small lamp to the floor and casting the room into harsh shadows. He reached into his pocket. Bixx felt his fingers wrapping around the butt of a handheld Light-Force. His index finger passed over the ID point, and the weapon whined with its charge-up.

"Carter!" Bixx yelled. "Do something!"

...can't connect. Can you try and...

Tamara had slid off the couch. She was on hands and knees, struggling to catch her breath. McCarris took aim. In the upper corner of his vision, the Light-Force's site monitor aligned with her left eye.

"Mommy?" Tamara's daughter appeared in the other doorway, rubbing her eyes. McCarris moved his aim, and Bixx watched in horror as the little girl's forehead appeared in the sight monitor.

"Nicole!" Tamara said, her voice hoarse and deep with fear.

McCarris swung back.

Tamara's eyes darted from her child to the weapon. They were filled with terror. "Who are you?" she begged. "What do you want?"

McCarris didn't answer, and Bixx could still feel Trumble's presence controlling him. McCarris pivoted the Light-Force toward Nicole.

"*No!*" Tamara screamed. "Please...no." She was crying now and pleading, her arms stretched toward McCarris.

Bixx could feel him struggle against the insurgent data.

"I-I'm sorry," he said painfully, as if he couldn't believe what he was about to do.

The insurgent data flooded McCarris's neural network, the last of his original programming transformed. He clicked off the safety.

At the sound, Bixx was overcome with a defining sense of purpose. "No," she whispered. "I won't let you."

McCarris flinched.

Suddenly, Bixx's spatial parameters returned and she was now physically one with McCarris. She felt the warm metal of the Light-Force in her hand and began turning it on him. In the sight monitor, his chest angled into view. He struggled with her, but Bixx didn't back down. She opened her mind and focused all of her will on McCarris's chi…

and pulled the trigger.

You better be worth it. 25

KORTEL drew the plastic curtain aside and entered the small area that had been set up for Bixx. The flight back from Paris had been delayed due to an atmospheric disturbance, and nobody at the Air France counter would give him a straight answer about it. The jump jet from New York was equally screwed up, arriving in Albuquerque 20 minutes behind schedule, which was unheard of. Now, he was looking down at the latest victim in a struggle that seemed to never end.

Bixx wasn't like the rest of her friends. She possessed a toughness Kortel had seen in many Russian Tel girls, a "screw it" attitude that got them through the chauvinistic Russian system. But now, lying there jacked into a mountain of Shoalburg's tech, Bixx looked more frail than he had ever seen her. A weird-looking interface hugged her head like it was about to crawl down her throat, and her chest was so crowded with medoptic cables that it was hard to tell whether she was a boy or a girl. The blunt pain of tired anger filled Kortel, and he began thinking of terrible new ways to kill Trumble.

Zvara glanced at him, his dark eyes more sunken than usual.

Shoalburg noticed Kortel over the top of his medpad and gave a slight nod. "When did you get in, Jonny?" he asked.

"Late last night. My flight was delayed." Kortel motioned at Bixx. "Armando filled me in on most of what happened. How's she doing?"

Shoalburg shrugged and set the pad down. "To be honest? Not good." His voice was heavy with frustration.

"She keeps calling out 'Anari,' " Zvara said.

The name sent a shiver through Kortel.

Zvara picked up on it. "Do you know this person?"

"Yeah. It was Tamara's best friend from the club. But Bixx couldn't have known her."

"Tell us about this Anari."

"She was a waitress. James was supposed to have erased her, but he didn't. He had a thing for her. They saw each other for over a year before I found out...." Although it had been years, the memory of McCarris convulsing in Kortel's telekinetic grip filled his mind afresh. He asked Shoalburg, "How did she end up like this?"

"Trumble was doing a damn good job of walling me up." Shoalburg looked down at Bixx. "She was amazing. I don't know how she did it, but she was able to affect McCarris's ability to process Trumble's downfeed. She has an incredibly intuitive gift that seems to be magnified by the Net. I could tell she was trying to stop McCarris, but Trumble's feed was too complex, so I jacked the connection and let her merge with McCarris's neural net."

"God, Carter. That's pretty radical."

"We were out of options." Shoalburg looked tentatively at Zvara.

"What?" Kortel asked.

"My interface—"

"Oh, Carter."

"What? It's been thoroughly tested. In trials, we never had any problems."

"But you did here, right?"

Shoalburg reluctantly nodded. "When Bixx merged, it didn't keep the streams separated. The peripheral interface VRMs didn't align with the local NNEs...."

"Just get to the point."

"I don't *know* the point."

"What do you mean?"

"When their streams merged, Bixx and McCarris became...one. I don't know how. It just happened, and Bixx took advantage of it. She turned the Light-Force on herself, I-I mean McCarris."

"She didn't—"

"No! I pulled her before the discharge."

"Wait a minute. How could the Light-Force discharge if you pulled her?"

Shoalburg and Zvara exchanged looks again.

The truth suddenly hit Kortel. "*James* pulled the trigger?"

"Yes," Shoalburg said.

Another shiver. "Jesus," he said to himself.

The area filled with an awkward silence. Kortel leaned down and inspected the interface.

"Why is she still connected?" he asked.

"I pulled her pretty abruptly," Shoalburg said. "We think that some traces of McCarris's neural net came with her. I'm not sure what will happen if I disengage it."

"God, Carter, what *do* you know?"

"We're in unknown territory here, Jonny. I've never worked with someone like Bixx. She's different. I didn't know you could even merge two personality constructs."

A small headache was building in the back of Kortel's head.

"Anari!" Bixx called out.

The area grew quiet again.

"What *is* that?" Kortel asked.

"It's not a what," Shoalburg said. "It's McCarris, or what's left of him."

"How long will she be like this?" Kortel asked, rubbing the back of his neck.

"It's hard to say...."

Just then, the plastic curtain pulled back, and Rocket was standing there. From the look of him, Kortel figured he hadn't slept for days. His mop of curls was flattened to one side, his eyes red and swollen. They shifted away from Kortel almost as soon as they took him in.

"Any change?" Rocket asked, walking over to Shoalburg. He dragged a metal stool next to the bed and sat.

"No," Zvara said.

Rocket stroked Bixx's forehead and whispered something into her ear.

Shoalburg grabbed the medpad off a side table. "Actually, there has been *some* improvement. Her theta waves are showing more activity, but it's her delta waves that concern me."

"Why's that?" Rocket asked.

"They're cycling erratically. Normally brainwaves run in 90-minute increments, but hers are all over the place. Something's going on in her head that I can't access through the Web or the interface."

Rocket looked up through his thick curls. "What if she never wakes up?"

"That would be unlikely. The real question is: what will she be like when she does?"

One of the monitors in Shoalburg's equipment chimed, and a holoimage of Richter appeared.

"Armando?" she asked, her arms folded tightly across her chest.

Zvara stepped over to the monitor. "Yes, doctor?"

Richter moved closer; her image loomed in the holoparameters. "It's the sun," she said gravely.

Zvara glanced first at Shoalburg, then Kortel. "It has begun."

Shoalburg quickly began reviewing some of the monitors hooked to Bixx.

Kortel started to follow Zvara out through the curtain, but a hand grabbed his shoulder and spun him around. It was Rocket. He started to speak, but stopped and glared. Kortel could feel the hatred radiating off of him.

Shoalburg pulled Rocket back. "Easy, there," he said.

Rocket shrugged off his grip. "Piss off."

"Hey, it's not his fault. Bixx knew the risks."

"How could she, Carter? You didn't even know them."

Zvara came up to Kortel's side. "Rocket, please. There are bigger issues at stake right now."

"Shut up, old man." Tears were welling at the corners of Rocket's eyes. "She could die for what? A *theory*? You don't even know if the sun will go Tsunami."

"Rocket–"

"No! You used her to get what you wanted." He passed his glare across Kortel and Shoalburg. "You're all *guilty*!"

Zvara stepped closer. "That's enough!"

Rocket froze. Kortel couldn't sense whether it had been voluntary or a result of Zvara's power.

"No one forced Bixx to go back in," Zvara said, his voice deep with authority. "She understood what was at stake...and didn't let her emotions get in the way."

Damn, Kortel thought. *Two contractions.*

Zvara stepped up to Rocket and took his shoulders. "Rocket, I need your strength now." His tone was softer. "This won't succeed without our best. You know Bixx would want you to do this."

Rocket broke from Zvara's hold and got in Kortel's face. "*You,*" he said, tears running down his cheeks, "better be worth it."

The bastard. 26

BIXX opened her eyes.

I'm alive.

She was on her back, staring through thick darkness at an old wooden ceiling. Some exposed ductwork was catching light, but she couldn't tell the source. She moved her hands to her stomach and discovered she was still in the same clothes. Maybe Shoalburg had taken her to an infirmary somewhere.

Bixx stretched. Her bare feet touched something cold and metallic. She recoiled, and her knees tangled in thin, crisp sheets that smelled vaguely of industrial cleaner. She sat up and bunched the sheets around her in a futile attempt at comfort. The room was cavernous and held hundreds of empty beds. The ceiling was taller than she had first thought, and there was a chill in the air.

"Hello?" she called out. *What's going on? Where is everybody?* "Dr. Shoalburg? Rocket?"

She swung her legs over the side of the bed and peered at the floor. It was soiled by years of dirt and traffic, and she wondered if the tiny octagonal tiles were as cold as the bed frame. Her attention went to the dresser that separated her area from the next bed.

"Oh my God," she said.

There, hanging precariously off the edge of the dresser, was her Bible from the orphanage. It was open, and Bixx could see the bookmark ribbon she had painted as a little girl. Its fluorescent yellow and pink flowers glowed faintly. Instinctually, she reached for it.

"Happy to see it again?" a voice asked from the dark.

Bixx yelped and slipped from the bed. As she fell, her hand hit the Bible and knocked it from the dresser. The sound of it hitting the floor echoed throughout the room. She snatched it up and backed herself into the corner created by the edge of the dresser and the bed frame.

"Who said that?" she asked, searching for details in the blackness. Her Bible smelled of old memories. Bixx held it close to her chest.

There was no answer.

Bixx peeked over the mattress, but the room was too large and dark for her to make out anything beyond the footboard.

"I asked if you were happy to see it again...your Bible."

A shadow shifted, and she caught the edge of a man's silhouette. He was standing in the aisle that separated her bed's row from the next.

Bixx hugged her knees. "Who are you?"

There was a laugh. "I don't think you could say that I am a who anymore – more like a what. Or maybe, a was."

The voice was familiar, but tinged with a techno quality. The inflection sounded whimsical, and Bixx took a wild guess.

"Mr. McCarris?" she called out.

"In the digital."

Bixx's heart was racing. "How is that possible? I thought I–"

"Killed me? Just the body, I suppose." The form moved toward her bed and passed through a shaft of light. Bixx caught a thin vertical slice of McCarris's face. "Kind of liberating in a disembodied sort of way." He raised his hands and inspected them. "Weirdest sensation I've ever felt. It's like having a lucid dream. I guess I should thank you."

"Why?"

"Because now I don't have to deal with my body. Being continuously jacked was no party. Sure, it had its advantages, but for the most part, it was a pain in the ass." He leaned against the footboard. "By the way, that was a brilliant move."

"Thanks," Bixx said, "but I don't think I did anything. I must have been pulled before I ..." McCarris's comment suddenly registered. "Wait a second. If I was pulled, then...did *you* fire the Light-Force?"

He looked away. "I was tired of dealing," he said.

Bixx's stomach tightened. "If you're dead, then am I?"

"No, you're still connected. This is the Net." McCarris gestured at the room. "It's synced with your brain. I guess it's creating this illusion from your memories."

Bixx felt the weight of her situation pressing down. She slowly stood and crawled back onto the bed. "Am I dying?" she asked, looking at her hands.

"Not from what I can sense. You're in some sort of coma, but I don't have any idea how you entered my consciousness, or vice versa."

Suddenly, Bixx's spatial reference changed; she was in the chaos of the Net, but before she could focus, another shift occurred, and she was back on the bed. She shrieked.

"You okay?" McCarris asked.

She didn't know what to say.

"Did you just *jump*?"

"Yes. I was back in the Net, but now I'm here again."

"That figures. I've been doing it, too. But for me, it's more like jumping into your memories." He folded his arms. "You've had a tough life."

Bixx's Russian heritage went up like the wall around Chernobyl. "No tougher than anyone else's."

"Not from what I've seen."

"Where are we?" she asked, changing the subject.

"Inside your head."

"No, I mean, what is *this*?" She shook the Bible at McCarris.

"You tell me. This is your memory."

Bixx stood on the bed and surveyed the room. "This looks like the orphanage were I was raised. But it feels different."

"Probably because it is."

"What do you mean?" She sat up and crossed her legs.

"From what I can gather, our streams have merged. I'm guessing that your mind has retreated to a place that represents safety to you. Your bed at the orphanage, for example. But dreams are full of metaphors. They're usually not exact. Kind of like when you have damaged data, and the program fills in the gaps. Your mind is doing the same thing, so it's not going to feel exact. Does that make sense?"

"Sort of. But how are you existing?"

"On the Agency mainframe...in the Net...who knows? Probably all of it, in some form."

"Do you know how long you'll be like this?"

Silence.

"Mr. McCarris?"

"I don't know." He walked into the middle of the aisle and motioned for her to follow. "Come on."

"Where?"

"Let's find out why we're here. Or actually, why you've put us here."

Bixx began to slide off the bed but stopped, remembering what a monster McCarris had been to Tamara.

"What's the matter," he asked. "You afraid?"

"No, it's just that you're a...I don't know."

McCarris walked up to the side of the bed, and Bixx could see his face in the dim light. His cheeks and neck had a light speckling of acne scars, which Bixx thought was odd, considering he could have had it all removed at any DermaBox. "I think the word you're looking for is asshole," he offered.

"I was thinking *govnyuk*."

"And what's that?"

"Shithead."

McCarris nodded. "I can't say I blame you. But if you were really connected to me, you would know I didn't want to kill her. My programming was being altered."

Bixx flashed on the moment back in Chicago when McCarris was about to pull the trigger on Tamara's child. He had said something about being sorry, and she remembered feeling his struggle against the rush of Trumble's data.

"I can feel you remembering." He leaned in, his breath non-existent. "I can see what you see."

Bixx studied his blue eyes. There was a faint pixeled edge in the makeup of his image – a rasterization of the detail. She wondered what sort of data was coursing behind his face now that he was nothing more than a logarithmic flow of ones and zeros.

"Then you know what I think of you," she said.

McCarris forced a smile. "I'm the one who should be scared." He straightened. "By the way, how did you hack Trumble's feed? That was the most encrypted stream I've ever seen."

Bixx shrugged. "I don't know. I felt the boost from Dr. Shoalburg, and then I just did it."

"Did what?"

"Listened. I can't describe it. It's like leaving my body. I open my mind and listen for the essence of someone. Their chi."

McCarris's face went blank. Bixx couldn't tell whether he wasn't getting it or something had disrupted his feed.

"Interesting," he said finally.

~

"Anything look familiar?" McCarris asked while they walked.

Bixx was intently studying the room, hoping that another jump would happen and she'd wake up from this psychotic nightmare, when she saw the light source that had illuminated McCarris's face. It was one of the round glass exit signs on the other side of the room.

"Some things do, and others, I don't remember so well." She stopped and pointed. "Like that sign. That never worked when I was here. But now it does. Weird."

"That's one word for it," McCarris said. He twisted to see what was behind them. "Was this place always so empty?"

Bixx turned in his direction, but the room dropped off into darkness so that she couldn't see the other side. "No. There were usually a couple hundred of us here. All crammed together. I remember…"

"What?"

"The smell." She winced. "It was awful. And they never did anything about it. We could only shower every third day."

McCarris made a clicking sound, like Bixx's grandfather had when he called his favorite horse. "And you could only shower for three minutes."

The whole thought of McCarris being inside her mind creeped Bixx out. Since his essence was a stream of continuously changing data packs, she wondered what would become of him. They started walking toward the exit sign.

"Do you think you have a soul?" she asked, turning down another aisle.

"I must," he said, sounding more like he was convincing himself. "How else could I exist?"

"Technology," Bixx offered. "Maybe controlled by the Agency's AI. How would you know? You would mistake its programmed promptings as your own will, your own thoughts. Can you feel your blood moving?"

McCarris pondered this. "Can you?"

"Yes."

"That's because you're still flesh *and* blood. I'm...." He hesitated.

"See?" she said. "That's my point. What are you now?"

McCarris didn't answer, and Bixx really couldn't blame him. As they approached the exit sign, she noticed it was casting an uneven light. Only certain things were highlighted by it, and she couldn't figure out if there was any pattern to it. Maybe there was a glitch in the programming.

McCarris's pace slowed, and he began looking around. Suddenly, he stuck his hand out and stopped her. This was the first time his form had made contact with hers, and she could feel the pressure of his hand against her shoulder. She could also sense his chi. It was warm, and there was an undercurrent of power that Bixx took for his connection to the Net.

"Hold up," he said, still glancing about.

"What do you see?" she asked.

McCarris whirled his face around, and Bixx noticed that the color of his eyes was deeper and had a liquid texture that was frighteningly real. For a second, her spatial dynamics wavered. Then she jumped and found herself in a kitchen. It was old, like her grandmother's, and a little boy was cowering in a corner. A man was standing over him, his belt drawn. The boy was terrified and crying.

Suddenly, the dynamics jumped again, and she was back in the orphanage.

"What just happened?" McCarris asked.

Bixx shivered; her tongue had a bitter metallic taste. "Ah, nothing...I mean, your eyes. They're kind of like water."

"Really?" McCarris studied her. "Hey, you just jumped, didn't you?"

"Yes, how can you tell?"

"Because your stream changed. Patterns merged, then separated. It was hard to look at. Where'd you go?"

"Nowhere."

"Bull. Tell me."

"I was in a kitchen, and there was a little boy with a man standing over him. The boy looked frightened."

"Did the man have dark hair?"

"Yes."

"Was he holding a belt?"

Bixx nodded.

McCarris shook his head. "Welcome to *my* childhood."

Bixx couldn't think of anything to say. His memory resonated with her; there had been many abused children at the orphanage who had told her their stories. "I'm sorry," she said after an awkward pause.

McCarris waved her off. "The Agency was the best thing that ever happened to me. My ol' man didn't understand our gift. He was an SP."

"What's that?"

"Sinless Perfectionist. The Church of the One-Way Ticket. There's only one way to God," McCarris emphasized this by pointing at the ceiling, "and in Daddy's eyes, that was to beat the living tar out of me after a night of drugging."

Bixx desperately wanted to change the subject. "Why do you keep looking around?" she asked.

"Because I see this differently than you. Since you're still alive, this all looks real, right?"

"Yes."

"To me, this is all code and shapes and colors. It's incredibly complex, but I recognize certain flow patterns. I used to do a little programming when I was younger, and this looks like a kind of imaging matrix. But this," he pointed at the exit door, "is different."

"Why?"

McCarris hesitated. "Because it's military."

The word sent another shiver through her, and Bixx began to feel cold. She folded her arms and hugged her Bible. "Military?" she asked. "What do you mean?"

McCarris walked up to the door and ran his hand across it. There was nothing special about the actual exit, from what Bixx could remember. Like the other furniture in the room, it was heavily stained, and its surface looked wet from years of repeated refinishing. McCarris's fingers seemed to meld with the wood, and Bixx couldn't tell if it was a trick from the light. He leaned in and raised his other hand.

"What do you see?" she asked.

He didn't acknowledge her.

Finally, McCarris removed his hands and slowly turned. The look on his face was serious, like he was processing the data and didn't like what he saw.

"How well do you remember your time here?" he asked.

The question seemed odd. "Pretty well," Bixx said. "Why?"

More of the concerned look. "All of this," he said, raising his arms to the room, "is a sophisticated layering program. I've seen this before in the wetware that was developed by one of our SBUs for the DoD."

"Your SB what's for the who?"

"Single business units. Real companies that our culture operates behind. Carter worked for one. Where do you think all the new implant stuff comes from? The Department of Defense has contracts with several of our companies. Back in the '80s, there was one that developed wetware that could mask a soldier's trauma. They used it in the China wars, and it made us a bundle."

"But I lived in Russia."

"I know. This is a bastard version of it. In some ways, it's better." McCarris craned to look at the ceiling. "Yeah. Not a bad rip-off. Amazing architecture."

Bixx was getting frustrated. "I don't get it. What's the military have to do with my memories?"

McCarris stepped closer and regarded her with care. "Whatever's behind that door is definitely not civilian. Part of what you remember of the orphanage *is* real. I can see that in the data. But this..." He stopped himself.

"What?" Bixx urged. "You saw something, didn't you?"

McCarris thrust his hands into his pockets and looked at his feet. "It's a masking program, used to block out severe trauma." He looked up. "Something's being hidden from you, and it's got a military signature. Do you have any periods of blackouts, lack of memory, stuff like that?"

Nausea was building inside Bixx. She found it hard to focus on the question. McCarris must have sensed it, because he took her shoulder.

"Are you all right?" he asked.

She wasn't, but she nodded anyway.

"Look, I've seen this kind of data before. Whatever's behind that door is very black – secret ops stuff. You've got a hell of an ability, and I wouldn't put it past the Russians to experiment on their young, especially the gifted ones."

Bixx fought to keep from puking. "You mean the Russian Command knows about the Tels?"

"Absolutely. We've been in partnership with governments for years."

Bixx's legs seemed to have transformed into something elastic, pliable. She found it hard to stand and leaned against a table.

"They did something to you, Bixx. Now, whether it was to enhance your gift or jack you for some agenda, that's hard to say."

"What do you mean...*agenda*?"

McCarris shrugged. "Could be a million things. Net projecting. Transcription coding. Even SIW."

"What's SIW?"

"Subversive Internet Warfare."

Bixx edged herself along the table and sat in a large chair. Her stomach was in knots. "Could you find out?" she asked. "You know, go in and see what they did?"

McCarris considered her request while his attention stayed focused on the door. "I guess I could try. What's the worst that could happen?" He laughed, but his demeanor shifted. "Weird thing is, I don't see any tech in you. Either what they did was totally organic, or the masking is hiding it." He shuddered, then started for the door.

"James?" Bixx called out.

McCarris turned.

"Thanks."

He smiled. "I've got a lot of bad karma to correct. It's the least I can do." He made that clicking sound and continued toward the exit. "Besides," he called back over his shoulder, "what else have I got to do, right?"

When McCarris reached the door, he positioned his legs like he was going to push on it. Then he gently placed his fingertips against the center panel and leaned in.

Suddenly, a bright light exploded from the point of contact. He screamed and stumbled backward.

Bixx launched from the chair and ran toward him.

McCarris held up his hand. "Don't!" he said.

She stopped about 10 feet from him. He was doubled over, and his form was degrading.

"What can I do?" she asked, feeling a strange compassion for him.

McCarris's image was now about 50 percent of its original quality. He examined his hands and arms. "The bastard," he said to himself.

"Who?" Bixx asked.

McCarris glanced up, his expression twisted in pain. "Trumble," he gasped, and then vanished.

Weird. 27

TRAILING Shoalburg down the narrow hallway, Kortel pondered the irony that the father of nano implants hadn't indulged in the cosmetic side of the technology. With bioaug basically a global religion, people didn't bother with diet or exercise; they just "restructured." Not that Shoalburg was fat, but he was, as Kortel's uncle used to say, carrying more than his fair share.

"Maybe we *should* fry," Kortel mumbled.

Shoalburg turned. "What's that?"

"Nothing."

"Gotta stay focused."

"Right."

They all cut hard lefts down another hallway. Zvara was leading and hadn't said a word since they'd left Bixx's med station. Behind him were Rocket and Shoalburg with Toffler bringing up the rear. She had appeared after they entered Richter's building, and Kortel could feel the heat of her vid lights on the back of his neck.

He leaned forward to Shoalburg's ear and whispered, "Why does Zvara allow her so much access?"

"Don't worry about that," Shoalburg said over his shoulder. "After we pull this off, you'll be famous."

Kortel didn't want to be famous. He didn't really want to be anything. If he had a magic wand, he would have waved it and wished for the way things had been when his biggest concern was whether the hostess would show for the night run at his restaurant. The thought of trudging through a sooty blanket of icy Chicago snow to the Wacker Street maglev sounded pretty appealing right now.

They approached two tall doors made of composite metal. They were windowless and looked out of place amid all the old wood and plaster.

Zvara swiped a pass card through an optical reader, and the doors clicked. He looked back at Kortel as if he had felt his gaze.

"This compound was a weapons lab during the China Wars," he said. "The technology is old, but it still works. Dr. Richter believes in security." Zvara raised a hand, and the door opened. It was odd to see him use his power so casually. Kortel almost said something, but then Zvara glanced over his shoulder, and it hit Kortel that this was it. Ever since he had arrived, they had been training him to use his ability on a colossal scale. Now the time had arrived, the nexus, where history from here on out would probably be referred to as post-Tsunami.

Kortel followed Zvara through rows of computer stacks similar to the ones in Shoalburg's lab. Unlike his intelligent chaos, however, Richter's maze evinced a distinct order. She was German, and Kortel had never met one who wasn't an organizational freak. The group came to a control bay that had a dozen lab techs huddled around a large holojection of the sun. Its surface was so stunning that Kortel imagined he felt heat coming from it. Richter was at the center of the huddle, her interface idly perched on top of her head.

She and Zvara didn't say anything; they just exchanged looks that said the shit had hit the galactic fan.

Shoalburg cleared his throat. "How bad?"

Richter regarded him as one who had asked the dumbest question in the history of their short-lived species before she resumed studying the holoimage.

"What is our time frame?" Zvara asked.

"We don't know," she said, pulling the interface into position. Its tentacles wrapped around her head, and she recoiled. The room became strangely quiet.

"Doctor—"

"Watch this," Richter blurted. She pointed to the projected sun and looked at them one by one as if she were making eye contact. A small flare erupted from the holoimage and engulfed her hand.

Shoalburg seemed unimpressed.

Then another flare, this one enormous, arched from the surface. It passed through Richter, Zvara, Kortel and Shoalburg. Rocket actually jumped out of its way. It fractured and disappeared just beyond a stack of Net processors.

"My God," Shoalburg said.

"Don't you see?" The interface was hugging Richter's head like a trained sea creature. "This is only the preliminary stage."

"How long until we all die?" Rocket asked Kortel. His voice was calm, but there was anger in his eyes.

Everyone turned.

Zvara intervened. "Doctor, please. What is the time frame?"

Richter faced him. "It could be any time," she said. "An hour? A day? We need to act."

"Does anyone not understand what you need to do?" Zvara asked to the room.

The techs remained silent.

"They understand, Armando," Richter said for them.

"Ready, Jonny?" Shoalburg's eyes moved across Kortel, and for the first time since he could remember, they seemed unfamiliar, even alien.

"Sure," Kortel said. "Let's get on with it."

Zvara motioned to seven chairs stocked with electronics and bioptic cable. They looked like dentist rigs Kortel had seen in one of Tarris's father's old medical catalogs. Tech guys were already sitting in three of them.

"I am sorry there was no time for all of you to train together," Zvara said. "Please, introduce yourselves."

One of the techs, an Asian, bowed slightly in his chair. His skin was deathly white, and his eyes were dark lines of concentration.

"Even in the face of disaster," another said through a thick beard, "there's always time for decorum." He had a distinct accent that sounded South African. He raised a hand, and Kortel shook it. "Ah, the famous Mr. Kortel. Thought I'd never see the day that I'd be working with you. My name's Bundles, Aubrey Bundles."

"Good to meet you." As Kortel settled into one of the chairs, Toffler stepped in for a close-up. He raised his hand, and she slid back, slamming against a computer stack. "Sorry," he said, "not now."

The move didn't faze Toffler. She sidestepped away for another angle.

The third tech leaned around Bundles and smiled. He had the Eastern Euro look Kortel had seen in Russia. His greeting was toothy, and his thick cheeks went almost to his eyes when he grinned.

"Isato is from Tokyo," Bundles said. "And Petrov here is from somewhere north of the Circle. Near the Kara Sea, I think."

"And you?" Kortel asked.

"Johannesburg."

"These are some of the best I could find," Shoalburg said, removing his eyes. His placed them on the tray next to his chair and slipped in his neural connectors.

Zvara was now in the farthest chair. He leaned forward and looked at Kortel. "Are you clear on what to do?"

The only thing clear to Kortel was that if this worked, he'd start believing in God again. Training with Zvara and Shoalburg had been one thing, but until he had looked into the faces now around him, it hadn't sunk in that he'd have to link with such a diverse group of Tels. The whole idea of a joined phase with more than 100 other telepaths was crazy enough. But the plan was based on a theory – a very loose, Shoalburgian theory – of doing it jacked and using the global network of the worldwide Web to create a grav phase so massive that it would strengthen the earth's gravitational field and deflect the Tsunami flare. Shoalburg calculated that linking through 3,000 or so satellites alone would do the job, but Zvara insisted upon using every jump point, relay node, and any other digital portal to ensure maximum coverage. When Shoalburg explained the theoretical physics of the concept, Kortel hadn't believed him. But when Zvara launched himself into the metaphysical passion of it all, Kortel realized that the whole New Mexico complex had been developed for one thing: to train him to be what Richter called a lens. He was to be the focal point through which all of their combined telekinetic power would be channeled. It would be a one-time shot: either he'd do it, or the planet would be destroyed...or maybe just part of it would; Richter didn't really know for sure. The flare might even miss the earth altogether, but who could say? Regardless, Kortel was now hours, maybe minutes, from stopping it. And how the hell was he going to do that...*exactly*? Even with all of the training, Kortel knew that when it came to the real thing, he'd have to improvise. He had asked Zvara, but all he could do was orate about Kortel's duty to mankind. Richter had been more fire and brimstone, opining that God would lead him, whatever that meant. Tarris's spin was a little more to Kortel's liking. He said to go in and let it fucking rip, which sounded like something he would have said years ago, when he was high on Jack. But there was still the "it" factor in Tarris's version, and Kortel was damned if he knew what it was. Bixx, though, seemed to have the best take on Kortel's dilemma. Listen to your heart, she had told him. It won't fail you.

Suddenly, one of Richter's computers chimed, and Kortel thought the holoimage of the sun had changed color slightly. A tech rushed over to the console, while the others scurried to their stations. Richter remained fixed on the holoimage.

"What is the situation now?" Zvara asked her.

Richter, still facing the sun, raised her hand. "Hold on," she said. Then her posture slumped and Kortel knew the answer.

A lab tech hurried to Kortel's chair and swung a diagnostic unit into place over his head. Similar techs did the same with the others.

Rocket was on Kortel's right. "Is it okay to be scared shitless?" he asked.

Shoalburg glanced over. "Way ahead of you."

A figure approached Kortel from the lab's darkness. "You better not be," Tarris said.

Kortel looked into the face of his old friend and smiled. "See you when this is over."

Tarris laughed and patted Kortel's shoulder. "My money's on you. Vegas has you at 2 to 1."

"That's optimistic."

Tarris leaned in. "It's realistic. Now get in there and stop this killer flare before it ruins my evening."

"Remember," Shoalburg said, "we're linking with over a hundred others. Don't go into phase until we're all connected. This trans-portal won't be like the one you had in training. It'll be more, ah, personal."

"Personal?" Bundles asked.

"Kick in ass," the Asian declared.

"On my mark," Zvara said.

Kortel heard the vacuum release of seven interface canisters being opened.

"Three."

His tech dangled the white disc inches above his face.

"Two."

It quivered imperceptibly, and he could almost feel it prepping.

"One."

"Shit," Kortel said when the interface's tentacles grabbed his head.

As his vision returned, Kortel felt the spatial nausea Shoalburg had warned about. Even though he had done hundreds of simulations, none of them compared to this. Every one of his senses was firing at what seemed a billion times the norm, and he was suddenly grateful for the comfort he received from the simple awareness of his body.

Kortel felt like he was standing on a tiled floor inside a large space. He flashed on the Hawaii memorial and how dark it became once the doors had closed. This was similar, but somehow bigger. When his eyes began to adjust, he could make out shapes and color. Gradually, the area took form, and he saw patches of detail in the faint light. He stepped forward, and his boot caught the edge of a table, possibly a chair.

Weird. This didn't look or feel anything like the simulations. Shoalburg had said it would be different, and Kortel was having trouble understanding why he would have simmed an old gymnasium for the trans-portal. And what gave with all the beds?

Seeing a ghost. 28

THE hair on the back of Bixx's neck bristled. McCarris's form had simply vanished. No pixel flux. Not even a hint of what Rocket called "data death." She glanced about. The room that had been her home for so many years suddenly felt strange. She had to remind herself that it was nothing more than photons and neural stimulation, that she was lying in a bed somewhere, that it was probably a sunny New Mexico day. At any moment, Shoalburg or Richter would bring her out of her coma. She began walking toward the bed where she had awoken, hoping she could fall back to sleep and not deal with this bullshit anymore. Maybe she'd wake up in Rocket's arms. Better yet, maybe none of this had ever happened.

Bixx sensed a ripple in the downfeed. A bright flash appeared on the other side of the room. She dropped to her knees and crawled behind the closest bed. The light died. Even though it was merely a simulation, she had to act as if it were real. Bixx was a pro at sim apps and figured this one was no exception. It would probably demand that she move through the space as if she were actually in the orphanage. Memory readers were tricky programs and could really mess with your emotions if you let them. Bixx waited, but nothing happened. Then she heard a table being bumped and a man swearing.

A figure slowly moved up the farthest aisle from hers. Bixx thought about making a break for it but didn't know if the app extended beyond the main room. If she wasn't careful, she could find herself opening a door to nowhere. The figure stopped and turned in her direction. Bixx hunkered down, barely able to see over the footboard. The man began cutting through the rows of beds that separated his aisle from hers. When he got within four beds, Bixx decided to take a chance. She sprang from her position and ran down the aisle toward the back of the room.

"Hey, wait!" she heard behind her. The voice sounded familiar, but she couldn't really tell.

Bixx skidded to a stop almost at the exact spot where McCarris had vanished. She looked back and saw the figure running toward her. His stride was athletic and smooth, and he was closing fast. She searched for the stairwell door that would take her to the ground floor. It should have been to her left, against the wall, but it wasn't there.

"Bixx, it's me!"

The sound of her name stopped her. She looked back and recognized Jonathan Kortel.

"What are you doing in the trans-portal?" he asked, trotting to a stop.

"The what?"

"The trans-portal. I don't know if you realize it or not, but you're in a med station. Shoalburg says you're in some kind of Net coma – something to do with your beta waves. He has you jacked into God knows what."

"McCarris said I was in a coma–"

"What? McCarris was *here*?"

"Yes. He said my mind created this sim of my old orphanage."

"I thought he was dead."

"It wasn't *him*. It was his residual personality data. I'd heard that if people died while jacked, their personality constructs might live on. Since McCarris's was already backed up, it makes sense. It's pretty cool, really. So what are you doing here?"

Kortel regarded her, his expression grave. "The Tsunami cycle has started."

The words invaded Bixx like a virus, needling through the fabric of her construct.

"Richter thinks it might start within a day," Kortel said, his voice edged with doubt.

"But you don't think so?"

"I don't know.... I can't imagine something like the Tsunami would sneak past the entire scientific community. Richter can't be the only one who's figured it out."

"Maybe she isn't," Bixx said. "What if the governments are keeping it a secret, you know, so the world doesn't freak out and get all crazy? And what if Richter's right?"

Kortel leaned in. "Then we better not screw this up."

Suddenly, Bixx sensed a tremendous surge in her feed. For an instant, she felt the duality of being in the med station and the Net. She gasped.

"You okay?" Kortel asked.

"I...I don't know. I could feel myself for a second...my real self."

"Maybe the drugs Shoalburg's been giving you are starting to work."

The surge happened again, and Kortel reacted. It drew his attention to the door below the exit sign.

"You felt it, didn't you?" Bixx asked.

"Yes." Kortel walked up to the door and ran his fingers over its surface. "I've seen this kind of programming before."

"It's military."

Kortel nodded, still examining the wood. "What's it doing embedded in your construct? Is it coming from your brain?"

"McCarris thought the Russian military might have tested on me when I was a kid, then used what he called a–"

"Layering program. I knew I'd seen this before." Kortel bent forward and examined the doorknob.

"Where?"

"In Russia," he said, straightening. "A couple of Tels I stayed with thought they'd been jacked with, too."

"McCarris thought they could have been prepping me to be some kind of weapon," Bixx said.

"Maybe. Anything's possible." Kortel began walking toward her. "I've given up trying to figure it all out. We Tels don't seem to have much say in our lives."

The comment sounded odd to Bixx, considering Kortel's power. "I'm nowhere close to your level," she said.

He gave her a knowing grin. "You're special, Bixx. I've seen what you can do. You're hyper-smart and have a gift for nav'ing the Net that most info jocks would die for. McCarris is probably right. The question is: What did they prep you for?"

At that moment, two waves of distortion cascaded through the large room. One wave rippled across the roof; the other traveled across the floor. It passed under their feet, causing their forms to waver below their knees.

"What the hell is that?" Kortel asked.

Bixx followed the upper wave as it moved down the back wall. The exit sign liquefied as it passed, then assumed its original shape. The door remained unaffected as the wave washed around it.

"Digital inversion," she said, and watched the two waves meet in the center of the wall and dissipate.

"Doesn't that mean—"

Just then, a blinding light consumed the room. Bixx covered her eyes, but her action was futile. The light penetrated her construct's reality parameters and blinded her.

"Shit!" she heard Kortel yell.

"Hold still!" she said.

"What is this?"

"A digital logarithmic spatial inversion code."

"A *what*?"

"An upgrade."

"You're kidding, right?"

The light withdrew as quickly as it had appeared, and Bixx's eyes instantly adjusted.

"Can you see?" she asked.

Kortel rubbed his eyes. "Yeah," he said, blinking. "But shouldn't I be blind for a couple of seconds?"

"Normally, yes. But I think this new code has rewritten the construct's parameters."

Both Bixx and Kortel were facing the back wall. The room's physical appearance hadn't changed: the wood and paint looked the same, and even the exit sign was still cracked. But something about the door didn't feel right.

"Does the door look different to you?" Bixx asked.

Kortel approached it, motioning for her to stay back. He got halfway and stopped.

"What do you see?" she asked.

"It's opened now, just a crack." He beckoned Bixx forward, but his attention went past her.

Instinctually, Bixx looked over her shoulder, but what she saw didn't register. The room, which had been disturbingly empty, was now filled with children. On top of each bed was a child sitting cross-legged. There were rows and rows of them, all roughly between the ages of 12 and 16.

"Okay," Kortel whispered. "Did you create this?"

"No!" Bixx shook her head. "I have no idea what this is. And why are you whispering?"

"Because." He pointed. "It looks like they're meditating."

Strangely, they did look like they were meditating. "So what do we do?" Bixx asked.

"I don't know. Our time's running out, and I'm supposed to be in a trans-portal, linking with a hundred Tels."

"Maybe the key to getting you into that portal is these kids." Bixx grabbed Kortel's arm. "Come on."

As they walked up the closest aisle, Bixx saw that Kortel was right. Each child's eyes were closed, and all of them were sitting in the lotus position.

"They don't seem to notice us," Kortel whispered.

"Or are choosing not to," Bixx replied.

"Is it me, or did the room get larger?"

Bixx studied the space. "I think it did."

"So how many beds are there?"

"When I was here, this room could hold up to 200, but I can't tell now."

They turned down the next aisle, and Bixx took in the faces of the children. There was a mixture of races and nationalities, and there seemed to be no pattern to their positioning in the room. They were dressed like they had just walked in off the street, and a small medpad hung at the foot of each bed. Kortel stopped and lifted one off its hook. The child, a slight Indian girl with long black hair and delicate features, didn't stir.

"Who is she?" Bixx asked.

"I can't pronounce her name. Tanvi-something. It says she's from New Delhi." He replaced the medpad, and they continued walking.

Halfway up the third aisle, Kortel pointed. "Look, an empty bed!"

They rushed over, and Kortel removed the medpad from the footboard.

"Well?" Bixx asked.

Kortel handed the medpad to Bixx and walked away.

She read the name. *Kortel, Jonathan.*

"What does this mean?" she asked.

"How would I know?" He faced her. "You created this, right?"

"Not this. I'm not sure what's going on."

Kortel came back and took the medpad from her. He scanned its files and shook his head. "Everything's here. Right down to my blood type and genetic profile." He tossed it on the bed, and immediately its image merged into the folds of the sheets. He stepped back. "What the hell?" He turned to the room. "Hey, kids! Wake up!"

None of the children moved.

"Maybe this *is* the trans-portal," Bixx offered.

"No," Kortel said, his attention focused on the Indian girl. "I know Carter, and this isn't it." He walked around the bed and reached for the girl's shoulder.

"Don't!" Bixx said.

He stopped in mid-reach. "Why?"

"Because."

Kortel rolled his eyes and continued.

"NO!" Bixx yelled. A distortion exploded in front of the girl, sending Kortel flying backward down the aisle. He landed on his back and slid to rest against the leg of a bed.

"See," he called out. "I said you were special."

Bixx couldn't believe what she had done. "I'm so sorry. I didn't mean to do that."

Kortel got to his feet and dusted himself off. He approached, but kept his distance. "I guess I'll have to be more careful around you. How did you do that, anyway?"

I...I don't know exactly. I just do it."

"You just *do* it?"

Bixx nodded.

Kortel raised an eyebrow. "Let's find your bed."

"It's over there, in the last row. I woke up in it...before McCarris appeared."

Kortel's attention lingered where Bixx was pointing.

"What are you thinking?" she asked.

"I've got to connect before it's too late."

"How?"

"I'm not sure. But if I had to guess, I'd say this bed is the key."

"Don't climb on until I get to mine." Bixx turned and sprinted toward her bed. The thought of jacking with the greatest of her kind was, well, unbelievable. It was a Net junkie's wet dream, and Bixx almost fell as she scrambled toward her bed.

"You need to concentrate on getting better."

"Do I look like I feel bad?" Bixx said, sliding past her bed.

"What do you think happened to McCarris's residual data?" Kortel's figure was barely visible in the darkness. Bixx could only make out his silhouette. He had climbed onto his bed and was looking back at her.

"I don't know," she said, crawling over the footboard. The bed was now made; the sheets felt cool and crisp against her hands.

"Did he say anything before he crashed?"

Bixx glanced at the two children on either side of her and crossed her legs to match theirs. The image of McCarris – his face flushed with shock, Trumble's name on his lips – flashed across her mind.

"He used Trumble's name," she said, hoping this wouldn't stop Kortel from jacking.

The silence was crushing.

"Great," Kortel said.

Listen to your heart. 29

KORTEL assumed the lotus position. He drew a deep breath and let his exhale linger. Surprisingly, he didn't feel nervous. In fact, he didn't feel anything. He had been through so much lately that this seemed a fitting end to a very weird ride. And if they did pull this off, he'd march straight back to Chicago and reconnect with Tamara. He checked his position relative to the boy next to him. The boy's legs were in full lotus, but Kortel's left foot was still tucked under his right knee. Ever since a biobike accident with a girl from Skokie, he had lost a lot of his flexibility.

"Screw it," he said under his breath.

He surveyed the room and wondered if this would work. Even if he did connect with the portal, what if Carter was wrong? What if he couldn't figure out what to do? What had Bixx told him, to listen with his heart?

He took another breath and closed his eyes.

Nothing.

"Hey, Bixx," he said, turning. "Is it taking–"

The shift hit him with such force that he thought his organs would explode through his skin. It took all of his will not to scream. The orphanage scenario began degrading, though not like the usual app flux. This was bizarre – similar to what he thought Riders experienced when they peaked on Jack. Tarris had tried to explain it once but had never found the words.

All the detail generated from the orphanage's matrix melted into itself, leaving the digi-frame exposed. And for a brief, astonishing second, Kortel saw the skeleton of the military program. In its raw form, it was an undulating pillar of crystalline black energy. It shuddered through Kortel's construct, and he fought the reflex to vomit. His visual range narrowed into a brilliant circle of white, and suddenly he was being transported through the chaos of the Net, falling through an endless black void, his arms and legs splayed. He landed on his stomach, and his face dug into something warm and gritty. The sound of waves crashing against a beach echoed at the edge of his awareness. He couldn't open his eyes.

"It's about damn time!" he heard. The voice was faint from a distance and sounded familiar.

Kortel coughed and spit and felt a thin layer of sand clinging to his face. He struggled to his hands and knees, and spit again. The rays of a high sun were burning the back of his neck, and there was a faint smell of bougainvillea and dead fish. A strong breeze tugged at the collar of his jacket, and he heard the sound of feet pounding against wet sand.

"Where have you been?"

"Carter?" Kortel asked, tasting bits of sand under his tongue. He opened his eyes to the sting of sunshine and watched Shoalburg's shadow grow around him.

"Get up; we're at the critical point."

Shoalburg's hands were at Kortel's shoulders, and then he was standing, wobbly, on a brilliant white beach. To his right was a row of people, 50 probably, dressed like they had been yanked out of their everyday lives and dropped into paradise. To his left was the same. He thought he saw the guy from Johannesburg.

"What the hell is going on?" he asked, brushing the crusted sand from his lapel. "Why the face plant after the shift?"

Shoalburg eyed him sternly. "This is your construct – your portal. It's not like the simulations we ran, but the protocols are the same, and they're set to your neural mapping."

"Then, where are you?"

"I'm in *my* portal."

"And all these people?"

"In theirs."

"But–"

"Jonathan! Richter says the Tsunami cycle is entering its final phase. You have to get connected and synced with the others. Come on."

Shoalburg pulled Kortel into position between an elderly black man and a teenage Asian girl. The man looked like a mid-level exec, and his suit's pattern shifted as he made room. He took Kortel's hand and laced his fingers in a firm grip. The girl was dressed like she came straight from the mall. She smiled politely from under a hood of black bangs and took his other hand. If Zvara had been successful, Kortel was now holding hands with a hundred of the most powerful Tels on the planet. He watched a wave roll in, its transparent arc catching the sun like green crystal.

Shoalburg stepped in front of Kortel, and his androidian eyes studied him. "Are you ready to play God?" he asked.

"Where am I, Carter?"

"You're in a lab."

"No, where's this beach supposed to be?"

A knowing grin formed at the edges of Shoalburg's mouth. "Turn around, Jonny."

Kortel complied and saw a set of old steps at an opening in the undergrowth. He immediately knew they led to the path that had connected his parents' home to the beach. Something shivered through Kortel, and the businessman squeezed his hand.

"Why here?" Kortel asked, his attention focused on the chipped whitewash of the top step.

"Because…"

Shoalburg's voice had changed, and Kortel sensed a shift in the construct. He turned back to find his father standing in front of him.

"This is *your* safe place, son," his father said. His hand went to Kortel's chin, cupping it with profound care. "Look at you…your mother would be so proud."

Kortel figured that the matrix's core had read his brain's emotional cues and conjured up a reasonably accurate image of his father. Anyway, how the hell would he know what his father really looked like? The last time he had seen his father, Kortel had been a child. He could barely remember his life on Hawaii, much less the details of his father's face. But rather than reassuring Kortel, the sight of his father standing there in his khaki shorts and lab coat made Kortel edgy, nervous. He knew this was an illusion and slapped the hand away.

His father didn't react.

Kortel got in the image's face. "Get the hell out of here!"

The businessman pulled him back.

"Who are you talking to?" Shoalburg called. He was leaning away from the line on Kortel's right, about 20 people down.

Kortel was suddenly confused. He looked into his father's eyes, and something fell away from his heart. Then the image slowly dispersed, and Kortel was staring at the ocean again. The waves were now only half their original strength and lapped the beach in a steady, hypnotic rhythm.

"We're connecting now," he heard Shoalburg yell.

About 50 feet from the beach, Kortel noticed a figure emerging from the surf. It was a man, and as he came closer, Kortel saw that he was dressed in a dapper gray suit, complete with a bowler and an umbrella hanging from his right forearm. It seemed he was walking up a set of sunken stairs, but strangely, he remained perfectly dry. When the identity of the man registered with Kortel, a spike of adrenaline coursed through his body.

"Trumble?" he whispered.

Jeffrey Trumble tipped his hat and kept walking.

Kortel let go of the people and tried to run, but his feet had merged with the sand. He glanced at the businessman, but he had already slipped into phase. The girl looked the same, along with all the others.

Trumble was making his way up the beach. He cavalierly poked the umbrella into the sand with every other step.

"Hello, Jonathan," he said as he approached. This was a younger Trumble, somewhere in his mid-40s. He was trim and proper, with a jaunty step. He removed the bowler.

"What the hell do you want?" Kortel demanded. The wind had picked up, and the collar of his jacket was slapping his cheek.

Trumble casually looked down both sides of the beach, then leveled his gaze at

Kortel. The classic British demeanor had been replaced by something darker, more sinister. "Surely you didn't think I would miss your big moment in history," he said.

"I have to connect with the group."

"That can wait."

"You don't understand; the Tsunami–"

"I know all about it. We have a few moments."

"No, we don't!" Kortel sensed a flux in the Hawaii construct and thought he saw the waves jitter.

Trumble eyed him.

"What?" Kortel asked.

"I was just thinking of the first time I met you. Cyril thought of you as a son, you know, but I couldn't get past your arrogance." Trumble looked away. The wind blew his hair across his forehead. "He always wanted a child."

"Jeffrey, look...I can't–"

"Do you miss them much?"

"Who?"

"Your parents."

Kortel hesitated. "Yes, very much."

Trumble's attention focused on something down the beach. "And I miss Cyril...*very* much."

A gust of hot wind blew between them, and Kortel's lapel slapped his cheek again. "So, what now?" he asked and glanced at his feet, or what was left of them.

Trumble returned the bowler to his head, cocked it slightly, and passed his fingers down its brim. He smiled softly and placed his hands on Kortel's shoulders.

"You," he said, with a wink, "get to see your parents again."

The comment didn't hit immediately, but the punch of raw energy to Kortel's chest did. The waves jittered again. He tried to speak, but those parameters seemed to have been altered. Trumble's hands squeezed tighter, and it felt like his fingers were digging to bone.

"You can't," Kortel said, barely finding the strength to get the words out. "The Tsunami!" He tried to grab Trumble, but his arms wouldn't move. Pain surged through his neural system and exploded inside his head. His legs buckled, but he didn't fall. The ocean and beach, even the sky were shifting, or maybe his vision was just collapsing. Trumble's eyes rolled back, and his grip tightened. A new wave of pain crashed through Kortel's body. He screamed.

The sun, whose warmth had comforted just moments before, now burned the flesh from his body.

"Jeffery, please," Kortel managed between gasps. "We have to save–"

The fabric of the idyllic Hawaiian matrix jumped, and Kortel felt himself back in Richter's lab. The horizon morphed into the underside of the interfacer. There was a strange smell in the air, like something burning. He screamed again, and the Hawaiian matrix returned. A pain shot up his right arm; a crushing pressure weighed upon his chest.

I'm dying, he thought as his mind raced through images from his life. Tamara's face flashed, and tears came to his eyes.

Part of Trumble's form had become a hideous collage of fractal swirls that Kortel had studied in his grade school computer class. But these were unbelievably more complex, and he couldn't look at them without feeling like he might fall into their centers.

Out of the corner of his eye, Kortel saw two figures standing at the edge of the surf – a man and a woman – and even though they were far away, he knew they were his parents. They stood motionless, the waves lapping their ankles. The rational side of Kortel knew they weren't real, that they were part of Trumble's deathblow, designed to send him over the edge. But another part of Kortel ached to join them, and he felt himself starting to let go.

Another surge of excruciating energy carved through Kortel's being. He could feel his heart failing. "The hell with it," he murmured.

Then, somewhere off to his left, there came a detached, murderous wail. Although he tried to look, his head wouldn't move. The pitch of the scream rose, and a figure entered the edge of Kortel's vision.

Bixx was charging up the beach.

She slammed into Trumble and drove her hands into the center of the largest swirl. Trumble didn't acknowledge her at first, but when she yelled something in Russian, his patterns coalesced back into the 40-something man. His eyes rolled forward and locked onto Bixx.

"Die, you asshole!" she screamed, and she jumped and wrapped her legs around Trumble's waist.

A look of astonishment came over Trumble, and Kortel felt his heart begin beating again.

Did we stop it? 30

THE energy coming from Trumble's avatar was beyond anything Bixx had ever experienced. She had sensed it before he had emerged from the ocean and didn't understand why no one had come to Kortel's defense. As they struggled, the fabric of her construct began to weaken.

Trumble removed one of his hands from Kortel and wrapped it around her neck. Bixx thought they had lost Kortel, but this move seemed to bring him back.

"You are very foolish," Trumble said, struggling to get the words out.

Bixx ignored him and tried to open her mind. If she could tap his core, she might be able to disrupt his feed and give Kortel an opening to link with the others. She channeled her energy toward Trumble's heart and squeezed his throat with all of her will.

Trumble's image wavered. "It won't work," he managed.

A tremendous force lacerated Bixx's construct. The duality she had previously felt returned. She could feel herself in the med station. Hands were holding her down, and a distant voice told her to remain calm. She sensed her eyes opening, and the ceiling of the med station appeared through the Hawaiian matrix. An unbearable pain coursed through her.

Shoalburg, she heard. It was Richter, cutting through the chaos of the Net. *What's happening? Why isn't Jonathan connected?*

I can't tell, Shoalburg replied. *Something—*

Static replaced the voices. A flash of ball lightning exploded in Bixx's vision, and she was back on the beach.

It's starting, Richter said. More static.

Kortel had his hands at Trumble's throat.

Trumble let go of Kortel and placed his other hand against Bixx's chest. Hot pain surged through her body. She could see Trumble's matrix in its raw form. It was like viewing all of his life at once, and the sight of it was almost overwhelming.

My God, she heard Richter say. *It's bigger than we thought.*

Bixx summoned all of her strength and unleashed it on Trumble. Her scream brought Kortel's attention around.

Trumble's image blurred.

"Let go and connect!" she yelled at Kortel.

He hesitated.

"Do it. *Now*!"

Kortel released Trumble and grabbed the hands of the businessman and girl.

Trumble watched him, then threw his attention at Bixx. His eyes filled with rage.

Bixx focused all of her power at the core of his construct and imagined it exploding. *"Paashol v'chorte!"* she yelled.

Trumble cried out and splintered into a million spiraling fragments of pixilated color. Another flash, and his form blew apart.

Bixx fell. Her elbow caught the brunt of it, but her face plowed into the sand. A gull squawked high above her. She tried to raise her head, but her construct was damaged. Her physical senses were off; the sand felt more like syrup without the sweet smell. A gust of wind passed over her back, and she tasted mint on her tongue. A deep ache throbbed through her body.

"Jonathan?"

Another gull squawked.

Bixx forced her head to turn. She tried to look at Kortel, but the sun was blinding.

"Jonathan?!"

The wind blew, and the minty taste returned.

Bixx struggled to her feet and searched the beach, but the people – and Kortel – were gone.

"Where are you?!" she yelled.

An odd shadow caught her attention, and she forced herself to look up.

"Oh my God," Bixx said. The line of people hovered hand in hand 30 feet above the beach. Kortel was floating another 20 feet or so above them. His arms were spread, and he was looking to the sky. Bixx thought of the Tsunami.

Suddenly, a flash of light obliterated everything, which reminded Bixx of the history vids that described what people saw at the detonation of an atomic bomb. A silent force slammed her to the sand.

It seemed like an eternity before Bixx's eyes would focus.... When she could, she saw bands of threatening clouds moving in slow time-lapse across the sky, and the wind whipping the palms and forming little tornadoes along the beach. She tried to wipe her face to no avail; the wind kept pelting her with gusts of fine sand.

"Jonathan?" she called out, shielding her eyes.

The people were still floating, but Kortel was gone. Their forms, glowing bright against the darkening sky, rippled for a moment before they dispersed into the wind. She heard a moan. Kortel was sprawled on the beach about 60 feet away. A rumble of distant thunder echoed off the ocean.

Panic cut through Bixx's pain as she ran to his side. "Oh, God, no," she said, dropping to her knees.

Kortel was on his back. His eyes were searching the sky. He looked desperate, like he had lost something he couldn't find among the clouds. There was another clap of thunder.

Bixx slipped her hand under Kortel's neck and gently raised his head. His eyes rolled, then focused, but he didn't seem to recognize her. His form wavered, and his digital framework showed beneath his skin. Bixx knew something was terribly wrong, but she didn't know what to do. Drops of rain began pelting the sand around them.

"Jonathan," she said. "I think your core is degrading. You have to disconnect now, before it's too late."

Kortel coughed, and his eyes went to Bixx. He smiled. "Hey," he said, his voice static and hoarse, "did we stop it?"

Bixx didn't know how to answer. Since their forms were still intact, she figured they must have stopped the Tsunami. Then again, they could be residual data themselves. "Yes," she said after some hesitation, "we did." The rain began to fall harder.

He nodded and coughed. His eyes went to the sky and began searching again.

Bixx gently brushed the sand from his forehead. Kortel took her hand. Another rumble of thunder came off the ocean.

"I'm going to miss that sound," he whispered, and his form vanished.

You believed in me. 31

THE jump jet smelled of stale air and Australian leather. It banked gracefully through a thin layer of clouds while Bixx studied the sun's reflection on the ocean. From this altitude, it looked like a blanket of diamonds thrown over a narrow stretch of the Pacific. She felt a hand at her arm.

"What are you looking at?" Richter asked. She was leaning on the armrest and peering out the window.

Bixx didn't answer.

"Beautiful, isn't it?"

"What is?" Bixx asked.

Richter leaned in to get a better view, and Bixx caught a hint of her perfume. It was clean and delicate and reminded her of something her mother had once worn.

"The ocean," Richter said, "when sunlight falls on it."

Seven months had passed since the Tsunami. Toffler's documentary had aired two weeks earlier and was still embroiled in a wave of media controversy. Much of the scientific community had dismissed Richter's work as fringe science. They argued that the earth's magnetosphere had been strengthened not by some secret cult of genetic mutants, but by a convergency of natural causes. All that Bixx could grasp was that it had something to do with the earth's core shifting, but the finer details eluded her. There had been a small group of influential academics who had predicted the flare, however, and they hailed Richter's achievement as nothing short of genius. Some media rumors even had Richter in the running for the Gates Prize, but she had laughed those off as being generated by her university's PR machine.

Toffler's promotional blitz had put her on all the big talk shows. She had defended her work as genuine and declared that the Tels would soon become a part of everyday life.

"Hey, Bixx," Tarris said, "where'd you go?"

Bixx pulled her attention from the view and turned to her friends. Zvara was seated in one of the chairs that faced the cabin and was deep in his netpad. Shoalburg was across the aisle from Richter, and Tarris was in the seat next to Zvara. He was facing Bixx and hugging Kortel's urn. Since they had left New Mexico, the only time she had seen him without it had been at the LAX security checkpoint, where he had been forced to turn it over for inspection. That fiasco had delayed their takeoff for more than 20 minutes.

"Everywhere," she replied. "Nowhere."

Tarris nodded and resumed staring out the window. His fingers played with the raised edge of the urn's keypad.

The leadership of the five world Agencies had viewed Toffler's documentary with great trepidation. They had acquiesced to its airing only after Zvara's relentless lobbying. They predicted the world would most likely lump their kind in the same category as aliens and relegate them to the tabloid media. Currently, the world was still reeling from the concept of the Tels, and since the broadcast, Bixx hadn't seen an info show that didn't have some panel discussing their possible existence. Conservative religious leaders claimed the idea was an affront to God, while many scientists believed the concept was ridiculous, reciting the accepted wisdom that the human brain was incapable of altering gravity. On one show, a Sinless Perfectionist almost strangled an MIT professor. Bixx and Rocket had laughed their guts out watching the show's security try and tackle the 400-pound woman. Tarris had even heard of a group in Nebraska that was already worshipping the Tels. They called themselves Kortelians and claimed that they had seen Kortel's image in a field of corn. Bixx had never heard of such a thing, but Rocket assured her that farmers had been seeing things in crops for centuries. Not a few corporations had jumped at the marketing potential. Action figures and virtual games were beginning to enter the Asian marketplace, and a friend of Rocket's had sent him a black net Bixx doll. Bixx had been shocked at the size of its breasts, but Rocket loved it and ordered a dozen. Because of the conspicuous timing, Bixx suspected Toffler had a hand in the merchandising push, but Toffler denied having anything to do with it. She had gone on about "intellectual property" and said her company had unleashed an army of lawyers to shut down any pirating. Sanjiv was pissed that there was no figure in his likeness. Nor was there a Kreet doll, but that had been okay, because he had disappeared after the Tsunami, and nobody really cared what he thought, anyway.

Bixx felt the craft begin to slow and sensed it was descending.

Shoalburg had brought her out of her coma a day after the Tsunami passed. She had asked about Kortel several times, but Shoalburg always dodged the question, saying he had to check on one thing or another. It had been Tarris who finally told her. He had come to her bedside and explained what had happened, or at least, what they knew about it.

Shoalburg's concept had worked. Kortel had channeled the combined grav force of the hundred most powerful Tels through every available satellite and had created a protective field that deflected the flare around the earth. The tech in Kortel's brain, his "soulware," as he called it, had merged with the blue mass that had puzzled Richter and Shoalburg. The combined tech had acted like a conduit for the grav wave. Richter was still processing the data, but Tarris figured the amount of energy must have been enormous. He had choked up when he described how Kortel, at the height of the phase, had burst into flames. It had taken four of Richter's lab techs with extinguishers to put him out. Toffler said she had captured it on vid, but had vacillated whether to keep it in the documentary or not. She finally decided not to air it out of respect for Kortel's memory. Bixx suspected that Zvara might have *persuaded* her into the decision, but she could never get him to admit it. There was also an awful rumor going around that the footage of Kortel dying had made it onto the black net, but Rocket had searched and never found it.

"Mr. Zvara," the pilot said over the intercom, "we'll be at the drop point in 10 minutes."

Zvara looked up from the netpad and glanced out his window. "We must be near the edge of the Hawaiian Zone." There was sadness in his voice, and Bixx thought he had aged considerably over the last seven months.

"We are being allowed only 15 minutes," Zvara said, his thoughts clearly somewhere over the water.

"How did you get permission to come out here?" Richter asked.

"There was a law enacted after the Event that allowed relatives access to certain areas near the Zone for services. I spoke with the department that handles this and convinced them we were as close to family as Jonathan had."

"Would everyone please fasten their seat belts," the pilot announced. "We'll be starting our vertical descent in just a few minutes."

"Tarris," Shoalburg said, "how did it go down with the lawyers?"

When the plane began banking, light angled through the cabin. It passed across Tarris's face.

"Pretty straightforward," he said. "Jonny's AI at his loft in Chicago had his will on file. He donated the bulk of his estate to the Hawaii Victim's Fund. The rest got split up."

The engines roared, and the jet's forward momentum came to a halt. It started to descend, and Bixx watched the ocean's glittering surface rise beneath them.

"One minute till hover point," the pilot blurted.

"I'm sorry Rocket couldn't make it," Richter said.

Bixx forced a smile. "It's okay. He falls apart at stuff like this."

The truth was that Rocket hadn't gotten past the idea that Zvara had used Bixx. Bixx had defended Zvara, saying he had to do what he thought was best. She figured her life was a small price to pay. Rocket said that was all bullshit, which brought about the worst argument they ever had. But in a way, this trip had been good for Bixx. She was using the time to reflect on the direction she and Rocket were headed. She caught Tarris staring.

"What are you going to do with that?" he asked, pointing to the miniature urn that hung around her neck. It contained a small amount of Kortel's ashes. Bixx had told Zvara she had one for each of her parents and wanted one of Kortel. He hadn't questioned her request.

"I'm working on a special place for it," she said.

Zvara looked up and grinned, and Bixx couldn't remember if she'd ever seen him smile before.

"There'll be a little bump as we level off into our hovering position," the pilot said, his drawl a little more pronounced. "Once we're there, I'll open the door. Remember, we have 15 minutes before the military will scramble some interceptors. And be careful. The winds out here can be tricky."

The jet rocked slightly and came to a halt. The door between Tarris and Bixx hissed, then slid into the roof of the fuselage. The Pacific looked surprising calm as it rolled 20 feet below them. The wind scattered napkins into every corner of the cabin. Bixx could barely hear the jet's engines and was amazed at how they could be muffled so well.

The sound of the ocean filled the cabin, and everyone stared at the opening.

"Tarris?" Zvara gestured at the door. "Please."

Tarris looked mournfully around the cabin, then at the urn. He entered the security code on the panel, and its top clicked. He raised the armrest and slid over in his seat.

The wind had died. The sun was beginning to set. It was a beautiful scene, and Bixx couldn't help but wonder if Kortel was smiling down on them.

Tarris knelt at the opening. "Jonny..." He tried to continue, but started crying. Zvara put a hand at his shoulder.

Richter took one of Bixx's arms.

"You were a brother to me," Tarris said finally. "I'll always love you." He lowered the urn to the edge of the door and tipped it. Kortel's ashes blew under the jet and over the Pacific. Everyone was dabbing at tears except Bixx. She wanted to cry, but the need had been purged back in New Mexico on a small mesa near the compound.

Tarris wiped his eyes with the sleeve of his shirt and returned to his seat. Zvara approached the opening and fell on his hands and knees. He bent over until his forehead touched the floor, and it struck Bixx that she'd never known what religion he was, if any. This looked like ans Islamic ritual, but she wasn't sure. Besides, it didn't matter. This was how Zvara wanted to pray, and that's what was important. His face was expressionless as he settled back into his seat. Shoalburg angled toward the opening and sank to one knee. He was quiet for a moment before he crossed himself. Zvara motioned for Richter, but she waved him off with a tearful smile.

"Three minutes to liftoff," the pilot announced.

"Bixx," Zvara said. "It is your turn."

Bixx unbuckled her seatbelt and went to her knees in front of the opening. A storm was building beyond the horizon, and brilliant rays of orange and pale purple arched through the clouds. Her thoughts went to what Kortel had said to her in the virt world of the orphanage. He had told her she was special, that she had a gift.

"You believed in me," she whispered to the ocean.

~

The hum of the maglev deepened, and Bixx looked up from her netpad.

"Next stop, LaSalle Street Station," a soft female voice announced. "Please stand clear of the sliding doors."

Bixx resumed reading about the mayoral race in the local press. She didn't care much for politics, and coming from Russia, had learned that politics was more about power than about helping the people. The article detailed the pros and cons of the challenger. It seemed she was a descendant of a famous mayor named Daley. Usually, Bixx would have clicked to the sports section, but this woman had vowed to fight organized crime, and any God-fearing Russian had to give it up for a woman who would go against the Mafia.

"Welcome to the LaSalle Street Station. Thank you for using the Chicago Transit Authority."

The maglev slowed to a stop, and the doors slid open. It was late in the afternoon, and Bixx followed the stream of commuters who made their way to the exits. She stepped onto the platform and waded into a current of business types who, according to her Chicago Guide, descended into this nine-block stretch of LaSalle every evening to decompress. She had read on the plane that this area had become home to the elite of the city's art crowd. Trendy galleries, haute cafes and couturier boutiques lined the crowded street. The guide's GPS indicated that the Pudder Gallery was two blocks north, on the left side. Bixx's coat had already sensed the cold winter wind, and its collar and cuffs had tightened to the point of pain. She was usually okay with apparel that thought for itself, but this rental seemed to have a mind of its own.

"Relax," she instructed. "Ten percent of current pressure."

The collar gave slightly, but the cuffs remained too tight. Her fingers tingled.

"Loosen the sleeves, or you're going in the trash."

The coat's waistband tightened around Bixx's hips.

"Pizdets!" she exclaimed, and pressed the emergency off button. The coat relaxed, and Bixx began feeling her fingers again.

She made her way up the street, stopping only to check out a pair of boots she knew she couldn't afford and to buy a Hydro Bite, which, depending how hard you shook it, could be drank or eaten. Bixx liked to eat them, and as she waited for the vending kiosk to prep her Bite, dozens of adverts demanded she buy everything from a space station condo to diapers that would eat a baby's waste. Two of the verts got into a fight about which had grabbed Bixx's attention first, when suddenly the BioDiaper advert morphed into the face of Jonathan Kortel. The image was so bizarre that Bixx didn't register it at first. She almost dropped the Bite when Kortel's smiling image said, "thank you," and called her by name.

That's impossible, she thought. She had seen Kortel's construct degrade with her own eyes, and there was no way that any part of his personality matrix could have survived. Yet…his image lingered.

"Hey, lady," a man said behind her. "Some of us want to eat in this century!"

"Back off, asshole!" Bixx said, turning into the face of a middle-aged corporate suit.

The guy stepped back, clearly concerned by the crazy bitch's attitude.

The BioDiaper advert had returned, and Bixx took her receipt. She slowly backed away from the kiosk, wondering.

"Are you okay?" the suit asked.

"Yeah," Bixx said, trying to wrap her head around what she had just seen.

"Damn Riders," the suit muttered as he slid his chip-card into the kiosk.

While Bixx walked away, she ran through Kortel's final moments on the beach. After two blocks, she finally shrugged the apparition off to exhaustion. After all, her flight had been in a holding pattern for over an hour, and the cab to the hotel had been a ride from hell.

It was 4:45, and the guide said the Pudder Gallery would close at 5. Bixx crossed the street, barely dodging a CitiCab that had an unusual amount of urban art attached to it.

The gallery's window had been converted into some kind of art installation. It looked like an enormous shadow box, and a crowd huddled in front it. Bixx caught the side of a woman's naked figure inside the box as she hurried through the building's weapons detector.

The interior of the gallery looked almost exactly like it had when she had been merged with McCarris. The sight of it was unsettling, and she stood for a moment remembering. The painting McCarris had commented on remained hanging on a far wall, which sent a chill through her.

"May I help you?"

Bixx turned and found herself face to face with Tamara Connor.

"Oh," she said.

Tamara smiled. "I'm sorry, did I startle you?"

"No, I just...never mind."

"Is it still cold outside?"

"Ah, yes...it is."

"Well then, we'll be closing in 10 minutes. If you want to look at the work, take your time. I'll be here for another half hour, at least. If you need anything, my name is Nicole."

She offered her hand, and Bixx shook it. Tamara was taller than Bixx expected and more attractive. She had looked pretty through McCarris's eyes, but in person, there was an innocence that hadn't translated. And her eyes were so blue they could have come from one of the mannequins in the shoe boutique four blocks back on LaSalle.

"Thanks," Bixx said, not really knowing how she would proceed.

Tamara smiled and disappeared behind a desk at the back of the gallery.

Bixx wandered the space and took in the various pieces. She rounded a large iron column and came upon a triptych of small paintings. They were hung in an alcove with a single spot illuminating each canvas. In the center of each painting was an amorphous figure depicted in aggressive strokes of dark colors. The figure looked like a man and seemed to be turning, so that by the third painting he was looking at the viewer. Bixx figured these were the ones Tarris had told her about. She had discussed her trip with him, sort of fishing for his approval. He had been unusually polite, saying that if this was what she needed to do, who was he to stop her? She stood silently in front of the third painting, captivated by its raw emotion.

After 30 minutes, Bixx was the only person left. She did a quick breathing exercise and approached Tamara's desk.

"Excuse me," she said.

Tamara looked up, and those blue eyes searched Bixx.

"I…" She hesitated.

Tamara's expression hardened slightly.

"I have to confess," Bixx said, her heart racing. "I'm not here for the work. I mean, it's pretty and all, but I don't know anything about art."

"You don't need to know much about art to enjoy it," Tamara responded.

"I know." Bixx glanced at the front door.

"Is there something wrong?"

Bixx caught herself trembling. "Look, I came to tell you something."

Tamara's eyes widened, and she nervously folded her computer and tucked it between two art history vid pads standing on her desk. One of them started to topple. "If you're from Family Services," she said, catching the pad, "you'll have to speak with my lawyer."

"Oh no!" Bixx said. "It's nothing like that."

Tamara relaxed and leaned back in her chair. "Who are you?"

"My friends call me Bixx."

"Really. Am I a friend?"

This struck Bixx as odd. She could feel the leftover emotion from Kortel's funeral rising. "Yeah," she replied, her voice cracking, "you could say that."

"Are you okay?"

Bixx nodded. "Could I sit down?"

Tamara motioned to one of the chairs in front of her desk.

Bixx sat and glanced over her shoulder at the triptych. "I've come here to tell you about the man in the paintings. The ones over there."

Tamara's eyes went to the triptych, and Bixx could tell she'd struck a nerve. "Really?" she said, folding her arms. "Tell me what you know."

"You're the artist, and you painted them from your dreams."

Tamara slowly unfolded her arms.

"Don't freak out," Bixx said.

"I'm not," Tamara said. "Quite the contrary; tell me more."

"You love the man in the paintings, but you don't know why, right? It's like you've been together before, but you have no memory of that time."

Tamara's eyes darted between the paintings and Bixx. Her face went pale.

"It all feels real, like you lived it once?"

Tamara cautiously nodded, her mouth open.

"Do the dreams happen every night, like a loop stuck in your head?"

"Yes," Tamara said, just above a whisper. "Almost every night. My therapist says it's my repressed anger toward my father."

Bixx shook her head. "But you don't believe that, do you, Tamara?"

"How do you know my real name?"

"I know a lot about you." Bixx twisted in the chair and pointed at the triptych. "Because I knew that man once. And he knew you."

Tamara's lower lip quivered as she stared at the paintings. Her eyes went to Bixx. "You said 'knew' him, past tense."

"Yeah," Bixx said, her emotions rising. "He died...several months ago." She started playing with the urn that hung from her neck.

Tamara's attention went to it. "That's an interesting piece."

Bixx reached back and unclasped the necklace. She held the urn for a second before placing it in the middle of the desk. "I lost my parents when I was a kid. I keep some of their ashes in something like this." Bixx touched the barrel-shaped pendant. "I think you should have this particular one."

Tamara stared at the urn and dabbed at the corners of her eyes. "Why am I crying?" she asked. "I didn't even know him."

"Actually," Bixx said, "you did."

Tamara picked up the urn and cupped it reverently in her hands. "What was his name?"

"Jonathan Kortel."

Her face was blank at first, but it quickly changed into a look of shocked recognition. "Oh my God, not the man from that documentary?"

Bixx nodded.

"He lived here, in Chicago. His restaurant is just a few blocks from the..."

Tamara looked at the paintings again, and Bixx could tell she was putting the pieces together. "Are you saying I'm the blonde woman?... The one they talked about?"

Bixx gave a faint smile.

Tamara shook her head. "I watched it, but I didn't believe it. I thought it was one of those shows that looks real, but isn't." Tamara glanced at Bixx warily. "And you're one of those...?"

"We're called Tels," Bixx said. "And yes, you're the one they called 'His Love.' They didn't use your name in the documentary because it would have made things hard for you."

Bixx couldn't read Tamara's expression. Either she was in shock or couldn't grasp the seriousness of her situation. "Listen," she said, "eventually some reporter is going to figure it all out and come looking for you. It's better that you hear the truth from someone you can trust and not from a stupid newscast."

"Why don't I remember any of it? I remember that time period, but not *him*."

"Well, you do...in a way. Your dreams are fragments of the memories. It's kind of hard to explain."

Tamara turned the urn over in her hands, and Bixx saw a shift in her. A look of acceptance had settled behind her eyes, and their crystalline blue seemed brighter.

"Tell me about him," she said. "Tell me everything you can remember."

A warm feeling of peace moved through Bixx. "Sure, I'd love to."

PAUL BLACK always wanted to make movies, but a career in advertising sidetracked him. Born and raised outside of Chicago, he is the national award-winning author of *The Tels, Soulware, Nexus Point, The Presence* and *The Samsara Effect*. Today he lives and works in Dallas, where he manages his graphic design firm, feeds his passion for tennis and dreams of six figure movie deals. He is currently working on a new book of fiction tentatively called *CoolBrain*.

IT'S A DARK NEW WORLD IN THE 21ST CENTURY North America is one union; trade in illegal cloning is thriving; and the Biolution has changed all the rules. National Security Agency profiler Sonny Chaco's latest assignment is Alberto Goya, billionaire CEO of global media giant AztecaNet. The NSA thinks Goya is involved with racketeering, but Chaco knows that he has ties to the Mexican Mafia.

Chaco's information is coming from Deja Moriarty, one of AztecaNet's brightest reality producers. Deja wonders if she's really helping her country, while Chaco seriously questions his feelings for his sexy informant.

Just when Chaco thinks he's got the goods on Goya, his superior assigns him to investigate a mysterious and powerful man. But everything goes sideways when Chaco discovers that Deja knows the mystery man. AztecaNet's head of security is soon on to Chaco and Deja, and there's nothing he won't do to stop them from bringing down his boss.

NOVEL INSTINCTS
www.paulblackbooks.com

Available at all online retailers including **Amazon.com** and **BN.com**.